BRUTAL DISCOVERY

In the sudden, welcome darkness, leaning forward, catching Maeve unawares, I grabbed the silky fabric in my left hand and gave it a hard yank. . . . The *swish* of it being pulled through the air sounded as if it were happening a billion miles away. Maeve was a pearly luminescence in the semidarkness, whitish in places where her slip stuck to her wet thighs, and—

—and then the light returned, without my hearing the thunder. And with the radiance came the truth . . . and after the brightness was gone, the image of it . . . oh, God, what I saw was burned on my eyes hotter than a brand on a hide. And every time the lightning flashed again, the image was seared in my brain, hotter and deeper, and she kept saying, "Oh, please, please leave," but there was longing, too, in that ragged choking voice, which only made it all the more awful. . . .

Also by A. R. Morlan

THE AMULET

DARK JOURNEY

by A. R. Morlan

BANTAM BOOKS

NEW YORK • TORONTO • LONDON • SYDNEY • AUCKLAND

DARK JOURNEY
A Bantam Spectra Book / December 1991

AUTHOR'S NOTE

During the research phase of the writing of this novel, one work in particular played a vital role in laying the background for the book (especially for the Prologue and Part Three), namely Harlan Ellison's "Gopher in the Gilly"; although the carnival setting used in my novel contains some deliberate inaccuracies that were in no way inspired by Mr. Ellison's work, but were instead utilized for reasons of convenience and/or brevity by the author of this book. What was actually lived cannot and should not be mistaken for the "realities" presented in the following novel.

In Memory Of

Fluffy (1984–1986), Louie (1984–1986), Huey (1984–1987), Heidi (1988–1990), Holly (?–1990), and Snowball (?–1990)—

Some were my "babies" from kittenhood to all-too-brief adulthood, some shared their lives with me for all too short a time before the end, but when love and memory remain, the end is never really an end. . . .

Acknowledgments

The author would like to thank the following people for their moral, emotional, and financial support during the nine years spent in the various stages of writing this novel; these people made a very difficult time easier to bear with their friendship, concern, caring, generosity, and simple kindnesses: my family, Ray Aldridge, Mark C. Anderson, Dean Paul and Gretta Anderson, Janet Fox, Harlan and Susan Ellison, Kathy Ptacek and Charles L. Grant, James B. Johnson, Jeanette Hopper, Dean and Gerda Koontz, Gary L. Raisor, Uwe Luserke, and last but definitely not least John S. Postovit.

PROLOGUE

Summer Shadow

"Thursday's child has far to go."

—Old nursery rhyme

"Didn't I think the Midwest was where reality was the thinnest, waiting for truth to erupt?"

—Peter Straub
If You Could See Me Now

Thursday, June 26, 1923

Come July, few members of the South-State Enterprises Carnival and Menagerie expected to be doing shows farther north than the southern-most tip of Indiana—until a Mr. Otis Ewert, banker, of Ewerton, Wisconsin, attended one of the carny's Indiana shows.

A good impression was made, an offer tendered, and after cash—equal to a week's salary for every freak, roustabout, and jointee employed by South-State—left Mr. Ewert's exquisitely tailored vest pocket to cross the palm of the carny manager, the carnies found themselves making a detour into the cooler, less humid lands of Wisconsin's north-central lumber country.

A three-day stint, providing entertainment for Ewerton's annual Water Carnival. (A few carnies speculated that Ewert simply wished to show off his prowess at the rifle-shoot booth before his cronies—as if the mold-grimed cache of Kewpie dolls and Teddy bears he'd won weren't proof enough.) And, because God surely had not *meant* for human beings to have to endure a deep-south summer, more than one South-State carnie's heart lifted upon reading the flowing script on the painted wooden sign posted at the outskirts of town:

Welcome to Ewerton!
Population 3,251 and Growing Every Day!

Those present during Mr. Ewert's assault of the rifle-shoot booth recalled his revelation that he was soon to be a proud papa, and wondered if he would personally amend the numbers on the sign after the blessed event occurred. He seemed the type.

Others, who had not seen Ewert (he of the icy blue eyes and pendulous lips), merely thanked Providence for a stint of coolness in the midst of a sweat-slippery summer. Even if Providence had had little to do with their current engagement.

But there was one carny who felt more than the coolness of the northern air.

What *he* felt was fear. Stone cold fear.

At first, Jonathan Quigley (aka "Monsieur Hypnotique—Mind Reader and Mentalist Par Excellence!") tried to dismiss the feelings, tried in vain to ignore the dreams. To neglect the baleful vibrations and hideous nightmares that began the night after Mr. Ewert cleared Dusty's rifle-shoot booth, then made his offer for the carny to head up north. The stirrings of ill will that Quigley attempted to attribute to old North-South "Damn Yankee" antagonisms; bad blood passed down like red hair and blue eyes in his family.

Quigley had been raised in the backlash of the Civil War, but with the coming of the new century he'd tried to put the soreness of the last fifty years behind him. It was his *parent's* war, not his—and yet. . . . There was something about the smooth-talking (yet distainful), watery-eyed Ewert that raised Rebel hackles Quigley had long since forgotten he'd had. Something that hinted at old danger, at clearly articulated *badness*, pure and . . . *less* than simple.

Quigley'd seen Ewert striding under the ropes of colored lights, arms loaded with prizes, before he'd dumped them in his Haynes Speedster; the yellow and blue bulbs cast oily reflections on those unctuous lips that had glistened in the darkness. "Cry-baby mouth, li'l baby wants his own way," Momma used to say when Jonathan was small. Ewert's lips glimmered like dull, uncut jewels set in a dough-pale face. And his eyes—vacant enough to be a fool's, but, behind the limpid blue, *waiting*—gleamed a light that told Quigley exactly how Ewert had conned a con like Dusty, beating a rigged game. Cry-baby gets *his own way*. . . .

The stirrings of *bad* began that night, after Quigley looked into Ewert's eyes. By the time the carny had finished its journey through Indiana, Illinois, and kitty-corner through Wisconsin, Quigley's feelings had grown less vague, stronger, more persistent. And the dreams . . . were something *more* than dreams.

Of that he was certain.

Driving his converted school-bus-*cum*-wheeled home north, he remembered times when his Monsieur Hypnotique spiel, designed to entertain and astonish, never to pry or hurt, got away from him. Despite all his Bible-learnin' back in Georgia ("No, Johnny, man ain't s'posed to know them things, or see 'em . . . kneel, son, pray to the—''), there continued to be times when his act went beyond his usual innocent revelations.

Kentucky, 1921. Two men fell, biting and punching on each other as their women screamed. All because he said the son of one man had a birthmark like his father's—Quigley hadn't known about the fooling around. Or that time in Georgia, last year, when that woman fainted. . . .

No amount of Bible-reading, quoting, or memorizing could stop what was to *be*, no matter how much or how little Quigley chose to believe. Not even if he wished with all his soul that he was wrong.

Sweat-slick palms gripping the steering wheel, Quigley was rendered cold down to his clammy toes by what he knew but *shouldn't* know.

Not that he knew, for certain, just what it was that he was afraid of. But he *felt* it, coiled around its *bad*ness like a pale grub under a flat stone. Biding its time. Inhumanly patient, growing. Quigley was positive that the worse-than-*bad* that awaited him was not a thing of the *now*, not in the "stop the car *before* you reach the washed-out bridge" sense, but something that was just reacing fruition even as he drove closer. Unstoppable corruption seemed to flow up through the tires of his bus, oozing through the spinning rubber, floorboards, shoe soles, and into his icy feet.

Then he rolled into Ewerton, population 3,251.

. . . two trunks, melded as one, rising from a single root, branches moving wind-slow under the low-domed sky, bloody sap showing black-red in the gloom, pooling around his wood and earthen feet. . . .

Jerking, heart lopping in his chest, Quigley clung to one last assurance as he traded a constricted land of wan yellow light and soaked pink-tan earth for the protective red-veined world of his inner eyelids—a fresh and unwelcome certainty. This doom was meant for him, too.

Snuggling his Bible against his chest, trying to will himself awake, alert, Quigley was nearly overcome by a sense of doom as yet uncoalesced, of added evil cosanguineous to that already waiting in Ewerton. Getting to his feet, pushing aside the paisley-printed curtain, he scanned the cars already parked

on the outskirts of the woods-surrounded fairgrounds, looking for Ewert's Haynes Speedster.

But Quigley hadn't heard Ewert's remark about his impending fatherhood, which put him in the dangerous situation
of *knowing* but not *understanding* what was really coming. . . .

Later, leaning into the tiny mirror propped on his knee,
Quigley drew palsied rings around his wide-pupiled eyes,
sighed, then darkened his fair lashes with burnt cork. Through
a curtained window (the majority of his windows were painted
over), he saw the row of cars outside grow long, dividing like
a one-cell thing gone malignant. Initially, all he saw were
Fords, most rusted-out and dust-grimed . . . then he spied
the showroom-bright cluster of cars: two Studebakers, an
Olds, a Case Model X, and a like-new 1920 Series 9 "Lex-
Sedan."

Pulling his lips taut, applying a fine sheen of color
("Frenchmen" were supposed to be exotic, especially to
these apple-knockers), Quigley was wracked with a spasm of
fear. He knew that this either was or had been a lumber town,
which meant good money for some, but . . . *but* . . . those
new cars had to have cost close to $3,000 or more. More
money than most men would see after a year of hard work.

Patting his lean face with rice powder, covering the trio of
dark moles on his left cheek, Quigley tried not to drop the
puff he held in shaking fingers. His eyes darted to the window, seeking the Haynes and its thick-lipped owner. The
sense of *dis*-ease he'd come to associate with Ewert and his
namesake town (funny, Ewert wasn't *that* old . . . certainly
not old enough to have a town named after *him*) was stronger,
a thickening of his blood that threatened to render him immobile; prey to the madness that permeated the air around
him. A feeling lacking *sensation*, a chill with no *coldness*
present. And the badness wasn't confined to a man, a fancy
car, or a mansion-size house (like the *huge* sage-green be-
hemoth he drove past that morning). It simply *was*, yet was
not of this place.

Running a hand over his slicked-back hair, Quigley pondered the contradiction: There was evil, impending wrong-
ness, infused in this town . . . while the actual *manifestations*
of corruption weren't within reach, or sight. *Yet.* Putting aside
his makeup, he told himself, *Three* more days, Johnny . . .
three more days, then you're free of . . . this, even though

he doubted his words as he thought them. Rising, he turned his back to the window, put on his suit coat . . . and missed the royal blue Daniels V8 Speedster driven by a man Quigley surely would have recognized. A man whose taffy-haired wife sat demurely beside him with her oval face half-hidden by a wide-brimmed hat.

A woman just beginning to be noticeably with child.

In her prime, Madam Zola had been a top draw on the South-State midway. But as the years pulled down the ersatz Theda Bara planes of her face, turning her into a Gorgonesque parody of a femme fatale, fewer and fewer swells, sharecroppers, and rubes lingered before her booth, seeking the answers to life's mysteries in her readings of the Celtic Cross, the Wheel of Fortune, or—for high rollers—the complex Tree of Life.

But as her youth and other charms ebbed, so had the interest of the hicks: Soon the Horse Shoe or five-card spread were too taxing for her customers' endurance. No more callused fingers shyly reached her way, seeking a bit more than the fortune her cards might reveal. These days she served as a moment's amusement no more significant that a cone of cotton candy or the toss of a softball at a painted milk bottle, and Madam Zola knew it. Novice-level four-card spreads satisfied those marks who did manage to overcome their Bible-belt mentality and wander her way. And if the interest in *that* spread waned . . . Madam Zola consoled herself that evenings spent in the ticket booth couldn't be too horrendous. But she prayed that that day was at least a summer or two in the future; the midway wasn't that bad, even when she was idle.

When she wasn't making predictions for the rubes, Madam Zola took in the *real* show. For her, the marks were the true attraction.

They were a show that never changed, no matter how often the carny moved; for all that the faces changed the show itself remained the same. . . . Oh, occasionally, a particularly fat or skinny or *different* individual was propositioned by the owner for a hole in the carny, but those marks bored Madam Zola to kohl-black tears. She relished the smug, "*I'd* never do *that*" smirks that never quite hid the longing in their eyes, the frantic laughter over the last lost dollar that couldn't erase the anguish over tomorrow's unpayable rent, or the mocking smiles saved for the freak top—the sneer of condescension given by the whole to the unwhole or *more* than whole. With the smiler no doubt using those same lips that curled to pray loudly in church the next morning. And the vacant, trusting ones, who sincerely believed and feared what they saw . . . for those last, Zola felt a mingling of pity and distaste. Sorrow for their ignorance, contempt for its duration.

So there sat Madam Zola on this balmy July afternoon. Her ruined face overshadowed by a turban adorned with a jeweled feather, deep-ringed eyes darting, taking in the parade of all-day suckers, chapped and reddened lips pressed in a knowing slit. Silent, yet patient, waiting for the apple-knockers to see and heed her sign, to succumb to its simple invitation:

FORTUNES

TOLD?

(Often she bragged to any carny willing to listen, "It's the question mark that reels them in, hook caught in bleeding lips. That, and the all-seeing Eye.")

But today, even the question mark and the fashionably bare-browed eye lured no fresh fish to her stall. Idly shuffling her deck of cards, rubbing the waxy surfaces with a bloodred thumbnail until a fragile mound of waxy shavings accumulated on the apron of her booth, she assured herself that unlike a Deep South crowd, these marks weren't likely to be half-illiterate . . . nor should they be *that* God-fearing. A Sunday school, quilting-bee, Norman Rockwell magazine-cover crowd. Unimaginative but harmless. Salt of the earth that gets ground down underfoot. Sighing, Zola decided that the ticket booth might not be too bad . . . until she caught sight of a small knot of people who seemed transplanted, alien in this crowd of farmers and small-business types.

The six couples, tied together by an invisible thread that Zola could *almost* see, were not coetaneous, as might be expected of such close companions. Two couples were a pair of in-laws; the would-be flapper hanging like lint on the arm of the blond man bore a most unfortunate resemblance to the oldest couple in the group.

Madam Zola had learned to quickly choose significators for potential customers—the King, Queen, Knight, or Page best suited to represent the mark in a spread—and now she dubbed Mrs. Vamp (vamp*ire*, she thought with a sudden shiver) the Queen of Batons, only reversed, to take that pouty, stubborn mouth and obstinate set of the jaw into account. As for her mate . . . he seemed intelligent; thoughts raced visibly across his strong face and lit up his green eyes. King of Swords—a fitting choice, especially the way he let the bib-haired harpy guide him like a spoiled brat pulling a balloon through the air. Perfect. Ultimately ineffective and unrealistic; a true Sword King.

Near them, a younger-looking, dark-haired couple (Slavs . . . high cheekbones), the woman's eye buried under a *very* thick coat of powder, which showed a hint of bruised flesh below. The younger man and woman were dressed like their companions—in a style much too sophisticated for their surroundings, too East Coast snobby—yet something in their garments spoke of a background more rural than that of their fellows. Her dress lacked the languid flutter around the knees; his flannel suit and white-collared Madras-plaid shirt was brash, uncouth. Farmer or lumberjack who made good, she told herself, nodding sagely at her own insight.

As the phalanx of improbably elegant (or nearly so) people came closer, Zola saw that one woman (a plump, reversed Queen of Coins with a silly smile that hung like bunting on her porchlike lower jaw; trotting next to her was a Knight of Coins clod who tripped over a discarded Goo-Goo Cluster wrapper) carried a child, a ludicrously jug-eared tot who brought to mind the *Yellow Kid* comic.

Getting over her amusement over the sorry-looking toddler, Zola assigned significators to the rustic pair—the bruised little thing was a Queen of Cups; good nature evident despite her downcast eyes, smile quick in coming, arms ready to carry the tot when his mother bent to pick a stone out of her shoe. The bruised woman's mate surreptitiously jabbed her with his elbow. (No doubt about who delivered her black eye!) A reverse King of Coins, the *only* fitting card for such a brute; no doubt a corrupt, unprincipled curr. His presence in the procession was an enigma—perhaps the *wives* were friends? Yet only the battered brunette, the tot's mother, and the dark-haired, almond-eyed woman with the jangling bracelets were even *speaking* to each other.

The sixth couple (Mrs. Bakelite Bangles, who walked with a wobble, had an equally unsurefooted mate) was boxed in the tightest by that ambulatory mass of party clothing. They puzzled Madam Zola more than the rural couple had. Only the dreamy blond man (who showed a spark of ire when he saw the hick jab his tiny wife's ribs) was better dressed or more obviously deferred to than this man was. Until she'd noticed them, Zola had thought that the old couple had directed the course of the stroll. But, she realized, the strings were pulled from *within*.

Then the group came close to the colored lights, and Madam Zola recognized "Mr. Sure Shot"—the man who'd hired the carny away to this godforsaken place. Ewert. King of Cups, she decided, crushing a mosquito onto the apron under her cards.

A thin smear of red and crushed wings clung to her thumb.

Any man who could outwit Dusty's gaffed joint could easily bamboozle a simple town and its simpler people. Yet, the minions didn't love their king. See them pass, nod, hurry on, breath held in fear. His companions don't realize the obvious . . . or they choose to overlook it.

Ewert pointedly eyed the new stock of prizes in the rifle-shoot booth (Zola remembered seeing the armload of toys he'd won two weeks ago tossed in a ditch near the site of that Indiana show), before he steered the group toward the beckoning eye of Madam Zola's sign. Then, dissension in the ranks.

The couple who thought little of the Eighteenth Amendment noticed the beano game across from Zola's booth. Pointing, the woman giggled, a shrill, jagged, painful sound, as she tried to drag her dazed mate over that way—until Ewert said, in a voice of oiled menace, "Waste time at a *beano* game? Gay*leen*, your sights need raising—" Ewert's wife (odd, she'd escaped Zola's scrutiny) broke free of her husband, saying, "Otis, Gayleen's sights are just *fine*. She only asked Porter to go with her . . . they'll be back." As she spoke, Porter and Gayleen timidly wandered off, toward the nearly full tent. The five remaining couples huddled close, lest a less suitable member of the community accidentally joined their select walking club, corrupting its purity.

When the tipsy couple left, Zola thought, These people have nothing in common at all. Age, breeding, their likely backgrounds—they didn't *fit*. Once separated, Porter and Gayleen no longer belonged with their compatriots. Yet the rest all clung together, like children on a playground following the self-proclaimed King of the Hill . . . *hurry after him, or be left out of the game forever*. Gayleen and Porter wistfully sat at an empty bench, cards of their former bench mates abandoned on the table before them. As the loudspeaker blared "Barney Google," Zola saw a liquid sparkle in Gayleen's rounded eyes . . . *lost your turn, children*.

Then the others were upon Zola, and their differences (the way seemingly uniform tree leaves reveal infinite variations when the branch is brought up close) became strong, and all the more unsettling. Their eyes alone were unified (save for the blond man and farm woman her husband called Treeva); a certain indifference, an acquired *coldness* linked them. Not animal cruelty, but a coastal decadence out of place in the Midwest, akin to trashy novels about flappers and sudden boot-leg riches. . . .

Wealth. Instantaneous, *immense* prosperity came to Zola's mind, but these were no mere nouveau riche. More like . . . bought-and-paid-for *riche*. As though they were *owned*. Heart sinking, Zola knew who had done the buying. Suddenly, the ticket booth was *inviting*. . . .

The blond in buff and peach silk—the others called him Wilbur—pushed forward, a lopsided smile on his face. A smile echoed in his eyes, thank God.

"Do you do card readings and palms, or just cards?" His wife edged closer, pup-eager to be first. Spoiled beyond rotten, she squeezed up to the apron. Ma-ma and Pa-pa nodded their approval, and urged their Hortense to get a "good" reading—as if the outcome of the cards was up to *her*, and not Madam Zola.

The fortune teller thumbed through her deck, until she located the yellow-robed Queen of Batons (the card said "Wands," but Zola thought that was Mr. Waite and his Golden Dawn cronies waxing eloquent), sunflower in one hand, leafed Baton/Wand in the other. Zola placed the card to her right—cloche-hatted Hortense's left—just as her neighbor lady had taught her long ago. Feeling the pressure of cold eyes—even the Yellow Kid did his best to stare her down—

Zola explained in her best sultry voice, "The significator . . . represents *you*, madame—"

"Look, Wilbur, a *throne*. I'm on a throne. Oh, a cat in front. Mona"—she turned to the tot's mother—"aren't black cats unlucky?" Mrs. Vamp's eyes were winter ice; Zola decided that if Death came up, she'd tell Hortense to pick out the coffin lining she liked best. But with the dealing out and turning over of all the subsequent cards, Madam Zola had little choice in *any* of the readings. Only the most negative cards showed their garish bright fronts (although the Lovers in Wilbur's present and the Moon in his future were an intriguing, if ominous, pair); as the cards told their grim tales, first the old couple—Horton and Myrtle—stalked off, to be replaced with the fuddled Gayleen and Porter, who returned to the fold, and then—

Zola had to restrain herself from pitching aside the deck and run screaming from the booth. Surely, most *assuredly*, the cards spoke the truth, revealing fortunes both accurate and hideous, with hints of *worse* to come. . . .

The cards *could* see into people; gaze unflinchingly at things best forgotten, best unknown by those with any shred of decency . . . illicit behavior, dark deeds performed in confused pasts, the entire repertoire of a showman's gloom-and-doom parade—but what was worse was what was *coming*. To *this* place. To *these* people before her. Even blond Wilbur of the lean face and kind eyes. Even timid, bruised Treeva, wife of the loutish Enoch. And more evil was revealed with each snap-flip of the oversize cards. . . .

That *Ewert* was almost inhuman, Zola could see. But when she turned over the Fool in his wife Abby's present, then *Death* in her future—

Abby Ewert looked at Zola steadfastly, unblinking in the face of such an obvious symbol of her current status—a Fool about to walk off a cliff. Under her brimmed hat, framed by unfashionably long gold-brown hair, her oval face and oddly colored eyes were serene, befitting a Queen of Swords (she hadn't blinked when Zola guessed that she had been widowed once, but admitted she *was* one, before her union with Ewert).

Abby had only folded her tiny hands against her swelling abdomen as Zola said, "I see an unexpected influence coming into play . . . something unlooked for . . . combined with your significator, whatever lies in the future may not be happy"—Zola flipped over the last card—"and your future holds—"

"Death?" finished Mrs. Ewert calmly, adding, "As in a pregnancy?" Ewert colored deeply at her unabashed tone.

"Like a pregnancy." If Mrs. Ewert was unafraid, more to her credit; Madam Zola met her challenge.

Shifting her sloping shoulders under whispering crepe de chine, she gave Zola a level stare, "Will my baby die then?" (In the background, Zola saw Treeva's bruised brown eyes water and widen in fear.)

"Perhaps not . . . but it isn't a good card. Maybe the *change* aspect will overtake the other meanings—"

"I've had enough of your 'maybes,' ma'am." Ewert flicked away his cigarette (behind him, Wilbur stomped it cold), and, eyes reptilian-blood cold, guided his wife away from the booth.

Nearly an hour after it had begun, Madam Zola's ordeal was over. The crepe de chine and summer flannel phalanx departed in search of the elder members of the unit. Glancing at her cards, Madam Zola felt the urge to burn then, smoke their waxy surfaces—abruptly she threw the deck of Tarot cards into the trampled dirt of the midway, reached over the apron to snatch up her Cyclopean sign, then fled the booth.

When she was gone, Wilbur backtracked to her booth, and scooped up the scattered waxy cardboard. Blew dust from the cards, shuffled them into a neat rectangle, and put them in his jacket pocket. And rejoined his companions.

Making the rounds of the darkening midway, pausing long enough for little Freddy Ferger's daddy to win him two new Teddy bears at the rifle-shoot booth, the six couples filed into the small tent near the northern curve of the midway, a tent fronted by a wooden sign reading:

MONSIEUR HYPNOTIQUE

Minds Read! Destinies Revealed!

(Adults 10¢ Children 5¢)

The six couples—upon seeing the group enter, their neighbors shied away from the tent—lurched around in the semi-darkness, patting their way along the last row of cheap folding chairs until all were seated. They didn't realize they had company until a male voice—cultured, resonant, accentuated with a slightly twangy undertone—cut through the musty silence:

"Lay-*deeze* an' gentle*mon*. Welcome to zee World of zee Mind, an' that which is Beyond zee Imagination!"

("They got better'n this in White City, in Chicago," Ferger grumped; his wife, Mona, shot back, "Fredric, pul-ease!")

Nonplussed, the voice droned on, "Enter into zee Realm of zee"—melodramatic pause—"Unknown!" Colored bulbs above and below the small, platformlike stage burst into brightness, weirdly illuminating the dark-caped figure before them.

Hair slicked darkly smooth, eyes raccooned, mouth a deep crimson slash, the mentalist stood before them. The marble smoothness of his face was marred by powdered moles on his cheek; the smile that swept up his face bypassed his eyes.

Quigley caught a liquid flash of red light on moving silver in the darkness, heard a gurgle and swallow, and then the dark moving figure blended once more into the surrounding shadows. Odd, how no one sat close to the stage. But there was no time for reflection; Quigley, aka Monsieur Hypnotique, launched into his spiel.

Extending a neatly groomed hand out into the audience—light caught his polished nails, made them scintillate like sunlight on new snow—he asked, "A leetle somethang from zee audience? A bauble, somethang per-son-*nal*—"

"You already got my dime, buster," was followed by a shower of rainbow sparkles arcing in the gloom, a soft thud, and a woman's inebriated giggle. Guessing he'd seen a beaded purse, Quigley persisted, "*Some*thang, for zee bodily emissions?" His rubbing palms produced a dry, snicking sound.

Two men whispered, one voice old, the other younger, then a soft, feminine protest: "Otis, what *are* you—No, Otis!" followed by movement, soft urgings. Then a little boy, pug ugly, toddled forward into the faint spill of light, an object held tight in a pudgy fist.

Something that glittered real gold.

The tot refused to give up the bauble, forcing a plump woman to crab-scuttle into the light, hissing, "Go *on*, Freddy, give the nice man the watch!" Porcine nose curling, he boo-booed, muddy eyes blinking back tears. But he dutifully held the watch aloft, recoiling swiftly when his gooey fingers made contact with Quigley's large dry ones. Booted feet *plock-plock-plocked* across packed earth, to a chorus of "Good boy, Freddy!"

The watch in Quigley's hands wasn't clammy-gooey like the boy's fingers, but *warm*, as if still worn on a wrist. Rolling his eyes upward, Quigley fixed his gaze on a yellow bulb as he tried to come up with an appropriate deduction (*married, called the man by name . . . oh, Lord, she said "Otis"*—) but the bulb *expanded*, filament white-hot and *writhing*, big and incandescent behind the yellow teardrop of glass. The filament was a live, *growing* thing coiled there inside the sallow, spreading, *encompassing*, jaundiced glow. It burned away the surrounding red and blue and green and clear lights, leaving only *yellow*—hazy, the edges pulled and ragged, bleeding into the dun sky above him. Only the squiggle of wormy white remained, a gnarled core of impure light, floating in the smear of rancid color.

Smarting from the glare, his eyes shifted downward—*to feet that were sinking into the floor below, planks gone crumbly soft, a fallow field of tan, sucked-dry earth covering his ankles with warm softness, pulling him down and in.*

Putting down his free hand, Quigley felt that the earth was shot down with subterranean rivulets of wet . . . a viscous damp that clung, too warm, too scented. A substance that enveloped his hand in a . . . personal warmth. Shaking his fingers, he sent fat droplets of viscid reddish matter flying through close, diffuse air. Then he saw the mound, a heaving mass of live ground that wasn't ground exactly. Even as the droplets flicked from his fingertips landed with moist plods before him, the rounded roll of . . . substance gave a wild scream and a shuddering heave; a blur of gooey fluid rushed out, leaving the mound cleft deep red and oozing. Until the pale, fleshy thing slithered out, like a peeled birch, twin-trunked yet one, a double-topped, living entity in a wasteland of blasted soil and fulsome air.

Then came the hollow blast, a muffled loud report, followed by a flurry of whitish ash falling from the low sky to touch and stick to the peeled birch thing. Filling Quigley's nose and throat with a dry taste that was so very familiar. . . .

Then the darkness, like a swift summer shadow falling across the sunset land, enveloped Quigley, until—

A sudden shine of brightness, a liquid silver thing that came and went, illuminating the ruined birch thing before him, its smooth skin rain-flecked save for the black-red ooze from the flesh cleft between its bent and writhing limbs. And the fissure widened, the pink-white flesh of the entity stained rippling carmine under the fall of rain . . . until a being of mud darkness and sharp woodiness came forward and rended the soft skin of the birch until the break was complete. Viscous sap flowed and ebbed, pumping like a slow, deep heartbeat until one writhing branch limb fell completely away—

Quigley raised both hands to cover his face, to stifle shrill screams—

Screaming. One woman, two; voices keen, ascending in the murk, a shrill descant to the urgent rumble of the man's voice—"Abby? Abigail, wake up!" Dazed, Quigley rubbed eyes still burning with the negative afterimage of the bulb filament . . . and, trying to swallow, found his throat raw, as if he'd been shouting—

The watch lay at his dry, black-shod feet, crystal shattered into icy shards, thin golden band coiled and twisted, the twin of the hot white thing he'd seen in the strange dream-world sky.

A crisp voice dominated the confused babble. "Otis, go away. She needs air. I'll carry her—*some*body open the damned flaps, *okay*?" A noisy scramble, then a triangle of light, quickly filled by a blond man carrying a blue-clad woman, her face turned away . . . but the fertile curve of her midsection was in plain sight for a second before the buff-suited man carried her off. A thick-set man began to follow, then paused a second to stare at Quigley.

The last light of the afternoon, orange-dark, coupled with the weak glow of the stage lights, was sufficient to illuminate the thick, glossy curves of the man's lips, the watery glare of his blue eyes—and Quigley, formerly Monsieur Hypnotique, Mentalist and Mind Reader Par Excellence, knew that the evil had found him.

And it knew *his* face and name.

Striding across the fairgrounds, ignoring the gawking on-lookers, Wilbur cradled Abby carefully, out of concern for the baby, not stopping until he neared their row of parked cars. Abby moaning in his arms, Wilbur bent down and fumbled with the keys of his Case Model X sedan, kicked the door open, then gently placed Abby in the backseat. He covered her with a blanket Hortense had left there, to cover their daughters when they wore their Sunday dresses. (Wilbur was glad that Ila and Koba were visiting his mother in Edina—at least they hadn't seen and heard those awful things. . . .)

Removing Abby's hat, pillowing the crown under her head, Wilbur jarred her hairpins; her sunset hair slid sensuously across his hands, onto the leather seat beneath her. The silky glide of her wavy hair (*Did your Zachary caress your hair this way before he* . . . *died? Odd, how that card reader* knew *about him* . . .) made Wilbur swell with shameful pleasure, which quickly withered when Ewert's strident bark, "Holiday! Let *me* at her!" came from close behind him.

Stepping aside, Wilbur Holiday assured himself that Ewert didn't *mean* to sound so crass (*Not* that *kind of fellow*, are *you, Otis*?).

Leaning against his sedan, Wilbur watched the others scurry toward him. *Dear* Hortense hobbled along, hanging onto Mr. and Mrs. Crescent's arms, her feet swelling out of too-small shoes; the Fergers took turns hauling little Freddy ("But, *Fred*, that—*ghoul* touched my little baby!"); the Winstons gamely wobbled forward, Gayleen's bracelets clanking in time with her jittering steps, and bringing up the rear, Enoch Nemmitz dog-dragged Treeva, who sniffed, "I just want to get home to Vernon and Vernilla—I don't *care* about 'dressing down' that horrible man!"

Swallowing down a backup of bile at the sight of his . . . *companions*, Holiday moodily drew a circle in the dust with the tip of his shoe, then reached into his pockets for a pack of cigarettes. Instead, he withdrew the deck of Tarot cards. On top was the Lovers, the man and the woman's plumpy naked bodies deep orange in the fading light. Grunting, Wilbur thrust the pack back into his pocket with such force he felt the silk lining pull and tear.

The Holidays took Abby home, and the other women likewise drove home, leaving Ewert's Daniels for the men, who promised to "have a word" with the carny manager over the incident in the tent. But by the time the action on the midway had wound down, the remaining five men had passed the gentleman in question a total of seven times, pausing only to tip their hats or cheerfully nod and smile when their eyes met his.

Arms cradling a veritable Sears catalog's worth of toys, the quintet left Dusty grumbling in his rifle-shoot booth, eyeing his empty shelves with distinct unease.

Near the Dean River to the west, the townsfolk assembled for the Water Parade, to be run in conjunction with the fireworks display at 10:00 P.M. sharp. Soon even the kootchie tent emptied, and the freaks sat in misshapen isolation. But as the carved horses and gilded posts of the merry-go-round made their last revolutions of the evening, the five men remained, ostensibly enjoying the graceful bob and dip of mirrored color before them. Occasionally one or another of their disparate yet oddly *unified* faces would tip back, silvery flask to lips, and then, in a mercurial blur, the flat bottle would pass from one set of hands to another.

A sleeve was pushed up to reveal a moon-watch; 9:52 P.M. Otis Ewert palmed his sleeve down, hugging his stuffed bears closer; to his left, Mr. Crescent glanced over a Kewpie doll to ask if it was time.

"Nearly, Horton. Figure out which one?"

Nemmitz answered; his voice was a low growl, barely audible over the mix of carousel music and "Swinging Down the Lane" coming over the loudspeakers. "I saw after the . . . old school bus. Blacked-out windows." His vacant smile failed to dispel the chill in his voice. "Saw 'im run out, go in there. Wish I seen where the old bitch went—"

"Now, now, Enoch, no sport in *does*," Crescent warned, patting his vest, feeling for a reassuring shape under the serge.

Goggling glassily at the river, Porter Winston observed, "Got the floats inna water . . . 'most time."

The five men strolled leisurely toward the parking area as the lights of the midway winked out behind them. The muffled thud of an expensive car door carried in the darkness. Headlights cast sparkling cones of light into the night, until blackness swallowed them. The footsteps of the men were sure, muffled by crowd sounds to the west, making little noise in the warm darkness as they circled from the parking area to where most of the carny's makeshift motor homes stood, dark and mostly quiet, their occupants at the river's edge for the parade and fireworks. The arms of four of the men were empty; most of their burdens left behind in the shining blue automobile.

Across the river, on the banks of Willow Hill, fireworks experts from Eau Claire compared watches, nodded, and started the show.

Next to the old school bus, ears listened, shoulders were tapped, heads nodded in near blackness. Behind them, a popping roar, followed by a simultaneous flash of sprinkling golden light, and a muted "ohhh" from the onlookers.

Their faces lit gold-white for a second, the men swiftly forced open the folding bus doors, just before the scramble, and the next, louder *boom*, and shower of scarlet sparks—

Which almost completely masked a muffled report.

Come late night, when all is starlit dark, the air comes alive with cool pin-points of greenish-yellow light. Fireflies dart and hover, swirling as they pen messages of light upon the shadowy tablet of air. They part, disturbed, as the blue car speeds down Wisconsin Street, across jolting railroad tracks, into the town proper. The windows are open; ruffling mussed hair, lifting points of shirt collars. The voices of the men inside rise and fall, soft and cigarette fogged in the cool air. Words are sucked out of the automobile, to hang for a moment, hovering with the fireflies, before dissipating:

"—beats a rif—"

"Two-legged's the best—"

"—ing him into that blan—"

"—worth your dime, Porter—"

"—keep this? It *smells*—"

The car rolls on, tires kissing the road, not slowing as it disgorges an object which shares the airborne state of the fireflies for a timeless second before descending with a muffled thud near a sewer grate in the street.

Lightning bugs swarm around it briefly, then soar away, uninterested in the discarded Teddy bear, its moundlike belly eviscerated, its back singed around the blackened, strong-smelling hole. Moist flecks of glittering blackness twinkle in the moonlight on its plush coat.

PART ONE

"Midnight Mayhem"
June 30, 1988

"Attention Shoppers! Midnite Mayhem—8:00 to Midnite This Thursday!"

> —Advertisement in the
> June 28 *Ewerton Herald*

"All we have to fear is fear itself."

> —Franklin D. Roosevelt

ONE

Flapping dryly, the canvas banner hung in the sluggish air, top half pulled taut by a wire strung across Ewert Avenue, bottom loose and dog-eared from over twenty summers of snicking in summer breezes. Flag blue letters hovered on a bed of cream: EWERTON WATER CARNIVAL—LAST WEEKEND IN JULY.

Below the insect-dotted banner, the six-block stretch of Ewert Avenue that comprised the business section of Ewerton was blocked off with several orange and white zigzagged sawhorses, surmounted at each end with yellow blinkers. The space between the sawhorses was filled with two or three hundred idly wandering people, who stopped at tables set up in front of stores whose windows promised MORE BARGAINS INSIDE STOP 'N' SEE!, or—most often—they grouped in bunches in the middle of the most narrow walkways, gossiping and effectively blocking the way of anyone who might want to slither past.

Brent Nimitz wished he had a dime—no, even a *nickel*—for each knot of people he had elbowed past. All of them no doubt neighbors who hadn't seen each other since at *least* two hours ago, and found it utterly *necessary* to fill each other in on all the latest. What they ate for supper, when they had a BM, who they met five minutes ago, and so on to maddening infinity. Squeezing by a phalanx of doorway gabbers, Brent saw that he was one of the few who had been willing to edge past to the interior of Clausen's Hallmark, now nearly empty save for a salesgirl.

As he gave the bored woman behind the counter a smile, Brent remembered the conversation he and his aunt and uncle had had over their takeout dinner from the DQ Brazier. Aunt Bitsy had said something about Midnite Mayhem being the biggest sale of the year, so big that the stores spent "all *year*" preparing for it. That prompted Uncle Palmer (brother of Brent's late father—Palmer still clung to the old way of spelling the Czech family name, *Nemmitz*,—which *itself* replaced Niemiec—instead of the modern *Nimitz*) to remark over his chili dog, "Least preparing for Midnite Mayhem keeps 'em busy . . . I'd hate to think they were drawing a salary for waiting on customers who don't come in the rest of the year."

Brent had feared another blowup between his elderly aunt and uncle, but Bitsy chose to ignore the crack and started in on the church bake sale she and some of the "gals" would run during Midnite Mayhem.

Palmer munched the rest of his hot dog in comparative silence before taking off from the DQ on foot—Doc's orders—for the ten-block walk to his friend Palmer Winston's apartment. Uncle Palmer was supposed to walk at least a mile a day, but seldom took fifty steps since his life-long buddy Palmer Winston (besides sharing the same first name, the old men shared fall birthdays a scant week apart) always seemed to be magically waiting for him at the next block, Olds Cutlass idling, Lucky Strike dangling from a chapped lip.

Bitsy didn't know about the ruse—Bitsy *being* Bitsy—and in the two days that Brent and his wife Zoe had been staying in the elder Nemmitz's farmhouse, Brent had gathered that the two old Palmers (each sixty-four come October) had been pulling the walk-then-ride bit for quite some time. He didn't have the heart to rat on his uncle, even though Bitsy said that old Doc Calder had demanded Palmer do a lot of walking, both to improve his sluggish circulation and to keep his bad leg limber.

But Brent figured that at *his* age, Palmer had the right to ride all he wanted. He'd managed to outlive all his siblings, most of them younger than himself, plus his parents, despite thick blood and a bum knee.

So when he'd looked out his bedroom window that morning and seen the ten-year-old Olds make a U-turn on the county trunk, slow down enough for his uncle to jump (!) in, and take off in a haze of tan dust for town, Brent only smiled and told himself that those two old bucks never would grow up. Hadn't his dad said that the two Palmers were like crossed fingers, one covering for the other no matter which way you looked at them? Lucky thing Zoe had been downstairs; she didn't like old man Winston, and might've kicked up a fuss over Uncle Palmer's joyride.

Wandering up and down the narrow aisles of Clausen's Hallmark and Gifte Shoppe, Brent peered at the back-

(a nearly scalped bugger who'd worn a baseball cap and an expression of eternal intestinal windiness), used to *share* the tiny bench with the two old Palmers?—Brent eased into a smile; no matter how cantankerous his uncle could be, Brent really loved the old guy. Not that his uncle was a *bad* man, or an ignorant, uncaring fellow. But even at his best, Palmer Edmund Nemmitz was . . . difficult.

He never hit or openly baited Bitsy (who—unknowingly and innocently—invited such treatment with her bird-brain mental state). As far as Brent knew, the old man had always been at *least* fair to his wife's daughter Angie (from her first marriage during WWII), and Palmer seldom went further than berating people he was ticked off at, yet Brent's uncle had acquired a reputation among the citizens of Ewerton (seemingly all 3,175 of them, if the sign outside the city limits was up-to-date) as a mean old fart who was to be avoided or quietly tolerated at all costs. Even his stepdaughter Angie had little to do with him.

But for all that, Brent genuinely liked and respected the man. It was an affection that had puzzled Brent's parents right up to the day they'd died in that car crash. On occasion it baffled Brent himself.

Palmer could be a caustic SOB at times; as he had been when Brent and Zoe had arrived at the farmhouse—no sooner had Palmer set eyes on them than he'd bolted from the house and trotted off for town. Zoe cried in their upstairs bedroom, telling Brent through her tears that his uncle hated her because his buddy Winston's wife Una had detested Zoe when Zoe had her for a teacher back in Ewerton High School. Even though Brent explained that Una Winston was long dead, and that Uncle Palmer never liked Winston's wife *any*how, Brent had a hell of a time getting Zoe over her crying jag. For a moment he hated the gimpy coot for his thoughtless exit.

But Palmer had been perfectly civil to Zoe (if distant) when he'd come back, so all was smoothed over—for the time being.

Pushing his way past the oddly empty-handed shoppers before him, crushing June bugs underfoot with small, chitinous smacks, Brent finally stationed himself before Palmer and Winston, fishing the Opus toy out of the bag as he spoke.

"You were right, Uncle . . . they never sell out anything here. Look at this"—he held out the six-inch toy proudly, wiggling it with his fingers so that the broad pink feet moved—"the first model, must be four, five years old." In the cold light, a nearly colorless puff of dust rose from the black and white and pinkish plush body.

Taking a drag on his cigarette, Winston drawled in his slightly monotone voice, "Probably been sitting on the same spot for all that time . . . you're Brent, aren't you? Grown a bit, eh?" then expelled a gray cloud of smoke through taut lips. His full head of iron-gray hair shone brightly in the harsh artificial light; his almond-shaped eyes were as sleepy as ever. And still coldly wary.

Next to him, Uncle Palmer (likewise blessed with a full head of gray hair, although his was partially covered by a limp fedora that cast a crescent-shaped shadow across the top quarter of his face) said, "*Win*ston, of course that's Brent Nimitz." He pronounced the latter carefully, the way his brother had insisted upon, Ni-*metz*; odd, he had never done that in Shirl's presence, always telling his brother it should be pronounced "the Czech way, N'nem-*itz*, no matter which asshole way it's spelled."

"Brent's staying with Bitsy and I, as I *told* you ten *times* already, he and his wi—"

"Married that Lawton girl, didn't you?" His blue eyes were moist and piercing under finely creped lids; old animosity brewed there. Brent recalled something Zoe had told him a few years ago, early in their marriage. "Una Winston crossed the line one day in school. Finally tripped herself up, and my parents got her fired. 'Early retirement' they called it, but *out* was *out*—"

While Brent hadn't managed to pry the exact nature of the incident out of Zoe (her parents were dead, too), apparently Una did something to Zoe that couldn't be swept under the rug. Something that demanded immediate attention on the part of the EHS school board, and ended the rein of Una-Pruna the Terrible, history teacher and student terrorizer of EHS.

Zoe wasn't the first student Una had "gone after" with her peculiar blend of favoritism/ostracism/systematic torture, but whatever she did to Zoe, it was the last incident. Uncle Palmer and Aunt Bitsy often wrote that Winston was simply *devoted* to Una, and was *so* broken up over her death by stroke a few years back that Brent thought he understood Winston's ill-concealed ire toward him . . . and Zoe.

Nodding, he replied carefully, "We've been together six

years . . . come August. We met in the Cities, working at this literary magazine—''

Almond-shaped eyes grew rounded, larger, surfaces glittering in the harsh pure light, giving Winston's seamed and sagging skin the appearance of a mask hiding the face of a bright-eyed child. Taking a drag on his Lucky Strike, letting the smoke out through his nose, he asked, ''Your wife, she ever tell you I was her high-school English teacher?''

That and so much more, you old diddler, Brent told himself, remembering Zoe's accounts of Mr. Winston's ''extra credit'' sessions after school . . . or *in* school, when he could get away with it.

Grinning, Brent replied, ''Seems like she mentioned something about you, and your *wife*, being her teachers.'' (*Some* teachers . . . *took her years to trust anyone.*) His uncle's mouth formed a moue, accompanied by subtle side-to-side movements of his shaggy head. Before Winston could reply, Palmer leaned forward and gave the Opus toy a pat on the beak, telling his nephew, ''Why don't you run on home and see if Zoe's headache is any better. Maybe this fellah''—he tapped the bird on the head—''will bring a smile to that face of hers. Nothing much worth buying around here . . . stuff'll be here next year, if it doesn't rot in the basements this winter.''

Hefting his lightweight bag of merchandise, Brent replied, ''Yeah. Looking but no buying—''

''Can't buy something with nothing,'' Winston mumbled between drags.

''—might as well get home to Zoe. Evening, Mr. Winston . . . Uncle Palmer, you tell Aunt Bitsy she'd better bring home the leftovers from that sale of hers.'' Brent patted his full midriff, and winked at Uncle Palmer, leaving after he received a barely discernible wink in return from the shadowy depths under his uncle's hat brim. Brent approached one of the sawhorses blocking off the end of the avenue, considered doing his macho sportsman bit by vaulting over it, then dutifully walked around it. He kept going down the avenue, bag tucked under one hefty arm, over to where his Pacer was parked.

From his spot on the bench, Palmer Nemmitz watched the younger man climb into his car, mouthing silently, ''You shouldn't have come back here, Brent . . . not with *her*, at least.'' Besides him, Winston echoed the same sentiment, muttering as he crushed a wildly flapping June bug onto the pavement in a scattering of hushlike brown wings and unidentifiable goo, "I don't know why those two picked this town to settle in, Nemmitz . . . not that your nephew seems to be a bad kid—looks rather *stupid*, though, toting around that tiny stuffed *birdie*, but—"

Palmer leaned over, to whisper in his friend's slightly overgrown ear, "Was playing with little stuffed *bras* any better?"

"—stupid for bringing *that* back here. She doesn't belong here, never has and never will." Hands shaking after his outburst, Winston lit a fresh smoke, puffed deeply, then went on, "Know what that little toy reminded me of? That old story Dead Fred used to tell, 'bout that time in '23, when he found that Teddy bear on Wisconsin Street, the one with all the stuffing torn out, and how he wouldn't let go of it. . . . "

Taking another puff, then grinding out another June bug, Winston sighed. "I'm just glad my Una isn't here to see that scutt traipsing back into town. Girl was the death of Una, to be sure—"

"Zoe wasn't in *town* then. Una had a *stroke*. Was building for years, you know it, I know it, and if Dead Fred was still sitting next to you, he'd know it, too." Palmer crossed his arms and leaned against the rough faux stone siding of the hardware store, resting his chin on his chest.

Winston lit a fresh cigarette, adding the long butt to the stamped-out collection at his feet, before continuing his harangue. "It was 'building for years' 'cause she was fed up with that girl. Her folks weren't even related to anyone, not so much as second hand cousins to *anyone* here in town, so why did they settle *here*? Wasn't as if the town sent out a written invite for them and that kid of theirs. Didn't make sense, old buck and bat having a kid her age—"

"Didn't realize that people had to take out a permit to live in Ewerton . . . get their heads examined, maybe, but *permission*—I dunno—"

"Palmer, I know you have to defend them because of Brent, but facts are facts." Stubbornly grinding down fragile June bugs, thin mouth sucked across crooked but still original teeth, Winston jabbed his friend lightly in the chest with a yellow-nailed finger. "That girl caused nothing but trouble. Couldn't catch on that people have a *place* in a town like this, be they born here or come here later—"

"*Oh?* Welcome to India . . . wait a second, and I'll go

rustle up a sacred cow, so you can shine it like you and Una used to shine those deer—''

"That's right, change the subject . . . you *know* what hard feelings that girl caused—didn't know enough to keep a low profile until she *settled in*—''

"Yeah, like settled down six feet un—''

"—wanted the *moon* right off, and for no good reason—''

"She's *smart*, Win . . . isn't that reason enough?''

"So? There's smart, and *then* there's smart enough not to *show* it. She didn't realize that kids born here had certain things coming to 'em because of their parents. They had a *momentum* going, like inheriting a family *name*, Nemmitz, involving *tradition* and *rights*. I'm sorry if you and your nephew's wife don't like it, but that's how it is. Hell, *you* know that from when *we* were kids. It *mattered* who our folks were, and *you know it*.''

Pausing to draw a deep breath of popcorn and sweat-scented air, Winston fished in his jacket pocket for a fresh smoke, while Nemmitz regarded him with pursed lips and delicately fluttering nostrils. Finally, he said, "If attending college on your precious GI Bill made everyone as asinine as you are, I'm proud to be an uneducated idiot.''

Palmer pushed his hat over his face, almost covering his eyes, staring through the narrow slit at the desultory crowd of people filling the avenue. Palmer was used to seeing the same people do the same slow shuffle down the avenue . . . during working hours, no less. Winston *was* partly right, for reasons that were definitely wrong. Zoe Lawton shouldn't have been part of this town; it was clear to Palmer that Zoe had potential (potential for *what* he was afraid to ask himself), while Ewerton had none.

"—Una *tried* sending that girl to the lower classes, so she'd get a sense of *place*, but it didn't work. Bounced right back up to Una's class. Una did her best to show the other students that that girl was no good, but Una couldn't get it through to those new pup teachers. *They* encouraged her, got her those scholarships, left the *town* kids in the cold—''

"Too bad most Ewerton kids aren't smart enough to hack it in college and become teachers like you did . . . what with all that 'interest' built up for them so they can succeed—''

"*That is beside the point!*" People halted in midstroll to stare at the pair of coots on the bench, but most remembered how Mr. Winston used to be in school, considered the source, and went back to nonshopping.

Once no more eyes regarded him critically, Winston continued in a cigarette-hoarse drone, "Once these teachers saw how 'bright' little Miss *Lawton* was, how she was outdoing her classmates, it was 'Zoe-*this*' and 'Zoe-*that*' and Una did her best to undo the damage, but the low grades she gave Zoe didn't help. Still graduated top ten. Una *bawled* when she read it in the paper. After what that little twit did to Una, complaining to the *school board* about how Una wasn't teaching history, but 'bragging' about how she and I used to go deer shining—as if it was any of the girl's *business*. Most of the kids were tickled pink to have a breather from the books . . . *you* wouldn't know about that, but *I* enjoyed the chance to lay my pencil down once in a while when *I* attended EHS—"

Stung, because Winston breached a taboo subject (Palmer's lack of a formal high-school education), Palmer tuned out the monotonous yet angry drone of his supposed best friend's voice. He was so intent on ripping apart a girl whose biggest "fault" was that she wouldn't let her English teacher slip his hand down her blouse for extra credit she didn't *need*. But when Palmer Nemmitz withdrew into his own thoughts, they, too, were of Zoe. . . .

As much as it pained him to admit it, Palmer was as unhappy to see Zoe and Brent return to Ewerton as Winston claimed to be. Not that *he* hated the girl; when she was living in town with her parents, Nemmitz hadn't even *seen* her up close, just a glimpse or two of her grainy image in Una's yearbook (a photo jabbed and scratched at with Una's pointed nails—"*That's* the one I was telling you and Bitsy about— pure trouble from the word *go*!''), before the annual was slammed shut with such vigor that Palmer wondered if Una was trying to keep the girl's image from escaping the confines of the page.

Palmer wasn't aware that Zoe had gone to college on scholarships until Bitsy finally told *him* that *Una* told *her* all about it (oddly, the *Ewerton Herald* never mentioned Zoe or her scholarships, most likely "losing" the news when putting together the final galleys . . . just as the drunk driving convictions of Ewerton's finest never appeared in newsprint). Bitsy had waited to tell him about it because the strident tones and harsh words her cousin used in regard to Zoe had upset

Bitsy terribly. At *that* point, even Una's faithful cousin Bitsy realized that Una was, indeed, losing it.

No, if anything (considering how much he disliked the woman his best friend had married when he'd come home from the Occupation Army in Japan in '46), all the things Una, and later Winston, said about Zoe should've made Palmer completely *adore* the girl, or at least feel sorry for her.

Yet, when he saw the wedding picture that Brent had sent to him (Bitsy was nursing a summer cold that August of six years ago; besides, Palmer didn't like attending weddings anyhow), he had felt such a chill, a sensation of reasonless *dread*, that he had purposely avoided any contact with the girl, and consequently all but ignored Brent as well.

What haunted Palmer most was that there was nothing *wrong* with the way Zoe looked, aside from that turned-out left eye . . . not that she was *wall*-eyed. Her pupil was just a tad off-center, so that her eyes appeared slightly out-of-sync. As if she was and wasn't looking at you, at the same time. But thinking about Zoe, as he had stared at the black-and-white studio photo with the artful soft-focus edges, which Brent sent special delivery, made Palmer feel like a dog with its forepaw in a trap. The only way out was to chew himself free. He was caught—stay in the old rusty trap, feel it twist and bite into his flesh, or gnaw his way painfully free, in all probability causing even *more* pain in order to win his freedom.

Staring at that low-gloss eight by ten, Palmer both wished and didn't wish it was in color—if it was, then he would've known, for *sure*, if her oddly set eyes were a *certain* color, and if her long wavy hair was really the color he prayed it wasn't. But what if her eyes *were* a concentric mix of pale brown bleeding into an outer ring of blue? And what if that glossy hair *was* a mix of soft taffy with gold and red and light brown threads woven in? There was no reason on earth why such a combination of eyes and hair couldn't happen again. Just as long as the person having those eyes, that hair, didn't look like . . . *her*.

Not Zoe, but . . . *her*, the *first* woman he'd seen, so many, *many* years ago, who resembled Zoe. Not that *her* face, with all its subtle differences, had been forgotten, or dulled by the passage of years. If Zoe had *truly* looked like *her*, Palmer would've known, would've cast aside the photograph in fear and loathing.

But only the eyes and hair seemed like *hers*; the rest of Zoe's face was and wasn't the same. Different, yet alike. Look here, look there, list the changes. What's missing, what's added. Yet, that very *difference* itself was maddening, tempting. . . .

But Palmer Nemmitz knew that dead women bear no children. And there was no way on earth that *she* could come back, could be young again. Yet, Zoe Lawton, who Brent **had** met and married (an irony, to be certain—Shirl had left Ewerton long ago, raised his son under a different name, taken pains not to have a "Ewertonian" son, yet said son fell for a girl raised *in* Ewerton), she too had those very eyes, **and** quite possibly the same hair.

A selective haunting . . . Look at me, my eyes, my hair, the hair you so wanted to touch, to feel sliding soft over splayed fingers . . . *look* at them, on a new owner. One you can *never* have, as you couldn't *ever* have me. . . .

From Palmer Nemmitz's journal
Hands. Opening, flowerlike, small fingers, small pink petals uncurling, only fast, like when a camera on one of those nature programs speeds up things meant to go slow. Her hands, that's how they opened, oh, dear God, wherever He was hiding that night—

Nemmitz pressed a set of shaking fingers to dry lips, watched people milling about tables of discount merchandise like flies around steaming dog stool, telling himself that some women were not *born* to wear shorts, before something Winston said penetrated his self-imposed isolation:

"—Una *died* with Zoe's name on her lips."

True. Lenny Wilkes, the county coroner, as well as part-time ambulance driver and owner of the garish bowling alley/arcade/video rental place out on county trunk QV, had told Palmer Nemmitz and Dead Fred Ferger all about Una Sawyer Winston's last night on earth over a couple of Buds at the Rusty Hinge Bar. And for once, Lenny's eternal refrain "I never seen nothing *like* it" was an *understatement*.

Lenny, Scooter Andersen, and Wayne Mesabi had sped in the ambulance to the converted house-into-apartments on Myrtle Avenue where the Winstons lived, in answer to the frantic call on 911.

And Lenny, Scooter, and Wayne had to have the front-of-the-house Komminskis' help to fit the stretcher into the Winstons' narrow back-of-the-house entry hall. What they all saw when the door was opened made Larry Komminski drag his wife Maureen away *before* she saw .. and got sick, as Larry soon was, all over the back lawn of the house.

"It was *real* bad, I personally never seen *nothing* like it, and I hope I don't again," Lenny had said, slurping down his sweated glass of beer. Beads of perspiration glistened in the stiff, waxed hairs of his crew cut, an echo of the moisture on his glass. "It was worse than old Gayleen Winston, and *that* wasn't no picnic. Una's face was like a wine grape, kind you see on a jelly-jar label. All swole up, too, like the blood had nowheres to go but kept on coming. We all knew she was a goner, but she was still *talking* . . . even bein' all puffed up. Layin' on the floor, drummin' the carpet with her heels and hands. Poor Winston looked like he'd just seen I don't *know* what. First time since I knowed him he didn't have no snappy comment on the proceedings. *He* had to be led away. Gettin' *her* on the gurney was a bitch plus two spare teats. Kicked and flailed like a tiger stuck in a birdcage. Ripped two straps off the stretcher, raked up Scooter's arms something bad. He got a fresh tetanus, just in case." Another noisy slurp of Bud, followed by a resonating burp.

"At first, we didden even notice what she was *sayin'*—thought it was just screaming crazylike, but then I made out what she was sayin' and let me tell you, it give me a *turn*. She was yellin' something 'bout a 'wall-eyed' whahoozis come to get her, mixed in with something about a *'dolly'* that seemed kinda awful, if you can imagine a doll being bad.

"And *then*, when she was finally on the gurney—most of her, anyhow—and down that narrow hallway . . . why they cut houses up like that *I* don't know—her voice goes from kinda slushy to pretty clear, and she says, 'That Lawton bitch, it's *her*, it's *her* . . . *her*, she's the one—*Zoe*!' ending real high and warbly. Poor Winston, he's dead quiet. Eyes real big like you seen 'em get, and Scooter had to take Winston's cigarette—somehow he lit one while we was there—out of his hand 'cause it was burnin' the old guy's knuckles. Oh, it was just *real* bad, guys.

"Hey, Nemmitz, I heard that your nephew *married* Zoe . . . I was just wonderin', uh . . . I mean, it was like Una was *seein'* Zoe right before her eyes, and after she said that

about Zoe, her face got all black and then her eyes . . . they
like sorta fell *in*—''

Over his beer, Nemmitz had replied, ''No. They haven't
been out of the Cities in quite a while.'' Dead Fred had been
all eyes and ears, nursing his beer between the other two men
in the back booth.

''Oh, no, Palmer, not to insinuate that Zoe *done* it . . .
but, uh, maybe she could've been in town *that* day, or called,
or—''

Or—The question had been there, in Lenny's moist bovine
eyes, and it was there in Dead Fred's pale blue ones . . . *did*
Zoe do *something* to Una, finally driving the last nail into the
coffin of the old woman's already dying mind? Impossible.
Zoe had wisely put a *lot* of distance between herself and good
old Ewerton. Brent wrote that proverbial wild horses couldn't
drag Zoe back.

Yet . . . here she was, back in town. Under Palmer's roof.
Zoe, with those light-brown-shading-into-blue eyes, and that
glimmers-of-many-colors hair. Alike . . . and *not* alike.

Like sisters. Like cousins, maybe. Palmer had purposely
asked about her parents after Zoe's arrival, when he left the
house in what he'd hoped only seemed like a *huff*. He learned
to his satisfaction and disquiet that Zoe's parents looked very
little like her, being thin, darkly colored people—yet they
were her parents, no secret adoption going on. Even Winston,
who had met them, was sure that the now-deceased Lawtons
were Zoe's folks. So, alike, yet different. . . .

Why Winston hated her, Palmer could understand. The Una
business, both in and out of school. The lost job, the pur-
pling, flighting death. Granted, her own imagination had
killed Una, not the living presence of the girl she had so
ardently and unreasonably hated, but *still*. . . .

Suddenly, Winston's dry rasp was directed at him. ''If I
were you, I'd give that little scut her walking papers, and that
a-hole nephew, too. Damn fool didn't know better than to
marry that out-of-town garbage—''

Leaning in close for the second time that evening, Palmer
whispered to Winston, ''If that 'out-of-town garbage' had let
you sharpen your *pencil* in her, you'd be singing a different
song, no?''

Winston found something different to talk about.

TWO

Brent Nimitz missed the left-hand turn where Ewert Avenue met Lumbermill Drive, and wound up taking a detour through what Aunt Bitsy called the "trashy" section of town; the cluster of streets near the Ewerton dump, southeast of town, lined with mostly darkened houses that exuded despair like a runner's sweat after a marathon.

Curling and uncurling his fingers on the wheel, Brent relived the events of the past few days, which had brought Zoe and himself back to Ewerton.

Monday, the twenty-seventh. He and Zoe were pink-slipped onto the Job Service Go Round; the literary arts magazine where he had been the art director and Zoe served as editorial assistant went belly-up, thanks to the government not renewing its grant.

Upon returning to their apartment that afternoon, they found a form letter in the mailbox; a cheery "Dear Tenant" notice informing them that the building was going co-op. Fifty thou for a bedroom and a bath and a half. On their two sudden non-paychecks. Zoe cried; Brent pretended he didn't need to.

After a long, nearly catatonic silence, Zoe abruptly perked up, asking where her *invitation* was. He was no less puzzled by her request after she explained that she meant her high-school reunion invitation. The one she'd torn up and flushed upon receipt in May.

She *had* kept the postcard her Class of 1978 secretary had sent, the one that urged Zoe to return her RSVP invitation.

Brent assumed that Zoe thought she wanted to attend the damned reunion because of the day's upsets, so he'd humored her, going so far as to call long distance to Ewerton, to ask Uncle Palmer if his long-standing invitation to summer at the farmhouse was still good . . . all the while wishing the old couple would rescind the invitation.

No such luck. Bitsy bubbled, she couldn't *wait* to meet Zoe. The next morning, they gave notice to the landlord, packed what they could into the Pacer, bought Duffy a traveling cage, stored what furniture hadn't come with the apartment in a friend's garage, and took off for Wisconsin, driving the two hundred-plus miles in under four hours. Zoe held the postcard from her former classmate in her fingers like a holy picture, not even letting go of it when she dozed off.

Zoe's gung-ho attitude seemed to wear off when they pulled into the city; she'd wrinkled her nose, saying, "My God, Brent, the place is *shrinking*—the population was larger than this ten years ago," as they passed the wooden sign on county trunk QV welcoming them to Ewerton. It was as if Zoe had been released from that mental coma and realized that she was someplace she had no *reason* to be—but being stubborn Zoe, she wasn't going to give Brent the satisfaction of knowing she'd made a mistake by coming "home." She *almost* cracked when Palmer gave her the cold shoulder, but by Wednesday morning, she was together enough to come into town with Brent.

Oddly, even though Brent's father was born in town, into a family area-born for generations, Brent was a stranger in Ewerton, while Zoe, daughter of consummate out of towners, had spent twelve years of her life here.

Twelve years. The first eight of them she was overlooked by many; Zoe was shy—aloof to those who misread her—but she'd coasted along, causing few ripples in the stream of the Ewerton school system. She was an only child, and her parents were company enough when the birthday party invitations didn't come, or when the other children grouped after school. to play. Good grades, a bookworm, with none of the highly prized athletic ability that was a desired trait in small-town schools. Passed over, not actually *shunned*. But everything changed come high school, for Zoe captured the automatic and lasting wrath of Mrs. Winston.

And for four years, Ewerton High School was Ewerton *Hell* School for Zoe; seemingly overnight, Una Winston changed Zoe's status in the already brutal caste system of high-school life—no longer simply overlooked, Zoe became the school mascot. As in goat.

Zoe had explained it to Brent over lunch weeks ago. Una Winston fervently believed in the "good ol' kids" system. Una's practice of grade inflating and deflating was long established by the time Zoe reached EHS . . . but when it came to Zoe, Una's smear campaign backfired, and the other teachers (save for her husband) tried to compensate—

"One of the teachers tried to get me a date for the prom, I'd never gone to any of them, but old Una-Pruna scared off any boy from taking me. . . ."

When pressed by Brent, Zoe elaborated partially—and in an unexpected way. Spooning up the last of her Yoplait, Zoe had said, eyes lowered and unreadable, "It was the beginning of my freshman year . . . during lunch I was outside, doing my usual solo stroll after eating, and from all over came, oh, ten or twelve of my classmates, mostly affluent twits of the year. All from my history class. Una-Pruna's class.

"They surrounded me, wouldn't let me pass. One chosen as speaker by the rest of the harpies asked me . . . if *I* . . . I . . . if I was *queer*, because 'if you are, we *have* to know . . . we have to take *showers* with you in gym, y'know.' Blood-sucking little bitches . . . as if it was a life-or-death matter, me not dating or not. I wouldn't answer them, and they only left when lunch was over—"

Midway down Roberts Street, Brent had to pull over, stop the car; unshed tears in his eyes made his vision too wavering for safe driving.

Not that it would've bothered him to hit and squash one of Ewerton's *non*-animal denizens.

Just *thinking* about that long-ago confrontation made Brent feel ill. The Papa Burger, box of popcorn, and slushy cone he'd consumed shifted and burned in his stomach. And he hadn't *been* there, impaled by ten or twelve sets of eyes, like a dying butterfly on black paper. Sitting in the Pacer, knuckling back tears, he remembered asking Zoe what she'd done *afterward*; how she'd faced those monsters without succumbing to the urge to drop her panties and get it on with some initially reluctant but ultimately willing dork, just to prove the bitches wrong.

Putting aside her Yoplait carton, Zoe had told him another story, of something she witnessed not very long after the lunch episode. Ironically, considering the concerns of her classmates, it happened in the shower room . . . and, as an added twist, it involved the girl who'd acted as spokes-creep for the others, as well as another girl from that ring of hate that had surrounded Zoe.

Brent's face still colored and warmed when he remembered .Zoe's matter-of-fact, slightly *gleeful* recounting of the inci-

dent. Leaning against the thickly padded car seat, he wondered if the lunchtime interrogation and the shower-room
peep show later on had anything to do with Una Winston—
for Zoe had been careful to note that the accusing girls all
came from her history class. Or if not that, perhaps it all tied
in with Zoe wanting to attend that blasted reunion. After what
had happened to Zoe, Brent couldn't imagine her *wanting* to
come back for the sake of coming back. Especially in their
jobless and homeless straits. When they were employed, they
weren't rich enough for Zoe to rub people's noses in it over
chicken and ham at the Hole-in-One Club come July.

Starting the Pacer's engines, Brent continued down long
and slightly winding Roberts Street, looking for any "For
Sale" or 'For Rent'' signs in front of the double row of elegantly decayed Queen Anne and Italianate homes lining the
street. The headlights picked up at least a dozen or more
metal signs in various stages of wear (including two designs—
one rusted, one streamlined and new—for the same realtor)
mushrooming on front lawns. If he and Zoe were staying in
town until her stupid reunion, they couldn't live with his aunt
and uncle for almost a *month*, especially the way Palmer was
acting so strangely around Zoe.

Slowing the car to a crawl, Brent peered up at likely pros-
pects.

THREE

9:16 P.M.

Palmer Nemmitz grew tired of Winston's lamentations, so he
got up, dusted off his trouser seat, and took off on a stroll.

Bitsy's bake sale wasn't due to shut down until ten, so he
was stuck. *Should've caged a ride with Brent and the bird,*
he thought, unobtrusively dodging the Happy Wanderer, as
those less tactful members of the town chose to call Ewerton's
most visible mentally deprived individual, who shambled
down the center of the sidewalk, humming and smiling to
himself. And stuffing his face with something chocolate and
melting, as well. At least the Wanderer was already supplied
with food tonight—usually he grabbed whatever he saw out

in the open, be it a kid's half-licked sucker, or something ant-encrusted on the sidewalk. Palmer pretended not to notice the round-faced, shaggy-haired Wanderer (he resembled a hyperthyroidal Rambo in his Army-surplus camouflage jacket, pants, and headband), and ignored the man's nod and brown-stained smile.

As Palmer passed by, favoring his bad knee, he watched his reflection glide beside him, air-swimming in a wavery, flattened world, first in the large windows of the Farmer's Co-op (which was, long ago, the site of the Founder's Bank of Ewerton, where Dead Fred's father tried to blow out his meager share of brains after the Crash of '29, but instead fashioned a circular window between his office and the wash-room next door). Next came the display window of the former Ladies' Room Boutique, which, decades before, had been Holiday's Grocery Store, which fed most of Ewerton when Palmer was barely tall enough to grasp and turn the brass door handle.

Stopping, Palmer watched June bugs flitter against the cool, clear surface of the greenish-tinted window, no longer paying attention to the abandoned bodies of the dismantled manne-quins with the chipped complexions and missing fingers, but instead seeing—through the totally clear glass of his mind—the interior of the Holiday store as it had been, as it still should be. Walls lined with jewel-bright canned goods and catsup bottles, pickle barrel tart spicy and full, and the saw-dust heaped fine-grained and fragrant behind the counter, bits of it tracked onto the hardwood floor when old man Holiday (Wilbur was so dubbed when still comparatively young) stepped out to get something off a high shelf for a customer. The air fragrant and slightly intoxicating, and cool in places, where the freezer stood, filled with bottles of soda, or Pop-sicles so frozen they felt cold like wet silk when you bit into them, sort of *meshing* between the molars. Not a plastic and cardboard scented store, like the IGA and other supermar-kets.

Bitsy thought Palmer crazy for mooning over the way the old grocery story used to *smell*; over more than one low-fat breakfast, she'd said, "Palmer, I should throw you in a time machine, shut the door, and set the dial for never-never land. You can't buck the tide. World's progressing whether you give it permission to or not."

Palmer walked past the old Montgomery Ward's catalog

outlet, the inside of the window black-papered with sheets of Monkey Ward's logo wrap, which created a deeply reflective, mirrorlike surface. In this ersatz mirror, Palmer saw almost perfect reflections of everything to his left: the strolling crowd, the opposite storefronts, the popcorn stand, the backward-lettered street signs, the pale oval of the woman's unsmiling face, her eyes locked on *him*. . . .

Stopping in midstride, Palmer held his breath until it pained his lungs; he was afraid to expel it for fear of not being *able* to take another breath. At first, he told himself it was only a shadow under the face, and the face itself was a reflection of a street lamp's globe . . . but the bit of darkness against the vertical wood siding of the Happy Step Shoe Store sign *spread*, clinging to the wall like a fragment of nightmare blown free of a sleeping mind. And the darkness-deeper-than-blackness became a definite shape, a certain form. . . .

Out of sheer agony Palmer exhaled, to stand fish-mouthed, his back to the dark vision across the street, unable to turn around and face her—for the simple reason of fearing that she would *really* be there. Better for her to be an image, trapped in the jet surface of the window before him.

Unnoticed by the people passing across the street, the dark shape crossed lower limbs of darkness that stood rooted in a slice of shadow, and raised just *one* flutter of hand to the smooth curve of cheek, pushing aside hair that fell long and finely waving to shoulders of ebony shadow. Something bright yet dark twinkled near her wrist, a wink in Palmer's direction, and he told himself, *Jet buttons . . . she had jet buttons at her wrist, her pocket flaps . . . oh, yes, how I remember . . . .*

From Palmer Nemmitz's journal—
No, that's not the way to put it down . . . not that part, not *yet*. But still, she deserves something more than a "he said," "she said," "I did" retelling of what happened. Not artsy-smartsy, like Winston might write. Oh, no, not for her. But she deserves something pretty, yet as full of horror (and awe) as she was herself. Seems as if she deserves more, or that I at least owe her—and her memory—more than lip service.

The darkness of her clothing, her stockings, her shoes, made her blend into the wall, the shadows, leaving her head and right hand to hover, seemingly unsupported in the cooling darkness. Even from a distance, he saw the glimmer in her hair where the moonlight and the street lamp's glow touched it. Hair such as hers he hadn't touched in many a year. Unable to stop himself, he ran a twisted fingertip along the reflection of her hair, and made a wet, strangled sound in his throat when she moved her hand as if to touch *his* hand. Faintly, he saw the slight breeze made the hem of her suit skirt flutter around her knees. With each breath her entire body rose and fell, as if taking in all of the night with each inhalation.

Rubbing his knuckles across chapped, cold lips, Palmer felt an intense itching-burning-*gnawing* sensation in his right forearm, a feeling abrupt in its intensity, yet teasingly *familiar*. Under the thin cotton of his shirtsleeve, Palmer felt the flow of blood begin . . . without needing to roll up his sleeve, he knew what the wound would look like. As if he ever thought that he'd be able to forget *that* wound. Or the one who made it.

From Palmer Nemmitz's journal—
Yet, Lord help me, it is not an easy thing to approach; the paths to the end are many, some plain, some so oblique I didn't see them for the paths they were until much, much later. When it was too late.

The only trouble is, it was so complex, but simple-seeming on the outside, and I was only sixteen when it happened. Fifteen *going* on sixteen to tell the truth, the age when it seems to hurt all the more, merely because a body hasn't become tough enough on the outside to shield the little child within. There's nothing more silly than a fifteen-going-on-sixteen child.

Opening his hand, caressing his cheek with the palm (friction between his hard dry palm and stubble-covered cheek produced a faint rasp), Palmer closed his eyes, trying to hide in a cave of inner darkness . . . but the image his memory chose to train onto the empty screen of his eyelids forced him to open his eyes once more.

She hadn't moved. Was still *looking* at him, as he told himself, *Steady, it's not her . . . . not* her *at all. Can't be her . . . no way, no how . . . no . . . oh, God,* no, *period. Take a closer look . . .* of course. *Should've known the girl would*

*play a trick on me for acting as I did when she and Brent
arrived at the house . . . you know yourself how Zoe looks
like her . . . Zoe's out there, playing a trick on you, you old
fool. She found that damn fool thing I wrote, she read it and
figured she'd get even with me for acting so strange . . . damn
near killed me, oh, you pulled a good one, but old Palmer
don't fool easy, girlie.*

As if aware of his thoughts, his seeing through her ruse, the
woman (*Zoe, has to be Zoe*) detached herself from the surrounding darkness, and walked, right hand swinging slightly as she
moved, left side still lost in shadow, into a cul-de-sac between
the Happy Step and the bakery, to vanish in a pool of blackness.
Palmer wanted to hobble across the street to tell Zoe that her
joke was a good one, but that he hadn't *meant* to offend her, not
at all . . . just a case of heebie-jeebies, a reminder of someone
else altogether. He wanted to tell Zoe that Brent was already
heading back home, that he'd brought her a nice gift, but a
nagging inner voice stopped Palmer.

A soft, insinuating voice, unlike his own thoughts, which
reminded him that Zoe didn't bring along a black suit; she'd
unpacked while Bitsy was around, and Bitsy reported to
Palmer exactly what the girl had brought with her. She mentioned no black suit, with or without jet-button trim . . . and
the voice that uttered soft words of truth whispered that last
night Bitsy had trimmed Zoe's hair, had taken inches off until
it just reached to just a whisper below her firm chin. He'd
seen the severed locks in the kitchen trash when he'd scraped
his leftover Hamburger Helper casserole into the bag.

And the hair of the reflection-woman had been long, flowing to a point below her black-outlined shoulders.

Shaking, Palmer hurried away from the charcoal mirror as
best he could with his aching knee, down the street to the
bake sale set up on the opposite street corner, not daring to
cross the street just *yet*. Under his breath, he mumbled, not
caring who heard him, ''*She* didn't get her hair trimmed last
night, oh, God, *she* wouldn't go and cut off that pretty hair
of hers . . . she knew how much I liked it that way, knew all
along I wanted to touch it . . . and her. Not Zoe. Not Zoe
at all . . . wish it were, but it wasn't . . . oh, Jesus on a
sidecar, she *found* me . . . came back from who knows where
and *found* me . . . all fresh and young and pretty . . . she
found me . . . her with that pretty hair, those eyes . . . Jesus,
my arm hurts . . . *again*. . . .''

FOUR

One after another, Brent studied and rejected each of the old houses bearing realtor's signs along the street. Despite the dim, diffuse light, Brent saw major flaws in each house he studied, and the occupied homes weren't in much better shape. Not that they weren't reasonably attractive, charming even. Beautiful as they might have been, these old houses were now tottering oldsters, empty in spirit as well as in substance. Gingerbread broken and never replaced, porch roofs sagging with dry rot, shingles forming lost-tooth gaps on roofs and turrets.

Brent wondered why no one seemed to *care* about the loss of Ewerton's past glory—these homes built of lumber money and hope. He spotted no Historical Register brass plates affixed to front walls. And as the town's past rotted, the businessmen hurried to cover over what little beauty remained with ubiquitous rough vertical siding and overhanging big-shingled false roofs. Pity was, they thought they were doing the town *good*, making it "modern" and "progressive." As Bitsy yammered on and on, Ewerton would be a "metropolis" someday . . . even as the population gradually declined and the streets were filled at all hours with young, walking men.

Frowning, Brent inched the car forward . . . then stopped, silent, in front of a gap in the sidewalk that wound in a gray snaking line along the grassy lawns. Opening the door, Brent moved to the passenger seat, feet resting on the grass in front of the sidewalk-less dwelling. Staring up at the sage-green *hugeness* of the house, he was overcome by the wild proliferation of turrets, columns, gables, gingerbread, curves, spindles, and multipaned windows topped with a widow's walk and massive chimney.

The Holiday house, three stories plus full attic, the biggest single-family dwelling in town . . . and no doubt the most expensive. Empty, silent, and—despite the froo-froos and patterned-glass windows—undeniably *masculine*. The house was empty, had been since old man Holiday died inside, a couple of years back. (Palmer had called Brent the day it happened, curiously choked up.) Yet it was as if the old man had never died—had never gone away, but sat waiting, lonely and alone, somewhere in that monstrous edifice, hoping that someone would drop in. Looking up at the house, Brent remembered seeing the house gussied up for the Fourth of July. Even now, the sight was so clear, so strong, despite the twenty years and more that had passed.

Brent had been hanging out with some local kids, their names lost to him, his head summer-scalped by Dad before they made the trip up here, so that Brent's ears stuck out like Dopey's in that dumb cartoon. And in the heat that shimmered up from the bowels of the earth, right through the sidewalk and the soles of his Keds, Brent and the other boys aimlessly strolled the streets, heading for the cool—if slightly scummy and stagnant—waters of Crescent Lake . . . until they passed the Holiday house. It was entirely draped in red, white, and blue bunting, each shade blindingly bright in the sunshine. Old man Holiday himself was on the porch, winding tricolor crepe paper around a thick porch column.

While Holiday wasn't stooped, balding, liver-spotted, saggy-jowled, or any of the things that boys Brent's age usually associated with decrepit old age and mean-old-man-ness (Brent figured that if he'd seen Holiday in '65, Holiday must've been close to seventy-seven, since Uncle Palmer mentioned yesterday that February 28 would have marked Holiday's centennial birthday), there was something about him that Brent found scary, strange. With his uncut, down-to-the-collar hair—which still retained a hint of brittle gold here and there, a memory of its former blondness—deeply bloodshot green eyes, and craggy, chiseled face, the old guy looked *unreal*, untamed by the passage of time and life.

The boys stared at Holiday a second too long, for he suddenly dropped his roll of crepe paper and, pointing a finger at Brent, yelled in a harsh, strong voice, "You! Bald kid . . . you Shirley Nemmitz's boy?" As his newfound friends giggled over his dad's *"girlie"* name, Brent yelled back, redfaced, "He changed it to Ni-*metz*, sir," and tried to run off, but the old geezer was already off the porch and coming for Brent, hand out at Brent's shoulder level, ready to grab him before he joined the others as they pounded down the street.

Then the hand with the yellowed, ridged nails was on his shoulder (Brent smelled a ropelike, funny odor, mixed in

with Ben Gay and musty clothes), digging in with strong
fingers. He realized in his fear that the old man was *talking*
to him, saying, ''—your Uncle Palmer that Treeva is all right,
tell him not to go worrying and getting all flummoxed about
her, she really is A-okay. Told me so herself . . . so you just
tell your uncle that, all right?''

Without waiting for a reply, Holiday let go of Brent. Holiday
briskly walked back to his porch, roll of tricolor paper in hand,
the long unwound tail of it fluttering behind him.

Brent shivered, even though the breeze was a warm one.
His Grandma Treeva was dead, ever since 1938. Old man
Holiday *should've* known that . . . after all, Treeva Nemmitz
died right in that very bunting-swathed house. Dad told Brent
that Mrs. Holiday cried and cried at the funeral, and bought
the blanket of yellow roses for the coffin herself . . . so
Mr. Holiday *had* to know Treeva was dead. If she really *was*
okay, wherever she was, it would've made more sense if
Mrs. Holiday came out and told Brent the good news, since
she took the death of her friend so hard.

Brent had mulled over the old man's words as he walked
away; it wasn't as if he'd *promised* to deliver the message. He
hadn't said anything after Holiday grabbed him. And the old
coot *was* strange, everybody said so—Mom, Dad, Aunt Bitsy
(Uncle Palmer was uncommunicative on the subject), and
Brent knew as well as anyone in the Nemmitz-Nimitz clan
that Uncle Palmer was a real swell guy, *unless* he got mad.
His temper, when goaded to a boil, was a sneaky thing, like
a bear trap open and waiting on a forest floor, hidden by
fallen leaves . . . one misstep and *bam!* So Brent never re-
layed the message about Treeva.

Now, sitting in the car tonight, feet touching almost the exact
spot where he and Holiday had stood, Brent remembered that
the old man had died in winter, alone in a cold house, lying on
a floor all frosty and stiff, a regular feast for the gossip-starved,
as Bitsy mentioned to him during a Christmas phone call last
year. Brent was only mildly surprised that the death wasn't labeled a suicide, which it may well have been. But then Holiday
was a Holiday, and married to a Crescent to boot. Local bigwigs
never committed something as base as *suicide* . . . ''accidental
shooting of the mouth,'' or ''accidental leaving-on of the gas in
an airtight room'' perhaps.

Feeling a small, sharp pang of guilt for never relaying Holiday's message to his uncle (*what the hell, might've been a*

code for *"let's have a beer at the Rusty Hinge," some harm-less shit*), Brent made up his mind to tell Palmer about that day, and the old gent's cryptic message . . . only *later*, over a glass of beer, right before he and Zoe and the cat left this sinkhole of a town.

FIVE

9:52 P.M.

Simultaneously taking a deep drag of his cigarette and splin-tering a June bug under his heel, Winston peered intently at his strolling friend Palmer Nemmitz, who seemed more in-terested in reflections in store windows than in keeping track of where he was going. Twice people had jostled into Palmer, almost knocking him down.

Winston wished Dead Fred were sitting next to him, just so he'd have someone with whom to hash over Palmer's odd behavior, but no one lingered near EHS's former "Teacher of the Year" longer than necessary. All Winston could do was watch his Lucky Strike ash into nothingness between fingers already burn-scarred, and slowly shake his head over Palmer's halting progress down the avenue.

Perhaps Winston should've followed his life-long friend; thirty or forty years earlier he *would* have—nearly fifty years before he *had* followed Palmer Nemmitz, literally for *miles*. In retrospect, that trip had only served to take Winston fur-ther away from Palmer than Winston had ever imagined was possible—but something told Winston that it was just plain foolish to go running after his friend every time Palmer was in danger of stubbing his toe on a raised bit of sidewalk.

In boyhood, Winston had dogged his best friend (Nemmitz was Winston's senior by a scant week) with a boyish mixture of love and trust and implicit faith that seemed at the time as if it were to be a lasting thing. With a snort, Winston re-minded himself that the damned war had changed everything between them, even as a *deeper* memory hinted that the sub-tle rift between them started shortly before the war, during a summer not unlike *this* summer.

The summer that Palmer Nemmitz ran away from home,

went south, stayed awhile . . . and trudged home, never to be the same person. But before that homecoming, Winston had followed Palmer, a tongue-lolling puppy after his friend, thinking that finding Nemmitz would make it all right again.

"Stupid fool," Winston said out loud, speaking for himself and for his wandering friend. Palmer was now inching across the street, close to Bitsy's bake sale, his eyes glued to the store windows. Why he didn't walk on the *other* side—it was obvious that he was looking *for* or *at* something on the opposite side of Ewert Avenue—was beyond Winston. But judging from his friend's halting steps, and tightly pulled-back shoulders, Nemmitz wasn't up to crossing that street. To anyone else milling around tonight, Nemmitz's gait may have looked only careful, and slow, but without having to see the man's face, Winston realized that his friend was *afraid*. Of what, he wasn't certain, but Winston guessed that it was on the other side of the avenue . . . only Winston saw nothing remotely frightening when he glanced that way.

Turning his attention back to Nemmitz, Winston was in time to see the small, neat man lift his head, turn it toward the little alley between the shoe store and the bakery, take a deep, nostril-quivering breath of night air, and, with aching slowness, gracefully *crumple* at the knees, deflating within his baggy clothes into a cotton and chino heap on the sidewalk.

Bitsy's screech was chalk gone wrong on a blackboard, all high notes with no sign of bottoming out. Winston's lips clamped down hard on his cigarette, the filter mashed to a flattened oval between his crooked teeth. People hurried over to Nemmitz, a murmur of voices trailing after them like exhaust issuing from a moving car. As he got to his feet and made his way to his friend, an incongruous thought passed through Winston's mind: *If only I knew what happened to him that summer, when he rabbited out of town . . . things would be the way they used to be between us again. . . .*

SIX

The honking car horn brought Brent out of his reverie; he looked around in time to see the blond woman driving the overloaded Ford station wagon wave as she sped past, and raised a hand in return before he linked a name with the face.

Sliding back behind the wheel, slamming the door, and starting the engine, Brent finally remembered her name: Sarah Andersen, the one who stood up at his wedding to Zoe, as one of her bridesmaids. He hadn't seen Sarah for six years, until yesterday, outside the IGA. He and Zoe had been on their way in, while Sarah and her brood of preschoolers were heading out. They'd all stopped in the narrow glassed-in entryway while Sarah pestered them with questions about them being back in town.

Unlike some of the other people who'd known Zoe whom they'd run into that day, Sarah seemed genuinely friendly.

On their way home yesterday, Brent mentioned to Zoe that Sarah seemed to be a nice woman and casually added that maybe the two women should spend some time together.

Zoe had shook her head wistfully, saying, "She only thinks she likes me because she doesn't really *know* me." Nothing Brent said afterward could shake her mood; as he now made the right-hand turn down Byrne Avenue that would lead him to the unnamed county trunk road, and home to Zoe, Brent reached over and patted the head of the Opus-Pathfinder toy, hoping it would bring Zoe out of her funk.

SEVEN

10:00 P.M.

Nemmitz kept protesting, "I'm all right, Lemme alone . . . just hot's all that's wrong," as strong arms lifted him to his feet, and Winston stood there staring at him from behind a scudding haze of cigarette smoke, his blue eyes gone round and glassy. Palmer found it hard to stand upright when unsupported, and let out only the mildest of protests when Bitsy propelled him to their Nash Rambler.

As Palmer shuffled along beside Bitsy, he kept snorting, trying to get the *smell* out of his nose, but the heady scent of mingled roses and jasmine and the subtle undercurrent of fresh blood lingered. Getting into the Nash, and slumping against the headrest, Palmer wasn't too worried about the blood odor. He knew where *that* was coming from; in the yellowish light of the car, he saw the faint double horseshoes of blood seeping through his right shirt-sleeve. But her *perfume* . . . it entered him with each ragged breath, lingering there, all around him. . . .

EIGHT

10:12 P.M.

Brent arrived at the Nemmitz farmhouse—an old-fashioned, white Prairie gingerbread-and-wraparound-front-porch style favored by advertisers of powdered lemonade drink mixes—parked the car in the cavernous garage-cum-barn, and quietly walked past the surrounding box elders and locusts to the porch steps, across the planked porch, and up to the spindle-decorated screen door, mindful that all the lights were out upstairs. Zoe must be sleeping.

The front door was unlocked, per usual (Brent told himself that *someday*, the wrong "neighbor" would drop in), and in the dim light of the table lamp that Bitsy never turned off, Duffy pranced about on the wool rug, mouth a pink maw as he cried out a greeting for his master.

As Brent shut the door behind him, Duffy stood up on his hind legs, raking the denim of Brent's jeans with dust-mop paws. Duffy was a gray long-hair, and Brent and Zoe always marveled over how well brushed he looked, almost too beautiful to be a tomcat. Brent thumbed some brownish gunk away from the corners of the cat's eyes, whispering, "Been coal mining again? Got coal dust in your eyes?"

Duffy smelled the catnip through the bag, so Brent extracted the box, ripping it open. "Shush, Duffy, don't wake Momma. C'mon, Daddy's bought you something good." He liberally sprinkled the dull green flakes and stems over the faded flowers on the rug. Duffy writhed and snorted the herb, tossing his belly-up body from side to side. Pausing a moment to tickle Duffy's tufted belly, Brent gathered up his goodie bag. He tiptoed up the stairs, wincing when he stepped on a creaker.

Ascending the stairs, Brent recalled the day when Palmer had told him that for several long years the Nemmitz family didn't even *use* this part of the house—after Treeva died, Enoch moved himself and the six children down to the basement . . . to *live*. He'd used already-tight money to put in a toilet, run extra power lines down, the works.

Of course, once Enoch volunteered for WWII (Palmer hinted that his father's action was a slap in the face at Palmer's 4-F status), Uncle Palmer, Winston, and their friends moved the family back upstairs, but it still puzzled Brent why anyone would move *down* there in the first place. Especially when the house above was so nice, and outfitted with running water and full power.

Standing in the dark hallway outside his bedroom door (the room had been his dad's when Shirl moved back upstairs) and listening for the sound of Zoe's breathing, Brent decided that it must've been the good old Czech mind-set; if you *have* it, you don't need to *look* at it.

Feeling around on the inner wall for the light switch with one hand, the Opus toy ready and waiting in the other, the bag at his feet, Brent whispered, "C'mon, Pathfinder, do your stuff—"

NINE

On the way to the hospital, Palmer gave a liquid snort, pinched both nostrils (*that* smell . . . *never smelled anything like it since her*—) and startled Bitsy by announcing, "You aren't taking *me* to no hospital . . . . just the heat, that's all." Still rattled, giving him an anxious look from behind oversize glasses with dipping bows that only accentuated her double chins, Bitsy replied, "Nonsense. You keeled over and the bank thermometer said it was only fifty-eight degrees. Cool enough, down twenty degrees from noon. Doc Calder's gonna look you over—"

"Clive doesn't work nights and you know it. Hasn't since that daughter of yours was at home. 'Sides, he might stick the depressor up my ass, to see if my tonsils are inflamed."

Arms tautly pushing out the fabric of her border-print blouse, Bitsy spun the wheel until the car stopped next to the corner. Her eyes wary yet kindly behind silly oversize frames, she asked, "Why *did* you faint?"

Glad that his hat shadowed his eyes just *enough*, he lied, "The old gut was rumblin' and Winston brought along *refreshments*, I took a few sips and—"

"Drinking on the *street*? After what Stu said to the City Council last week, how they're going to be vigilant, and enforce—"

"Bitsy, since when has your cousin Stuart the Sheriff ever gone after a *Winston*, huh? Or a Nemmitz? Sawyer sheriffs have looked the other way when it comes to certain folks doing whatnot for *years*—"

"But Stu said—"

"Stu says a lot he don't mean. And even if he does, you think his deputies or the goomers on the police force are gonna arrest someone who's their wife's cousin twice removed, or an in-law of their dad's second-cousin's uncle? Man's hands are tied, Bitsy. Besides, no one saw us."

Bitsy opened and closed her mouth quickly, before starting the Rambler and making a U-turn into town. Slumping down in his seat, hat almost tipped over his eyes, Palmer thought, *Too bad she was walking in* that *direction . . . if she'd been going the other way, I'd have known, been sure about it once and for all.*

TEN

10:18 P.M.

Pushing the stuffed Opus into the doorway, Brent found and clicked on the light switch, saying from where he stood in the hallway, "For *you*, madame, your *dream date* . . . smugglebunnies always welcome!" Puzzled by the lack of reaction, Brent assured himself that Zoe must have taken a sleeping pill . . . only *those* made her snore. Then, he looked in.

The bed was empty, still made, its quilt-covered surface marred only by Zoe's carelessly tossed halter top. Her shortie nightgown hung over the back of the desk chair, where she left it that morning. Telling himself that their mattress was, after all, too soft for Zoe's bad back, Brent—Opus still in hand, bag now tucked under his other arm—stepped softly up to the other bedroom doors, peering into the murk with dark-accustomed eyes, his way faintly lit from behind by the light spilling out of his empty room.

Spare bedroom, plastic on a bare mattress. No Zoe. Bitsy's room (she and Uncle Palmer were long past nights of sharing a bed) equally empty, the ruffle of her canopy hanging limp and pale in the eldritch light. Another room, next to Brent's, occupied solely by a covered sewing-machine table.

Last stop, Uncle Palmer's room. Faintly, Brent made out the spindled footboard, and behind the finely turned uprights a pair of bare feet splayed out in repose. Zoe's feet. Beyond them, almost melting into the blackness within, the twin mounds of her breasts, half rounds that caught the faint reflection of the distant bedroom light.

Cautiously feeling for the light switch, hoping that his uncle didn't have any geegaws hanging on the wall that might fall and shatter under his blind touch, Brent positioned Pathfinder in front of his face, like a three-dimensional tribal mask. In the moment before finding and flipping the switch, Brent intoned, "And now, Lad-*eeze* an Gentle*mon*, straight from Clausen's Hallmark and Gifte Shop*pee*, your very own dream lover! No hickies, pulh-*lease*!''

Brent saw the fuzzy outlines of the room from behind the stuffed toy; the desk topped with an ancient typewriter, the neat stacks of magazines, the quilt-topped bed, the tips of Zoe's fingers, and the reddish stains on the gaily printed pieces of the quilt. . . .

In the silence, it seemed as if every sound were magnified, huge. The crinkle of the torn bag as it slithered down his side and fell to the floor. The tiny, smacking sound as Brent's lips came together hard in fright, then slackly opened. And Brent imagined that he could still hear her blood, the gentle flow of it as it trickled down the long, fish-gill slashes on her forearms, but Zoe was so *white*, marble pale and so, so *still*— any blood that had flowed from her had stopped its meandering trickle hours ago.

ELEVEN

10:20 P.M.

Palmer hoped that Bitsy wouldn't notice him itching his forearm, wouldn't see his fingers scrambling the thin cloth, drawing blood as they scratched. If she did, it would mean another U-turn, and a drive over the bridge that swayed no matter what those lowlifes on the city crew said about the bridge being perfectly safe—even though the ambulance never used it.

As the car wound around the corner where Lumbermill Drive met Ewert Avenue, Bitsy asked, ''Mind if I stop back at the bake sale? I left my cake servers, and I better pick them up before they wind up on the kitchenwares table at the next church rummage sale. *You* know how Emma Clausen is. You name it, she'll squirrel it away until the next sale. Emma even put out a half-*used* tube of Preparation *H*—Palmer, you want me to pick up something for that arm of yours? No? Well, I hope it itches clear to the bone . . . person tries to help.''

Bitsy circled the car around until she was only a block's walk from the dismantling bake sale. As Bitsy drove, Palmer lowered himself farther into his seat, until only the tip of his fedora was visible, and his spine cried out for a *little* consideration.

From Palmer Nemmitz's journal—
Thinking on it now, if *hurt*, pain, ache, what-have-you, wasn't so smart, it would be constant, so a person could get used to it, and finally ignore it. Just get on with life after a spell. But, *being* smart, it lays low for a time, sometimes short, sometimes long. Let's you think it's gone, dead, finished, healed over. You start to breathe easy, relax.

Then it goes right for the nuts, talons clutching, crushing until you can't hardly *see*.

And pain is pain, be a body sixty-three or fifteen, only, oh, Jeezus, to feel it then—

There . . . she can tease me, she can do this to me—he scratched his thin forearm, felt the rich wetness of blood under his fingernails, saw it glimmer black in the dim light—*but I won't let her gawk at me like some sideshow freak . . . oh, shit, that's a good one.* Bitsy, standing and gossiping with her lady friends at the nearly empty bake sale stand, never heard Palmer's strained, verge-of-tears laughter, bottled up inside their hot car.

If she had, she would've jumped back into the Rambler and driven him to the hospital immediately . . . to have him committed.

TWELVE

10:35 P.M.

Opus, aka Pathfinder, almost-gift to Zoe, watched impassively from the top of Palmer's dresser as Brent slowly circled the bed, wanting to, yet unable to touch the still, pale form that lay there.

For how long he couldn't even remember later, Brent had stood in the doorway, staring at Zoe, until he finally asked himself, *This what "scared stiff" means? I can't fear Zoe, not my Zoe. But if I'm not afraid, why can't I . . . touch her? Go make sure she's really . . . aw no, that can't be my Zoe, she only had a* headache, *just a headache, so she wanted to sleep, said to wake her up when I came home . . . Zoe, don't do this to me . . . why, Zoe, why?*

But there was no answer to the *why* of it all, none at all. . . . Yet Brent's mind obligingly ran the horrible home movies taken but a few days ago; the firings, the co-op notice, the second class reunion reminder card held tightly in sleeping Zoe's fingers.

That was when he was able to move, to mechanically put Pathfinder on the dresser, set the bag on his uncle's desk, before slowly walking over to the bed. To gaze down on Zoe's nearly luminescent nakedness, marred only by those gaping, lipless mouths, opening on toothless darkness down each arm. Her fingers were lightly curled, not clenched, not flat and stiff. He gingerly extended one of his own fingers to touch hers; mere centimeters away, he detected no warmth radiating from her hand. He withdrew his and shoved it in his pocket.

Brent felt a small twinge of comfort; her wedding band was still in place—she didn't do this with splitting from him in mind, or so he chose to believe.

And she hadn't died on *his* bed, his dad's old bed, as if realizing that Brent would have to sleep *somewhere* tonight. As if wanting to spare Bitsy the trouble of making up the plastic shrouded bed, but Christ, why Uncle Palmer's bed? Wasn't he entitled to a good night's—then it hit Brent.

Sick to the core of his being, wishing he'd better explained to Zoe that his uncle didn't *mean* to seem cruel. *(Oh, Zoe, he's just different, just an old fart with a lot of bad memories and nothing to look forward to. He* didn't mean it, *oh, God, not like this—)* Brent couldn't look at her anymore. Casting his eyes down to his Reeboks, he mindlessly watched his toes wiggle under the leather. The rug underfoot was dark, maroon and navy blue; he hoped no blood dripped there, even if it was a dark rug—

That was when he saw it. It had fallen to the floor and bounced partway under the dust ruffle of the bed. Funny that he hadn't seen it before, but there was Zoe, and the blood . . . Brent forced himself to take it easy, calm down; after all, no one was watching him, or his reactions, then bent down. He recoiled from the coolness of the plastic camera body, then gently probed the surface for any broken edges or loose parts *(first she dies on his bed, then she breaks his camera—).* He saw an instant photo jutting out of the bottom, like a stiff, blackened tongue.

Brent pulled the photo free, set the instant camera on the desk where he *guessed* his uncle kept it, and peeled off the photo's protective cover sheet. He wondered if there'd even *be* a picture underneath, but within seconds an image formed on the small piece of emulsified paper. No face, just a pale background, crisscrossed with flat blue lines, a tangled abstract.

Deep blue lines against creamy pinkish white, like sunlit birch bark. As he held the snap between thumb and forefinger, Brent glanced at the photo, then at Zoe. Within seconds, he found a match of the picture.

There, just above the rise of her left breast, in the hollow formed by the upward curve to her shoulder and the ridge of her breast bone, a creamy patch of skin that just barely covered the muted neon tracery of her now-still veins. Darker than he remembered, as if drawn on the flesh with a runny Magic Marker, yet her fine-textured skin shone *over* the lines. None of her other veins were so deeply colored, or so visible.

As he stood there, eyes darting back and forth between the picture and the reality, a wild fear entered Brent's mind: *Suppose Uncle Palmer and Aunt Bitsy come up those stairs, tiptoe in, not wanting to startle me, then see me with* this *before they see Zoe . . . they won't think* she *took it, oh, noooo . . . they know who the artist is in the family*—so he suddenly, guiltily, stuffed the picture into his jeans back pocket.

Not wanting anyone to know that Zoe had, indeed, chosen *this* bed out of all the beds in the house to . . . on, Brent swallowed down a mix of popcorn and slushie-flavored bile, and forced himself to reach down, down . . . and *touch* Zoe's hand.

Downstairs, Duffy was too stoned on catnip to hear his master's stifled wail of anguish.

THIRTEEN

10:40 P.M.

Sensing that this was not to be a productive Midnite Mayhem, most of the merchants began to pull in their display tables. One store window after another became dark glassy mirrors facing the opposite sides of the street. And in turn, sensing that the night's shopping was over, most people quit the blocked-off street and walked to their cars. No one bothered to glance in the direction of the little cul-de-sac near the bakery.

Where the darkness was *deeper* in one small, woman-sized spot.

FOURTEEN

10:58 P.M.

Panting, arms aching, Brent stood in the doorway of his uncle's now unoccupied room. The fresh quilt (an almost perfect match of the blood-soaked one now gracing Brent's bed—Bitsy was attached to her Lincoln Log pattern, and churned out dozens of nearly identical quilts—Brent hoped Palmer wouldn't notice that the binding on this one was a deeper shade of blue) was spread taut over the wooden bed, tucked down at the footboard as it had been before. Luckily the . . . hadn't seeped through the quilt; whatever Bitsy used to fill her coverlets, it trapped . . . *fluids* like a sponge. A weird thought flashed through his mind— *"Miracle Fill" takes in blood and locks it in tight!*—and he let out a shaky giggle. It felt so . . . sacrilegious, sniggering in the hallway not twenty feet from the place where Zoe was, but Brent didn't, *couldn't*, care less.

After what he'd done in the last twenty or so minutes, it wasn't as if he didn't deserve a break. The old hamburger chain jingle revved up in his head, "You *de*-serve a—" along with the memory of him carrying Zoe's already . . . *firm* body (*stiff* sounded so crass) wrapped in the quilt came back to him with savage force . . . along with the lunatic image his imagination had supplied him with when he first tried carrying Zoe out the door with her head over one arm and her legs slung over the other. A cartoon scenario of her . . . *firm* body grazing horizontal *gashes* in the sides of the doorway; he'd wound up taking her out of the room sideways, head first. . . .

Remembering that he'd left Pathfinder on the dresser, Brent forced himself back into the room. As he walked around the foot of the bed, his nostrils widened, trying to sniff out blood. Once he had Pathfinder tucked safely in his waistband, Brent noticed that a pile of magazines had spilled over, glossy covers glaring under the harsh ceiling light.

Bending down to straighten them, trying to push the *Sports Illustrated*, *Popular Mechanics*, and *Midwest Hunter* issues into some semblance of order (most likely gift subscriptions, none looked read), he saw that one of them wasn't a magazine at all, despite its glossy cover.

It was a manuscript, a few dozen closely typewritten pages bound in one of those plastic binders with the separate hard spine that slipped over the back to hold the pages together. The cover was deep blue, such a dark hue Brent could barely make out the typing on the first page . . . nor could he see the deep splotch that marred the surface of the page.

Remembering that his aunt and uncle would be home any second, he shoved the plastic-covered manuscript into the pile of magazines, patted the sides of the stack reasonably straight, then, before leaving the death room, spotted the dull sheen of the razor blade. It had fallen and stuck nearly upright in the bedside rug. Holding the sticky blade between thumb and forefinger, palming off the room light with his other hand, Brent quickly forgot about the typewritten, blue-bound sheaf of papers.

But, if—

If he hadn't been in a hurry, he might have lifted the thin booklet to his nose, taken a deep sniff—

—and caught a fresh blood odor, mingled with floral perfume. . . .

FIFTEEN

11:07 P.M.

Exasperated, spine throbbing under the strain of being tightly edged almost on the horizontal, Palmer reached over and laid on the car horn, a series of long and short honks. Bitsy was slow to leave her friends, but the honking kept up until she said a last good-bye to the group of women she might not see or talk to for seven or eight hours.

Tossing her Tupperware into the backseat, she scolded, "I hope you're happy, Mr. I-Can't-Wait-to-Get-Home-to-an-Empty-House!"

"Kids are there, Bits. Probably wondering where we are, 'specially since the bake sale was supposed to end an hour

ago—'' The itching in his forearm was maddening, insistent
. . . *notice* me, *notice* me, it bore down into his flesh, deep
into his arm—and psyche.

"They don't give a toot where we are. Probably in *bed* doing
what young couples are supposed to be doing . . . probably
wouldn't notice if the world came to an end.'' She pulled away
from the curb, and only then did Palmer pay attention to his
protesting back, easing up into a normal sitting position. He
refused to look at the blind alley, refused to give *in*.

As Bitsy drove slowly down Seventh Avenue East, Palmer
answered, "Of course they'd notice if the world came to an
end . . . bed would shift. Break their concentration.''

"Palmer Nemmitz! I don't know how I ended up with an
old scamp like you!'' Bitsy fussed, unaware that she had
brought up the subject of copulation. While he didn't give
voice to his sentiment, Palmer told himself that Bitsy wasn't
the only one wondering how he wound up with her.

SIXTEEN

11:15 P.M.

Having been assured by Stu Sawyer that the sheriff would be
out soon—along with Lenny Wilkes, period, no one else—
Brent hung up the phone. He wandered upstairs, the Opus
toy still stuck in his waistband a comforting presence.

Taking a last look at Zoe, wishing he'd been gutsy enough
to slide on her shortie nightgown, and hating himself for not
being able to touch her any more than necessary, Brent
touched the carmel taffy waves of her hair. He reached for
the tip of one breast, before settling for a pat on her nearest
hand. He told himself that it was *okay* for her fingers to be
cool . . . the upstairs rooms were cool; Uncle Palmer had
had the place well insulated.

Then he remembered the razor blade. Wiping off his prints
(he was still out of town to these folks, even if he had Nemmitz blood in him and a Sawyer in-law), he coaxed Zoe's
prints onto the blade, then let it drop from the fingers he'd
laboriously pressed together. As they slowly moved back into
position, Brent rushed away, overcome by an intense urge to

relieve his bladder. If the moisture wouldn't come out of his eyes, it had to come out somewhere . . . and Brent's eyes were dry to the point of being painful.

Leaving Zoe in their room, Brent left the lights on, before making his way to the downstairs bathroom, the one with the coy "Necessary Room" ruffled-edged oval sampler on the door. (He couldn't use the upstairs toilet; Bitsy filled it with old-lady things, zippered girdles, chopper hopper, and whatnot piled on the tank lid.)

Pushing past the blue embroidered sign, Brent recalled the sampler hung above his uncle's bed, a yellowed linen birth announcement, "Thursday's Child Has Far to Go," in blue cross-stitch, framed in birchwood. Funny, today was Thursday, too.

Brent lifted the seat and lid, but as he began to unzip, he saw that Zoe must have felt the same way about using Bitsy's bathroom, before padding upstairs, lying on Palmer's bed, and—

A long twist of red dental floss floated lazily on the clear water, moving slightly from the vibration of the lifted seat and lid, fuzzy in spots where it caught and pulled between Zoe's tightly packed teeth. She'd done that in the Cities, threw the used strand in the bowl so Duffy couldn't fish it out of the wastebasket and play with it. She always worried about him, treated him like a baby . . . only now she wouldn't have to worry about Duffy getting his plush paws on the scented strand of floss, because Brent used a Water Pic, and . . .

. . . and Zoe was *gone*, gone for a long, long time, and wouldn't use any more floss, and—

—Brent reverently lowered the seat, then the lid, patting the blue tufted cover. Taking Pathfinder out of his waistband, he hugged the toy close to him as he slowly backed out of the room.

SEVENTEEN

11:40 P.M.

Winston was a few steps from his apartment door when he heard the double *whoop-whoop* of ambulance and squad car sirens. In the jaundiced glow of his next-to-the-door light, the old man's mouth sucked in, forming a crooked, almost-lipless line across his pale face. Mumbling, "Can't be Nemmitz . . . he'd never get into a goddamn sick wagon,'' Winston fumbled his key into the lock.

Wistfully, he wished he'd see some fireflies, instead of the nervous flutter of pale moths around the yellow bulb, but the fireflies seemingly vanished long ago, along with his youth.

And his innocent times with that old fuck Palmer Nemmitz.

EIGHTEEN

12:19 A.M.

Stu Sawyer and Lenny Wilkes had come and gone, taking Zoe with them, after Lenny had stood over her and whined, ''I never seen *nothing* like this,'' prior to authorizing Zoe's removal to the hospital morgue.

Lenny drove back to the house after taking care of Zoe; at first, he sat in the kitchen with Palmer and Bitsy, but eventually Lenny felt that he was intruding on the couple. He searched the house for the poor girl's husband—widower, now—finally finding the young man on the front porch.

Brent was curled up in one of the porch swings, holding that stuffed bird Palmer had said he'd bought for his wife. Brent stared at the dirt road that ran past the house, eyes dry and fixed. His bulk made the swing lean sharply to the left; the chains that held it up meekly protested when Lenny settled his girth on the other end of the wooden slat seat.

Lenny sat quietly for a few seconds, then began, ''When I was a boy, used to be the sky would just dance with fireflies this time of night . . . yellow-green so bright your eyes hurt. Don't know where most of 'em went, but I miss 'em. Haven't seen 'em in *years*. . . .'' His voice trailed off nostalgically, wistfully (as his nemesis Palmer Winston's had done less than an hour before), but it was a long time before Brent said something—and not in reply, either.

''Almost took a leak on her floss . . . there, in the bowl, she dropped it before she . . . *before*—'' and as his voice dissolved into giggles, Lenny cautiously leaned over to pat Brent's broad back, ''there, there''-ing the young man. Lenny had seen just about every post-death reaction, and heard just about every deathside statement known to man, but this one was a new one to Lenny, who thought, *Don't they have a wastebasket in their biffy?*

As he tried to puzzle *that* one out, Lenny's eyes wandered down the road, which ran past the Nemmetz farmhouse in a northern direction. Suddenly, the road was lit by low beams, twin pools of deep golden light, followed by a car . . . the likes of which Lenny hadn't seen since he was a small boy, back in the late thirties. Back in the days when this car had been new.

Long, sinuous, sleek, full-moon white, and rust-free along the running boards, the Pierce-Arrow moved slow and stately down the county trunk. In the window, lit faintly greenish-yellow by the swirling luminescence of fireflies, which circled the head of the driver, Lenny realized—for the first time in a long side career of looking into hundreds of slack, unbreathing faces—that he was witnessing the impossible.

A *dead* woman, driving a classic car down a dirt and gravel road under the pale blind eye of the full moon.

A jolt of fear shot through Lenny's penny loafer–shod feet, and raced through his portly frame . . . but he refused to shiver, refused to show his fear before the giggling young man sitting next to him. For Lenny had *seen* the blood, the gill-gapes in the pretty woman's arms. She was *gone*, unquestionably dead . . . but if so, what was she doing behind the wheel of a white Pierce-Arrow, animated as you please *(Jesus sitting in a rumble seat, did she* smile *at me?)*, so *alive*, her face all glowing with that shifting, living light?

As if sensing Lenny's thought, his intent to get up and run to the edge of the road, just to make *sure*, the white dream of a car picked up speed, and vanished into the early-morning darkness.

PART TWO

"Waking Slow"

I wake to sleep, and take my waking slow.
I feel my fate in what I cannot fear
I learn by going where I have to go.

—Theodore Roethke
"The Waking"

NINETEEN

With the sawhorses across the ends of Ewert Avenue removed, the Happy Wanderer strolled the predawn street un-
impeded, not bothering to lift his feet the extra six inches
necessary to mount the sidewalks. Heavy feet shiff-shuffled
through greasy popcorn bags, candy wrappers, and a brown
mush of spit tobacco and June bug carcasses, parting the
oceanlike drifts of litter like the keel of a ship, leaving a
permanent wake behind. It was so quiet he faintly heard the
delicate crackle of insect hulls grinding to powder under his
thick boot soles.

Happy—given name: Cooper Reish, uncle of the present
head undertaker at the Reish-Byrne Funeral Home located at
the intersection of Reish Street and Byrne Avenue—hummed,
a high-pitched warble rising to dog-disturbing shrillness.
Happy was used to getting by without talking; he was labeled
as having ''low verbal functioning processes'' so most people
assumed he couldn't talk, and didn't expect him to speak. He
was willing to go along with the misunderstanding, if it made
people happy.

Not much else he did made people happy. The store man-
agers didn't like him humming in their shops (no better
method of clearing out a store short of lobbing tear gas
through the windows), they didn't like him walking out with
pockets full of candy and gum or the way he bypassed the
checkout counter as he left. His nephew Craig didn't like it
when the phone rang during a visitation, and they chewed
Craig out about Happy's latest binge (and gave Craig the es-
timated totals of his uncle's sweets haul—with a ten-percent
markup).

The couple who ran the group home on Crescent Street
were *never* happy when Happy wandered home come suppertime, chocolate rimming the tips of his stubby fingers.

So, Happy didn't talk, which seemed to make all the things
he'd been pulling for the last fifty or so years tolerable . . .
better than if he further annoyed people by babbling. Happy

didn't need to open his mouth for purposes other than shoving food in or letting a burp out. Craig paid for what he took, so Happy felt no need for remorse . . . the Wanderer was retarded, not *dense*.

Feet churning the trash-covered pavement, he halfheartedly looked for remains of candy bars, or flavored water in paper cones to slurp down. Then, it came to Happy: He already *had* a candy bar, the one he got last night. Not breaking stride, he dug a grimy hand into his jacket pocket, bringing forth the slightly melted, misshapen deep blue-wrapped bar.

Pausing in mid-avenue, feet planted on either side of the yellow stripe, Happy laboriously unwrapped his treat. He tore the Stardust Bar logo neatly in half, before extracting the long oval-shaped bar inside. Biting into the confection, Happy's lips were sticky-brown-coated. The creamy swirl of white nougat surrounding the crisped rice dipped down and around on his chin, leaving a white tongue-shaped outline.

Lips smacking, Happy resumed his trot northward, dropping the wrapper on the street. There was just enough of a breeze to lift the tossed blue wrapper end over end, until it came to rest along the gutter near the Coast-to-Coast store . . . only four feet from the bench unofficially "reserved" for the Palmers Nemmitz and Winston.

Because he couldn't eat and hum at the same time, Happy's ears picked up the delicate snick of the wrapper, and suddenly curious, he shambled back just in time to see it come to a flattened stop against the gutter.

Glancing from the brown-smeared blue wrapper to the old men's bench, he scrunched up his brown eyes. Through a feathery rainbow of enlarged lashes, he almost saw the bench occupied, as it was in the days when the three old men sat there—Mr. Winston, Mr. Nemmitz, and Mr. Ferger, only nobody ever called him *that*. Ferger was Dead Fred to everybody, a blubbery, pasty-faced old coot in a mesh baseball cap, big lips always flap-flap-flapping, whether a person talked back to him or not.

Dead Fred's skin always looked . . . *funny*, like he'd been dead long *before* the cops found his body over in the woods across the river. Happy had seen it, a big shape covered with wiggling flies, like the old man's skin had sprouted lots and lots of glittering blackish wings, only he stayed on the ground without taking off. Happy's nephew did something strange after Dead Fred was brought in—he called down to Eau

Claire, where a crematorium was, and had them come get what was left of Dead Fred. Happy remembered Craig telling his wife Susie how Dead Fred was so "inconsiderate" to go off and have his heart attack in the woods. In the *summer*. Craig didn't tell anybody that he'd had Dead Fred burned up and then put the ashes box in the closed coffin (plus some bricks)—except for his Uncle Cooper, and *he* wasn't expected to spill any family beans.

Happy didn't really miss Dead Fred, burned up or not, any more than Happy missed hearing a radio station playing that he hadn't really been *listening* to.

Setting his imaginary sights on Mr. Nemmitz, Happy smiled inside. He liked the short man with the gimpy leg and green eyes; Mr. Nemmitz always winked at Happy when the hardware store manager tried to shoo Happy out before he could get in the store and visit the candy counter next to the cash register. The Wanderer liked that—the wink, not the shooing away part. But as for the *other* Palmer . . . Early on—before earning an ubiquitous EHS "Certificate of Attendance" at the age of twenty-nine, before the school board made the Reishes face facts (as in Cooper wasn't just a "slow learner" or "too shy to talk"), and allow him into special education classes—Cooper had vegetated in *regular* classes, in the days when Mr. Winston started to teach English.

Staring at the vacant bench, Happy easily pictured chain-smoking Mr. Winston there, and he remembered how Mr. Winston snuck *peeks* down the girls' blouses . . . even if Mr. Winston didn't *think* Happy was looking. Happy had *seen* . . . seen a *lot*. Mr. Winston always ignored Cooper Reish, sitting in the back row, but Happy wasn't comatose in that last row . . . the memory of those days made Happy's face flush. Before swallowing the last of his Stardust bar, he spit a gob of chocolate-nougat-rice-and-phlegm near the spot where Mr. Put-His-Hands-*There* usually rested his feet.

Patting his pockets, listening for the jingle of loose change (kids usually caged what coins he had), Happy found them all empty . . . but he wasn't sad for long. He knew where to find more Stardust bars . . . but they weren't in any store in Ewerton.

That didn't bother the Wanderer . . . he *liked* to walk. Buoyed by the prospect of filling his pockets with creamy candy bars, his step unusually high and light, Happy set off on an angle across the street, toward a narrow alley on the opposite side of Ewert Avenue.

Minutes later, as the sun rose buttery and sizzling bright, it touched the rough bricks of the empty cul-de-sac near the bakery, where, for a few wavering moments, the shrill tuneless hum of the Happy Wanderer could be heard . . . until it, too, faded away.

TWENTY

. . . runt, little runt *she hissed, as the trailer went pink-white for a shuddering second, then it was, oh, please again—*

When his alarm sounded at 7:00 that morning, Palmer Nemmitz was grateful for its strident buzz. If an A-bomb had dropped miles away, shaking the land and filling the sky with a blinding flash of horrible light, Palmer still would've been grateful for its wake-up call.

Anything to stop those dreams—his mind betrayed him, letting him suffer through it, without the luxury of a waking scream, or a roll off the bed to the maroon and blue rug below—those movies shot many years ago. In living, pulsing 3-D; vivid shades, hues and shadows razor sharp and merciless . . . with him the star of the whole shebang, mouthing lines with a painfulness honed by repetition.

Under the sheet, he felt her hate-kiss on his forearm; without looking, he knew it was open again, fresh and rippling into his flesh. He wondered, if he was both fast and careful, if he pulled out his arm, held it to the light . . .

For a few merciful seconds, he forgot about last night; what had greeted him in the yard, the house, the way the ambulance and squad car lights cast whirling, bright splashes of color on the white clapboards of the farmhouse. But mercy wasn't in great supply that morning, and Palmer wasn't *able* to forget for long.

Abruptly, he swung his thin, neon-veined legs out from under the sheet, hurried his bent toes into his sheepskin-lined slippers (something seemed . . . *funny* when he looked at the quilt scrunched up at the foot of the bed; closer inspection served only to confuse him, so he let it rest). His slippers were placed with the left positioned at cross angles to the right—his mental shorthand for remembering to do something come morning. Staring down at the tufts of the rug, rubbing sleep grit out of his eyes, Palmer waited until it came back to him.

Call the crematorium in Eau Claire, have them come up for Zoe as soon as possible. Brent—before Bitsy's Nytol took effect—had said that Zoe wanted to be cremated, it was in the will she'd brought along with her, picked up from their Cities lawyer before they left. As in cremated *before* being embalmed; through his bubbling laughter, Brent had insisted on *that*. Something about Zoe calling Craig Reish a jackass.

Palmer had promised to make the arrangements, prior to leading Brent off to the hastily made up spare bed, but now he regretted his promise. Brent hadn't seemed to be all *that* clear about his wife really being *gone*, as in for *good*—suppose he came to later, unsure of her death, wanting to see her one last time? *Then* what?

Feeling queasy, Palmer hurriedly dressed (forcing himself not to peer down at his itching forearm), but when he went downstairs, Bitsy was already up, fixing cold breakfast.

"Remember about making that call? To Eau Claire?" she said, seeing him walk into the room. "Number's on the message pad." Palmer knew he was trapped, misgivings not withstanding.

Long after he hung up the phone, and sat down to his bowl of soggy shredded wheat, island of Sugar Twin damp and semiclear in the sea of milk, Palmer couldn't shake the feeling of *bad*, of having done wrong in the very act of doing what Brent requested of him. Mechanically shoving food he couldn't taste into his mouth, cud-chewing it with his remaining back teeth, Palmer forced himself to act *normal* between joyless bites, just as Bitsy was doing across the table from him.

"Palmer, keep playing with that and I won't buy it anymore. . . ."

Neither of them looked at the empty place near the stove where Zoe had sat during her few meals with them.

No Brent at the table, either; Bitsy claimed she heard him snoring when she rose at six. Albeit unvoiced, there was a tacit agreement between them, to treat Brent as gently as possible, to be as undemanding of him as necessary. Bitsy took it upon herself to feed Duffy, nicking her finger with the lid of the pull-top can ("Poor thing's so quiet . . . think he knows, hardly touched his Fancy Feast"). Palmer did litter-box duty, twisting shut the piece of newspaper surrounding the offal before dropping it in the wastebasket. He almost tossed his cereal when he saw a lock of Zoe's hair there.

Although Brent lost his parents years ago, it had been an accident, a quick hurting that carried no stigma. But what Zoe did . . . Palmer's lips curled in unconscious disgust. He could imagine what Winston would say—not to mention the rest of Ewerton.

When he thought of *other* people, he remembered what he saw last night in the Monkey Ward's window. Bitsy asked, "Are you all right?"

Waving his hands, he said, "Touch of indigestion, that's all," his mind going two-forty: *If Zoe was already . . . gone —she must've been, or else Lenny wouldn't have said, "try to bend her arms in"—she wasn't out there by that store . . . unless all the dead walk—*

Gulping down lemon-lime flavored Alka-Seltzer, wincing at the faint aspirin aftertaste, Palmer hoped his voice didn't waver as he told Bitsy, "Better get my behind into town before Win starts spreading God knows what about this. I'd better take the car—gonna be a scorcher out. You be all right here, with Brent?"

"Fine. If Winston's heard anything, he's worse than a party line and twice as fast."

He leaned over to offer her a parchment kiss and settled for a smile instead, then placed his fedora on his head and went out, mindful not to slam the door. Bitsy pretended to busy herself until the Rambler disappeared down the road, dust dogs nipping the rear bumper.

After she could no longer see the car, Bitsy hurried to the black wall phone near the broom closet (it replaced their candlestick phone in the fifties), dialing her cousin Stu's number from memory. As the line beeped, she traced the outline of a bird on a 1986 calendar towel, laying out her conversation as if readying an outfit for Sunday services at the Methodist church. Then:

" 'Lo?"

"Stuart, this is your cousin Bitsy." Stu had only one relative named Bitsy, but she dutifully added "your cousin" whenever she called.

"Oh . . . yeah"—sound of a hand rubbing stubble close to the mouthpiece—"damned sorry 'bout last night. How's he taking it?"

"Who?" At times, Stu found Bitsy's guilelessness disarming, even cute, but this morning was not such a time.

"Aw, Bitsy, use your—Brent. How is *Brent* taking it?"

"Oh, *him*. Still resting. Snoring like a snow blower in the spare room. I fed his cat this morning, cut my thumb on the can top—"

"Sorry 'bout your *thumb*, Bitsy, but did you wake me for—"

"Oh, no, no, *no*. It's about . . . *her*. Zoe. Have you, um . . . filed a *report* yet?"

"Yeah, last night. What there was of it." A pause, then, warily, "Why do you ask, Bitsy?"

"Stuart, put yourself in my place. In *Brent's* place. Can you imagine spending the summer with all those *rumors* hanging over your head? With folks tsk-tsking and shame-shaming? The poor boy lost his job, his home, and now—"

"*Beatrice*, are you suggesting I—"

"Does it *have* to be in the *paper*? It's not like *not* putting it in would *hurt* anyone—she isn't . . . *wasn't* a city resident, only passing *through*, so to speak—"

"Bitsy, you've been living with Palmer too long. His mean and nasty is rubbing off. Oh . . . all right. Not that it'll do much good, because tongues flap regardless. Don't go bothering Lenny now, hear? And if people get to asking *me*, or Lenny, we can't hide the truth—"

"Only until Brent leaves. Like I said, he's lost his j-o-b, and hasn't a place to stay—"

"Please, Bitsy, one hard luck story before breakfast is all I can take. I'll *try* to keep it under my hat—only until Brent's gone, okay?"

"Oh, Stuart, I'm so glad I voted for you—Stu? Stuart?" she chirped into the dead line, before hanging up with a smile. All that boy needed was some reasonable persuasion.

Minutes later, when her daughter Angie called, asking if what she'd heard from Millie Wilkes was true, about someone *dying* in the farmhouse, Bitsy was ready with a tale of a terrible spat ("—they had this argument, it got pretty nasty, blood and all—''), further setting in motion events beyond her constrained imagination. . . .

TWENTY-ONE

"Brooke, put down that bottle or I'll *brain* you! Sorry, Heather, Brooke was gonna pour OJ on L'il Scoot's head—'' Cradling the receiver between her head and shoulder, Sarah Andersen slid barefoot along the slick kitchen floor, snatched the bottle of generic orange juice out of her daughter's hand, then slid back to the counter, before asking Heather Wilkes— who lived only three doors down on Hemlock Street, but was as housebound as Sarah this morning, with *five* kids to run after—''*What* did your mom-in-law say about Zoe?''

"Millie *said* something happened out there last night, but Lenny didn't say just what before he came home, cuz he was tired. But before Lenny got up this morning, Stu called, wanted to talk to him. Millie heard some of it on the extension, Stu was calling about Zoe, and how *he* was 'keeping a lid on it,' but that Lenny was on his own, and that was when Len told Millie to get off the living-room phone. As soon as he left, Millie called Angie Calder-Bettinger, but *she* didn't know didley, but Lenny *is* the County-You-Know-What, so it's pretty obvious. I'm listening to WERT, see if they announce—''

"Jeezus, I *saw* her the other day. She was fine, asked about the kids and—''

"I'm just betting nothing's gonna be in the *papers*. You know how those *Sawyers* are—''

Winding the phone cord around her free hand, Sarah fought back a blur of tears that turned her kids into runny caricatures as they sat around the kitchen table. When Blaine asked, "Mommy, why you 'fying'?" she raised the cord-wrapped hand to her lips, forefinger lifted. . . .

TWENTY-TWO

By nine-thirty, the pair of Palmers were in their usual places on "their" bench (Winston cussed after stepping on a glob of brown and white macerated candy, doing an exaggerated rooster strut and scratch to scrape it off his sole). Today their faces wore looks of grave concentration as Nemmitz gave a *Reader's Digest* account of Zoe's demise; cut the nudity (no use getting Winston *excited*, his old brain needed all the blood his body could spare), shorten the razor slashes (blood only needs a small opening to come out, right?), minimize the blood loss (only one quilt was dirtied, and Bitsy *had* sewn in both a blanket and one of those silver survivalist things that repels moisture)—like Bitsy before him, Winston accepted Palmer's lies.

Finished, eyes blurring under the shade of his hat brim, Palmer sat quietly on the uncomfortable bench—the fools in the City Works Department couldn't keep the old, comfortably angled wrought iron and wood slat benches that had graced Ewert Avenue for seventy-some years—nodding automatically as he listened to Winston stick his two cents worth in. Another Zoe harangue: "his" Una always said Zoe would come to a bad end.

If Zoe were buried, she'd be spinning in her grave—or so Palmer thought, watching the Yingley clan (Pap Yingley, Momma Yingley, and Baby Bear Pete Yingley, who was forty if he was a day) toddle down the avenue en route to the Wooden Keg, which opened at ten sharp. In midshuffle, Papa Bear dropped something that flashed silvery in the sun, keys, most likely. Palmer watched with mild disgust as Papa Bear waited for his unsteady wife to hunker down, pigtail askew, and pick them up. Baby Bear stood on the sidelines, cigarette ashing onto his improbably dirty raincoat . . . and the revolving thermometer clock jutting out from the nearby bank read seventy-five degrees.

Watching the trio shuffle into the Wooden Keg (the owner of the Rusty Hinge threw them out years ago), Palmer sighed. Things were deteriorating in Ewerton faster than the flesh of a camp deer before hunting season. He wasn't sure which had come first; the peeling-paint neglect of the homes (thanks to higher property taxes for those who fixed up their houses), the ugly revamping of the storefronts, or the influx of out-of-state welfarettes lured by Wisconsin's promise of easy dole for themselves and their litters of kids. No matter which had come first, decay was decay.

"—getting my poor Una fired over something *that* trivial. Una wasn't the first teacher to lay hands on a student, and she wasn't the last. All for a goddamn *list* tacked up on a bulletin board. Twit should've left up what Una wrote after her name . . . Una had every right to deck her after she ripped down that list—"

Palmer gave a phlegmy snort. "What 'list,' Win? You haven't told me *that* story at least fifty times—" then pointedly turned his attention elsewhere. Winston placed another Lucky Strike in his mouth, lit it, blew the smoke in Palmer's direction, then went on, "All Una did was underline *her* name on a mimeographed Honor Roll sheet tacked up in the hallway. On the cork board. After Una underlined it, she added an . . . appropriate *notation* after Zoe's name. Nothing that people didn't call Zoe in private, so I don't know why she—"

Tuning out Winston's smoky tirade, Palmer noticed the Happy Wanderer trotting down the avenue, oblivious to the cars that swerved to miss him as he approached the bench from the north. Happy was filling his face, cheeks war-painted brown and glistening in the hot, clear sunlight. Soon the Wanderer ambled past, chewing a brown-covered white nougat bar whose odd contours stirred an old—yet very *fresh* memory in Palmer Nemmitz . . . a poignant, very terrible memory.

From Palmer Nemmitz's journal—
". . . did you ever do this trick with a Stardust Bar? My father showed me when I was . . . tiny. Said stardust was a cousin to gold dust, only silvery, and that you had to 'mine' for it. . . ."

Cramming the last of the oval bar past his brown lips, the Wanderer pointedly dropped the deep blue wrapper in front of Palmer, as Winston finished, "—so when that little bitch tore the sheet off the board, Una *had* to get it away from her, put it back up. I don't care how many kids said they saw Una

land the first punch. Just lying through their teeth to get rid
of—''

Unable to sit through a recital of the Martyrdom of St.
Una, Palmer got up—knees popping—and walked the short
distance to where the wrapper lay.

When he saw the twin of that wrapper crumpled in the
gutter, Palmer squatted down to pick up both wrappers. He
crammed them in his trouser pocket with such a furtive yet
painfully obvious motion that Winston interrupted himself
with the question, ''What are you doing, trying to make that
Indian on late-night TV stop crying over how dirty our streets
are?''

Palmer fought back blind panic—he hadn't seen a wrapper
from a Stardust Bar since . . . since . . . (*Oh, sweet Jesus,*
no) Feeling his crusted-over wound open, begin to seep and
itch again, Palmer mumbled without thinking, ''Candy . . .
gather up wrappers, send 'em for a free bar.'' He stood up
quickly, head swimming.

Winston puffed silently on his cigarette, almond-shaped
eyes narrowed. It wasn't until Palmer sat down again that he
drawled softly, his voice an echo of the way it *used* to sound,
long before . . . a *lot* of things happened, ''You want we
should go into one of the bars? Cool down? I suppose it was
a shock . . . what happened last night?''

''Umph . . . mighty hot out,'' Palmer mumbled, leaning
against the rough exterior of the store, letting the street sounds
of cars and talking pedestrians wash over him. He pretended
to doze, hat tipped over his eyes, mind running in five different directions at once.

It had to be *her*, not Zoe, but . . . *her* last night. The candy
wrappers cinched *that*. True, in the past few years they'd
brought back Clove and Blackjack gum, but Palmer didn't
think they'd brought back the Stardust Bar. No, he would've
noticed.

No Stardust Bars, the ones *she* had liked so well.

Clamping his left hand over his right forearm, Palmer let
his mind drift . . . he hoped that Zoe's death didn't have
anything to do with *her*. But Palmer knew in his all-but-
withered heart that it did, oh, most *certainly* did. . . .

*Oh, shit, I hope Zoe didn't find that crazy paper of mine,
and read it before she died . . . in my room. Don't care what
Brent claimed about where he found her, that was* not *my*

quilt on my bed this morning. Man should know his own quilt, on his own bed.

Snapping out of his semidoze, Palmer looked down in awe and dread at the crimson oval of blood ringing the bite. The more than *forty-eight*-year-old bite, a deeper than the skin wound. Pooled blood made the fine lines in his left palm shine deep red. Crossing his arm, trying to hide the spreading stain, Palmer wondered how he could sneak into the house without arousing Bitsy's attention. . . .

TWENTY-THREE

Stomach rumbling in anticipation of a late breakfast as he drove down Lumbermill Drive, Coroner Lenny Wilkes marveled over the autopsy he had just witnessed over at the hospital.

It had been little more than a formality, a quick look-see done over that Lawton-Nimitz woman's body. Heck, it wasn't even a *proper* autopsy . . . but Lenny never did expect much from Clive Calder. Perhaps he really did mean it when he said, "No need for the saw . . . obviously the poor girl bled to death, no use messing up the table." Lenny never could tell with Clive Calder. He had more fuzz in his head than a jar of cotton balls.

Although he never dared to say it, on account of not being sure if he was or wasn't speaking to some distant relative of the Doc who might take offense, Lenny was convinced that Doc Calder—who had delivered Lenny's son, and his son's kids—was losing it.

Lenny had bumped into the steel table before the autopsy began, causing the dead woman's left arm to flop off—and reveal a paper-cut thin separation of near-ruler straightness that began at her armpit and ended nearly at her waist. No blood flowed from the slit; it had eluded Lenny's attention last night, but that morning he pointed it out to Calder. Unfortunately, he and Clive—and the body—were the only people in the cool steel and white tile room, so no saner head could back Lenny up on what happened next.

Calder ran a gloved finger along the gill-like slit, then seemed to forget about it. He went back to oogling the dead woman's undraped chest, poking a finger at the dark veins over her upper left breast.

Clearing his throat, Lenny asked, "Clive, don't that"—he pointed to her side—"look sorta strange to you? I don't see no blood—"

" 'Course not . . . didn't you see all that blood on her arms? On the quilt? Body's only got so much blood," Calder snapped, indicating the discussion was *over*.

As Calder finished his half examination, prior to writing out the death certificate needed for her transport down to Eau Claire (the man from the crematorium had been waiting for them when Calder and Lenny arrived around eight), Lenny fumed and stewed. Though he lacked the formal training for his job, just as his grandfather and father hadn't been trained as coroners when *they* held the office, Lenny did his best to know *something* about human pathology.

He had those two books that Japanese coroner from L.A. wrote, and he dutifully read *Reader's Digest* articles about Joe's body, and watched *The Body Human* whenever it was on TV. Despite the handicap of his Ewerton education, Lenny prided himself on knowing the basics about the life and death of the human body.

As he had stood next to the grooved stainless-steel table, its occupant silent and still, Lenny remembered reading about postmortem wounds being different from those inflicted before the heart stopped beating . . . they *didn't bleed.*

Zoe's arms bled; she *had* found and opened veins. After Doc Calder rinsed off the blood, Lenny could still picture it there. *Yet her side was so bloodless he had almost seen no wound there.* But being self-trained, Lenny wasn't going to argue with Clive about it—it wouldn't bring her *back.*

And that crematorium guy was sitting in the lobby, waiting, signed papers in hand. The young redheaded man with the trio of raised moles on one cheek (sorta like the guy who played The Sundance Kid in that movie) had a slight southern accent—and he made Lenny feel vaguely *guilty*, although for what reason Lenny couldn't begin to imagine. The fellow surprised Lenny by calling him "Coroner Wilkes" instead of plain old "Lenny," as he'd requested before shaking the redhead's oddly clammy hand.

But politely formal as the man was—he gave a name, but Lenny was too distracted by his unaccountable guilt to catch it—he gave Lenny the willies. One thing; for being at least thirty-some years old, the man had a . . . *different* way of speaking. Not just a matter of accent, but a carefulness, a precision no longer part of today's speech. The way Grandpa August used to talk, no "y'knows" peppering his speech; only good pronunciation and odd turns of speech such as "it is I." Lenny assured himself that kids might be taught differently down South . . . but deep inside he *knew* that wasn't it, at all.

Doc Calder seemed to like the redheaded man, so Lenny convinced himself that his dis-ease stemmed from hunger. He needed Millie's good flapjacks, with apple hunks . . . but as he drove, Lenny's mind looped back to that long silver table—

He couldn't figure out how Zoe cut her own side without dripping blood on her midriff; stopping at an intersection, Lenny traced a blunt fingertip along his own left side. Even though he didn't have a prominent set of man-titties, he wound up making a crooked line down his body—nothing like the arrow-straight slice he'd found on her. And she had had no blood at *all* on her middle.

Starting the car, Lenny decided that Stu Sawyer would know how she did it—he'd seen his share of dead bodies in Korea as well as back home. Stu and Lenny could hash it out over a Bud or two.

A station wagon darted across Share Avenue; the long, lean whiteness of it reminded Lenny of the Pierce-Arrow he'd seen last night. The one with the girl inside. The one that had prompted his decision to oversee Zoe Nimitz's autopsy in the first place.

Pale hairs rose on his sunburned arm—*goose walking over my grave*—Lenny assured himself that the car was from out of town, someplace where—

Braking hard, he almost ran over the Happy Wanderer, strolling down the middle of the street.

Fuming about the Wanderer jolted the autopsy out of his mind; hoping that Millie might make some caramel nut rolls, too, Lenny pressed on the gas.

TWENTY-FOUR

JULY 2

Friday was a lost day for Brent—curled in the darkness of the spare room, he ignored offers of food, numbly signed *something* that Bitsy shoved under his nose, and spent hours thinking.

Bitsy and Palmer kept whispering about Zoe being *gone*—gradually, the images of Thursday night became more and more surreal, with each odd detail becoming magnified, farcical, until Brent came to a conclusion: Zoe had up and left him. The cruel sight that had greeted him Thursday night was nothing more than that—a nasty, unforgivable *joke* on Zoe's part. After all, Brent reasoned in his dark cave of bedclothes, Zoe couldn't be *dead*—the apparition that greeted him in his uncle's bedroom had been board stiff. Nobody gets that stiff that fast, not in less than three hours. And there were no accompanying rings of lividity—Brent had taken art and anatomy courses. He *knew* about such things, even more so than that silly slob Lenny Wilkes.

If Bitsy, Palmer, Stu, and Lenny wanted Brent to *think* Zoe was dead, Brent didn't want to spoil their plan . . . *Ewerton's an old-fashioned kind of town . . . women who run off are frowned on.*

Brent was not a sobber or chest-pounder by nature; he hadn't shed a tear when Mom and Dad died in that car crash. Not that he didn't *feel* it, but Brent by habit poured his feelings into a deep well within him. The pains of the living hurt him more than sorrow for the loss of life . . . or the loss of a straying wife.

If the others wanted to play their little games, Brent was willing to go along—rather than let himself *believe* what he'd seen in his uncle's bedroom.

Saturday morning, the third, Palmer and Bitsy were relieved to hear Brent say, "C'mon, Duffy, let's fatten you up some," before pounding down the stairs to the kitchen. Bitsy doubted that anyone could feed up that poor, quiet kitty, but she was happy that Brent was up and around again.

Brent said little, and his aunt and uncle avoided talk of Zoe. Bitsy ached to tell Brent about the redheaded fellow who stopped by the house with the cremation papers; the *nicest* fellow, but he did give her a turn . . . he was so intense, as if trying to stare into her soul. But Brent didn't speak of Zoe at all, as if wishing to put her departure behind him.

After breakfast, Brent cradled Duffy in his big arms and asked, "Does he look sick to you or what?" Duffy looked kitten-small in his embrace.

Putting down a potato among the fleshy pairings on the counter, Bitsy cooed, "Kitty don't feel good? Lemme see, Duffy." Staring into his green eyes, she said, "Third eyelid's out . . . could be upset, but he's been droopy since—don't eat worth a poop, either—"

"Vet's office open?"

From his place at the table, as he worked his crossword puzzle, Palmer thought Brent seemed more upset over his cat's illness than the death of his *wife*, but didn't comment about it.

"Not until Monday—"

"Shit. I don't suppose they do house calls for small animals, do they." Brent cradled Duffy's fuzzy head against his chest; the cat tentatively brushed the pad of his gray paw against Brent's chin. Cradling Duffy's head under his own chin, Brent turned and left the room. Heavy footsteps pounded up the stairs.

Bitsy searched the cupboards under the counter, until she found a can of evaporated milk. Scooping up a can opener and a small saucer, she said over her shoulder, "Angie's Mingie perks up when she gives him this . . . worth a try." Her lighter footfalls ascended the staircase.

Feeling the prickle of tears forming behind his eyelids, Palmer put aside his *Milwaukee Journal* "Green Sheet" crossword, unfinished, and plucked his hat and light jacket off the rack near the door.

Walking out to the Rambler, Palmer told himself it wasn't so bad with the girl. At least she *chose* her way to go. But the kitty was a goner. Palmer could see it in his eyes. Then, the image of another set of eyes came to him . . . *goner* eyes, in a face twisted in a rictus of tear-stained fear and something *worse*—

From Palmer Nemmitz's journal—

. . . I saw her face crumple as she cried; her mouth was saying what she'd said before, "Oh, please, please, don't tell." And then . . . I could look no more.

Shaking, trying to keep his mind a blank, he climbed into the car and revved it up . . . while the open bite on his arm, now covered by gauze and tape under the sleeve, burned and bled.

"Guess what I heard last night at the Rusty Hinge?" Winston blurted out his question without so much as a "Good morning" as Palmer made his way to the bench. Winston's eyes were eager, darting, as Palmer asked, "What'd they do, wash the glasses for a change?"

"I was sitting in a back booth, and in the one behind mine Lenny and Stu were drinking and talking. About Zoe. Seems there was a long slit in her side, not bloody at all. Doc Calder didn't pay it any mind, but Lenny called it a 'postmortem' wound; Stu said it sounded *pret*-ty weird, and wanted to take another peek at her, but Lenny said it was too late, that *you'd* insisted she be—"

Instead of being angered by Winston's thoughtless recitation, Palmer grabbed the other man's shoulders, hissing, "*Which* side?"

Disappointed that Palmer *wasn't* angry with him, Winston took a drag on his cigarette, coughed, and said "How the hell should *I* know? Lenny didn't get specific, after a few beers he's never accurate. Doesn't matter which side. As I was saying, Lenny said *you* requested cremation. Stu thought it strange, her not dead two days and already ashes. No funeral, either. He was already ticked at Bitsy, for calling and making him keep it out of the paper, since she didn't mention *cremation*. Want to know what *else* Stu thinks?"

"Even if I don't, you'll tell me anyway," Palmer said with false mildness, regarding Winston through hooded lids. Winston was nonplussed.

"Stu *said* he thinks this whole business is fishy. Said it struck him funny that Zoe was so *stiff*, 'specially since the rest of you left the house at six, seven that night. She was like a *board* by midnight. Takes a few hours to bleed to death, let alone stiffen up. Even if she did it as soon as the cars pulled out of the driveway, it didn't leave her much time to die, let alone firm up. And Stu wasn't sure when Brent *did* get home—''

''He insinuated *Brent* did it?'' Rage glittered in Palmer's eyes; Winston backed off, saying quickly, ''I think he meant he was confused by the whole evening. And pissed 'cause the report pictures he took didn't come out.'' Lighting a fresh smoke, Winston started again, ''If my Una were here today, she'd be vindicated at last . . . girl wasn't any good, not to insult Brent, but she caused a lot of grief—''

As Winston played the worn record one more time, the grooves nearly static, Palmer realized something that had been staring him in the face for as long as Winston had been harping on and on how he ''detested'' Zoe.

Lips parted in a smile that hurt his jaw, Palmer rocked back and forth on the bench. He'd finally seen through Winston; his realization based on years of association, observation— and dumb luck.

''Taught literature, didn't you, Win?''

''Of all the damn-fool ques—yes, I taught *literature*.''

''Shakespeare.''

''Yes, him, too, now what—'' His eyes narrowed behind a haze of blue smoke.

''Well, when I was listening to your comments about Brent's wife, I was reminded of something I read in *Hamlet*. Remember when the Queen says the Player King 'doth protest too much'?''

''The Player *Queen*—oh, you son of a *bitch*!''

Palmer got up and walked to the Rambler; focusing on the deep blue solidness of the car, he shut out Winston's rumble of protest. But the very blueness of the car reminded Palmer of Stardust Bar wrappers. . . .

TWENTY-FIVE

Entering his one-room-plus-bath apartment on Railway Drive, Winston slammed the door. He headed straight for the whiskey bottle hidden under the bathroom sink, next to a bottle of Lysol. Taking the cap off Jack Daniels, pouring five fingers worth into a tumbler, Winston decided that he'd do himself a favor if he took a pull from the Lysol bottle. End his misery for good.

Sitting on the unfolded sofa-sleeper, the rolled metal frame biting into his unpadded thighs, Winston didn't think of Zoe Lawton . . . at least not *immediately*. His mind instead jumped to a time long before Zoe was born . . . his stint in the Occupation Army, in Japan.

Forty-two years later, he still shuddered when he realized how close he'd been to busting rocks in an Army jail. He'd signed away any chance at a life away from Ewerton with the discharge he'd got. And he'd been on the verge of another promotion, too.

Draining his glass, quickly refilling it, Winston couldn't get over how Palmer had psyched him out. A *mind trick*, something a shrink might play . . . Winston flinched; staring at the burned-out TV tube across the room, he thought of his honorable discharge, given after all charges leveled against him were dropped, before mulling over the miserable performance he'd just put on uptown.

Not to have seen it *coming*—that hurt worst of all. Not being able to deflect the remark, turn it around, jab Palmer with it. Balancing the nearly empty glass on his bony knees, Winston decided that he was rattled because of the drink. *Drink* was the reason for all of *this*. Like that bitter, clear sake in Japan. All to blame . . . but certainly not *him*.

Rising from the hard bed, legs already stiff and cramping about the calves, Winston reverently stood before each of the shrines to his lost youth and manhood that dotted the room.

The Army shrine, safe within a rectangular memory box; bars and ribbons from his uniform, his achievement medals, a few bluish-tinged photographs of him alone, with his buddies, and with his C.O., and the lone netsuke he'd kept for himself. The inch-high ivory beggar man looked reproach-fully at him, as if to say, "Look what you screwed away."

Walking unsteadily from the hanging shrine, shrinking in-side under the glare of the netsuke, Winston moved to the School shrine—a joint one to Una and himself.

Thirty-six yearbooks, dating back to 1950. Engraved plaques declaring him Teacher of the Year for '54, '55, '60, '62, '64, and '66. The last year, he told the students assem-bled in the gym for Awards Day that he was touched by their support, but followed his words of thanks with a request that they no longer elect him Teacher of the Year.

But after carrying out Una's angry request that he eliminate himself from the running, Una never did win one of those small wood and engraved metal plaques.

Una never got a "Favorite Teacher" ornament, as Winston often did come Christmas; taking a long pull directly from the bottle, making Jack Daniels do a headstand, Winston thought, *See, your pupils hated you all along.*

One by one he pulled annuals from the shelf, leafing through the slick pages until he found his photo, which for twenty-eight years was placed next to that of Una. Like the picture of dissolute Dorian Gray, Winston saw bitterness and old age cover his previously open and amiable features. A succession of thin, adhering masks fashioned of fine spider-webbing, layer after layer of clinging lines.

Until one morning he'd awoke to see an old, wrinkled man, nose big and veined, ears oversized, mouth a raised scar, eyes clouded over with cataracts of self-pity.

Looking into his frozen yesterdays captured in two by two and a half inch black-and-white, tears welled behind his lids, spilling over the webbed flesh under his eyes. He wondered if he'd won his Teacher of the Year plaques out of love or fear, or a mixture of both. None of the girls minded his at-tentions, and all initiated it in the days when he'd been young and good-looking. By the time his looks were warped, tra-dition among the girls, along with his reputation and author-ity, were well in place. Unless a body did something so obvious it couldn't be overlooked *(like you, Una, naughty girlie)*, having tenure covered many a sin, both inflicted and sought-after.

Yet, after seeing his visage disintegrate in the acid of acer-bity, Una's pictures had a *sameness* about them. True, her hair grayed, and lines formed on her pinched ferret features, but *Una* didn't change. The bitch-in-heat look never left those darting eyes. Bottled-up rage shone in them too—even in grainy black and white.

Mr. Daniels blurred his eyesight, but Winston's inner sight was clearer now, much more so than when he neglected Mr. Daniel's, and protective words and thoughts covered Una's memory like battered armor. He'd been compelled to defend his choice of a bride (an experience common to men who wed town whores); soon the need to explain and defend her became a second personality for Winston, a persona designed to deflect ridicule and speculation by good people who couldn't believe that a good-looking, smart ex-Army officer like Palmer Christian Winston could marry some*thing* like Una Sawyer—be she related to the sheriff's people or not.

And as Una began to . . . act up, the lie absorbed his life, became engrained in his moral fiber, distorting what *was* with a false face, an untrue voice spouting unbelieved catch phrases. During his years with Una, her sickness—she was nothing but a she-devil, a split-tongued screwing, hurting, and hunting machine whose own son hated her—seeped from inside Una into Winston. Seeping as they slept and lay with each other, like air inhaled after being exhaled by the other.

Leaving the yearbooks piled on the floor next to the bookcase, swinging the bottle like a railway lantern, he visited the Baby shrine, a pitifully small collection of framed photographs, too few to fill a dime-store montage frame.

Baby Arlin in his stroller, Una standing by; Arlin alone, scared in the photographer's studio despite the Teddy bear he clutched; little Chester and little Clarence, in a hinged dual frame, both snapshots taken shortly before their successive deaths in the same crib. Una blamed it on the time Winston had spent in atom-blasted Japan. He never *was* sure if she was right. (As an afterthought, there was a tiny framed snap of Arlin's girl, Devorah, whom Winston hadn't seen since she left town not long after Dead Fred kicked off. She didn't like Winston all that much, and he never read the stories she wrote and published.)

Having paid homage at each shrine, Winston went back to the extended daybed. He stretched out on it, spine propped against the back of the couch, thin legs splayed out over the rumpled blankets, unmindful that his shoes were still on. Draining one bottle, he dropped it to the floor, to bounce on the candy-stripe indoor-outdoor carpeting. Pushing aside flat pillows, he reached into the empty cavity under the bed, where bottle number two was stashed. Winston slowly filled his glass so as not to slop any onto his bedding.

He reflected, not for the first time, that no matter what he had done with his life, his decisions pleased no one—not his parents, not his wife, his wife's son, his son's child . . . or himself. Between sips, he gave voice to bitter thoughts he dared not express on the bench; a slurred monotone addressed to the walls, the dead TV, the radio, the shrine, all of whom listened in respectful silence. And in return for its attentiveness, the room learned things that even the sober Winston might've been taken aback to hear plainly stated:

"Bad mistake, marryin' her. All 'cause of that Army head-shrinker, what *he* said . . . didn't help with Palmer marryin' Una's *cousin* . . . that shrink, he didn't have to write that about me, didn't have to say . . . *that*. Drove me right to her . . . cover up, cover up Una's ass for her. Smooth things over, tell 'em how good she is, 'cause *Una* says the girl's a monster, with an evil *eye*"—he showed horned fingers for the benefit of the draperies, the ceiling—"didn't matter how nice the kid was, no way, no how. I liked her, no matter what Una said. Smart kid . . . Una didn't like 'em too smart, 'cause Una wasn't so smart herself . . . *thought* she was, but she wasn't. Lays eyes on Zoe, starts rantin' and ravin' 'bout Zoe's devil eyes, how Zoe reminded her of something *bad* she saw when she was little . . . sheesh! Didn't explain, just kept talkin' 'bout 'devil eyes,' 'wall-eyes' . . . got Una in a pickle, didn't it? You *deserved* it, Una.

"Funny thing, Zoe wasn't wall-eyed, one eye was just set off kilter. Her eyes—hurt and innocent and knowing all at once—drove me nuts, but not *crazy* nuts. Not like that girl down in Georgia . . . *her* eyes were something *else*. . . ."

Voice cracking from hoarseness, he took a deep pull from the bottle, no longer caring about his bedding when the amber liquid splashed onto his sheets, his pillows. Sliding down to a prone position, Winston's mind went back to that night in Georgia, him driving on that back road close with trees, moon and starlit; his headlights had offered only a gold-tinged illumination that cast odd shadows on her face. Shadows that distorted her features, yet turned her taffy hair into a halo of spun gold. When he lay on top of her, her face was no clearer to him . . . but he'd seen her eyes plainly, briefly, when moonlight hit them before hiding behind a scud of cloud.

One of her blue and brown eyes—tan circled the pupil, blue filled in the rest of the iris—turned out slightly, giving her a guileless stare. A stare that suddenly, inexplicably, turned gleefully cold and cruel. Just as the pain started, and he felt himself falling into her. It was as if she'd swallowed him alive with those eyes. And he'd heard an inner voice unlike his usual thought-voice say, *See what it's* like . . . *feel how it can be on the* other *end of the situation?* And he *had* felt, and having experienced it, he was never to forget it . . . or replicate the feeling, which, although painful, was also intoxicating.

Afterward, she'd said what she said to him, and he'd made tracks away from her in his borrowed car.

. . . and even though he'd been searching for Palmer Nemmitz, he failed to find his friend. But Winston came away from the trip with something he didn't know he was seeking . . . and later skirted the fringes of insanity to find again.

Draining the bottle, half hoping he'd puke in his sleep and end the whole mess, he decided that he'd been lucky to escape *her* night embrace with no outward scarring other than a slightly bitten lip . . . not realizing that along with a dribble of whiskey, a drop of blood from a tooth tear on his lower lip slid down his chin.

TWENTY-SIX

No sooner had the Rambler pulled into the driveway than Bitsy's tirade began; she stood in the darkness of the huge garage where she had waited since after supper, sputtering, "Some *thanks* I get around here, *Mr.* Nemmitz. Ask you *special* what you wanted for supper *last* night, so's I'd know what to make *today*. Fixed macaroni and cheese the way *you* like it, baked in the *oven*, with Velveeta on the *top*, and then you don't come home to eat it once I fixed it! Macaroni and cheese binds me something *terrible*, but who had to eat it?"

Bitsy tailed Palmer into the kitchen, where Brent sat finishing his coffee, keeping up her harangue as Palmer hung his hat on the rack, but kept on his jacket. "*We* had to eat it, me and Brent, even the *cat* don't want it. It's awful reheated, so what do you suppose I had to *do* with it, hmm?''

"Put it in the trash with the rest of the meals no one wants to finish?'' he asked mildly, before adding, "Can't a man spend the day with a friend and have a bite to eat uptown afterward? Or do I need a note from home? And I *am* sorry about the macaroni and cheese. With Velveeta on top. Good *night*." With slow, deliberate steps, he left the room.

Climbing up to his room, Palmer heard Bitsy tell Brent, "Mr. Smart-Pants don't know I was on the phone with Pearl Vincent, who just *happens* to live in Winston's apartment house, and *she* said he was jabbering and throwing things on the floor from early morning *on*. Either Mr. Popularity has friends I don't know about or he ate a take-out burger over Dead Fred's last resting place—Palmer sure don't have that many *friends*—'' before he shut his door on the rest of her rant.

Palmer took off his jacket, hung it over the back of his chair, then took something out of one pocket—a Stardust Bar he'd bought from a boy who caged one off the Happy Wanderer, not long after Palmer left Winston. The candy bar was warm, slightly melted, the rich blue wrapper adorned with white script letters and stars adhered to the surface of the confection below in stiff wrinkles and peaks. Longing to rip away the wrapper, Palmer used all of his willpower to leave the star-sprinkled paper alone. Intact. Reverently, he placed the bar next to the instant camera on his desk.

Staring at the bar, at the innocuous yet ominous paper wrapper (when was the last time he'd seen a *paper* candy-bar wrapper?), Palmer wondered if he should look for that manuscript of his, see if it was still hidden between the unread stacked magazines near his bed. He decided he couldn't bear to look at it tonight, let alone open the blue cover and re-read—*relive* what he would find within. Besides, if it *had* been moved, it would only confirm his fear that Zoe *had* read it . . . a suspicion somehow more awful than her death.

Unbuttoning his shirt, Palmer did not look down at his forearm, nor did he check the bloody bandage held in place with two rust-brown stained strips of adhesive. Better to do that come morning, so he could pretend that he'd scratched it open himself, made it bleed . . . his nail tips were vaguely crescent-shaped, weren't they?

The warmth of the night air pressing down on him like a

blanket, Palmer kicked his way out of his trousers, then lay on top of his quilt—as he was sure Zoe herself must've done—thinking, *What did you see, Zoe? Before Brent carried you from here. Does* she *still hate me? Did she slice you up for* her *sake . . . or for mine . . . ?*

TWENTY-SEVEN

JULY 5

Sunday evening, Duffy began breathing noisily and deeply, and nothing—patting his sides, bowls of milk, catnip—seemed to help; Bitsy and Palmer feared that the ''Nothing's wrong *here*'' facade with which Brent was shielding himself would give way under the strain of his cat's illness (a Monday morning call to the next nearest veterinary clinic was useless; all the doctors were out for the Fourth), but come Tuesday morning, Brent was together enough to scoop up Duffy, and nuzzle the cat's soft gray fur, while Bitsy watched through tear-fogged glasses.

Putting Duffy in his carrier, Brent took cat and cage out to the car. Only when the Pacer's engine revved up did Palmer remark as he filled in his crossword puzzle, ''Poor kitty's used up the last of his nine lives . . . see how blue he is? Like the cat's getting punished for what that girl did—''

''Palmer,'' Bitsy admonished, huffing between strokes of the pliant bread dough, ''has nothing to do with *her* . . . she did what she wanted to do. Poor kitty looked sickly when they brought him—''

Her breathy outburst was abruptly punctuated by the slam of the screen door as Palmer left the house.

The veterinary office waiting room was post-holiday crowded; hounds with quills in their muzzles, hissing cats, and a ferret writhing like a huge worm in a pillowcase. Brent realized that something *was* bad-wrong when the assistant came out from behind her desk and offered to take Duffy to an examining room, to wait in quiet. By then, Duffy was huffing openmouthed, gums and tongue bluish. Occasionally, he let loose with a yowl.

Sitting in the small room in the back of the clinic, Brent held Duffy in his lap, and stroked his thin, quivering ribs. Breathing in the vaguely animal scent of the room, Brent brooded, *Did I offend someone up there so much to deserve this?* He thumbed dried matter out of Duffy's eye, mumbled "Coal minin' again?" then thought, *No one mentions Zoe at all . . . almost like she is dead—but no, it didn't really happen that night . . . it was so damned weird, it had to be something I dreamed up . . . Zoe wouldn't do that to herself, not like that . . . oh, damn, Duffy, why did you have to get sick. Why?*

Brent reached into his back pocket for a handkerchief—and found the wrinkled instant snapshot . . . of Zoe.

It was all true . . . not a bad dream, not a sick joke of Zoe's. And the paper Bitsy had shoved under his nose—he and Zoe had brought along their wills, with the bit about cremation—Brent's panting mimicked that of his cat, as he thought, *Zoe was right, this place is bad . . . but why'd she ever want to come back? Oh, Duffy, I don't understand anymore—*

Then the vet rushed in, explaining that he could only spare a minute until after the other patients were attended to. Brent put on a shaky smile, before putting Duffy on the cold Formica-topped table.

"They say when they'll call back about Duffy?" Bitsy eyed the date on the paper-wrapped piece of meat she'd taken out of the freezer, and shuddered because it read 8-17-87. She threw it into the sink to defrost for supper, while Brent kept an eye on the pot of water Bitsy had boiling on the stove.

After a shot of cortisone, Duffy had calmed down gradually. The vet told Brent that he suspected either complications of feline leukemia or heart muscle disease. If it wasn't either illness, cortisone might help, but it would take a few hours to know for sure. Brent reluctantly agreed to leave Duffy in isolation, until the shot took full effect—*if* it was going to help.

Brent asked to use the back door to exit; the thought of all those strangers, with their healthy animals. . . .

Upping the heat under the pot, Brent said, "Not exactly, but he only got the shot an hour ago, so. . . ."

Taking another paper-covered piece of meat from the freezer and placing it in one of two paper bags on the counter, Bitsy asked, "Did they say why his *gooms* are so blue?"

Wondering if he'd misunderstood, Brent asked, "His *whats*?"

Bitsy pointed to the pink line above her artificial teeth, saying as if Brent were dense, "*Gooms*. What teeth are set in . . . don't people have them in Minnesota?"

"Oh, his *gums* . . . Dr. Mertz said he wasn't getting enough oxygen—"

"You talk like Palmer . . . he mispronounces it, too," she said over her shoulder as she dug around in the frost-encrusted freezer. Brent felt a dual stab of pain, for her ignorance, and for Palmer's having to put up with that ignorance. It was as if everyone here spoke poorly because one teacher mispronounced something, then taught all the students to say the word wrong.

Having cleared the freezer, Bitsy put in a pot of boiling water. Putting a second pot to boil, she then sat down with Brent to await the first breakup of the ice. Brent pretended to be absorbed in his cup of coffee until Bitsy cleared her throat, then asked about something Brent hadn't been able to . . . *believe*, let alone *accept*, until an hour ago, in the veterinary office.

"I don't know if this is the right time, but . . . have you decided what to do with . . . her? I mean, she's welcome to stay on the mantel, but I was just thinking—" Bitsy traced the outline of the roses on the oilcloth with her fingernail while Brent absorbed what she'd just said.

The small metal tin had come on Monday; Palmer was out, and Brent was upstairs with Duffy when the redheaded fellow knocked on the kitchen door and left the tin box with Bitsy. Supposedly he assured her that she "needn't worry" about payment, that her husband had taken care of everything. Brent hadn't been able to ask just what was in the tin, although, he realized now, the answer had been lurking in the back of his mind. As Bitsy waited for his reply, Brent *did* forget the odd exchange between Palmer and Bitsy. Palmer had mumbled something about not having given so much as a credit-card number to the man who delivered the tin, but didn't repeat himself as Bitsy said, "Come again? I didn't hear you—"

"I dunno . . . her folks, they're buried in Illinois, but . . . Zoe didn't have close ties there. I . . . suppose I'll take them—*her*—back to the Cities . . . haven't given it much thought . . . sorry. Should've handled it myself, but . . . I'm glad you and Uncle Palmer did it for me. No problems, were there? I seem to remember signing something—" he remarked casually, while inwardly he pleaded, *Tell me I didn't sign her cremation release—*

"Oh, yes, that was the slip from the crematorium. The young fellow was so nice, he didn't want to disturb you himself, being a stranger and all, so *very* considerate. And he didn't insist on getting paid in advance—"

Visions of fly-by-night medical supply houses and Zoe's student-dissected body flashed in Brent's mind, as he asked, "He show you any identification? Any proof about working for a—"

"Now don't go worrying, he had an honest face. And he brought back her ash—*cremains*, so no need to get all flummoxed. And no need to pay us back, you're family—"

Trying not to sound as panicked as he felt, Brent took one of Bitsy's puffy white hands in his and asked, "I'm just curious . . . was he driving a car labeled as being from the crematorium? Show you *any* ID card—"

A chunk of ice dislodged and crashed in the freezer, making both of them jump in their seats. Bitsy replied, "There was some lettering on the car, but these bifocals are impossible—but he was so officious, polite, like I *told* you. No reason to panic."

The subject settled to her satisfaction, Bitsy got up and unwrapped the piece of meat in the sink's draining rack—a pot roast. As Brent sat, hoping that the "young fellow" *was* as sincere as Bitsy considered him to be, he told himself that it was okay, that Lenny Wilkes had had to sign to authorize the release of the . . . Lenny had to check things out. He wouldn't want to screw up and lose his cushy job.

Suddenly, Bitsy broke his concentration. "Could I borrow the Pacer? I have to go uptown for some chili sauce, Palmer won't eat pot roast unless the top is coated with chili sauce while it's roasting."

"Steering pulls to the left, think you can manage that?"

"I dunno . . . Brent, you'll be going uptown soon, could I hitch a ride? We could stop at the IGA, then head for the vet's—"

Brent got up, shut off the stove burner, and reluctantly followed Bitsy out to the garage.

TWENTY-EIGHT

After the trip to the IGA (where Bitsy made a scene when an obviously blitzed food-stamper with improbable orange-dyed hair paid for a twelve-pack of shortie beers with a crisp C note), Brent saw that two hours had passed since Duffy's shot; he drove down Wisconsin Street until he hit Fourth Avenue, made a right, and headed for the clinic. As they approached the building, Bitsy sniffed, "I wish that boozy food-stamper had had to go through what my Palmer did, back in '40 . . . coming home, he had to eat whatever he could find, be it in a garden left to rot, a garbage can, or what*ever*. And him with a hurt leg—"

While Brent was aware that his uncle had "gone South" for a summer long ago, that's *all* he'd heard from Dad, no particulars offered. He'd assumed that Palmer had had the wanderlust, done his wandering, and headed home come fall. And hurt his knee on the way. But eating *garbage*—

Parking his car under the sign on the side of the building that read, "Vet Clinic Parking—Violators Will Be Neutered!" both wanting and not wanting to go in to see how Duffy was (*Doc had said a heart-lung transplant, then shook his head "no"*), Brent stalled. "What happened? Couldn't he work for food? Odd jobs? Or was he too young?"

"Oh, he *couldn't* work. On account of his *knee*. That's why he limps now—didn't rest it then. And he *was* underage, so he ate what he could, making his way north. Must've been *awful*, but he never said much about it." Bitsy opened the car door, face wrinkled with concern. "Come on, let's see how that little boy of yours is."

Brent made a mental note to ask more about Palmer's trip south—something didn't sound *right* about what Bitsy said. Something seemed left out, or unknown.

Burdened with this new puzzlement, on top of everything *else*, Brent followed Bitsy into the clinic.

TWENTY-NINE

"You'd be doing him a favor. . . . If I could pull him through—which I doubt—it would only happen again. Worse." The vet stroked Duffy's arched back, grime-nailed fingers lingering over each knob of the fleshless spine. When his eyes met Brent's, they were apologetic. Glad that Bitsy was in the waiting room, not clucking and fussing over Duffy, Brent hunkered down, head level with Duffy's pink-lined ear, and mouthed silently, "Be good, boy, hear? Look for . . . look for Momma. She'll take care of you."

Duffy's eyes spoke of such tiredness, such pain, Brent said, "All . . . right. Put him down. I can't stand seeing him like this."

Nodding, Dr. Mertz filled a syringe from a bottle marked "POISON" and other things Brent couldn't read through the tears in his eyes. Gently, he said, "You'll have to hold him," so for the last time, Brent picked up Duffy, hugged him tight, soothed him as he yowled when the needle went in. Then, the wait. . . .

Bitsy peered out the office window, trying to see where all the squad cars were going—in the distance, she heard sirens toward the northwest part of town where her Angie lived— revolving colored lights flashed on the hoods of cars as they sped down barely glimpsed streets. People stood around, pointing to the Willow Hill area, just as an ambulance whooped by, heading north; Bitsy considered stepping out to ask what was going on, but Brent came into the waiting room, white plastic-bagged form in his arms, followed by the vet.

Brent paid no attention to the prolonged whoop and drone of the mixed sirens; despite Bitsy's obvious glances in that direction, he turned onto Ewert Avenue, and went south, away from the unknown accident, driving slowly with Duffy flopped across his lap. Listening for the siren, Bitsy started to say, "Maybe I should drive—" but Brent, speaking in a strained, repressed voice, asked, "Just what happened to Uncle Palmer

when his leg got injured? Dad . . . never said. I knew he was
4-F, but what went down?''

Turning around with a sigh (the cars and the ambulance
were at their destination, sirens shut off), Bitsy hoped that
Pearl Vincent might fill her in once she got home, as she told
Brent, ''All he said was he fell off a moving train. Landed
funny, messed up his knee something awful. Took him months
to get home afterward. His daddy was terribly ticked off when
Palmer pulled 4-F, so *he* signed up, went to fight the Jerries.
Palmer ran the farm. After my Tommy bought the farm in
the Pacific, Palmer married me. Didn't insist on making Angie
give up the Calder name, which comforted Tom and Clive's
folks—not that it made 'em any fonder of Palmer. I've a lot
of pictures in the family album—did Shirl ever show you any
he had? Of your grandpa Enoch the war hero, or—''

As if slowly coming up through a deep sea for air, Brent
collected himself, saying, ''No, Dad didn't keep any family
snapshots. Wasn't good with cameras. Specialized in photo-
graphic decapitations . . . Mom was spooked by appliances,
let alone a Brownie. The flashing bulb 'scared' her. . . .''
Voice trailing as he neared the Coast-to-Coast store, Brent
stared at the empty bench.

Bitsy remarked, ''Must've been something pretty unusual
to tear those two away from their bench this time of day,''
but Brent didn't take the hint. Mechanically he turned down
Lumbermill Drive, taking the same route he'd taken the night
Zoe . . . *died*.

Bitsy chafed in her seat as the car crawled down Roberts
Street; she remembered the bread dough that must've tripled
in volume, and the long-cooled pot of water in the freezer.
But she didn't notice that the Pacer was being followed, at a
long distance.

The white Pierce-Arrow matched every turn of the Pacer,
its taffy-haired driver steering slow and stately, almost as if
she *wanted* the Pacer's occupants to notice her.

THIRTY

The Palmers, Winston and Nemmitz, grew tired of watching the clumsy combined efforts of the Ewerton police force (all four of them) and the Dean County Sheriff's Department (six strong, including Stu Sawyer, who looked pretty damn silly standing in the shallow waters of the Dean River, trouser legs rolled up, his saggy bottom hanging wetly flat) to pull the lone occupant of the blue Mercury out of the flooded car. After ten minutes, they decided that the person inside the Mercury was a goner. Heading for the Rusty Hinge—which was considerably cooler than the banks of the Dean River—Winston snorted, "Any *fool* could see that orange head bobbing behind the windshield—nothing alive lolls like that."

Each nursed a single beer as they sat at one of the round tables that commanded a murky view of Sixth Avenue West—just in case the floundering water-logged lawmen managed to get the body out of the half-submerged car. A heap of crushed Lucky Strikes filled the black plastic ashtray at Winston's left elbow.

Puffing his newest smoke, the tip flaring grainy orange in the ceiling fan cooled darkness of the bar, Winston said to Palmer at his right, "True, Ewerton's had her share of crazy doings, before *we* were born, even, but you've got to admit things have gone from bad to worse since Zoe showed up in Ewerton."

Changing the position of his beer can, forming interlocked circles of moisture on the wood-patterned Formica tabletop, Palmer replied, "Are you implying that Zoe had something to do with old Alvin Miner axing his wife to death in the *thirties*? Or maybe with the Komminski girl who used to live below you and Una going crazy? Hell, just cabin fever, pure and—"

"Got to admit, nobody that young went loony that way before the Lawtons came to town—" Winston leaned back in his chair and blew smoke at the lopping blades of the fan below.

"Zoe was out of *town* by then, you numbskull . . . Una

was already dead, too, remember? Wait, I see it coming, so don't go into all that about Una, I'm not in the *mood*—''

"Wasn't going to talk about my girl at all . . . touchy, touchy, aren't we?" Winston blew smoke into the face of the Indian maiden on the Leinenkugels can, before going on, "Had Maureen Komminski in English . . . can't recall her maiden name offhand, but she was a nice kid—"

On the bar radio, one of the WERT announcers babbled, "Oh, Stu, *Stu*, how *awful* . . . like your own daughter, Stu, oh, *Stuuuu*—" while Stu Sawyer tried to give some live information about the drowning that morning, but no sooner did he say two words than the announcer moaned, "Ohhhh, Stuuu—like your own—" before his mike went dead. Palmer muttered, "Most important broadcast since the Hindenburg, mark my words . . . probably play it back fifty times today alone."

Both men finished their beers, setting the cans down on the table with simultaneous *thunks* of aluminum on Formica, before Winston remarked, "I haven't thought of the Hindenburg since the time when old Wilbur Holiday pulled Civil Defense duty and used his widow's walk for an airplane observation post."

Palmer's answering silence was masked by the gibber of the WERT announcer until Arnie the bartender switched off the radio and turned on some TV game show. The dry rasp of a match scraped along Winston's shoe sole. Waving the nearly spent match in the air before placing it in the ashtray, Winston watched his friend squirm—as he always did at the mention of Wilbur Holiday—and cough in the sulfurous air. Winston added for spite, "Old man Holiday was really a weird one . . . cripes, by now his house would be done up tricolor. Remember the year he had the *chimney* painted red, white, and blue?"

Leaning back in his chair, pleased by Nemmitz's stricken expression, Winston drawled on, " 'Course, his *house* wasn't the only thing that set Wilbur apart . . . wasn't he the one who delivered Abby Ewert's baby, right behind the *counter* in his store? Winter of '24, if I remember what Mother said correctly. Mother *also* said Abby got a bad scare at that damned carny the year before, prior to the City Council outlawing carny trash from coming here anymore . . . like that Elephant Man movie, where his momma saw an elephant, and the baby was—"

"You sound just like what you are, an asshole—" Nemmitz let his friend talk. He didn't remember hearing this story before.

"Mother even said that Wilbur had to write out the death certificate for the baby on the spot—"

Shaking his head of gray hair, until some slid into his green eyes, Palmer said, "Since when was Wilbur a *coroner*? Wilkses have been in the job since before the fucking glaciers—"

"*Dep*-u-*ty* coroner . . . winter that year most folks were down with influenza, Auggie Wilkes included. 'Sides, Wilbur only let himself be assigned the job 'cause of Hortense. *You* remember how *she* was. I can't believe *you* didn't know about him being . . . oh, never mind. Anyhow, once he wrote out the certificate, the Ewerts shipped the body south, Madison or thereabouts. Mother said it was all on account of some mind reader taking Abby's watch and—"

"What happened, he see his time was up?" Palmer attempted to be jovial, but Winston was unstirred.

"No, he got vibrations from her watch, and then had this *fit*, shouting strange things—*hell*, your parents were in the tent, too, their whole crowd was there—Mother said it was awful. He foretold a horrible—"

"Never heard of it from my old man, or our Ma—"

"Oh, is that so, Nemmitz? Too *bad* your mother didn't tell you about that, considering she was so *close* to that crowd . . . heard tell she and Wilbur had this fine customer-grocer relationship—"

As Winston crossed the line between playful banter and vicious attack, Palmer crushed his aluminum can, twisting the middle until the thin metal tore and the jagged edge almost ripped his fingers. He felt an itch on his forearm, a moist burn that set his remaining teeth on edge.

Glancing over at Winston's nodding head and hooded, distant eyes (he was saying, "—ber, how Wilbur's eyes went bloodshot later on, all Christmassy-looking—") Palmer was unable to take it anymore. Dropping the can to the floor, anger rose in him like hot vomit. Unable to keep it down without choking, *dying*, Palmer got unsteadily to his feet.

In a piercing whisper that cut through the soft bar noises like a wet knife entering skin, going to the place where *bone* lies, he said, "That's funny, Winston, 'cause *I* heard tell about *your* mother being Abby Ewert's *best* friend and 'bosom' buddy.'' He left the bar with quick strides, slamming the door behind him. Arnie actually took his eyes off the game show to watch Palmer's departure, shrugged, and went back to watching the show in mid-contestant squeal.

In the lull after Nemmitz's angry quitting of the bar, Winston sat staring down at his knobby, high-veined hands, not noticing that his Lucky Strike had burned down to flesh until he felt the heat . . . and then took his time pulling the spent butt out of his hand.

THIRTY-ONE

''—says she's a bar-hopper who blew into town last year, only Stu says her friend, the one she left her kids with, wasn't sure what state she's from, so Stu sent a diver down to try and find her purse, in case it's still in the car or under it. Woman's neck was broken—probably didn't feel the water—but Stu couldn't find a witness to what *happened*. Oh, Mrs. *Yingley* had some cockamamy story about seeing the woman's car drive off into some sort of monster *heat* shimmy. Stu just ripped up her statement and left the bar. Drove right off Seventh Avenue into the river—missed the bridge by a good five *feet*. Stu's waiting on the autopsy to see how drunk she was—''

Bitsy paced around the kitchen as she listened to Valerie Sawyer, keeping one eye on the two huge loaves of bread baking in the glass-doored oven. Brent could hear Val plainly from where he sat, and wondered if Stu's wife shouted like that during normal face-to-face conversations. With lungs like that, she didn't need a phone—sticking her head out the window would've sufficed . . . *Brent, you think mean thoughts, you get punished*—

After a futile search of the walk-in pantry that Bitsy used as a catch-all closet, Brent found no suitable boxes for burying Duffy.

He found it ironic—less than five hours ago, the drowning victim had been alive, no doubt looking forward to her next drink, his Duffy was still alive, perhaps wondering why it hurt to breathe, Brent was still clinging to the vague yet com-

forting hope that Zoe really *hadn't* done *that* to herself. . . .
Now, everything was different, changed.

Strange, how Brent felt nothing for the dead woman in the
river, yet for Duffy . . . Even Zoe had chosen to go—*why* he
didn't know, might never know. If it was because of Brent,
he was sorry; he'd have to deal with it when the time came—
if, indeed, he ever felt more than the utterly unfamiliar, sucking void yawning inside him when he thought of her.

But Duffy was another matter. He was only a little over
two years old, for Christ-all-Friday. And with no idea of what
was happening to him, not even at the end. Not the way the
cat cried, paws wrapped around Brent's arm. His eyes didn't
close, as if he didn't want to go without *seeing*. . . .

He was Zoe and Brent's *baby*. *If this is what losing a kid
is like, I hope I die without heirs*. Blinking back tears, swallowing the liquid that blocked his throat, Brent opened the
basement door and marched down the wooden steps, his
weight making the boards sigh discordantly.

Pausing at the bottom step, Brent surveyed the cardboard
boxes, wooden crates, and the old play kitchen that must've
belonged to Angie Calder (at least Palmer bought her nice
toys, his child or not). Looking around, he again asked himself why in the world Grandfather Enoch *wanted* everyone to
live down here. The walls weren't even finished off.

He poked into some boxes set up on wooden blocks against
the mildew. Old newspapers, rags, plastic flowers. He told
himself he was being stupid; doing the sort of thing people
wrote to Dear Abby about: "My wife died the same week
my cat did, and all I can do is cry about the cat . . . people
act so *strange* when I mention it—"

Leaving the boxes, Brent approached the furnace (hidden
by a wooden partition put up in '39 or '40), and saw trunks,
both civilian and army-style, resting against the makeshift
wall. Opening the first, a soft brown one with brass fittings,
he saw it was lined with rose print paper, feminine but faded.

The top tray held delicate underthings, lacy trimmed che-
mises, teddies and panties *(Zoe would've loved this—)*, all
slightly yellowed with age, smelling of mothballs and pine
soap. Figuring that the dainties must've belonged to his
grandmother, Brent lifted out the first tray and set it aside,
revealing outer clothing below.

A winter coat and an over-the-head opening dress, both
stained brown, despite obvious efforts to clean them. Lifting

up the dress (thin wool in a soft tan with white trim), Brent smelled strong unperfumed laundry soap under the mothball stink. The coat bore the same odd scent, along with the faintest iron whiff of blood . . . the same smell he now associated with Zoe.

Hastily replacing the tray and shutting the trunk—a cloud of dust rose from the falling lid—and he moved on to the next one, likewise unlocked, only black-covered. There was no tray inside, only a jumble: old school books, from the twenties and thirties, inside the front covers the name Palmer C. Winston was written in a neat, childish hand; three photo albums, pages rusty black under the harsh light of the basement's naked bulb, the top pages filled with photos of Gatsby-esque couples; three folded Army uniforms wrapped in blue tissue, one of which belonged to a higher-ranking officer, as near as Brent could determine *(Three? Didn't only Enoch and Uncle Vern serve?)*; and at the bottom of the trunk lay an old knapsack, the big, roomy kind popular with Boy Scouts years ago. It was both full and closed; listening to Bitsy's faint chatter above him, Brent lifted the knapsack out of the trunk, set it down on one of the locked Army trunks, opened the sack, and began pawing through its contents.

A long, yellowed envelope, gummy flap gone cracked and orange, filled with an assortment of cut-up Hershey bar wrappers, separated into the words "HER," "SHE," "HE," and "HEY"; yellowed strips of cellophane tape clung to the tops. A cheap Shirley Temple doll, dress crumpled and the slip hanging lower than the dress hem, perky smile still dimpling merrily.

There was more at the bottom of the knapsack, but as Brent reached down, to feel the smoothness of something celluloid under his fingertips, he was startled by Palmer's voice, shouting down the stairs, "Brent? Need help? I'm coming down."

Brent crammed the odd items back into the knapsack, and tossed the filled bag into the trunk as the old man's arrhythmic clumping grew louder and louder—then Palmer's voice was in his ear. "Find yourself a box yet? Bitsy . . . told me. Sorry." He gave Brent a pat on the shoulder as Brent slammed shut the lid of the trunk, sending another puff of dust into the musty basement air.

Brent nodded, unable to speak for a moment, hoping his uncle wouldn't realize that he'd been snooping into that knapsack *(wonder if it went south with Palmer?)*. Abruptly, Palmer said, "There's nice boxes in the garage. I'll go get one while you . . . get him ready. Say good-bye. He was a good cat. I'll miss seeing him. He . . . didn't suffer, did he?"

"No . . . went pretty quick. Just awful confused . . . you see him yet?"

Nodding, Palmer said, "Went up to your room, didn't think you'd mind. Looks like he's asleep, dreaming . . . well, c'mon." Palmer pointed Brent toward the stairs. Brent made a mental note to ask his uncle about the bloody clothes and strange items in the knapsack—not now, but later, over a beer before Brent blew town.

But Brent had other things to attend to first.

THIRTY-TWO

Poking around in the garage, Palmer was in a panic—not only was he sure that Brent had found that old knapsack, but Palmer suspected that Brent had . . . maybe found some of the "souvenirs" from that exquisitely horrible time, down south in '40. When it all . . . happened. Hoping that Brent hadn't had the time to dig down to the bottom and find what rested there, Palmer came to a reluctant decision, there in the oily mustiness of the cavernous garage.

He had to get rid of the knapsack. He kicked himself square in the keister for hanging on to it for *this* long. *Should've tossed it in the Dean River*—yet, if he had, he couldn't prove to himself that it really occurred, that she was really *real*. Without the *proof*, it might all dissolve into a distant nightmare, a dream that outlived sleep.

Craning his neck, trying to see if any of the boxes he'd promised Brent *were* up on the shelves above his seldom-used workbench, Palmer's mind hammered at him. Getting rid of the bag, and what was inside, would make him *really* lose her; then he'd be losing what good there was along with the badness . . . because of that hour of awful glory, he'd be giving up her sweetness, too, and if he lost *that*—it would mean losing everything inside him that made him *feel*, made him human . . . even if she herself wasn't quite human. . . .

No matter how much it hurt to hang on with slipping, bloodied fingers, he clung to her . . . *remains*, because he had so little else to hang on to in his life. And even less to look forward to. He *needed* what little he had of hers, those pitiful reminders, even if he had to hide his treasures. If she wasn't real; he'd have to write everything off as a result of drunkenness and thwarted lust. *But that was Winston's trick, wasn't it?* he thought, lips forming an unconscious imitation of Winston's crooked grin.

Uncomfortable with his near-alien thoughts, chafing under the harshness of his suddenly active conscience, which spoke so stridently to him, as if sitting on his bent shoulder, scolding him while whispering in his ear, Palmer forced himself to remain outwardly calm. Spotting a box resting on some old paint cans that looked to be Duffy's size, he dumped the few remaining paintbrushes inside, then, box tucked under his arm, went back to the house.

Palmer hoped with all his heart that Brent would be so upset about his cat that he'd forget about the knapsack and its contents . . . because *explaining* them was something Palmer wasn't sure he could do. To Brent, or himself. The setting sun turned his silvery hair tawny gold, and temporarily erased the wrinkles from his cheeks, making him look almost as he had in 1940.

THIRTY-THREE

Past sundown, the sky still held an eldritch light, sourceless yet *there*, a dim illumination that turned dark colors blackish, and whites and lights gray-tinged. Behind the farmhouse, away from the road, Brent dug a hole, the mound of dirt behind it crumbled dry and loose on the nearby grass. Duffy, wrapped in one of Zoe's sweaters, its flat arms cradling him in a fleshless embrace, was sealed inside the small cardboard box, which Brent gently placed in the rectangular hole. Before covering it over, he placed an even smaller tin, roughly six inches all around, into the hole next to Duffy's impromptu coffin.

Scooping up the wormless soil, he let it pour through his fingers onto the grave, a crumbling soft brown rain in the last warmth of the evening. Afterward, he patted the dirt down with his palms, until he was startled by his uncle's voice from above and behind him: "Think the city will issue me a cemetery permit?"

Ready to erupt in harsh words, Brent turned around without getting up—then he saw the trickle of tears on Palmer's cheeks.

Brent attempted a smile, before returning to his self-appointed task. Hunkering down beside Brent (knees popping loudly with the motion), Palmer handed him something heavy and tissue-wrapped—flat rocks and a few pretty stones. He explained, "Bitsy's girl had this half-assed collection, but she left 'em here. There's quartz, granite, and I dunno what else, but they're kinda pretty. . . ." Palmer's voice trailed off into uncomfortable silence as he stared at the dusty circle of disturbed earth.

Brent nodded his thanks, then, in explanation, said, "Bitsy was wondering when I'd . . . move her. I didn't open the tin, just in case. . . . Don't tell Bitsy *where*, she'd be kinda spooked—"

"It'll stay our secret. Besides, Zoe was attached to that cat." Palmer shifted the stones around on the flowered piece of tissue. "I didn't think a headstone was right for the backyard. . . ."

Brent picked up one, placed it on the smooth bare earth, and motioned for Palmer to do likewise. In a couple of minutes the grassless earth wore a pattern of small stones, arranged in a random yet meaningful design, each rock fitted in place with care.

Once they finished, Palmer offered to take Brent for a ride. "Clear your head a bit . . . fresh air." Brent agreed.

As he washed up, Brent heard the Rambler idling in the garage, and thought, *He must be* really *anxious to get away from Bitsy tonight.*

Speeding down the county trunk toward the last of the vanishing light, Palmer drove with an elbow hanging out the window, knobby hand lightly guiding the wheel.

"—sorry 'bout the way things . . . turned out. Bitsy and I want you to know that you're welcome to stay here for as long as you want. No talk of rent now, hear? I haven't much family *left*. . . ."

"Glad to for now, Uncle, but come fall, it's back to the Cities, *somewhere*. Not because of you two," he added quickly, noting the stricken sag of Palmer's jaw, "it's just this *place*. I wasn't crazy about it when I was small, and now . . . I dunno, it's just not a place to *grow* in, become a better person. Oh, *some* people do all right here, but they'd be the kind to make a go of it in a moon crater.

"And it's not what those clods did to Zoe, but . . . It's just that folks here don't seem to *care*." Looking out the window in disgust, Brent saw a hillside dotted with the most lovely older homes he'd seen in years. Gathering shadows hid whatever flaws the homes might have possessed.

As Brent stared, Palmer said, "Things deteriorated when they tried to make the town more 'modern'—Chamber of Commerce got the notion twenty years ago that Ewerton needed 'upgrading.' Pretty soon you couldn't tell what was new-new or fake-new."

"Too bad they threw the town's only asset down the toilet. And flushed twice. Looks like most of this place was built yesterday . . . it has no memory, no past. Only halfway human street is Roberts, and that's falling apart . . . oh, and this place. Could we drive up?" Brent pointed to the next street on the right.

In answer, Palmer swung the Rambler around, pointing to the white on green street sign—Fredric Street. "City Council named it in honor of ol' Dead Fred himself, back in '22." Heading north, coaxing his car up a steep ascent, Palmer explained, "This hill was settled in the mid-teens, after Otis Ewert, the fella this place is named for, came to town. Pumped it full of new money. He and Winston's old man Porter, Fred Ferger, Sr., my old man, old man Crescent, planned out the streets, and the Founder's Bank approved the loans for building the homes. Some Sawyers lived here, too, and the Wilkes clan, plus the Andersens—"

"You mean Andersen as in *Scooter*? Sarah's—what the hell happened, inbreeding? Nepotism?"

Smile bitter in the faint light, Palmer said, "Bit of both. Folks out here are worse about 'marrying in the circle' than some religious sects. Lots of couples are distantly related, or in-laws before they sign the license. Wasn't that bad when I was young, but it was starting. People here take less store in strangers than the folks down in Appalachia. It's as if you have to be related in six different ways to every local family before you're accepted. The few bright ones here get out, like

Scooter's brothers, which leaves the yo-yo heads hell-bent on making the town over in their own image."

Palmer braked across from a lovely frame and brick house that topped the hill like a turreted crown. As they took in the curving brick porch, delicate shutters, and stained-glass windows, the street lamps came on with a faint firefly sizzle, bathing the house with a cool glow.

Brent saw that the cream paint was flaking, and also noticed the empty windows unsoftened by curtains. Sighing, Palmer pointed to the top dormer, "I spent many a night sleeping in that room. This was the old Winston place, Palmer's house until he married Una Sawyer. It's been empty since the fifties, when his ma Gayleen died. Always wondered why he didn't move back, or buy it later on. Beautiful inside. Wainscotting and stamped tin ceilings. Three fireplaces. Now Winston lives in a one room plus bath. Nuts."

Brent asked, "Is it sold? You could convince him to move back in—"

"Not for sale. Most of the empty houses on the hill aren't either. One good thing, the city can't rush in and buy them up, turn it into another empty industrial park or apartment buildings. You've seen the empty stores, the drive-in closed in '86—"

"Drive-ins closed all over the nation. VCRs—"

Palmer waved his hand. "I *know*. Don't you *see*, losing the drive-in, the Soo Line, all the fly-by-night stores that open and close in the space of a month, a year . . . it all *means* something? Ghost towns have the sense to know they're dead, capitalize on their ghost-hood. But a *corpse* just lays there, stinking. Attracts flies, who feed off dead meat—oh, Brent, I'm sorry—"

"It's all right." Eager to either leave this place or change the conversation, Brent asked, "The Winstons must've been pretty well off, owning such a fancy house . . . wasn't his dad a teacher, too?"

"Porter worked his way up to superintendent when Winston got to high school . . . special kid, Winston was. Not like now. . . .

"He and I had this relationship going ever since we were in the cradle, practically. After the Depression hit my old man harder than it did Porter, Winston stuck by me. Looking back, I think that the Crash was the start of the double standard in town—rich children assumed to be smart, and the poor—''

Hearing the echo of Zoe's story of Mrs. Winston's teaching methods, Brent felt the hairs on his arm rise, and was glad of the darkness in the car.

''—pattern was in place by the late thirties, but I didn't get sucked into it the way the other poor kids did. Because of how Winston stuck by me. Him treating me right made others do likewise, even after my siblings got sucked under. It was good between us until, oh, 1940 or so, maybe a bit beyond . . . but then, things got messed up. Don't know exactly when or how,'' he quickly added; his tone suggested that he did, indeed, know. ''Used to be a *hell* of a lot better between us.''

''Yeah, I figured that,'' Brent said, then added, ''What I could never figure out was why you two put up with Fred Ferger . . . he was so cantankerous—''

Shifting around in his seat, until he faced Brent, Palmer explained, ''We put up with him on account of our parents. Lemme backtrack a little.

''See, my parents, Fred's, Winston's, the Crescents, the Holidays, and the Ewerts were very *special*, in the early days of this city, when it was rightly called a town. Those six couples were the cream rising to the top of the town, their reward for all they'd done to make it more than a whistle stop.

''Otis Ewert bailed them out when the lumbering failed, but money wasn't enough . . . town needed *people* to get it going again. Those couples pitched in to help. So they were *quite* respected, considered *important* in the scheme of things.

''I learned most of this secondhand, though—the Ewerts moved away before I was born. Then the Crescents grew too old to take an active part in city life, and as I said, there was the Crash. But the feelings people had for our parents extended down to Winston and I. Suppose you could've called it a dynasty.

''And as people expected a lot from our elders, they naturally looked to Winston and I to come up shining later on. Some thought Winston a natural for mayor, and more than once I was told Ewerton could use someone like me for city government. Don't look at me that way, it's true.

''After the farm nearly went bust and once the elder Winstons' health declined''—he mimed a bottle tipped to his lips—"people still thought we both had promise. War changed a lot of that. Blunted the edge off both of us. Considering the heavy loss of Ewerton recruits over there, we should've had it made. Things just fell apart though.

"Ironic, he and I marrying Sawyer cousins, considering how the Sawyers were second-string important around here. Think two cream-of-the-crop kids marrying Sawyer girls all set to take the city by storm. But it didn't happen. We were taken by the city, steamrolled over both of us—"

"Ever wish you could've met all those couples, when they were in their heyday? Sounds fascinating, the roaring twenties, Great Gatsby, all that," Brent said, trying to make his uncle lighten up. "Y'know, when the town was still young, when the buildings were new. Wish I'd had a camera, to capture it. Or at least my sketchpad—"

"Did you ever see old man Holiday? He was alive the last time you were here. Tallish fellow, with blond—well, gray—hair—"

Before realizing how awful it sounded, Brent blurted out the tale of his meeting with Wilbur Holiday, finally giving his uncle Holiday's odd message. There was just enough light in the car for Brent to see the stricken expression on Palmer's face; visibly shaken, yet silent, Palmer backed out onto the street, and headed for the business district below.

Ultimately, the Rambler braked in front of the Rusty Hinge. Inside the warmly lit bar, a few couples sipped beer and mixed drinks. To his relief, Brent saw that Mr. Winston wasn't among them.

Palmer toyed with the ignition key, flicking the glow-in-the-dark plastic keyholder, his mouth a taut black scar that alternately puckered and pulled out. Finally, yanking out his keys, Palmer asked, "Did you . . . think he was just mouthing off, crazy?"

Remembering Holiday's solemn tone, his rational green eyes—the *gravity* of his request—Brent decided to cover his faux pas. Opening his door, Brent said, "Yeah, he was whacked out . . . I don't think he *meant* it. Probably wanted to get a rise out of me."

His lie was rewarded with a smile from Palmer, who suggested, with a nod toward the bar, "How 'bout a wake for that boy of yours, a toast to a good kitty?" He led Brent into the fan-cooled interior of the Rusty Hinge, where brightness obscured all shadows.

THIRTY-FOUR

While Brent and Palmer kept vigil at the old Winston house, mulling over irrevocable losses, Bitsy watched the news, *Wheel of Fortune*, gossiped with Angie on the phone (that rude, boozy food-stamper in the IGA *was* the drowning victim) and decided to make an early night of it.

By 8:40 she was in bed, false teeth bobbing in their bath of Efferdent on the toilet tank, face religiously creamed with Night of Olay, hair wound around soft curlers, snoring like an idling chain saw. In her deep sleep, Bitsy didn't hear the gentle *scree* of the screen door opening.

Or the muted *click* of the front door, followed by the muffed thud of footsteps across her good wool carpet, which changed to sharp taps as the steps crossed the kitchen floor. Bitsy's snores almost masked the sounds of the basement door opening, the light clicking on, and the footfalls down the steps.

Nor did Bitsy hear rummaging down there, and she didn't stir when the footsteps ascended the stairs, crossed the kitchen and the living-room floors, to make their way up the stairs . . . growing louder, closer, going past the room where the old woman slept so soundly, so peacefully, wrinkled lips fluttering in a discordant night song. The footsteps stopped; from Palmer's room came further sounds of searching. . . .

Later, when a car revved up in the driveway, Bitsy dreamed about the car her future husband Tommy and his brother Clive once had. An old roadster, with "Catch me—I'm Dillinger" crudely whitewashed on the doors. Oh, the *fun* she and Tommy had, driving down dirt roads outside town. Clouds of brown dust settled in their hair, in their bright faces; he said, "Want to?" and she nodded, face flushed. . . .

When the car outside the farmhouse pulled away, Bitsy dreamed that the Dillinger roadster put on speed as Tommy gunned the engine, while Bitsy's brown hair floated behind her lolling head like a swarm of bees—

When Palmer and Brent came home, to stumble up to bed, Bitsy didn't notice at all, so deep in sleep she was, dreaming of her Tommy. . . .

THIRTY-FIVE

The next two days erased the clamor over the Dean River drowning and the did-she-or-didn't-she "death" of Zoe Lawton Nimitz ("Guess who I saw, driving around in a long white car, alive as you please—"), and replaced the disruptions with the swing of familiarity and forced repetition of the ordinary. Yet, under the placid exterior of Ewerton, ripples of unease spread outward, to touch people before moving forward.

Palmer Nemmitz forsook his daily tussle with the crossword puzzle; he fixed his own breakfast before taking off in the Rambler, leaving Bitsy and Brent with vague excuses about getting "a good spot on the bench," even though he spent his days cruising around, searching for the Happy Wanderer, as his arm itched like crazy and his mouth pulled into a white-lipped grimace.

South of town, on county trunk QV, Lenny Wilkes sat behind the counter of "Lenny's Place," making change for crumpled dollar bills, getting out the booklet listing his XXX-rated videocassettes for those giggling, snorting snot brains Dusty Parks and Bob Gray, all the while kicking himself in the butt for not *insisting* that Doc Calder do a proper autopsy on that Nimitz woman. Calder didn't even take *pictures* of her—Quincy on TV was never that sloppy.

Dark thoughts crept into Lenny's usually uncluttered mind, stained deep by the crazy *things* he'd been hearing lately . . . some people claimed they'd seen an old white car driven by a woman with long, caramel-colored hair. And the way the crematorium fella struck Lenny all funny when they met. Worse, Lenny had begun to think about *comas* and *zombies*, not to mention *dummies*.

The last notion came to him while watching that *F/X* movie; the hero made dummies that seemed so real they *bled* . . . didn't old Nemmitz say something once about Brent being an *art director*, whatever that was? The only magazines Lenny read cover to cover didn't have much need for art directors (just someone with an airbrush or who made sure the photographs were printed right side up), but Lenny *assumed* they supervised what other artists did.

And Zoe *was* board stiff, which was weird once he thought it over. Lenny watched a bunch of greasy-haired guys who should've been at work this time of day as they tilted the pinball machine trying to get a better score, and wondered if Brent had *directed* someone in the construction of a Zoe dummy. For a joke. Scare the hicks . . . stranger stuff went on all the time. Millie read *The Star*, showed him the juicier articles over dinner. So, Lenny could either believe his new-formed theory, or admit that he was going bonkers, seeing dead women drive classic cars.

At the opposite end of the city, Stu "Satchel Ass" Sawyer, Dean County sheriff, enjoyed a couple of days of relative quiet, since most people were too busy hashing over the strange deaths last week to get themselves into any *new* trouble. True, Dusty Parks and Bobbie Gray got reported for yelling filth out their car window at a group of ladies waiting for the senior citizen bus outside the IGA, but those two never did grow up.

But Stu was disquieted when he tried to find the file on the Nimitz woman's suicide. After cleaning out his file cabinet, he was faced with the sick realization that he'd either round-filed the report or shredded it along with the reports his deputies filed on people who didn't *need* any trouble right now. Like Scott Andersen, who ran another stop sign near the middle school. Scooter worked two jobs, tried to keep his family off the dole, when only two thirds of Ewerton even paid city taxes. Stu hated to see good guys pay through the nose, while the deadbeats took a free ride, past Go, collect $200.00 in county money . . . and Scooter pulled "Go to Jail."

Only this time, Stu had turned more than a traffic violation into cat box filler. Or he'd out and out pitched the Midnite Mayhem report. Garbage day had been Friday, meaning that the report was long buried in the stink of the Ewerton dump.

Rifling his rifled-through files again, sweat a dark skunk line down the back of his uniform shirt, Stu cursed himself for giving in to Bitsy. *Should've given the report to the* Herald *editor, or that gibbering jerk at WERT, or had 'em run an obituary of* some *kind.*

Even *Val* doubted him; she'd wheedled, "Couldn't you and Len have made a boo-boo? It *was* late, honey—"

But what worried Stu, even more than having done an Ollie North on the Zoe Lawton-Nimitz file, was that he'd *seen* the phantom "long cool car" his deputies were jabbering about. Not the whole car, not a glimpse of who was driving it, but Stu Sawyer knew all the local cars in Ewerton, either by sight or by plate number. *Nobody* he knew drove a white Pierce-Arrow. With odd, peach-decorated tags.

"*Damn,*" Stu growled. He hoped things would stay quiet until the Water Carnival came up—*then* people could go utterly bugshit, like they were *supposed* to each year. Maybe they'd forget this whole Zoe Nimitz business while having a good time.

A good time was the furthest thing from Winston's mind after he found his Army uniform hanging in his closet. He distinctly remembered Una donating it to the Methodist rummage sale the year before she died . . . yet there it was, neatly pressed, clean, neutral-smelling (no hint of mothballs or mold, as if freshly issued by the quartermaster), and complete down to the dress hat and matching tie. Every button shiny, every stitch perfect, each crease iron-sharp. And hung on a wooden hanger—not a black metal one like those supporting the rest of his shapeless clothes.

After finding the uniform, Winston hid in the darkness of his apartment, which reeked of stale bedclothes, warm whiskey, and molding food on takeout plates. He wasn't quite able to *believe* in the reality of what hung on his closet door, yet he was unable to drink it away.

Likewise unhappy, the usually Happy Wanderer (now plain Cooper "you are *grounded*" Reish) sat on his lumpy group-home bed, tried and found guilty of staying out too late. And pigging out on candy. Moping, the Wanderer wished he didn't have to rely on his doorway or window to leave his room.

And for two days Brent and Bitsy holed up in the farmhouse, cleaning. Methodically, they started with the pink insulation-blanketed attic, and ended up in the basement by Thursday.

Standing on the last of the basement steps, both of them wondered where to begin. Brent spread his arms wide, suggesting, "Would a fire hose do the trick?"

Shaking her head, Bitsy sighed, "We'd only end up with a lot of wet junk, 'stead of dry junk. Oh, well, s'pose we'd best move it away from the middle, then wash the floor."

Brent asked, "Uncle Palmer ever say why his old man

moved the kids down here to live? It's been puzzling me . . . this isn't the most cheerful place, he didn't bother to paint or—''

Bitsy stopped pushing a big box marked ''Entertainment Center—This Side Up'' toward the wall, sat down on it, and patted the place next to her. Fearful of spiders crawling into his shorts and beyond, Brent gingerly rested some of his weight on the paper-filled box as he listened to Bitsy's story.

''I don't know if Shirl told you this, but Enoch and Treeva didn't . . . get *along* after the Crash—not that they got on well *before*, but worse was worse. When Treeva died, Enoch's mourning took a strange turn. Got it into his head he didn't want to be *reminded* of her, but not wanting to move outright, 'cause money was tight—''

(*Not so tight he couldn't afford a bathroom down here*, Brent thought, glancing over at the small enclosed area where the sink and toilet were hidden, and at the old-style sink in the south corner of the basement.)

''—the next best thing. By living under her house, he didn't have to see the walls that reminded him of her . . . didn't have to clean them, either! Maybe that made the move worth it . . . *anyway* what was worse was what he done to the older kids. Made 'em quit school. Palmer was so smart, too. Him and that Winston, such bright boys—not that you'd be able to tell nowadays, but then! Wish you'd've seen them.

''Winston was such a good egg, tutored Palmer himself, on weekends, after school, whenever. Nowadays how many boys are willing to do that? Gave Palmer all his school books . . . now that's friendship. I was a couple of grades ahead of the boys, but I remember what Winston did. Taught Palmer 'most everything he learned, 'cept ROTC, which didn't interest Palmer like it did Winston.

''Winston had hopes of being a career man. Army. Wouldn't think it now, way he slouches . . . guess it didn't work out. But that's a story your uncle knows better than *I* do.

''Never saw two boys closer than the two Palmers, more like kin than my Palmer and Vernon were. Poor Winston was an only child. Know something, Brent? I do believe God made a mistake by not letting those two be brothers.'' Letting her bespectacled gaze wander, Bitsy's eyes lit on the black trunk near the furnace. She hurried to it, followed by Brent.

He hoped that she wouldn't notice the mess he'd left in the trunk on Tuesday.

Throwing open the lid, Bitsy plowed through the old books until she came back up holding the three photo albums. She failed to notice that the trunk wasn't as full as before . . . nor did Brent see that there were only two Army uniforms under the books now. Hugging the albums to her ample chest, Bitsy said, "The basement isn't going anywhere. We can look at these upstairs, sit on the couch." Brent followed, cheered by the thought that there were no spiders in the couch.

THIRTY-SIX

Quickly, Bitsy hurried through the pages of the oldest album, the one containing faded photos of the six "cream" couples Palmer had mentioned, despite Brent's voiced interest in it. Bitsy's people weren't among the cloche-hatted and white-suited people, so she skimmed the small images, pausing only when she came to those that featured the two Palmers and their parents.

Brent noticed that Winston inherited his mother's eyes, but received nothing from Porter, save for his dour late-life expression. Literally seeing his grandparents for the first time (Dad had been reluctant to discuss his parents, save for "our old man wasn't one to waste affection"), Brent saw elements of his own visage mirrored there; their dark hair and eyes, Enoch's chunky frame and broad shoulders, and Treeva's rounded, Slavic face.

Bitsy kept flipping pages, not anxious for him to see a crowd that had excluded her family during Ewerton's halcyon years. Later on, he'd have to look over the book, paying close attention to those semimythical couples.

Bitsy picked up and opened the next album ("*al*-bee-*uuum*" as she pronounced it), and showed Brent crinkle-and-pattern-edged photos taken in the thirties and forties, when the two Palmers were growing up.

Brent was astonished how much the two boys resembled each other, both thin, compact, not very tall (Winston overtook Palmer only in the later photos), with identical slightly wavy, dark hair, light complexions, and pale eyes. There were dozens of shiny snapshots of the two of them, interspaced with photos of two tall, dark-skinned teens posed by a rusted-out car with "Catch Me—I'm Dillinger" white-lettered across one door ("My Tommy and Clive, he's the doctor who—*imagine*, seventy and still practicing!")

Pointing out a photo of Winston, looking collegiate in an argyle sweater, cuffed pants, striped shirt, and saddle shoes, lopsided grin on his lean face as he slouched, hands in pockets, against a brick storefront, Bitsy said, "Some folks called him 'little Gatsby' after some fella in a book he used to tote around. Dressed so *snappy*, like his folks used to before the Crash . . . his father's cream suits, all that. Looked sharp on him, went with that *hair*—

"All us girls had crushes on him . . . I tell you he was valedictorian and top-ranking officer in the EHS ROTC? Folks just *adored* Winston, 'specially Wilbur Holiday. That was on account of him having no boys of his own. Wilbur liked my Palmer, too—there's Wilbur, I didn't know Palmer had hung on to *that* shot."

Brent stared at the small photo, made even smaller by the wide crinkled border surrounding the image; a younger version of the man he'd seen outside the Holiday house, now standing in front of his store, arm around the shoulders of one of the Palmers. No matter how hard he looked—glare from the lit table lamp didn't help—Brent couldn't figure out *which* dark-haired teen was standing next to the blond man. Bitsy changed the page before he had a chance to ask about it.

Pausing at a hunting picture of Porter Winston and his son, she said, "Winston's daddy was a crack shot, taught Winston so he'd be first in rifle shooting in the ROTC. Strange, Porter used to shake so bad he could hardly drive his Oldsmobile, but put a rifle in his hands and *wham!* bull's eye. My papa said the last time they had an outside carny group come to town for Water Carnival, Porter hit every target, bam, bam, *bam*, yet couldn't hardly walk from booth to booth. I was there, but I don't recall *that*. Dead Fred was on hand, too, he was only two or so, like me. Poor Freddy, he had Buster Brown bangs and big jug ears."

Pointing to a summer snapshot, her Palmer and Dead Fred standing, beer bottles in hand, outside the curving brick porch of the Winston house, she said, "Those scamps! Not of age and slopping it up. On the school superintendent's lawn no less! Winston took this—see him in the next one? See what's in his hand? Already smoking Lucky Strikes at fifteen or so. Wonder he didn't get mustered out of ROTC—oh, would you look at *that*? Still can't *fathom* why Fred put up with that foolishness,'' she exclaimed, tapping a picture of Palmer Nemmitz pouring out a bottle of beer over Dead Fred's head. Palmer's grin crinkled his eyes, and Dead Fred's mouth hung open, as if someone had whacked him upside the head with an ax. Brent commented, ''Must've liked it, he didn't move.''

Adjusting her glasses, Bitsy replied, ''Was a glutton for punishment . . . I often thought my Palmer had something on him, after the war. Never found out what . . . at first I thought it was just that no one wanted anything to *do* with Fred, on 'count he was a pain in the keister, but after the war . . . it was *different*. Palmer found some real deep hole to fit the screw in, and pleasured himself by turning it every once in a while. Like he did with poor Wilbur,'' she added sadly, pausing at a portrait of Holiday that occupied half an album page. Judging from the thirties cut of his clothes and the width of his neatly knotted tie, Holiday was in late middle age, perhaps fifty.

Mentally, Brent compared his severe, yet kind-eyed visage, hair neatly combed, corners of the tight-lipped mouth slightly upturned, with that of the wild-eyed and shaggy-haired old man outside the sage-green house. Brent decided that the years between the photo sitting and the sticky summer day twenty-some years ago had been neither kind nor pleasant for the ruggedly good-looking Holiday.

''I saw him, last time Mom and Dad and I were up here, but I didn't realize he looked like that—not exactly *handsome*, but—''

''A lady-killer, right? Wish I had a color photograph of him. Beautiful green eyes, something like Palmer's. Nice teeth, only his teeth were set funny in his gooms, would've needed braces, I suppose, but in those days . . .

''That wife of his, Hortense, never knew what she had in Wilbur. She didn't have brains enough to fit in the hole in a spool of thread, while Wilbur was so *smart*. Had degrees from a university, and he ran a grocery store. He did read a lot, lent out books to both Palmers. *That* was years ago.

''Wilbur could charm the pants off a person, too. Didn't have many men friends his own age, though. Jealousy on their part, I suppose. He was looked down on for not having any business sense—he wasn't cut *out* to be a merchant, but he managed to make a lot of money . . . *how* I'm not sure. . . ."

Bitsy ran a fat finger along Holiday's strong jawline in the picture, adding, "He did buy up a lot of property . . . most of it was worth a mint later, after the Second World War. Folks thought he was crazy for buying up this and that—did you know he bought up most of those heaps up in Little 'Frisco?"

" 'Little—' "

"Ewert *Hill*, the crazy streets—"

"Oh, *those*—no, I didn't. Nice houses, though," Brent said, fidgeting from hunger, yet not wanting to disturb Bitsy's narrative for one of her grease-laden fried hamburger and pasta meals.

"You *think* so? Rat traps is what they are—would you believe, Wilbur set up trust funds, for the *houses*? Put money into bonds, so the city could use the interest to pay for the taxes. Didn't leave diddley to his surviving daughter, poor Koba went all but loony before she died, trying to break his will, but you know those big-city lawyers . . . I guess Wilbur *liked* eyesores, but it seems a waste of good money to *me*. Now if he'd spent money to *modernize* those wrecks, make them into nice efficiency apartments—"

Unable to hold his tongue any longer, Brent said, "*Bitsy*, the current trend is to either renovate Victorians or build—"

"Big-city silliness," she sniffed. "You sound like *Palmer*. Why shouldn't Ewerton smarten herself up? This isn't 1928, it's 1988. Who needs an ugly run-down old town? I've been after Palmer for years to put up some aluminum siding. Brent, you're a young man, wouldn't you rather live in a *young*-looking town? Clean lines, no muss and fuss? *No?* I must be the only forward-thinking person in this house.

"And that *bathroom*"—she glanced in the direction of the downstairs "Necessary Room"—"I've been after your uncle to put in a new toilet. Old one has a cracked bowl. I've had my eye on one of those marbleized streamlined ones. Palmer *knows* how to install them, so that's not the problem. He just won't pick one up. Brent, could *you* twist his arm, next time you two go out driving? Would mean the world to me," she wheedled, making blinky eyes at Brent, who thought, *First you tell me how you want to rip away the last bit of grace this town has, and now you want me to force Palmer to cor-*

rupt his own bathroom? *C'mon, Bitsy!* but said, "Sure, next time we go uptown, I'll mention it." Then he noticed a bizarre snapshot—

Wilbur Holiday stood in front of his house, which was decked out with every Halloween geegaw known to stationery stores—die-cut witches, curved-back cats on fences, jack-o'-lanterns—and next to him was a tiny girl dressed up as a gypsy, holding a paper sack of goodies. Pointing to the small face forever frozen on the verge of tears, Brent asked, "Who's *that*?"

"Oh, here's my Angela," she cooed, oblivious to the pained expression on the tot's face. "Palmer took her trick-or-treating and brought along the Brownie. See his shadow there? Poor Angie was so *scared* of Wilbur . . . she never went trick-or-treating with Palmer again. Let's see, that's her fortune-teller outfit, which would mean she was—oh, here's the date on the edge! 1948. Don't the house look awful? No wonder she was terrified, all those ugly witches. . . . That was the last year Palmer and Wilbur were on speaking terms, I think, or was it *later*—"

"What was the falling out about?"

"I'm not sure . . . some flap about the land surrounding this house, acreage Wilbur bought up during the war . . . he came back around the fall of '48 or so to sell the land back to Palmer. After a lot of shouting in Palmer's office—that back parlor he don't use no more—Wilbur left in a huff. Palmer *did* buy the land back, but from what I heard uptown, *Wilbur* came out on the steaming brown end of the deal. Yet Palmer acted like *he* was stung."

Lapsing into silence, Bitsy watched darkness pool in the deep corners of the room, hands resting on the rough black pages of the open album in her lap. Abruptly, she switched gears. "Since Wilbur died, the house don't look like some exotic gussied-up roundheels. Old eyesore. People laughed at the place, like it was some kind of joke—"

THIRTY-SEVEN

A frosty white car, failing sunlight glinting off the sweeping curves of its wheels, the polished chrome trim, slowed to a stop before the Holiday house. The driver slid over to sit on the passenger seat, opened the window so she could lean out. Rich sunlight caught her hair, setting the long locks aflame with burnished red-gold fire.

She continued to stare up at the Holiday house, cocking her head from side to side in an intensely feminine gesture.

A tall figure in a baggy sweatsuit jogged toward the Holiday house, his expression a mixture of shock, wonder, and more than a trace of fear as he padded close to the white car. "Miss? Excuse me, but I must speak with you—Miss, you bear a most striking . . . *resemblance* to—"

Clive Calder stopped a few feet from the car, squinting at its occupant, as he rubbed his palms up and down the side of his legs.

Even in the deep, last light of day, Clive Calder's normally dark face was pale, drained. . . . He stepped closer to the car, close enough to almost reach out and touch the hair of the young woman, who had yet to move from the passenger seat.

When the fair-haired woman cocked her head, Clive wiped his mouth over and over, pulling down the slack skin.

Calder said something softly to the woman. She daintily shrugged, let loose with a tinkling laugh, and slid over to the driver's seat—*after* opening the passenger side door and letting it seductively swing open.

Clive hesitated a moment; warm night air lifted and tossed his limp white hair, but as the street lamps went on in a sizzle of dead white-green, he climbed into the car. And said something loud enough for anyone to hear:

"Miz . . . Lawton, is it? Or do you prefer Mrs. Nimitz?" Calder's voice shook, a thin, falsely brave tenor floating down the nearly empty street like an airborne dandelion seed. Once again the woman's laughter danced in the warm air, but the sound of her mirth was now a cold, cold thing. . . .

The Pierce-Arrow's engine came to life with a mute roar. The car then glided up the street heading north.

THIRTY-EIGHT

Feeling as if his behind had merged with the cushion on the couch, yet not wanting to offend his aunt by getting up to stretch, Brent listened to the tale of Wilbur Holiday's last years in the Holiday house.

"Stu went in after the postmaster called his office. Wilbur's mail hadn't been taken in for a week, yet he'd left no notice asking the post office to hold his mail.

"Bone cold in the house, Stu said his breath followed him through the house like a lost puppy. Not a stick of furniture was there, save for the big stove in the kitchen. And the pump sink. Stu never saw the *likes*. And the walls had ice runnels all the way down to the floor that sparkled like a tumbler of lemonade held up to the sun . . . after the first look-see, Stu was *sure* Wilbur'd up and gone days before. Nobody can *live* like that. Not in a house so cold your lungs turn to slush. Stu's toes were ice stiff, and he was wearing thick stockings I'd knitted for him. And Stu *is* chunky—don't tell him *I* said that—while Wilbur never had an extra ounce of meat on him he didn't have immediate use for."

Brent noticed that the colorless hairs on Bitsy's plump forearms were rising, each hair rooted in a dimple of gooseflesh as she dutifully recited Stu Sawyer's winter's tale.

"Stu said he was ready to give up, but a little voice told him the old man might be *upstairs*, so up he went. Later he said he had bits of ice trapped in the hairs of his nose by the time he reached the second floor. Rubbing his nose was like 'grinding it in a snowcone.'

"Most of the doors were open, showing nobody inside. He almost didn't spot that little room under the stairs. Door was shut, but Stu saw a sliver of light under it that made the frost on the threshold sparkle like crushed bottle glass. He tried the door—he swore the cold of the knob went right through the palms of his Welles Lamonts—and it swung open with this *scree* he claimed made his filling ache. Then Stu looked in. . . .

"Wilbur was there, on the floor, near the only window. Stu said he was just *lying* on the floor, a half smile on his lips, showing his crooked teeth. Stu was shook up by that, more than there being no furniture in the place, or by the coldness.

"Later he told me, 'Bitsy, it was like Wilbur pulled one over on all of us, him lying there grinning away . . . holding that postcard in his hand, like he'd *planned* it all.' And my cousin is *not* a man to spook easy. Marine in Korea, he was.

"Once he saw how Wilbur was all coated with frost—stuck to the floor, bound to the boards with *ice*, clothes and hair just *stiff* with it—well, Stu *knew* Wilbur was dead. He ran downstairs into the street, looking for a house where he could call—"

Brent had seen Stu Sawyer, on the night Zoe . . . The man was built like a denuded grizzly, crew cut and flat-assed, with a saggy pap of a belly. It was all Brent could do not to laugh at the thought of Stu pounding icy pavement, frantically searching for a phone. Especially since his car had a two-way radio inside.

"—didn't think of the car radio until he got back to the house, poor Stu was so *rattled*, he swore it was worse than Korea. But Stu went back in. He stood watch over Wilbur, as if Wilbur were about to get up and head downstairs on his own.

"*Any*way, Stu bent down, to warm the face of the postcard, see what the picture was . . . there were *naked people* on it! Stu said there was a third person on the card, a yellow-faced man with wings, sitting in a gray *cloud*. Stu thought it was *pre*tty *kinky*, so he looked at the back as best he could, but couldn't find no message. He pried it out of Wilbur's fingers and tossed it aside just as Lenny Wilkes and Craig Reish came upstairs, carrying a stretcher. They didn't see it, so at least *that* didn't get spread around town. People considered Wilbur strange enough—not that he didn't give 'em some *cause*—but to die holding on to a dirty *picture*? Stu looked for the picture later on, after Wilbur was taken away, but someone must've tracked it outside on the sole of his boot."

While Bitsy prattled on, dentures clicking softly in the dimly lit room, oversize glasses bobbing in time with the rise and fall of her voice, something nagged at Brent's memory.

An image hovered just out of inner sight—"*naked people . . . a yellow-faced man with wings. . . .*" Somewhere, Brent had *seen* that picture.

Then it came back. Not a *post*card, but a *Tarot* card. His roommate's girlfriend at the UM had a deck. Used to give bullshit fortunes at parties. Depending on how good the grass had been, the bright colors on her cards' faces looked fluorescent, after a couple of joints, the people and things on the cards actually *moved*. After years of employed, respectable life, the memories of his college days made Brent wince.

Finally, Bitsy said, "Was that your stomach or mine? Goodness, look at the time!" peering at her Timex through her bifocals.

Brent felt as if he were walking on a field of needles as he followed into the kitchen on his sleeping feet.

"—didn't have a crumb of food in the house, either, just a postcard in his hand. Man must've lost his *mind* . . . you want chicken or tomato?" she asked, not missing a beat between her death tale and her question about the soup cans held in pink-nailed hands. Brent pointed at the chicken noodle.

While Bitsy opened the can, Brent realized that old man Holiday must've been trying to leave a message. When coupled with his strange communication about Treeva twenty years earlier, it wasn't too hard to guess what Holiday was trying to admit to the world. Brent mulled over the name of the "postcard"—The Lovers.

And then Bitsy had put two and two together for him, by saying that her husband and Wilbur Holiday had the same green eyes. Suddenly, he was glad that he'd told his uncle about Holiday's strange words while they were alone.

As Bitsy stirred the soup on the stove, Brent got down a couple of soup bowls from the cupboard; smiling sadly as he placed the bowls on the table, he thought, *No wonder Dad said Palmer had no right to the family name.*

Bitsy kept stirring the bubbling, foaming yellow soup, humming as she did so.

THIRTY-NINE

Warm night air reverberated with a high wavering hum, announcing the coming of the Happy Wanderer on Hill Road—an escapee, via a slit screen, of the Crescent Street group home. The Wanderer's shamble gradually took a winding course, matching the shallow S curve of the street as it wound past the paper mill. Behind him, the Wanderer heard the displacement of air as a car sped toward him, and saw his bulky shadow—gold-edged and fluid on the pavement—grow tall, taller. As Happy studied its amazing growth, the car came to a stop, and a voice called out, "Come here, Cooper!"

The Happy Wanderer, who seldom heard his real name except when someone was angry with him, made a simple assumption on the dark road—he'd been caught by the group-home leaders. The shouting continued, but in his panic, the words were garbled, meaningless.

Happy ran, his hum replaced by ragged, hard breathing. His shadow ran before him as the car followed, a liquid black thing that bled off into the darkness between the street lamps. Happy's eyes filmed over with a red-black haze; as he reached the second shallow curve of the S a single thought pulsed through his mind—*hide*.

Behind him, leaning partway out of the Rambler's window, Palmer Nemmitz kept shouting, "Cooper, come *here*! I only want to talk—*Cooper*, please stop, it's *me*—Cooper!" before the car came to a neck-snapping halt on the street, the engine flooded. Palmer directed his attention to the dashboard for no more than a few seconds, but when he looked up again . . . the Wanderer was *gone*.

And he hadn't been moving fast, no more than a labored *trot*. Street lamps and lights from the mill yard flooded the last stretch of Mill Road with crisscrossed pools of light, not to mention the bridge lights. There were no trees or high grass along this last bit of road. No Happy Wanderer, either.

He wasn't across the river, or still crossing the bridge.

The Happy Wanderer could never move that fast, under any circumstances, eluding someone in a matter of moments.

Moving lips unaccustomed to prayer both by heritage and

personal choice in a chilling plea *(Please, God, let him have run fast, that's better than any alternative—)*, Palmer felt frigid, teeth-chattering fear grip him. Making a Y-turn on the narrow street, he found it hard to grip the steering wheel.

Somehow, he made it down Mill Road to the point where it joined Lakeview Road, then speeded until he hit the county trunk, where the shakes hit him so bad he barely sputtered along at ten miles per hour.

FORTY

Placing grease-rimmed bowls into the sinkful of rainbow bubbles, rubbing them until they squeaked under her wet thumb—"No squeak, no clean," Bitsy solemnly told Brent as he dried the dishes with a lamb-embroidered dishcloth—she told him of the double wedding of the two Palmers.

A marriage and a half, actually; Bitsy and Palmer were already hitched, but willingly renewed their vows when Winston returned stateside after the war and proposed to Una. Bitsy hinted that Winston needed someone to prop him up during the exchange of vows.

While Bitsy chugged a dish rag up and down in a tumbler, Brent recalled Winston's photo-frozen expression of being cast alive into the pit—on his *wedding* day, no less. Brent had thought only nineteenth-century virgins looked that soul sick.

Considering that Winston was fairly good-looking, an ersatz Errol Flynn (thin mustache, back-combed waves of hair), he found it incredible that Winston had settled for some*thing* like Una Sawyer.

Brent wasn't callous enough to condemn all unattractive-to-ugly women to the "you've a better chance of being attacked by a terrorist" club, but Una Sawyer *was* the Wicked Witch of the East, squashed down by Dorothy's house. "In the eyes ugly," as Dad used to say. Not so much a state of *physical* unattractiveness, but an inner repulsiveness that might've rendered even the Mona Lisa horrible to behold.

The phone rang. Drying her hands on a rooster-print towel draped across the handle of the oven door, Bitsy hurried to the phone.

When her plump face sagged, Brent stopped drying the

bowl in his hands, suddenly tense, alert; the stresses of the past few days welled in him, ready to spill over. A litany ran through his mind, *Not again, not again*. Faintly, he heard the sharp gabble of a woman's voice coming from the receiver—the *worry* in the voice was unmistakable. Bitsy tried to talk, but was repeatedly interrupted. Unobtrusively, Brent walked over to the table—ostensibly to pick up a spoon lying in a thin pool of yellow broth on the oilcloth—and listened to the faint stabs of anguish coming over the line:

"—*is*. Uncle Clive . . . *hours* ago, he's . . . so *prompt*. I called the . . . and he's *not* at home, and—"

"Angela, have you called *every*one?"

The voice was brittle ice, shattering. "*Yes!* I even . . . *nothing* . . . that *cousin* of yours . . . person's report can't be filed until twenty-four—"

"Did he have someplace to go? A doctor's convention? Maybe he lost track of time—"

"*. . . got* a watch!"

"Oh, Angie, haven't you and Dick ever missed a dinner date, 'cause something else came up—"

"*. . . this* late, or . . . calling first!"

"Now, now, do you know where he usually took his walks?" Bitsy had a big curly bracelet of phone cord wrapped around her wrist as she stood staring at the cloth calendar on the wall nearby.

"Along Roberts . . . view Road—long, uninterrupted streets—"

"Did Dick drive out and check, see if he's hurt—"

Reluctantly, his spoon in hand, Brent went back to the sink and dropped the spoon into the lukewarm, semibubbly water. What Angie had said about Stu Sawyer sounded par for the course in Ewerton; don't bother with anything until it was too late.

The good old "twenty-four hours" b.s. . . . as if Stu had a big-city lawman's enormous pileup of cases taking up his precious time.

Behind Brent, Bitsy soothed, "Have you called all the bars? Maybe someone invited him in for a few—you know how Clive tries to please people, be polite. It's only after nine, I'd wait until, oh, say, midnight, just in case his watch ran down or something. Angie, you realize Clive *is* getting on—"

Angie's anguished blast hit Brent's ears at a distance of five feet—"*Only in his seventies! He's* not *fucking senile!*"

Winding down, Bitsy tried to make her daughter share her own lack of concern. "Now, hon, Clive always was a bit wild, *you* remember that car of his—stop *worrying*. He's a big boy and it really isn't *that* late. He probably has some friends you and Dick don't know about, and is with them now. Heavens, this is *Ewerton*, not some big dangerous city—really bad things like that don't *happen* here. Clive can take care of himself. Come morning he'll be all apologies for missing the meal. You'll see . . . now good *night*, Angie. Come morning he'll be home . . . yes, now good-*bye*!"

Uncoiling the cord from her wrist, she told Brent as the Rambler's tires crunched faintly on the gravel drive, "Clive didn't show up for a six-thirty dinner date at Angela's house. Can't scare him up on the phone so she's out of her mind. Next thing Dick'll call the National Guard—"

Brent wanted to say, "Maybe she's right, he is an old guy—" but his uncle walked into the kitchen, and Bitsy snapped, "Diner's closed . . . I hope you had enough sense to grab a bite uptown." She huffed into the living room.

While his uncle hung his hat on the wall peg, Brent filled him in on Angela's call. All Palmer said was, "Clive must've taken the long way home," but Brent saw concern in his green eyes, and echoed, "Yeah, the long way."

Bitsy reappeared in the doorway, saying, "See, I said there was nothing to worry about. Girl of mine is nothing but a worry wart. Going to be a mass of wrinkles come morning." Yawning, showing her bubble-gum pink upper plate, she concluded, "If you gentlemen don't mind, I'm calling it a night." Glancing at her silent husband sitting at the empty table, she added, "Some people work hard enough to *get* tired out."

Palmer ignored her as she clomped upstairs. Instead, he stared at the refrigerator door, covered with magnet-held snapshots and the ubiquitous foam, sequined animals.

Noticing the barely perceptible tremor of the old man's blue-veined hands as they rested on the slick surface of the table, Brent let the water out of the sink; over the *chug-chug* of dirty suds spiraling down the pipe, he asked, "Think Clive is all right? Bitsy seems sure, but I dunno . . . Angie sounded awfully upset—"

"Angela vacillates between indifference and overreaction, like someone we know"—he aimed a knobby finger at the ceiling where the faint give and pull of footfalls was followed by the muted rush of water filling a basin—"but in this case, I think she is right to be worried. She call Stu?"

"Gave her the 'twenty-four hours' song and dance—"

"Figures." Palmer sat rigid, both shiny palms touching the oilcloth, eyes still fixed on the humming refrigerator. Wiping his hands on his shorts, Brent asked, "Think we should look for Clive? We can take both cars—"

Shaking his head, Palmer instead asked, "What do *you* think happened to him?" in a tone that clearly told Brent that he had already weighed the options—and come out in favor of a dead weight.

Taken aback by the leaden query, Brent sat down opposite his uncle and said softly, "Who knows? I've seen some of the local color around here . . . anything for kicks. Courts let them off with a fine they pay for with beer money, lay some probation on them. I hate to say it, but Clive's an old, old guy, and—"

"Yeah." Interlocking his fingers, Palmer rested his chin on his crossed knuckles before rambling on, "Ever see the Happy Wanderer? Big guy, dresses like G.I. Joe? Hums a lot—"

"You think he hurt Cl—"

"Nah. Not *him*. What I mean is, have you *seen* him? He walks around town, eating candy bars. Drops the wrappers . . . you seen what *kind* he drops?" Gaining momentum, he prattled on, "That Wanderer, sure drops the oddest—"

Reaching over the table, Brent took Palmer's shoulders in both hands until the old man let out a gasp of pain.

"Uncle Palmer, what's *eating* you? If you're that worried, we'll look for Clive. But I can't follow this crap about the Wanderer, and his *candy* bars. What's *wrong*? You're not yourself at all. Ever since Zoe, you've been rattled worse than you were after Dad died. You didn't even *know* Zoe. I'm—I was her husband, and even I'm too numb to feel it all yet. C'mon, what's *wrong*?"

When Brent let go of his shoulders, Palmer stared at the patterned oilcloth, mouth slightly open, eyes heavy-lidded. After a lull filled only by the whooshing hum of the fridge behind him, Brent said, "I have a bad feeling about Clive, too. In my guts. Bitsy thinks it's wild oats or something, but . . . Bitsy's *Bitsy*. I just know it's . . . bad, and that Stu's an asshole. I'd go look for him now, but . . . I think it's too late—"

"You mean that, what you just said? How you *felt* it, that he's—" Palmer's green eyes never left the table; Brent reached over and, after giving his bony hand a squeeze, said, "To Bitsy I'd lie, 'cause with her you have to fib a little. But you know me better. Wish I could say different, but when the cat walks over your grave, you *feel* those paws . . . I *am* sorry."

Digesting that last remark, Palmer slowly lifted his eyes until they met Brent's. "I'll tell you what's what, what it is that's bothering me, but first *you* have to come clean with me 'bout something. Just where did . . . she, uh, Zoe . . . die?"

A wave of shame hit Brent—he may've fooled Bitsy, but Palmer *never*. Face coloring, Brent tried to buy time by cracking his knuckles, but Palmer's expectant gaze forced him to haltingly tell the truth. He even mentioned the part about finding the camera on the floor, photo sticking out like a rotted tongue.

"—she'd done a really bizarre thing, not like Zoe at all—"

Palmer cut in, "I know all about that cut on her side, Lenny saw it, but Clive, he didn't give it a second—"

"That *what* on her—"

"The *slice*, on her—didn't you *know*? Oh, Lord, I thought you—"

Feeling soured soup shoot back into his throat, Brent poked at his burning eyes with blunt fingertips while Palmer rattled on, "I half expected she'd do something like that, I would've been . . . disappointed if she hadn't—"

Unable to speak, Brent reached into his back pocket for the instant photo he always carried with him (for fear Bitsy might find it otherwise, wordlessly he handed it to Palmer, who fell silent when he saw it. Holding it out of the glare of the ceiling light, Palmer peered at it expectantly, mouth silently working, until he asked, "Where's the names of the towns, the county trunks?"

Stunned, Brent reached over and took back the photo . . . seeing it for the first time for what it was.

A map, composed of wide blue lines. A road . . . but to where?

Lips quivering, Palmer backed away from the table. The chair legs made a low scudding sound on the linoleum. "Lemme go upstairs . . . come morning, I'll tell you. Everything. Now, though . . ."

After he had left the room, Brent silently sat at the table, not aware of Palmer's heavy steps up the stairs . . . nor was he aware of the car that kept making passes by the farmhouse, its interior firefly lit against the blackness beyond.

FORTY-ONE

JULY 9

By Friday afternoon, Clive Calder did not return home. After a worked-up call from Bitsy ("Stuart, what's the *matter* with you? Any *fool* could see something was wrong last night, you should've looked right off!"), a missing person was filed— "White male, DOB 9-17-15, white hair, blue eyes, 5'11½", 160 lbs, last seen wearing—"

Once the investigation was under way, Brent realized that now was not the time to press his uncle about the way the old man was acting—or about Zoe's death. While his aunt and uncle fretted over Clive, Brent took to eating at the Dairy Queen, or the A&W.

He ignored the way some conversations going on inside the eateries would *stop* when people finally realized who he was. He no longer expected condolences from anyone over what happened to Zoe. He knew Zoe wouldn't appreciate their false sympathy and reptile tears anyway.

What *did* bother Brent, as he munched chili dogs and slurped down Blizzards, was the nagging horror of what Palmer had implied Zoe had done to herself. *Slitting* her side. And Palmer had mentioned that he'd been expecting, *anticipating* that act. . . . Just thinking about it nearly made Brent vomit up his sodium-rich meals, but self-preservation prevailed, and the food stayed down, digested, and turned into extra inches around his midsection.

It also niggled him how he wasn't *sure* that *Zoe's* ashes had been returned. At any rate, no body to exhume, no way to find out if her side *was* cut.

The autopsy report or her death certificate might say something, but considering Doc Calder, he may well have stated that Zoe died of a sore throat, or caught cold. With Calder missing (dead?), obtaining the report might be a bitch and

Brent hated to make a fool of himself by asking Lenny Wilkes about it.

His nights were so restless he sweated through both his pj's and his sheets. By Saturday, he'd gone through all the spare sheets in the upstairs linen closet. Not wanting to bother Bitsy with questions about how to operate her antiquated wringer washer, Brent scooped up the dirty bedding, added some clothing (including Zoe's shortie nightie), and drove up to the Super Suds Launderette early Saturday morning.

The launderette was a long, narrow building, brick and peeled-board fronted; a brick propped open the glassless door. The space where the glass had been was covered with an unpainted sheet of plywood, on which the words "Satchel-Ass Sawyer Sucks" were penciled. The last word, "Cock," was scribbled over with blue pen.

Approaching the building, Brent heard children inside, yelling. A girl screamed, "Mommy! Blaine's puttin' my barrette down the drain hole!" A voice shouted back, "Stoppit already *both* of you! Gimmie that *now*—oh, *hi*, Brent, how ya doin'?"

Turning around, full basket of clothes held in front of him, Brent saw Sarah Andersen sitting in a yellow, scooped-shaped plastic chair, wrinkle-backed romance novel held in one thin hand. Sarah's other hand was firmly clamped on the shoulder of a preschool-age boy who held a red duck barrette in dirt-tipped fingers. Brooke snatched the hair ornament and put it back in her hair, albeit upside down, before plopping down on the white chair next to her mother's.

Letting go of Blaine, Sarah patted the white seat on the other side of her. "I haven't seen you since—c'mon, sit down. I'm going *nuts* in here. Need to talk to an a-d-u-l-t!" She widened and rolled her eyes until Brent laughed, despite his thought, *Can't anyone say they're sorry about Zoe? Even you?*

Hefting his brown clothes basket, he demurred, "Got to get my clothes in the machine." Fishing quarters out of his cutoffs' pocket, Brent shoved the sweaty clothes into a machine, poured in Bold 3, and selected "Warm" before thumbing in his coins and slamming the lid.

While water rushed into the machine, he sat down a couple of seats from Sarah, crossing his legs and leaning back into the chair. Sarah fiddled with a blue plastic hair clip before saying in a voice that carried as much uncertainty as sympathy, "I'm really sorry about Zoe . . . I hope everything is okay now."

The last sounded like a question; it took Brent a few seconds to think of an appropriate response.

Sarah did seem sorry, but not *sorry*-sorry. Itching his bare knee, Brent slowly replied, "Thanks . . . Uh, she's in a better place now. I think she's happier now . . . it still hasn't sunk in, y'know. Guess now's not the time or place." Concentrating on his knee, he nodded while Sarah said, "I understand . . . this isn't the best place, for you or her."

There was no rancor in her tone, yet Sarah's words hit Brent the wrong way. Letting it pass, he gave Sarah a quick smile. "I really needed to get out of the house, you've heard about Clive, I sup—"

Shaking a twirling finger next to her temple, she said, "All that's been on the scanner is that Clive 'hasn't been *seen*'— my ass! Either he died from the heat or someone rolled him and hid the body. Didn't anyone call the cops right away?"

Brent leaned over and told what he knew.

"I *knew* Stu didn't deserve to win the election!" she said, crossing her legs nervously. Her wiggling toes made the thick rubber soles of her flip-flops *swack* against the sole of her foot as she fumed, "Where'd he think an old fart like Clive would *go*? In a jogging suit?"

"I dunno, I think Ewerton is after blood this summer." After speaking, Brent felt exposed by voicing a fear so deep he'd scarcely been able to think about it.

Sarah nodded, her words punctuated by *swacks* of her thong, "Know what you mean . . . first Z—then that drunk drove off the bridge, or missed it, or what*ever*, and now Clive. 'Course it doesn't help that Police *Chief* Bib Stanley chose *this* week for his vacation, as *usual*—"

" 'Bib'?"

She traced the outline of a bib on her bony, freckled chest. "Eats like a pig. His wife Rhonda makes him wear a napkin 'fore she puts his plate on the table. Anyhow—maybe if he'd been around, he'd of been more help."

Sarah went on, "If Clive wasn't a Calder, and an in-law of Stu's, no one would do anything to find him. Way it is, they're avoiding bad press, on 'count of that stupid Water Carnival coming up. Big tourist attraction, or so the Chamber of Commerce and Shitty Council think. Me, I don't see that it brings in *that* many people. . . . Say, how's that cat of yours? Zoe said you brought him up with—''

"Dead. On the fifth. Had him . . . put down. Bad heart."

Sarah grabbed Brent's wrist, gave it a squeeze. "Oh, I am *so* sorry . . . was he sick for long? Oh, that's a blessing. Poor kitty. We used to have a cat, Chewie . . . beautiful cat, dark gray, with huge ears and dark green eyes. Like an Oriental shorthair. Either ran off or somebody stole him . . . if they took him for stud they're in for a shock. Had him fixed last year, but the sack hung down, so maybe they thought. . . . '' Sarah's eyes watered as her voice trailed off.

"Hit me pretty hard with Duffy, too . . . if your Chewie ran off, I hope someone who really wanted a cat found him.''

Sarah sniffed, "Or I hope if he got car hit, he didn't feel it. Either way, that's it. Chewie was too cute to just go out and *replace*.''

"Same with Duffy.'' After a beat, Sarah asked, 'I know it's none of my business, but when I was talking with Zoe, we never got around to why you guys came back up here. . . . ''

Figuring *Why hide it?* Brent told her everything, until Sarah interrupted, "*Zoe?* At the reunion? After the way those girls and Una—well, Mrs. Winston is gone, so maybe it wouldn't be *too* bad—''

"Sarah, was *Mr.* Winston as rotten to Zoe as his wife was? The night I spoke to him he mentioned that he'd taught Zoe—''

"Scooter said he's a letch. Used to peek and feel if the girl was willing and he could get away with it. Winston might've been interested in Zoe, but his screwy wife put paid to *that*. They were just a *fucking* weird couple—*literally*—''

"What do ya mean, 'literally'?'' Brent was startled by the voice; looking behind him, he saw a man in his late twenties wearing faded jeans, a long-sleeved shirt with the sleeves rolled up, work boots, and a red and white mesh baseball cap on his tangled light brown hair. Narrow blue eyes regarded Brent from under bushy brows, and an equally bushy mustache covered a mouth full of yellowed teeth.

He looked vaguely familiar—Scooter Andersen, one of the few "sort-of'' friends Zoe had had at EHS. The kids busy shoving bits of crayon into the floor drain resembled him. Scooter swatted the nearest one's behind, yelling, "Don't *do* that, ya hear? Go outside, but don't run into the goddamned street.''

As the shrieking kids scrambled out the door, Scooter sat down in a chair opposite Sarah and Brent, and pulled out a pack of cigarettes, generic menthol, offering the pack around. He put it back in his shirt pocket after Sarah took one. Soon a crisp burning odor cleared the cloying fabric softener sweetness out of Brent's nostrils. Between puffs, Sarah said, ''Brent was asking about how the Winstons used to treat Zoe, and I was saying—''

''*That*. Oh, yeah, sorry 'bout Zoe . . . we meant to call or something, but . . . anyhow, Zoe was okay. We weren't that close, but we'd talk in study hall, that sorta shit. Some of the kids were jealous, on 'count she was smart, but once Una started in on her—whoooeee! Hated Zoe like something else. I was in class with Zoe the first time Una saw her, and right off she says, 'I will *not* have you making *eyes* at me! Uncross that eye right *now*.' Sure as shit, bitches in our class, all the twits, picked up on what Una said 'bout Zoe 'making eyes' and thought the old bat meant Zoe was on the make. Only I don't think that's what the old prune had on her mind. She freaked over how Zoe *looked*, period. Like she reminded Una of someone she hated.

''Never noticed her eye myself, until Una brought it up. But after that, *everybody* noticed—''

As Scooter drawled out his story between puffs, Brent thought, *No wonder they ''had'' to know if she was queer. . . .*

''—if she'd done something like that to *me*, I sure as hell would've done more than rip the sheet off the bulletin board—''

''What *was* written on that sheet? Zoe never told me—''

Exchanging a look with his wife (who shrugged, as if to say, Go ahead, *tell* him), Scooter stretched out, booted foot almost touching his wife's rubber-soled thong.

''Saw the sheet myself . . . I was the one who called Zoe over, so she could do something about it before the whole school was laughing behind her back. Old Una wrote 'Wall-Eyed MONSTER!' in that scribbly-scrabby writing of hers, with her fine-line red pen. Like she was correcting a paper. Zoe went white, and ripped it down, only Una-Pruna was comin' down the hall—when she saw Zoe do that, she let out this *whoop*. Face purpled, and she came storming through kids milling in the hallway on account it was between classes, and she whacked Zoe upside the head. Sounded like someone getting aggravated at a melon. Heard it ringing in my head for *days*—''

Wondering if Una Winston had been delusional, Brent began to ask what Una had said in defense of her actions, but a wailing siren shattered the low easy sounds of the day, setting Brent's teeth on edge.

''What the hell . . . sounds like the tornado warning—bet someone needs the cops real bad.'' Throwing his cigarette into the street as he ran out of the launderette, Scooter stepped on the butt as he got into his parked station wagon. Brent watched him switch on the CB, and turn the knob slowly up and down the band, until Sarah yelled into his ear, ''If this is something good, you wanna come with us to see?''

Brent shrugged. ''Why not?''

''I'll take your stuff out of the washer, someone'll swipe it if you leave it here.'' She threw her nearly dry clothes into a basket, then opened his machine and placed the spun-dry wash in his basket, Zoe's nightie topping the wet clothes.

Sarah's kids clustered around the wagon, watching their dad play with the CB, until Scooter found the frequency in use, and listened intently. Nearby stores and bars disgorged curious people, who looked up and down the street, and pointed in every direction.

Sarah poked Brent in the back; turning around, he saw that her arms were straining under the load of two stacked baskets. Sheepishly, he took his off the top.

Clive. They've found him, I knew I should've gone out looking for him that night, why didn't Bitsy get worried *for Chrissakes*—

Scooter leaned over and yelled, ''Something happened out by the fairgrounds.'' As Sarah, her brood, and Brent piled into the Andersen car, Scooter turned on his red ambulance dashboard light and took off down Wisconsin Street, the in-town road leading to the fairgrounds, rolling up the power windows to better hear the tissue-crinkle CB static.

Brent thought the noise gibberish, but Scooter translated as he drove.

''They aren't even using *codes*, for Chrissakes! Do we actually pay these boobs to *protect* us?'' The wagon plunged into the cool green tunnel of a grove of trees that overhung the street on either side; behind them, Brent saw a growing line of cars following, which seemed to inspire Scooter to drive even faster.

Outside, the siren blat died away to a residual ringing in Brent's ears. Scooter opened the windows, letting in a rush of air—for which Brent was grateful. The car smelled like rancid french fries, bubble gum, and sweat, undercut with old cigarette butts.

Luckily, the fairgrounds were unfenced, for Scooter tore across the pounded dirt surface, sending up clouds that hung over the area long after the last of the cars following the wagon squealed to a stop. Through the dirt haze, Brent saw the red and blue swirl of lights near the storage building, a huge sheet metal and wood edifice standing near the northernmost corner of the grounds.

While Brent rubbed grit out of his eyes, Scooter exclaimed, "Look at them squad cars! Even rounded up Bib Stanley—must be important shit."

Succeeding in only further irritating his eyes, Brent stared blearily at the cop cars parked at crazy angles near the front of the building. Lenny Wilkes pulled up, waddled over to the only occupied squad car, then went into the partially opened building. The rest of the civilian cars—including Palmer's Rambler and Winston's Olds—were parked a few yards behind the Andersen station wagon.

Suddenly, Stu Sawyer's bullhorn-amplified voice blasted, "Stay out! Authorized personnel only! Go home now!" The Andersens were trying to keep their kids within grabbing distance, so Brent took off at a run for the building, entering the dim interior close on Lenny's penny-loafered heels. Behind him, he heard Winston drawl, "If you didn't want company, Stuart, why'd you advertise?"

Turning around, Brent saw Mr. Winston moving at a speed he never would've expected from a man his age. Uncle Palmer puffed as he trotted to keep up with his friend. The rest of the dozen or so people who'd followed Scooter stood around uncertainly in the harsh sunlight, not wanting to defy the sheriff, yet too curious to leave.

"OUT! That means you, too, Winston!" Stu bellowed, while Winston, who stood at Brent's elbow, flicking ashes into the top of an empty Leinenkugels beer can, said, "I fully expected Stuart to take out an ad on WERT, just in case no one showed up . . . otherwise, he never gets to play with that damned bullhorn we taxpayers bought for him."

Brent's uncle pushed through the large wood and metal door, blinking in the grainy half-light. He panted as he reached Brent and Winston. "Made Bitsy stay home. She's close on a heart attack the way it is—what the hell's going *on*?''

A hulking shape detached itself from the darkness and approached the trio. "You all get the hell out, hear? Police business, OUT!''

Brent's eyes became accustomed to the darkness, augmented by faint half-light coming from plastic-covered windows set high in the walls of the musty-smelling building. He saw men poking around piles of . . . *junk*; pieces of things jutting out at odd angles, darker shadows against patches of mere darkness. Suddenly, someone banged a flashlight against a wall, sending up a dull, echoing throb before the cone of gold light finally lit the interior of the building.

Then Brent saw the hacked-apart jumble of split wood and painted, shining surfaces, before his line of sight was obscured by a thin silhouette that pleaded, "C'mon, you guys, clear out. If there were any footprints you've trampled them— somebody find the light switch, huh? Or a better flashlight?''

"Bulbs are broken,'' came the reply from the rear of the building, and another officer yelled, "Flashlight don't work, batteries—''

"Aw, *screw* the batteries,'' Thin-Silhouette sighed. Someone came into the building with a battery-powered lantern, shutting the door behind him. In the cavernous building (a good fifty by one hundred feet), the lantern had the illuminating power of a stove bulb in a dark basement, but it was better than a single weak flashlight.

By now, Brent recognized Bib Stanley's voice ("This is Chief Stanley, with a radio reminder for all skateboard riders—''), and thought the man's five o'clock stubbled face didn't match his nasal voice. He nearly laughed at the thought of Stanley's nickname; sure enough, there was a spot of something on the man's light tie, but it was hard to tell what in the yellow-tinged light.

Palmer poked his nephew in the ribs before saying, "Oh, c'mon yourself, Bib, not after you all but put it on Radio Free Europe how you got trouble here—''

"Palmer Nemmitz, you shut—'' Bib's stubble-coated Adam's apple bobbed behind his tight collar, but Winston stepped forward, tip of his smoke glowing deep orange-black as he tapped ashes into the white can, "Considering that you had to come out from under your rock, Brian, we might as well get a look at our lawmen in action. I was beginning to think you were just a voice on the radio—"

"Palmer Winston, you shut up, too. Do I have to put both of you under arrest?"

"Convenient time to do it," he drawled back; while the argument between the two Palmers and Bib dragged on, Brent finally took a look around him. At the carnage. . . .

What surrounded the dozen or so men in the storage building was utter destruction, annihilation . . . a silent testimonial to an orgy of violence, of gleeful rage.

Brent remembered his dad telling him that the city of Ewerton owned its own amusements, booths and rides, and never had to spend money on hiring any outside amusements for its annual Water Carnival—when not in use, the rides and booths were stored in this building.

Nothing remained whole, nothing had escaped whatever instrument of destruction was employed to wreak this terrible damage. Near Brent's feet was the decapitated head of a merry-go-round horse, gilded bridle nicked and chipped, large painted eyes staring into his own.

The wire mesh of a dunk tank was twisted, warped into a free-form sculpture àla Calder. The dusty floor sparkled with fragments of funhouse mirrors, which sent odd chunks of reflected light onto the walls, the twisted hulks of ruined equipment.

At Brent's elbow, Lenny Wilkes suddenly blurted, "Did you ever see the *likes*? Officer in the squad car said the place was shut tight . . . locks wasn't busted—"

"Huh? Sorry . . ." Brent apologized, staring into Lenny's darting brown eyes. The older man looked fit to cry as he whimpered, "The *lock* wasn't busted. And them windows is twenty feet off the ground, none of them broke neither. This stuff, it's all we *got* . . ." Lenny made a moist, gagging noise deep in his throat as he raced out of the building.

Palmer came up to Brent and led him out the now opened door. "Nothing we can do here . . . someone did a *sick* thing. End of the Carnival this year, for sure." But his uncle's tone struck Brent as odd. The old man seemed *glad* about the probable cancellation of Ewerton's only tourist draw.

Brent's eyes pained him so much when he stepped into the sunlight he forgot about Palmer's strangely jubilant tone. He hurried over to the Andersens' station wagon, quickly filling them in on what he'd seen as he picked up his laundry basket.

When he reached the Rambler with his load, the sound of Stu's bullhorn carried harsh and exasperated in the hot air— "Winston, I said *scram*! You'll read about it in the paper. Now *out* 'fore I arrest you!" Putting his laundry in the back-seat of the Rambler, Brent heard Scooter shout back, "Yeah, we'll read it—*if* they decide to print it!"

Stu heard Scooter; he appeared at the door of the building and bullhorned, "Next joker who pipes up is gonna get arrested! I want this parking lot cleared out in *five minutes*!"

Palmer had the car rolling before Brent closed the passenger side door and settled down in his seat. Sighing, his uncle said, "Thought for sure they found Clive—Lenny must've had the same thought. Damned idiots. Don't want people at the crime scene, so they blow sirens so everyone and his second cousin comes out here outta sheer curiosity. Shit for brains, every last one of 'em." Before Brent had a chance to remember or to remark about his uncle's inexplicable exhilaration over the eminent shutdown of the Water Carnival, the older man asked, "You want Bitsy to run them wet things through the drier?"

FORTY-TWO

For an event that quickly got out of hand, the discovery of the fairgrounds break-in had begun simply, innocently.

Gordy Gray, owner of the Super Suds Launderette, and chairman of the Water Carnival Committee, decided to stop at the storage building to check which booths needed to be refurbished.

But Gordy, having unlocked the big padlock that secured the door of the huge building without incident, realized something strange was going on when he flipped the light switch inside the door—and no lights came on.

His subsequent call to 911 was more frantic than even this grave event might have warranted.

Local law enforcement personnel were already under the pressure of the Doc Calder case, so when Gordy shrieked,

"Fairgrounds! Disaster: *Hurry!*" followed by a dead line, no one could really be blamed for overreacting—"

But Stu Sawyer was nonetheless in the mood for *serious* blaming. Morosely shredding bits of paper as he sat at his desk, Stu again and again asked himself, *What the heck* happened? Within less than a couple of weeks, Ewerton had gone to shit—a suicide, a drowning, Clive, and now the fairgrounds building.

Luckily, Stu *had* thought to look outside the building, but he wasn't cheered by his findings—or the lack of them.

No ladder impressions under any of the high-set windows. Not so much as an indentation. Gordy swore up and down that the lock was whole, untampered with when he came to the fairgrounds. The question of footprints *inside* the building was a moot one; Bib's boys had been tromping around in there before bringing any illumination into the building. (Bib had made one discovery—the bulbs had all been broken, on the *ceiling*, leaving claw shards of glass and ruined filament in the screw-in sockets.

After shooing out that old pervert Palmer Winston, and coaxing Bib into taking his men outside before they pulverized what little was left of the ruined booths and rides, Stu wasn't able to find so much as a dropped ax or a forgotten baseball bat. Whoever had done this had taken his, her, or *its* instruments of destruction along, before exiting a locked, high-windowed building. And not only did the windows lock from the inside—making entry impossible without shattering the panes—but they were covered on the *outside* with storm windows, which were secured from the outside.

No digging at the base of the building. The ground was packed down, hard, all along the foundation. No one could pack it down so perfectly, so quickly.

As the hungry shredder devoured and spit out the remains of an old memo, Stu rubbed his slack cheeks with a paw of a hand.

Then there was what that old fart said; Stu had caught a fragment, but just enough, of Palmer Nemmitz's words—he was *glad* the Water Carnival was doomed this year. "Old spoilssport," Stu grumbled, remembering how Palmer never showed up at a Water Carnival since after Pearl Harbor, when Stu was young. Not *once*, even when Bitsy had to tote Angie around during the festivities. Like Palmer was too *good* for a small city carnival.

"Spoilssport," he repeated . . . since the Palmer Nemmitz *he* knew was nothing but a crab-ass since the forties anyway, it never occurred to Stu that his cousin's husband might be *afraid* of Ewerton's annual Water Carnival.

FORTY-THREE

JULY 10

Sunday morning, Brent planned to sleep late, but dreams of merry-go-round horseheads trailing sawdust mingled with sticky, viscid blood onto his bedclothes woke him up; heart thumping, breath coming hard in the humid morning air.

Downstairs, the sound of WERT came up, faintly, something about a "Summer Sizzler Sale" at the Happy Step Shoe Store. Bitsy had already left for church; for once the kitchen smelled *good*, not of burnt toast and overboiled coffee. Butter, egg, and bacon odors hit Brent's nostrils; he shook a finger at Palmer. "Didn't Bitsy say the good stuff's out for you? Where's that dry toast, hmmm, mister?"

Leaning back in his chair, Palmer nodded toward the stove. " 'Been in the kitchen *all* day, working on that' . . . yours is still in the pan. And to answer your question, no, I'm not supposed to eat eggs, butter, *or* bacon, doctor's orders, but considering that, said doctor up and got himself lost . . . hope you like lots of bacon. Fried some in with your eggs."

Walking over to the stove, nearly tripping over one untied shoelace, Brent scooped up scrambled eggs dotted with bits of crumbled bacon onto an ironware plate Palmer had warming in the oven, then sat down next to his uncle. A scraped-clean plate sat defiantly next to his Sunday paper. Mouth nearly full, Brent managed to ask, "Bitsy take the Rambler?"

"Nah, one of her church ladies picked her up." Suddenly, Palmer got up, asking, "Got any plans for the day? Wanna hitch a ride into town with an old heathen? I . . . have something to tell you." Without waiting for an answer, Palmer grabbed his fedora off the rack, while Brent gulped down the last of his eggs before running his plate under a spray of water in the sink, hoping that *now* he'd find out why what Zoe did to herself was so important, so scary to the old man . . . and to Brent, too.

Once the Rambler was speeding down the county trunk (the last time Palmer had taken his doctor prescribed walk was the end of June), Palmer spoke of Enoch Nemmitz, not of Zoe.

Guiltily, he began, "Dunno if I mentioned this before, but my old man—your grandpa—and his cronies, they thought of themselves as . . . very special men. Above it all. When I was a pup, people remembered, and some *talked*. Wives were no different, including Hortense Holiday.

"That whole crowd—well, not our Ma, or Wilbur Holiday"—Brent hoped his expression didn't betray his realization over why his uncle singled *those* two people out— "held themselves up above *normal* law. As if they were better. And folks just took it, on account of what they'd done for this place," Palmer added, as he chewed dead skin off his lips. "You know, give and take, they gave, but the town had to take in return."

Turning right onto Byrne Avenue, in the shadow of the Little 'Frisco homes, he continued, "It all hasn't changed too much since then. There's still a bunch with their noses up in the air, that Willow Hill crowd, and there's still the common folk, only not as hard-working now as they used to be . . . and the welfare ones who settled here. And the kids of those who *used* to work, ones who slobbed up. And then there's the drifters, work 'cause they have to, and learn to like being trampled down by those on top. They don't strive, but they don't slob out, either. Just drift along like seeds from a dandelion.

"I don't know how well you knew your wife's folks, but from what I heard about 'em, they drifted, didn't make waves. Tried to live what life was left to 'em undisturbed—"

Palmer was right; Brent had met the Lawtons—both in their late sixties when Zoe left Ewerton—shortly before Joe Lawton died, when they were living in Minnesota, near the North Dakota border, in a village ending in "tonka" or "tonna." He and Zoe never went back there while the gray-haired couple still lived.

The Lawtons were working-class people to the bone, no pretensions and little aspiration; dark-skinned, thin people who seemed uncomfortable with their late-life only child—just as Zoe was uncomfortable with them. The Lawtons were good people, but unprepared for a child like Zoe, with her high sense of self-worth, despite no urging toward that mindset from them.

After his chat with Joe (Winnie Lawton kept a vauge nodding silence most of the afternoon), all that Brent could gather was that the man used to be a camping nut before Zoe came along. That was it; no hopes, no dreams, no desires, just memories of a few good camping trips in the Wisconsin Northwoods. Zoe bit skin from her lips during the entire edge-of-her-seat-stiff visit.

Next to Brent, Palmer went on, "—would've faded into the woodwork if it wasn't for Zoe. Wasn't *like* her folks, was cut from a whole 'nother cloth. Instinctively knew she wasn't cut out to be a baby factory, knew she was heading for something *different*—"

As they passed a sign reading Polk Avenue, heading south, Brent casually said, "I thought you didn't know Zoe when she lived here."

"Heard tell of her from the Winstons, few others. And those new, out-of-town teachers at EHS, they'd talk her up around town. Never saw her in the *flesh*. Funny, but I don't think that her not conforming was the only reason Una didn't take to her. Went deeper than that," he added cautiously, turning from Polk Avenue onto Mill Road for a short distance, before heading north again on Linden Avenue.

"After asking around, it struck me that *she*, the way Zoe was *Zoe*, and not anyone else, *that* made her someone to hate. Someone to . . . forgive me, I can't think of a better word, *fear*. As if being *herself* there was this potential for trouble, at least in the eyes of some folk." He let his voice trail off as he sped down empty Linden Avenue, then crossed Lumbermill Drive on a slight angle before heading up Share Avenue to the north.

Brent waited for Palmer to finish before mentioning what Scooter Andersen told him about Una's horrified fixation on Zoe's eyes, but the Rambler came to a lurching stop and Palmer was out of the car, leaving the engine idling, heading for a pile of scrap paneling, old pipes, and wallboard near a freshly remodeled house on the left side of the street.

He shouted over his shoulder, "Make a U-turn and park on this side," before stepping up onto the browning lawn next to the pile of refuse. Reluctantly making a Y-turn (the street was exceptionally narrow), Brent parked near where Palmer stood, pointing excitedly at something in the scrap heap.

Turning off the engine, Brent got out and looked in the direction of his uncle's knobby finger—at an antique pearly white toilet and tank, and matching pedestal sink. While dirty, the pieces were intact, although the chipped seat and broken lid were beyond salvation. Hazy sunlight shone on the mother-of-pearl sheen of the creamy white surface, highlighting the raised beaded trim under the rim and around the outer edge of the sink. Even the fancy metalwork taps and faucet were intact, waiting for a good scrubbing—

"Bitsy will *kill* you," Brent warned, realizing what the elderly man had in mind . . . and liking him all the more for the idea. Shading his eyes as he stared longingly at the cast-off fixtures, Palmer said, "When I was a kid, we had a set just like this in the upstairs bath, before the old man tried to lift the toilet off the floor with his bare hands because he was drunk and wanted to show our Ma how strong he was . . . broke the bowl clean off. . . . This set'd go in good with the old-fashioned radiator in there, no?"

"*I* think you've got a death wish . . . Bitsy told me to make you pick up a streamlined—"

" 'Streamlined' my ass. You take the toilet, I'll get the sink." Grunting—but smiling—under the weight of his load, Palmer staggered to the Rambler. Feeling like a jerk—an *elated* jerk—Brent grabbed the toilet. He saw a white curtain ripple, then heard a shrill, "Mommy! A man's taking the toidy!" A tired voice yelled back, "So fuckin' *what*, Ginger? Eatcher cereal!"

It took a few minutes to fit the pieces in the trunk, and the lid wouldn't close all the way, but the parts were safely stashed. Once they were rolling again, Palmer bubbled, "I know how to install this, I did it before. Be a snap. They have seats and lids that look old-fashioned at Gambles—they're open today. . . ."

Heading for the north-of-town hardware store, Palmer eyed the siding and shingles make-overs on either side of the street with distaste, grumbling, "Damn idiots think they can improve the town by robbing it of its age. Like coating the Liberty Bell with spray enamel, plugging up the crack on the side. Not realizing it is what it is *because* it's dull and cracked.

"People like Bitsy miss the point. This is an old town, lots of water under the dam. Least old man Holiday had some sense. Knew this town would go to hell once you took away what was old. Folks laughed at what he did to his house, but at least he didn't go covering it up with fake brick and plastic siding that *looks* like plastic siding—houses can't *breathe*—"

"Not to change the subject"—Brent smiled to soften his interruption—"but before we stopped, you were saying about Zoe—"

"Ah, Zoe . . . wasn't the first maverick this town has seen, a body not living up to expectations. Winston and I, we both shocked this town once upon a time, and what we did made it worse because it wasn't expected of us." Then, to himself, Palmer reflected, "Odd, no matter where he and I found ourselves, this town always had a hold on us . . . a pull that kept a certain mind-set in both of us. May've been well and good for *this* place, but it wasn't always right for other places, other situations—"

While Brent listened, puzzled, Palmer shifted gears. "Hope you have some money in that back pocket of yours—Bitsy's got the credit card." Brent was so confused by Palmer's shift from introspection to exuberance all he could do was numbly nod assent.

Resembling a boy let loose in a Toys "Я" Us with a hundred-dollar bill in his hand, Palmer scurried up and down the aisle of the plumbing supplies, settling on a new seat and lid combo, flange bolts and caps, a wax ring, and a copper riser with a bright chrome finish, plus a cake of Bon Ami and a canister of Zud. Helping his excited uncle out to the car with the brown-bagged items, Brent wondered if *he'd* be this way when he reached sixty-some, getting all hepped up over a used toilet.

As they approached the farmhouse Palmer offered his services as ersatz Master Plumber, *if* Brent would shut off the water valve in the basement. And stay out of Palmer's way. "Can't abide anyone breathing down my neck while I work."

Once home, Brent helped to carry the fixtures upstairs—his protests that Bitsy wanted the *downstairs* toilet replaced fell on conveniently deaf ears. After telling Brent where the water shutoff was located, Palmer shooed him down to the basement, saying, "Gimmie an hour or so to change this, then come on up."

A heavy *thump-thump-crash* resonated above; Brent mumbled, "Bye-bye, old toilet. . . ." Shaking his head, Brent wondered if he and Zoe would've reached this point eventually. Bitsy pushed, Palmer pulled, and installing those ancient fixtures was an outward manifestation of the couple's "failure, to communi*cate*" as Strother Martin said in *Cool Hand Luke.*

Standing in the basement doorway, waiting for Palmer to tell him to turn on the water, Brent wondered if it was a failure to communi*cate* that messed up things between Zoe and himself. She could've left a note—not a whacked-out photo that had meaning only for his *uncle.*

Leaning back against the door, the knob digging into his back, Brent thought, *Suppose she* didn't *take the* —until his uncle shouted for him to start up the water again.

After turning on the water, Brent headed upstairs—stepping over the broken-in-two sink and deeply cracked toilet and tank resting at the bottom of the landing, promising himself to think things through later on . . . if only for the sake of his own sanity.

Outside, in the hallway, Palmer had neatly stacked his tools and the opened Bon Ami and Zud against the wall.

Not only had his uncle professionally installed the pearlescent fixtures, he'd lovingly cleaned them until the surfaces glowed like the inner lip of an abalone shell. He'd scrubbed out the bowl, and lifted the lid to show off the clean interior.

"All they needed was some care, little elbow grease. Don't they look better than those institutional things?" Agreeing, Brent began to say, "But this isn't what Bitsy—" but Palmer persisted, "Don't they just *fit* in here? Look at them and the junk downstairs. No comparison."

"*I* like them, *you* like them, but you know what *Bitsy's* going to say. You'll be back at Gambles buying a new set just to stop her yelling and screaming—"

With a determined glint in his green eyes, Palmer crossed his arms and asked, "She going to *pay* for her aerodynamic crapper? Give that woman a dime and she buys ten bucks worth of Tupperware. Or takes off to play Bingo. I'm not buying her some fancy-dancy stool and sink. And as for—"

" 'As for' *what*? You old—old—*worm!*"

Bitsy's voice shook at the bottom of the staircase, followed by the sensible clump of her Pillow Soft shoes. The two men exchanged looks: Brent anxious, his uncle both amused and indifferent.

Bitsy's curly head appeared at the stairway landing, quickly followed by her border print top and polyester slacks. She glanced from man to man before adding, "Oh, Brent, you convinced him to—this isn't the right room, but let me see anyway—" Brent retreated to the safety of his room before Bitsy squeezed past Palmer into her bathroom, but her wail was no less upsetting—

"Ohhhhhh . . . how *could* you? Wipe that smirk off your face and put my old fixtures back! Picked these off a *trash heap*, didn't you? I'm supposed to set *my* fanny on—I don't *care* if the 'seat is new'! It isn't *white*—it's all swirled and ugly, like an oil spill—*get out of my way!*"

From the still confines of his room, Brent heard Bitsy *clump-clump* to her room, pull open a dresser drawer with a rending *scree*, followed by soft sounds of tossed clothing, hangers clicking as each item landed on the quilt-covered bed.

From the hallway, his uncle asked, "Hey, wanna flip a coin, see who gets to christen it?" Under different circumstances, Brent would've laughed, but now his stomach was awash with bile. From where he lay lengthwise across his bed, legs dangling over the side, he replied, "Aw, Uncle Palmer, knock it off. Hasn't *enough* gone down?" Grabbing a pillow, he pressed it over his head, nose filling with the overpowering smell of sweat and fabric softener.

His uncle said more, but Brent couldn't make out the words. Faintly, Bitsy's voice shot back in sharp retort, followed by stomping down the stairs. A few minutes later he heard a car start up after a door slammed shut; rolling over, he craned his neck until he saw the road through his window. A car he didn't recognize, driven by some white-haired lady, was heading into town, Bitsy inside. The Chevy was trailed by a billow of exhaust.

Shifting position on the bed, until he lay on the diagonal, Brent stuffed the pillow under his head. Scrunching up his eyes, he tried not to let a rush of memories engulf him; memories he'd mostly been able to keep at bay, held back with that almost stereotypical Minnesotan sense of stability, and the promise of *later*, when he was free of this *sucking* town. Yet, the images came, unbidden . . . *why did you* want *to come back* here. . . . *I have* nothing *left here, not even peace*

*in my own family home. . . . Zoe, please, come back, tell me
. . . please, Zoe. . . .*

*. . . But she wouldn't listen to him, no matter how slow he
drove the Pacer down back roads whose deep blue pavement
twisted and turned under his tires, heading first this way, then
that through creamy pale dead grass. And the trees lining
both sides of the road pressed in, keeping Brent's eyes away
from the dun-colored sky above. As the road shifted, the
branches moved accordingly, hovering, bending low to scrape
the roof of the car. Zoe knew in advance which way the road
would writhe before her.*

*In the quiet he heard the slap of her bare feet on the pave-
ment, a sharp counterpoint to the steady, muted splashes of
blood droplets hitting the ground as she walked from him,
leading him deeper,* deeper *into the tunneling overhang of
sheltering trees. Blood formed a stripe that shimmered and
pulsed as it ran down the whitish curves of her waist, her
hips, thinning and pinking out where it clung to her moving
legs.*

*Blood dampened Duffy's gray fur where she held him. He
watched Brent while riding in her copper-iron scented embrace, green eyes wide-pupiled as he yowled silently, bluish
tongue and gums framing creamy white fangs.*

*The wound on Zoe's left side shone deep, black-centered
as she turned to the left, the edges of the slit flesh flapping in
time with her steps. As before, her thick taffy hair rested over
her face, obscuring everything above her neck.*

He called for her to come back, please *come back, he didn't
care if she took that picture of herself, he didn't care how she
got the quilt all bloody, it would wash out, just please come
back—he'd even let her go to that reunion, just please turn
around, Zoe, I need to see you once—*

*And then she slowly turned around, shifting her body with
exquisite playfulness, not breaking stride, yet moving her head
in his direction, ever so slowly, until he saw the rounded swell
of her left breast, curving in and up to her neck, and her
face—*

*—which hung white and gelid, a glistening mass of adipo-
cere flesh, features lost in that lard-soft surface, until white
bone thrust forward, forward . . . a long protrusion of bone
decorated with a bridle of gold, ending in yellow horse teeth.*

Blood oozed around each tooth, welling up from the gums,
and Brent tried to back up and pull away, but when he looked
around to the road behind him, it—

(From a distance longer than long, his uncle's voice rose
and fell in a keening siren wail, urgent yet faint, "Oh, no
. . . no, it can't *be*—")

—had disappeared, leaving him only one way to go . . .
where she slowly walked backward, finally letting him see
her—

("Jeezus, I should've known she's behind all this—")

Chest pounding, Brent sat upright, then swung his legs
onto the floor. At the doorway, he heard one of the WERT
announcers reading a statement: "—Gray said in an ex*clus*ive
statement that the Ewerton Water Carnival *will* go as sched-
uled. I repeat, Water Carnival Chairman Gordy Gray *has* secured rides and amusements for this year's festivities. Under
the circumstances of the break-in at the fairgrounds, the city
ordnance prohibiting out-of-town amusements has been re-
scinded. This year Ewerton will host the South-State Enterprises Amusements. According to Gray, they—"

Downstairs, Palmer—unaware that Brent had tiptoed out of
his room, into the hallway—let out another anguished moan,
"She *is* here, back *here*. . . ."

Uncertain what to do—go down and embarass the old man,
or pretend he'd been sleeping—Brent rubbed his rough
cheeks, whiskers raking his soft palms, and listened to his
uncle's deep mourning below. Finally, he yawned loudly,
hoping the sound would carry, and plodded heavily downstairs, asking in a pseudo-groggy voice, "Uncle Palmer? You
down here? I must've dozed off—you eat yet?"

Palmer stood in the kitchen doorway, eyes blank as he
rubbed his thumb along the side of his nose. For the first
time, Brent noticed that his uncle wore a large gauze and
white tape bandage on his exposed right forearm.

Brent stepped up to him, asking, "You okay?" when the
phone rang, an insistent shrill intrusion. Coming to his senses,
Palmer mumbled, "Might be Bitsy . . . you mind, Brent?"

He padded past Palmer into the kitchen, but before he could
say "Hello?" Winston's cigarette rasp cut in "Nemmitz
there?" Pressing the receiver to his chest, Brent yelled for
Palmer.

After he shuffled into the kitchen, taking the phone from
Brent, the younger man made his way to the front porch.

Behind him, his uncle said, "Yeah, who *else* would it be? Who? Oh, *him* . . . hasn't he a family? VFW elected you to do the honors, eh? Yes, I'll go. But I don't relish the thought of seeing that Reish pup—"

FORTY-FOUR

JULY 11

Palmer and Winston hated the green-carpeted reception room at the Reish-Byrne Funeral Home; their intense dislike of the place nurtured through many a visit paid to loved and not-so-loved ones they'd left in the dubious care of the Reish and Byrne families. The night before, the commander of the local chapter of the VFW called Winston, asked him if he'd mind doing the funeral arrangements for Bertram Hagg, Ewerton's former oldest citizen and only surviving WWI veteran, who died at the Ewerton Nursing Home without a single relative to his name.

Palmer was more than glad to let Winston take over the details of the funeral; he'd had his fill of them when his siblings died years before. Watching Winston examine the sample cards, haggling about the number of cards he had to order to qualify for a discount, Palmer leaned back in the uncomfortable imitation wood-grain and oxblood plastic chair, deep in thought.

He'd overreacted when hearing that name on the radio last night; surely, "South-State Enterprises Amusements" wasn't the same outfit as the "South-State Enterprises Carnival and Menagerie"—it just *couldn't* be. It had nothing to do with *her*, not one thing . . . but *yet*—

Palmer was still half-certain he'd seen *her*, on Midnite Mayhem night. For Zoe *was* dead, stiff, back at the farmhouse . . . with that *slice* on her side. The left side, the important one. That brought *everything* under suspicion.

Including the Wanderer, and those candy bars of his. *Her* favorite, a bar not manufactured for more than forty years.

Palmer hoped that Bitsy was happy, staying with *Tommy's* daughter and her family. He certainly didn't miss Bitsy . . . or the still-vanished Clive, for that matter. True, he did wish

Clive would show up again if he was capable. Not *knowing* was a killer, but Palmer's mind taunted, You *didn't come home, turn back when things got bad. You went farther south, deeper into it, until . . . she . . . and only then did you go home, but it was way too late, wasn't it? And now the Wanderer has those candy bars of hers, had to get 'em somewhere. And that somewhere wasn't the IGA . . . no, not at all—*

A million miles from the tortured voice in Palmer's mind, Winston asked Craig, "How's that Susie girl of yours, huh? Good girlie, that Susie . . . had her in English three years running. Oh, my, *what* a girl." (Under the expanse of his fake oak desk, Craig Reish's spongy-soft fingers balled into fists—even as Craig nodded and smiled unctuously.)

Winston made Reish give him a special deal on Hagg's funeral, knowing full well that Craig cut costs only in order to get Winston and his taunting about Susie (even if she *had* been a most willing pupil!) out of the office before Craig planted his fists in Winston's tight-lipped mouth. Winston felt justified in his efforts; Palmer had been no help whatsoever.

After he "nailed down" the funeral package with Reish, Winston was mildly surprised when Palmer invited him to the Nemmitz farmhouse. After a silent, bumper-to-bumper drive, Palmer no sooner parked the Rambler than he disappeared into his house, leaving Winston to come in alone.

He stood in the kitchen with Brent Nimitz, who all but ignored him as he drew something on a large sheet of white paper with a stick of wrapped charcoal. When Winston edged closer to see what Brent was drawing, Nimitz flipped the paper over, casually asking if he wanted coffee, soda, or Postum, playing damn-fool airline host in his cutoffs and polo shirt.

Knowing full well that his presence was unwelcome, and deciding to rub it in, Winston stood against the sink, tapping ashes into a used saucer on the drain board. Tersely he replied, "Just waiting for Palmer to come play host."

He didn't have long to wait, for by the time Brent had helped himself to a diet Coke, Palmer limped back into the kitchen, holding something curled up and shiny blue in his right hand, as he furiously itched his forearm with his left hand. Winston noticed Brent staring at his uncle—and then Palmer thrust the blue object at Winston.

A bound manuscript, resembling term papers he'd graded during his latter years at EHS.

Disregarding Brent, Palmer said quickly, "Before you do anything else today, you've got to read this—should've given it to you a long time ago. I was hoping it wouldn't be necessary. But you have to read it before things *happen* again." His face was drawn, white-lipped, green eyes glassy; he licked his lips before continuing, "Before things happen to the rest of us . . . I know what happened to Una, and this boy's wife, too. It's . . . *her*. She followed us here—"

A ripple went through Winston, ice cubes dropped melting down his back; hiding behind a screen of expelled smoke, hoping his voice was a casual drawl, he replied, "Palmer, sure you haven't a touch of heatstroke? You aren't making a bit of sense. Don't look so *stricken*. I'll read the damned thing . . . want me to correct it, too?" He added an approximation of a smile.

Swallowing hard, fleshless Adam's apple working above his clip-on tie, Palmer said, "Just read it, then crack jokes. It . . . explains a lot. Read it and see."

Not liking what he saw in his friend's face—an echo of the fear he himself felt—Winston let himself out, rolled manuscript in his free hand. Walking out to his Olds Cutlass, he paused only to stomp out his cigarette before leaving. He pushed the manuscript far away from him on the passenger seat.

Palmer was about to follow Winston out the door, wanting the last word, when Brent grabbed him by the left arm.

"What in hell was *that* all about? You *both* flip out, or does this have to do with what we were talking about. Last week, when Clive—"

Struggling to free himself from his nephew's grip, he quickly said, "If things progress the way they've been, he'll be needing that more than you do right now . . . besides, that thing's death to anyone who reads it who shouldn't. I know you were trying to help that night, sparing my feelings when you took her out of my room, but it *did no good at all*. Not for Zoe, not for Clive, not for me . . . I just hope you *never* have to read it."

With that cryptic remark, he pulled free and hurried outside to start up the Rambler. Brent stood numbly, sweating can of soda in one hand, tears stinging his eyes, muttering, "Hey, old man, she died on her *own*, didn't need any prompting from your stupid *story*—" until he remembered the last time he'd seen the blue booklet.

He scooped up his charcoals, his half-completed drawing of Zoe holding Duffy (her face her own, not a slush of rotted flesh, or a blood-toothed *thing*), and ran upstairs to the relative sanity of his room, thinking that the time for leaving the farmhouse was definitely at hand.

FORTY-FIVE

JULY 13

The morning of Bertram Hagg's funeral dawned hot and promised to become hotter by the time of the noon service. Not a cloud in sight, not a breeze to stir the stifling air.

The *Ewerton Herald* carried a photo of Hagg slumped in a wheelchair, peering groggily at a sheet cake covered with a hundred swirled candles that dripped wax all over the frosting—not that Hagg's taste buds were up to detecting any sort of flavor when the picture was taken—over the caption "Oldest Citizen Dies Peacefully."

Reading over the accompanying article in his office, Stu Sawyer muttered, "How was he s'posed to go? Humping some waitress at A&W?" Feeding the paper into his shredder for lack of anything better to do, Stu again cussed out Bib Stanley for letting his yahoos trample the interior of the fairgrounds building last Saturday.

At least that Gray kid—the clean-cut one—managed to round up another set of rides; so far nobody called on "Speak Your Piece" to bitch about the possible *cost* of such an equipment rental.

But Stu no longer felt as if his ass were being chewed by fifty sets of teeth over the break-in. The damaged rides had been carted off to Ernie Shipman's junkyard as scrap, although the ruined booths—unsuccessfully dusted for prints—remained in the building. So far no leads panned out, either.

Dusty Parks and Bob Gray had been at the beer-tasting contest at the Wooden Keg the evening before the break-in (no one forgot Dusty's puking fit after his twenty-first shot of beer), if, indeed, the break-in *had* occurred right before it was discovered.

If it *hadn't* . . . then the case was shot. Nothing was *taken*, which left out a trail of stolen goods. Reluctantly, Stu was prepared to file the case as "Unsolved". At least he wouldn't have to answer some very *difficult* questions about the modus operandi of the vandals. . . .

What *did* annoy Stu was that he'd gotten so little cooperation in Clive Calder's disappearance. Damned shame, in Stu's opinion—Clive had delivered most of the same people who didn't give two squirts where he'd gone, or what had happened to him once he got there.

Nobody claimed to have seen Clive. When Bib Stanley finally did decide to mount a search party to look through the various patches of wooded land around town, some yo-yo had phoned WERT with the suggestion, "After this long, a person could just *sniff* 'im out—" before the radio station's call-in line went dead due to "technical difficulties."

Donning his dress uniform prior to leaving for the Hagg funeral, Stu hoped that he wouldn't pull funeral duty for quite some time . . . preferably not until the day when the Palmers Winston and Nemmitz were planted six feet under.

When *that* day came, Stu was willing to shovel out the graves himself . . . with his bare hands.

Judging by the spread of flowers surrounding Hagg's coffin at the cemetery, Pearl Vincent, Winston's landlady and Ewerton's official mourner and prayer card collector, would've dubbed Bertram Hagg only middling popular on her "How-many-flowers-did-he-get" scale—had she not been sitting at home, icy handkie on her forehead, feet on the ottoman, watching game shows with the sound turned off. Hagg was lucky to get what flowers he did; the wilting spray from the VFW came too late for the brief visitation, and the nursing home only chipped in enough for some daisies and mums in a low dish. The two Palmers bought the coffin spray out of their own pockets, a blanket of yellow roses and baby's breath.

In the withering heat, the roses didn't stand a chance; by the time the casket was suspended over the freshly dug grave, the outer petals were blown wide open, ready to drop at the slightest vibration.

Winston and Palmer decided that no church services would be held; making people sit in a nonair-conditioned church was criminal, especially for services for a man few had seen since 1973.

Metal chairs formed two rows near the grave; ten mourners sat placidly under the shield of a striped canvas awning, listening to Winston read his eulogy of the dead war hero.

Taking a deep breath before launching into the last paragraph, Winston wondered if this would happen to *him* someday—him lying in a webbing-supported box, while some fool he didn't know in life read a cock-and-bull story of what a great old guy he had been.

From his seat Nemmitz stared up at Winston; as he delivered the final line of the eulogy, Winston realized that he couldn't afford to stall his friend. He'd have to tell Palmer that he hadn't been able to read that damned manuscript.

For after one page, he discovered it wasn't a *story* Palmer had cobbed together.

And Winston couldn't tell Nemmitz he was *scared* to read further.

The Ewerton cemetery was located a few miles south of "Lenny's Place," near enough to the river to be bearably cool, and tree-surrounded enough to be almost unseen from the nearby road. The two Palmers didn't stick around to oversee the filling in of the grave. Both had been to enough funerals to have total faith that the job would be completed without their supervision.

Slowly, in the way of friends who know each other well enough not to need to fill every second with needless talk, the two elderly men walked to familiar headstones; sharing the duty of standing for a few seconds in front of each stone, before moving on to the next site.

First, the Winstons; Porter and Gayleen side by side under granite, and Winston's infant sons, their markers bearing delicate angel babies etched in marble. They glanced at and quickly passed Una Sawyer Winston's stern flat brass marker; hers was a single plot, with no room for a mate in her eternal rest.

A few rows down, past Weiss and Yingley plots, and a few Sawyer stones, they stopped before a large marker; "Nemmitz" was chiseled over a row of smaller names and dates: Treeva, 1898-1938; Vernilla, 1923-1945; Effie, 1926-1951; and Merle, 1930-1946. Without asking, Winston knew that Palmer had other names, other dates carved in his mind: Enoch, 1896-1944; Vernon, 1923-1944; and Shirley (Shirl), 1932-1982. Although Shirl rested in Minnesota, there was no reason why the bodies of Enoch and Vernon couldn't have been buried here, instead of in that French cemetery.

Winston watched as Palmer put a yellow rose, plucked from the edge of Hagg's coffin blanket, under Treeva's name; he took a second to stroke the silken, dying petals before rising and wordlessly heading for the Crescent Mausoleum, down by the river flowing west of the graveyard.

Palmer, despite his bad knee, made good time; Winston—dying for a cigarette—huffed after Palmer, calling out, "It isn't going to up and walk away . . . slow down for Chrissake!" Reluctantly, Palmer turned, saying, "If your mother could hear you, she'd be twirling in her coffin . . . taking the Lord's name in vain in a *cemetery*. And Gayleen a Sunday school teacher."

"Since when were you born again? Never saw you set foot in a church save for weddings and funerals." Once he caught up with Palmer, Winston figured that no one could see him behind the walk-in Crescent tomb. He took out his pack of Lucky Strikes, shaking one out with nervous taps of his hand. Noting how Winston's fingers shook, Palmer snapped, "You read it yet?"

Winston—lit cigarette firmly clamped between dry lips—took off for the highest, fanciest grave marker in the entire cemetery, a ten-foot-tall pillar two rows away, close to the river.

Luckily for the decedent entombed in the above ground vault next to it, the marker in question had been bought and erected twenty years before the Cemetery Ordinance of 1983. ("The city reserves the right to limit the size of monuments and markers to a height of no more than three feet, in keeping with the uniformity of the grounds.")

Winston stared at the name carved on the small square of white marble set into the front of the granite marker:

WILBUR W. HOLIDAY
1888–1986

And in smaller script, below the pair of dates:

"I think, therefore I am."
Rene Descartes

Behind him came Palmer's soft voice, "Ever figure out why Wilbur put that on his stone? Seems he studied philosophy, but . . . he could've come up with something more *serious*. He was a strange duck."

Moving closer to Winston, he asked again, "You *read* it? I wouldn't ask if it wasn't important—"

Pinching off the hot end of his cigarette, before storing the butt in his pocket, Winston—never taking his eyes off Holiday's odd marker—said, "I haven't, but I will, starting this afternoon. For *you* . . . otherwise I'd never bother. Last thing I need is to pore over some old *goat's* ramblings—"

"It's true, every word of it. Some concerns you, some concerns me, and some of it concerns someone we *both* knew quite well—"

Praying Palmer was wrong, Winston snapped, "I never told you about her . . . least I don't think—"

"You were *awful* soused the day you phoned me after the Army let you loose . . . was surprised you knew your name, let alone *my* number." As Winston stared, shamed, at his shoes, Palmer went on gently, "You didn't say much, but it was enough. I knew . . . *her*, too. Better than you did. When you read it, you'll understand. Give me a ring once you're done . . . we've got to plan—"

Listening to Palmer, Winston decided, *Must be in the blood . . . Palmer's gone as crazy as Wilbur used to be*, but when he spoke, his lips formed a reluctant promise.

"Can the speech. I'll read the damned thing," to which Palmer answered, "You might think 'damned' is an exaggeration . . . you'll think it an understatement, afterward."

With that he limped away from Winston, sun shining hard on the silver-gray flatness of his hair. When Winston turned to watch him leave, for a second he thought he saw Wilbur Holiday slowly walking away . . . filled with sudden thought, and renewed life.

FORTY-SIX

After giving his manuscript to Winston, Palmer forsook his search for the Happy Wanderer and his Stardust Bars. Visiting Winston's apartment was also too obvious, too . . . *pleading*. And the fourteenth became the fifteenth, which in turn became the sixteenth. . . .

It took Winston nearly that many days to drink his way through Palmer's blue-bound, closely typed pages. Over three days since he spoke to anyone or anything, save for the dingy walls of his room. He didn't even want to *think* about the slightly puckered deep brown stain on the first page, resisting a strong urge to smell it.

Just as he resisted the overpowering urge, voiced in thoughts seemingly not his *own*, to call Palmer, tell him he'd read it, and understood the danger.

Both the peril they'd narrowly escaped, the wrath waiting for them, hidden in the utter blackness of late-summer shadows, so deep and depthless compared to the brightness of hot summer sunlight. But, fearful that calling and *talking* about her would make her all the *more* real, Winston disconnected the phone, pulled the rectangle of clear plastic and copper wire out of the wall receptacle, and then did the same in the back of the phone. But he still felt no safer, and nothing Mr. Daniels under the bathroom sink had to say helped either.

Sitting on his unmade daybed, staring at the small framed sampler hanging just within his sight on the bathroom wall, he read the cross-stitched words aloud, dismayed by the quiver in his voice, " 'Thursday's Child Has Far to Go.' "

No kidding. He'd traveled miles and miles, only to end up right where he started . . . knowing less and having nothing to show for all his years spent searching for whatever men his age were supposed to have found by now. Una's son was a better old man than Winston's could ever be. Arlin was *born* to be an old man. Suited, somehow—

"Oh, shit," Winston drawled, "got to get out my suit for that damn wedding!" He'd almost forgotten about the Mesabi wedding at the Methodist church come four o'clock. And his invitation was propped up on his dresser, where he could see it, too.

Getting to his stockinged feet, he saw that it was only a quarter to two, plenty of time to shower, dress, and get to the church. He *had* remembered to buy a gift (a card to put the check in, actually). Now it was only a matter of getting ready. Taking off his shirt, revealing a sunken chest lightly tufted with crinkled gray hairs that thickened as they reached his belly, Winston stepped into the bathroom.

Soaping up under the jet of lukewarm water, Winston wryly reflected that this was his punishment for paying "attention" to the willing EHS girls—when they married, they inevitably hit him up for a generous wedding gift. Hot-to-trot Heather Thorn Wilkes mailed off birth announcements every time she shat out another brat. Lately, these girls expected a C note or better . . . inflation, he supposed.

Drying himself, he slipped into a worse-for-wear terry-cloth robe, then padded barefoot to the closet, trying to ignore the Army uniform hanging there (Una *had* given his away, he was *sure*). He took out his good suit, the one he'd worn Tuesday, only to stare at it in dismay. The cigarette he'd snuffed out and placed in his pocket hadn't been fully extinguished. He was lucky the apartment hadn't caught fire, for there was a large hole, singed a brittle brown, on the front jacket pocket. And his suit was dove gray.

Sickened, he pawed through his closet, but thanks to Una's weeding of his wardrobe, nothing he owned matched. Mates to jackets and pants were gone; everything left clashed enough to look idiotic when paired.

Wistfully, he remembered when he was the sharpest-dressed young man in town. Before the war, before Una . . . before *everything* else.

He also remembered the RSVP note he'd sent back to the soon-to-be Mrs. Thorn. If he didn't show, especially after appearing at all the other weddings, people might talk, say he was slipping.

Holding the ruined jacket up to the light, wondering if he'd have time to patch it, he noticed the Army uniform, hanging dark and bright-buttoned on his closet door.

Go on . . . you looked so handsome in it. Like Errol Flynn . . . go on, see if it still fits. Bet it does. . . .

Trying to drown out the unwelcome thoughts, he said out

loud, "I'll buy a new suit at the Haber-Dashery. Three piece. Very dignified—"

But with what? You only have thirty dollars left in checking, and your pension check isn't due yet. All they have are leisure suits at that shop. You don't want one of those. Go on, see if it fits . . . for the heck of it. Just try and see. . . . Reaching for the uniform, he remembered the notes attached to the bottle and cake Alice found: "Eat Me" and "Drink Me," only . . . he didn't *think* Ewerton was Wonderland.

Winston didn't need to suck in his stomach; his regulation trousers fit easily—*with* his shirt tucked in his pants. The whole uniform was there; when he'd looked for his good shoes on his closet floor, he wasn't surprised to find his regulation dress shoes there, too.

Perhaps Una missed them . . . but Una never lived in *this* apartment. The shoes were spit-polished; Winston may not have been an Outstanding rating soldier during his *last* months in the Army, but right up to the day he left Japan, his shoes were inspection-polished. He found a pair of Army-issue dark hose stuck in a corner of his dresser drawer, as if his past was seeping into his present through odd cracks and dark places.

Completely dressed in the uniform, save for the hat he held in trembling hands, Winston stared at his reflection in the mottled mirror. Softly, in case Pearl Vincent had her ear to the wall, he said, "Looking swell . . . *Lieutenant.*"

Saluting, he put the hat on his full head of gray hair; if anything, he looked more distinguished than ever in the uniform. Exchange the bars (from the Army shrine) for stars, and there's General Winston. He could've done it, if he hadn't screwed up.

Impulsively, he sniffed the cuff of his jacket; no mothball odor, none whatsoever. Funny. Licking his lips, noting that he'd better get moving if he wanted to arrive on time, Winston had a strange thought, *Maybe it's fitting I look the way I did back then. If what Palmer wrote is all true—God knows the man has no imagination—it's too late for me anyway. Perhaps* she'll *leave the suit alone . . . so I look nice in my coffin. . . .*

Giving himself a last salute, Winston picked up the invitation and the gift envelope, then left his apartment.

Never to return again.

FORTY-SEVEN

Beginning at three, and trying twice each hour after that, Palmer dialed Winston's number, but was rewarded with a dial tone and the familiar ringing sound—nothing more. At the top and bottom of each half hour, Palmer got out of his chair in the living room, shuffled into the kitchen . . . then shuffled back to his chair, and his newspaper.

But while Palmer supposedly sat reading, Brent noticed that he didn't hear the dry rustle of pages being turned.

Brent lay on the floor, knees supported by a throw pillow, watching cable TV. He rolled over on his side, to stare up at Palmer, who sat half-hidden behind his still newspaper.

"Can't you get through to whoever you're trying to call?"

Silence and stillness. Brent resumed watching the flickering set. His uncle made his umpteenth visit to the kitchen. Brent's throat caught each time the dial rotated.

Brent positioned himself in the doorway while Palmer stood expectantly, receiver in hand, staring at the old wall calendar. Hanging up after at least twenty rings, Palmer blinked when he saw Brent.

"Sorry if I've been ignoring you, but c'mon, what's up?"

Motioning to the phone with his thumb, Palmer replied, "Winston. Can't ring him up. Told him to call me soon as he read it, couldn't have taken him *this* long—"

"That blue booklet you gave him?"

Nodding, Palmer ordered, "Turn off the TV and come with me. I need to find Winston *now*." He headed for the hat rack, grabbed his fedora, and left the kitchen. Wondering what bug got under the old man's bonnet, Brent dutifully switched off the set, then followed Palmer out the back door, letting it swing shut with a deafening crack behind him.

During the drive to Winston's apartment, all Palmer volunteered was a mumbled comment about it being "*her* time," whatever *that* meant. It was well past seven by then; shadows welled depthless and pure behind buildings and under trees, *too* deep for this time of evening. A strange notion came to Brent: A man could get swallowed up by a shadow that thick.

He wished he was home watching USA's *Saturday Nightmares* horror flick and *Alfred Hitchcock/Ray Bradbury Theater* combo, but there was a Saturday nightmare brewing in Palmer's wide green eyes, the pupils dark and darting under the half shadow of his hat brim.

Outside the frame house where Winston lived, his Olds was parked under the enveloping shade of an elm, but Palmer dismissed the car. "His night vision isn't the best. Can't drive come dark, 'less it's a full moon."

The entire house was dark ("Pearl must be at Bingo," Palmer whispered), but when they tried the back door that led to Winston's room, it was unlocked. After knocking one last time, Palmer asked in a voice meant to be casual, "Win? You doze off? *Winston?*"

Feeling along the door frame on the inside for the light switch, Palmer flipped it on, revealing brutally lit-from-above squalor. Repressing a shudder, Brent remembered his similar action on the night he found Zoe . . . *Please, God, don't let the old drunken fuck be dead in there, Amen.*

Clothes crumpled in heaps on the floor where Winston stepped out of them, or draped across chair backs, like memories of bodies sitting there. A muck-coated tongue of a daybed stuck out of the tweedy couch; Brent flashed back to the photo sticking out of his uncle's camera. Closet doors stood ajar, revealing the pitiful wardrobe within.

The place smelled like the bottom of a wet laundry hamper, with a whiskey-scented Stick-Up on the underside of the lid. Pastel food containers bloomed on tables, and white Leinenkugels cans rolled on the floor.

From where he stood, Brent made out something on the bathroom wall, a framed sampler like the one hanging over his uncle's bed. He started to point it out to Palmer, but the older man, after surveying what was in the closet, said, "His good clothes are still here, and he hasn't bought anything new in ten years. Must've gone for a walk, or bar-hopping. Should be back soon."

Brent noticed the blue-bound booklet resting on the dresser . . . as well as something more ominous. The phone sat on a nearby table, disconnected from the thin gray cord linking it to the wall outlet. A quick glance at the floor revealed the fragile connector, resting on the dusty carpet under the ivory connector box.

Waiting until Palmer took another peek in the closet, Brent reconnected the cord to the phone. Knocking the blue manuscript to the floor, he inched his hand over and plugged in the phone jack, before standing up, booklet in hand. Palmer whirled around in time to see Brent waving the rolled pages in front of his face. "He left this . . . maybe he finished it, and went for a drink before calling you."

Glancing about the room, Palmer reluctantly said, "Could be . . . perhaps he's calling from wherever he is now. Maybe his phone didn't work, could be, couldn't it?" His green eyes were childlike in anticipation. Putting his arm around Palmer's bowed shoulders, Brent noticed that the wound on his uncle's arm had seeped through the gauze bandage.

"We'd better get home then, in case he's trying to call you—" They were almost out the door when Palmer made a break for the room, mumbling, "Better leave a note, case he comes back here first." Grabbing and old newspaper, he tore off a strip; using the ink pen he found near the phone, he scribbled a short note—"Call me, P.N."—which he rested across the dial of the black phone.

Watching his uncle, Brent hoped that the old lush would be *able* to return the call.

FORTY-EIGHT

At the Hole-in-One Club, Winston sat at the end of the bar nearest the rest rooms, downing his fifth (sixth? seventh?) whiskey sour of the evening. They didn't sit well on the meal he'd eaten. Raw ground round surrounded by an eye-moistening ring of chopped white onions, ham slices, baked beans (the ubiquitous Ewerton wedding staple), plus sticks of cold vegetables and melon balls—served *cafeteria* style.

His ears were assaulted by the *thrum-thrum* of amplified bass notes from the jukebox in the corner of the dance floor, not to mention the resonant *thrumb* of the bass player in the live band noodling through a lazy waltz in the opposite corner of the dance area.

Close to the band, oldsters bounced around the floor, well-padded fannies touching when couples got too close. The last time Winston dizzily looked over his shoulder at them, a few women were dancing together, without fear of ridicule, as women did in the days of his youth . . . the days of *her* youth, too.

With each sip, it was as if Winston swallowed down the wrinkled coating that separated the young Palmer Winston from the grizzled buck who stared at him daily from his bathroom mirror. When he glanced at himself in the bar mirror five feet away, it was as if his wrinkled flesh was only a mask shielding the tender heart and fresh face of his boyhood from the callousness and harshness of the world.

Draining his glass with a tip of the wrist and a leaning back of the head, Winston nodded for the harried bartender and asked for a refill—hold the sour. The girl hurried back to the other end of the bar after slopping some liquor into his glass, leaving a trail of droplets that shimmered under the bar lights like molten gold.

There were three empty seats on either side of Winston. When he'd walked into the church, decked out in his uniform, people had been polite enough not to say anything in the church itself, but here at the reception, word was out—old man Winston finally flipped his lid. Arlin Winston and his wife were so embarrassed they left after nibbling some steak tartar and sipping a glass of free beer.

The bride—in true Ewerton fashion, just the slightest bit *snug* around the let-out bodice—gave him a barely concealed glare undiminished by the size of her ex-teacher's check. Mrs. Thorn was close to tears, as if Mr. Winston had shown up looking like *that* just to ridicule her.

Winston didn't mind the stares—he looked *damn* good, no potbelly or leisure suits for him!—now that he was nearly blotto, the stares of his fellow revelers were a *comfort*. They proved he wasn't like any of *them* . . . he never was. Just like that poor Zoe girl; *she* knew she was better than these clods, these mothers-to-be in veils with hair on their upper lips. Different . . . the way *she* must've been, when first Palmer, then Winston, knew her. . . .

Turning gingerly on his bar stool (a black, padded contraption that squealed infernally) Winston blearily watched the giggling little kids dancing on the fringes of the crowd by the jukebox. The miniature bride's veil and tiara were gone, and the flower girl had kicked off her tiny pumps, while the older children bobbed and weaved in parody of their older siblings and parents. As if stuck, the jukebox played the same song, endlessly: "I Knew the Bride When She Used to Rock and Roll."

Facing the bar again, clunking his empty glass on the wet bar in time with the record, Winston reflected that he'd always wondered what happened to Palmer down south—only now that he knew, it made things worse. Yet, it *did* put so *many* things into perspective. The reflection in the bar mirror nodded in agreement with his bitter revelation.

"You okay, Mr. Winston?" Next to the hatted image in the mirror, a young man, tuxedo unbuttoned and hanging open to reveal a ruffled peach shirt, leaned over the bar, face flushed from downing one too many plastic glasses of Bud, tapped Winston's shoulder before he sat down next to him. "Like your getup. VFW meetin' today or something?"

Winston realized that the peach-shirted apparition was speaking to *him*, not to the guy in the mirror. Slushily he replied, " 'Or somethin' . . .' Forty years, still fits." He patted his flat belly for emphasis; the youth shamefacedly thunked his own baby beer gut.

"Nice 'ception they got going, huh? Getcha some chips? Her old man's donatin' 'em. For free. Corn curls? Rippled? Ol' Wayne brought a station wagon full. Not too far past the due dates." Motioning to the bartender, the young man yelled, "Hey, Betty, park it here! And bring me some nachos!" then turned his attention to Winston. "Dance with the bride yet? Band's playin' a waltz . . . or you could boogie with the kids—"

Noticing that the Infernal Song With No End was winding down, he dug around in his pockets for change. Pressing a quarter into the boy's beer-sticky fingers, he carefully said, "Another *song* . . . not *that* one. *A*nother song, *any* song. Hokay?" Making eye contact with the youngster, Winston gave the boy a frantic stare.

The peach-shirted apparition nodded cheerfully. "Gotcha. No sooner said than done, pop." Grabbing the package of chips Betty tossed to him, he vanished into the wiggling crowd by the jukebox. After the last perky chorus of "I Knew the Bride . . ." faded, the machine let out a moment of silence. The kids moaned as one when a slow, yet urgent song came on; an eerie ballad-paced rocker Winston hadn't heard before, yet found himself liking:

Returning to the bar, the youth paused by Winston's elbow and shouted in his ear, " 'Fade Away' all right with ya? BoDeans, from down-state," then faded away himself into the swirl of people milling on the hardwood dance floor.

The kids had deserted the jukebox to hover around the live band, which blatted out a polka. But the song on the machine drowned out the *oomph-pa-pa*; its title formed a haunting, rhythmic refrain to his thoughts.

Better get this over with . . . nothing left for me here, better to die than live this way. Never mind what Palmer *has in store . . . I never did anything that* horrible *to her. Except leave. . . .*

He nearly jumped out of his clothes when he heard the soft voice in his ear, a modulated purr, " 'I like large parties. They're so intimate. At small parties there isn't any privacy.' " He heard gentle breathing, a faint undercurrent to the din of the record, the band, the people crowded into the Hole-in-One Club, the bass notes pounding through the floor into his feet as they touched the bar itself.

Winston moved his head—eyes still shut—toward the far end of the bar, and opened them. Betty and her customers had drifted away, a bright-colored knot of drinking, laughing people, a million miles away from him, paying him no heed.

Only then did he turn his head in *her* direction. Her words he knew; lines from his favorite book, *The Great Gatsby*. Her voice he knew, albeit dimmed by the passage of years, the false acoustics of memory. But those eyes, he remembered.

His lips began to form a name, a short, short name, but the word remained unvoiced, unsaid, as he freely looked at the woman sitting next to him, the black gabardine of her suit almost touching the crisp serge of his uniform sleeve.

Yes, she *did* resemble Zoe Lawton . . . up to the point where the slight differences began. The same long, softly waving taffy hair; bar lights picked up highlights of gold, red, softest brown, and silvery blond. He'd never been certain of the exact color until he read of it in Palmer's painfully written remembrance of her. Nemmitz's memory had been all *too* clear, to the point of obsession . . . tempered with not a little fear and guilt.

But . . . *she* was *here*, sitting next to him, the soft curve

of a black coat or cloak thrown over her left shoulder. Her
odd eyes stared at him with a mixture of pity and amusement.

Do you toy with a man, before . . . you're done *with him*?
He tried to swallow; phlegm caught in his throat as he real-
ized what a *beautiful* angel of death she was. *Just* the way
Palmer had described her.

Jet buttons on her suit caught the dim bar light, reflecting
pools of golden luminescence, while her creamy beige Bakelite stickpin, studded with dozens of rainbow-fire rhinestones,
cast dots of prismatic color onto her strong chin, her smooth
cheeks. And that hair, the kind that would shift and cascade
through his fingers if only she'd let him push his hands into
that waving mass . . . such hair he seldom saw anymore,
certainly not on permed, bleached, blow-dried, and moussed
Ewerton women.

No matter how close death—or something worse—might
be, he felt that old tightening in his groin, a tingle running
up and down his thighs, coming higher and higher. His lips
formed a jerky smile, cracking the taut dry skin, making an
old sore there bleed.

She said no more, but smiled at him sadly, her two-color
eyes lowering.

Fear churned in Winston's stomach; his breath came short
and ragged, yet the old thrill, the long-gone excitement, was
there, too. He decided, *If a man must die, let him* die *in
style*.

Unsteadily getting to his feet, Winston faced the woman,
noting that her curved calves were covered in black hose, the
seam-up-the-back kind that women, alas, no longer wore.
Her ankle-strap shoes would've done Joan Crawford proud
. . . so shiny, so delicate.

Slowly, he extended his arm, right hand reaching for her
red-nailed right hand. The dark button on her braid-trimmed
cuff winked in the light as her hand met his.

The *coolness* of her touch, as her fingers daintily curled
around his blue-veined and liver-spotted hand, made his teeth
come down hard together, pinching the tip of his tongue between them. As her hand gently gripped his, Winston felt the
tingle, a needle-prickle sensation that both hurt and tickled
. . . as if the shape of her hand was but a temporary thing,
subject to unexpected change.

Determined not to disgrace himself or his uniform *this* time,
Winston helped her to her feet. Swaying slightly in place, he

was suddenly aware of an urgent sensation in his lower abdomen—the eight (or nine, or ten) whiskey sours wanted out, *now*.

Bowing slightly at the waist, he mumbled, " 'Cuse, me, please," then scuttled with a tight gait for the men's room, vaguely aware of the woman's sharply ringing footsteps behind him. They echoed the beat of the song on the jukebox as it faded away to hissing silence . . . a silence made larger by the utter lack of *any* sound coming from behind her black-suited form. . . .

Winston made it into the rest room just in time to position himself in front of the urinal as he unzipped. Eyes hazed over with crawling crimson and ebony filigree that waxed and waned like clouds scudding over a full moon, he reached for his member, aiming it at the porcelain. A shuddering stab of pain ripped through his body; his eyes snapped open as his mouth gaped silently. The burning started in his organ and radiated outward; rippling waves of agony buckled his knees. Mind racing, Winston realized that he hadn't felt such agony in decades . . . over four of them, to be exact. Since that one-two bout of clap he'd suffered from in Japan. When he was twenty-two, and the uniform he wore now was new.

Painfully shaking off, he examined his organ. Through his drunken stupor, he saw that it was deep pink, inflamed; he knew what that puslike discharge meant without much reflection. But what he *didn't* understand was the way his hand looked.

The puffiness in his knuckles was *gone*; Winston knew he couldn't be *that* drunk and live . . . but weren't fewer liver spots dotting the thin skin covering his tarsals? His veins no longer popped up, but were smooth and pale blue under spot-*free* skin, *which was covered with fine* dark *hairs*.

Hastily zipping up, Winston was aware of a different, insidious pain . . . a crawling, *shrinking* sensation. As if his skin were drawing in tight, tighter against his bones; his muscles cramped in his calves until he did an impromptu, skittering dance away from the urinal.

Somehow, head bent down, arms wrapped around his churning stomach, he made it to the nearest washbasin. Turning on the water with fingers that grew smoother and firmer by the second, Winston thrust his unfamiliar hands under the jet of water, to let the rush of warmth ease away some of the strange pain.

After shutting off the water, he reached over for a towel—and stared, openmouthed, at the ghost in the mirror. A ghost of the Palmer Winston he'd once been, pale face and shocked blue eyes framed by wavy dark hair. As he stared, his face *itched*, gently, and the last vestiges of wrinkles vanished into the smooth planes of the skin of a man in his twenties.

While the last of Winston's pain became a terrible memory, he remembered what Nemmitz had written about the small, yet pivotal role Clive Calder had played in all that had transpired in the summer of 1940. *Did she find Clive, do* this *to him, before whatever* else *happened to him?* The soft, small voice in his mind, a voice not wholly his own, replied, *Would she waste this on* Clive? *Was he what you are to her?* Shaking his head, seeing his image do likewise, Winston tentatively touched the reflection—which in turn raised a hand whose forefinger met his, separated only by cool, slick glass.

His now-moist, soft lips moved, formed words, "Then it's true . . . if *I* can be young, then *she*—" Abruptly, he ran for the door, young muscles pumping under firm flesh. When he opened the door, *she* was still standing there, waiting . . . even though the hallway around her had changed.

The floor, the color of the walls, were all different, yet . . . *familiar*, too. He had seen, walked upon, that same dark-stained floor, and bounced after many a round off those same damask-papered walls, much more dignified than the nubby-textured beige paper he'd seen only minutes before. Face darkening, he remembered . . . the Hole-in-One Club looked this way *years* before, when . . . *when* . . . when he came home from the war and married Una—

—Una wasn't here, but *she* still stood there, face gently expectant, mouth open slightly, showing a glint of ivory teeth. Suddenly, he did not want to go. He wanted to return to the noisy wedding reception, wanted to plant a boozy kiss on the ugly bride's fat rouged cheek, wanted to go back to his smelly, messy apartment, wanted to hide in his old wrinkled skin. . . .

Winston flattened himself against the door, tried to back into the bathroom—there was a rustle of movement, a slow, busy motion under the draped blackness of the coat thrown over her shoulder. Winston heeded the words his best friend had written . . . words that told of something best not revealed under that draped black fabric.

A thin whimper escaped from the depths of his throat, as a feeble trickle of blood fell from the open bite wound on his lower lip. When he tried to push open the door, he suddenly felt *solidness*, unbroken by *any* opening.

Extending her right hand, lacquered nails glinting near black against her pale skin in the murky light, she said in that movie-star perfect voice of hers, "Give me your hand, Winston . . . we've a way to go, and you don't know the road yet."

FORTY-NINE

Palmer Nemmitz's watch hands read 12:31, moving dark against the greenish glow of his watch face as he stood in his dark bedroom, staring out the open window. The lights of Ewerton shone faint beyond his neighbor's field of corn, random blinks in the distance.

If it had been lit from within, Palmer could've seen the interior of Winston's old bedroom. The one in his boyhood home, on top of Ewert Hill. From the depths of the basement, Palmer used to see the light from his bedroom; Winston used to signal with his window shade, whenever his parents were asleep. He'd drive out to see Palmer, case of squaw piss—Winston's favorite Leinenkugels—in the trunk, and wait for Palmer to sneak out of *his* home.

Remembering, Palmer brushed a tear from his eye. Ever since slightly past midnight, he had felt . . . *empty*. The closest Palmer could come to describing it would be to say it was as if a part of him had been sliced off, yet continued to live . . . even though it wasn't *one* with him anymore. *There*, but not *quite* there.

He hadn't felt that way when Clive vanished, even though he knew the old Doc would never return to Ewerton alive, or whole. Tonight, the empty sensation was enough to wake him up, make him crawl out of bed to stand before the deep blue-black rectangle of the open window.

Winston still hadn't called, hadn't let Palmer know he'd come home and seen the note propped up on his telephone.

Yet . . . it was as if the message *had* gone through; a wordless, thoughtless presence invading Palmer's being, without telling him anything coherent. There, but *not* quite *there*.

Palmer whispered to himself, and the starlit darkness, "May God help you, Winston, *wherever* you are . . . if you're with *her*, I can do no more for you," as he scratched at the fresh, open bite wound with blood-crescented nails.

PART THREE

The Ones Tod Browning Missed

When you are old, and full of sleep,
And nodding by the fire, take down this book,
And slowly read, and dream of the soft look
Your eyes had once, and of their shadows deep.

How many loved your moments of glad grace,
And loved your beauty with love false or true,
But one man loved the pilgrim soul in you,
And loved the sorrows of your changing face;

And bending down beside the glowing bars,
Murmur, a little sadly, how love fled
And paced upon the mountains overhead
And hid his face amid a crowd of stars.

—William Butler Yeats
"When You Are Old"

"Real isn't how you are made. . . .
It's a thing that happens to you. When a child
loves you for a long, long time, not just to play
with, but really loves you, then you become Real."

—Margery Williams
The Velveteen Rabbit

"We accept you, we accept you."

—*Freaks* script, 1932

FIFTY

JULY 18

When Arlin Winston reported his father missing, Stu Sawyer wasn't having another Clive Calder case on his hands; no belligerent relative's "I *told* you so," no lingering feeling that he shouldn't have been so quick to follow the letter of the law in missing person's cases.

Not that Stu would have an easy time of it; Arlin last saw Winston on the sixteenth, at the Thorn-Mesabi wedding. It took Arlin all of two days to figure out that his father's behavior had been a little *strange* at the ceremony and reception—never mind that the old dipso was wearing an *Army* uniform.

But all Arlin found in Winston's apartment were smelly piles of clothes and mossy food—and Palmer Nemmitz's note. *Then* he called Stu.

Stu checked the apartment himself; plenty of stink, but no wrinkled corpse moldering under the daybed, or slumped in the grimy shower stall. He called every wedding guest, as well as the Hole-in-One Club bartenders, hoping the old tosspot went home with someone to sleep it off. He hadn't.

As morning turned to afternoon, and afternoon shadows grew long and deep, spreading out from the buildings and trees like old stains, Stu's worst worries coalesced into stomach-twisting fear . . . for not only had the former teacher disappeared, but if the witnesses could be believed, he'd been *taken* somewhere.

And worse, everyone agreed about who had done the "abducting."

Flipping his notebook pages, Stu reread the scribbled statements of those who saw Winston after Arlin and his wife left the reception:

BETTY PERKINS—He was downing whiskey sours like they were going out of style. Had on a uniform, shoulder things and metal buttons, stuff on his breast. And a hat. Then it got busy at the other end of the bar. When I got back, I saw him leave with a woman—yeah, I know her. She was a couple of classes ahead of me at EHS. The one Mrs. Winston beat up in '78. . . .

DARRYL DOYLE—Gave me a quarter for the jukebox—yeah, he was drunk, that something new? Looked sharp, though. Thought he'd been to a VFW meeting, but I'd had a few myself. Last I saw him, he was sitting next to a woman in a black suit. Long hair. Young, even for him.

HEATHER WILKES—He was there, and so was his girl-friend, I guess you'd call her. Zoe Lawton, who else? Yes, Stu, I heard, but I know how you Sawyers and Nemmitzes—

At that point, Stu's pencil had snapped, but there had been no mistaking the certainty of Mrs. Wilkes's snotty tone. Stu had flinched from the unvoiced question in her voice, in her slightly bulbous blue eyes—why *is* Zoe alive when you claimed she was dead?

Too many people had seen the same chain of events; Winston sits at bar, Winston is joined by woman in black, Winston gets up, helps woman off stool, before heading for the can, then Winston is followed by said woman . . . who happened to remind people of Zoe Lawton Nimitz. But the scenario *always* stopped there. No one saw either Winston or the woman again that evening. A fractured Cinderella; at midnight the handsome prince and the beautiful stranger change into a couple of field mice who scurry away unnoticed. But in fairy tales, the beautiful stranger wasn't already *dead*.

Stu had *seen* Zoe Nimitz, dammit, *she was dead*. Cold and almost bloodless. People don't live through such wounds. Not with all that sticky redness on Bitsy's Lincoln Log quilt.

Cursing Bitsy for her "let's keep it quiet" phone call, Stu tried calling the Nemmitz place again (his morning call had gone unanswered), until his least-favorite in-law answered. But Palmer volunteered little, only admitting that he'd "dropped by" his friend's apartment "sometime Saturday." He claimed to know nothing of Winston's whereabouts, although Stu caught the stammer in his voice. Before he hung up on Stu, he blurted out that Bitsy was staying with "that girlie of hers," but didn't elaborate. Not in a mood to listen to Bitsy's babbling anyhow, Stu instead dialed the hospital.

But a search of their files resulted in no autopsy report filed on the Nimitz woman. Stu drove down there to help look for the report, with no better luck. By then, Stu felt ready for an autopsy himself.

Driving back to his office, Stu prayed that the poor girl *was* dead when she was shoved into that oven—which reminded him to make an important, albeit delayed, phone call.

He hoped he didn't sound as stupid as he felt, asking about the Nimitz woman in the most roundabout, nonaccusing way possible. . . . Afterward, he prayed that he hadn't sounded as shocked as he really was upon hearing that no individual from Ewerton, let alone Dean County, had been cremated in Eau Claire within the past thirty days.

"Aw, Stu, can't this wait? There's a movie on HBO—" Lenny's voice was a metallic whine (damn cheapie modular phone!), ready to launch into the blow-by-blow synopsis of the film in progress. Stu cut him off—mouth dry, heart a muffled jackhammer—with a cautious, "When Doc Calder did the autopsy on the Nimitz woman, are you *sure* she was dead? Yeah, you told me about that cut on her side, what I'm asking is, are you *positive* she was dead before . . . she was picked up?"

"Sure looked, y'know, dead, but . . . I got doubts, Stu. Had 'em since the thirtieth—"

"*What?*" Stu reared up, head clunking the frame of the Ollie North poster in his basement den. "And you *signed her fucking death certificate*? Why didn'tcha grab a stethoscope, give 'er chest a *listen*? Hell, you didn't mention any 'doubts' in the Rusty—"

"*Then* I thought I was . . . y'know, going a little nuts. She didn't get up or nothing like *that*—it was just something I *seen*, on the road that night after you left, and her body was gone—"

Listening in lip-chewing silence as Lenny recounted his vision of the dead woman driving past the farmhouse, Stu wanted to ask, "Did the license have a *peach* on it?" but that would've made it all *too* real.

Long after Lenny hung up—after giving Stu a cock-eyed theory about rubber dolls and "hick tricks"—Stu sat in the quiet of his paneled basement warren, safe from Val's bright-eyed questioning and the distracting noise of the TV.

Once he saw a segment on *60 Minutes* dealing with insurance-scam "deaths"; no bodies, but plenty of funny paper claiming the insured person was dead and gone. Lots of "proof" for the sake of a claim . . . but Stu was faced with an inversion. No body, save for ashes—*if* Zoe had been taken to a crematorium other than the one in Eau Claire—no autopsy report, a death certificate that held water like a wire basket, and no obituary or suicide notice in the paper. Plus the report he'd shredded.

And *he'd* seen the same car Lenny saw that night, the one his officers had casually mentioned seeing in the past few days. Stu wondered how he could politely ask Palmer for proof of payment for Zoe's cremation, then decided he didn't *need* to be polite when it came to Bitsy's old man. Granted, Stu had to do a little more investigating before confronting Palmer, but when the time came to do so, it would be rubber hoses and lights in the face all the way.

Rubbing gritty crusts out of his eyes, Stu vowed that he'd get to the bottom of this whole mess . . . and find the fairground vandals, too. Preferably *before* the Water Carnival—the festivities would take up more time then he could afford to lose.

At least Gordy had replacements lined up for the ruined equipment . . . although, for *some* reason, the *name* of the replacement amusement company had a familiar ring to it.

FIFTY-ONE

After a Sunday of strange silence—Palmer stuck close to his room, puttering noisily while Brent ate solitary meals and watched TV, hurt by Palmer's withdrawal—Brent was surprised when he came downstairs Monday morning to find Palmer sitting at the kitchen table. But his eggs were untouched, and he stared not at his Green Sheet, but at the blue-bound manuscript they'd retrieved from Winston's apartment.

With a birdlike jerk of his head, he looked up when Brent entered the room, yet said nothing while the younger man fixed a pan of eggs. Protectively, Palmer rolled up the booklet, holding it next to his sunken chest.

Not until Brent ate the last forkful of gooey yellow eggs did Palmer speak, with a simultaneous thrusting-forward of the booklet.

"You'd best read this . . . once you do, you'll understand what happened to your wife"—the phone rang, but he ignored it—"I can't . . . guarantee that you'll find her once you're done with it, but . . . don't count it out."

Brent guessed Palmer had rehearsed his little speech for many hours—even so, the words fell flat as he uttered them. Not even the ringing phone distracted him, as if Palmer had but one chance to make his pitch to Brent.

Reaching across the table, Brent took the sweat-slippery booklet from Palmer. "This will tell me what you can't?"

Haltingly: "Pretty damn close. About Zoe, about *her*, about Winston, Clive. When I wrote it, I didn't *think* it meant all that much, but since then . . . You'd better read it, kid. Read it and understand why I'm . . ." Voice trailing off weakly, Palmer looked every one of his sixty-four years. And then some.

Brent understood the unvoiced "scared," and nodded, wishing to God he'd thrown away that second reunion notice of Zoe's. Her coming here had set this all in motion, even if he couldn't understand the *why* of it.

The blue plastic cover glinted harshly in the overhead light; that same cruel illumination brought out every wrinkle and age spot on his uncle's frightened face. On the tinny kitchen radio, the WERT morning announcer began speaking about the Water Carnival, and its featured amusements. Palmer got up, saying, "I'd best be going uptown . . . you read that, son. That wife of yours did." With that he plucked his hat off the rack and slammed the door behind him. The Rambler revved up, then pulled noisily out of the garage; the dry crunch of gravel was audible through the window screen.

Brent put the dishes in the sink, then picked up the manuscript and carried it upstairs. The cover felt obscene, slick and greasy, as if handled by dirty fingers.

Raising his shade to let in pure light, Brent thought of the hands that had touched those pages before his—Palmer's knobby and high-veined, Winston's yellow-tinged and shaking, and Zoe's. . . . Sitting on the edge of his bed, Brent was reluctant to open up the booklet—on one hand, it might bring him closer to Zoe, but on the *other* hand. . . .

After a moment of painful indecision he bent back the blue cover. Sighing when he saw that the thin pages were typed single-spaced on *both* sides, he slowly began to read the jammed elite type on the almost marginless pages.

And found himself in another time, another Ewerton. . . .

FIFTY-TWO

From Palmer Nemmitz's journal—
Hands. Opening, flower-like, small fingers, small pink petals uncurling, only fast, like when a camera on one of those nature programs speeds up things meant to go slow. Her hands, that's how they opened—

(As he read on, Brent thought, *Never would I have thought Uncle could express himself like this . . . whoever or what-ever "she" was, she must've been* something. . . .)

. . . pain is pain, be a body sixty-three or fifteen, only, oh Jeezus, to feel it then—
—her hands looked . . . all wrong—
Facts. Background. Fifteen and then some. 1940. The farm. The old man. That snipe hunt. She deserves to have the stage set just *right*.

After our Ma died, it was bad, especially after the old man moved us down to the basement to live, shunning our Ma's house; like grubs, squirming around under a mausoleum. Come each May, the old man would get near to impossible, though.

May was the anniversary of the time in '35, when the federal government, under the New Deal, offered northern Wisconsin, northern Minnesota, and Upper Peninsula farmers the chance to homestead in the Matanuska Valley Colony in the territory of Alaska. The old man's cousins in Sheyboygan let him in on the offer, since Ewerton wasn't within the offical boundaries. The old man's cousin Emman wrote and said the deal was intended to take folks off the dole; give farmers a chance to start fresh with one cow, a horse, plus New Deal supplied clothing, food, furniture, the works. FDR was going to supply new houses, churches, and schools in the settlement.

Everything but the church part impressed the old man

mightily (he wasn't too keen on churchgoing after what happened in Czechoslovakia; his father was put in public stocks for planting crops on a Sunday), and considering how the farm had been steadily failing and shrinking since the Crash, the old man saw this as his chance to start fresh. He was all set to write back to Emman, when our Ma told him, "You go, Enoch, you go alone. I'm not going and neither are the children. Remember the bird in the hand . . . we lose the farm, we can't come back if it doesn't pan out up north."

That didn't set so well with the old man. For a week our Ma didn't dare go uptown, until the swelling went down. But we didn't go to Alaska, either.

Every time Emman's letters came in the mail, the old man read them aloud during dinner. Our Ma sat barely able to chew as we heard about the fine house Emman and his family had picked out from a choice of five designs offered, and how things grew big and healthy, up there in the valley.

And he'd emphasized the name of Emman's new town, *Palmer*, on account it was my name (chosen by our Ma, instead of the old man's choice of Albert), until our Ma's face would alternate red and white from the upset.

After each letter, he'd go into his same old spiel. "Should've taken Emman up on his offer, Christ-all-Friday. Should be up there, in a new house, 'way from *this* place, but oh, *no*, I'm still *here*, busting my prat, with nothing to show for it. All because someone didn't want to leave her *friends* . . . bet I know who her *best* friend is, don't I? Old 'green eyes,' eh, Treeva? *Palmer*? I *should've* gone, taken *my* kids with me. Leave you and *yours* to fend for yourselves. Maybe your *friend* might've helped you—" On and on like that, a broken record, grooves worn down to hissing static.

All the while, the others would snigger, even the little kids too young to understand what the old man was insinuating about our Ma. And I'd look at our Ma, and she'd look at me, sadly, as if to say, *If I'd only known, I never would've had you*. But there was affection in her eyes, too. That kept me going, kept the old man's hate and fear at bay.

And then she died, and we went underground, as if she were still alive and well upstairs and we were hiding from her . . . no, the *old man* was hiding from her.

So without fail, if the mailman left a letter from Palmer, Alaska, in our mailbox, I invited myself to Winston's house for supper. And stayed overnight if the meal stretched out too late. Without our Ma there to give me that sad, apologetic look over the remains of dinner, I couldn't face Emman's letters alone. By then, Effie, Merle, and Shirley were old enough to *know*.

But as welcome as the Winstons made me feel at their table and no matter how well I got on with their son, I couldn't live there twenty-four hours a day. Sometimes, there was no escaping the hiss of a blunt needle dragging through those worn grooves.

Like that morning in May, Sunday, the twenty-ninth. The day the wheels were set in motion; the day I became aware that they'd been set to spinning out of control. The day . . . my *future* died.

It was before seven, and we—the old man, me, and my brother Vern—were shoveling out the cow barn, which was one of my least favorite things to do outside of getting my back teeth drilled until my tongue smoked. And we only had three cows left out of the herd the old man had when I was born—back when he had hired hands to do his mucking, and wore cream-colored suits and a straw hat when he and our Ma drove into town.

Since it was May, he was telling us how he belonged in Alaska, living in a new-built home of *his* choosing, but our Ma hadn't wanted to leave "her" home, "her precious, *damned* sweet *home*." Vern and I were so used to his story we knew when to nod and when to shake our heads, not taking our eyes off what we were doing lest we toss a shovelful of green-brown flop on each other. Only, when I'd sneak a peek at Vern, his brown eyes would have this smirking look. I missed our Ma's soft brown stare something terrible.

Then the needle hit a fresh groove, startling me. "—and then I heard someone name of *Palmer*'s been doing what ought not to be done in public with the Byrne girl, and it better *stop*," and when the needle slipped back in the fizzed-out "Emman sez the soil's better up there" groove, I noticed Vern edging over to the barn door, getting closer and closer to the sweet-smelling opening, prior to dropping his shovel into an empty stall and running off. He could smell a fight brewing like animals sense a thunderstorm on a sunny afternoon.

I tried to edge off toward the door, too, but it didn't work. In the distance, I heard the thud of Vern's boots against wet grass, and wished to God he'd slip and break his rear end.

When a record goes around, there's a chance the needle will skip a groove and end up in a place it's been before. Sure enough, the old man goes in a voice that's *way* too calm, "Heard 'bout you and the Byrne girl in Holiday's store Tuesday last. Rest of the folks in the store heard it, too. Fred Ferger Junior was telling ol' *Wilbur* what he'd *seen* one night, and it was *real* amusing. Know what Freddy said? He knew what you and that girl was up to. Why do you persist in *embarrassing* me, Palmer?"

He *never* called me "Palmer."

It was no use, but I started, "Fred didn't *mean*—" but I was cut off before I could say "me" with a slicing swipe of the shovel, which narrowly missed my knees. I went backward, shaking my head, while he went on in that too-calm voice, all the while swinging at me with his shovel, "Fred said he saw 'Palmer and Betty Byrne having an *assignation*' in an empty Soo *boxcar* sitting on the sidings near the *depot*, Friday night two weeks *past*, saw moonlight on naked *skin* inside that car. Sound familiar yet, *bastard*?"

I was so used to him calling me "bastard," "cottage colt," and "*friend's* boy," what he was calling me now didn't make me blink twice, but the "Friday night two weeks *past*" part did—I knew when he said it that the old man would take my startled reaction all wrong.

Fred'd found a way to get even with me for that snipe hunt, only he wound up tarring *me* with a brush that had Palmer *Winston's* name all over it. And I'd tried to talk Winston out of taking Fred on that damn-fool "hunt." Not that Dead Fred at eighteen should've fallen for a *snipe* hunt.

His father should've taken him on one of those two, three years before, when he was younger than Winston and I were in '40. Even my old man, who hardly thought the sun rose and set in my rear end, took me and Vern out together. Afterward, the three of us had the only mutual laugh of our lives over it. Winston's dad took him to the Rusty Hinge to celebrate afterward; that was nothing out of the ordinary for a Winston to do, but Porter *was* Winston's old man, and Winston was thrilled by his gesture. Maybe it was that Porter took the *initiative* that took Winston off guard.

That's what we were discussing that early May Friday night while we sat on out favorite bench uptown. Mind, this wasn't one of those butt-breaking flat things the city works men put in a few years back. We sat on a real *bench*—thin slat seat tilted at a comfortable angle, curved metal armrests, and a back to support your own. A few blocks down sat the "old women," as Winston and I called them; gas-station geezers who whistled at girls, slapping their knees in delight when the ladies spun around to see who'd wolf-whistled.

Winston and I, though, didn't intend to spend the whole night there, chewing the fat; we had plans for the rusted-out Studebaker truck Porter picked up for a song for his son to drive around in come night. (Not that Winston had a driver's license yet, but old Sheriff Sawyer and Police Chief Weiss understood how disasterous it was for Porter or Gayleen to drive, so heads turned the other way when Winston sat behind the wheel of the Winston's Woody or LaSalle coupe.)

That old truck was parked in front of us, case of Leinenkugels—to be dipped in the cold waters of Crescent Lake—resting under the seat. As Winston downed his bottle of Coca-Cola, and I slurped the last of my Pepsi (I had to make my nickel stretch further than Winston did), we both thought of the good time we'd have by the lake that night.

Swallowing the last of his soda, Winston went on, "Night of the snipe hunt, Dad took a milk-bottle holder, put a few cans in it, and dipped it in the water for half an hour. They were cold by the time he came and got me out of the woods, but we still opened up the Hinge come morning—"

"Didn't the cans do it?" I burped from the heavy carbonation of my soda.

"He only drank a little. Dad swears it's skunky in cans. No use arguing, I was shocked he *decided* on the Hinge once he came for me—jeepers, I already sound like a broken record and I haven't even used *this*." He held up a church key plucked from his shirt pocket, grinning that lopsided grin of his.

Winston was a good-looking kid, but his smile made all the difference. But he was ashamed of the way his teeth rode up deeper in his gums on one side; his dentist told him there was nothing he could do to fix them, so usually Winston kept his lips sealed tighter than a scared girl's legs on her first nighttime date.

"Win, didn't your dad *tell* you?" I leaned back, waiting for him to take the bait. He sat there, face serious under the golden glow of the corner street lamp, eyes dancing behind the pair of $3.25 Ray•Ban cheaters he wore even though there wasn't any sun out to need protection from. Maybe after pay-

ing thirteen times the price of ordinary sunglasses, he wanted
to show off his investment. But I could tell, sunglasses or
not, Winston was stumped. Setting his swirled bottle down
on the bench with a hollow *thunk*, he leaned back, asking, in
a "you *win*" tone, "*What* didn't Dad tell me?"

Placing my larger bottle down next to his, I said simply,
"Snipes are *scared* of cans." Winston shook me by the shoulders, until we were both laughing so hard we had to blow
our noses and wipe the tears from our eyes. Putting away his
hankie, he glanced down and moaned, "Aw, look, I killed a
June bug. Poor thing's all squashed to hell—"

"How will you survive in the Army with that attitude?
Gonna stand over a Hun and say, 'Aw, I shot him'? If there
would've been a snipe out there, you'd've bawled buckets if
you shot him—"

Winston looked my way, about to reply, when he heard the
blatty muffler of Clive and Tom Calder's car thump down the
street. We stared as the Calders cruised by. Tom was perched
on the radiator, like a living hood ornament, posing. Dead
Fred jogged after them, panting, "You said *last* week I'd get
a ride, c'mon, you two, fair's *fair*—"

In answer, Clive honked the horn and stepped on the gas,
taking off so fast Tom almost toppled head-over-ass off the
hood. Clive was planning to be a doctor; a man you'd really
want poking around in your insides. . . . Dead Fred stood
there in the dust, lippy mouth gaping. When he saw us on
the bench, he did his best imitiation of the *Jack Armstrong,
All-American Boy* announcer: "Palmer Winston . . . Palmer
Winston . . . *Palmer Winston, the All-American Boy*!"

I was fit to toss my cookies. Winston leaned over, whispering, "Offissa Pup *lives*!" before rolling his eyes in disgust. Winston was one of the few people in town who both
read and *understood* George Harriman's *Krazy Kat* comic
strip—Ewerton was *Gasoline Alley* country—sure enough,
Dead Fred *did* resemble the dough-faced Offissa Pup, down
to his blue cap and shirt.

Dead Fred—Winston once claimed he looked like an un-
fried fritter, dead white, and the name stuck—was six feet
away and gaining on us. No time to run for the truck and
work the clutch furiously, as the Calder boys had done.

And I just had this *feeling* Dead Fred was listening in on
us, even from a couple of blocks away. That was Offissa Pup's
trick, perfected in the days when Winston and I used to sit

on the front steps of Holiday's Grocery Store, sharing Eskimo Pies, PK Candy-Coated Gum, or the two Twinkies in the pack, talking over important things like Tarzan Pop-Up books, and radio serials (I followed *The Green Hornet*; Winston was devoted to *Jack Armstrong*), when, suddenly, like a bad smell wafting into a room after the cake's burnt in the oven, there would be Dead Fred, asking for licks or bites off whatever we were eating. And woe to us if we happened to be arguing when he showed up. He'd pick the other guy's side, and get a person so mad they'd scoop up their marbles and run home, and it wouldn't be until later that it dawned on us that Dead Fred had done it, *again*.

If our folks and his folks hadn't been close friends, we wouldn't have given the time of day to Dead Fred. But our folks *had* been, so we had to put up with Fred.

So, we sat on our bench, awaiting our doom. Fred came to a titties-shaking stop, all but glowing where light hit lardy flesh. Without preamble he asked, "What's this 'bout cryin' when you shoot a snipe? It helpless, like a doe?" (How he heard us blocks off was something even Charles Fort couldn't have fathomed.)

I didn't know whether to laugh or cry over Fred's sheer *stupidity*. Dead Fred, serious as all get-out, asking if a *snipe* was something *real*. His father hunted, so there was no excuse for him not *knowing*. I'd thought every boy raised in a rural area got hauled out to the wood some wet, shivery night, ordered to sit and wait, gun poised on his knees, until the great and fearsome *snipe* came tearing out of the dark cover of the trees, nostrils flaring, hooves pounding bits of mossy earth up into the air . . . and the kid would wait, and *wait*. If his dad was mean, he wouldn't go back to pick him up, but if he was good-natured he'd return to the woods, fetch the red-faced kid home, and come morning they'd both have a good belly laugh over it.

It was a *growing-up* thing to endure, like taking that first nose-curling sip of beer, or blowing cigarette smoke out your nose and coughing until you heaved. Silly in retrospect, but we grinned and bore it and dreamed of the day when our own sons (God willing) would be left out in the woods some soggy night, alone with the rustles and the slithers and the moist plopping sounds—and his imagination. Cruel, but life wasn't always a trip to the soda fountain. As I said, the old man and I only laughed together over the same thing once.

I was fixing to ask Fred, "Your dad hasn't taken you snipe hunting *yet*?" but Winston beat me to the punch, speaking in that flat drawl of his as he tapped a smoke out of his green Lucky Strikes box, "Not at all, Fred . . . don't you *know*? Snipes"—he paused to light up; in the glow of a close-held match his face was calm, no twitching cheeks or shifting mouth, then shook out the match, dropped it to the sidewalk, ground it out, and let out his first puff before continuing— "are bigger than a moose. Huge antlers, sharp-tipped instead of rounded. Tear your innards out if you come too close. Long, yellowed teeth, curved so it's hard to pull out of its jaws. Covered with slick fur so you can't get a grip on them for all the grease. Only one vulnerable spot on its whole body."

Winston let his sunglasses slip to the tip of his nose; with his cigarette-holding hand he pointed with his forefinger to the spot between his eyes, almost grinding his Lucky Strike into his right eye. "Spot so small only a BB gun will get him."

Offissa Pup was *real* impressed. Rocking back and forth on his heels, hands in pockets, he looked up and down the length of the deserted street—even the gas-station sitters had shuffled off—an awestruck expression on his moon face. While Fred was busy giving his brain cell a good runaround, I leaned in close to Winston, whispering, "*Not* a good *idea*, Win," but he gave me a wink before pushing up his Ray•Bans.

Dead Fred exclaimed, "Something that dangerous ought not to be let run around. Might *get* someone. S'pose they don't advertise 'bout it for fear of folks getting killed hunting it?" I wanted to take little Freddie by the arm and lead him home, making sure his mommy tucked him in with his Teddy bear, but Winston was on a roll.

Getting to his feet with a fluid grace I admired but couldn't emulate, Winston stuck his smoke in his mouth at a jaunty angle, just like FDR in publicity stills, and slapped Dead Fred on the back. "C'mon, Fred, this town shouldn't be menaced by such a beast. You've a good idea, and *I* just happen to have my BB gun in the truck. What do you say, huh? Do we rid Ewerton of the snipe, or do we sit in darkness and fear? What shall it be?"

Dead Fred's face lit up. Clambering into the truck after Winston, he shouted, "Let's *kill* it!"

I should've reached in and taken the truck keys, or just

walked home. But Dead Fred really *believed* Winston, and his father *should've* explained to him about snipes—

So, I climbed in next to Dead Fred. We were cramped in tight, barely able to breathe, our sneakered feet resting on the white beer cans. Winston drove fast down to the bridge next to the small hill to the south (where the drive-in hadn't been erected yet), crossing the plank bridge with a merry rumble, then headed north for the long drive—some of it over places with no real road—to the Ewert Woods, past Willow Hill.

I'd hoped that if Winston was damn-fool enough to do this, he'd at least have the sense to dump Fred in the *fairgrounds* woods, so his trip home would be short—but Winston was giving him the *full* treatment. (Years later, they put a bridge near the sash and door, close to Seventh Avenue West in the business district, but in '40, Dead Fred was doomed to hoof it home but *good*.)

As Winston drove—how he saw with those cheaters at night I have no idea—he elaborated on the snipe, adding sharp hooves of white bone, red-rimmed eyes "so deep black you'd best not stare into them or you'll be hypnotized for sure," and the ripe smell of the beast, until I was certain Dead Fred would ask, "This is a *joke*, isn't it?" *But he never did.* The fool bought it lock, stock, and pickle barrel. Winston wouldn't have spoken to me for a year if I'd ratted on him by then.

It was too late to say *anything*; we'd bumped and rattled our way over bare ground right up to the lip of the woods, under the solid black shadow of Willow Hill. Winston didn't use his flashlight, claimed it might frighten the snipe—*then* he dropped the bombshell on Dead Fred.

Handing him the BB gun in the firefly-lit darkness, dots of chartreuse luminescence reflected double in his Ray•Bans, Winston solemnly began, "Fred, I've a confession to make"—*Please tell Fred it's a joke!*—"Palmer and I, we've already tried to hunt the snipe. He has our scent. If we step into those woods, he'll be halfway up to Canada in a jiffy. Remember, his eyes glow in the dark. All you have to do is aim for the spot between them, okay?"

Winston had no business giving Fred that BB gun. But he did it anyhow, and me, dummy that I was, said nothing to him until the slithery sounds of Fred walking into the woods grew dim, and his plump silhouette vanished into the greater darkness of the woods.

Once Fred was gone—he had more guts than I'd credited him with—I turned in the direction of Winston's lit Lucky Strike, hissing, "You a-hole! Our fathers will tan our behinds for us when they find out!" "I didn't think he'd go in . . . I laid it on thick, so he'd back out." A match bloomed into flaring color in the darkness. In the small circle of light, his mouth was all puckered, like it got when he was worried or upset, before he sucked the fire onto the tip of his new smoke and shook out the match.

So he hadn't counted on Dead Fred's bravery, either. That made me feel better as I followed him back to the truck. Sitting in the cab, watching tiny motes of queasy green light dance outside the windshield, we passed the church key back and forth. The Studebaker filled with the tangy aroma of Leinenkugels while we waited for I don't recall how long for Dead Fred to come out.

My eyes weren't too bleary to read the luminous dial of my watch the last time I remembered to look at it—9:57. By then, we'd been maybe half an hour in the truck.

Getting home late was no worry—ever since moving down to the basement, Vern, Vernilla (his twin), and I discovered that once the old man dozed off come eight or earlier, he was out, until the double-bell alarm by his bed rang come dawn. Ever since our Ma died, the old man didn't want us around unless it was time to do chores, cook, or be of some earthly use; what we did otherwise didn't seem to concern him.

Vern seldom shimmied out the window, while Vernilla sometimes crawled out, legs thrashing in her skirt and slip, to see this or that boy (she spent some of that time with Winston, but the subject of just what he and my sister did was taboo). I crawled out of the dank basement into the fresh coolness of the night so often that Vernilla joked that my name ought to be carved in the molding around the glass.

Winston's folks were usually "sick" after supper, so he could've led a fife and drum band through the house from basement to attic and they wouldn't have missed a beat in their snoring.

So there we sat, getting pie-eyed and giggly, swapping Dead Fred stories. As the evening went on, we'd hop out of the truck, let the squaw piss turn to brave piss, then hop back into the truck. Winston hung his cheeters on the sun flap, so he could see the wheel when he steered, never mind the road.

I can't recall how, but I made it through the window and

into bed—I didn't *think* about how we'd left Dead Fred out in the woods all night until two days later.

When Winston and I were in town, shooting the breeze near Holiday's store, Dead Fred acted as if nothing unusual had happened when we walked by. Neither of us brought up the hunt, thinking the matter was over. I hadn't asked Winston what he did after dropping me off at the farmhouse . . . but Dead Fred didn't *have* to ask. He'd seen; or if he hadn't seen Winston and Betty Byrne *that* night, he knew that mentioning the date of the hunt plus Winston's nocturnal activity would be enough to get at least one of our mutual gooses cooked. And he still had the BB gun with "PCW" branded on the stock.

So, standing in that manure-redolent barn, cows moaning low behind me, I swallowed hard, telling myself, *I get my hands on you, Winston, you won't have anything left to put in a girl, never mind what no-balls Fred has coming*. The old man swallowed, too, before saying, "I didn't *appreciate* hearing about your little *tryst*, 'specially in front of that green-eyed *buggerer* . . . ain't enough you do *dirt*, like your *mother*, but I have to hear *tell* of it in *public*!"

He dropped the shovel he'd been swinging at me, and, moving like Fred Astaire despite his girth and weight, stepped over to the wall near the door—where the pitchfork was. Grabbing it by the handle, pointing the business end at me, sharp points glinting in the dimly lit barn, he seethed, "I only put up with Treeva 'cause she was mother to *my* children. Not that she didn't deserve what happened to her, but you're asking for a lot more than she *ever* got. Bastards can't *ever* go to heaven, no matter how good they are in life, so I suppose I shouldn't be surprised at how rotten you are. Considering Hell's your final whistle stop," advancing at me until I backed into an empty stall, with nowhere to hide from his fire eyes and the tips of the pitchfork pressing my chest though my work jacket. As he went on, he slowly pressed the tines in deeper.

"Maybe your *daddy*'ll protect you, eh, *bastard*? Hung like a rabbit, just like him, goddamned *bastard* son of a *bitch*—"

I still had my muck rake in my hand; when the tines began to hurt, I clipped the old man in the legs. He dropped the pitchfork with a yowl, but by the time I made it out of the stall, he was after me, hands going for my neck, yellowed teeth clenched behind white lips. I put my foot between his legs and hooked my right arm around his left, sending both of us sprawling into the last vestiges of muck on the straw below, me falling back-first while the old man fell sort of sideways, hitting his head against a post next to a stall. I shucked out of my jacket, leaving it stuck in the shit and the straw next to his shuddery-breathing form.

Favoring the leg I'd twisted as we fell down, I ran as fast as I could for the house, heading for the north window. Luckily, the younger girls and Shirl were off jumping rope by the old pump house, so they didn't see me painfully squeeze through the window, landing hands-first onto the big bureau.

The basement was dark, as usual; the lone bulb cast odd shadows among the hodgepodge of furniture we'd hauled from downstairs.

I didn't know if I was alone down there or not; I was too shook up to care. Knowing the old man, this wasn't going to be the last of it, so I got my knapsack out from under my bed—the sack had been the old man's when he was a Lone Scout, or so he claimed. Yanking open my drawer of the bureau, I shoved handfuls of underwear, socks, shirts, and jeans into the roomy confines of the bag, helping myself to some of Vern's bandannas because he'd run off.

As the sack grew from canvas flatness to Christmas stocking fullness, I breathed like a normal person again. By the time I stood up, placing my arms in the straps, I was thinking clearly again, too.

I was *glad* I wasn't the old man's kid—otherwise, I'd *be* like him, or like Vern and his stupid "wall dictionary." I glared at the cut-apart Hershey bar wrappers Vern had separated into "HE" and "HER" and "SHE" (no "HEY" yet; Vern wasn't a scholar), and taped to the wall with that sticky tape the WPA workers used to repair frayed documents over at the courthouse.

Vern was glad when the old man took us older kids out of school after our Ma died; his burning ambition was to be Old McDonald on his farm. The "wall dictionary" was reading matter aplenty for *him*. But I'd been neck and neck with Winston in school, and to me, what the old man did to us was like living in Hell without benefit of death. As if I'd had any chance of getting the farm anyhow, or even sharing it with Vern. *Bastards don't inherit anything but shame*, I told myself, fighting the urge to rip down Vern's handiwork.

But if I did that, he'd only make me buy him new bars, for new wrappers, and since my life's savings consisted of three dollars and seventy-nine cents, with most of *that* in nickles and dimes, I had to conserve my cash for as long as possible until I could earn some more.

Moving past islands of furniture to the kitchen area, for a heartsick moment I had no idea *where* I intended to go, let alone *do* once I got there.

Reaching the kitchen (ancient gas stove, icebox, chipped sink, oilcloth-covered table, and beat-up chairs, ringed on three sides by shelves of food and dishes), I forced those worries from my mind, and set about gathering up as much nonspoiling food as I could lay hands on. I found an uncut flour sack Vernilla was saving for dishcloths, and threw in this and that—a box of raisins, a can of peaches, a half-empty jar of peanut butter—but just as I wrapped my fingers around a can of chicken noodle soup (I liked it cold) I heard Vernilla from above and behind me: "Whatever you take, leave the soup. That's *supper*."

I whirled around so fast the heavy sack of food whacked me in the thighs. Vernilla was coming downstairs from the upstairs kitchen (the only part of the house we saw on a regular basis; the old man had yet to install a door to the basement from outside), a "you're gonna *get* it" look on her face.

She was only seventeen, but she was already coarsed-out. Put a baby on her hip, she'd have passed for thirty. Vernilla was dark-haired, like all us kids, big-boned without being fat, so all the bones stuck out hard and mean on her. I loathed her, and the feeling was gleefully mutual.

As she clomped down the wooden steps, she told me she'd been in the barn and seen the old man, who was "just *fine*, but you ain't gonna be once he gets his hands on you." It was plain she couldn't wait for the moment. I kept throwing things in my sack, until the veins on my hand and wrist stood out when I tried to heft it.

Vernilla positioned herself by the table, assembling the fixings for a pot of chili; then, bemoaning that she was nearly out of Gebhardt's Chili Powder, she added slyly, "Maybe you can stop at your *father's* and buy me some?"

I bit my lips and said nothing, having remembered that I'd be needing some Absorbine Jr., for sunburn and athlete's foot alike. I was fixing to do a lot of walking. So I stepped into the board-walled bathroom cubicle.

I'd half expected to see the old man waiting for me when I came out, but only Vernilla was there. The air was sweet with the smell of browning camp meat from the old man's out of season hunting trip.

Vernilla heard me step out, and started up again as she drained the fat into the coffee can of old grease Vern used to fry potato chips in come fall. The grease in that can was three years old, and smelled it. (Once, during a fight, Vern threatened to heat it up and pour it down his twin's throat.)

"You deserved what you got from our Pa. Should've whacked your kneecaps off, then went for what's above 'em. Doing *filth*, like our Ma—in a *box*car. Rutting dog—"

I couldn't take it. The old man was bad enough, but he wasn't my *flesh*. Vernilla was. Not taking my hand off the railing, one foot poised on the bottom step, I replied, "For your information, *sister*, it was Palmer *Winston* Fred saw with Betty . . . you jealous about her, or doesn't Winston screw you in that *nice* a place?"

I was nearly to the door when she collected herself enough to shout, "*Me*, jealous? Your best buddy isn't *that* good— *I've had better*!"

Before I turned the knob, I looked down at her. "I'm so glad you put quality before quantity."

Striding across the kitchen upstairs (sadly dusty and mud-tracked), I heard her ragged shout, "Don't let the screen door hit you in the ass!" then I was out of that place, heading for the road. I bypassed the barn, where the old man was waiting for me to come back and take my medicine—or prepare for a coffin-fitting. He still had that pitchfork.

That's how the old man was; it was beneath him to come *after* a body. *That* would've signified a loss of power, the authority of saying, "You come when *I* call, or else!" Like when he went after our Ma; when she ran, it was worse. She'd have to hole up longer; whenever Mr. Holiday saw me up-town, he'd pester me with questions about her, and slip me arnica and aspirins to take to her on the sly. And I brought them to her, even though I knew old Wilbur was the cause of her condition in the first place . . . but damn, my father was a nice fellow.

I was almost to the road when I heard Vern's shout, and the earthy plods of his boots as he ran to catch up with me, his voice breathy.

"Pa . . . gonna getcha . . . waitin' . . . the barn. Said to tell you . . . forgot your jacket. He's got the pitchfork,'' he ended on a teasing note, brushing the hair out of his narrow eyes. Cradling the sack of food like a baby, I ignored him. Vern tried to keep pace with me, but I had motivation on my side. He began huffing again, mottled face growing redder by the second.

"Palmer . . . you ain't fixing to *leave*?"

I tried to keep my voice even. "Why not? I don't have anything here. 'Bout time I left."

Vernon stopped in his tracks behind me. "But who's gonna help me mow the *grass*?" His voice would've done a hungry baby proud, a fussy and wet baby at that. As I trotted away from him, he wailed, "This mean I gotta cut grass all summer?"

I never turned back to answer him. The sun came up warm and clear; I adjusted my cap so it shaded my eyes as I walked the three miles into town proper. I sorely regretted not ripping Vern's candy-bar wrappers into brown and silver confetti.

Making the turn from the country trunk onto Byrne Avenue, I almost was run down by the Winston's LaSalle coupe. Winston was at the wheel, dressed in a white flannel suit of his father's, three-spike hankie sticking jauntily out of his breast pocket, brown hair combed just *so*.

When he stopped, braking so hard he sent his parents lurching forward, I saw that he wore his *matching* tie and hankie, the picture of fastidiousness. I was so mad at him by that time, I was close to puking all over the coupe. Him and his goddamned *snipe*—

"Need a ride, Palmer?" Winston was all good manners; his parents must've been semisober. They smiled and nodded hello to me; Porter slack-faced as usual, Gayleen—clutching her Bible and Sunday school things in a beringed and bangled pair of hands—made "googly" eyes at me, a coquettish thing she'd done since the late twenties. For a second I almost stopped being angry with Winston; he wasn't their *son*, but an unpaid baby-sitter, cook, chauffeur, and wet nurse combined. And official excuse-maker to boot.

But he never complained about it. *He* would've got along just dandy with my old man if he were in my manure-caked shoes. But looking at him, sitting pretty behind the wheel of that blue coupe, smelling of bay rum even though he didn't shave regularly yet, then looking down at the flour sack of food in my hands, feeling the press of the knapsack on my back, I couldn't work up *much* pity for him. Then there was the matter of Dead Fred—

Leaning out of the car, he touched my arm, blue eyes concerned. "Sure I can't give you a lift?" Then he noticed the knapsack, and the bundle in my arms; he began to say something else, but I shook off his hand.

"No, I think I'll take a *boxcar*, Romeo . . . by the way, Vernilla says that she's had better," I snapped, stalking off and breaking into a run when I hit Roberts Street. Behind me, I heard him stammer something to his folks about me being "out of sorts." When he started the coupe, the engine flooded.

I slowed to a fast trot down the street; it looked so beautiful in the morning sunlight. Houses tall and fresh-painted, trees and lawns jewellike, still bearing the last prismatic drops of night dew. People driving or walking to church nodded and waved to me, and I nodded in return. I didn't notice that Wilbur Holiday was heading across his lawn in my direction. I turned around and we almost collided.

Wilbur didn't have his coat or tie on yet; his shirtsleeves were rolled up to the elbow, which made him look younger than his years. That yellow-blond hair hid whatever white was creeping in, too. His eyes squinted against the sun; bright green, but light, too, with hints of yellow. Startling, especially when the thread-thin lines in the whites turned red. Uncommon eyes . . . like mine.

(*I love you, Ma, but damn you, too. . . .*)

"Palmer, you aren't leaving?" His brisk voice tried to sound casual but failed. He placed strong hands on both my shoulders; his eyes seemed to beg, *Please don't go . . .* no.

I swallowed; bile backed into my throat, made me wince when I didn't want to show *any* emotion. Finally: "Yes. Time to set out on my own." I shook his hands from off my shoulders; Wilbur let them drop to his sides forlornly. A slight breeze ruffled his light hair; in the places where the sun shone through it, it resembled pale fire. Craggy features crumpling around the mouth and eyes, he jammed his hands in his trouser pockets and fell in step alongside me as I walked south.

When we'd passed a couple of houses, he said slowly, "Palmer, I think I know what's wrong. I think it best we go back to the house"—he glanced at his huge sage-green mansion, then in my direction again—"I'll put on a pot of coffee, and we'll talk. The situation can't be *that* bad—"

He said more, but I was thinking again, and my thoughts weren't all that pleasant. Our Ma *died* in that big green house. And the wife of the man she'd *been* with was right there when it happened. I hadn't been inside there since I was a baby; now wasn't the time to pay a return visit. Especially with the old man still in the barn waiting for me.

First I'd come in, then Wilbur would get on the Ameche, tell the old man where I was, and three days hence Mr. Byrne and Mr. Reish would be plugging up pitchfork holes in my chest. No *thank* you!

The more I reflected, the stranger my thoughts became; my eyes watered, my throat grew full, then I wheeled around in my tracks and faced Wilbur, staring at him green eye to green eye. "Why don't you follow Dead Fred? He just *loves* to talk. Go ask *him* why I'm leaving."

I broke into a run, away from Wilbur and his pleas to "please come back, it isn't that bad," for it *was* "that bad." Nothing he could do or say would make it better. *He'd* done enough already, nine months before our Ma had me.

I didn't stop running until I nearly doubled over from a cramp in my stomach. By then, I was out on county trunk QV, headin' out of town, looking the wrong way at the "Welcome to Ewerton" sign . . . with the added smaller sign "Jobless Men, Keep Walking!" tacked on beneath. After the cramp subsided, I walked until my shadow was a small puddled thing at my feet, and my arms felt hot and dry. I wished I had one of those Jack Armstrong Hike-O-Meters, like the one Winston got in exchange for cereal box tops. He hardly ever *walked* since Porter taught him to drive.

And so began my journey south—out of laziness, I kept heading down, instead of branching out east or west. By evening, I reached the place where Dean County left off and Taylor County began. Cottage colt that I was, I slept in the woods, hoping as I drifted off that Winston's snipe would get me and end my misery.

Looking back at that time, seeing it as a whole from the distance of age and experience, I tell myself that *maybe*, if I'd swallowed my anger, taken that ride with Winston, or *maybe*, if I'd taken Wilbur up on his offer of coffee and a heart-to-heart talk, things would've turned out very different. But that morning, nothing on earth could've kept me off that road because, perhaps, nothing *of* this earth *made* me keep walking away that day.

FIFTY-THREE

When Winston opened his eyes, the *grass* wasn't right; he blinked owlishly at the isolated, *intensified* blades, which tickled his nose as he lay prone on the ground, moisture seeping through his serge uniform trousers and jacket. He gave up trying to figure out why the grass looked wrong, and squeezed his eyes shut again. Bright sunlight turned his eyelids into richly patterned red window shades; not wanting to bury his face in the odd-looking grass (*funny, it feels all right*), he rubbed his face with his palms, pressing fingers into each eye, flooding his pounding brain with darkness.

The blackness within was quickly replaced with an inner fireworks display; pulsing chartreuse, crimson, and electric blue kaleidoscopic bursts of color. Interesting, but devastating while he was hung over. And famished, too.

Winston heard his stomach rumble over the faint insect sounds of the morning, if early morning it was. He wasn't sure, be it of the time of day or the day itself. Rolling onto his back, feeling gentle bumps and grassy knots of earth below him (but keeping his palms pressed over his aching eyes), his sigh trailed off into a low moan.

Drunk. He'd been drinking . . . somewhere. That much he was reasonably sure of; but as for the rest . . . at least he knew his *name*. It came to him in pounding waves, the way the announcer of *Jack Armstrong* . . . used to thunder his way through the title credit of the radio show. A building rush of words, "Palmer Winston . . . Palmer Winston . . . *Palmer Winston*—" until it was almost as if the words were being spoken aloud—in Dead Fred *Ferger*'s voice, no less!

He shifted his hands to his ears, masking out the reverberating tones, eyes recoiling with searing pain when the eyelid-filtered light hit them. He spoke aloud, his reedy voice not *quite* familiar to him, or perhaps familiar so long ago that it was once again strange.

"Oh . . . *damn*."

How long he lay, he couldn't be sure. Nor was he sure of just *where* he was. Somewhere grassy, that much was certain. And he was hot in his shirt and uniform jacket. Fumbling his tie loose, he then unbuttoned the top button of his shirt. A slick, slightly greasy pool of sweat welled in the hollow below his Adam's apple.

As he rubbed his fingers together afterward, the tips felt *hard*, the skin taut and firm over the bone. For a reason that eluded him, that in itself was all *wrong*. . . .

Eventually, he sighed, then sat up at the waist, propping himself up with his elbows, legs splayed out in front of him. In that position, the sun wasn't directly in his eyes, so he opened them slowly—and squinted almost immediately.

He'd been right about the grass. There was plenty of it . . . all as strange as it had seemed upon first glance. The field was luminous, each blade quivering and shimmering in bright sunlight, double-edged with a delicate multihued coat of frost. A sudden freeze that hadn't blackened or rotted the grass, but *beautified* it. As his eyes painfully focused, Winston saw that the whisper-thin edges of each blade of grass were infinitesimally beaded with slivers of prismatic color. His hand, with its lack of scintillating ruddiness, looked dead in comparison.

With that observation, he got up suddenly and unsteadily, almost falling down with the effort. Once on his feet, Winston halfheartedly dusted off his Army dress uniform. His hat lay, as if suspended, on the sparkling, nearly *moving* grass. Yet, when he bent to pick it up (and was rewarded with a stab of pain behind his eyes for the effort), the grass beneath the hat slowly sprang up, as if it were writhing, after being bent down for who knew *how* long.

Despite its strange appearance, the grass felt fine underfoot; no snaking movements under the soles of his polished black shoes, no crunch of frost. And the grass had been warm under him, he recalled that much. Jamming his hat on his head, Winston stumbled away from the disquieting spectacle, heading for the single line of trees growing in a direction he *thought* might be west.

The row of trees—elms, by the shape of them—stood fence close, the branches of each tree intertwined with those of its neighbor, the trunks closer than slats. After covering a distance of thirty unstable yards, Winston saw bits of color and shape between the mossy grayish trunks. As he walked, it came to him, at last.

The Elysian Fields. Heaven. Happy Hunting Ground. He was *dead*; finally gone on the ultimate bender, slopping it down until his body said *no more* and he threw up in his unconscious state and gagged on his own vomit. Like Mother and Father had done. Too much *sippie-sippie*, no more *wakie-wakie*.

As he picked up his shambling pace, the spaces between the trees enlarged, the colors taking on true form and definition, until he stood next to one of the middle trees in the row. Resting his left hand on the bark of the nearest elm, he tried to ignore the cracks in the bark as they grew large, then thin and tight . . . almost as if the skin of the tree was *breathing*. Then he gazed in stunned awe at the panorama before him.

It was either Heaven or the world's worst hangover. Gulping down sour phlegm, leaning his whole body against the firm tree trunk, he mumbled, "If Heaven doesn't look like Ewerton, I'm going to be a laughingstock when I come marching home." But . . . he was wrong on both counts.

As Winston approached the backs of the homes on Lakeview Road, no one looked out of windows at his swaying approach, no catcalls reached his pounding ears, and no one came running out to welcome him home. Cutting through the yard of a fine brick and frame two-story home that appeared sugarcoated in the bright light (each brick seemingly pressed from ground glass and quartz flakes), he made a beeline to the gently lapping waters of Crescent Lake. The shimmering, rippling surface didn't deter him from dipping a hand into its waters, then slurping up a palmful of cool water.

Sitting down next to the lake, Winston looked up at the Holiday house, which sat on a slight rise to the northeast. The sage-green edifice was gaily festooned with tricolor buntings that flapped crisply, independent of the direction of the breeze. Hearing the snick of stiff fabric against freshly painted siding, he watched the house ripple and glow in the sunlight, as a soft voice inside him said, *Father always did go overboard for the Fourth of July, didn't he?*—and a shuddering chill ran from his aching head to the soles of his tired feet.

Getting up, he told himself, *No, no, not right . . . Father died in his sleep, after I came . . . after I . . . no, think about the house, the house hasn't been decorated in years, not since Fath—NO already! Old man Holiday* died *that winter, he died, and . . . and—*

A calm, soothing drone overrode his panicked thoughts, *Doesn't the house look* nice, *Winston? Wilbur's been so lonely—*

Both hands clamped over his ears in a vain attempt to shut out the dulcet, yet alien tones, Winston stood twenty feet from the back of the house that loomed sage-green and luminous before him. If he were to go up to the front door, and just *touch* it, there was a good chance the voice would still itself, leave him alone—

Raw, high-pitched, his scream filled the crystalline air, echoing down the perfect, unblemished streets of a Ewerton he thought he'd left very far behind him, in a sealed past. Yet, the notion persisted that all he had to do was go up and touch the doorknob.

Hands sliding over his eyes, Winston doubled over in nausea and fear . . . and didn't see one of the frosty lace curtains on the other side of a many-paned window move aside, then silently fall back into place.

FIFTY-FOUR

Palmer Nemmitz eased the Rambler down Roberts Street, its old homes tomblike in their creeping gray stillness. Sullenly, he glanced up at the Holiday house, home of his father—for all the good it had done him to have Holiday blood in his veins. He cursed Wilbur in the stale warmth of the car, mostly for not trying to *do* something for his irregular child once Treeva died. Wasn't as if what they'd done was a state secret. People only had to look Palmer in the eye to *know*. . . .

Licking his lips, Palmer queasily wondered if Brent had reached the part in his manuscript where he and Wilbur came close to talking. Palmer knew that Brent had been present during that last argument he and Shirl had—the one about the "right" to use the precious Nemmitz name. At least Brent had tact enough not to mention it—then Palmer braked hard, until his hat brim almost touched the windshield. He'd almost run over the Happy Wanderer, who was crossing from the straight, southern end of Roberts Street to the curving, northernmost part, across Lumbermill Drive, carrying a burnt sparkler in one hand and something melted and chocolate in the other.

Feeling like a hunter who spots a ten-point buck after spending all but one day of hunting season sitting in cold wetness, *waiting*, he told himself, *Easy does it . . . don't scare him off like you did the last time . . . smile, act as if you couldn't care less when he doesn't want to talk—*

Shutting off the engine, he opened his door, calling out in his gentlest, most nonthreatening voice, "Why, hel-*lo*, Cooper! Awful hot day to be out walking, isn't it?" The Wanderer stopped, regarded him with a good simulation of thoughtfulness, then ambled over to the Rambler.

He wanted to get in through Palmer's door, so he obligingly slid over, got out through the passenger door, walked around, then nudged the Wanderer out from behind the steering wheel—then had to get out again to shut the passenger door, since Happy had both hands full, and seemed reluctant to let go of either item. By the time Palmer got back to the driver's side, the Wanderer was wedged behind the wheel again. Palmer thanked God no one was watching as he eased the heavy man over to the passenger side again.

Driving down the rest of Roberts Street, Palmer cast sideways glances at his guest. He was eating what looked like a Stardust Bar. Grinning until his cheeks ached, he asked, "Candy good?" An emphatic nod, as the Wanderer tapped his burnt sparkler on the dashboard.

Licking his lips, trying to ignore his itching right arm, Palmer continued, "Been looking all *over* town for a candy bar like that . . . can't find 'em nowheres. Sure do miss that kind of candy . . . newfangled ones taste like chocolate-covered air. Nothing to 'em."

Happy's attention picked up; Palmer sensed that he was listening closely to him.

Choosing his words carefully, Palmer went on, "After I looked all over for that candy, know what I said to myself? 'Cooper Reish didn't get them in *town*, no sireee-bob!' But you got them somewhere close by, 'cause Lumbe is eight miles away . . . too far to walk in this heat, right?" Happy's head-banded head went up and down warily; cautious eyes regarded Palmer strangely.

Gulping, Palmer asked, "You just pick 'em up, or . . . does someone give 'em to you? Uhm, what I mean is . . . someone who knows you like Stardust Bars gives you some, doesn't she?" Worried that he'd almost shown his hand, Palmer held his breath until the Wanderer nodded with vigor, light dancing in his usually vacant eyes. Suddenly, his mouth opened, letting out chocolate-scented breath. *"There,"* came the high-pitched whisper.

Excited by the enigmatic admission, Palmer forgot himself: "Is she still pretty? Where is 'there'? You walk, or does she pick you up?' . . until he noticed that the Wanderer was looking out the window, ignoring him.

Realizing that he'd bollixed things up, Palmer headed for the group home on Crescent Street. The delicious scent of roasting hot dogs wafted into the car; he heard faint sounds of celebration from the back of the house. Palmer leaned over the Wanderer's girth to open the passenger door; he didn't want chocolate smeared all over the handle.

Pushing it open, he boomed in falsely hearty tones, "There you go, Cooper . . . better get home 'fore all the chow's gone." Gently, he pushed Happy out of the car. The Wanderer's legs were out the door when he suddenly dug a brown hand into his breast pocket, extracting something deep blue and star-covered that crinkled. . . .

Placing the Stardust bar on the dashboard, he made a curious motion over the Bar; it resembled a peace symbol, but with the fingers pointing downward, straddling the piece of candy. Like a dowsing rod, seeking out—

"Chocket-dust," he said knowingly, winking at Palmer, unaffected by the old man's fearful reaction. Happy then stepped into the hot sunshine. Minutes passed before the car door slammed shut, and the Rambler gunned away from the curb.

FIFTY-FIVE

Glad that he'd picked up and put on his uniform hat, for the protection it gave him from the blazing sunlight, Winston trudged past empty houses on Crescent Street. His nostrils were maddeningly, all too briefly tickled by what he thought was the aroma of roasting hot dogs, and—*Father used to roast them on a Sunday, give them out to the neighbors, the Woodards brought over lemonade, and— STOP IT! That was Holiday, not my father!* But even after the phantom odor dissipated, the rumbling in his stomach persisted.

Reaching Linden Avenue, he crossed over to Myrtle Avenue, the site of a dignified yet elegantly plain house that tugged at an old memory—he should *know* the place, yet—

Then it came. The house was altered, that's why he didn't recognize it right off. The added-on fiberglass-shielded staircase was gone, as were the two extra sets of house numbers over the two mailboxes that weren't there now. Now you see it, now you don't.

But Winston knew this house; he'd *lived* in it. His last years with Una, after she'd forced him to sell the old house on Ewert Hill. Looking at the pale blue siding, shimmering like sunshine on dry fallen snow, with rainbow chips between the boards, he still remembered the layout of the back-of-the-house downstairs apartment he and Una shared, containing the stairway to nowhere that formerly led upstairs.

Nearly faint from hunger, Winston found himself reliving the day Una died, in bright flashes of color and sound that still made the inside of his skull throb.

Him in the bathroom, still fastidious after decades of marriage, taking a leak. Then her screams, about a "wall-eyed *creature*!" Him thinking at first that the sleeping Una was having another Zoe Lawton nightmare. Washing his hands, he heard something odd through the wooden door. *Una*, clomping around in her thick-soled sensible shoes. Not, not walking, *running*. Between footfalls, he made out the dainty *trippy-trip* of cleated shoes. Coming *down* a flight of stairs. Then, the chuffing thud of Una's heavy, lumpy body hitting furniture, then floor. Try as he might, his damp hands wouldn't turn the knob. Had to cover it with a towel. Outside, Una burbled and moaned, "wall-eyed" and "devil dolly"—he couldn't make out what else. Finally, the knob released, and he was out in the hallway, moving as fast as his arthritic knees would carry him, but it was too late. Much too late. Una was bruise-faced, getting darker, fat-ankled legs kicking, drumming the floor. Her hands rose up partway, in the direction of the empty stairway ending in a plastered-over doorway. Her voice bubbled thickly in her throat as she demanded that Zoe come back, *now*. The wall-eyed tormenting monster was unseen by Winston, who had to shout into the phone after dialing 911 because the dispatcher couldn't understand him over Una's screams.

Right up to the time Lenny, Larry Komminski, and Scooter hauled Una out of there, she kept looking at the empty wall at the top of the stairs, screaming for Zoe to return. Winston didn't want to know what Lenny had thought, what he'd said uptown. And Arlin didn't comment on the incident while moving Winston out of this house, into the apartment at Pearl Vincent's place.

In his current state of being, Winston wasn't able to get a handle on the incongruity of his memories; here he was, young, fresh out of the Army (why else the uniform?), but he was remembering a son who wasn't born yet moving him out of this place, which he hadn't moved *into* yet. Trying to figure it all out only made his headache worse.

But one thing was certain—he had to eat, *now*, or faint in the sun. Striding onto the front porch supported by five wooden posts, he assured himself that breaking in was all right, since he'd be living here someday, taking comfort in his roundabout logic as he tried the front door. Locked, but it opened easily after he leaned against it while jiggling the knob.

Heart fluttering, he swung open the door, peering at the semi-darkness within until his eyes adjusted. The furniture within sat at seemingly impossible angles to the walls—close, yet not even near to touching, despite there being no *space* left between wall and furniture. The pieces were in the popular styles of his boyhood, yet, they too were *wrong*, a quality of line and padding too elusive to pin down, yet *there*.

Still, where there was furniture, there might be food. Winston tried not to notice the odd arrangement of mahogany and chintz sofas, chairs and tables, as he made his way from the room to a hallway, walking until he saw a Universal range in the last domed doorway.

The kitchen was dustless, spotless, clean-floored. On one of the counters he saw an ice-cream maker. Raised metal lettering stated it was a Peerless Freezer, like the one his parents used to have.

The pantry door was open; as he walked inside, he let out a soft "Ooooh" of surprise. A dozen shelves lined with jewel-deep, sparkling Kerr, Ball Mason, and Schram jars, full of every canned food imaginable . . . each jar seemed to whisper, "Eat Me," just like in *Alice in Wonderland*.

There were cans, too. Del Monte and Campbell's. Bottles of Heinz catsup, jars of Beech-Nut peanut butter. Plus boxes of Jell-O that carried the promise of fruity sweetness inside.

Staring goggle-eyed at the cache of food before him, Winston became aware of the humming Frigidaire in the kitchen behind him. He thought of Eskimo Pies, the ones Mother bought for him. Special deep dark chocolate that just didn't *taste* the same once he reached adulthood, and that creamy whiteness inside (like those Stardust Bars he also enjoyed). He wondered if there were any Eskimo Pies in—

There were. A whole unopened box of them. And lemonade in a tall clear pitcher, chunks of ice bobbing lazily among the lemon slices. A bowl of quivering red Jell-O. Slices of ham fanned out in marble swirls on a bone china plate.

Winston made several trips back and forth to the table. Coolness tingled on his hot face and hands; he left the door open as he ate, barely pausing between bites and swallows, the Frigidaire humming merrily as he threw the food into himself. Even the Jell-O was his favorite, cherry.

He was afraid to pull a chair out from the table—since they all seemed to be and *not* be pushed all the way under the table itself—so he stood on his tired dogs, filling his stomach until it complained for a different reason.

The food was wonderful—it felt *good* sliding down his throat—so he didn't mind the way it was brighter-hued than normal, edges twinkling like stars at midnight. A delicate show of light, true, but still faintly visible.

Chewing the last of his ham, Winston remembered how his mother and father (*your mother and her* husband insisted the inner voice) used to point out this house to him long ago, telling him how it used to be the home of some friends of theirs. They mentioned this *particular* house, he was sure. They must have visited here a lot. Or something.

Finishing his second Eskimo Pie, Winston assured himself that who *used* to live here didn't matter now, since no one seemed to be in the house anymore. Washing his hands at the gleaming enamel sink, he was glad that the water behaved normally. He then set off for the back of the house. For that staircase leading upstairs.

Standing at the foot of the stairs, which were now covered with a wool runner tucked in at each step with a brass rod, hand resting on the cool carved bottom post, Winston's eyes teared a little. He was sober enough again to throw up his defenses, and thought of his poor Una, dying like that while staring up at nothing as she breathed her last. But now, instead of a pale plastered wall, Winston saw an oval stained-glass window, a glowing on-end eye set into the wall at the top of the landing. Puzzled, he didn't remember seeing *that* when he lived here—not from the outside of the house, at any rate.

Deep reds, blues, and greens of glass throbbed in black-leaded frames, a rose pattern, with white-blue drops of dew dripping from the petals . . . only, as he watched, the chunks of glass burned bright; he saw the drops *move*, sliding bloody red off the rose. He started to climb up, for a better look—until he heard the faint, resonant sound of mattress springs, *shifting—*

—under the weight of a moving body, followed by a softly articulated "Whaaa?" from above. But Winston never heard the voice's query. The stillness outside was shattered by the pond of his footfalls on the pavement as he ran down the middle of the street, unable and unwilling to look behind him.

Swiftly and silently, the front door closed itself.

FIFTY-SIX

Upstairs, in the bed . . .

. . . she raised her body on one elbow, before falling back from exhaustion—she was not ready, yet, to venture forth. Head flopping almost spinelessly onto the pillow, she cast her eyes up to the ceiling. Opalescent light touched the molding; gentle pure colors that soothed her tired eyes. So very tired, almost to the death. . . . Her lips formed an ironic smile at that.

Old memories, stored here, in this room, this bed, against her inevitable return, came rushing into her. . . .

A winter morning, the edges of the window frost-swirled, rhinestone sparkles in pale winter-morning light. Outside, she knew the air would be crisp and dry in her nose, painful yet exhilarating . . . only Otis told her not to go walking about in her delicate condition—Suddenly, she felt her stomach, slightly rounded, yet not really rounded enough but she wasn't sure what should be resting in her abdomen.

Odd, she weakly told herself, I know no man named "Otis" . . . she remembered someone lying next to her, the mattress sagging in his direction—but this "Otis" had no face, no voice for her. . . .

But the memories had been waiting for a long, long time, breeding patience. Eventually, "Otis" would become familiar to her once more. . . .

FIFTY-SEVEN

From Palmer Nemmitz's journal—
Once I found myself in southern Indiana, it was halfway into June. My flour-sack food-carrier had long ago been torn into handkerchiefs. My Kleenex—last reminder of the days when the Nemmitzes had been wealthy enough not to carry a cold in our pockets—was long gone, too, as was most of my Absorbine Jr. I was used to walking, so my feet didn't bother

me overmuch, but the tops of my arms and hands, as well as my face, burned despite the Absorbine Jr. I'd smeared on them. And I hadn't enough money to buy more.

No one was hiring boys, when grown men were still turned away. I couldn't depend on finding unmowed lawns on every block I passed in the succession of blink-and-you-miss-'em towns I wandered through. Some old ladies paid in glasses of milk and a cold sandwich, period. (When the lady in question was wearing a patched Hooverette, I would've been an ogre to demand *cash*.)

A few times I hitched rides with drummers or plain old folks who thought I looked trustworthy enough to let into their Fords or DeSotos. One fellow—a vacuum-cleaner salesman who actually sang the old "Hoover Song" in his car, for courage, before each stop on his Illinois route—gave me a sawbuck because he claimed I brought him good luck. He sold three Hoovers while I was out waiting in the car. Come to think of it, considering the scraggly kids playing outside weathered gray houses on his route, the fellow may've been right.

That was my problem—my luck shed onto *other* folks; I didn't have much of it for my own use. Some farmer with crates of chickens on the back of his pickup took me southeast, into Indiana, when I'd been hoping to head due south, to see the Mississippi. (I'd declined to march along Highway 66; every Tom, Dick, and Fairy was on *that* road.)

Once I hit Indiana, I did a lot more hoofing than before; I missed the many trees clumped together where I could hide out and sleep. The part of the state where I was dropped off was *flat*, flatter than Illinois, flatter than an old maid's chest when she lies down on an ironing board.

It was rough, trying to walk and keep an eye out for cars, while all I could see were heat shimmers dancing and wiggling as high as a foot off the pavement in places where the road was hard—and even above places where it was choking dirt. All I had for company were the signs that gradually segued from "Burma-Shave" to "Jesus Saves."

Once I got my fill of *those*, I took to looking at the stiff bundles of ratty fur. After looking at the road signs every hundred paces or so (I counted the steps between each one), I'd cast my eyes down; soon I was an expert of sports on car-flattened dead things. Some rabbits would lie still and open-eyed, save for the telltale crimson spot of blood dribbling out of an elegant ear, while farther on, I'd see something all twisted, bones-out and eyes-on-stalks, a creature out of *Lights Out* on NBC's Red Network. Once I saw a toad whose lungs had burst out of its sides, two moist, floppy wings; I hoped the poor thing would make use of those wings where it was going.

Those pink deflated lungs poking out of that mottled greenish skin stayed with me for some reason, as if it was *important*. Then, I supposed it was an indication of my boredom and highway fever; thinking fondly of some toad Vern would've swerved the lawn mower to run over back home . . . but later, I wished I'd heeded the symbolic warning of that toad, and turned tail and run—

—*oh, please, don't tell, oh, please, please, she said, until she took to looking at me eyes all hateful and said, little runt, runt bastard, feel powerful now? then it was, oh, please, go, please go now, all over again*—

—but at the time, I thought that running home, tail between my legs, was an invitation for the old man to come at me with the pitchfork, so I kept moving on.

While I walked, between the occasional full day or so I spent in some pissant town, doing odd jobs or mowing lawns, staying on the lookout for gas stations where the attendants looked charitable enough to let me wash up in the rest room, despite my scraggly appearance, I tried hard to keep track of my days, not letting one or two catch up on me unawares, until I wouldn't know my Saturdays from my Mondays, and never mind about Sundays. So, even though I hadn't brought along a notebook or scribble sheets (something *Winston* would've done), I knew exactly what day it was when I walked into that sleepy little village in southern Indiana—itself indistinguishable from nearly every other piddling village I'd already passed through in that flat state—but it was a milestone, nonetheless.

Thursday, June thirteenth, 1940. Eighteen days on the road. My third state of the union. And I had thirty-six cents, exactly. Luckily, no squad car had stopped, the officer asking if I was a vagrant. If a man had less than a dollar to his name in some states, he could be hauled in. I wasn't a man yet, so I had no idea what might happen. Probably get tossed in the hoosegow, where some four-letter man would make me feel "welcome." I needed money, a one- or two-day job. I'd al-

ready thrown out a pair of toe-and-heel-gone socks, and I felt
a blister forming, hot and tender, on my left heel.

I can't recall the name of the village anymore; I do remember the welcome sign said something about a "city," which
was quite the thing then. If you had three people and a spit-
toon next to a pup tent, it was considered "progressive" to
consolidate and dub the place a "city."

No matter what the name, this "city" was a twin to most
of the post-Depression towns I'd passed through. Co-op, couple of diners, gas station with the multibrand pumps, grocery
store with a red, white, and blue Pepsi-Cola sign attached to
the front wall, a public telephone denoted by a blue and white
Ma Bell sign hung on the front of a building, maybe a bakery
or shoe store, plus the ubiquitous Monkey Ward's or Sears
catalog outlet. Bars with dying neon beer signs in the window, if the town wasn't dry. Church or two, and a house with
a VFW sign posted out front. And the houses and farms, few
if any kept up proper, not when there were kids to feed and
clothe first.

And always, be they in front of the Co-op, spilling onto
the front steps of a grocery, or gassing behind the filling
station pumps, there were the "old women," phlegmy-
voiced, wrinkle-jowled, all-knowing pensioners. Blowhards
and pains-in-the-keisters who'd flock together for support and
protection. It was like staring at a piece of Ewerton each time
I wandered up to them, asking where the best eats were, or
who needed odd jobs done. (Old farts or not, they *always*
knew everybody and his second-cousin-thrice-removed's
business, and relished telling a new set of ears just what was
what, and where to go to get in on it.)

That June day, I found them on a long straight bench behind the four pumps of a filling station. Four of them, too,
living representations of the Mobil, Texaco, Wadhams, and
home-brand gasolines lined up on that strip of concrete before them. A sign in front gave prices for each brand per
gallon; to this day I remember that the Texaco (big gold "T"
flashing inside the red star) was 20.3 cents per gallon.

One of the gassers behind the pumps was younger than his
mates, his hair only nipped with frost. "Hank" stitched above
his breast pocket, and he wore the leather-billed hat and bow
tie of a service station attendant. I decided to ask him where
to get a cheap bite to eat; he had to answer the same question

for scores of motorists. And he appeared to be middling kind—the older men looked washed-out, past caring.

Tilting my cap forward so that I could look "Hank" in the eye without squinting and coming off as being distrustful, I nodded to each fellow in turn before asking, "Sir, uh, Mr. . . . Hank, could you please direct me to a place to eat? Good and ch—inexpensive?"

"Hear that, Leo? Kid wants to eat '*in*expensive,' must be a college boy, eh?" a grizzled fedora-hatted man nudged the almost identically grizzled and hatted gent to his left, who chuckled in return, "You a Minnesota, Wisconsin boy? From up that way?" Both of them spoke the fastest I'd yet heard in Indiana.

"Quit badgering the kid," Hank said, tugging at the knot in his tie with a grease-crescented nail. Smiling up at me, he advised, "Don't pay them, no mind. Or their friend, either. Don't have to say where you come from, *ain't none of their business*"—he glared at the trio of coots—"and if you want cheap food that's good, you go down the street a ways, to the Blue Tulip. Minnie serves the best food this side of—"

"What 'bout the Red Dot?" Leo chided; the one who hadn't talked yet piped up, "Food's no good since Howie tossed out the old grease."

"True, true, not the same a'tall—"

"Leo, only reason Hank's recommending her place is 'cause he's fixing to get hitched to—"

"Shaddup, Chet." I took a step forward when Hank motioned for me to come closer. Pulling a dollar out of his pocket, he reached up to tuck it in my shirt pocket (my pants pocket would've been handier, but men who didn't know each other didn't go sticking their hands too close to each other's business). The one he'd called Chet chortled, "Now he's paying folks to eat there, drummin' up business any old way—"

Winking, Hank got up, whispering, "His son-in-law works at the Red Dot and it's true what they say about the grease. You tell Minnie Hank said—"

"Speak up! Speak up!" Chet cupped a hand to his ear. Leo chided, "Hank's askin' the kid to tell 'er to keep them headlights covered!"

"Nope, tole him to tell 'er to keep them knees to-gether—"

"*Shaddup*. Don't pay them no mind. You *tell* her"—

speaking loudly this time—"that Hank says 'Hello.' That suit
the three of you?"

All nodded, clucking like chickens pecking grain out of
gravel. Hank whispered, "Get going before you get trapped
here all summer," then waved me off as I trotted off in search
of the Blue Tulip.

When I'd left Ewerton in May, I thought it the cesspool of
the world, but since then I'd seen places ten times more run-
down and Depression-flattened. This town was clean, but
more washed-out and threadbare than a thrice-laundered piece
of Kleenex. Sad, considering how so many towns tried despite there being no factories or the like to support them.
Compared to the town I was walking through, Ewerton
should've been a little Minneapolis or Madison—the mill and
the sash and door were still running—but it *wasn't*. I mean,
Ewerton wasn't too run-down, but it seemed like it *should*
be; as if the place had no *right* to be as well off as it was.
Like a corpse looking good in the coffin with nowhere to go
but down after the funeral.

Still, *this* town was starting to show bare bones. The Pepsi
sign all but had the color worn away, and the checkered-pants
and derby-hatted fellow on the Kayo Chocolate Syrup sign
hanging in front of a grocery store sported a beard and shirt
of pure rust. The barber pole was pink, white, and baby blue
striped, peeling and sun-faded. My hair curled down longer
than usual, but I didn't want to waste the thirty cents the
fellow had advertised for a haircut under his "Tonsorial Studio" sign. (I pitied the man, considering how people hadn't
called a barbershop a tonsorial studio since the time when I
was a very small boy—I suppose he couldn't afford to repaint
his window.)

One door down from the barber was an Ace Hardware,
then Hank's girl's place, and I smiled in spite of myself. The
cafe was an oasis in a street of warped boards and crumbling
brick.

A white half store with thick paint across the bricks, and
blue trim on the door and window frames. Blue-check curtains hung in the window and the top half of the door. A
wooden Dutch boy and girl, the kind folks used to put in
their gardens or flower beds (before daisy wind spinners and
bend-overs became the rage) were propped against the door
on either side. They looked fresh; someone cared enough to
tote them in each night, and when it rained. And the place

didn't smell like the old grease Howie threw out before the food stopped tasting good at the Red Dot (or like Vern's can of potato-chip grease back home). I caught a whiff of cinnamon and apples, and then I went inside.

After days spent walking where the sun beat down yellow-hot through occasional baby-green trees, and the roadside was baked yellow-tan, walking into that cafe was like standing under an icy winter sky. I almost expected my breath to billow out when I exhaled.

Two round tables close by the door were covered with real cloth tablecloths, not oilcloth. A blue glass Bromo bottle filled with white tulips sat on each table. The enamel on the chairs wasn't chipped too bad, and the seat cushions were blue check. A long counter, snowy and sparkling, and five blue-topped stools. On the right-hand wall was a collection of signs and such, mostly in blues and whites. The little girl sitting on the bar of "White-Pure-Floating" Fairy Soap, and the cone-hatted Woman on the Moon toasting Miller High Life beer. Also a poster for "Madison's High Quality and Tested Seeds," showing a pair of Dutch children holding hands. I hadn't seen one of *those* in years; not since Mr. Woodard tore down the one in the Co-op window in favor of a Burpee's poster and a red and yellow "Lay or Bust Poultry Feeds" sign, back when I was in the first grade.

Staring at the happy, plump faces of the children, who clomped along in wooden clogs as if they hadn't a care in the world, I compared them to myself, tromping around once-removed from a bum, until a woman's quickly paced question startled me.

"Be wanting something, young man?"

Before I forgot, I said, "Your beau Hank says 'hello' " which tickled her no end. Minnie was a thin, flat-chested woman of thirty-some years; she had smile wrinkles deeper than the Grand Canyon on either side of her mouth. Her hair under the little white cap was done up just like the picture of Betty Crocker General Mills put out four years earlier, only Minnie wasn't sour-pussed like Betty. I could see why Hank was sweet on her, even if her legs had no calves to speak of. Man could snare a worse-looking woman, with *no* smile lines.

I asked her if her pies were good; she nodded, adding, "Hank all but points folks' cars this way and gives 'em a push." Stepping behind the counter she yelled toward the good-smelling rear of the diner, "Fella this morning leave us any pies?'' A muffled voice shouted back, ''Just the Dutch apple and last night's pecan.''

Pointing a bony thumb over the printed handkerchief pinned points-up on her shoulder (any fool can guess what sort of flower was on there, and what color, too), she explained, ''My brother cooks, I bake. Feller came in this morning, wanting pies on 'count the bakery's closed for the owner's mother's funeral. All but wiped me out, had to whip up a couple for the noon rush. They're baking now.''

''Must've been real hungry.'' Looking over the neatly typed menu resting on the counter, I tried to figure how best to spend the dollar Hank gave me.

''Wasn't for *him*, he said they was for someone who worked for him. In his carny.'' When she saw my eyes light up, she went on, ''Aren't from here, are you? Carny's been the talk of the town for the past week—didn't you see them signs posted? Camped out north of town, in Marvin Higgin's pasture. Don't have fairgrounds 'round here. Use Marv's field come revival time, too. You ready to order?''

I ordered two cups of coffee, a slice of apple pie, and a glass of milk, too. I'd get some change back from my dollar. It tickled me to hear her yell the order to her brother—who stood all of five or six feet away—especially the ''pair of overalls'' part about the two coffees.

While I ate, she hung around, talking, showing off the plain gold ring with the tiny diamond precariously balanced on top—I'd seen a flake of snow give off more sparks when the sun hit it. I told her the ring was lovely. When she leaned over to give me a better look at it, her dress top came down in a deep enough V for me to almost see her titties, if she'd had any. Hank was getting himself a nice gal.

After hearing of their August wedding plans, I asked about the man who'd cleared her out of pies—did he happen to say he might be *hiring*?

''Oh, yes! Be wanting a refill on that? You're *not* from here—I mean Indiana—'round *here* folks say 'I don't care' when offered food or drink. But that's okay, kid—okay, Palmer. You don't *have* to say it, it's just I'm not used to customers taking up on my offer right off. Where was I? See, this hefty young man comes banging at the door 'fore I had it unlocked, wanting in. Said he needed some 'sweet, gooey pies' on the double, for one of his side show people. Fat lady's my bet. Well, any*who*, he said his helper up and quit two shows ago, north of here, and he needed someone to help out—take 'er easy, you're gonna *choke* on that! Carny's gonna be here till tomorrow morning, plenty of—''

Wiping the last of the crumbs into my mouth with the back of my hand, I pushed the dollar bill toward her with my other hand. ''Awfully good pie, ma'am. You keep the change.''

She smiled, becoming pretty in the way of plain, yet happy women. As I headed for the door, she leaned over the counter. ''You tell that beau of mine his gal says 'hello,' Palmer. And good luck with that job.'' I thanked her and was out the door, into the eye-hurting sunshine and yellowness, and partway down the sidewalk before I realized I was going the wrong way.

I doubled back so I could pause by the gas station long enough to stand, breathing hard, by one of the glass ball topped pumps and tell Hank Minnie said ''hello.'' That tickled the three coots no end. Then I waved and took off in search of Higgin's pasture; after a few blocks I saw fragments of a poster someone had almost ripped off a telephone pole, leaving only a few flapping tatters:

> ****** PRES   G! ******
> **SOUTH-ST   RISES—**
> **CARN   GERIE!**
> Thrills   ls, and
> Excitem   All!
> One Night   ly!
> Bring the Fa   y!

Shifting my knapsack into a more comfortable position, I set off for the north, passing the last of the weathered houses that ringed the business district, until I reached open land bisected by a single dirt road, covered on either side by scruffy grass.

After a half hour's walk, I found the carny, hidden from sight first by a barn and a couple of outbuildings. It was strange; one second I saw a barn and not much else out of the ordinary for a farm, yet walk a few steps forward, and there it was, a carnival coming to life in a field. Step backward, and it was *gone*. Forward, *there*. Like that trick drawing, the one advertised for years in the back of ladies' magazines my wife still reads. The one of the pretty woman sitting at a dressing table who turns into a grinning skull once you give the picture a second look. "All Is Vanity," I think it's called. First beauty, then death in the bone.

But *then*, as I walked toward the carny, I had no reason to fear it, as I'd feared that woman/skull picture our Ma used to own; both the farm and the tight circle of tents, booths, and rides were normal, everyday things—useful to the living, not white bones freed from the flesh by death.

I still had a lot to learn about what was truly fearful and what wasn't.

FIFTY-EIGHT

The closer I came to the big white trucks that had carried the carny riders into town, the better I could read the lettering on their sides—which wasn't in much better shape than the words on the remainder of the poster I'd spotted. The only set of red-lettered words that were readable against that dirty cream background said:

SOUTH-STATE ENTERPRISES
CARNIVAL AND MENAGERIE

I didn't care overmuch about anything but the "SOUTH" and "CARNIVAL" parts—the latter was self-explanatory, and the former was a boon granted by an angel. I'd wanted to head south since the second day of my trip, and now I'd found a meal ticket.

The rides were being erected as I arrived—their tenders seemed to have no trouble assembling them—but there wasn't a hell of a lot of progress being made with the last booth when I reached the edge of the pasture and sat down, cross-legged, to watch the proceedings. A cluster of five men tried to pull up the sides of a big booth with ropes, but the booth didn't want to stay erected. Its sides kept falling down like a card house in a tornado. It was such a good show they should've sold tickets to it.

As I said, there was a handful of men. The tall, husky one I took to be the one Minnie mentioned; an older—forties or so—redheaded man with pale skin, like milk poured over blueberries; a fellow with slicked-back hair (a leftover sheik

from my babyhood); a really tall, skinny fella with a deep
tan and a bare scalp; and a dwarf who stood, oh, maybe as
tall as my little brother Shirl. Not so small you'd risk stepping
on him, but not tall enough to be of serious help, either.

From the way they were doubling in brass, I figured they
were in dire need of more hands, but I decided to make them
ask me instead of the other way around. I didn't want to blow
my chance by seeming overeager.

When I sat down, they'd almost propped up the walls and
attached them together, but no sooner did they let go than the
sides lost altitude, like man's best friend when the wife says
her head hurts. The redheaded man's cheeks and nose turned
bright red when he looked behind him and saw those walls
collapsing.

"Ohhhh, *sheeeyit*! Look at that—Hold it *up*, do I have to
tell you when to *breathe*? Get under that—Larry, *do*. Look
later. Am *I* so funny? Should I put on a *clown* suit?"

The hefty fellow Mr. "Ohhhh, *Sheeeyit*!" addressed stood
wiping his eyes with a frayed bandanna, laughing, "Oh, Harold, that joint don't need proppin' it needs choppin' up and
bein' burned f'kindlin'! Damn-fool boards is warped, no
'mount of nails'll make it stand upright. Want for it to fall on
the marks like it did day 'fore last? Nice out, we could set
up the stock unner the stars—"

" 'Nice out' my *be*hind, I'm not standing out there without
a joint," Mr. Slicked-Hair grumped. Sun glinted off his hair
oil in white flashes. The thin man piped up, "If we ain't
puttin' it up, I'm taking a nap—"

Harold snapped, "Nobody's going anywhere until this joint
is set up. Marks pass good money across the apron—*with no
apron they don't pass no money*! And I *can't* do this myself.
Hear, Larry? No chopping up the boards, no hanky-panky
under the stars—"

"Well Harold, you *do* suck the fun outta livin'," Larry
drawled, itching his shoulder, exposing a wide band of white
flesh when he moved his overall strap aside.

Harold's face was a pot-roast mottle of red and white as
he bellowed, " 'Fun' my"—(some foreign word, "too-kiss"
near as I can remember)—"what am I paying you for? To
have 'fun'? Either the joint goes up or *you* go—"

His remark jarred me. Minnie seemed to think the beefy
young man *owned* the carny, but looking closely at Larry, I
noticed he didn't seem the type to want to hand out money

once it crossed his own palm. Like as not it pained him to peel off the bills to pay for those pies. But Larry did appear jovial, like Winston back home, only not as intelligent. Larry was sneaky bright, not book-learning bright. Sometimes sneaky bright's more useful, though. . . .

"—same goes for your *buddy* in that pen of his. And another thing—"

"You suggesting the *geek* lend a hand?" the dwarf asked from where he rested on the prone booth. Harold's face twisted, like he'd bit down on a lemon without peeling it.

"I don't want to *see* that—that—*creature*! Don't want to *hear* about him, either! All I want is—"

"The money be brings in?" Larry finished, thumbs hooked behind his overall buckles, looking for all the world like a Normal Rockwell *Saturday Evening Post* cover; all he needed was a can of worms and a bamboo fishing pole. Poor Harold had *his* fingers hooked in his hair as he stood there unable to speak, eyes blazing. With his pale blue eyes and freckled snub nose, and that hair and funny way of talking, I had him pegged for Irish, maybe first generation. Irish or not, he was *awfully* mad.

Before Harold could sputter out something (like "You're fired!"), Larry spotted me sitting on that trod-down pasture. "Hey, we don't need the services of my buddy after all . . . bein' eyeballed here. Kid, you wanna pitch in or you just enjoyin' the show?"

Getting to my feet, dusting off my worn pants, I replied, "Little of both, mister."

Before they'd let me join them in their labors, I had to answer a volley of fired-off questions: What was my name, where was I from, where was I headed, and did I *need* the work? For some reason, my knapsack met with their approval. Maybe it made me look desperate. Either way, I helped them get the warped booth set up, and as we struggled with the heavy wooden sides and canvas back flaps, the men chuffed out introductions: Harold Shea, owner of the carny; Larry, no last name offered, ran the Mystic Tarot Wheel of Fortune and "owned" a geek, the mention of which made Shea grimace and roll his eyes; the tall man was Bones, the Living Skeleton; the Sheik was Tony, who ran the one-ball joint, which "used to be Dusty's Rifle Shoot, till his stock got lost and he got nothin' after his fifty-fifty split"; and the dwarf was Longo, who took care of the menagerie—which consisted of a few small animals.

When the booth—or "joint"—was up, the six of us turned our attention to setting up a medium-sized tent nearby. That went a lot easier; soon it was standing upright, with the six of us inside, hidden by undulating canvas, almost like being in a womb hidden from the outside world, and being able to hear only snatches of noise without. Inside, the tent—it measured only fifteen feet or so around—smelled like week-old dog shit baked to powder in the sun. We all cleared out of there, leaving the flaps up to air the canvas out.

Larry protested, "Lissen, once them kadoodies come trompin' through the midway in their cow-shit boots, they ain't gonna notice a little musty stink. 'Sides, Moby Jackie'll smell up the midway soon 'nough. Pours toilet water on herself 'fore each show, gallon per wrist."

"She the one you bought all those pies for?" I asked, then explained to Larry about Minnie saying he needed help—only I didn't mention the part about him being the "owner," instead of a geek-sitter.

Larry shouted at Shea, who'd stalked off after we righted the tent, "Harold, you want I should hire this kid? Good worker. And I need the help with my—"

Stopping in his tracks, Shea shouted back. "If you want, hire him, you do what you please regardless! Just make sure he *works*," then strode off for his trailer—a beat-up Airstream—slamming the door behind him with a teeth-jarring metallic *blam*! Cheerfully nonplussed by Shea's words, Larry explained, "Shea don't like the geek, but he likes breakin' even every night on 'count of him. Harold's a good ol' boy, even if he ain't from the south. Does all right with what he's got to do it with. C'mon, lemme show you where to stash that pack. You bunk with me, I got me two beds. Five-inch mattresses. Better'n most 'round here."

Larry had a camper, a Zagelmayer that was almost as old as I was. A canvas-sided thing set on a base of dark green, with a green door in the back. Compact on the outside, but inside it was surprisingly roomy. Two on-wall beds, with the thick mattresses he'd mentioned, plus shelves and a fold-up table. Plus about as many beer cans as I'd seen in one place outside of the night of Dead Fred's snipe hunt. No empty Squaw Piss cans, but lots of Krueger's "Finest Beer" and "Cream Ale," plus practically every brand of beer ever brewed, except Leinenkugels. He must not have gone that far north. The cans were lined up on the shelves, resting on the fold-out table, and piled in a "His Nibs" packing crate. Larry didn't share Porter Winston's contention that canned beer was "skunky"—the watermelon poking out of his overalls proved that he'd drained his collection of cans himself.

Also, the camper was littered with greenish-fuzzy cans that once held rattlesnake meat, if the labels could be believed, as well as a few dog-eared Tijuana Bibles.

He showed me which bed was mine, and promised to find me a blanket. I stashed my pack under the bed as Larry explained that his were "de-luxe" quarters, a far cry from the joint benches or platforms where most "agents" or "jointees" (booth operators) like himself slept, or the back of a pickup truck or prairie schooner, where some of the carnies camped out when they couldn't afford an "in town" hotel room. My "privileged" status made clear, Larry led me out of there and steered me to his joint.

His Mystic Tarot Wheel of Fortune was nothing like that tomfoolery on the TV nowadays, with a vacant clotheshorse flipping letters on a board after someone spins the numbered wheel, then jumps up and down and screams for five minutes. Larry's wheel was bigger than a wagon wheel, with a real deck of Tarot cards affixed along the edges. Some he called "Major Trumps"—those were all brightly colored pictures under tiny numbers, with names underneath like "The Fool," "The Lovers," or "The Tower." They reminded me of the pictures Winston's mother Gayleen once used for children's Bible class (she did a dry run of her lesson on us when I had supper there). Strong colors and wimpy, wispy-looking people standing all stilted against strange backgrounds.

Only, these cards were *mean*. The Fool was set to walk off a cliff, and those poor men were falling out of the lightning-struck tower. The Major Trumps were spaced out between what Larry dubbed the "Minor Trumps." Thirteen-card suits (Page as well as a King, Queen, and Knight) of sprouting twigs, swords, golden cups, and star-emblazoned golden disks. Every numbered card had a different picture on it. The court cards had full people on them, not two heads and shoulders stuck middle to middle, like the pasteboards I was used to.

It would've taken me all the rest of the day plus the night to study each card, but Larry wanted to show me how he'd "gaffed" the wheel so it would stop at a certain suit of cards when he put his foot on the right lever. Like playing the organ without the two keyboards.

He explained I was to "shill" for him that night ("don't go tellin' Shea 'bout this, 'cause he don't actually *approve*")—step up to the apron, win enough to get the marks interested, then call it quits and let the marks play to lose. Then slip behind the joint and shove my prizes up under the canvas flap.

Larry explained that he didn't like to waste his voice "working the play," and my shilling would save him from having to talk up the game too much. He capped off his lecture with a hand signal he'd give me when business was slow, and he needed to attract marks to the joint. Larry was pretty raspy and wheezy by the time he finished, so it was a good thing I picked up on shilling fast. His voice wouldn't have held up for a second run-through.

I should've balked at shilling, but that was the whole *point* of a carny. You paid your money and you took your chances. No promises about even breaks. Larry claimed the other agents had stronger voices to pull the suckers in and make money across the apron—I'd be doing a *visual* spiel. Make his joint look good, the way the picture of the tomato on the can always looks bigger and redder and more perfect than what could ever be inside.

Besides, if the marks saw some *stranger* (Larry warned me to keep my trap shut, lest the marks "get the heebie-jeebies from your accent") win everything, and weren't suspicious, then it was their own fault. Paying good money at a booth was like flushing coins down the toilet just to hear them rattle. Either way, the money was *gone*. *I* couldn't force people not to waste their money if they were of a mind to do so.

In addition to Larry's joint, the midway was comprised of the one-ball joint (milk-bottle toss with weighted bottles), a Palm Reader, Dunk the Darlings (a floating duck game using Kewpie dolls instead of ducks), Add 'Em Up Darts (Larry scornfully referred to *that* joint as a "flatter," as in "Flatten the marks"), a baseball shooting gallery, the balloon stand, hot dog, cotton candy, and just plain candy stands, the kootchie dancer tent, a freak top, a cluster of animal cages flanked by painted canvas screens depicting none of the animals on display, and a small tent off away from the rest of the midway, which Larry simply called "The Tent," before pointing out the rides and giving me the names of the jockeys.

Shea owned the rides, the food stands, and a couple of the joints, plus the animals—the other joints, including Larry's and the dart one, were owned by the jointees; they tagged along at their pleasure. Larry hinted that such joints came and went, on the whims of their agents. And that was the sum total of the South-State Enterprises Carnival and Menagerie. Hardly seemed worth all the effort of putting it together and knocking it down come midnight. But I didn't say so to Larry, not when I was getting room, board, and a little pay (two bucks a week, take it or get lost).

Before chow was served at noon, Larry invited me back to his camper, adding, "Got me some Lone Star Beer, from Texas. Not too warm, but be careful not to go shakin' up the can." Soon we were comfortably stretched out in the slight shade of the camper, watching the other carnies sit around on fold-up chairs or on the ground, talking, or hanging out bits of wash on hastily strung-up lines. Nobody seemed terribly excited about that evening's show.

When I asked Larry about it, he shrugged and replied in his softly inflected voice, "You could light a bonfire and be roastin' marshmallows for an hour unner their asses an' they'd only think it a bit warm in the shade. Lost whatever spark they had years back. But 'fore I joined up, this outfit was a sight to see. In the days 'fore Shea bought it. Saw 'em perform myself, down in Georgia, when I was, oh, somethin'-teen. Had a Jim Dandy freak top, fat lady w' a belly out to *there*, thin man so starved he'd swell up if you gave 'im a Tootsie Roll. Frog lady, an' pinheads—whole passel of *those*—an' a bearded lady, only I ain't too sure 'bout *her*. Beard was hangin' lower come the end of the show than when I first showed up. Pegged her for a fake. But the mentalist—real copacetic. Didn't take no stock in his Frog-man accent, but he made Beulah Dunn start screamin' in the back row—*that* was a real knee-slapper—"

I figured Larry was in his early or mid-thirties, so the heyday of the South-State Enterprises Carnival had been in the mid-twenties, or thereabouts. I wondered what had happened to make the outfit sink so low. Between sips, I asked him about it.

"Hollywood. Most of them freaks took off when word got out that *Dracula* guy, Tod Browning, was gonna make that

Freaks film. Ain't never seen it myself, so I dunno if any South-State freaks made it or not. Either way, they musta found themselves somethin' better'n they had here. Heard 'bout the exodus from the cook. Hired on just as the last of 'em left. Tole me 'bout the *Freaks* movie. But even if they wasn't good 'nough for Hollywood, they had to be a *hunnerd* times better'n what's traipsin' 'round now.''

Having finished his beer, Larry picked up a second can and opened it, the church key pressing down and rending the top of the can with a hiss and fine mist of beer that hit my forearm. After glugging down half the can, he resumed his wheezy speech.

"Bones, f'instance. Know how he keeps that tummy so flat?'' I shook my head, and Larry mimed sticking a finger deep in his throat, exposing a coated tongue and gray-decayed teeth, making an "aaaawwwaaakkk" noise deep in his throat. The subject of his demonstration was sitting on a lawn chair two hundred feet away, puffing on a Camel. It was all I could do not to laugh.

"An' wait'll you see Moby Jackie—lazy gobblin' fat, that's all. Be kicked out w'out her daily pie ration . . . blows all her pay on 'em. You seen Longo—iffen you wanted to see *short*, you should've—''

As he spoke, a person with canary-yellow hair done up in a gauzy head scarf tied in the front tottered behind the midway on a pair of high heels, a silken kimono wrapped around a slightly plump body. I saw the face plain; bee-stung lips, dark-lined slightly pop eyes, and rice-powder white skin. Hortense Holiday looked like that when I was a boy; Theda Bara gone to seed. Only this carny was younger and better-looking. The pale eyes behind the rings of kohl blinked seductively, then focused on the movie magazine held in a pair of red-nailed hands, as the carny leaned against one of the big trucks.

Nudging Larry's elbow with mine, I whispered, "What is *that*?'' He snorted and took a sip before answering. " 'That' is Mr. or Miss Daisy-Denny. Never seen a half'n' half 'fore? Really *is* a 'he.' First came to work in the same sorta hole you're in now—shillin' an' cleanin' an' the like. Joined after we played near his hometown of Memphis. Old man ran a Piggly-Wiggly, but Denny didn't want no sucker job. Must've smelled work. Anyhow, Denny came one night an' left with us come sunup. That was, oh, lemme see, '32 or

'33. 'Round the time the Depression's teeth was sunk down deep in people's asses, an' it was painful to scrape up the thirty-four cents it took to have a middlin' time on the midway, 'specially when a movie an' a short an' two cartoons cost a dime.

"At first, I couldn't figger out why in hell Denny gone done that. Findin' hisself a hole in a droopy carny like this, 'specially after all the freaks drifted off like dandelion seeds on a good stiff wind. Him with a cushy daddy's-boy job waitin' back home. Come workin' time, he did as little as humanly possible without a body already bein' dead an' smellin'.

"But I figgered out what he had up his sleeve one hot day when we was settin' up the freak top. Us men stripped to the waist, an' when Denny peeled off his shirt I seen them floppy man-nipples of his, like somethin' off a baby's bottle. Took to *jerkin'* them as he worked. First one, then the other, an' all this aimed at Harold, who's got this *concentratin'* look on his face. When we was through, Shea whispers somethin' in Denny's ear, an' they set off for Harold's trailer. Only Shea put his shirt back on, though.

"Shea's wife set to work on Denny, an' that night the top had itself a new attraction—'Daisy-Denny, the Fabulous He-She, the Anatomical Wonder, the Hermaphroditty!' Damned so-an'-so found hisself a way to have his cake an' eat it, too. Slugs down orange Crush an' gets cash money for the lack of effort. Marks watch him flappin' his *kee*-mo-no open an' shut. *Coolest* goof-for-nothin' 'side from Bones, though. Don't have to worry 'bout trousers or nothin'—hardly moves 'nough to work up a sweat. Lookit him flippin' them pages like they weigh ten tons each—hey, Denny, don'tcha go droolin' over Clark Gable, pages'll stick together."

In a bray that would've done a hog farmer proud, Daisy-Denny trilled back, "I'm droolin over Cary Grant, sweet-ums," before blowing Larry a kiss. He flinched to avoid it, which made me laugh behind my teeth.

As Larry swore at Daisy-Denny under his breath, a sudden metallic *blam*! caught my attention. I stared off to the east, where a new, iridescent Airstream trailer and white Pierce-Arrow had parked while Larry and Denny exchanged gibes. I'd just missed seeing the driver of that sweeping automobile enter the trailer, but a second later, I saw a flicker of movement in the window nearest the door. A quick lift and drop of the pink, ruffled curtains, revealing a woman's face. All I took in was a spill of taffy hair and darkish eyes, then the pale fabric was back in place.

My eyes darted to the Pierce-Arrow. It was the *cleanest* car I'd seen in my life—not a dot of rust or daub of mud marred that snowy paint job, or the shimmer of the chrome trim. And the interior was, of all things, *pink* leather.

No one back home drove a car quite like that. It was a Hollywood movie-premier car, something a starlet might show up in. Car like that wouldn't last one winter in Wisconsin, or a summer for that matter.

"Who owns *that*?" I pointed at the Pierce-Arrow with my empty can. Again, the curtains rippled. Larry spit off a ways from me before replying.

"Cotton-candy car belongs to Maeve. Puppet Lady. Taggin' after the carny goin' on a year. Showed up last July, came one night an' did her act there an' then. Harold snatched her up like *that*." Snapping black-nailed fingers, Larry continued, " 'Course, Harold ended up makin' concessions to her that if you ask *me* I wouldn't've made at *all*. Shea's the type, you kiss his ass, he'll say you didn't pucker up right. F'*her*, he'd kiss his own behind. An' her a stuck-up bitch. Not *carny*. You work here long 'nough, you'll see, you're *carny*. Stick close, gas a little 'bout each other, but still *carny*. Unnerstand? You will, you will.

"But *Maeve*"—he gave her name a singsong snarl—"don't want to *eat* with us *carny* folks, so *Maeve* don't *have* to. Has the chow brought special to her *door*. Shea sez it's 'cause she's on her dogs all night.

"*Maeve* don't want her pretty hands chapped, so she gets one of the girls to wash her clothes. Must've been born w' a gold-plate spoon in her craw, never mind silver.

"That car o' hers? Drove *in* with it, trailer, too. Has clothes like nobody's business. Dresses her *puppet* like a round heels, too. Spangles an' diamond stickpins, oh, that one is *somethin'* all right. *And you know it*, don't *you*?" he snarled at the now-lifted curtain and the pale face behind it.

I wondered if she knew what Larry thought of her, what he was saying. I hoped she couldn't read lips, but Larry's expression told the story plain enough.

I couldn't make out her face clearly, but her hair hung down long, like Veronica Lake's, and had waves that didn't look as if they came from a machine in a beauty parlor. I wondered if Larry hadn't taken a shine to Maeve when she first drove up—her trailer would've been an improvement over his dinky camper, and of course there was that *car* (*pink* upholstery!)— maybe he asked her to hold hands, or something more, and she rebuffed him. Bad feelings like his didn't sprout full-grown and bearing fruit overnight.

When Larry said something about "like to pull them knees apart," I almost regurgitated beer bile, hoping that Maeve had good locks on that metal trailer door.

What I *should've* wished for her was a padlock and an iron bar . . . but not on account of Larry.

FIFTY-NINE

Dragging his feet with every step he took, Winston came to the conclusion that he *had* to be dead, and that this place was his own special *Hell*. Oh, it was a very *crafty* place, so pretty and freshly new, every house in spit-and-polish condition, with all those glitters of colored light flickering around the edges of things. Winston's mother hadn't been a Sunday school teacher for *nothing*. She'd gotten it across to him long ago, when he still wore woolen playsuits and assembled Tinkertoys on the front parlor floor—Hell was a *cold* place, yet fire-filled, too, with flames lapping at the wicked. He knew that a flame was more than one color—there was red, orange, yellow, blue—the same colors he'd seen wavering around *everything* in this place. Yet, when he touched things, they weren't *hot*. Cold fire. As in Hell. (Still, Mother *had* claimed that the flames lapping at the skin of the damned *hurt*— otherwise, what was the point of it all?)

Winston didn't recall dying, just as he wasn't quite sure why he wore his Army uniform . . . but wouldn't they lay him out in his uniform for his funeral? If that *was* the case, and people wore what they were buried in the afterlife, Gayleen must be *very* upset—she was never fond of her blue-flowered Vionnet. He hoped he wouldn't run into his mother just *yet*—she wouldn't appreciate that he'd allowed Una to pick out something from Gayleen's closet in which to bury her in. But so far, he'd seen *no* one walking on any of the streets.

Hugging the meager shade of an elm on Evans Street, which lay between Dean Avenue and Share Avenue in restored splendor (*when I walked the school census route, this part of town was a dump*), Winston shook his head, muttering, "Hope it wasn't Mother in that house . . . maybe it was the timbers settling. But . . . what about all that food in the pantry? Everything I like, too . . . if I hadn't heard that *noise*. . . . '' His voice feathered into inaudibility, even as he kept moving his dry lips.

Hell or not, this place *did* resemble Ewerton . . . but not the town he'd watched wither and die, pulling in on itself over the last forty-plus years, like a rotted jack-o'-lantern eating its own nose. Being a tricky, deviously deceptive Hell, *this* Ewerton was the one he'd left behind him, along with his youth and optimism. After donning the mask and costume handed to him by Fate during his last weeks in the Occupation Army. The role of Unassuming, Unproductive Citizen, his dreams shattered by that damn Army shrink. Now old Major Herman Taub, M.D., *he* was the one who deserved to be double-stepping through Hell. *But not* my *Hell*, Winston decided—this Hell was too beautiful for the likes of Major Taub.

Ewerton hadn't been this clean, this fixed-up since Winston's boyhood. Not a board hanging loose, not a flake of paint missing, not an unraked bit of garbage left to clog the storm drains. A perfect postcard begging the viewer to "Come to Ewerton!"

As he walked, unwilling to risk shelter on another front porch, Winston gradually realized that this was *literally* the town of his boyhood—across the river to the southwest, that horrid cluster of Monopoly houses and broken plastic tricycles was *gone*.

Same thing with the hospital—the *new* one, not the small resolute structure that once again overlooked the Dean River. Also vanished.

Stopping under the considerable shade of a far-spreading oak that marked the end of the junction between Evans Street and Fifth Avenue East, Winston wondered what had happened. Not to himself, but to the town he'd so recently been living in; hating it, yet unable to tear himself away from the memory of the pleasant place it once *had* been. Somehow, it had rotted away, without benefit of a funeral or wake. His town was decomposing in the open, a car-hit rabbit left to fester, worm up, then melt into a furry patch on the side of the road.

And those he'd left behind didn't realize they were worms, as they swallowed dead flesh.

"Pack of fool maggots," he said aloud when a thought came to him, born of hours spent walking in a place of cold prismatic fire and *House Beautiful* dwellings—suppose this *was* the real Ewerton? Dorian Gray and his picture, hidden away to fester . . . the notion *was* more optimistic than his other option. Maybe the real Ewerton got fed up and left, letting the alterations and ruinations happen to its alter ego.

His fears slightly dissipated, Winston longed to sit and talk over his theory with someone—just to find out if, along with dying, he'd gone bug shit, too.

Almost like spending eternity with a hangover . . . which happened to be his immediate problem. The food had settled his stomach, but his head still felt as if a tornado was going two-forty under his hat.

Resuming his foot-dragging pace down the street, he wanted nothing more than to *talk*—discussing anything, with *any*body. Almost as good as having sexual relations, even though he'd painfully discovered after ducking behind a hydrangea bush a few blocks ago that not only was he in Hell, but he had the clap, too. . . .

Yet, though urinating, or even walking, was an agony, Winston felt the return of his old urges. Guiltily, he asked himself if he hadn't punished himself enough already. Hell or not, he had no reason to behave like a rutting bull in a barnful of cows . . . no matter *how* he'd acted when he was a kid.

And afterward, the small voice reminded him; before he thought of the consequences, he smacked himself upside the head, to quiet the soft pure voice. Fresh waves of agony shot behind his eyes. He kicked himself for not looking for some aspirin in that house, before he got all misty-eyed over Una and took a peek up that staircase.

He told himself that the squeaking he'd heard was the result of putting his foot on the first tread of the staircase. Old houses made strange noises when you stepped on the wrong floorboard. Still, the staircase had been irresistible . . . for that rose window *did* seem to be bleeding.

This is silly, *I'm dead.* No bogeyman was going to slither (*trippy-trip, I heard cleated shoes*) down the carpet, leaving tatters and moist bits of itself in its wake. Nothing could get him because he *was* dead—bad things only lay in wait of the *living*.

Reaching the end of the street, he had a clear view of the river, and of Willow Hill beyond, where all the swanky homes were gone, too. He took off across open ground, unmarred by the crackerbox law and fire buildings. The *real* firehouse sat close by the depot. The bridge was gone, as it had been when he and Palmer took Dead Fred on that snipe hunt.

He'd only fed Fred a line of baloney to get *rid* of him—either scare him off or make him scoff. Winston didn't realize that Dead Fred was that stupid. He wished it hadn't gone so hard on Nemmitz. After Palmer took off that Sunday, Winston had a sick certainty that Palmer was in trouble. Yet there was nothing he could *do*.

Watching the sinking sun turn the surface ripples of the river into a gold-green moifé ribbon of shifting, subtle color, Winston felt like he did that May of 1940—cut off, adrift, *lacking*. He'd even risk returning back to the living, just to talk to Palmer again—

Then, as if in answer to his mental plea, he heard a faint sound float across the river. A soft crooning of his name, echoing in gentle parody of the strident reverberating voice he thought he'd heard that morning.

"Paaa . . . lmer, Paaa . . . lmer." He scrambled down to the bank of the river, where the sound was louder, more identifiable. Growing certainty turned to increasing fear, yet there was an element of desire, too. Suddenly, the idea of crossing the river to investigate the voice's source was both tempting *and* terrifying.

Winston paced the marshy riverbank, lost in indecision and creeping dread, *listening*.

SIXTY

From Palmer Nemmitz's journal—
Five years or so before I joined the South-State carny, when I was in school, Miss Holiday brought Wilbur's old magazines to class, when we were cooped up during rainy recesses. I pulled a copy of *American* out of that smooth-covered pile of reading material; inside was Don Marquis' "Willy Takes a Step." The story didn't stick with me, but oh, this one illustration—

It was a Rockwell. This big derby-hatted fellow introducing a skinny kid to a table of seated circus folks. There was a girl in a filmy getup, a fat lady, a thin man, a bearded lady, a clown, and a scruffy, no-good ruffian at the table, and all but the last-mentioned man looked happy to see this kid join their ranks.

I carried that image in my mind for years; when Larry said it was time for lunch, I thought he or Shea would introduce the new kid to the old hands, everyone would smile or wave a fork in greeting, and then I'd be *part* of it all. But thinking isn't the same as doing; when Larry put his hand on my shoulder and told the twenty-some people assembled around a makeshift board and sawhorse table, "Here's Palmer, got his hole here today," I was lucky if two or three people looked in my direction before shoving hush puppies, fried okra, and some sort of fish into their mouths. (It was stupid to give them my right name, but I doubted that the old man had sent the Pinkertons sniffing after *me*.)

So I ate in silence, trying to figure out how to tell Larry thanks, but no thanks for the job. I decided to wait until after I took in the show; the only carnivals I'd seen were Ewerton ones, and those weren't the *same*. I wanted to know what my town had been so eager to keep away.

The midway didn't open up until dusk, the time of mottled grayish light and thick shadows. When ugly becomes exotic, the plain, mysterious. Once they started up the generators, and the rides and the colored lights strung between the joints came to life, there was an atmosphere of suppressed tension and anticipation that had been lacking in the daylight.

Seeing dots of glowing color suspended against the night sky, like teardrops from a rainbow, I was hit with memories of home. For my town changed come nightfall; the street lamps and house lights made the night friendlier; when Winston took to driving like a bat out of Hades down some street, the lights would streak past, flit-flit-flit of rich gold, fireflies strung together like popcorn and hung on the branches of the night air.

On the midway, I liked the way the globes of bright color made faces go all odd-shadowed, weird-toned. White hair turned to banks of sunlit snow, all twinkling in warm and cool hues. For me, the ropes of colored bulbs were the best thing about the midway.

It was a let-down to admit it, but the amusements at home were better than those in this carny. The sum total of the "menagerie" was a listless chimp, a big bobcat billed as a "Mountain Wild Cat" who was friendlier than most cats who lapped cream from a saucer (later I learned that the worst thing Chatty would've done if she escaped would be to *love* some mark to death), a pair of molting tropical birds in washed-out colors, and a llama who created the most excitement of the bunch when it let loose with a steaming stream of piss. It was shameful how some of the women carried on. *Disgust* crept into my perception of those people after I heard the snickering over that damned llama, while Longo—dressed in tights and a spotted animal skin—cracked a tiny whip and looked just plain stupid.

Around then I began to see Larry's side of things, why he'd rigged the wheel, and looked down on the marks. My disgust turned to disdain once I took in the girlie tent. All that *ooofing* and *eeefing* by grown men over the same thing the girls in Ewerton used to do for free on a Saturday night.

The ride jocks wanted me on their rides, for *free*, but Larry warned me about them ("They'll stop the ride with you hangin' upside down just f'the *heck* of it"). Besides, I got dizzy easy, and I needed a clear head for shilling later on.

One-ball did a brisk business; Tony played the crowd well. Milk bottles weren't all that intimidating. But folks were shying away from Larry's wheel, despite his persuasive spiel. I suppose the pagan look of the pictures turned them off—we *were* near the Bible Belt. Larry gave me the hand signal, and

I ambled over, pushed forward his coin (marked with black paint, so he could reuse it), then pointed to one of the suits on the wheel.

Usually, I couldn't win a fart at a bean-eating contest, but damned if the swords didn't come up *three* out of three times after he spinned.

After I had a couple of Shirley Temple dolls in my arms, six, seven people showed up to watch me win more. When Larry leaned over and whispered, "Get lost," it was time for me to play the gracious mark, let the next sucker lose a few bucks on a doll he could've ordered for less straight from the catalog. I shoved the dolls under the canvas flap in the rear of the joint, but then, figuring that the marks might wonder what happened to those dolls, I ducked into the freak top, so they'd forget my face.

The tent no longer had that dried dung odor; the air was now ripe with the scent of cotton candy, Cracker Jacks, and Goo-Goo Clusters. And Stardust Bars, a favorite of mine from the late thirties.

The fragrant air was filled with a gabble of voices, almost reverent in awe. These folks seemed *desperate* for entertainment; then I recalled that I'd seen no movie house here, not even a closed-up one like in Ewerton.

So I milled around the marks; I watched them as they eyeballed the freaks; faded eyes glittered at things no good person should've enjoyed. Finally, I forced myself to stare at the freaks, just to clear my head. This show could've graced a Sunday school picnic, excepting Daisy-Denny, and *he* would hardly cause a ripple at a stag party.

When a body first stepped through the tent flaps, there was Bones, standing almost buck naked save for a loincloth over his privates and keister. All his body hair gone, too, so as to better show off that bony physique. While the barker (a wrinkled old buck with a gimpy leg) jabbered, "While you and I live on *food*, he lives on *air*!" Bones struck little poses, sucked in his flat gut, to display his cage of a rib frame. All the while puffing on Camels; the pack sat on a stool next to him, along with a box of matches. I recalled Larry's fingerdown-the-throat with a wry smile before passing on to the next attraction.

Moby Jackie. The Fat Lady. The poster outside billed her as "Half a Ton of FUN!" Oh, she had three chins, and a spare tire big enough to shore up a John Deere tractor, but then X-ray glasses *are* glasses.

She was housewife heavy. But that would've been forgivable if she'd *looked* the part of a Fat Lady. Dead Fred had lovingly recalled one he'd seen at White City for our benefit—not just fat, but *sexy* fat. Inviting, the way a mound of rising dough in the bowl smells so good you want to eat it raw.

The only *more* on Moby Jackie was more sallow skin than I'd ever seen on a live body before. Sitting on a stool built short-legged to make her look bigger, she spooned quivering pudding into red-smeared lips, rouge-dotted cheeks working as she moved the cud around in her mouth before swallowing. Like something bloated, swelling up before the final death rattle. No merry jelly flesh, waiting for a caress. Just hanging slabs of lard bulk, slack and dead-colored, the skin mottled and jaundiced. Most of her skin was visible—her sailor dress with the anchor-trimmed collar came up to the pocked flesh of her thighs, and the tight puffed sleeves rode up above her elbows, which were little more than greenish-gray scaly patches set into the spongy flesh of her arms. Finger holes in clay.

Frantically I thought, *Get on top of* that? *You'd sink in it like quicksand and* die, as men tried to hide boners by pulling their pants forward, fists stuck in pockets. They couldn't have noticed her *face*.

She wore a wig. During lunch, I saw her thin hair, balding above the hairline, a filthy stringy pale brownish no-color. The corkscrew cascade of fake curls was cheerful, but her face was pure vinegar and piss. Those men with the hard-ons were either just plain addled or horny enough to stick it into a cow.

I quickly passed the pretty, tired-looking woman with the faded smile who showed the marks her six-fingered hands, and her nail-painted toes—even the tiny sixth ones jutting off to the sides. When she held those hands to the light, you could see membranes there, too. I exchanged a quick up-turning of the lips with her and hurried away.

The fire-breather didn't impress me, but the marks lavished attention on him and his feathery plumes of flame.

The last freak sat behind a screen embellished with a garish representation of a human hybrid of dual gender, bisected at the waist. Curls and cleavage above, a manly loincloth below. The face didn't resemble Daisy-Denny's. Since there weren't

enough barkers to go around, there was only a sign next to
the screen, admonishing, ''Men and Boys Only!'' but I saw
many an arm-in-arm couple (including Hank and Minnie, who
didn't see me) go around that screen, followed by the bashful
giggle of the woman before her husband or beau whisked her
away.

After Hank and Minnie exited, I went behind the screen to
see if Daisy-Denny came up to the level of the half and halfs
I'd heard about. They were *vertically* half and half, with a
butch on one side of their heads and long waves on the other;
the differences continued on down the body.

First I found another screen, which wrapped around in pan-
els. A light glowed behind the screen, casting a distorted
silhouette shadow of Daisy-Denny across the peachy-pink
fabric. I was followed by an old man and a skinny young
goomer in overalls and a work shirt. The three of us rounded
the screen, to view Daisy-Denny.

With the kerchief off, and more makeup on, Denny sure
looked like a girl—a million times prettier than Moby and her
green elbows. Golden hair flowed down past his shoulders in
deep waves; a lock of it strayed accidentally-on-purpose over
one black-circled gray eye. He was so powdered and rouged
I couldn't make out any beard stubble. His lips glistened wetly
in the light of the tiny boudoir lamp with the frilly shade he
had on a bamboo table next to him. One red-nailed hand held
a bottle of Orange Crush with a lipstick-smeared opening.
As he sat on a dainty vanity chair, he tipped the bottle to his
lips and chugged down half the contents, Adam's apple barely
rippling. Up until then, he had his kimono closed—raw
silk, clinging deeply pink to his padded shoulders and hips—
holding the neckline shut with his free hand. When he decided that the three of us was all the audience he was getting
for a while, he took the bottle from his lips, licked them with
a slow, tongue-curling motion, and let go of the kimono. His
man-titties weren't much bigger than Dead Fred's but he'd
rouged the nipples.

Once he had our complete attention, he did what passed
for an act. By moving muscles in his upper arms, he made
his chest bounce. First one teat, then the other, until the mark
in the overalls gulped loud enough to hear, and the old coot's
wrinkled face broke into a picket fence toothed smile. He'd
noticed me by then, and gave a slight nod of recognition. In
answer, I made my chest jerk, as he'd done. My shirt was

just tight enough for him to notice my efforts easily. Slippery lips puckered into a moue. As if to say, *Can you top this?* he pulled open his kimono wide enough to show his hairless armpits and shaved lower chest, jerking his muscles harder, making the nipples contract to red raisins on creamy flesh. I made my shirt strain. *Like this, mister?*

He took another sip of soda before giving me an arch, "But can you top this?" stare, flipping aside his kimono *all* the way, revealing what had lain quiet until then, under the folds of silk. The hick whistled. Holding a hand under it, to better show off the merchandise previously stored under the counter, he smiled as I shook my head. *Not even with both hands working.* He shrugged in reply, running a painted fingernail up and down the length of his shorn torso, *We can't all have the luck.* He may've been blessed in some regards, but I wondered if any girls would've wanted him—especially since he was prettier than half the ladies I'd ever met. Pretty like Errol Flynn was one thing, but how many women would've bedded down with Jean Harlow if she was equipped like Denny?

After arching forward so we could see everything out front, Daisy-Denny sat down again, flipped the silk over his white body, and drained the rest of his soda. Show was over.

As we filed out, I was embarrassed to discover it was rather *painful* to walk. Noticing my predicament, Denny blew me a kiss before reaching under his chair and pulling out a full bottle of Crush. Popping the crimped top with a church key extracted from the pocket of his gown, he made lazy circles in the air with the tip of his mule-shod foot. As a parting shot, he made the pink fabric dance over his left breast. I was too humiliated to do the same in return as I crept out of the freak top into the safety of the rainbow-shattered darkness.

The first thing I noticed was that the small tent Larry called The Tent now sported a huge silvery sign out front. The last survivor of a family of fun-house mirrors. A few people drifted off toward the sign; I followed them until I read words painted in deep vermillion on the wavery reflective surface, as if written across the warped faces and bodies of those reading the sign:

!!THE MISSING LINK!!
The Most SHOCKING Display of Human
ABERRATION

Know in the WESTERN Hemisphere!
ADULTS ONLY!!
Limited Viewing
7:30, 8:30, and 9:30 ONLY!!!
50¢ Admission
Pay As You Go In Please!

Larry's geek, no doubt. The creature that provoked such ire in Harold. "50¢ Admission"—no wonder Larry taunted Shea about the money his "buddy" brought in nightly. Fifty cents bought a good meal; add a bit more and it bought something to wear. Enough money for two gallons of gas, or to go to five movies.

I started for Larry's joint, wanting to ask him about the sign, but his booth was closed, dark, a sign posted on the apron:

Back in 20 Minutes

According to my watch, it was close on 7:30. Marks were already clustered around the closed flap of the tent, standing in place like obedient cattle, not attempting to open the flaps. But when I joined the crowd of twenty or more people, I sensed a mood not usually associated with cows. Growing urgency, tinged with blood hunger.

The closest I can come to the feeling surging through those marks was how the people had acted at a county fair I attended close to thirty years later. My wife, her brother Buddy (God rest his simpleton soul) and I went down state to this fair, a few years after people in Plainfield found out how their neighbor Ed Gein obtained his supply of deer liver and custom-made night clothes, plus things folks don't mention unless they're cracking sick Ed jokes.

Some enterprising man bought Ed's old maroon Ford, the one he used to transport the last "deer" he'd shot. Just the car, mind, a plain old maroon, 1949 *Ford*. No body, no blood . . . just a used *car*, one you'd be likely to see on a highway or street *anywhere*. But the fella made the most of his purchase; put it inside a canvas fence with three little skull and crossbones-decorated flags on top, and strings of lights between. You had to climb up a ladder to look down into the tableau of the car and a used window-display dummy curled in the trunk. You had to *pay* to climb that ladder.

And there were signs—four of 'em, side by side, surmounted by a long narrow one. As Buddy climbed the ladder, I copied down what the signs said on a couple of matchbooks. Bitsy clucked on about how *awful* it was, while I scribbled in hand-drawn boxes:

Remember	ED GEIN Of Plainfield, Wisc.	See His Grave Robbing & Murder	CAR $1,000 Reward if not true
Read LIFE	*It's Here!* Ed Gein's crime CAR $1,000 Reward if not true!	The Plainfield WISCONSIN Crime That shocked the Nation	Look! See the Car that Hauled the Dead from their Graves

Some of the words slanted, some were big. The sign promised a lot of excitement. Bitsy jabbered a blue streak, how embarrassing it was, how folks from Wisconsin shouldn't have to witness such terrible things, how she was glad Angie wasn't with us, and how I should be ashamed of myself for writing down what was on the signs. This was while her brother was up on the ladder, ass skyward, hanging over the canvas to get his money's worth. I didn't go up, but not because I took what old Ed Gein did personally, like Bitsy and most Wisconsinites did in '57 and later. He was soft in the skull—it's the *sane* killer you got to be wary of. . . .

I didn't pay to see the car because I figured, why not display the shoes Ed wore while digging up or shooting those poor ladies? They took him to the scene of the crime same as the car did, and on a more personal level. I wasn't scared of the car, nor did I hold it in the same breathless awe Buddy did. He nearly broke his pratt climbing up those rungs; I never saw a man move so fast unless the booze was free or the food served buffet style.

When he clambered down, his fat face sagged in abject misery, as if he'd reached the toe of his Christmas stocking and found a lump of coal instead of a walnut. When asked what was wrong, he sighed, "Wasn't no good, dummy's *head* was still on."

That's the only way to describe the marks by the Missing

Link tent is that they wanted heads *off* and blood flowing red-hot. I'd never seen a geek myself. It had to be disgusting, considering the way Shea carried on about it. But . . . pretty *good*, too, from the anxious ants-in-the-pants way people waited for those flaps to open.

Under the colored lights, I saw the glint of more than a few quarters and fifty-cent pieces held in work-worn hands. Whatever the geek was like (he or it lived in a horse trailer hitched to the back of the llama cage), these folks were willing to shell out hard-earned money just to take a peek at it.

It was 7:31 by my watch when the flaps opened, and Larry's face appeared, but no one said, "You're late!" They just herded in, dropping coins in a little metal box sitting on a spindly plant stand. I passed my empty hand over the box and tapped it with my thumb, simulating the sound of a coin being put in.

Larry winked at me, face all pasty-pale in the blue light that suffused the interior of The Tent. The place reeked of sewage, tangy preserving alcohol, and something earthy, yet not-earth itself—straw. Once my eyes were accustomed to the dim light, I saw that Larry had strung just enough blue and green lights in there for the marks to see their way around without stepping on each other's feet.

Half of The Tent was curtained off with a blanket strung between a pair of poles stuck into the sparsely tufted soil. Through the blanket, and over the top where the blanket didn't reach the tent's peak, I saw a dim reddish glow. A few people headed for the blanket, but as soon as the tent was elbows-rubbing full, Larry dropped the flaps and warned, "That's f'*later*," before launching into his spiel as he guided us to a long table at the back of the tent.

"Ladies an' gentlemen, you are about to see the most *shocking*, ob-*scene*, an' *primitive* example of *Homo sapiens* alive *to*-day—"

"Didden pay four bits to see no *homo*," a man growled, but Larry overrode him, wheezing, "But *before* we can gaze upon the eighth wonder o' *nature*, contemplate the *early* stages of this creature's life *cycle!*" With a flourish, he removed the cheesecloth that had covered the objects on the table. From the aqua school of faces around me came a sucking in of breath; many pairs of eyes bugged out as they stared at the big jars.

Each was sealed with cord-wound cloth, and contained . . .

something that floated and bobbed and shifted under the murky light, the water green- and blue-flecked where reflections of color hit the surface. The *things* were soft, formless, yet vaguely suggestive of things familiar (here an eye, there a waving nubbin of flesh), and the water was snot-thick, cloudy, churning when someone bumped the table.

When Larry decided we had our fill of the jars and the mysteries within, he intoned, "This is the creature in its *infancy*—b'hold the full-grown speci*men*!" Holding aside the blanket, he waved the marks into the other half of the tent. I hung around until the end, whispering as I passed Larry, " 'Speci*men*' my be*hind*." All he did was push me into the crowded spot where the rest waited, by the red-lit pit.

At first, in that bloody light, I thought there was only a mound of straw in the small pen set in the middle of the floor . . . but the mound *moved*, slowly at first, a rustle of bristly straw and a scrabbling sound . . . then the straw mound grew to a point and broke open, like a festering wound. Then the bad stink came, worse than dog, horse, cat, cow, or pig shit, coming so hard and so fast more than one handkerchief was pressed in haste over a fluttering set of nostrils.

The geek. Eyes squinted black in the lurid glow, face shapeless and stubbled, hair standing up every which way, dirt-blackened body bent and shaking. He—*it*—wore caveman rags, so matted with encrusted manure and embedded bits of straw that the thing crouching in the pen resembled a mutated porcupine. Its prickly costume hardly covered its runs-darkened rear end, or flopping balls and water hose. I saw more than one long-lashed pair of eyes hone in on what peeked out from under its rude scrap of clothing.

The ladies' faces were off in that carmine light; eyes glinting black jet, rouged cheeks leeched of color. Beard stubble on the men resembled pepper flecked over lean cheeks and hard chins, like bad guys out of *Dick Tracy*.

The more the marks watched the frantic paddling about of the thing in that double-bed-sized, wood-sided pit, the more the thing's ugliness and lack of humanity seeped into *their* faces. And what was worse was that they *liked* what they saw. . . .

When it let loose with an invisible cloud of poison gas, bent double from the pain of its cramps, they all *liked* what they heard, what they saw, even what they smelled. Fifty cents worth, and more to come—

Frenzied padding around the pen. Came close enough for the nearest people to *touch* it. Bare feet made harsh sounds as their thickened surfaces came in contact with the straw. Hugging its guts with filth-swirled arms, it squat in the center of its pen, and shat out ropes of steaming brown. I tried worming my way out of that place, but the press of bodies around me was too tight. I looked for Larry, but he was gone. Swallowing down vomit that wanted out, *now*, I glanced at the thing in the crackling pen. Rolling like a dog in its own dung, bent legs and inward-curled arms up in the air, all it needed was a tail . . . then I saw what it had in its *hands*—

Clenching my teeth, I clamped my hands over my mouth, for fear the marks would toss *me* into the pit, wanting me to roll in it if I puked in front of them. Unable to face that mockery of humanity writhing in the pen, I looked around . . . but in The Tent, there *was* no such thing as humanity. Only tongue-lolling glee, high-charged excitement. Like a passel of kids, waiting for their first pony ride. Or as if they'd caught Santa Claus under the tree. And the *women*. . . .

While the thing rolled and smeared and licked, in subanimal frenzy, a sound rose up in the tent, starting with one voice, adding voice after voice until it became a single sound, a reverberating chant—"Chick-*en*, chick-*en*, chick—" The marks stared toward the blanket flap, at Larry . . . and the squawking, flapping hen he held by the feet.

They parted to let him through; reaching over the four-foot-high wooden slat walls of the pen, he tossed the bird to the creature. Which caught it with dark-smeared fingers. The bird's tiny eyes were pools of terror; soon its feathers were stuck upright with smeared offal.

I got on my hands and knees and dove through a forest of blood-tinged trunk legs; gabardine and chino and nylon and denim brushed my cheeks like rough leaves. I butted calves and kneed insteps along the way, but no one bent down to investigate. No one noticed at *all*.

I found the edge of The Tent and lifted it, emerging from that stinking blood-walled tomb into the cool, sweet darkness of night. I was in back of The Tent, away from the noise and candy smell and colored lights. I kept crawling on my knees, cough-hitching until the hot tears came, and nose drippings ran salty into my quivering mouth. Behind me came this swelling *whoop* from the marks; imagining the coppery-hot blood reek, I prayed the chicken didn't feel *anything* any-more—

A guy yelled, "There she goes, the Headless Wonder!" *Then* I let loose with everything I'd eaten since noon, maybe since I was *born*. It splattered my hands, my shirt, steaming in the darkness, a reflected heat that beat against my skin. I hitched and hitched until nothing but bubbly spit and forced air came up, burning my nose and throat. Behind me the lights of The Tent grew dim, but I kept coughing, trying to vomit up the horrible memory. But I couldn't bring *that* up and out, no matter how much I tried.

A creature doing *things* was bad enough, but to sic it *on*—

"Are you all right?"

Oh, shit, oh, Jeezus on a boxcar, oh, *damn*, now *I* had an audience. And I had no idea how long she'd been watching. Brushing grass, trash, dirt over what I'd done, I hoped she'd go away.

"Mister, are you all *right*?" Spoken slow and careful, as if I were either drunk or half-dead. She wouldn't leave until I answered. My mind raged, *Didn't you get a good enough show in The Tent?* But I brushed off my shirt, wiped spittle and vomit off my chin, before getting to my feet and turning around to face my audience.

She stood ten feet from me, back-lit by the midway lights, in the space between The Tent and the balloon stand. From her shape and stance, I knew I hadn't seen her milling around earlier. She was a near-black, featureless cutout, legs spread apart enough for me to see how shapely they were, balanced on those high heels. *She* saw me just fine.

Deciding to even the odds up a little, I moved closer to The Tent, so she'd have to turn partway into the light to speak to me.

My maneuver worked; her head was no longer a golden-brown haloed shape, but a face . . . the same face I'd seen earlier, peering out from behind pink, ruffled curtains. I began talking, hoping to distract her from that puddle of vomit and bile on the grass, the mess I'd been unable to cover.

Clearing my burning throat, I began, "I'm . . . fine, miss."

Her carefully worded reply was slow in coming. "Did it have . . . something to do with The Tent?" She said it the way Larry did, with emphasized capitals—only with added disdain. I nodded, then, unsure that she'd seen me, added, "I didn't expect . . . I've never *seen* one before."

"You mean to say you don't think you got your fifty cents worth?" She said that so harsh and fast I didn't notice her lips moving, but even when she spoke slowly her mouth didn't change position very much. Seen up close, or closer than I'd previously seen her, Maeve had a set, immobile face. Solid, with a good strong jaw, a no-nonsense expanse of forehead and a slightly wide, round-tipped nose. Maybe pretty if she smiled, but the lack of smile or frown lines by her mouth indicated that she seldom made either expression part of her daily routine. The lack of wrinkles also made guessing her age impossible.

Past girlhood—under her crossed arms I saw a set of headlights pushing out the top of her peplum-edged black suit jacket—and the curve of her hips under the gently flared skirt indicated what the old man used to dub "a breeder."

But . . . there was something *lacking* in her, that child-on-the-hip quality even Vernilla possessed.

A sterile, hope-lacking way about her, which eschewed flirtation and coyness, as if she'd given up on sex long ago, or never looked in the first place. Maeve spoke like a salesclerk who just came upon a patron who slipped and fell in an aisle. Concerned on the part of the store and nothing more. Remembering what Larry'd said about her, I wondered if her refusal was coldly correct when he'd no doubt asked her to do whatever it was he wanted to do with her.

But the disparaging way she said "The Tent" made me suspect that she'd been less than polite with him . . . not that I blamed Larry for *trying*. Blame him for the geek and the chicken, yes, but for wanting her . . . never. As my eyes swept her face, taking in little things—the soft curve of her hair, the way one eye turned out a tad (not wall-eyed, but as if it had flirted with the notion), or the way the small raised mole under her lower lip on the left side of her chin cast an infinitesimal shadow across her rounded chin—I realized why Larry hated her, too. Anything worth wanting is later worth getting all worked up over, be it a good or bad direction.

While we stood there, awkward, caught in a moment of uncertainty, the liquid jet buttons trimming her right cuff and the mock flaps of her jacket pockets winked at me, and I noticed that she wore dainty ankle-strap shoes, their patent surfaces forming a twisted mirror of the midway lights above and behind her.

She was sweating in that fancy black suit (the likes of which

I'd only seen worn by Bette Davis or Joan Crawford, in my sister Effie's movie magazines); her perfume wafted toward me. Real *perfume*, not the delicate toilet water women back home used. Mingled roses and jasmine, a heady, heat-borne scent, which drifted my way, clearing the bile odor from my nose.

Maeve may've had the frost of autumn in her set mouth and strained neck cords, but there was a hint of spring, of blossoms and *life* clinging to her—and I knew I'd either have to say something, *anything*, or hang my head out and cry out of sheer frustration. It was like wanting to keep a snowflake, or preserve a rose petal without allowing it to fade or wither.

Clearing my throat again, I went on, "Thanks for asking how I was . . . I . . . didn't *pay* to go in there. I work here, joined this afternoon. I help . . . him." Shamefully, I jerked my head in the direction of The Tent.

Her carefully composed face never moved a muscle, but her eyes told the whole story. She'd seen me sitting with Larry before lunch. I sensed her pulling away before she took her first step toward the midway. When she spoke, her voice—a softly muted alto, clear yet laced with a purring undertone— was neutral, dismissing.

"Then I mustn't keep you from your work." Uncrossing her arms, she revealed that her left hand was shoved into a big puppet, likewise dressed in black, with a honey-colored wig and black veil. I remembered Larry calling her the Puppet Lady. I wondered where *her* tent was located; the midway was already full, with no empty spot in the freak top, either.

Walking away from me, into the midway, Maeve adjusted her puppet's sequined hat and veil. Dangling shoe-clad doll feet hung down from the skirt of the puppet—or dummy; by the size of it, I suspected it was a Charlie McCarthy type of puppet.

Its head was the size of a honeydew melon, with a wig of human hair (growing up with three sisters, I knew rayon or mohair from the real thing). I guessed Maeve had paid a pretty penny for the dummy. Either that, or she'd carved it herself and used her own hair clippings for a wig. I caught a glimpse of its face, and it was a far cry from that Appleton Wisconsin ventriloquist Bob Neller's Reggie (I'd read that Neller's sidekick could assume four thousand expressions, thanks to several moving parts in its face). This face was flat and hard, like celluloid or enameled metal, as if Maeve had used a doll head.

Once Maeve became a doll-sized figure in the crowd, I scraped at the ground with the sides of my shoes, more or less covering the mess I'd made. After checking myself over, finding I wasn't as filthy as I felt, I hawked up the bitter bile spittle in my mouth, then dug around in my pockets for the pack of Clove gum I'd bought in Illinois. Shoving the fragrant stick into my mouth, I dropped the flattened-out wrapper on the grass-covered pool of vomit.

Hoping I didn't look as wrung-out as I felt, I reentered the midway, ignoring Larry's signal to come liven up his mark-less joint. Composing a resignation speech in my mind, I searched for Maeve, until I saw a knot of people walking in a slow phalanx near the merry-go-round.

Two voices, both female, only one was higher-pitched, were talking a blue streak inside that cluster of marks—Maeve, doing her act. She didn't sit jabbering with her dummy, like Edgar Bergen did with Charlie and Mortimer Snerd, but walked as she talked, steering people in her direction as she did so. I nearly jumped out of my skin when I saw the dummy's hands *move*, as if by themselves, but close up I saw how she held a pair of thin black wires, from metal coat hangers, manipulating them with her rolling fingers. The other ends of the wires were attached to the tiny gloves the dummy wore. Move the wires, and the tiny hands moved, too. Against the black of Maeve's suit, the wires were almost invisible.

And like most puppets, this dummy was able to say certain things that most folks wouldn't tolerate coming plain out of the mouth of a comedian. Charlie McCarthy got away with things that would've resulted in a yanked sponsorship for, say, Jack Benny. Yet Bergen made raunchy or just plain insulting remarks through Charlie's wooden lips, and folks listening to their radios all over the country roared with laughter.

Besides being tart-mouthed, Maeve's dummy was done up like a little-girl version of Maeve herself; same mole painted on her chin, same almost wall-eyes. But flat and slick, with no pores or imperfections visible. And her nostrils didn't flare like Maeve's did when she breathed. Maeve manipulated its mouth from within; red lips opened and closed stiffly, and darkness gaped within. Like Maeve, the dummy was tight-lipped, but oh, did she have a mouth on her.

In Betty Boop tones, she squealed, darting those big eyes

from side to side, "Ooooh, lookit that *man*," as gloved hands pointed to a mark stuffing a hot dog into his mouth. Maeve asked, "Mae, do you think he can really get *all* of that into his mouth?"

Head tilting, Mae replied, "If he does, he'll have to piddle through a straw!" I almost choked on my gum when I heard that, but from the way the marks carried on, they'd never heard anything so rib-tickling in all their born days. While the man turned red, barely able to swallow what he'd bitten off, and his buddies said, "Better check t'barn, see if the horse is gone," Mae whipped her head around, tiny hands pressed near her head, then trilled, "Ooooh, I *hate* it when men talk dirty!"

I can't recall what cracked up folks more, the hot-dog bit, or the talking dirty part. What put the icing on the cake was the way Maeve stayed straight and serious, not laughing at her own joke.

Maeve's jacket came down in a low V on her chest, exposing her short neck and delicate collarbones—yet when Mae "spoke," neither Maeve's throat or mouth moved. *No wonder she never moves her face,* I thought—

—*through the rain I could see her face, working as she cried, and her mouth was saying what she'd said before, Oh, please, please don't tell, and her face was wet behind the window, working and*—

—then she moved on, toward the hot-dog stand. A couple of fellows chided their girls, "C'mon, Sally, Jessie, want something warm and pink in a bun? W' horseradish on one end?"

"Only if we don't have to swallow it." One of the girls giggled, and then *I* blushed for real.

I suppose there would be such girls wherever I went. But I thought, *If that's the only kind of girl I can find, I'd rather be a bachelor sitting at the kitchen table in long johns and slippers, drinking Green Drops in sugar to ease the indigestion from my own bad cooking.*

It was depressing. Everywhere I went, girls talked crude and acted worse. But I considered myself too hick for a city girl; even Winston had little luck in the Twin Cities when he and his parents visited friends there. For us, it was worse than being stuck between the rock and the hard place.

By the hot-dog stand, the two couples ate their weiners; the men went "Ow!" as the girls bit into theirs. I shook my head, sickened. Even though Maeve's dummy brought up the subject, it was just an *act*, meant to get a rise out of hicks. But when Maeve spoke to me, it seemed as if she brooked no hanky-panky on the part of *any* man. There and then I decided she wasn't country-raised.

Maeve and Mae rambled on; letting ladies know that their slips were showing ("Cotton's low," Mae drawled in a mock-southern accent, pointing a wire-controlled hand at a lacy slip peeking out from under a dress hem), asking a mark, "If fish gives you brains, did you eat a sardine?" and the apple-knockers roared while loading up on cotton candy and Goo-Goo Clusters.

Buying a bar for myself, using one of Larry's black-marked coins, I followed Maeve, and caught her eye as she led the crowd, Pied Piper style, away from the food stands. As she neared the wheel joint, where Larry sat eyeing his wrist-watch, waiting for the half hour to roll around again, the edges of her mouth turned upward, briefly. At *me*.

When she smiled, her face took on a whole different char-acter. I smiled and waved back. Maeve turned away, but over her shoulder Mae's head peeked at me; a wand-manipulated hand waved at me. Mae resembled a child hanging over its mother's shoulder, waving bye-bye at someone walking be-hind her parent. I was charmed; my rehearsed speech for Shea and Larry faded away to static on a distant radio station. I wasn't *told* to go into The Tent . . . and I doubted that the marks who took in such a show could be easily corrupted by what they saw.

So, I decided to stay on. At least until I got another chance to talk to Maeve, find out a bit about her. Despite her often blue routine, Maeve was one of the first decent girls I'd come across since I realized that there was more to girls than middy dresses and pigtails.

That's how I felt about Maeve, even though I'd only talked to her for a minute or two, and had watched her for less than an hour. There are some things, some people, you just *know* are special; no need for confirmation. That time, that place, with Maeve, was such a situation. She was unlike any girl I'd met in terms of looks and actions—unlike *anyone* in Ewerton. But attracted to her as I was, I was also in total awe of her. That near-worshipful feeling kept me from approaching her during her act. Tapping her on the shoulder, making some sassy remark for Mae to answer to, then add some tart rejoinder to put the crowd in stitches—I knew I'd wither inside if I was even half-sure that she really *meant* whatever jab she had Mae send my way.

Hanging back in the fringes of the crowd she led from joint to joint, I realized that she too was a shill, feeding the marks to the agents and ride jocks, letting them snare a few customers without putting themselves out too much—and the marks were all jollied up, ready for more fun. She lost some audience to Larry's joint, the one-ball and the carousel, but picked up more outside the kootchie tent and the freak top.

Funny, Maeve never went *into* the top, just hovered by the flaps until she latched on to some marks. Only when the half hour approached did her loyal audience forsake her, to join the large, anxious crowd by The Tent. By the second show, close to fifty marks clustered tight and wiggling in anticipation near the mirrored sign.

When she found herself alone, she rested her dummy across her chest, its head balanced on her right shoulder, arms hanging down limply, wires dangling. Maeve held on to her left shoulder with her right hand, as if shutting herself up between shows. It *should've* been the perfect time to go up to her, strike up a conversation, offer her a candy bar . . . but when I ventured close enough to see her eyes plainly, I saw how distant they were, shut off from all human contact. Mirrors facing mirrors; all you see is a tunnel of mirrors, each facing the other, extending off into another space beyond the back of the mirror.

If I stared into those blank, self-reflective eyes, they would've sucked me in, trapping me in that diminishing world. I wandered away from her, stopping by the freak tent. I could see her, but unless she shifted her eyes in my direction, she couldn't see me.

So, I watched her, as she stood still and silent, the blackness of her suit and shoes merging into the patches of blackness beyond, her face and stocking-covered legs disembodied, surreal. As if they were the only live parts of her. When she breathed, the jet buttons on her suit twinkled like far-off stars. Her cloud of hair, the color of freshly pulled taffy, picked up the distant colors of the ropes of lights, a nimbus shimmering around her head. And her face didn't shift a muscle; the mouth never formed a smile of remembrance or a frown of regret.

Yet hers was not a peaceful isolation; I sensed a wary tenseness in her legs, in her short, solid neck, like a rabbit who sensed my presence, but couldn't flee. Trapped . . . yet this rabbit had run *to* this place, had entered the trap with both eyes open.

I wanted in the worst way to go up to her, tell her that the trap hadn't sprung yet, that she was too good for this pitiful mockery of a carnival—but I knew my thoughts would sound crazy if voiced. Forward, too. I stood there in confusion, staring at her until her image was burned in oddly colored reverse negative on my eyelids when I blinked—

—oh, God, what I saw was burned on my eyes hotter than a brand on a hide; every time the lightning flashed pink-white the image seared into my brain hotter and deeper, and she kept saying, oh, please, please leave, but there was longing, too, in that ragged, choking voice—

—until the sound of release, of gibbering reward, came from The Tent.

Seconds later, the marks streamed out, looking like they'd all had a ten-buck time in the sack. With the return of her audience, Maeve came out of herself, and arranged her dummy in an upright position. Striding purposefully into the crowd, she began her teasing banter anew. Again I tagged along, oblivious to Larry's come-here gesture, mindless of Shea trying to wave me over to the cotton-candy machine.

I had that swimming-inside feeling I'd get when I thought I'd seen or done something before, but couldn't *possibly* have, as I followed Maeve and Mae around the small oval of the midway. The marks were different, a few of them at least, and the jokes were new, too ("Ooooh, if he noses around me anymore, I'll—*I'll*—'' "What, bite it *off*, Mae?'' "And risk getting lockjaw?''—then Mae's gloved hands reached for the mark's face, a move so quick and fluid it was scary). But, in a way, it was all *exactly* the same, a mocking repetition that reflected no heat on Maeve's part; no involvement, only an eerie semblance of interest and forced humor. And the hicks lapped it up, hanging around for more.

When the last geek show started, she shut herself up again, an automated figure able to fold into herself with a turn of her key. And able to turn that key again and come to life at the close of the show in that terrible tent.

Close on midnight, the carny wound down. The marks wandered off to their Fords and battered DeSotos, revved up, and left. Shea emerged from the cotton-candy stand, signaling to the ride jocks that the rides should be shut down—

horses hanging in midprance, Ferris wheel baskets shuddering from the cessation of motion, all lights winking off, a last moment of color to flare against the eyelids.

With the passing of her followers into the darkness ringing the midway, Maeve flopped Mae onto her shoulder, and took off for her Airstream without a backward glance at the rest of us. I was set to gather what little moxie I had and ask her if she wanted to be walked to her trailer door when Shea intercepted me. Scolding me for not helping him earlier, he produced a flashlight before giving a short speech he must've given to each and every gofer, agent, and ride jock his last-legs carny had ever employed.

"I run a clean carny, ain't the best, ain't the worst. Dunno what you may've heard or seen elsewhere, but no man or woman who's ever trod my midway got his pocket or her purse cleaned out without his or her knowledge or consent. Understand? No dipping from pockets or purses. No paper hanging. Don't need no iron door swinging shut after *me*. No spreading your legs or ass for money. You don't need the marks, and they don't need what you got in your pants. You want it, you go with a carny. Don't want no Poppa here come sunup, claiming his daughter's bust. Running a clean carny's got its disadvantages, I'd earn plenty more by helping myself instead of waiting for it to get paid out, but I get caught, I loose more than plenty. So I don't, and you don't either. I don't pay *nobody's* bail. But what they *lose*, I take."

He switched on the flashlight, banged it against his thigh to shake the batteries; it sent a cone of light across the bent-down stubble of the pasture.

Handing me the light, he went on, "You don't know how to slough the joints and rides, so you keep out of the way. Look for dropped change. Be careful of spit, light makes it shine like a quarter, so don't feel 'less you're sure. Bring me what you find, I'll settle up later. Now scoot."

He left me to walk around bent over, scanning the ground with slow-moving arcs of the rancid yellow beam. Sure enough, I spotted perfect round glints of copper or silver, and my pocket grew heavy. As I looked, I'd sneak a peek at Maeve's trailer, whose curtains glowed pink from within. A dusky pink that made me quiver inside, almost instinctively. When I saw her wavering shadow, I almost took off at a run for that radiant window; if I ran fast enough, and quietly, I could've made out what was behind those rosy curtains. But

Shea was everywhere, yelling, pulling, giving orders, occasionally lapsing into his Gaelic lingo.

Dutifully, I ran the beam over every trod bit of grass; every so often I pocketed a penny or nickel. It wasn't until about twenty minutes later that I managed to work my way to her trailer—just as her light winked off, leaving a patch of blackness against the silvery shine of her Airstream. I couldn't resist running my hand along the length of her cool white car, the paint skin-smooth under my fingers. Then Shea was pounding sod behind me, demanding the change and the flashlight. He made me turn out both pockets; they hung limp and defeated in the moonlight. I'd found $1.35—Harry let me keep two bits.

There and then I decided to slip a dime or two into the sides of my shoes when I searched out change the next night. *And* to start looking a little closer to where Maeve parked her trailer. (Lord, the things ignorance can fool a body into being party to. I looked *forward* to standing next to her trailer while those pink curtains were lit from behind—but then, it wasn't *July* yet.)

After Shea left for his trailer, I went to Larry's camper. On the way, I heard the kootchie tent girls doing a little after-hours *entertaining* in the beat-up old school bus they used as a trailer, and hoped for their sake the men were ride jocks. When I saw my mattress flopped out onto the ground next to the camper, and listened briefly at the screen door, I realized that what Larry was doing would make Shea *awfully* unhappy if he were to find out about it.

Sighing, I stretched out on the mattress, and pulled the blanket crumpled alongside it over me, hoping that no from-town woman had seen fit to sneak into the *geek* trailer . . . but not willing to discount it, either. But, as I said, ignorance can fool a person into doing almost *anything*.

SIXTY-ONE

Haunted and obsessed with the crooning voice that floated across the river to him, Winston was afraid to cross the water unless he could find the means to become less than sober. If he were intoxicated, and whatever was waiting for him *was* too awful for belief, he'd be armed with the comforting option of not *having* to believe what he saw. Considering that this *was* either Heaven or Hell, liquor should've been available— either for his reward, or to further his degradation.

But after Winston wandered the quiet and murky streets, peering into the bars he'd frequented all his life, no window revealed the amber or clear wink of bottles within. A new fear gripped him—suppose this place was *dry*. As in the Prohibition times of his birth? When the old saloons served soda and sandwiches. The irony made him laugh, a keen, bitter cackle that echoed the uninhabited streets, providing an eerie counterpoint to the cries northwest of him.

Not quite wanting to do a hands-on search of each house or bar, he ambled down the center of each street, eyes locked on the forward movement of each foot, reminiscing about the good old days . . . with Una. Not only had she shared his passion for . . . passion, but she'd lifted her glass with the best of them. Which happened to be him.

Una . . . his perfect soul mate. Drank like a man, screwed like a whore, and even liked to shoot and hunt. But . . . Una shot to *kill*, he remembered with nose-wrinkling distaste. Not just shooting to break apart clay pigeons at the gravel pit south of town, as Winston liked to do.

Unfortunately, Una loved to kill small animals when the urge took her; being a woman who was slave to urges of *all* sorts, she paid little or no attention to the dictates of the law when it came to shooting game. She loved to see the light go out in the eyes of living things . . . be it by crushing the spirit of a hated pupil, or by using her rifle to rob the very life of soft-furred things in the woods.

She was the only *girl* ever taken on a snipe hunt by her father . . . and come sunrise, she didn't want to go home. Her father bragged uptown that Una was "real disappointed" that no snipe existed. She'd been itching to see and smell the blood running out of the bullet hole.

Years later, long after the fire of passion between Winston and Una was doused with liquor, she still ached to slash and kill. Loading the Olds with flashlights and spare batteries, plus rifles in the trunk, they'd take off down Maple Road, just like Winston and Palmer had done many a night before. Whenever their lights caught the reddish coin-shaped glow of frightened animal eyes, Una would suck in her breath, muttering something about "wall-eyes" as best as Winston could make out. He never asked her to repeat herself.

But when shots were fired, they were never fired from *his* rifle. He didn't enjoy it, but went along to keep Una from decimating the entire woods.

Una was unable to resist bragging about her nocturnal adventures. One night, as Una trained her beam on a pair of wild eyes, the woods lit up with a rotating red and white glow. Making tracks to the Olds, they pulled away at eighty miles an hour. As he drove, headlights off, until the flashing lights became Christmas-tree tiny behind them, he laid down the law. No more shining, shooting, or even sighting with an empty gun. In the faint glow of moonlight, Una's wrinkled puss puckered with displeasure. "You're no *fun*," she pouted, then crossed her arms and sat in strained silence all the way home.

Two months later, after the bulletin-board incident, the school board had to say, "Enough's *enough*."

Now, as he reached Lumbermill Drive, Winston waffled over whether or not to head for the bridge nearby, or keep walking to the end of the street. He said aloud, "Damn kid didn't realize she only made things worse by telling the cops . . . drove Una *crazy* when her shining was taken away."

SIXTY-TWO

From Palmer Nemmitz's journal—

Five-inch mattress or not, I didn't get the world's best sleep that night; when I wasn't batting off mosquitoes, I was dreaming of Maeve. But every time I approached her—just to talk, mind—Mae pushed me away, jabbing me with little fingers that poked like sharp sticks. Just over Maeve's shoulder, I saw the geek, loping and slobbering, leaving a trail of runs in its wake. No matter where Maeve carried Mae, the geek trailed behind, a shadow with form and dimension. As the geek reached for her with brown-caked fingers, I woke up. My mattress was the lone dry spot on the ground; all around, the rough, flattened grass was beaded with tiny drops of dew, and in many places there were finely woven canopies of dewy webbing, resting in patches on the ground.

When Winston and I were small, he used to peer under the white patches of dew-embroidered mesh, believing that Teenie Weenies (of funny-paper fame) camped out under there. More often than not, he demolished the delicate water and webbing fabric, yet he kept searching, always sure that he would capture a Teenie Weenie of his own; put it in a card house when he got home. After he discovered girls, the Teenie Weenie hunt was forgotten.

I wished that *I'd* forgotten about The Tent, but come morning, Larry made me take a plate of fried oatmeal and a bottle of rye to the horse trailer where it slept. Breathing through my mouth, peering through an obscuring veil of lowered lashes, I could barely make out the geek—or smell his ripeness—when I slid the tin plate and opened bottle into its den. I ran back so fast even the kootchie girls laughed.

It was all I could do to swallow down that pancake-shaped mass of oozing oatmeal; eating, I kept my silence, as did most of the bleary-eyed carnies at the plank table. Then it was time—this was close to dawn—to sweep out the animal cages, feed and water the animals prior to going on the road. Chatty the bobcat nearly licked the skin off my arm; she liked me that much. The carny was ready to roll come quarter to six. I'd thought farm chores were hard. At least no one had insulted me yet, called me a bastard, so I figured things could be a lot worse—

—*little runt, she said, glaring at me, and I couldn't back away fast enough . . . then it was oh, please, please all over again*—

—and before we left, Larry sent me into town to buy some pies for Moby Sourpuss. When I reached the Blue Tulip, Minnie was just opening up. Her supply of pies was almost wiped out again, but she was nice about it, asking me if I liked my job. Wondering if *she'd* liked the geek, and dreamed of his smearing embrace, I told her things were fine—I had a five-inch mattress.

Funny, how that's the best thing about the job that came to mind.

After I left, pies balanced on my arms like a waiter at noon rush, I kicked myself for not thanking her again for the job tip. Once the summer was over, she was lucky I didn't return to her safe little cafe and kick the carp out of her for bringing up that carny job—even if I *had* wormed the information out of her.

My arms ached by the time I reached the Fat Lady's converted pickup truck home (blue curtains and plants in the makeshift windows); she took the pies with nary a thank you. It was a relief to climb into Larry's battered Ford, lean back and rest while he pulled out of the pasture, closely following Maeve's Airstream.

I'd caught only a glimpse of her, while washing up at the Higgins' pump; her left arm was in a sling, with the tips of her red-nailed fingers sticking out. After seeing Mae last night, I figured the dummy was a real armful. Massaging my aching forearms, still tense after I balanced four pies for over a mile, I wished I had a couple of slings myself. Larry watched Maeve step out of her trailer and get into her car, her dark blue flower-patterned skirt billowing out around her calves, and remarked, "Always wears that sling . . . claims the puppet weighs a ton, an' she can't rest it on her knee like Edgar Bergen. Should see how she steers single-handed. Uses her knees to guide the wheel while she works the clutch. Easier to slip that sling off f' a few seconds, but if she does *that*, folks'll quit *doin'* f' her. Might chip off that purty nail polish. *Pays* one of the girls to do laundry for her . . . some folks is just *mighty* special." He said more, but by then we were passing through the town whose name I've forgotten.

The gas-station gossips were in place behind the pumps; I waved to each in turn, and then we were on a flat road leading south. The sun beat down in yellow-hot waves, making the inside of the Ford an inferno, even with the windows down . . . like a preview of Hell, before death and damnation claim a soul forever.

Brent's vision was swimming with greenish, tightly packed letters against fuzzy blackness when he closed his aching eyes. He heard Palmer yell, "Food's done . . . I've been in the kitchen *all day*, so you'd better appreciate it," in a wicked parody of Bitsy. For a second Brent was disoriented; he'd expected his uncle to sound like the teen he was in the summer of '40—not like the old man calling him to come downstairs. An old man who never really grew up.

Over their bowls of chicken and rice soup, neither man spoke, but Brent noticed that Palmer was keyed up over *something*. He kept missing his mouth; his faded blue plaid shirt was soup-dotted by the time he was halfway through the meal.

Tipping his bowl to catch the last spoonful, Brent casually asked, "What's new uptown?"

Swallowing loudly, Adam's apple bobbing under the slack covering of crepe skin, Palmer remarked, "Would you believe, Winston wore his old Army uniform to some wedding on Saturday? 'Fore he took off?"

Wondering if his uncle had gone heat-crazy, he carefully replied, "Oh? Someone tell you that?"

"No no no. Went to his *apartment*. With one of Stu's boys. Wondered if I could tell if any of his clothes were gone. Winston broke into his memory box, one with his Army medals in it. Didn't tell the deputy, though. *He* let it slip about Winston being in uniform when he—"

"If it has you this rattled, why don't you ask Stu about—"

"He and I don't get on." Palmer helped himself to more soup.

"Then have *Bitsy* ask him," Brent said, annoyed by the whole conversation—as if what the old letch wore when he left really *mattered*. He could've been buck naked for all Brent cared.

"Not talking to her either." Palmer's mouth was set in a

hard line. In exasperation Brent began, ''Then I don't see why it matters what he was wear—'' when he realized how very important it was what Winston wore that night. Pushing himself away from the table, Brent said, ''Those Army uniforms in the trunk—the ones covered with Winston's books—''

''Wait—before I say more, how much of *it* have you read?''

Feeling as if he were trapped in an inane game of Twenty Questions, Brent told his uncle where he left off reading (resisting the urge to shake him by the shoulders and shout, ''What the hell *did* you do to that poor girl?'').

''Just keep going. It's told better there than I can tell you in person. I'm going downstairs . . . scat.'' Puzzled and miffed by the childish treatment he'd received, Brent clomped back upstairs, to the waiting manuscript.

Palmer's footsteps were loud, raspy on the concrete as he walked to the black trunk. Tossing aside school books, he searched the trunk until his fingers met the paper lining on the bottom.

There were only two uniforms, Enoch's and Vern's. The dress uniform Bitsy had bought on impulse at the church rummage sale the fall before Una died was missing. Shirt, tie, hat, all had vanished. And she'd bought the whole outfit, hating to see it get tossed along with all the other unsalable things, with the best pieces stuffed in boxes bound for missionaries in Africa, and the worst hacked apart for quilts or braid rugs, also mission-bound. Winston's uniform had rested untouched, and unseen in that trunk for years. Only the Nemmitzs knew of it; Palmer hadn't told Winston of Bitsy's purchase, hadn't wanted to dredge up bad memories.

Brent, snooping around down here, had seen the three suits, but was too good a boy to mention his find until minutes ago. Palmer doubted that Brent had given the uniform to Winston—Brent obviously hated the old man. Without asking, Palmer knew that Bitsy hadn't touched it since placing it in the trunk.

Replacing the contents of the trunk, closing the lid with a muted bang, Palmer scratched his forearm, musing, ''She must've thought you'd be needing it, old friend. Wonder what *you* did to her.''

SIXTY-THREE

As the sun slid gently into the far shore beyond the river, Winston was overcome by a crying need for liquor—whiskey, beer, cough medicine, his body wasn't choosy anymore. A live, coiled thing writhed in his guts, sending tender shoots of pain into his limbs, his head. From where he stood, propped up against the fire hall, Winston saw the thumblike protrusion of the Winston house up on Ewert Hill. Inside, there would be liquor.

In a private haze that obscured his vision, he lurched up the hill, cutting across lawns, until he reached the long set of steps leading to his boyhood home. The slope of driveway that would've brought him up to the brick porch was insanely, impossibly slanted, more so than he remembered it from his boyhood. Winston swayed in place before the first step. His feet were leaden, unable to lift high enough off the ground for him to mount the first step.

"One, two, uh . . . *one, two*—" he tried, but the words Porter had taught him were gone. Biting his lips, Winston stared up at the house. Redoubled fear gripped him when he remembered what waited within the house on Myrtle Street, competing with his gnawing booze-hunger. Able to climb the stairs or not, he could no longer face the thought of entering his former home, to perhaps hear something he *couldn't* explain away . . . a gurgling death rattle, or the thrashing of his parents in their urine-sodden beds. Noises not easily attributable to squeaking stair treads.

When a lull in his dual pain allowed him to walk without falling to his shaking knees, Winston went back into town, pausing to peer through windows again, as if a second go-around would reveal liquor he'd missed before. But all he saw was clothing, shoes, and merchandise, all predating 1940 or so. It was hard to tell; Ewerton was usually years behind when it came to fashion, especially after the Crash.

Leaning against darkened windows, leaving hand prints that hung, ghostlike, on smooth glass as he passed on down the line of stores, he decided, *If this is Hell, wouldn't a run-down Depression Hell be more appropriate? This place isn't as gone-to-seed as I remember it. Whatever this place is, it isn't a place of punishment . . . not in a self-deprecating sense. It likes itself.*

Street lamps winked on, and prismatic outlines reappeared around each object and building touched by the golden glow. Winston's shaking fear returned. For the coaxing voice, silent for many hours, came again to lull him into a lustful stupor. Fighting the urge to head for the woods, to find the source of that siren call, he took off instinctively for Roberts Street.

His knee-quivering trek came to an end only when he stood in front of the Holiday house. *Father's house*, came the tiny, soft voice, with unexpected insistence, drowning out his attempts to quiet it.

In the street lamp's glow, the house was stately, grand, bunting hanging down in sweeping curves against the porch railing. Between the strains of the *Father's house* litany, Winston recalled how the house had been ridiculed for years. But even in boyhood, Winston had loved the Holiday house, found it irresistible in its oddness and extravagance.

Unable to stop himself, he stepped onto the porch; after touching the cool brass knob, he jumped back a couple of steps when the stained-glass insert lit up in a jewel-bright blaze of color. Panting, Winston glanced around. *All* the ground-floor windows on his side of the house were yellow-white with light, bright rectangles topped with glowing bands of colored glass. No shadows moved within, but he pounded on the door anyway, until both fists ached.

Resolutely, he fumbled with the knob, leaning against the door as he attempted to pry it open, as the nagging voice repeated the same gentle message, until—"All *right* then . . . Mother wasn't any better than Nemmitz's mother . . . *satisfied*?"

His voice was ragged, mocking, but as he tried the lock, it *gave* under his shaking fingers, as if in reward for his admission. Just as the bolt retracted, he added, "Like hell he's my—" The bolt snapped back with an audible *click!*

Frantically, he twisted the knob, rattling the heavy door, then rested his forehead against the carved varnished wood. Faintly, he heard someone moving behind the closed, locked door, inside the house . . . followed by heavy, slow footsteps. Almost *sad* in their steady plod away from the door. No squeaking stair caused *that* sound.

Again he pounded the door, trying to look through the

thick chunks of colored glass, but his vision was obscured by gathered curtains hung on the other side. Only when his knuckles hurt to the point of making him cry did he stop his frenzied knocking. He'd been too proud to beg with the unseen occupant, but now, rubbing his aching fingers, he sobbed, ''Open up . . . *please*, oh, please, *please* . . . I can't *stay* out here!'' But all he heard was the faint crooning of his voice from far away.

Sniffing back tears, wiping his nose on his sleeve (the row of buttons on the cuff raked his sore nostrils), Winston stumbled off the porch, back toward town. Behind him a window shade was pulled aside upstairs.

Winston sat on the bench he used to share with Palmer, curved back slats supporting his slumping spine, eating a candy bar from the lobby of the movie house up the avenue. The doors had been propped open—by whom he didn't know, or *care* to know—the lit marquee surrounding an empty space where the name of the feature should've gone. In the frosty lobby, he'd spied a counter loaded with candy bars. Hunger got the better of him; he ran in, grabbed a bar, and ran out, before he had the time to hear anything he didn't want to hear. He'd ripped the wrapper off before reading the label, but thought he was eating a Stardust Bar.

As he chewed, barely able to swallow, he was serenaded by the singsong voice, each syllable of his name drawn out, faint. To distract himself, he looked up and down the well-lit street, noticing for the first time the cars parked along the curbs. Odd, he didn't remember *them* before—he used to love to drive for miles without stopping. Before old age ruined his night vision.

But now, his eyesight was just fine in darkness, as good as it ever was. *So* good, in fact, that he observed something that sent out an alarm that spread through his entire body, leaving him tense, doubly alert. None of these cars were later than '23 or '24 models—not unusual in itself, since few families in town could afford new cars each year—but as he scrutinized the license plates, he saw that he'd been off in his estimation of the era of this place. In 1940, Wisconsin plates were light-colored, with only four numbers instead of the usual six for the previous years. Light-on-dark skinny plates with the numbers ''23'' and ''24''—his night vision was nothing short of *miraculous* now—stamped into the thick metal, along with only *five* numbers. The last time he'd seen a license plate with only five numbers was when he was about five years old.

Gulping down the last of his candy, Winston saw Wilbur Holiday's 1922 Case Model X Sedan parked near his store. Getting to his feet, rocking slightly, Winston took a second look in the storefronts.

The clothing in the windows was different. From the twenties, when he was a baby. He'd seen photographs of his parents and their clique dressed in such attire; some of those pictures were taken the summer *before* the year of his birth. Summer of 1923, to be precise.

The concrete beneath his feet felt as if it had turned to quicksand between one step and the next. Winston slumped against a cool window; where his cheek rested on the glass, a slick chill rippled through his shaking body.

It all *changed.* As he'd wandered, the rest of this . . . *place* had altered. Subtly, years had rolled away, stripping him of all that he vaguely remembered, snatching away the remotely familiar, the *comforting.* Anything he could cling to in hope of keeping his sanity.

While the far-off voice gibbered, wailing his name, Winston tried to breathe evenly, telling himself, *It's trying to remind me of something. 1940 wasn't right . . . it's like . . . this place wasn't* satisfied *somehow. . . .*

But it wasn't *fair*—how could he be expected to remember something that happened the year he was *born*? Or before his birth? Smart as all those Army IQ tests said he was, wasn't that expecting an awful *lot* from him?

It was just too much to try to puzzle out in his condition— he needed a drink so badly his teeth ached and his bones jittered in his skin. Not to mention his need for a smoke, even a smashed butt. And that *voice*, calling, calling. . . . He'd figure this mess out later, when he wasn't torn apart in a dozen different directions by pain, need, loneliness, and fear. When the tumult of emotions gripped him in the midsection like the hard pinch of a vise, he hugged himself, rocking back and forth as fireflies circled his bent form. They made lazy circles around the strange being whose cries tore the air with a forlorn, keening howl, in discordant harmony with the wails drifting across the cold, lapping river.

SIXTY-FOUR

From Palmer Nemmitz's journal—
If anyone knew the worth of that carny (*excuse* for a carny
was more like it), it was Harold Shea—and *he* bought the
whole shebang for a song himself. According to Larry, Shea,
his wife, and her brother purchased the carnival, thinking it
would be an idyllic, playful pastime well suited to three
middle-aged people. Having bought it in the depths of the
Depression, from an owner very anxious to sell out, Harold
was led to believe that he was getting a bargain.

By the time I'd found my hole there, Harold was in a state
that bordered on not caring about *anything* anymore, save for
his fervent desire to keep on the good side of the law. Larry
claimed that making bail for any malcontent in Shea's employ
would've broke the bank. Shea's brother-in-law was the advance man, making the arrangements for where we'd play,
and Harold did what work he did because he was short-
handed, a situation that didn't improve after we did our last
show in Indiana before crossing over into Kentucky. The ride
jock who manned the merry-go-round took off, and once we
hit Kentucky, the six-fingered and -toed girl, Nancy
Something-or-Other, left in the middle of the night, taking
only her valise and bottle of nail polish.

That Kentucky show was the first one I worked as jointee
in Larry's booth, working the play and manipulating the G's
(gaffs) on the wheel, so Larry could do back-to-back shows
in The Tent. He and I cut what I earned in the joint fifty-fifty,
which amounted to him *still* earning something from his joint,
plus what his geek pulled in. And that meant I was getting
more cash, too. Often enough to rent myself a cheap room
in whatever rooming house was close by the carny. I could
wash up, buy new underwear and socks. Enough to stay human, enough to keep me from going totally carny. Also, talking the game took my mind off Maeve. I could no longer
follow her around. And, taking Harold up on his advice, I
managed to find some comfort with one of the kootchie girls.

As we passed on the diagonal through the thickest part of
Kentucky, Larry asked me if I knew how to drive. I'd driven

the old man's John Deere, and taken turns behind the wheel of Winston's truck, so I agreed to take control of the wheel—and avoided unfolding and refolding those road maps Larry had stuck up under the sun flaps.

He had half a dozen of them tucked up in there; not the kind they sell *now*, but the *old* kind of state road maps. The big ones, that *came* wrinkled and thumb printed, with frayed creases just where you needed to find the name of a town. The kind that never folded up flat, but assumed puffy shapes unknown to geometry or nature. The ones with the main roads in a tracery of red, like a frayed body lacking skin to cover its network of veins and arteries, and the back roads in blue.

Mainly, the carny followed the blue roads, going from hick town to hick burg to hick flyspeck on the side of the road, always a couple of days behind the advance man, with his crudely printed set of posters stashed in his car, setting up and moving on until winter came, and the carny bedded down in Florida.

Whatever Harry paid his brother-in-law, the man deserved double; he managed to drum up enthusiasm and anticipation among people who could've put on a better show themselves for half the cost. The midway was always midling crowded, and the marks seldom left disappointed—why they *weren't* was beyond me.

Actually, since Larry never drove lead, he didn't *need* any maps to guide him—Shea led the carny into each new town—but nonetheless, Larry pulled down the maps each morning, pouring over them as I drove, recounting the memories associated with each town. It became a ritual; me steering, and him unfolding one of those fine-lined maps. Patting the folded and creased paper out nearly flat against his ample lap and the dashboard, he traced lines with a dark-rimmed finger, reading off town names with the fond nostalgia of a schoolgirl looking over prom mementos. And each town came with a story.

Take down the map of Kentucky—

"See Broadwell, south of Cynthiana? Was *near* Broadwell, pissant burg couple o' miles out, we picked up Moby Jackie. Was *Miss* Lynne B. Jackson, then. Come to the carny fresh from gettin' the lock picked—what s'prised me was some fella found a way to fit his key in all that flab in the *first* place—least that's what she tole one o' the girls. Joined on when the cotton-candy lady quit. Ate her way through what wasn't sellin' too good. Then the 'riginal Fat Lady, Ju-Ju-Bee—wore Mary Janes big 'nough to use f' canoe paddles—got hitched to some skinny mark who followed the show six nights runnin'. Harold decided *Miss* Jackson would make a dandy Fat Lady. Force-fed her chess pies an' Mississippi mud pies an' whatnot. F' while a ride jock bedded with her, but one night she poured a whole bottle o' Pepsi-Cola on the fella's head while he was dozin'. Seen the bottle an' soaked pillow in a ditch.''

Pull down the map again, farther down-state—

"Morris Fork's where I picked up the geek. Shea had a conniption fit when I brung *him* back in the opened truck o' the car on 'count I didden want him pissin' or pukin' on the 'pholstery. Shea was fit to be tied, how I couldn't *do* that, his show was *clean*, f' the *family*, but I tole him I'd pay f' the chickens an' shine outta my own pocket, kick in f' his chow. Money it earns I share w' Harold, mind, to pay f' The Tent, an' pen, but if I gave him the money on a silver *platter*, he'd say the platter needed polishin'. Keeps tellin' me, 'Larry, my carny needs a *real* freak, a *good* one. So people won't want your *buddy*.' But he ain't never found hisself a *good* 'un. Somethin' Tod Brownin' missed. Harold's hadda make do, havin' his wife paint up Daisy-Denny.''

Peer at the map of Tennessee, as low-growing trees lining the narrow dirt road slap the windshield—

"See the city north of here? Knoxville? When we pass a big city, I gots to go an' find a real newspaper for Jomel, that creamy-faced kootchie I seen you eyein'—don't deny it, I seen you lookin'—that's why I took off last Wednesday. Buy her that paper. She's innerested in what Hitler's doin' over in Germany. Claims we're gonna get sucked in the mess real bad. Like the fate o' the world 'pends on her readin' 'bout somethin' that don't concern her.

"Them folks had the chance to immigrate here, an' if they liked where they was, that their fault. Maybe Jomel can stop ol' Adolf by shakin' her privates in his face. But I heard he likes 'em *blue*-eyed—''

Skirting the Appalachian Mountains, trace their outline on white-whorled paper—

"Was near Chattanooga Maeve latched on. Drove up, trailer attached to her car like she'd been travelin' 'round on her own an' planned to keep doin' so. Got outta that car come the start o' the show, in that black suit. Stickpin in her lapel,

coat draped 'cross one shoulder. Like Joan Crawford steppin'
up the front walk o' Grauman's in Hollywood-land. Had her
figured for a kootchie girl—that slow sway to her ass.

"Didn't look like nothin' else in that crowd, didn't talk
like no one, either. All of a sudden, she goes into her act,
w'out preamble. Not five feet from my joint, I hear this nasty
little voice sayin', 'Don't *I* get a chance to look around?'

"In a sugary voice, Maeve sez, 'Of *course*, Mae,' an' off
comes the coat, an' out comes the puppet. Thought Harold
was gonna swallow his tongue an' wisdom teeth when she
started jabberin' with that puppet. Shea hired her on the spot,
but 'stead of jumpin' f' joy at gettin' herself a job, all she
done is give 'im that smile that *ain't* no smile, sayin', 'I won't
work the *freak* top, or that tent over *there*.' Harold was
pantin' like a puppy dog 'cause *he* hired hisself a top-rate
draw f' peanuts an' didden want her drivin' off outta pique.
Could tell there an' then she didden think her shit 'tracted
flies. Like she's doin' him this *big* favor by joinin' on. Harold
claims she keeps the marks from wanderin' off too soon.

"*I'd* make her shake that rear end for cash money . . .
make her puppet do a little shimmy, too—"

Driving through the Appalachians—

"Not two miles from here, some snake worshipers tossed
a live rattler in the pit, tryin' to put the Lord into the geek.
Nearly tanned their hides after makin' them crawl in there t'
get that rattler outta there."

Take down the map of Georgia, point at a certain spot—

"Sonoraville's where that mentalist I tole you 'bout hailed
from. Monsieur Hypnotique was his stage name. Ol' hag used
to own the Tarot readin' joint, 'fore I bought it an' changed
it to a wheel joint, name of Madam Zola, *she* tole me the
mentalist's name as Quigley. Redheaded fella, whiter skinned
than Harold an' not freckled, neither.

"Had *moles*, three o' 'em, right *here*.

"Talked Frog talk, all 'deeze' and 'zee'—folks didden mind
long as he was good at what he did.

"When I joined the carny, it hit me real sad t' find out he
was long dead. 'Cause I seen him once, back home.

"Zola claimed he blew his brains out, somewhere north,
real north, like where you come from—

"Oh, I *know* you only tole me 'north.' I got ears—

"Sure, I been up *north*, think I'm *chained* to this carny

come winter? I got ears, I remembers—dialects is somethin' of a hobby w' me, kid.

"You talk like folks from Minnesota, Wisconsin. *Think* Zola said it was up Minnesota way. Claimed it was a real bad place, an' tried to rid her mind of it once she left. Said the town *felt* wrong, an' the people were real strange. 'Specially a few she done readin's for. Cards said they was *no good*. Threw out the deck 'cause the cards was *tainted* by them. " 'Fore she took off, Madam Zola tole me the carny went sour on 'count of Quigley dyin' in that town up north. Left me her other cards, couple of packs. Gaffed the wheel myself . . . even Harold don't s'pect all the G's on it—an' don't you go tellin' him, neither—"

Larry didn't have to worry about me informing Shea about the gaffed wheel; if Harold wanted to live with the illusion of innocence, it wasn't up to me to demolish his fantasy world. Sometimes a body has to act blind to keep sane. Shea and I stayed out of each other's way, except for our nightly exchange of flashlight and coins. And he never noticed that I walked sort of funny sometimes, because of the coins I'd tucked in my shoes when his back was turned. The knotted sock at the bottom of my knapsack held over three dollars in change by the time we reached Georgia in July.

Shoving the odd coin in my shoe wasn't the only trick I'd learned by the time I reached Georgia—by then I was smart enough to place myself close by Maeve's trailer and luminous white car after each night's show; after Harry gave me the light I lingered near her pink-curtained window for a few minutes . . . long before the light winked off inside. As we went farther south, and the heat grew solid, oppressive, Maeve began opening her windows to let in the cool night air (leaving her curtains pulled, though). Sometimes I heard her practicing her routine, her voice slipping from Mae's treble to her own alto, a fluid verbal ballet that was truly something to hear. Only she did it soft, so as not to keep folks awake.

The changing flow of her voice reminded me of my sisters Effie and Merle exchanging sister talk under the covers of their shared bed. That was the only time I heard Maeve speak anymore. The rest of the time she kept to herself, occasionally talking with Jomel, the newspaper-reading kootchie girl (who also washed and hung out Maeve's lovely, lacy clothing). Maeve only appeared at meal times long enough to open her door and accept the plate and cutlery Jomel brought her.

She didn't sit in the shade after lunch, and she didn't venture into town. I don't know how she got her woman things, maybe Jomel bought them for her.

I'd been with the carny for five weeks, and Maeve hadn't talked to me once since that first night. Yet, that short conversation had been enough to sustain me; keep me tagging in her shadow, hoping against hope that something would happen to make it natural, even *necessary* to talk to her again. It wasn't as if she were the most beautiful girl I'd ever met— there were girls in Ewerton who were prettier in that fleeting, fast-blooming way that fades before a girl reaches twenty or so—but the play of sunlight on her hair was a *magical* thing.

Turned it into a blaze of mixed browns and blond and red and near-white, the strands shifting color, depending on what direction her head moved. And her turned-out eyes were strange, ringed in blue *and* brown.

And I'll admit, even for a woman of her times, before it was fashionable to look as gaunt as a plague victim, Maeve was a well-built girl. Not *fat*, but well fleshed, the kind of girl who withstands more than a slight touch. Yet refined, not rawboned, or coarse. like Vernilla.

There was a certain *something* in the careful way she walked, and held herself, that suggested a different sort of upbringing than her fellow carnies had experienced—the kind of upbringing that makes jealousy blaze like a cat's eyes caught in the beam of a flashlight. Despite her quiet demeanor, she didn't hide her light under a bushel. Not the way she'd hurry out of her trailer to wipe away whatever dust or mud dared adhere to the running boards or fenders of her Pierce-Arrow. Not with a rag, but a good washcloth, followed by a drying rub of a towel with colored bands along the edges. Only well-to-do people used to buy *those*. And she did that in a carny where the sides of the trucks hadn't had the letters freshened in years.

Every time Maeve darted out of her trailer, towels and washcloth tucked in her sling, Larry would snidely remark, "Wonder if she rubs that ol' washcloth all over *herself* in her trailer? Or is that her *car-washin'* set?" I don't believe Larry had more than one washcloth to his name, and *it* was packed away under his beer cans and Tijuana Bibles. A splash of cool water on his face and under his arms from a gas-station sink was enough to suit Larry. At least the stink from the tents and animal cages made him bearable—compared with a walk downwind of the geek trailer, Larry was a bed of roses.

From the time I hired on, Larry had me feed the geek, shoving plates of food and the obligatory bottle into the open end of the trailer, and reclaiming the empties in an hour. Larry ordered the geek into its filth-matted costume each night—how I never learned. There are some things no person should *have* to learn.

So, I'd assumed that my geek duties were merely to sweep out what filth I could reach with the animal broom, and let Larry handle the rest. After all, the geek was his find. But all the times Larry'd talked to me over his weathered highway maps, giving me the history of the carny, he did neglect to tell me one *little* detail. *I* was supposed to make the geek's open pen clean enough for an animal to live in, let alone a booze-sweating thing that decapitated live chickens with its mossy teeth. And as luck would have it, I found this out courtesy of Harold Shea. . . .

It was the morning of the eighteenth. A Thursday—my special day because I was born on a Thursday one week before Palmer Winston's Thursday arrival.

The eighteenth was the sixth Thursday I'd spent at the carny, the fifth since Maeve last spoke to me. It started out like the other days had begun: breakfast of fried oatmeal and biscuits, washed down with oily coffee; then set up the tents, the big diesel generators, and the like. But I never got a chance to help out that morning, for Shea caught me by the upper arm just as I was leaving the plank table after breakfast. Dragging me in the direction of the geek's trailer, he asked, "Kid, you been cleaning that . . . *trailer*?"

I nodded, but he shook his head. "I don't believe it, and *this* is why!" We stood in front of the dark, pitlike opening of the horse trailer, and even with the partial door latched, the smell was so fierce I almost upchucked there and then. Shaking my arm, Harold yelled, "When was the last time you got in there and *cleaned*, huh, kiddo? When? Yesterday? Last *week*? Last *month*? EVER?"

As his voice rose, his cheeks flamed under the dusting of freckles covering his nose and upper cheeks. People made themselves *real* scarce. It was as if there were nothing in the universe but me, Shea, and the geek. Staring at the scuffed tips of my shoes, I shook my head, eyes watering from the ammonia reek of the green-painted trailer.

Harold gave me a warning shake that sent hair spilling over my eyes, saying, "You wait *here*!" and strode off in the direction of the animal cages. I breathed through my mouth until he came back and shoved a pail and an animal broom into my hands. Pointing to the pump at the far end of the abandoned schoolhouse playground where the carny was set up that day, Shea barked, "Fill this bucket and leave the bar of soap in the bottom so it suds up. Give that trailer a good washing out, and if my eyes water the next time I pass by here, you'll scrub it out with a toothbrush, *understand*?" Without waiting for an answer, he stalked off, sending up little puffs of dust with his pounding heels.

I didn't look back at him while the bucket filled, but watched the water churn up oily bubbles off that white bar of soap. I stopped pumping when the water reached the rim, close to the wire handle. All the way back to the trailer—half expecting the waves of stink to ripple like heat devils on pavement—I thought, *Barn, a little, smelly barn.* . . .

I held on to that thought as I opened the half door, shedding light on what lay sprawled on a bed of soiled straw. The remains of its last bottle rested on its dirt-stiffened shirtfront, glinting in the morning light. *A barn, a small barn* . . . .

I mucked out that tiny barn, careful to avoid physical contact with what lay supine and reeking before me, slopping water onto it with the wet animal broom, half noticing that it never flinched when the cold water hit it. The rag it wore for its shows hung on a bent ten-penny nail.

I was getting dizzy from trying to hold my breath.

So far, so horrible, I thought, sweeping up the last of the waste. But what I'd seen was a *cakewalk* compared to what happened next.

Jumping into the trailer for the last time, I noticed the shine of sunlight on the bottle the thing held in grime-embedded fingers. It clutched the slimy bottle the way a baby holds its nighttime bottle. I saw that the geek had the mouth of the bottle about an inch from its own mouth, and the two openings were joined by a suspension bridge of fulvous thick drool—which *also* caught the sun's rays. I watched in sick fascination as the chain of slurpy, semi-opaque drool *swayed* slightly; movement made the rope of spittle grow longer, slack, until it reached the thing's chest, a viscid umbilical between man and bottle.

Then—its faded, vacant eyes rolled away from the focus

point of the bottle, until they met mine in all their pale blue-white unholy glory. Wide pupils almost obscured colorless irises. Abruptly, something hideous dawned in those blasted eyes. *Recognition.* It was looking at me, making eye contact with *me.* I walked backward until I felt the edge of the trailer beneath my heels, but I wasn't fast enough. . . .

Its mouth parted, spittle hanging on the lower lip like viscous egg white clinging to a broken shell, as *sound* came out. Not the guttural cry the creature usually made before cracked, bleeding lips encircled the jerking, living neck of a chicken . . . but the sound of a *word.*

"Want?" I almost fell backward jumping out of the trailer, missing the steps altogether. I threw the bucket and broom to the ground before running off for the narrow gully I'd seen when we'd first come to this show's site. Bile-laced oatmeal was in my mouth, straining at my hand-shielded lips, trying to free itself. I barely ran into the deep-walled ditch, nearly tumbling head over ass as I did so, before my hand reflexively left my mouth.

I vomited all over the lank grass and large stones and rusted beer cans covering the floor of the gully—thankfully, the ditch was deep enough to hide me when I bent over. I heaved until my chest and throat hurt; so much puke came through my nose I hardly got a breath of air in my lungs. I heaved until nothing but clear bubbling spittle came up. Hot tears scalded my cheeks while I coughed. The tops of my shoes, my pants, everything was splattered with half-curdled oatmeal and coffee.

I wished I were dead; no, I wished I'd never been born, or thought of. I'd assumed that what reclined in that trailer was a thing devoid of thought, conscience, or regrets, a drinking and shitting contraption Larry wound up each night with a secret key, so it would prance and crap and kill chickens for a fifty-cents-a-head audience.

But it talked *to me. Asked* me if I *wanted* what it had in its *bottle.* That drool-encrusted Siamese twin cradled on its dirty chest.

But as I slid to my knees, trying to spit up the memory of what I'd seen and heard, my nightly prayer of the last five weeks was answered. Maeve's voice floated down to me. "Are you all right down there?"

God must've hated me something *awful.*

Part of me was wondering why the sky wasn't pitch-black,

why the air wasn't filled with merry-go-round music and the
cloying smell of candy and hot dogs . . . the only thing that
was the same was the puddle of vomit at my feet, and her
eyes boring into my back.

Her voice came from directly behind and above me. If she
wore her black suit, and carried that damned hunk of carved
wood, I was ready to scream like a woman.

I rubbed the tips of my shoes in the damp grass and tore
up handfuls of it to brush off my pants as best I could. I was
wishing with part of my soul that Maeve would take the hint
and go away, back to her silvery bullet of a trailer, yet another
part of me said, *Once you've puked in front of someone—
twice—you haven't much to lose.*

As I tried to make up my mind what to do, what to say,
Maeve spoke up again. "Would a Bromo help? Bottle of 7-
Up?"

With "now or never" desperation, I unsteadily got to my
feet and turned around. Maeve did stand above me, but far
enough back so that I couldn't look straight up and under the
skirt of her dark blue nylon dress. She had her sling on, made
from an old bedsheet, and tied in a knotted bow at the shoulder. Two points stood up like angel wings. Her expression,
while not openly amused, seemed *bemused* by my condition.
But her eyes were kind, not condemning. She extended her
right hand to help me out of the ditch, and I almost forgot to
check mine for throw-up before grasping it and climbing up
the wall of that gully. Her fingers were small, short, attached
to a tiny palm. The inside of her hand was smooth, yet dry,
Just warm enough to suit me. I never could stand sweaty
palms, or clammy fingers.

After she helped me out of the ditch, I stood downwind of
her, so as not to be offensive. I rubbed my tongue over my
teeth, trying to get rid of the vomit before I opened my mouth.
I wished I could dart back to the camper, to get my toothbrush out of my knapsack. Even with that bile smell lining
my nose, I caught a wiff of her perfume, the same heady
scent she'd worn that first night.

Her dress sleeves were short, puffed, with blue polka-dotted
cuffs (matching the collar of the bouquet-sprinkled navy
dress). In sunlight, her right arm was a creamy pink-peach
color, with an underlay of muted bluish green where the veins
were visible under her delicately textured flesh. The way apple blossom petals look in sunlight, smooth yet finely grained,

with minuscule patterns on their surfaces that catch and hold the light in ways your mind never expected.

I didn't realize that I hadn't let go of her hand until she asked, "Would you care for something? To make you feel better? I have 7-Up, it's warm, but I could run some pump water over the bottle." For the first time, I noted an anxious undertone in her carefully modulated voice. When I looked into her eyes before replying, I saw that her pupils were large, despite the morning brightness. Deep pools of darkness in the middle of those strangely colored eyes—I saw tiny reflections of myself in her eyes, and wondered how I *really* looked to her. I wanted to slink away, but she suddenly smiled. Squeezing my hand, she asked, "Don't you want to talk to me? I won't bite—"

—I clutched my arm, feeling the sharp soreness there, and she said through lips red-black in the abrupt white light, runt, *little runt—*

That brought me to my senses; I pulled my hand away, saying, "Sure, I don't mind *talking* . . . uh, I didn't mean it to sound like—oh, damn it, I don't know what I mean. Sorry, pardon my Fren—"

Really grinning now, she took my hand again and led me to her trailer, taking care to walk as far away from the rest of the carnies as she could.

"Come on, Palmer, I'll get you something to clear your head." As I followed, her perfume swirled around us, cleaning the horrible odors from my nose.

When we reached her trailer, she said, "Wait here, be back in a minute," before disappearing into her Airstream. She reemerged with a bubbling glass of water; an Alka-Seltzer tablet fizzed on the bottom. I'd been expecting Bromo, with her shaking the mixture from glass to glass, but I figured her wrist was still sore from toting that dummy. At any rate, it wasn't polite to ask about it.

The Alka-Seltzer tasted like dead aspirin floating in rainwater that has been in a barrel for a month, but I did feel better. Stifling a burp, I handed back the glass as I excused myself, then waited in awkward silence while she reentered the trailer.

Coming out, she had 7-Up in one hand, and a second bottle tucked into her sling, the green neck and crimped cap barely visible behind the ample opaque folds of her bulky sling.

Maeve said, "There's a few trees in the back of that old schoolhouse. Shall we sit there?"

Five weeks of yearning, and now *she* was asking *me* to come sit in a private place with her. But she wasn't some girl back home, all but pulling her panties down before a boy had a chance to say "Why not?"

She had *asked* me, not told me to come along. But looking in her eyes, I realized that my not following would bother her as much or more than it would give me cause to kick myself later on. So I followed as she walked to the run-down wreck of a schoolhouse and the nodding trees beyond.

The motion of her legs made the tiny bouquets sprinkled on her dress dance and weave against the blue background like flowers blown in the wind. I was taken with her, more so than on that first night. Then, her black suit and Veronica Lake hairdo were sophisticated, movie-star glamorous and forbidding all at once. But that morning, Maeve wore her glossy hair in a simple tail down her back, and her dress was schoolgirlish, with those dotted cuffs and long collar.

I believed she might be a teenager. But unlike any teenage girls I knew. If I'd had the chance to walk hand in hand down the streets of Ewerton with her, the other girls would've wilted before her. As I said, she wasn't pretty-pretty, but had the promise of something better than prettiness, something more lasting. Yet—there was an undertone of sadness, of uncertainty, which put her at odds with herself. Sure, but not sure of herself. She never made a wrong move, but I sensed her wondering every second if she might not do something unseemly.

There was cool shade under the trees growing close to the schoolhouse. Gossamer tents of dew and spiderweb fineness dotted that shady grass where she and I sat down, each of us holding a bottle of 7-Up. Pointing at the nearest round of webbing, I told her about Winston's childhood desire to capture a Teenie-Weenie under such a "tent," as I used my church key to open my bottle, then reached over and opened hers without asking.

"He catch any?" Maeve took a deep sip of her soda, hid a burp behind her hand, then smiled to me. I wasn't sure if she was poking fun, so I took a long pull of my 7-Up (an image of the geek came and went, and my soda almost shot back into the green bottle), until she added, "When . . . *I* was a little girl, I used to think they lived in my mother's sewing basket.'' When she said that, the last of my guard came down.

Instinctively, I knew I could say *anything* to her, without fear that she'd laugh. As much as I'd talked to Larry over the past month and then some, I'd never been able to say the silly little things a person sometimes *needs* to tell another person. Things you *have* to let out, in order to be whole again. That jumbled mix of the crazy and the dead serious I used to tell Winston; the kind of things he'd tell me back. Unimportant necessities, with a little of the painful mingled in, too.

So as the shade pulled away, leaving us half in sun, half in cool shadow, we sat talking, draining our bottles and leaving them like carved vases of emerald in the shaggy grass.

Some of my jumpiness eased away for the first time since the old man aimed pitchfork tines at me. Apart from admitting that she came from a ''good'' family, Maeve volunteered little more than that she found it amusing how people dutifully sat *watching* the radio as it played, ''as if they expected to see Lamont Cranston or Jack Armstrong jump out through the speaker,'' while *I* wound up talking at great length, pouring out all the things that had remained unsaid between Winston and myself . . . including a few things I never should have said. About Ewerton, my family, my parentage.

Everything, including the truth of how Lamont Cranston's original alter-ego Orson Welles had killed our Ma, back in '38. . . .

Ma should've realized that the old man was ticked when he smashed our Kingston-Selecto-Matic against the parlor wall after Welles came on at the end of ''The War of the Worlds'' and sardonically admitted the broadcast we'd just heard was a fake, *after* we'd huddled in fear in the basement for half an hour, listening through the cracked-open door as the Martians blasted half of New Jersey to floating ash. Our Ma realized that it was a Halloween sport, but the old man didn't, even after she ran up and switched back to Edgar Bergen and Charlie McCarthy. (''Enoch, if the Martians *were* coming, wouldn't Edgar know?'')

When Welles chuckled about it all being a prank, the old man beat our Ma with his fists, anything that he could find that fit in his split-knuckled hands, and *then* he got mean. Sometime in the night she left the house, taking off for the home of my father, and the next thing we kids knew, she was dead. Within twenty-four hours she was buried—the old man was too niggardly to have her embalmed.

Maeve's kind eyes and nodding head kept me going after *that*, until I wound down by telling her how much the geek frustrated me, along with Harold's inability to make Larry get rid of the stinking thing.

Only when I reached that point did she interject something, pointing out, "Mr. Shea has little choice, Palmer. He hasn't the manpower to run this carnival half right, you see that yourself. He needs barkers in front of every freak, and we need to do shows every night, not jusy every other night or less. Most office men would've given up on this carny years ago. The geek isn't . . . *right*, but I can understand why Mr. Shea accepts the money it brings in. It's either give in a little, or have the whole carny—his entire *life*—die under him."

"If he can hire, he can fire, too," I insisted, turning over on my back. The knobs of earth under the rough grass poked my ribs and spine. Maeve's upside-down head shook as she replied, "Larry's the one who should be fired, if there's firing to be done. *He* lured that creature out of some alley with a cheap bottle. Once the geek started making money, it put Mr. Shea in a tight spot. A run-down carny has to have either a swell freak top or a geek to bring in enough money to survive, and when you're stuck with substandard freaks. . . ." Her voice trailed off as she leaned against a tree, closing her eyes.

I rolled onto my stomach, to get a better look at her while she was unawares. Her lipstick bled along the edges of her mouth, fine feathery lines of red leading away from the main color like the way her smile itself bled off into nothingness.

As if feeling my stare on her soft skin, she opened her eyes, continuing, "Mr. Shea hasn't *any* choice. His whole freak top *is* phony." The way she said "freak top" sounded like she'd bitten into something sour or spoiled. Without waiting for my opinion, she rambled, "And it's not the lack of fat or lean that makes them fakes. It's the way they don't act as freaks should. People who are . . . *different* band together, for companionship and sameness in a world that's not like them. These . . . *clods* chose to be freaks. Like Dennis. Doesn't want to work, so he lets his hair grow long and sits on his dead bottom, sipping soda all night. Nothing keeps him from being normal but bone-deep sloth. Same goes for the others, Moby Jackie, Bones, too. Poor Nancy was the closest thing this carny had for a freak, and she took off. Can't blame her, no one talked to her. Not even the ride jocks. Her life was hard . . . none of those *impostors* knows what it's like. It's so awful they can't ever begin to comprehend it—''

Anticipating that I was fixing to ask her what made *her* such an expert on the subject, she added, "Have you ever seen the film *Freaks*? By Tod Browning? Sorry, I forgot what you said about your movie house being closed. I doubt they showed it up your way anyhow. The studio pulled it quickly, but it ran where I grew up. I saw it. I was around—I was really young when I went, but I still remember it clearly. More so than *Dracula*. The freaks Browning found . . . Pinheads, three or more. A man, bisected *here*"—a red-nailed finger "cut" her across her pelvic bones—"who walked on his hands. Midgets who made Longo look normal-sized. And . . . others . . . so pitiful. Distorted, yet . . . they all *cared* for each other. Protected and accepted one another. As if they alone could comprehend their humanity even if their appearance made that humanity hard to accept.

"It was heartbreaking, how they wanted this one character, a normal woman who married a midget, to be part of their special world. I'll never forget the scene. All these people at a long table, for the midget's wedding feast. The freaks began chanting in all these odd voices, 'We accept you, we accept you.' The woman—Cleopatra—was *sickened*. But it was so touching, these freaks wanting to be one with a woman who only emphasized their strangeness. Accepting *her* into *their* fold. Ironic, for she'd never do that with them. It . . . showed who was really the better person, or persons, if you will."

She paused, throat too full to speak. Smoothing out her posy scattered dress against her extended crossed legs, she finally spoke both to and past me.

"But the most horrid thing about the movie, apart from the climax, of course, was the realization I had when I left the theater with Daddy. When *Dracula* was over, Bela Lugosi washed off his makeup and went home.

"The freaks had no makeup to remove. But *inside*, they were trapped behind the most elaborate masks in the world, hiding human souls . . . but the world couldn't think of them as human because they didn't look the part."

"I know what you mean—" I began, trying to tell her that that was *sort* of the way I'd felt at home; wanting ever since

I could recall to just be one of the Nemmitz kids, but ending up set aside because I had the eyes of a man not married to my mother. Always called "bastard" and "unnatural child" by the old man. I had all that waiting inside me, waiting to be said and heard by Maeve, but she snapped, "No you *don't*—you don't know at *all*—" and then she had this *look* on her face, as if she'd said something too deep and personal for even her ears to hear. She closed her mouth, pressing it into a wrinkled, tight line.

Before I thought of something apologetic to say, she breathed deeply, and continued in a light, casual voice, "When you and your friend Winston were small, did you ever do this trick with a Stardust Bar? My father showed me when . . . I was tiny. Said stardust was a cousin to gold dust, only silvery, and that you had to 'mine' for it—silly, isn't it?— well, it really *was* something like dowsing. I had to close my eyes, and wave my hand over the candy display like this—" Her hand shook, as if she felt water—or stardust—then swooped to the imaginary bar. With that she laughed, a hitching, bubbling sound that seemed to fight its way past her own guard to escape.

As she quieted down, I was about to ask her more about the *Freaks* movie she'd seen, hoping to gently pry out of her the reason why it upset her so much, but Larry's voice, shouting my name, shattered my chance forever. Maeve started to get to her feet; I went over to help her, but as if she was afraid of seeming too dependent, she was already standing, dusting off her skirt before I reached her side. I carried the bottles as I followed her, until she stopped, pointing at the pump I'd used earlier that morning.

"I wish this pump had a pipe so the water spurted out like a bubbler. I'm still thirsty."

I offered to pump if she held her hands under the spout to catch it; while I pumped, Larry's voice grew more insistent, but I was still seething about the geek, so I took my sweet time. Maeve cupped her free hand under the spout, until her pink palm was filled with a shimmer of water. When she slurped it up, she splashed her white collar and dark bodiee, then dried her hand on her skirt. As we walked back to her trailer, I recalled how Larry'd looked at me as if I were crazy when I used the word "bubbler" for "water fountain"— Maeve said "bubbler," too. Which meant she *might* have come from Wisconsin. I hadn't heard the term anywhere else I'd visited that summer.

In the distance, Larry kept yelling, "*Paaa*-lmer, *Paaa*-lmer"; when we reached her trailer, instead of me asking her if she was from Wisconsin, too, all I did was stammer, "M-maybe . . . we could talk again? I—I enjoyed it. With you."

By then, I was so warm-faced I wondered if my cheeks were glowing like neon. *Her* palms may've been dry, but mine were salty-slick. Placing the two bottles at her feet, I backed away, saying, "I've got to go, Larry's gonna have a fit." All Maeve said was, "Palmer, you *watch* him," before picking up the bottles and placing them in her sling. Then she went into the trailer, shutting the door quietly behind her.

I *wished* she would've said, "Yes, Palmer, I'd love to talk with you again," but at least she *hadn't* told me to get lost. Unfortunately for both of us, I completely ignored her warning about Larry.

During her routine that night, Maeve was perky, making the contrast between herself and Mae all the more obvious. Mae would've made Charlie McCarthy blush. W. C. Fields and all the Marx Brothers, too, I supposed it was our talk that morning that put her in such a tizzy. There was hardly a break where she left off speaking and switched to Mae's voice. I was jumpy myself; while running the wheel, I goofed and let two marks win Shirley Temple dolls. But I was in such an expansive mood I would've gladly given every damned mark a doll.

It had felt good to really *talk* to someone again, let alone a girl like Maeve. It made me feel things in places that didn't come alive when I had heart-to-hearts with Winston, and I'm not referring to what was stored in my shorts, either. Judging from her routine that evening (and how she hung around the wheel joint) Maeve must've felt things that were new, too . . .

When the midway wound down and Larry bawled me out for losing stock (this would be a sleep-outside night), I made my coin rounds with Harold's flashlight. As I picked up the dropped coins, I heard Maeve practicing her new act. I told myself she wasn't changing on account of *me*, that *I* couldn't have had an effect on *her*. The new routine was just that, a *routine*. An act. Fake, like all the fake freaks in the freak top.

But, later . . .

All I can say in my defense is that part of me knew that I often played the fool, but how much of one didn't occur to me until way too late. *Much* too late.

SIXTY-FIVE

Winston didn't realize that he'd dropped into a troubled, dream-infested sleep until he tried to run away across pale tan earth that sunk beneath his feet—and fell off the bench, onto the hard cement of Ewert Avenue. Blood from his scraped palms hovered on the scintillating porous surface, each droplet rimmed with rich purple-blue fire. When he stood swaying on his feet, Winston saw that the knees of his uniform pants were darkening, a spreading stain that turned the fabric a liquid black in the street lamp's glow. Raw knees shaking, he sat down hard on the bench. The force of his action jolted his bladder, reminding him that he *had* to urinate. No matter how much it hurt.

Tears hung in his lower lashes when Winston emerged from the narrow alley. As he sat down on the bench, Winston said, "I wish I was dead if I'm not . . . if I *am* dead . . . oh, *shit.*"

Raising his burning eyes, feeling hot moisture run down his sunburned cheeks, Winston noticed that everything had *changed* again. The cars were models from his late boyhood and early teens. Boxy Pontiacs, Willis-Overland 8's, and Fords, the names so reassuring when whispered aloud, like automotive prayers. And all adorned with four-numbered white-backed plates, with the new slogan stamped on the bottom, "America's Dairyland." 1940 plates.

Closing his throbbing eyes, Winston felt cravings ripple through his body—the intense, muscle-jerking *need* for something warm and burning to drink, followed by a carton or two of Lucky Strikes. Then, as if he'd needed the prompting, he remembered that summer when Palmer went away. . . .

Not until a week passed did both Winston and Wilbur Holiday grow worried—Winston asked Vernilla about her brother during a midnight tryst; she closed her legs with a scissoring of her thigh muscles, slapped his cheek, and hissed, "If you're so interested in Palmer, go have your fun with *him*!" Later on, Winston learned that Holiday had actually phoned Mr. Nemmitz about the missing boy.

Wilbur never revealed what Enoch had said; all he told Winston as they played a game of chess at his store counter was, "I don't think Palmer will have to worry about the Pinkertons tagging after him. . . . Check and—*mate*."

It shocked Winston, hearing his own thoughts echoed without first voicing them. During the week Palmer had been gone, Winston spent many an hour in the sawdust and produce-scented coolness of Holiday's Grocery Store. He felt more at home in that dim establishment than he did in the prismatic brightness of his mother's front parlor at home.

Besides enjoying Wilbur's company (he was better-read than Porter, more lucid), Winston appreciated that Wilbur had kicked Dead Fred out of his store the Monday after Palmer wandered out of town.

Still it made Winston uncomfortable at times, how Wilbur intuited his thoughts, his feelings . . . and articulated them better than Winston could himself.

Studying the board, wondering how Wilbur beat him *again*, he cautiously asked, "Did you hear what Mr. Nemmitz said to Mr. Woodard at the Co-op? 'Bout Palmer?" He hoped his voice didn't quiver as he spoke. Winston didn't dare look Wilbur in the eye.

"When a man has sons to spare, maybe he doesn't miss one. I suppose Enoch considers Vern and little Shirl to be enough. I don't happen to share his sentiment, but unfortunately, Palmer isn't my legal responsibility." Wilbur set up the board with deliberate precision, likewise avoiding Winston's now-upturned eyes.

"Your move."

Winston was tempted to push the board onto the floor, bury the pieces in graves of sawdust, and scream, "But Palmer *is* your responsibility!" Yet, he liked Holiday too much to rub salt into old wounds. Besides, Winston was afraid Wilbur would have an excuse to rub in how it was partially Winston's fault that Palmer took off.

Not for the first time, Winston bit his lip in shame over his actions; "hung like a rabbit" was a phrase he'd heard the girls whisper admiringly about him often enough.

"Your move, Winston." Holiday tapped him on the shoulder. Halfheartedly, he advanced the first piece at hand, the King's pawn. By one space. He didn't notice which pieces Wilbur slid forward; mechanically, Winston advanced all his pawns by one space, and was caught unawares when he heard, "Check."

Wilbur's Knight was one move away from capturing the White King. Unwilling to protect his King, he nudged his last pawn forward, not caring when Wilbur said softly, "And mate," before scooping up the pieces and placing them into the fitted, felt-lined box.

Holiday stepped out from behind the counter, bottle of 7-Up in one hand, an unopened one for Winston in the other. Smiling weakly, Winston accepted the offered bottle. Removing the crimped cap, he realized that he'd been second-guessed again. Winston *was* deep in the dumps and Holiday swore by 7-Ups restorative qualities; *he* practically lived on it.

Winston chugged down the contents of his bottle, setting it on the counter behind him when he was finished. It did make him feel slightly better.

Pointing to the advertisement-plastered window, he asked Wilbur, "Would you look at *that*? Dead Fred was hanging around the barbershop when I came *in* here. Think if I camped out in here he'd wait outside all night for me?"

Before draining his bottle, Wilbur replied, "Wouldn't doubt it. He sat out all night in the woods."

Touché, Winston thought, humbled. Wilbur gave him a fixed stare, green eyes impaling Winston. Hanging his head, Winston mumbled, "Just wish it never happened . . . that snipe hunt with Dead Fred. It was a *joke—*"

"It wasn't just you. That night put a head on the situation. Fredric only speeded things up a bit."

"Still, Dead Fred didn't have to go saying that . . . he *knows* what Mr. Nemmitz is like." *And so do you,* Winston mentally added.

Placing his empty soda bottle next to Winston's, Wilbur said, "The older Fred gets, the more he looks like his father . . . uncanny." Winston wondered if Wilbur'd gulped down too many bottles of 7-Up; Fred Ferger, Sr., was a thin, florid, sharp-featured man, nothing like his pasty, thick-lipped, and chunky son.

But Wilbur's opinion about Dead Fred's looks was unimportant—what bothered Winston was that Palmer hadn't so much as written since he left. With Mr. Nemmitz unwilling to look for him, Palmer could be anywhere by now.

Taking out his pack of cigarettes, offering one to Wilbur, Winston walked to the front of the store, away from the sawdust near the counter, and lit up, exhaling in Dead Fred's direction. From close behind him came the snick of a safety match striking a shoe sole, followed by Wilbur's voice, "Palmer, if this is eating you so bad, why don't you go and try to find him? Take the truck, head south for a week?"

Winston tapped ashes onto the floor, crushing them to cold dust beneath the sole of his shoe. "How do you know he went south? He used to talk about wanting to go to the Dakotas, see Mount Rush—"

Holiday shook his head behind a cloud of hovering smoke, pale hair shifting dryly across his forehead with the slow movement of his head. Pushing back his hair with his free hand, Wilbur explained, "Too close to Wisconsin. Down south is different. And *I* heard him say something about the Mississippi. He was walking south the last time I saw him. Easy to keep going that way."

"It's easy to talk, too. I can't go, even if I could take the truck. For one thing, I'm too young—"

"You'd pass for a good eighteen to twenty, easy. Especially the way you've been worried. Porter can get you a driver's license—and you *can* take care of yourself—"

"The taking care of myself part isn't the problem." Winston lit a fresh cigarette off the end of the spent one, crushing the old butt into a frazzle of loose tobacco and shredded paper on the wood floor. Wilbur nodded, began to put an arm around Winston's shoulder, but stopped in midair, letting his arm fall heavily to his side. Sighing, blowing out the last wisps of smoke from his lungs, he replied, "You've *two* problems. If you could arrange something with them, going south would be a picnic for you. . . ."

"Mr. Holiday, you should go. Your wife could take care of—"

"*My* wife? Or are you speaking about some other wife of mine who *likes* to work?" There was no rancor in Wilbur's voice, only the sadness of truth. The two men stood looking out the store window, each locked into inactivity and worry, unable to find release.

It wasn't until two weeks later that Winston was unexpectedly presented with his key to freedom. Gayleen's sister Eileen came to visit, along with her husband, three children, and her husband's unmarried sister Joyce. As large as the Winston home was, it had but two bathrooms, making things diffi- cult—plus each visiting family member came with his or her own collection of suitcases, hat boxes, and shoe trees. Plus their appetites.

Winston's parents were touched by his generous offer of his bedroom to Joyce; readily they agreed to his suggestion about going down to Eau Claire, to visit his great-aunt Charlene, during the fortnight or so company would be staying. It was also tacit family knowledge that Winston and his cousins couldn't abide each other, and Aunt Eileen *was* miffed that Winston was headed for class valedictorian (not to mention being the youngest ROTC leader in Dean County) while her Roland was in his second year of the ninth grade. Winston's driver's license came through the day before he left Ewerton.

On the morning of June twenty-seventh, Winston drove down the steep incline of Ewert Hill—putting as much dis- tance between himself and his family as possible without driving the Woody into the intersection fast enough to kill someone.

Before leaving town, he used one of the ten twenties in the envelope of "spending money" Porter had given him that morning to buy a case of beer, thought about it, and made it two cases (he didn't know how long it might take to find Palmer). Cache of Leinenkugels safe in the trunk, he stopped by the grocery store, to say good-bye to Wilbur. Holiday was so busy with customers, though, that all he did was wave over people's shoulders, mouthing, *Good luck, son.*

That made Winston feel a little sad; Wilbur was always nicer to him than his own father, despite the money Porter lavished on him. The envelope of twenties Porter tucked in his jacket pocket gave him less of a thrill than the bottle of 7-Up Wilbur handed to Winston when he *needed* it.

On his way down-state, Winston *did* stop to see his Great- Aunt Charlene. He even stopped at a florist, for a bouquet.

As he rested it by her tombstone, he hoped that his parents

wouldn't mention his destination to their company until he was well out of the state.

Luckily, Winston brought along his own tightly rolled wad of bills, using those to pay for his nights in lonely motel rooms off the main highways, or noisy evenings in the YMCAs he occasionally ran across as he drove deeper and deeper south. He stuck to the red-marked roads at first, close to the Mississippi initially, then eased to the southeast after remembering that Palmer didn't like to *swim*—in Winston's opinion, that made a prolonged stay by the big river a somehow less likely option.

Winston's newly acquired southern road maps grew soft-edged and strangely wrinkled. By the time he grew sick of the sight of bunched stucco and concrete cabins along the roadsides, each fronted with signs inviting him into "Nice Clean Rooms!" with "Private Showers!" he was faced with the sick certainty that he was nowhere *close* to Palmer. And it wasn't just that no one recognized Palmer from the year-old snapshot Winston showed around at every motel desk, diner counter, or gossip's spot in very faceless town he drove through. It was because he didn't feel the *presence* of his friend in any of the places he'd passed through so far.

What Winston missed was a sense that he was seeing a place *after* Palmer had done so, as he used to feel in Ewerton. Ever since the two Palmers were small, Winston was convinced that since Nemmitz was a week older than he was, Palmer had a week's jump on things. From the time when they wore bangs and woolen playsuits, Winston had decided that he couldn't really *see* something unless his "older" friend saw it first. A silly notion, magical thinking. But his childish conviction told Winston that he was on the wrong track. And no one *had* seen Palmer; they'd remember those green eyes if they'd seen him, Winston was sure of that.

After pulling the car alongside a road in southern Mississippi, Winston sat rubbing his eyes behind his Ray•Bans, smudging the dark lenses with the tops of his fingers. He'd reached the point where he either had to go home, or light out in a new direction. But he meant not *knowing* . . . while going on and not finding Palmer was something Winston hated to contemplate. Trouble was, Palmer could be *anywhere*, in any town, on any road—

Suddenly alert, he pawed through his worn collection of maps, seeing what he'd missed before—the *blue* roads. Roads without the lure of garishly painted motels, roadside diners, and other ways of getting money from a guy's pocket. Sheepishly, he reminded himself that Mr. Nemmitz hadn't given Palmer an envelope of new twenties and the use of the family car—Palmer was *walking* all the time. He probably wasn't this far south yet.

Realization galvanized Winston into action. After polishing his sunglasses, he started the car, made a U-turn, and headed north, going down the first blue-marked line he saw on his service station map.

The trek northward, toward Kentucky and finally Indiana, lulled him into a cocoon of self-pity and introspection. He spent less time waving the now dog-eared picture under people's noses, choosing only individuals he was sure would remember a lone traveler hoofing it south—service station attendants, old bench-sitters who knew directions that might be asked by a young walker, waitresses in hole-in-the-wall diners.

And when not showing the photograph (two Palmers, Coke and Pepsi bottles in hand, in front of Holiday's store) to strangers who shook their heads before asking, "He your brother?" Winston spent his days driving.

Alone, as he'd been for the past few days, Winston was forced to pass the time with himself, his own mind . . . and not long into the trip, Winston discovered that his traveling companion wasn't the most pleasant fellow. Not that he could *help* but be an unhappy wanderer on life's road. No red-blooded American boy should've had to be both nursemaid and parent to his own folks. Cleaning up messes he could tolerate to a *point*—sick-up was sick-up, be the person really *ill* or just "sick."

Guiltily, he heard the remaining cans of beer rattle in the trunk, but he assured himself that it was very hot, which made him thirsty. Besides, *he* didn't mess his pants or bed, didn't lie for whole weekends in soiled bedclothes, spilling the bottle onto his chest, then crying because his hootch was gone. He wasn't *that* bad.

As he drove, hands white-knuckled on the wheel, Winston dismissed that he was hard-pressed to remember a day when his parents didn't help themselves to the "medicine" from the thin silver bottle or, after Prohibition was repealed, from the big bottle. Nor could he remember when *he* hadn't smacked his lips in anticipation of his nightly beer, or shook all the Lucky Strikes from his pack before lighting up after school let out. No, he wasn't like *them*, he assured himself, *I'm* not, *Oh, please, not like them*, but bit his lip until blood came while he turned the wheel to the left.

What steamed him worse than baby-sitting his parents was how they *did* manage to plan out his whole life for him—even as they sat in their own filth in bed. Realizing that their only child was better than just bright, really *special* upstairs, they'd awaited his impending manhood with an anticipation that out-did that of a child waiting beside the fireplace for Santa Claus on Christmas Eve. And hurried him along when they thought he was holding on to childhood for too long a time.

Taught him to shoot when he was seven, not just BB guns, but Father's deer rifle. Winston's shoulder was black and blue for weeks, but he'd shot the bull's-eye of the paper target Father tacked onto a tree in Ewert Woods. After hours of trying, of wanting to please his father, just so he could go home and hide under his bed, far from the stinging stink of gunpowder and the huge noise and bone-jarring report of the rifle. But he forced himself to love shooting, later.

Taught him to drink, watched him as he sat puzzled at the dining-room table. The funny medicine smelled warm but stung as it slid down his throat. Mother said, "Maybe he needs some seltzer in it," but Father said, "Nah, he's a beer man," and all Winston wanted to do was spit up the foul-tasting golden liquid . . . until his tummy began to *glow*. After that it was a "funny" when company came and Father poured out a thimbleful of "medicine" into Winston's glass after supper. But he learned to love the sound of the can spurting open under the pointed pressure of the can opener, and the sight of the first escaping bubbles coming out of the twin triangular openings.

Taught him about girls; sat him down in the parlor, Father's face red under the rainbow slash of light from the sun-catchers as he told Winston what went where. Only Winston didn't tell Father that he'd already *seen* when Una Sawyer led him out behind the sand pile in back of the elementary school. Taught him a game called "doctor."

By his twelfth birthday, Winston had been taught all his parents deemed necessary—even if it hurt (bleeding animals on mossy ground), even if it confused him ("medicine" making him sicker *after* he swallowed it). He was their bright boy, their *only* boy, destined to show everybody what it meant to be a Winston.

True, he *was* smart. Brighter than his classmates, unquestionably brighter than his elders, which was the difficult part . . . for his folks, already considered to be *something*, wanted to be thought of as something *better*. Through Winston, they saw a chance to step up into *real* power.

By 1936 Porter let Winston in on the Plan. First, graduate top of his class in 1942. An officer's high ranking in ROTC, "To show 'em what a real man you are." Then college, a teacher's position—show people how respectable he was. Then, a run at City Council, service organizations. Then the mayor's office—the final feather in Porter's cap.

Trouble was that Porter explained as Winston listened, never thinking to ask his son if *he* was the least bit interested in the Plan.

Needless to say, he wasn't. Teaching was the only thing his parents did that Winston respected, but he wanted none of the responsibility of the position, the opportunity to dominate others as *he'd* been dominated.

Speeding along the blue roads, occasionally glancing at the "Burma-Shave" and "Jesus Saves" signs lopping past his car, Winston wondered when the roles of parent and child had become subtly mixed up in his household.

But there was no question in his mind as to where his path *out* lay, how he could bypass the Plan. Porter took three newspapers; and Winston read the headlines about the war in Europe with a fascination that verged on the stomach-twisting. That wildly gesturing little Austrian was going to get FDR mad enough to climb into the ring of war—unless the Japs beat Hitler to it.

Pulling into a little town in southern Indiana, heading for the four pumps of the service station, Winston decided that the *only* chance he had to get what *he* wanted out of life—without an obvious show of disrespect—was to be drafted and shipped out of Ewerton. A draft was inevitable; with it he could break free, honorably. Once safely out of town, he'd become a cog on the wheel, not singled out for a prearranged future. What he achieved, he'd achieve because he wanted to.

In any case, Winston knew he couldn't remain forever linked to Ewerton. Not if he was ever to become anything that *mattered*.

But when the service station attendant and the geezers sitting with him said, "Sure, we seen *him*, July it was—" "Nah, early June—" "Hank sent him to see his gal at the Blue Tulip," Winston was so stunned he let his cigarette burn down to his knuckle. After thanking the men, Winston sucked on his burned finger as he walked to the Blue Tulip, thinking as he saw the weathered storefronts and rusted signs, *Palmer would compare this to Ewerton.* Seeing the world through *other* eyes again was a comforting sensation.

It was as if he'd seen it all before; the "Fairy Soap" sign, the seed poster, everything. And Hank the gas jockey's girl told him that Palmer had ordered two cups of coffee, then left after hearing about that carnival needing help. . . . For some unfathomable reason, the news made him feel as if a cat had walked over his grave. An impression stronger and darker than his "Palmer's seen this first" feeling. He'd been tempted to tell the spare, wrinkled waitress, "No, my friend wouldn't do something like *that.* Everybody in our town knows carnies are no good," but said nothing. Not being raised in Ewerton, she wouldn't *understand.*

Funny feelings or not, Winston's journey suddenly had focus; instead of "Burma-Shave" or "Jesus Saves" signs, his eyes were alert for tatters of carnival posters, an outfit called "South-State Enterprises Carnival and Menagerie." Finding a telephone pole or signpost bearing the sun-bleached fragments of the carny posters made Winston's heart leap. He hurried into each run-down town or village, picture in hand; after learning that his friend *had* passed through, he'd speed down the next blue road.

He first learned of the carny on the eighteenth, so Palmer had been on the road for *weeks*, if the men in Indiana remembered correctly. With luck, Winston decided he'd find Palmer by the end of the month.

With the "am I on the right road?" worry gone from his mind, Winston mulled over a fresh dilemma . . . his *problem*, as some called it in more delicate moments.

Often, he found himself thanking God for the most awful thing: his parents were usually too blotto to know *everything* he'd been up to lately. If they knew, Porter would've nailed him to a tree and used him for target practice.

As he crossed from Tennessee into Georgia, and saw car

license plates embellished with glass-bead peaches (something *sure* to catch Palmer's eye), Winston's perverse thoughts made him laugh bitterly in the dusty confines of the Woody. He'd foil Father's elaborate plans, simply by getting on a party line, and telling someone, anyone, on the other end just a *few* of the things he did on his nights out. If only a handful of people overheard of nights spent with the daughters of Ewerton's finest citizens, his fate as mayor would be forever banned. And, if he told the person on the other end of the line what he sometimes *thought*, they'd string him up from the post-office flagpole. While *some* sex among the teens was tolerated, tacitly encouraged as a way of ensuring a wedding for less desirable girls, he doubted that *anyone* in town would be able to understand, let alone condone, his untried fantasies.

Winston knew what happened to old man Thorn when he did what he did to Becky Wilkes during last summer's Water Carnival. Even after he paid her a nickel first and didn't do much before he got caught. Winston remembered how people looked daggers at the Thorn clan.

All he'd need to say over some party line was, "Sometimes, before I go to sleep, I think about being with a girl who's so . . .'' but even putting what he wanted, what he almost *needed*, into daytime, lucid thought was too humiliating. His late-night special fantasy was something he kept close to his chest, not telling Palmer or *anyone*. Admitting it to himself hurt.

Going with the girls he knew in town was one thing; they were his age, or older, and knew their minds. If a girl said *no*, Winston never forced the issue. He'd put it back in his shorts, button his shirt, and drive the girl home. He wasn't desperate enough to *need* to force or hurt any girl. He had that going for him, but it didn't make him feel any better about his night fantasies, the barely voiced, always *pictured* desires.

When awake, he'd look at young girls, little ones of ten or less, and that near dream would return. Winston didn't want *those* girls, dressed in their Sears HoneySweets dresses of lacy dimity or poplin, who played jacks or jumped over hopscotch board chalked sidewalks.

Their *size* was right, but their faces, the curves of their bodies, were all wrong. The . . . *female* of his night thoughts (if he dared call that near memory of warm curves and soft secret spots a *woman*) wasn't a child, yet when he was fully awake, he invariably compared her to a child. But the *almost* memory of her was so strong, yet so vague.

Ever since his first memory of that queasy desire, when he was twelve, he'd tried to recapture the feeling, to quell his urgent wanting. Falling into every soft opening he could find, or wrapping his arms around a willing body beneath his. For a few minutes, he'd drive away the night want, but as hunger returns once food is digested, so his fantasy returned.

Once, he remembered that there had been snow falling, landing without melting on their intertwined bodies; a slow-descending fall of gray-white flakes covering the tan earth below them. Afterward, he forced himself not to look at little girls during winter days, when large flat flakes of snow drifted down in lazy spirals, to land and slowly melt on the shoulders of pique and princess coats. Out of fear, perhaps, of finding what had been eluding him. . . .

True, even if something unseemly happened, his father would smooth it over, hush it up, but Winston still shook inside when he pondered the whole dilemma. On one hand, being from a good family had its advantages, but on the *other* hand . . . Winston wondered if the pressure of always being expected to be the future of Ewerton was worth the cost.

If Palmer hadn't been growing up with him, another bright, up-and-coming youngster, Winston was sure he would've crumbled under the weight. The thought of life in Ewerton without Palmer was just too much to contemplate without at least searching *one* more town, *one* more state.

The deeper into Georgia he drove, seeing whole, unripped South-State posters, knowing he was only a show or two away from his friend, Winston promised himself that once he caught up with Palmer, he'd tell him *everything*—even about the dreams and the way he looked at little girls. Palmer would put it all in perspective—he'd been around this summer, he'd know what to do, what to suggest. Then . . . Winston hoped he would stop *hurting*.

His thoughts made him pull off the side of the road near strange trees unlike those at home. He panted until the tears stopped and he could concentrate on the road again.

For the first time, Winston admitted to himself that he not only missed his friend—he missed a part of himself. The past few weeks had been like coping with one hand in a two-handed world.

By July 24, Winston was within driving distance of his friend; some codgers he spoke to one morning *definitely* remembered seeing the dark-haired, short teen in town not two days before. One old man said around his plug of chaw, "Him, he said he an' his outfit be headin' down by Athens way. Doin' a show one, two days hence. You get goin' now, you can catch up with 'im 'fore the week's gone." Thanking the man, Winston ran back to the Woody and jumped in. By nightfall, he made it halfway to Athens, despite reading the map wrong and going twenty miles out of his way. He was so *close.* . . .

"So close," Winston whispered softly, to himself, to the distant voice on the wind that blew slight and fitful down the avenue, passing warm against his sweat-shiny skin while he huddled on his bench. In the past hour, as his mind traversed the blue roads of memory, nothing had changed around him; the cars still bore their four-digit plates, the dress-shop dummies still wore their Vionnet crepe dresses, and the shoe store down the street still advertised huarache oxfords for $2.95 a pair . . . just as it did when he was sixteen. No cloche hats for sale, or cars bearing long, thin plates. *That* sight had been an illusion, a dream—and the same sentiment went for the voice. A self-punishing dream, he assured himself through his blinding headache. He thought Hell *had* to be as bad as he'd been taught it should be . . . or at least as bad as he deserved.

Curling up on the uncomfortable bench, resting his head against the iron arm, Winston pressed his eyes shut against the glare of the street lamp. He tried to disregard the waves of pain that washed over every cell of his body.

Palmer. He had written all this down. What he did, while Winston was searching for him. Where Palmer had been, who he met . . . Winston was sure *he'd* read about it. *When* he wasn't certain (something about a wedding hovered at the far periphery of memory, almost within recall), but he *did* read *something* Palmer wrote—

But, as if to distance him from that inner revelation, the river voice called louder, its tone sweet, coaxing, as the last of the wedding memory slipped from him (*not my wedding, but I left with a—*), and he realized that he *did* know the voice that called to him. It was his *wife*, his *Una*. His dead wife, but he was dead, too, so it was all right to want her. Maybe she'd been waiting for him, in this strange Hell, for so many years. Loneliness? Winston couldn't begin to comprehend the full import of the word, not after only a day spent here.

Forgetting the pain of his last few years with Una, the embarrassment, the rages, her blackened face, Winston hurried for the bridge south of town, legs rubbery as he ran to his Una. His *girl*, or at least he hoped she was a girl again—didn't he wear the skin of a younger man? As he hurried in the dense, streetlight-dotted darkness, to the woods beyond Willow Hill, Winston admitted that once Una let herself go, he *had* dreaded her touch. But he'd shed his mask of bitter age, anything *wonderful* might've happened to her.

Breathless, Winston found the strength to run to the source of that haunting call.

SIXTY-SIX

From Palmer Nemmitz's journal—
July 26 began as a hot, sunny day; early morning dew was sucked away from the blades of grass underfoot.

The kind of day when the hollow under your Adam's apple is pooled with sweat by seven A.M., and your underarms feel like someone's squirted them with motor oil.

The kootchie girls wore play shorts and rayon blouses tied in bows under their breasts, exposing sweaty midriffs. The backs of their maize and lime-green blouses were dark, clinging to their spines. Daisy-Denny donned a terry-cloth robe and men's latex swim trunks, bitching that he wanted to chop off all his yellow hair with a butter knife—when Denny forsook his clinging silken kimonos, it was *real* hot. We'd been through heat such as I never *imagined* in Wisconsin. Like soggy blankets sewed to your skin.

Much too hot to walk, so Larry unhitched his car from the camper and let me drive into town for the morning's supplies. I wasn't worth more than five bucks, but I felt like a million that morning. There I was, employed, money jingling in my pockets, sitting behind the wheel of a vehicle folks didn't have to know wasn't mine.

I wiped out the village bakery and the general store had plenty of kidney beans. If the geek didn't *perform*, the apple-knockers were unhappy.

After making the carny purchases, I took out my own money, and parted company with a good deal of it.

Maeve hadn't ventured out of her trailer except to appear at the door when Jomel brought her her food or took Maeve's soiled clothes to wash. (Maeve was fussy about her clothes; she put the costume her dummy wore in with her own, as if she couldn't bear to smell whatever sweat came off her onto that tiny black dress.) The heat hit Maeve worse than any of us. She could hardly breathe. When she came out come nighttime, she was pale, all big eyes in dark circles, and her mouth twitched under its coating of red.

She didn't seem to be hiding from *me*; she'd smile at me in passing, mouth a faint "Hello." Knowing how she liked chocolate, I bought some Tootsie Rolls and Tootsie Pops. I asked the old buck behind the counter to put a piece of string around the white sticks, and tie the end in a bow. So they'd look pretty.

I was glad Maeve wasn't out when I returned; it was awfully hard concealing those ten wrapped suckers in the crook of my arm as I carried the crate of kidney beans to the camper. Shea didn't want the geek's chow anywhere near everyone else's food. But when I came out of the camper, after hiding the spiky bundle of candy in my knapsack, I found out that Harold Shea had other problems on his mind besides the geek.

His voice carried in a fit-to-be-tied screech from his trailer parked fifty feet away as if he stood five inches from me.

"Goddamn *whore*! How long? How long's *this* been going on? Huh? Nothing but"—he shouted something that sounded like "noff-kehs" but it was impossible to ask him to repeat himself—"every last one of them!"

Then came a lull, as if Harold had burst a blood vessel or swallowed his tongue in rage. By now all the carnies were milling in back of the midway, save for the kootchie girls, who vanished in that beat-up double-deep orange school bus they shared. Even Maeve ventured out, dressed in a pair of gracefully weathered rose-pink overalls and matching blouse, both piped in white, matching her ever-present sling. She was wan, as if still needing sleep, breathing through her mouth in deep, ragged spurts.

While the others watched Shea's trailer, I moved nearer to

Maeve; the air around her bore the sweat-intensified odor of roses and jasmine. I wished I'd brought along that candy; it would've been the perfect time to give her that sweet bouquet, while the others were distracted. Out of surprise alone, she might've invited me into that pristine trailer—

—*get out, get out, she hissed, and I stumbled when walking backward over one of her shoes, unable to turn away from the sight before me, yet wanting never to see again if seeing meant looking at that*—

—for maybe she'd have 7-Up in there, and we'd talk some more, until talk turned to something better, something as deeply shared as a heartfelt talk. I'd reached the point where I found myself anxious each morning until I saw her white-slinged figure appear at the door of her trailer; each night I prayed that she wouldn't up and leave in the star-flocked darkness, as six-fingered Nancy had done.

Each morning, seeing her brought on a mixture of relief and renewed longing. Just her smile was enough to make me all jelly and sparklers inside. And whenever her odd-ringed eyes met mine, I got the impression that she liked my green eyes as much as I liked hers. In that second of contact, the look of hurt she carried in her eyes was gone.

All this had been happening with no need of conversation. Talking would've been superfluous, ruining a perfect bubble of time between us. But I wanted to go beyond smiling and staring, beyond that point in anticipation of what should come next. My eyes were satiated; the rest of me said, *Our turn now.* I hoped and prayed Maeve felt likewise, that the rest of her wanted to share what her eyes had been enjoying.

She didn't break away when she noticed my presence; which confirmed my feelings. I was about to say something to her, tell her how pretty her getup looked, when whatever had been keeping Shea quiet released his tongue. "She *what*?"

Maeve jerked within her clothes, giving me a puzzled stare before the next outburst.

"I don't have to—where is she? This business will stop *now*—" Everyone was suddenly very interested in the dust and trampled dirt at their feet when Harold stormed out of his trailer—Maeve and I were no exception.

She made lopsided circles in the dust with the toe of her white huarache, which was tied at her ankle with a dainty leather bow. Slowly, I moved toward her until my foot touched the edge of one of those dust circles. We looked up at each other at the same instant; she lowered her eyes first, coloring slightly about the tops of her cheeks. The ghost of a smile played at the corners of her lips. I asked, "Think he'll DQ her?"

It was obvious what Shea was fuming about; what was puzzling was that he hadn't noticed what was going on sooner than he did. I often heard goings-on in that old school bus. Some nights the moon was full enough to see the marks as they hightailed it into town after getting their share.

Shrugging her shoulders, Maeve said, "I don't know what he expects to do come show time," but her voice shook a lot more than necessary under the circumstances. As we stood there, near enough to touch without extending a hand more than an arm's length away, a current passed between us, a shaking of the air, a tingling of the skin.

Around us, the sky took on the most unusual color, a pure yellow-green, a shimmer that made the tree leaves seem lit from underneath. Each blade of withered grass was touched with inner fire, as if the sun had fit itself into the earth, and shone up through the reddish soil. The sky was opaque with scudding piles of dingy clouds, as if all that was cool and blue and gentle to the eye had vanished.

When our eyes met again, the eldritch light turned hers a strange muddy color. I could only imagine how *mine* looked. The weird light made her hair a shining, live thing, taking on the color of fall leaves and dried corn silk.

It was a brief slice of time that seemed not of this earth, not of the life I'd known up to that moment. The sun was below us, the pale earth hung above, surface scudding like drifts of begrimed spring snow, and we were trapped between, in a pocket of air and light unshared by the rest of the sane world. If there were sounds in the world outside ours, I didn't hear them. Reaching out my hand, I let it come slow and open-palmed toward her cheek. I felt soft down on her cheek under my fingertips, as her eyes swept shut with a feather-gentle motion. Her breath quickened, and then—

—the whole world jangled and crashed in around us, an explosion of sight, sound, smell, and sensation. The bus door opened; I felt the reverberation in my teeth. Male and female voices screamed unintelligibly, followed by the low babble of the carnies. Rain sheened over skin. A cut-grass tang flooded my nostrils, overpowering Maeve's rich perfume. Her eyes were fo-

cused on something behind me, pupils black and mirrorlike under
the runnels of water dripping from her tight cap of wet hair.

I turned around in time to see Shea chasing Jomel, the
newspaper-reading kootchie girl, out of the school bus. But
Jomel didn't *look* right, for a reason I couldn't grasp at first
glance. Only when I saw the limp brown curls dangling from
Shea's fingers did I realize that Jomel's head was smaller,
covered with a springy, butch-short coat of black hair. Hair
like I'd seen on the colored folks who showed up at the midway some nights.

"Goddamn *passing* whore slut! How *dare* you work my
show? Marks don't pay hard-earned money to see a *nigger*
'less she's a pinhead or got four arms an' three legs like Betty
Lou Williams! Folks down this way could've *bought* you a
while back!"

Shea waved around the wig he'd no doubt torn off her head
in a fit of anger; its long curls flopped, stuck together under
the shimmering rain.

The object of his wrath stood defiantly before him, hands
on the hips of her soaked shorts, legs spread, forming a triangle of wet milky tan and rain-drummed earth. But her expression was elated, as if she were glad that her kinky-haired
scalp was bared to the elements. Her smile was awful, for it
held back words *no one* wanted to hear.

Shea ranted on, a bitter tirade made all the more pathetic
because what he'd discovered *really did disappoint him.* He'd
fooled himself into believing that he ran a fairly clean, if dull,
carny, marred only by the thing in the horse trailer.

He screeched under the rain's steady drumming: "I don't
run no glitch carny—*this is all I* have, *can't you see that*?
Not so good, but I try to be halfway honest to scum who
don't *deserve* fair 'cause they're so gone on ugliness and that—
that—*thing* in the pen. No screwing them more than what's
up front. No trouble. No law chasing us. *I-have-tried!* And
now, *this!*" He shook the sodden wig.

As he paused for a heaving breath, Jomel stepped forward,
hands still on her hips, ugly grin still strung across the bottom
of her face. Speaking in an exaggerated parody of colored
speech, unlike her normal voice, she taunted, "Wassa matta,
Massa Shea?'Fraid them white sheets'll pay you a visit come
sundown 'cause one o' dey number dipped his wick in a
*dark*ie?" Her voice flattened, shifted, "You motherfucking
sanctimonious *bastard.* As if those white knights wouldn't be

interested in *you*, too! Maybe they'd want you as much as a
'passing' whore—I heard tell they don't like Jews, either—''

From the way Harold Shea's face fell, shapeless and whey-
white, it was plain Jomel struck a nerve. Shea's skinny wife
held her hand tight against her mouth, as if afraid her chin
would slide down to her flat chest, while Jomel snarled, ''I
may be one-quarter 'nigger' but I'm not *dumb*. I read, I listen. I put two and two *together*. Red hair and freckles don't
fool me, Ellis Island Irish, put down Shea 'stead of some Jew
name. You may've fooled the rest into thinking you were
spouting *Gaelic*, but I've been up north, I've *heard* people
speaking Yiddish! And them white sheets are kissing cousins
to the Nazis—you're damn lucky your folks took the boat over
here, 'cause your kind back home is gonna get *fried*. Just like
what's gonna happen to your stinking carny one night! I only
hope it stops raining by then so the fire burns nice and
bright!''

Yanking her rain-saturated wig out of Shea's limp fingers,
she marched back to the school bus, pulling the door shut
with a thunderous noise. As if in divine answer, a clap of
thunder followed by an arc of lightning made very last one
of us who'd witnessed the fright jump and shudder in place.

That was when I noticed the Fat Lady, doughy face twisted
with inner meanness, as she joined the loose circle watching
the argument. Her thin hair was still mostly dry, and her lardy
body was close by Shea's trailer. Smug satisfaction covered
her raw-dough features like melted butter.

Unable to look at that sneering expanse of dead flesh, I
turned my gaze to Maeve's face. I was shocked by how distant and unconcerned she was by the ruination of a man who'd
babied and coddled her instead of making her work the freak
tent, and pull in real money for her act. Not to mention the
humiliation of Jomel, who'd willingly done Maeve's laundry,
saving Maeve the pain and bother of using her sore dummy-
toting arm during the day. Her eyes were blank, guarded, her
face devoid of feeling, as if she'd seen an accident on a city
street, calmly observing the blood of strangers form coppery
puddles on the pavement.

Shea's voice, strong but shaky, rang out across the wet field
where the carny was set up, ''Show's off tonight! We slough
now. Tony, go into town, tear down the posters. We move
out after the rain stops.''

Behind him, the school-bus door opened, and out stepped

Jomel, dressed in a cheap cotton percale bolero dress, head wrapped in a turban-tied scarf, flimsy suitcase in hand. Without a word, she walked past Harold; not until she was well down the road into the tiny Georgia hamlet did she turn around to yell, "I hope you *all* fry in fucking Hell! Till your skin is burned blacker than mine'll *ever* be!"

After giving each of us a hard stare (my cheeks burned when her eyes met mine), she turned and walked down the dirt road, wobbling slightly when her heels sunk into the mud, shoulders set and straight, head held high. Rain turned her dress into a soaked shroud wound around her legs before she was out of our sight. Once she was no more than a thin, wavering line far, far down the road, the attention of the carnies turned to breaking down the rides and joints. Before going to help them, I turned to Maeve and asked, "Didn't that *bother* you at all? Christ, for all she knew Harold could've been Jewish *way* back, and just kept a few of the old words. And Jomel, she can't help what her relatives did way back. Maeve, she was *nice* to you. Aren't you afraid of what she might say, in town? Of what might happen?"

Maeve only said, in a voice of dawning awareness, "I should've *known* . . . you slept with her, didn't you?"

"W-what?" I sputtered, then protested, "That doesn't have anything to do with what happened just now—"

As if speaking to me through a thick fog, lost in her own world, Maeve said, "Do you really think she'll do what she threatened to do? Her being what she is?"

"None of us could tell," I said before I realized how stupid that made *me* sound, adding as she wheeled around and walked back to her trailer, "For cryin' out *loud*, Maeve, she did your *laundry*, she didn't *have* to bother—"

Without turning to face me, she shot back in a tight, venomous voice, "Doing laundry comes naturally to *her* kind."

I strode up to her and spun her around before she could open the door, saying in a shaking voice, "You *bitch*. Jomel called the wrong person 'sanctimonious'—I suppose *you're* so lily-white and *perfect* the thought of being *scared* never *occurred* to you! What smart-aleck remark do you have about *me*, knowing I'm a bastard? Does being a lowly *jointee* come naturally to 'my' kind?"

I had my hand on her arm, holding her soft skin with tense fingers. Her eyes grew wide; for the first time I saw fear in them . . . fear of *me*, I guessed then. I was so worked up I couldn't think straight. As if what *I* was had anything to do with the secrets Jomel and Harold had kept.

Seeing two good people demolish each other was worse than any geek show could ever be. Ugliness charged the air with malignant energy, touching me, finding hidden ugliness within, sparking that dormant repulsiveness into new and hideous life. Two people who had previously meant little to me parented an oversensitive monster within my soul, a being that fed on all the bad things I'd ever heard said about myself; all the hate I felt for what I was, and for the two people who'd so carelessly created me; áll my doubts and inadequacies, real and imagined that lay within me, unvoiced and undealt with. And that newborn monster squalled at Maeve that morning, holding on to her silky arm. Under my fingers, her skin gleamed blood-starved white.

Struggling not to give in to her pain, Maeve said in a voice that blended into the gentle purr of the rain around us, "Palmer, you have no *idea* what real *fear* is like." She shook her arm free and ran into her trailer. Only a trace of her perfume remained.

My left palm and fingertips burned; I'd held on to her *much* too hard. The way the old man used to do to our Ma, grabbing her when she'd least expect it, not letting go until she'd cry, silent tears falling down her stiff and hate-glazed face, but she'd never give in and sob loudly, like a child. There had been a glitter of tears in Maeve's eyes, but her face had been set, strong.

Even though none of his blood flowed in me, I'd inherited something from the old man—*meanness*. At that moment, part of me cringed, ashamed, but the rest of me was seeing-blood mad, nearly puffing smoke from the nostrils in rage. If Larry hadn't called me, I don't know *what* I might've done that morning.

Looking back on it all, safe behind the barrier of years and time, I know that only the time of day would've been different. What was going to *happen* would've taken place under a harsh yellow-green sky—instead of under a no-color blanket of darkness. Only, maybe, if I'd been forced to really *see* everything, all in a piece, instead of in pink-white flashes, things *might've* been different.

Perhaps I would've run away before the real horror began.

• • • •

Later, Tony came back from the hamlet, after spreading word that the carny was canceled for the night. On account of rain. Tony said Jomel was nowhere to be seen, which was either a good or bad thing, depending on how you looked at it. But Shea breathed easier, and decided it best to stay put for the night. Back roads *could* wash out, or be blocked by trees during the storm. Since the rain showed no sign of letting up, no one argued with Harold.

Thunder and lightning followed each other closer than a male dog scoots after a bitch in heat. The sky went pure slate-gray, and the eerie green-yellow light faded to murky blue-gray. Carnies huddled in trucks, or wherever they could find a bit of dryness, while the animals were frantic in their cages. The bobcat's wails were pitiful, sirenlike. Longo had to pull canvas over the cages, so the menagerie would calm down.

Larry had a battery-powered lantern in the camper; while rain made the canvas walls shudder and flap wetly around us, Larry and I were snug in that beer can-lined place. Yellow light made the brightly colored tin surfaces wink and sparkle like dusty jewels around us. Larry lugged in a case of shine, potent stuff he'd bought off the back of a truck that pulled into the midway three nights back.

There were six bottles of the stuff left (Larry said it made the geek do things "Satan hisself ain't dreamed up yet"), and Larry fished one out of the crate.

Holding it up to the maize light, he solemnly asked, "Look good to you? Or is it spoiled?"

That was our ritual; be it a pie bought for Moby Jackie, or a freshly opened bottle of gin or whiskey for the geek, Larry'd hold it up and ask those two questions. I'd supply the rote answer, "I dunno, Larry. We'd better try it first." Which we did; inevitably the item in question would be pronounced "spoiled"—meaning that no one but us could be expected to eat or drink it. It would be a *crime* if the carny lost its Fat Lady or geek on short notice. Better that two easily replaced jointees got sick.

The way that shine burned our mouths and singed our throats, the cork should've dissolved days ago. It made my eyes water and my nose run—before I swallowed it. It was surprising that the geek didn't grab hold of himself and turn himself inside out after slurping down a bottle. Larry and I only managed a swig or two each, then switched to beer.

Larry wanted to play cards, but after rooting around among

his dirty comic books and beer cans, all he found was a spare deck of Tarot cards. Tossing aside the named picture cards, and the Page from each suit, we had ourselves a serviceable deck of pasteboards, even if the full-figured King, Queen, and Knight had to be turned upright before we knew what sex they were supposed to be. The number cards were tricky, with only tiny Roman numerals on top.

Between the lantern light, the flashes of lightning, and the way runnels of rain made strange moving patterns on the canvas camper walls, it was surprising that either of us kept track of how many cards we were holding, let alone knew what they were.

But it was either play cards in that drumming downpour or worry about a visit from the men in the bed sheets and soft dunce caps. I knew about the KKK, despite living up north all my life. In the twenties, there were clans up Ewerton way. Did crazy stuff, like burning a cross on the lawn of the Catholic hospital in Ladysmith, or hanging an effigy of the pope from the Dean County courthouse flagpole. *Not* people to fool with.

Looking at the small screen set in the door, Larry said, "Shit, they ain't comin'—rainin' too hard. How they gonna keep them crosses lit?" So there we sat, each seated on the edge of his respective bed, the spare cards laid out on an upended crate between our knees.

We tried gin rummy, but the cards were too big, and hard to hold, so we switched to five-card draw, playing game after game and not keeping score. Just deal out cards and throw away cards, trying to match the strange symbols to come up with flushes and pairs.

I was fascinated with the pictures on each card, for at last I saw them up close. In the joint, I was too busy to scrutinize them, but in my hand, the figures and scenes looked so *rounded*, as if suspended above the paper, that I was tempted to scrape the surfaces, to see if the tiny bodies bled or screamed out in pain.

That's how drunk I was. But it was a different kind of drunk than the time of Dead Fred's snipe hunt. That night with Winston, I was blotto, floating on a haze of forgetfulness. Hunched over those nearly moving cards, nose filled with the mingled aroma of beer, mildew, and Larry's stained overalls, my eyes alternately blurred and focused in on things so sharply that I was afraid the little card people might pop up and stab me in the eyes. I still felt my face coloring from what I'd said to Maeve after what *she* said to *me* about that bump-and-grind girl. Everything seemed so real, so extra alive. So embedded in my mind, right up to this day. That's the worst part of all. . . .

"Dealer takes two," he said, thumbing the cards off the top of the pink-backed pile between our knees, adding, "Either shit or get off the pot . . . you flummoxed over that bitch?"

"Which bitch?" I giggled over my impromptu rhyme.

"It matter? The one you was tryin' to get a feel off of 'fore Shea an' the coon started in."

"I dunno. Everything's got me pissed now. Gimmie three, four cards. What the hell." I slapped the discards onto the illustration that covered the end of the crate. The boy behind the wheel of the car in the drawing reminded me of Winston. I was torn between an impulse to run home and give that so-and-so a bear hug, or spit in his big blue eyes.

Larry passed me four cards, looked at his hand, mumbled, "Aw shit, where are the pairs?" then continued sagely, with a nod of his haystack of hair, "Blimp did this carny a favor, riddin' us of that coon. Ain't no coloreds fit for a carny since Betty Lou Williams—"

"Who was she? Pair of nines, sticks and swords."

"Got them swords hid in your lap or somethin'? Betty Lou played circuses, better'n *this*. Had a doo-hickey growin' right *here*"—he indicated his left side, above the place where his waist would've been if he hadn't been potbellied—"tangle of funny-shaped legs an' an arm . . . or two arms an' a leg. All black, anyhow. Like her. Somethin' to see, no lie. Harold'd give his eye teeth an' tongue for a freak like her. Tole me he wouldn't need no geek—"

"It gonna get sick? This kinda rain?"

"Nah, any gets in'll hose him off good. Gimmie two cards. Ever see a *real* freak? Kind that don't walk around 'cause they can't? Like Daisy and Violet Hilton? Asses was joined. Limped around. Or Myrtle, with four legs? Pinheads? Albinos? Armless, legless—"

"I seen farmers with arms torn off—"

"Cut off don't count. Stump ain't smooth. These cards you give me are no good, what'd you take for yourself? Lemme see—" He tipped down my fanned-out hand of cards, whistling when he saw the spread of swords in my hand.

"Goddamn kid dealt out a flush. Sonna*bitch*!'' He slapped his knee, until his hand stopped in midslap and he said real fast, and funny-sounding, "Don't put them cards back in the deck. Let's see 'em again.''

I handed over the ten, nine, eight, seven, and five of swords. Larry studied them intensely, frowning, he went, "Uuuummmmmm,'' in a way I didn't like at *all*. Uneasy in the near silence, I said, "Still don't think Moby Jackie had no right ratting on Jomel. Wasn't like *she's* some angel sitting on a cloud.''

"Moby's jealous 'cause she's so piss mean an' ugly no man wants her no more. Done scared off the only ride jock dumb 'nough to stick it up in 'er. Only Fat Lady men don't pant over in the whole south an' she knows it. But she done us a favor 'bout that picka—'' As he spoke, Larry still pored over the cards, so I got up and looked out the screen door.

Surrounding trees swayed and tossed like live, hurting things. Dainty ripples of illumination and shadow resembled rain pattering on the surface of a pond. It was disorienting, as if the world had tilted again, and I stood in a direction that should've left me prone, not upright. My knees were rubbery, as if my thigh and leg bones met in nothingness. But I was alert, too. *Real* alert. My mind raced like a locomotive on greasy tracks.

What had happened that morning was like a string of boxcars linked behind an engine going full stroke. The marks screwing Jomel led to the Fat Lady, who led to Harold, who led to Jomel, who led *back* to Harold, and finally, riding the caboose, was Maeve, with her crack about poor Jomel. True, *my* train had some cars in two places at once, and it kept going nowhere on an empty track. But to me, the Fat Lady had set this whole thing in motion.

Women. Just because they possessed the only place where a man fit naturally and could lose himself totally, they thought themselves goddesses on earth. And since only they bore young, they were insufferable. Our Ma had been that way; she did what she did with the man who sired me, yet the old man kept her around because he'd married her, and she had his place of refuge hidden inside her, under the folds of her slips and dresses and long aprons . . . the place that belonged to *him* by word of God and law. The secret place that she'd opened elsewhere than her bed at home. The place that brought forth me, and set me loose into a world that didn't give two shits from a cow's behind for me.

Jomel, Moby Jackie, silent six-fingered Nancy, the wives of Harold and the cook, the rest of the kootchie girls, and Maeve, oh, *especially* Miss Expensive-Clothes-and-Spotless-Car—all of them were the same. Slits suspended on legs with something on top to fondle.

I never realized I harbored such *anger*. But as the rain shifted direction, hitting the screen to hang in square-boardered droplets on the wire mesh, spraying my hot face lightly with cut grass–scented moisture, all I wanted to do was lay hands on the nearest *female*; squeeze all the pride and fiestiness and life out of her . . . until she became the way I felt inside.

Back home, I'd missed our Ma, but now, I wanted to kill her—bring her back to life just so *I* could kill her—the way I figured Hortense Holiday must've done. One bitch getting back at another bitch. Women—they had stuff in them to drive men to all sorts of craziness, always making themselves all the more alluring, to make us men all the more insane with the wanting and needing of them. Like Maeve splashing on that heady perfume, dressing in those pretty clothes I couldn't *help* but notice, and wearing that soft shining hair of hers long and gently waving—as if she knew how I liked girls' hair hanging down long and touchable, not all curled and waved and marcelled into tight ridges that might give me something akin to a paper cut if I touched it all wrong.

Oh, not *obvious*—she never pushed herself on me, as poor Jomel had done; but by hanging back she made me all the more insane with the need to touch her, to hold her and die in that embrace. As if she'd tuned into my liking girls who held back a bit, just to make me wonder and want all the more. Like twisting the dial on a radio until the music suited her ears. Maeve knew how to make me do what *she* wanted me to do. . . .

While I stood by that screen, my face damp from rain spray, everything good that had passed between us was twisted into a distorted reflection of reality. My mind went and changed parts, ruining those moments we'd spent together.

Finally I said, not turning around to face him, "Larry, why in *hell* did God go an' make woman? Been nothing but trouble since He stole the rib." Behind me, I heard the dry snick of pages being rifled in a real book, something alien for Larry.

I turned around to see him paging through a frayed cloth-bound volume, then looking at my cards placed face-up on a dirty blanket. Glancing up at me, he said, "God got addle-paddled after all that creatin' in such a short time. If He'da' thought it through, He'da' given a man a box an' been done w' it. Saved a lot o' trouble when it come time to put extra rest rooms inna fillin' station. Never found a woman worth more'n one, two rolls inna hay. Drive you up a tree an' make you shake till the leaves fall off. Ever notice how some ladies start to droolin' an' goggle-eyein' the geek? Like they just been diddled w' a ten-inch corn cob? Women *like* a man t'be a *man*, none of that Errol Flynn fancy-ass women *say* they like.

"Know what I think? I should find a mate f' him in that trailer there. Aw, don't look so *mortified*, it'd give the men folk somethin' to drool on, too. Marks might pay a buck for that. Save on chickens, too."

As I sat down on the bed opposite Larry's, I mumbled that Harold might not like it, as I tried to read upside down what was in the book. There were drawings of Tarot cards inside, plus a text. Larry traced under the words with his fingers, saying, "I don't think he's gonna have much to say 'bout what I do in The Tent. Not tomorrow—if he has a show left come then. Goddamn Ellis Island Irishman. Never heard the likes." He went back to reading and frowning; I didn't tell him how my father changed our name from the old spelling of Niemiec to Nemmitz, for fear of Larry accusing me of being some nationality less favorable than a Jew. The Czechs were in hot water themselves over in Europe.

Then Larry snapped the book shut, keeping his place with one grimy thumb, and I saw the lettering on the worn cloth cover. *The Pictorial Key to the Tarot, Being Fragments of a Secret Tradition Under the Veil of Divination.* By Arthur Edward Waite. Quite an eyeful, but I was so *on* I could've memorized the whole of the Declaration of Independence if Larry had fanned it in front of my eyes.

Larry tapped the cover of the book; his blunt fingertip made a dry *pocking* sound as he said, "How many times them same cards come up f' you tonight? Too many times to be happenstance. Like the cards is tryin' to *tell* you somethin'. Madam Zola, she left this, used it herself 'fore she took off. Book says you're in bad trouble, kid. Some wicked cards you keep drawin' out of the deck. Last hand of yours is somethin' awful. Wanta hear what the cards is warnin' you?''

"Sure. Things can't get much worse for me." I leaned forward, upsetting the crate and the rest of the cards with my splayed legs.

Larry gave me an "Are you *sure*?" look, but I nodded. Picking up the five of swords, which depicted three men (the redhead in the foreground was looking back at the others) under a dirty scud of clouds covering a blue sky and sea, Larry tapped the front of the card. " 'Cordin' to the book, this un's failure, dishonor, degredation an' . . . discouragement." He repeated the words like a child at a spelling bee, reciting material by rote. "Says it means 'triumph of enemies,' bein' poor an' anxious, bad stuff like that. Some troublemaker is doin' things to you. Nasty goin's on. Wanna hear the next card, or do you wanna pile into bed an' sleep it off?''

Not realizing that I'd pushed away a lifesaver on the sea of agony that surrounded me, I lifted the next card. "What's your book say 'bout this one?" It was a seven; a red-hatted man toting five swords and looked behind him at the pair planted upright in the soil. Behind him, three gaily patterned tents topped with flags stood in the distance, before a glaring yellow sky.

Swallowing, Larry recited from recent memory, "Uh . . . uncertainty, failure at the last second by giving up too quickly . . . vac-vac"—he opened the book to laboriously read—'vac-ill-ation,' " then closed the book, going on without the text. "Unreliability, an untrustworthy person or situation is loomin' . . . you'll travel by land, an' get hurt on the road. Real upliftin' stuff, kid. Jeezus on a hay wagon, lookit them tents. Three, like our three. Madam Zola, she said them cards talk, an' she weren't lyin'. This next card was upside down when you handed it to me—''

" 'Cause it was easier to count. Knobs on the hilts confused me." I opened a can of beer and slurped it down to cover the twitching in my mouth and throat. The card lay on Larry's blanket, a patch of smooth bright color against the roughly matted wool. The woman with the tied-down arms and blindfold over her eyes (her hair was long, wavy, but I didn't dwell on *that*) hung upside down, surrounded by eight swords driven into an oily swirl of black, green, blue, and yellow. In her orange gown, she resembled a finger pointing at me against a field of gray.

Larry rambled, "Turned around like this means there's an 'unfore*seen*' event, somethin' surprisin' or accidental's gonna happen. Plus treachery, frustration, anger an' despair an' danger," he added, ticking off the words as if trying to remember the names of Snow White's seven dwarfs.

I sipped my beer in silence; the bitter tang burned my raw throat. I indicated the next card with my eyes—the one dealt to me many a time that afternoon and evening. I didn't need a book to tell me the card was a loser. The way the blond man in the bed sat up holding his face with his hands told it all. And the nine swords on the black wall behind him weren't for decoration.

Touching a fingertip to his knee as he rattled off the words of gloom and anguish, Larry mechanically droned, "Disappointment, misery, death, desolation . . . sufferin', mis-mis-*carriage*, failure . . . resignation, martyrdom or . . . or"—slightly sheepish, like a boy who has to cheat on the last exam of the semester, Larry consulted his book—"implac- able re-*venge*."

Finishing my beer, I crushed the can at the middle; it resembled a stout steel hourglass, hiding time inside, keeping it prisoner. Without waiting for me to ask, Larry gingerly picked up the last card, saying fearfully, "This un's the worst card inna whole *deck*."

All those swords driven into the prone man on the beach didn't mean he was taking a nap, waiting for the tide to give him a free bath. Black sky above him hovered over a thin band of chrome yellow. Blood pooled black around deep puncture wounds.

"—death, ruin, disaster, failure of hopes, plans. Leadin' to desolation an' grief. Says here you gotta be careful, an' trust *no* one. It did say that 'death' *could* mean the end of somethin' untrue you believed in, if that helps—"

"Long as it don't say 'Go buy a headstone,' I'm not worried." I tossed the twisted-apart pieces of the can to the floor, where they landed next to the chess pie I'd bought for the Fat Lady. The one set aside for after the evening show. Moby Jackie claimed she slept better on a full stomach, but she couldn't have been that deep asleep, not if she'd seen marks going into the kootchie girl's bus. How she'd known a mark went in to see Jomel was anyone's guess—maybe a spite choice among the girls.

Pure spite, like what Maeve said about "*her* kind" knowing all about laundry. Maeve's words, her tone, had burned me up; all along she'd acted as if she *cared*, as if she alone realized that true carnies and true freaks should band together, support and shore each other up—then she said what she did and brought all the good I'd thought of her crashing to the ground. All that big, heartfelt *talk*, about *caring*—what kind of caring did she show to Jomel? Calling her only female confidante something akin to a *nigger*? As if Jomel had stepped down, hoop earrings swinging, off an Aunt Jemima syrup bottle? I was torn to ribbons because of it all.

Larry glanced down at the pieces of the can where they fell close to the creamy sweet pie, saying, "Almost got beer on it. Next thing, you'll be steppin' in it, makin' a mess. Why don't ya run it over to the sow 'fore it winds up spread all over the floor? I'm not expectin' the maid to come in till next week," he joked, trying to get my mind off what he'd said about the cards.

Refusing his offered slicker, I said with false brightness, "Need a shower anyhow, be back in a minute." The screen door *thwacked* behind me as I tried to shield the gooey pie with my upper body for the thirty-foot walk to where Moby Jackie's truck was parked.

With every soggy footstep, I pictured her slack fat face and pig-mean blue eyes under that balding fringe of no-color hair. Even Jomel's wooly hair was an improvement over that stringy mop. No wonder she'd tattled on Jomel like an overgrown schoolgirl. Just jealous because she was built like an upright piano only twice as wide. No roundness, no shape to that boxy lardish mess; a creature not worth the breath she sucked in.

Moby Jackie's truck had a half house built over the back of it, like a big dog house with a crude door set into the rear over the tailgate. Pounding on that door, the wood cold and slimy under my fist, I told myself that it was *her* fault, all her fault. Maeve was starting to come around to me, letting me touch her cheek without pulling away—until Moby Jackie stirred things up, ruining it all. Then the door swung open, nearly knocking me off that slippery extended tailgate before I inched over to the far end of it.

Miss Lynne Jackson was dressed in a light blue silk crepe

negligee trimmed in *ostrich* feathers, of all things. Cape
sleeves surrounded bluish-white forearms and hands, like a
person about to keel over from a bad ticker. Seeing her flab
spill out of that shiny, much-too-tight robe, I almost heaved
up the beer and shine roiling around in my stomach. The tips
of her nails were long, almost transparent in the glow that
spilled from the interior of her makeshift trailer, like sun-
hating things coiled near the foundation of a house. Those
horrible hands reached for the pie, fingers spread obscenely,
as if it were an upright dick. I imagined that shapeless, blue-
tinged thing wolfing down the pie once I left, cream and
saliva running down her triple chins in strands. I didn't blame
the marks for spurning her feather-trimmed flab for cream
and coffee skin and a cap of kinky hair.

Moby Jackie said in a coaxing, come-hither voice, "Want
a little something in return for the pie, boy?" She let her
robe fall open, and I had to struggle from aiming hot puke
at her buried eye of a navel, or her shadowed overhang of
gut. I said nothing, so she kept wheedling, "Pie's gonna get
all wet, boy—" *that* reminded me of poor Jomel, walking
with her skirt flapping wet and cold around her legs, as she
turned into a sliver of color on the horizon.

Everything swam red-black before my eyes as I snapped,
"Not was wet as Jomel got today, you-you-*you*—" Words
failed me, so I *acted*. Threw the pie at her, aiming for the
narrowing pig eyes and pouting mouth, but I hit her square
in the bust instead.

The pie *hung* there, a spare brown teat, cream smeared on
her feathers and smooth blue robe. Her face mottled bluish
red and dead gray-white; in a strident bellow, she shouted,
"This is a ten-dollar robe! Come morning you're DQ'ed!
Harold will *kill* you! Hear? You *bastard*, look at my *robe*!"
She said more, but I was off, running away from her, heading
away from Larry's camper, praying no one had heard the
three-teated sow roar through the drone of the rain.

As I ran, pants legs slapping cold and heavy against my
calves, I imagined it all. Shea yelling and screaming at me
in front of the others, with me unable to stand defiantly, as
Jomel had done. I knew I'd crumple if he said "bastard" to
me even *once*.

What was worse, I'd already babbled like a fool about my
dubious parentage to Maeve. She already took potshots at
colored people; making a crack about me being a *bastard*

would be nothing for her. It would be worse than all the taunts and jabs at the dinner table because these carnies weren't kin enough to know when to let up before I sprang up to fight back. Only this time, I had no farmyard weapons handy. I had one option—run away that night. Into the rain, into the dark, with no sense of where I was headed.

Women . . . damn *them*, I thought, as I found myself standing before a trailer whose window glowed deep pink. And I decided that if *I* had to hurt, I might as well share the feeling, pass it around until it was gone—even as a last drowning part of me asked, *Why* her? . . . which I answered with a petulant, *Why* not?

SIXTY-SEVEN

Walking quickly down Maple Road, his way lit by a dusting of stars and a sliver of moonlight, Winston's thoughts kept him company, kept the night fears brought on by the close press of trees on either side of him at bay. Calves cramping slightly, Winston remembered the twenty-sixth of July, 1940, the stormy day he was *certain* he'd catch up with Palmer.

The last poster he'd seen promised that there was to be a show that evening, in a small hamlet outside of Athens. There were no rooms to let in the hamlet, so he'd driven to the first seedy little roadside rooming house he could find.

The place was a two-story frame house, paint peeling away and gutters leaf-glutted, but a sign promised clean beds and a meal for under a dollar, and there was room to park the Woody alongside the house. Despite the misgivings he felt over the signs over the *two* front doors, one labeled "Whites" and the other "Coloreds," Winston decided to wait out the storm there.

From the way the rain had been drumming steadily since midmorning, he feared a hurricane or worse. Besides, he reasoned, he didn't want Palmer to think him overeager by coming out before the show and all but dragging him home. The thought of Palmer knowing just how much Winston had missed him amounted to a show of affection Winston didn't think he could deal with comfortably. Better to just "happen by" and invite Palmer to join him on *his* "trip."

But after putting his suitcase in his narrow one-bed room, and splashing his face with water poured from a cracked bedside pitcher, Winston supposed he could pretend he was interested in the setting-up of the carny, and snare Palmer before the midway opened. He had the money to spare for an extra room once they returned to the rooming house.

Filled with resolve, he started down the threadbare carpeted stairway—but when he reached the lobby, Winston forgot all about Palmer. Standing in the cluttered hallway that served as the "White" lobby was a dripping young woman, battered valise in hand, long brown curls dripping audibly on the warped linoleum at her feet. When Winston looked into her dreamy, dark-lashed eyes, letting his gaze wander freely over her smoothly tanned skin and what lay under the trickling folds of her bolero dress, he found himself a *new* friend.

Winston hadn't actually been *lonely*, exactly when it came to feminine company during his trip. But this young lady was . . . different.

Her name—Jomel—enchanted him; at home there was a preponderance of Beatrices, Merles, Effies, amd Bettyes. Serviceable names all, but not melodic or bell-like on the tongue. And Jomel's room was also on the second floor, two doors down from his.

Carrying her valise up the stairs, Winston turned on his usual charm; Jomel blushed demurely at all the right times. Once he reached the top step, Winston found it difficult to walk without discomfort. Intuiting his predicament, Jomel whispered as he set her bag down next to her door, "We'll have to see whose bed is softer," then let herself into her room, softly closing the door behind her.

Cradled on her bed (the softer, less squeaky of the two), him behind her, they watched lightning turn the room bright pink-white, then saw everything go darker than the pupils of their eyes—all in the space of a few seconds. Jomel rubbed her head against the front of Winston's neck, her short hair tickling him. He was shocked when her brown wig slipped off, but understood when told that the woman at the beauty salon used too much heat while waving Jomel's hair.

But once the lights went out, that was the last thing on his mind. For once, *he* tired out first, rolling away from her with ragged breath. Later, as they watched the storm rage outside, she asked Winston his business in this part of the country, " 'Cause you don't talk like the locals.''

Guiltily, Winston remembered what he *was* doing here, and reluctantly got off the bed. After turning on the light, he rummaged in his pockets for the photograph of himself and Palmer, while Jomel sat up on the bed. Sitting next to her, Winston handed Jomel the ragged snapshot, watching her face as she stared intently at the picture. But her dark eyes were unfathomable.

Without a tremor in her voice or hand, she gave him back the photograph, saying, "Sorry, I'd remember him if I saw him. Anyone ever tell you he's cute but you're better-looking?" Winston persisted, "He's traveling with a carny, they're camped out east of here—"

"You're a Pinkerton, aren't you?" There was an edge of trepidation in her liquid voice. Shaking his head so that the dark hair would fall boyishly over his forehead, he replied, "Hardly. I'm just looking because"—*I'm lost without him? She'd think me a four-letter man if I said* that—"I needed someone to pal around with in my hometown. Not many fellows our age, that year was a bumper crop of girls. No detective stuff.''

That seemed to reassure her. Resting against the headboard, she said, "I didn't see any carny, and I pass—went around the only big field around here. Maybe they canceled, on 'count of rain?" He had to concede it sounded likely, but disappointment must have been obvious on his face. Suddenly Jomel leaned forward, harsh overhead light making her crisp hair twinkle on her rounded head. "I can't offer any cotton candy or Goo-Goo Clusters, and you've already had your ride, but I can tell fortunes. That 'carny' enough? I've some cards in my satchel.''

Gracefully, she tumbled out of the bed, padding in stock-inged feet to the valise that rested open across a cane-bottomed chair. Pushing aside dainty items of clothing, including a blouse and pair of shorts that looked as if they'd been washed and hastily wrung out, she found a rectangular box. Sitting on the edge of the bed, she fanned the cards in her hands, looking for one in particular.

As she did so, she apologized, "I'm not good at this, but a long time ago I saw a carny woman who did readings. After

I hung around a couple of hours, she offered to show me how it was done. Later on I bought a book and this set of cards. Lost the book, but I memorized most of it anyhow.'' Having found the card she sought, she held it face forward before Winston. ''Knight of cups . . . it stands for you during the reading. It goes *here*''—she positioned the card near his thigh on the ripple bedspread—''and next I shuffle. You touch it now, no, left hand, that's it. Here's the card of your past—''

''Wait, why is this card for me?'' He pointed at the armored knight seated on a gray horse, yellow chalice in hand, running a finger over the card's waxy surface. Aside from the straight nose, the figure on the card bore little resemblance to him. Jomel shrugged. ''Seems right . . . it's a good card, means you're pleasant, *romantic*. . . . Not a bad card, if that's what you're worried about.'' Jomel thumbed the top card off the pile and put it on the bedspread next to the Knight of Cups.

Winston started to move the card into a right-side up position, but she brushed his hand away. ''No, no, card's *supposed* to be that way. If it comes up like that, it stays. Affects the meaning—uh, oh, you've been a bad boy.'' She smiled, wagging a slim tan finger at him. She tapped the card; a medieval couple stood facing each other, golden chalices in hand, under the watchful glare of a winged lion's head floating above them, or, rather, as when viewed upside down, rested *under* their flower-wreathed heads. Winston saw nothing implicitly wrong with the scene, a couple toasting each other didn't *seem* ominous, but Jomel went on, ''You've done something silly . . . someone close to you backed away because of it.''

Winston crossed his arms over his chest, thinking of the snipe hunt and the drunk afterward, hoping that his cheeks hadn't reddened—but Jomel was able to read him *quite* well.

In answer to his unspoken thought, Jomel said, ''Nothing that a body does the cards don't see. May *look* like cardboard, but they're more than *that*. Same way a Bible is more than paper and cloth binding. Not alive, but they see, they hear . . . they *know*.''She mouthed a spiel heard when she was a child, to give him a good show. Winston relaxed—but only slightly.

Slapping down the next card, also reversed, she smiled. ''Two of Wands . . . this way it's a *good* card. You won't be punished for being a naughty boy—least not *soon*.'' Winston couldn't understand how a purple-robed man holding a small globe in one hand and a leafing branch in the other meant something good, but he sat back and let Jomel explain, as if she really knew its meaning in the first place.

"Something sort of strange, but nice, is waiting . . . could be scary, but it sure will be *different*. Lemme see what your future holds. It changes this card—oh, I'm so sorry." The last part came out flat and mechanical, as if Jomel dared not reveal her true feelings. And this time, even Winston saw that the card carried no happy omen. Three of the black-robed man's five cups were overturned; red and green liquid gushed on the yellow soil. The man's face was hidden by his hunched shoulders, but his hair *was* dark . . . The gray sky behind him was devoid of clouds, birds, or a sun. Simply a flat gray *blankness* that made Winston feel both weak and *familiar*, for reasons he couldn't and didn't want to understand.

"It's . . . not good. A loved one will disappoint you . . . something you're looking for won't be what you hoped it'd be. You'll feel anxiety, sadness, regret, for unexpected reasons. If you treat someone nice, they won't be nice back . . . even your friends will betray you. I wish it were a better reading, but the cards, they *know* even if—"

"Maybe the cards were thinking of someone else." He swept the four cards in a pile, the five of cups on top. He thrust the cards into the deck she held loosely in her left hand, burying them in the middle.

Shuffling the pack before putting it back into the box, Jomel, not raising her brown eyes to meet his blue ones, said, "There's something else the cards say about you." She waited for him to reply, but he lay back against the headboard, the clammy metal chilling his ribs and spine. She began again, "When more than one card from a suit shows up in a reading, like the three cups in yours, it means the message is . . . real *strong*. That it's almost sure to happen. I don't know if that's what you want to hear, but the fortune teller I knew said to be sure to tell the client—it's his dime. Oh . . . I suppose I should've told you sooner, but . . . well, it's a dollar, two if you want to again—"

In answer, Winston got up and took a crumpled dollar bill out of his jacket pocket, then, thinking over what she'd just said, pulled out a dime and wrapped it in the dollar. He tossed the bundle on her lap before slipping on his pants, shirt, and shoes. Rolling his underpants, T-shirt, and socks into his jacket, he left the room without another glance at Jomel.

Winston splashed himself with cold water from the bedside pitcher, washing the girl's scent off his body, then redressed and made his way downstairs, suitcase in hand. Rain turned his hair into a dark skullcap by the time he'd climbed into the Woody. For a few seconds he shivered behind the wheel, before turning the key in the ignition, working the clutch, and pulling away from the house.

Between the steady *slap-slap* of his wipers, and the bowing and bending of the trees lining the road, Winston found it difficult to see, driving almost by feel, his headlights all but useless in the shimmering downpour. As he passed a telephone pole, something clicked in his mind; he backed up to take a better look at the denuded wood. The South-Side Enterprises poster he'd seen there hours before was gone. The carnival had no doubt canceled on account of rain, which in turn meant that the carny—and Palmer—could be long gone.

Winston pulled over onto the soft muddy shoulder of the road, under the dripping trees, and took his last quarter case of beer out of the trunk. Quietly and determinedly, he downed half of it, shedding silent, wracking tears as he crumbled each drained can. He couldn't face the prospect of losing Palmer's trail and returning home alone both defeated *and* sober.

Looking at the twisted cans at his feet, Winston felt slightly better. He knew he'd suffer come morning, a fitting punishment for not going to his friend when he had the chance. Failing his own expectations hurt, but letting his only friend down verged on the unforgivable.

Yet, tonight his drunk was . . . different. Instead of becoming cozy and sleepy, sinking into oblivion for a few nightmarish hours, Winston felt as if his brain were peeled like a grape; every thought, every sensation, every stimuli, was incredibly sensitive and sharp. Like a bizarre punishment meted out to an evil-doer on "*Lights Out*," a penalty carefully tailored to custom-fit his particular crime. Winston sought forgetfulness, hence he was cursed with hypersensitivity.

And that newfound perception told him that he was insane to sit in a car, under a *tree*, during an electrical storm. He pulled back onto the road, cruising slowly down the narrow stretch before him. Then the road didn't look familiar at *all*.

SIXTY-EIGHT

From Palmer Nemmitz's journal—
Standing there, watching the lightning turn Maeve's trailer into a luminescent bullet, until rainy darkness obscured that unearthly glow, my mind was a whirl of voices not my own: Larry's, Harold's, Maeve's, Moby Jackie's, and poor Jomel's. Everyone and no one was to blame for the way things had fallen, but I was sure of one thing—someone was going to hurt *worse* than I was hurting, worse than *anyone* had hurt before. It was either release the pain or allow it to rot me through from the inside, an acid of such power even Arch "Lights Out" Obeler would scream his throat bloody at the thought of it.

Maeve was moving inside that trailer, the shadow of her right arm near her lamp shade was a dark lurching thing that rippled across the pink curtains, almost scaring the piss out of me. But my hurt was stronger than my fear; as her voice echoed in my mind (*comes naturally to her kind*), I mounted those rain-slippery metal steps leading to her door. Inside my pants, I was all hard and anxious, from the memory of how I'd wanted her before. But that desire was now tempered with *knowledge*, by the spoiled way things were now.

Lord help me, I found the handle on that rain-cold door, and covered it with my shaking hand. The firm metal steadied my trembling fingers, before I tried the lock. Under the muted metallic drum of the rain on her Airstream, I heard Maeve slam against something with her passing, but she didn't cry out.

Rattling the locked door, pounding it with my free hand, my knees, I heard myself saying, "Open up, bitch. *Now*," and it was strange as if my mouth and brain were working independently; my conciousness a child cowering in a darkened room, eyes riveted to the glowing dial of the radio, listening as poor Sidney Ellstrom was done in in yet another gruesome manner on "*Lights Out*," *I* could do nothing at that point. The part of me that *counted* was raptly watching that golden dial . . . only this time the horrible mind-pictures were going to be *real*. My *body* pounded on that door; between the dull thud of flesh hitting metal, the cowering boy in me heard Maeve talking to herself in there, small, gibbering, panicked noises in a voice gone strange with terror.

She *knew*. She realized who demanded that she open the door. But she couldn't stop the inevitable, couldn't keep that lock on her door from giving way under the repeated shaking and jiggling. She couldn't *do* a thing . . . but she was smart nonetheless.

When the door finally gave, and I plummeted into that flowers-and-sweat-smelling trailer, Maeve snapped off her lamp. My eyes stung from a sudden exposure to bright light followed by abrupt darkness. A swimming mixture of blackness and blooming lime-green afterimage filled my line of vision. All I heard was the sound of her moving swiftly in the darkness to a place well away from me, scraping a chair along the floor before stopping.

Her breath was a labored wheeze, the suffering sound of a hurt thing. Gradually, my vision cleared. I made out dim shapes in the murk of the trailer—a bed, small stove, a table, a sink. And a vanity table in the back, behind which Maeve huddled, back pinned to the wall, something pale and slightly luminous thrown over her body. Only her head and clutching hand were visible. Lightning bloomed outside; for half a second I saw her room clearly.

Woman things, frilly pillows, china dolls, the shine of silver trinkets on the vanity before her. The spread-out whiteness of her sling on the bed. Her wide-eyed stare of terror, mouth open slightly.

But just as the brittle light from without died away, I turned my head back to the bed, for there was something there besides the sling—

In the darkness that followed, Maeve spoke, her voice breathy and thin.

"Palmer, you're drunk. Get out and I won't say anything to Mr. Shea. Just *go, please*, Palmer—"

Funny how the waspish rasp was gone, as if it had never been, replaced with a contrite, pleading little-girl voice. Funny how she forgot so soon.

The moist tear of her breath was masked by a bone-shaking boom of thunder; vibrations shot into my feet, my manhood, making me ache and *ache*, all at once. Waiting for the lightning, I trained my eyes on the barely visible whiteness of her discarded sling, listening to her babble, "Please, Palmer, you haven't done anything yet, just go and everything will be all—"

When the light came I was ready, eyes fixed on the bed. In that moment of sizzling brightness, I saw what lay on the narrow bed . . . I saw, but I didn't *believe*. I shook my head, feeling myself go soft and limp from terror.

Maeve's *hand*, her left hand, *lay on the bed*. Bloodless, fingers red-tipped and curling, it rested on the blue-white folds of sheeting, curled fingers beckoning to me. A peachy-pink solid thing, totally separate from Maeve. My breath hitched; I covered my face with my hands before I turned to face her. My consciousness was no longer a terrified child, but a part of *me* again . . . only I was too frightened to ask *"Why?"* as Maeve said, "It isn't what you think—

That was the second *out* that I passed up that night. First I spurned my own bed, and in that terrible moment, I spurned the door behind me, choosing to stay. I walked toward her, right arm extended, shaking fingers aimed at her exposed face and trembling body under the pale silken robe she'd covered herself with in haste. She tried to back away from me, but the wall stopped her. Before her was the vanity table—*her* only way out was to run past me. I was taller and faster than she was, and she knew it. In the hazy darkness, I saw fear on her face, and smelled the animal scent of desperation coming off her in waves, a sick, perfume-tinged odor.

Faint light from the right-hand window cast blue-gray shadows across her face; a breathy bubble issued from the liquid darkness of her mouth, "That . . . on the bed . . . not important, oh, Palmer, you don't *want* to know, oh, please, just leave, come morning . . . I'll tell you everything, oh, please—" Her voice cracked; I heard tears welling up in her throat, and imagined them spilling from her beautiful eyes.

But the image of that hand lying on her bed came back . . . her disembodied *hand*, from which no blood flowed. I moved over, legs like wooden stumps beneath me, so I almost fell onto the bed when I leaned over to feel for the hand. Then my legs went hot where the piss leaked down, for my warm hand touched not a dead hand, but a plaster hand, one that had *never* felt the flow of blood under fine-grained skin. Only cool stiffness. My fingers found the rough porous place where it had been detached from the arm of a store-window dummy.

To my left, Maeve tried crawling under the vanity table, but she didn't fit. In a voice that rose higher and higher, she gibbered, "Palmer, I won't kick up a fuss if you *leave*. Put it down and there'll be *no trouble*. If you don't go I'll scream, Mr. Shea won't like it, there'll be trouble—"

My tongue came unstuck from the roof of my mouth. "I'm already in so much trouble a little more might feel good." Tossing the plaster hand to the floor, where it shattered chalkily, I came closer to the vanity table. Its rounded edge bit into my thigh. There was a small *pocking* sound I couldn't identify, followed by a quick flurry of movement—then something hard and smooth hit my jaw. The table lamp. Seconds later it shattered to the floor. Searing pain made my eyes water. I leaned forward, blocking Maeve's path of escape, hands cradling my aching jaw—just as light blossomed outside the window.

My face was close to the vanity table, close enough so that I saw *everything* there in that flashing instant. Bottles of perfume; a rose-enameled compact; a china hairpin box; silver-topped comb and brush set with initials swirling on the shimmering surfaces, strands of hair twisted in the brush; hair ribbons twisted around an empty bud vase, and *under* the ribbons . . . a mask. A tiny celluloid face, split along the mouth and cunningly hinged so the lips of the wearer made the molded lips move. *And the face was Mae's.*

Steadying myself, I put both hands on the table, and upset the milky hairpin box. Hairpins scrambled across the embroidered runner like long-legged ants. In near blackness, I strained to see the small oval mask . . . as I realized I hadn't seen Mae *anywhere*. . . .

"Please leave now!" As she cowered in her tight corner, Maeve's voice was warbly, tear-garbled. The soft shining surface of her robe was quicksilver thing, catching what weak light came through the small window. The silky fabric moved, sometimes fluid, sometimes quick and jerking; odd shadows rippled across its finish. "I won't tell, only *leave now*!" The implicit agony of her voice made my head pound; *"Now!"* rang in my ears like the shatter of glass.

Still leaning on the table with my right arm, I reached for her tear-hot face with my left hand; her skin twisted in a rictus of fear under my fingertips, her breath warm and moist on my wrist. Out of the corner of my eye, I saw movement under that pink robe. Heard the susurrus of silk being pushed back. Saw the flowing advance of something too dark to make out clearly emerge from under the robe, close by my right arm. Then I *did* turn to look, in time to see, and feel—

Pain. In my forearm.

Where *teeth* sank in.

A soft, tickling sensation of hair brushing my burning skin, as the teeth relinquished their hold.

And the onyx trickle of blood from my savaged arm—on Mae's mouth and chin.

As I clutched my arm, *she* said through red-black lips in abrupt pink-white light, "Little runt bastard."

She said that. *Mae.*

"Little runt," she said again, voice sharp and taunting, as tiny hands wiped blood from her lips. I couldn't back away fast enough. Then it was the "Oh, please, *please*" part again, only that was Maeve—*and she wasn't talking to me.*

In the sudden, welcome darkness, I thought, *No, no . . . can't be it can't be . . . her act, she's doing*—leaning forward, catching Maeve unawares, I grabbed silky fabric in my left hand and gave it a hard yank. . . . The *swish* of it being pulled through the air sounded as if it were happening a billion miles away. Maeve was a pearly luminescence in the semidarkness, whitish in places where her slip stuck to her wet thighs, and—

—and then, the light returned, without my hearing the thunder. And with the radiance came the *truth* . . . and after the brightness was gone, the *image* of it . . . oh, God, what I saw was burned on my eyes. And every time the lightning flashed again, the image was seared in my brain, hotter and deeper, and she kept saying, "Oh, please, please leave," but there was longing, too, in that ragged choking voice, which only made it all the more awful—

I *understood* now, comprehension made it all plain. *Sickeningly* plain.

Mae was not a puppet. And . . . she was not a midget. Nothing as *sane* as that. Maeve had hidden it well, but in a mind-shattering second, I *saw*—

They were twins. Only . . . Mae was tiny, malformed . . . *and growing, like a branch, out of Maeve's side.* Larry had mentioned the black girl with the three arms and four legs, but that poor girl didn't have to cope with a *live head and two arms coming out of her.* A thinking, *speaking* head, and arms that reached out and hurt with tiny red-tipped fingers.

Wedged in that corner, Maeve was on reluctant display, standing upright, back against the wall, chest shuddering under a filmy white slip—no wonder she couldn't breathe. Mae was *in* her chest. And her hands, or, rather, *hand*—her left arm and hand were tiny, a stunted dead branch where her shoulder ended prematurely—opened and closed, like petals on a flower that couldn't decide whether to bloom or wither. From where she jutted out of her sister's side, Mae tried to lean her naked, twisted torso against the wall. Tiny doll hands scrabbled to cover the minute buds of her breasts. And *both* of them were staring at me, one twin tearful, the other bitter . . . then both spoke:

"Oh, please don't tell, oh, please, *please*," she said, until *she* took to looking at me, eyes all hateful, and said, "Little runt, little runt *bastard*, feel powerful *now*?" then it was "Oh, please, go please, go now," all over again, their voices overlapping like raindrops on a pane of glass. And all I could think in my beer and shine stupor was, *A tree . . . a birch, a stripped birch split by lightning. Winston would say that if he were here . . . Oh, Winston, where are you when I need you?*

The twins tried to blend into the wall behind them, hands unconsciously working like blossoms on a nightmare tree— even Maeve's stunted, gnarled hand. Between flashes of searing light, I saw how Maeve slit her slip to allow space for Mae's pygmaean jutting torso that emerged from Maeve parallel to her partially uncovered left breast. *Had to sew up the slit before Jomel did her clothes . . . hide, hide, cover it all up—*

Hideous . . . not only what they *were*, but *living* like that. My conversation with Maeve zipped through my brain, each word taking on different, darker meaning—especially since a silent, hidden third member listened to every word we both said, contorted body concealed in that white sling, fake hand carefully positioned as a subterfuge. Showing only enough to make people think there was a real hand and arm inside . . . and it worked, worked so well that Maeve passed for "normal." Irony welled bitter inside me.

Then I remembered what Larry had said about Harold Shea needing just one super stupendous freak, one so strange and wonderous that the carny could do away with the geek. The same geek that had sickened me, twice, humiliating me before the very *freak* whose unveiling could've spared me that

suffering. Not to mention poor Harold, and his suddenly suspect religion. And not to mention *all* the carnies, who made
do with meager wages and not enough hands to do anything
properly.

Worst of all, Maeve *knew* . . . and she *hid*. In the most
obvious place. The sheer *gall* of her actions both astonished
and horrified me. Maeve, in her quest for normalcy, had
turned her own sister, flesh of her flesh, into a puppet, a
masked, veiled *thing* exposed only in the shadows of a summer night, never to see daylight, or feel anything but cloth-
filtered sunlight on her white skin.

And Maeve knew Harold would've treated her like a queen.
With her, he could've run the "decent" carny of his pipe
dreams, not a childish, makeshift parody of a carny.
Nothing about this pitiful carny *had to be*. All that held Shea back
from the dignity he craved was a white sling. And Maeve
spoke disparagingly of the pitiful has-beens and never-weres
in the freak top. They could've bought her for what she was
worth and sold her for what she *thought* she was worth and
retired on the difference. *Bitch*.

When my eyes met Mae's the light of hate in them was
awful to see. Those eyes had been hidden behind that doll
mask, but the thought that they'd always been there, looking
daggers at the world she could never be a part of, made my
stomach roil and my knees buckle.

When I put my right hand over my mouth—the bite on my
forearm stung worse than a swarm of hornets, a spreading
fire that consumed my flesh from elbow to wrist—something
cold and hard met my lips. The mask. I didn't remember
grabbing it off the vanity top. But when I saw it, looking as
if it grew from my own hand, something inside me said
Enough.

I stumbled backward out of there, unable to tear my eyes
from that pale-fleshed living tree, that grotesquerie shuddering and sobbing in the corner. Only when I felt wind and
fresh rain hitting my back did I turn around and jump to the
ground, running as my feet hit the mud. Behind me, I faintly
heard mingled curses and pleas from the twins, but I ran until
their voices merged with the steady drum of the rain.

The lantern was still lit in the camper, but Larry was gone.
The Tarot cards lay on the rumpled blanket, the sword-
tortured figures glaring bright and sick-hued under the yellow
glow. Breathing in hard, jagged gulps that felt like razor

blades slicing my lungs (*oh, Jeeze, Mae's in her chest*), I kneeled down and pulled my knapsack out from under my bed. Cramming in whatever clothes of mine I could find scattered on the camper floor, I reflexively put in Mae's mask, too. Plus something long, thin, and golden I'd snagged along with it. The bouquet of Tootsie Pops resembled a prickly mace; the sight of it made bile flood into my mouth. I flung that across the length of the camper.

Packing my rumpled belongings, I realized that waiting around to be fired was worse than just up and quitting. I slung my full knapsack onto my shoulders and ran out of the camper, slamming the rickety door behind me. With all my heart, I wished that I'd listened to Larry and called it a night long ago.

But the summer of 1940 was not my time to listen to anyone. I headed past the dark, hulking shapes of the dismantled rides and big trucks, running for the grove of trees north of our encampment. A voice inside screamed at me, *The trees are worst of all . . . lightning likes trees!* By then, I cared little if I lived to see the morning. I hoped that I would die. I *deserved* to die. After what I'd seen, death was my only fitting punishment.

But to reach the swaying blackness of the trees, I had to pass by Maeve's trailer. Suddenly, I heard her, pleading, "Palmer, wait, maybe we can explain . . . please, Palmer." I spun around, nearly dropping to my wet knees in the mud, and stared at her Airstream, its window now a dark, all-pupil eye. Then the door blew shut; and her face appeared in the window, a pupil of white in the darkness. Through the rain, I saw her face crumple as she cried; her mouth was saying what she'd said before, "Oh, please, please don't tell." And then there were *two* faces in that small window, and I could look no more.

I ran all the way to the trees, not stopping until they stood thick and strong-smelling around me, filling my nose with a pungent, earthy-green odor. Sinking to my knees, I cradled my hurt arm against my shirt, leaning over to vomit up all that I'd drunk earlier, until my mouth and nose burned. This time, there was no concerned voice behind me, asking if I was all right. No more 7-Up, no more talks under the cool shadow of a big gnarled tree, no more *wanting* her until I could cry. All of that was gone and dead, never to be again.

And because of that loss, part of me mourned, and died in turn.

Hawking until the taste of spit-up was gone, I told myself I was drunk, bad drunk. Crazy, seeing-things drunk. God, no one could *live* like that. No one could *survive*—but as if to contradict me, pain pulsed in my arm, *squirming* in the flesh, as if tiny teeth still lingered there.

High above, scudding, swirling storm clouds parted, enough to cast feeble light down through the mix of broad-leafed trees. In that faint illumination I could just make out my arm, and the round kiss of blackness there. Too small for an adult's mouth. And too deep and *hurting* to be imagination. Probing the bloody place with my fingers, I felt the open spots where skin had been pierced. Touching the bite only made it worse. I doubled over in a rain-soaked lump of pain. All around me, the wind blew in howling, speaking gusts; in my agony and confusion I swore that the wind spoke to *me*. Called my name.

When I felt the hand on my shoulder, I almost popped out of my skin. Burrowing into myself, I pulled my body into a tight ball—until Larry said, "What in fuck *happened*? I saw you runnin' when I come back from feedin' the geek but you didden hear me callin'—hey, what you doin' with your pack? You ain't goin' off *tonight*—lemme see that arm. Saw blood in the camper, was hopin' it wasn't yours—"

He pried my arm away from my body, scanning it when an obliging lightning bolt struck. When all went dark again, Larry whistled. "Somethin' caught *you* good. Bobcat?" Overcome by shivers, I shook my head. Larry poked the wound with dirty fingers. "Looks like a people bite. Some-one mad at you?" Through teeth that wanted to do nothing more than dance independent of my gums, I told him what happened, up to the point of breaking into Maeve's trailer, but before I went further than "I luh-let myself in," Larry whistled through his stained teeth, saying, "Never figgered *her* f' the bitin' type." I said no more.

Pulling my arm out of his grasp, I stammered, "Hu-hurts real bad. G-g-got anything?" Grunting in the affirmative, he was off running for the camper before I got out the last word. Rocking back and forth, I hugged my arm. Cold rain pum-meled deep into my bones (*Jeeze, her skeleton, all twisted—*), as my eyes added more moisture to my face. Only the tears were hot and salty, stinging when they slid into my mouth.

Then I heard the pound of heavy footfalls, and saw Larry running back, beer belly flopping under his soaked overalls, a shirt wrapped around something in his hand.

Crouching down next to me, Larry grabbed my arm, saying, "This'll sting," as he poured shine into my wound. I bit my lower lip and scrunched up my eyes to keep from screaming out loud. Recorking the bottle, he said, "You drink some, an' put the rest on the arm. Piss'll clean it out, too. You try that if it gets to smellin' bad. Pee'll kill any damn thing. An' I got somethin' for that sister of yours. One you said liked Shirley Temple." As I kept biting my lip, tasting saline warmth, he fiddled with my knapsack, pushing a doll inside. "There. Ought not to get wet. Sis of yours should like 'er. Found some candy, it yours?" Shaking my head, I saw Larry's broad shoulders shrug. " 'Kay, I'll use 'em f' prizes. Now, what the hell *happened*? Gals don't go 'round bitin' fellas f' *nuthin'*."

What Larry said spun around in my head for a few seconds. Everything I'd wanted and hoped for and desired that had gone sour welled up in me, until the mass of confusion and hurt imploded, leaving a tiny core of pure *mean*, pure *bad*. In those rain-scented woods, I told Larry something, a reason for what had happened . . . a false tale that came from a well of badness I didn't realize I possessed before.

It tickled Larry, made him grin. Patting my shoulder, he said a last good-bye, then got up and left me to my evilness and agony. Rain and cold dug like little fingers—white, shaking, red-nailed fingers—that curled and uncurled inside me. Shivering, I watched Larry leave, picking his way over fallen branches. I got up to follow him a ways, until I could just see the Zagelmayer, and the golden square of the screen window. Larry was moving inside, then emerged; when I saw where he was heading, I could look no more.

Charged by fear, I bolted through the trees, ran and stumbled and fell once or twice until I was racing across open ground on the other side. I put as much distance between myself and that carny, away from *them*, as I could. I was glad for the rumble of thunder, knowing it could drown out the screams.

But all I did was put physical distance, a matter of a mile or so, between myself and what was happening behind me. When a person does what I did back there, there aren't enough miles in the universe to keep it away. . . .

SIXTY-NINE

Velvety-lush blackness surrounded Winston as he walked the last mile to the Ewert Woods; thick, scented, close-set with mixed trees, dense enough to shelter almost anyone or anything within its spike-branched depths. And Una's voice was strong, calling him, *begging* him to join her in that rich-smelling place of needle and leaf-cushioned green-black. There was the promise of enjoyment in her voice, of refuge from the strangeness that surrounded Winston . . . her voice carried undercurrents of peace, of calm, of forgetfulness of all that was, and would be.

Cold sober, only slightly sick, Winston walked on, knees sore, soft fluid blisters forming on his heels; as he trudged on, he relived old memories—not those of Una, but of an earlier, bittersweet time, the night he'd lost track of Palmer, and found himself on a strange, rain-patterned road. And the more unfamiliar the road became, the *drier* it was . . . bone-dust dry, in fact.

Winston didn't notice when glittering rain first gave way to residual droplets on his windshield, but gradually he realized that the Woody's tires were no longer splashing through moisture on the dirt road before him. Shutting off his wipers, rolling down his window, Winston no longer smelled the watermelon tang of rain. Ahead, the road was narrower, a thin, winding curl of brown ribbon, overhung with jutting black-leaved branches that smacked the roof of the Woody with odd sounds. Like fingers drumming on an empty beer can, only *sharp*.

It was like driving through a tunnel, only scarier—for smooth tunnel walls wouldn't have scraped the roof of his car, or slapped moistly against the windshield with a slimy, slithering whisper, producing weird echoes.

Moonlight shone in shattered fragments on the road, the hood of his car, revealing only enough to confuse and trick him, not enough to allow him to make out anything clearly.

And the sounds outside his opened window went beyond strange, *or* identifiable.

Despite the muggy warmth of the night, Winston rolled up his window. The trapped wheeze of his breathing only further unnerved him, so he opened the window to begin the cycle anew. That he had no idea where he was made little difference. His tank was almost full. Come morning he'd puzzle out his location, drive around until he found a town. His mind insisted he was in Georgia, so Georgia it was.

As he drove down a road that seemed to loop back on itself, Winston studied the trees that hung down. It puzzled him that the dark-leafed branches tossed so much . . . when there was so little breeze to propel them. When a branch smacked the arm Winston had hanging out the side window, he yelped—the leaves felt both sticky-wet and prickly, too, like the underside of a geranium leaf. No leaves like that grew on any tree *he* knew about.

Winston tried looking for a cutoff, but the road wound before him, as appendageless as a snake. His mind didn't register the white car until he'd almost passed it. The leaf-shrouded blur was moth-pale, hidden in the deep shadows of the roadside. Something about the way the car was parked was . . . *odd,* but the prospect of finding out from the driver where another road might be made Winston brake to a neck-snapping stop.

He fumbled in the glove compartment for the pack of Clove gum he kept there. Chewing furiously for a few seconds, then swallowing the tough lump of gum before stepping out of the car, Winston told himself, *No need to rush . . . Palmer isn't waiting for you anymore.*

Finger-combing his drying hair, Winston nonchalantly strolled over to the white Pierce-Arrow that rested, lopsided, on the shoulder of the road. Winston peered into the interior of the car—no one inside. Perhaps the owner was as lost as he was, and had gone off on foot in search of another road. He almost turned around and left himself, until he heard the woman's voice. "Could you please help me? I'm new here, and don't know my way."

Winston didn't see her until she moved against the darkness of the surrounding trees, and even then, she seemed so *far* away from him. Small; a delicate thing half obscured by wedge-shaped shadows. Her spun-taffy hair formed a halo around the pale oval blur of her face in the weak moonlight.

Having caught his attention, she went on in that small, modulated voice, "Please stay here with me? I'm so lonely . . . you're the first person I've seen in, *oh,* so long." Unable to speak, Winston found himself edging closer to her car, keeping the auto between himself and the woman. Her car was utterly spotless, save for a fine beading of raindrops on its surface.

Before she came close enough to touch him, he smelled her, a mix of roses and jasmine, the way some of the gardens down this way smelled, an intoxicating mingling of wild scents. Her perfume made him dizzy; he leaned against her car, eyes closed, breathing deeply. Faintly, he heard the scritch of fabric rubbing against fabric, a skirt against stockings, but it wasn't until much later that he realized that he'd heard no footsteps coming through the grass.

When he looked up, she was standing just out of his reach, still merged into the leafy darkness. Above them, clouds obscured the moonlight. Her scent cut through the wet, green odor of the foliage, and the earthy tang of the red dirt beyond.

She moved closer. Faint light from the Woody's headlights cast weird shadows across her features; one second she was a childish parody of a woman, then she became a goddess wrought of molten gold.

As she approached Winston, something about her refused to register. . . . Over in the trees, she'd seemed so *short*, yet only a couple of steps brought her up to a height of at least five feet four inches. How she'd managed *that* puzzled him, until he reasoned that summer shadows do strange things to a person's eyes. Any alternative was unthinkable, even in his still-intoxicated state.

Winston reflexively shoved his hands into his pockets, saying with a shaky smile, "I'm a stranger here, too . . . sorry I don't know the way out. But I'll stay with you," hoping she wouldn't find his implied suggestion too forward.

The long-haired woman chose not to speak, not to thank him. Unable to stand the silence that hung between them, he blurted out in what he hoped was a bantering tone, "I don't suppose I should be expecting any thanks for staying—" instantly regretting his choice of words. She wasn't a dollar-a-throw roundheels, but a young *lady,* perhaps of means (he'd seen the luscious pink upholstery in her car)—yet, to his utter shock, *she* reached for his hand with her right one.

Grasping his fingers firmly (her touch stung, dotting his

skin with the tips of a million infinitesimal needles), she led him deep into the trees and tall grass, away from the tilted car and the dusty shoulder of the road.

And as they walked, her in the lead, the grass grew tall, taller, and the branches no longer scratched Winston's face or arms. Something told him that they really hadn't gone very far . . . but when he glanced back at the Pierce-Arrow, it was both far away and absurdly large. Shuddering, he focused on the back of her head, on the shifting waves of gold-brown hair that moved slightly, gently, as she walked before him. The rest of her—save for her hands—was sucked into darkness.

But when she stopped to kiss him, her face bloomed soft and luminescent beneath his; kissing her was like getting his nose tickled by beer bubbles. An insubstantial, yet stinging sensation. Her lips were warm, yet there was coolness within. Her mouth *was* cool, tasting of chocolate and something else, a flavor that during his childhood, he would've dubbed "green." His name for the taste of green gum-drops and ju-ju bees; a refreshing, cool piquancy that transcended spearmint or wintergreen—more a *sensation* than a mere flavor. Her teeth were smooth nubs of ice, sending shivers throughout his mouth and tongue. Their lips parted with a moist, softly smacking sound.

Without need for words, they urgently removed each other's clothing, sinking slowly to the ground after their garments crumpled on the grass—a dreamy ballet of movement without *feeling*, for Winston knew not what clothes he had taken from her body, as if his fingertips had failed him. Then, they were prone, sealed against each other, apart from the damp grass and uneven surface of the ground below.

And in his excitement, Winston found himself growing sleepy, that utter relaxation of mind and body that came before sleep, before his special dream. Only this time, there was no need to fantasize about *her*, the small love of his dreams . . . for at the instant of letting himself into the dream, his moment of waking *was* the dream.

For the woman in his arms *shifted*; not so much a matter of movement, but a complete veer into another *scale* entirely. Beneath him, her movements were not those to which he'd become accustomed during encounters with others. And his being *sunk* below the level of comprehension, to a point where he was acutely aware that something was wrong, yet blissfully right, too.

She was in control—not only physically (he'd never before imagined the sense of being *entered*), but *totally*. Thoughts beyond his own wants and needs flashed through his mind so quickly he had no opportunity to reflect upon them. With the passing of each alien desire, he was carried along on a tide of something that did not resemble the death he'd experienced in the arms of other girls, but instead shot through his entire being—mind, soul, body, and beyond.

When he reached a point where he feared that all of him would be forever devoured, he found himself flipped over on his back, looking up at the sky . . . a strange canopy of woven whiteness, laced with sparkling prismatic dew of shocking size. Then, he found himself in the place of his mind, the place he'd visited many a night before . . . that time and space of dry crumbling tan earth, under the fall of warm gray ash. The arid, warm spot, with *her* beneath him. His tightly small woman, the childlike being long past childhood, long past all future maturity of body or mind or experience, only *this* time he was alert. His eyes opened wide, taking in the deep gritty texture of the soil, the low leaden sun that cast light but no heat, and the huge visible motes of gray ashlike dust swirling and drifting down, as if trapped in the interior of a paperweight. And he looked down at her, under him— then closed his eyes tightly, wanting this dream, this living fantasy, to end, *now*. For he'd seen blood oozing blackish and twinkling on what should have been her—

Frantically, he tried to break the warm connection between their bodies, even as *his* entire body stung and itched wherever it touched hers. And then his being, even as he squeezed his eyes tight, was flooded with the taste/sight/sensation of *green*, of rich chocolate and the now-cloying reek of jasmines and roses, intermingled and refined, with undertones of something *sweeter*, yet slightly fulsome. . . .

After a million suns exploded in his brain, leaving wavering afterimages floating before his eyes, she allowed him to withdraw his shriveling limpness. He felt the dribble of warm blood on his lower lip, dimly wondering why he hadn't noticed the pain of the bite when it happened. But the gentle slide of blood down his chin renewed him; he entered her once more, feeling the intact warmth of her body beneath his, and the dewy coolness of the grass below. And the clouds opened above them and let moonlight filter through, enough to penetrate the moving trees. Enough to touch her face.

Later, all he remembered was that her eyes were blue and brown, in rings of color around each pupil. And that one eye wandered. When he was deep within her, those eyes turned from gentle to sharply cruel; he fell into her again, so far that only the pain kept him afloat. Her eyes bored into his, asking, *Feel how it is on the* other *end of the situation?* Then came a sensation he couldn't describe later on, but oh, while it *happened*—it was purification, rapture, purging, and agony, all blended into a single nameless emotion, a sentiment of such exquisite refinement and awesome power Winston was unable to resist it . . . once it was over, he couldn't explain or recapture it. It was both completion and dissolution; one part of him sought to forget it, while the other part longed to reexperience it.

Afterward, Winston still felt the pain, but there was a longing, too. For more, and more. . . .

Yet, what had happened to him was as if he'd been starving, and had finally eaten his fill, never to hunger again. There was something frightening about that realization; the "never to need again" part was too much to contemplate at his age. The implication was staggering, overwhelming; as if his life had been firmly guided, and all *he* needed to do was glide along, mindless, unexpectant. The woman who could give him all that he'd ever want was his for the taking, he sensed, but the notion gave him no comfort.

It was too much like life at home with never a thought about Winston's need to think for himself, to try and maybe fail and try again before getting life right. He'd already rebelled against an easy, sure path—and now he was presented with an equally alluring, albeit repelling, fate.

For he *knew* that the woman-child he still held in his arms, whose delicate places still sheltered him, was *all* he'd ever need in life, all he'd require to be satisfied—all that *would* sate him, from now on. But to have . . . *this* thrust on him was too much to bear, no matter what she could be to him. The lack of *choice*—of seeking, then finding—wounded his pride.

Staring into her eyes, Winston saw that she *liked* doing this to him; offering pleasure, agony, and confusion that came with *everything* she gave. Her fantastic eyes were triumphant, sated, yet curious. Overcome by shame and bewilderment, he left her body, the sound of their parting shockingly loud in the darkness.

Winston felt around for and put on his clothes; he tried to hurry but only slowed up because he kept putting the wrong limbs into the wrong openings. She lay smiling up at him, taffy hair a waving spill around her face, arms circling her head in a relaxed position. Unable to speak, Winston hurried to his Woody, getting in without shutting the door as he gunned the engine, but he still heard her say in a low, yet distinct voice, "Take me with you . . . make me real and you'll never want again—" Slamming the car door, Winston told himself that he'd only imagined that she'd added his name at the end of her sentence.

He pulled away, driving until faint sunlight shone on damp road mud, and the trees stood tall and indifferent to his passing. White signs dotting the road assured him that Jesus would save him—but Winston now doubted that otherwise reassuring sentiment. Mingled shame and pleasure stayed with him; for a week he sought no female company. He barreled through each small town, pausing only to eat or drink, not even touching the remaining cans of beer in his trunk, not after he'd learned that next morning that no one, no where, had heard tell of a South-State Enterprises Carnival, nor were there any new posters slapped on any signposts anywhere. . . .

Then, he was back in Wisconsin, in Ewerton by late evening, and Porter and Gayleen welcomed him home. Their only comment was, "Great-aunt's phone out? We called, but couldn't get through." He assured them that the dear old lady *was* having phone problems, but not to worry, she sent love and kisses—then he *did* need a couple of beers, to prepare him for the rubbish heaps that masqueraded as his parents' beds. And to cope with Wilbur Holiday's disappointed tone when he called Winston the next morning, asking if Palmer was home.

Then he learned that his friend hadn't returned . . . but he was unable to go back and look again. There were no visiting relatives to nursemaid his parents, and school was starting within a month. Remembering how he'd seen no more carny posters after the twenty-sixth, Winston felt dead inside, but told himself Palmer was a big boy. For Winston had his own problems. *She* might be out there on some blue road, waiting for him. A fear darker than the prospect of never seeing his only friend again. . . .

• • •

Shuddering with the memory of those long-ago days, Winston found himself within touching distance of the woods. Taking a deep breath, Winston dived into the dense trees; branches slapped him in the face, clung to his jacket, as if silently imploring, *Stay out, stay away.* . . . But he pressed forward. The sharp tang of oozing sap made his nostrils flare. Needles and dead, brittle branches poked his eyes, his hands.

Deeper into the woods, Una's voice became clear, ringing, so close he heard the gentle sound her tongue made as it touched her teeth. Propelled by the promise of sweet escape, Winston pushed on, on, until he . . . *saw* her white limbs against a tree, and—

Noticing him, she stopped her crooning. And the silence of the woods was a palpable thing, alive in itself, broken only by Winston's dissonant breathing . . . until his eyes made sense of all they saw, taking in *all* that waited in the clearing before him. He thought, *Lord . . . looks . . . like . . . yarn, wet, on hands, big spread-out hands. . . .* ohmigod *Una, I can't* I can't! The pulsing echo of his screams shattered the silence of the forest, until he could scream no more. His footfalls reverberated through the trees like the beating of a terrified heart, but still, *still* he heard her laughter behind him . . . satisfied laughter, commanding him to return, yet not really caring if he did or not.

For Una's needs were being satisfied.

Huddled under a sprinkle of winking stars, Winston tried to make himself comfortable on his bench, before giving up entirely. Rattled by what he'd seen in the woods, he was torn; spend the night exposed on his bench, or go into a building, to perhaps find something *worse* than what waited in the woods. But one thing was clear as he hugged his shaking knees and nursed his aching head—this place was *not* Hell. What he saw out there smacked of something more ancient than a Judeo-Christian Hell; more pagan, violent . . . and tailor-made. There was a hint of just desserts, even *reward* unrelated to mere retribution.

Wanting—*needing* a drink very badly, Winston tried to think of who'd want to *do* that to Una. Curled up on his bench, Winston gradually recalled a newer memory, a secondhand recollection. From Palmer Nemmitz's past. He too met a girl like Winston's white-car girl, but oh, with such a difference. A huge, unmistakable dissimilarity, something Winston *surely* would have noticed. But the similarities between the two women were uncanny. And there *was* that car—

But if they were the same person, how could a *freak* have felt so normal at the start? Then, remembering the stunted, vicious twin, comparing her to how *his* girl had changed, Winston began to shake.

SEVENTY

Brent lay across his rumpled bed, near the open window, wiping his tired, watering eyes. *The cut, on her side . . . no wonder Uncle Palmer didn't want to tell me . . . it was his damned fault. A damned* symbol, *that's all Zoe meant to whoever did that.*

As he pressed the manuscript against his chest, Brent stared up at the plaster-caked painted ceiling. *But what would* you *have done, hotshot? If you were in* his *shoes? You freaked at the sight of Zoe's* body— Drifting off to sleep, mind numb from the assault of his uncle's narration, Brent felt weak and helpless in the face of such cruelty, such inhuman superiority. No matter what Palmer had done to the twins, what right did they have to kill an innocent woman, then slice, photograph, and *arrange* her? Brent seethed with rage as sleep overcame him. Below him, sleeping before a television screen, his Uncle Palmer made half-accurate motions with his left hand, against the bleeding, itching open wound on his right forearm.

Brent woke up sometime past midnight, the glare of the overhead light in his eyes. Propped up on his elbow, he again turned the pages of the manuscript in search of the awful thing his uncle had said to Larry that night, the terrible thing that brought the eternal wrath of Maeve *and* Mae upon him . . . and which had sucked in Zoe.

From Palmer Nemmitz's journal—

. . . stuck to the blue roads, mostly, walking until I saw enough men and boys hopping freight and felt confident enough to try it myself. For a week, maybe more, I made good progress. Common sense told me to stay clear of the hoboes who hugged the dark corners of the cars. Likewise, I knew better than to fall asleep in a boxcar.

The worst hop was my first—my heart was in my cheeks until I knew I'd made it into the slowly rolling car without slipping under it and getting both legs lopped off by those silver wheels. Luckily, my arms were strong; hoisting myself into the open cars with a single easy motion became second nature to me. The times I found myself in an occupied car, I sat as far away from my "companions" as possible.

Once, I got into a car occupied by a rail man who lay on a pile of wood chips, along with Mr. Jack Daniels. He yelled that he'd turn me in, but I yelled back that I didn't think sleeping on the job was standard Chessie System practice—after that we both quieted down until I jumped off before the next stop.

And all the while I traveled that first week or so, living off Pepsis and Moon Pies (the cheapest meal possible), which I bought in general stores, I told myself over and over, "You were drunk, you were scared, you were drunk, you were—" until it ran around in my head like some rhyme.

Still, what I'd seen that night stayed with me, plastered on the insides of my eyelids, not even granting me peace in sleep. True, I *had* been drunk, but it was an odd, alert drunk. Everything stood out clear and isolated in my head, all the better to drive me crazy with the remembering of it.

And, worse, I had proof of what I'd seen. How many ventriloquists dummies need to wear a mask? In full light, it was obvious that a live person had worn it, for the back of it carried a residue of greasy sweat. The mask had been cut from a doll's head, one of those cheap ones sold in the Wish Book. For attaching to a stuffed body. The edges were jagged around the outside—Maeve's knife had wavered. And wound around the mask was something else, but not of Mae's. An add-a-pearl necklace, a special necklace given to a girl at birth and augmented each year with a new pearl. One for each year of life. The necklace intertwined in Mae's mask bore sixteen pearls.

Maeve and Mae were only sixteen years old . . . scant

months older than me. For some reason, knowing *that* made me hurt all the more.

What I'd *done*, back in those woods, made me cringe and cower inside. I was of two minds; what would be worse for the twins—losing their livelihood, or *keeping* their job . . . after their secret was known?

And as if my memories weren't enough to sicken me, I had a reminder of that night *on* me. The open bite wound wouldn't heal—no matter how much shine I dribbled on it, until my eyes watered and my lip ached from being bitten. No matter how often I peed on it, to cleanse it. No matter how many plantain leaves I crushed and laid across it—*the damned bite wouldn't heal.*

Not that it was infected. No pus oozed out, and the skin around it was a healthy tanned pink. It just *bled*. When I awoke after a night curled up under some tree, or behind some barn, I swore that I saw the faint shine of fresh spittle around the perfect teeth marks. Once, the sheen of spit was so new, so *real*, I scrubbed my arm against my pants, until my thigh was smeared reddish brown, and my arm bled freely.

I reached a point where I feared letting people see my arm, for fear they'd get overinterested in me. More than once, I wished I'd asked for those Tootsie Pops when Larry asked me about them. But thinking of food and Maeve (I wondered with revulsion if Mae ate too) sickened me so much I barely had an appetite anyhow. The closer I got to Tennessee, the less I wanted food, save for my occasional smiling Moon Pies and Pepsis—both of which made me light-headed, and a bit foolish. . . .

Early in August, I hopped a boxcar one afternoon. Before I realized it, it was morning. The burlap around the big open door of the boxcar hung down in places, like big filmy curtains. Outside that big window, the sun began to rise out of pink and orange and pale golden-tinged clouds, with a ribbon of mauve on the horizon. When the sun moved up, the clouds became light-edged, glowing, with a rose-colored shimmer where the sun came through the strongest. It was so beautiful I wanted nothing more than to be swallowed up in that beauty. But then the light grew pure and pale in color, and something about the goldness of it reminded me of Maeve on that last day when the gold came up from the ground to caress her pink outfit as I'd touched her face. All of a sudden, the memory wasn't *good* anymore; it filled me with a panic that worked

badly with my light head and fluttery, empty stomach. Then
. . . then the faint scent of jasmine, and roses, filled the boxcar; it became too confining, too much like the geek's trailer—
or Maeve's trailer. All I knew was *I want out, now.* Swaying
dizzily, I got to my feet, and before thinking it through, I
moved to the edge of the opening and jumped—

Right into nothing. My fall was broken ten feet down the
embankment, as I came to rest on rough stones and rusted
beer cans. And for the first time since I was bit, I forgot all
about the searing pain in my arm—for the agony in my right
knee was enough to make me bawl.

Waves of pain shot up to my groin and down to my toes,
cramping the entire leg. I couldn't stand up, let alone hobble stiff-legged, for hours—how many, I couldn't tell. My
Ingersol watch was broken in the fall. Funny, even though
I could've *sworn* I'd smelled jasmine and roses (neither
flower was uncommon in the Southeast), there wasn't a rose
or jasmine bush anywhere within smell or sight.

I can't recall too much from that day . . . or the next or
the next. I found sticks somewhere, and ripped up Vern's
bandannas, using them to tie the sticks to my swollen knee.
The top of it was an ugly shifting purple-green-blue, like a
housefly. Painfully easing my pants back on, I lurched my
way north, not seeking medical aid. Aside from not being
able to pay for a doctor's services, I was afraid of being
tossed in jail—I was both a minor and a vagrant.

So I traveled at worse than a snail's pace. I had plenty of
time to see the flattened husks of sun-baked dead animals by
the roadside, forever frozen in horrible, pathetic positions,
until the dirt and mud covered them come fall. Many a time
I wished I could lie in the middle of the road, letting passing
cars and trucks flatten and dejuice me, until I was a dry husk
with no memories and no regrets. Just a thing lying sun-
blackened and quiet along the soft shoulder.

But a man can't die a roadside death, like a small hopping
animal. I thought hard as I hobbled, biting skin out of the
insides of my cheeks until I hawked bright phlegm, remembering the lung-winged toad I'd seen earlier that summer,
finally seeing it for what it was, a premonition of that rain-
drumming night in the trailer. I wondered what it was like,
to have to live with something *live* growing out of you that
wasn't *you*. Living a lie in order to live a half-way normal

life. And Mae had only a midnight, masked life, mocked by the rubes, and mocking in return.

Half of me was glad I didn't have to experience their pain, but the rest of me remembered that I'd been dealt a losing hand myself. At least the twins had money; *that* made people turn their heads and look the other way when it came to a lot of things.

Take Winston; everyone and their uncle's uncle knew about his drinking and smoking—yet Winston was the boy most likely to be king of the hill. Nobody with eyes could ignore his parents either, but Porter remained superintendent, and no one suggested that Gayleen wear fewer jangling bangles to Sunday school class.

That was the worst thing about small towns; they coddled and protected their trash—provided they were home-grown trash. Not a week went by when the Yingley clan didn't have a member enjoying a week's free lodging in the "Ewerton Hilton"; the Winstons bought their "medicine" at the same tavern, but Porter's and Gayleen's faces never peered out from behind vertical bars—all because the Yingley's were from out-of-state. And the police did *nothing* when Porter uprooted the parking meters on the east side of Ewert Avenue—he didn't even notice until the last meter crashed through his windshield.

Money. It was the sole thing that made me quit kicking myself in the seat of my shabby pants over what happened to Maeve and Mae—and it was the only thing that let that bite on my arm heal and scab over.

After my watch shattered, I lost track of time—not only the hour of the day, but whole days themselves. I'd limp past a town on what I thought was Friday, only to see folks in their Sunday best filing into churches. No matter how I tried to keep track of my days, they lagged behind me or ran ahead of me, until I gave up altogether and just *trudged*.

Hip sore from walking the wrong way, feet too tender to walk over rough stones without making me sniff back tears, not looking up or down—just *ahead*.

No one stopped to give me a ride—and looking as I did, I didn't blame a one of them. My hair was too long, my clothes were filthy, my flesh piebald with dirt, and my left shoe sole was loose, letting in dirt and grit and adding misery to each step I took. *I* wouldn't have given *me* a ride.

So I walked, unable to bend my knee, unable to give my

burning hip a rest, just inching north along America's blue roads. The weight of the pack on my back decreased as the days and nights grew colder. Pretty soon it wasn't apparent that I was losing weight; my form was plumped out with layers of clothing, some mine, some plucked from early-morning clotheslines or pegs in open sheds. I couldn't even leave a few coins for what I stole. I felt no guilt over the food I snatched from gardens or garbage cans—if people left food on the vine after harvest, or tossed out edible bits from last night's supper, they needed no compensation for the little I took to survive. I would've killed for some of that greasy but clean fried oatmeal or okra at the carny. I didn't need to wipe the coffee grounds off it.

Once I reached the southernmost tip of Illinois, I was too ashamed of my appearance to ask service station attendants for the key to the men's room—and baring my behind to the elements only intensified my embarrassment.

Inching through Illinois, I saw geese fly above me, headed for where I'd come from, and I realized that I'd lost more than a few days during my journey home. The layers of thin clothing I wore didn't insulate me from the cold. Many a day came and went when I debated whether to turn myself in to the nearest county sheriff or police chief. The fear of them saying, "Missing? No one's reported you missing . . . you wanted for some crime, son?" kept me on the road.

I dragged myself forward a few miles each day. By that time, my fingertips were usually bluish and hurt like the dickens. It's been so long since I washed that the dirt kept some of the cold away; when I rested alongside the road, under orange- and yellow- and brown-leaved trees, I easily rubbed cigar-shaped bits of shed skin and dirt from myself. I wanted my hands and face to look slightly clean, in case someone took pity on me and offered me a ride. No one did, but I didn't attract the attention of any squad car riding cops, either.

Soon my path was softened by the fall of leaves along the road, and on side streets of the towns I reluctantly passed through. I wanted to cry when I saw little kids skipping off to school, snug in their princess coats and sturdy school boots. Back home Merle and Effie and Shirl would be in school, and Vern and Vernilla were doing my chores as well as theirs, listening to the old man's noon gripes. Or maybe since the most important member of his audience was gone, he just ate his food without raking me and our Ma over the coals for dessert.

Near the Illinois-Wisconsin border an idea came to me, something I thought just might work. That mix of pain and guilt on Wilbur Holiday's face still hung in the back of my mind. He knew, and I knew, and three-fourths of the town knew, so why shouldn't I try to get something more from the man than his green eyes? No blackmail; just help, anything to keep me away from the old man until I was twenty-one and free of Enoch Nemmitz. Holiday had scads of money. Surely he could afford a helper in his store? Or recommend me to another businessman for a full-time job, maybe with room and board thrown in? I knew his wife wouldn't like it, but after what she did to our Ma, I didn't think she'd have much to say in the matter. She may've been a Crescent by birth, but that didn't give her the right to kill—even if she was never charged or punished for what she did.

The hope of getting help kept me going for those last six hundred miles or so; by then my knee had healed to a stiff numbness, enough to let me hobble faster through Wisconsin. Up through Rock, Dane, Columbia, and Marquette counties, then Waushura, Portage, Marathon, and Taylor counties, until I was close by Dean County . . . and home. The closer I got to Dean County, the warmer it became, until the morning of the glorious sunrise, when it was warm enough for me to unpeel a few layers of clothing and toss them into a ditch. I didn't want the old man to know I'd stolen anything. Running off was one thing, but stealing was another.

I knew it was Monday; I'd heard bells and seen a few rusted-out cars shuff down county roads to church the day before. Of course, the piety of the drivers didn't extend to the young man limping his way painfully down the road. Piety was for *inside* the church, not to be wasted on strangers who might appreciate it. But what I saw the next morning, come daybreak, was enough to make me forget all the badness I'd seen or done in my life.

Nothing before or since was that beautiful, be it man-made or a product of nature. There were shades of red, orange, and purple that painters don't have names for, let alone the pigments to recapture them. The clouds glowed gemstone bright, each hue layered and intertwined; the shades both blended and apart. All were lit from behind with a light both pure and wild in its intensity. A voice in my mind whispered,

*Nothing truly good can come of such glory . . . there's no
humility in beauty,* but my eyes appreciated the show. The
shades faded a bit by the time I reached county trunk QV,
but were still bright enough to reflect on the homes around
me, turning white and yellow clapboards to butter-blushing
hues.

I was down to my bottom shirt—the one I'd worn the day
I left Ewerton. My collar and shirt cuffs were frayed white,
but I could do nothing about that. Around me, the temperature was at least in the fifties, warm enough to turn my grimy
fingers a normal pink.

Limping along Mill Road, close to Roberts Street, I saw
something that made my heart thud sickly in my chest. Some
houses had carved pumpkins rotting on their front porches or
beside their compost heaps, faces leprous with mold and
black-freckled with frost. Collapsed mouths devoured cut-
open noses, and the eyeholes drooped, showing rotten white
within. Tossed-aside jack-o'-lanterns meant one thing—
Halloween was over. Moving faster, ignoring the protesta-
tions of my tender hip, I crossed Lumbermill Drive and
walked along the curving stretch of Roberts Street, until I
looked up at the Holiday house. It was November all right—
as in Armistice Day.

The black and orange bunting was gone from those sage-
green columns and porch railings, to be replaced with tricolor
bunting, flags, and balsa-wood rifles propped up against the
house. The same decorations Wilbur brought out every Sunday before Armistice Day since *I* could remember, and reverently took down come the day after the holiday. So this was
November 11 . . . which meant that I was no longer sixteen.
I had been making my way home for close to four months.

The thought of it all made me stop in my tracks, to run
dirty fingers through my lank greasy hair in mute amazement.
I'd been gone close to six months, a lifetime, yet I hadn't
learned a thing about myself—save for discovering a secret
core of badness inside me that almost (if indeed it hadn't)
killed someone—make that a *couple* of someones.

I was so lost in shock I didn't notice Wilbur until he stepped
across his porch, making a board sing loudly. When I looked
up, he was coming across his lawn, a smile lighting up his
usually dour face, his eyes huge with surprise. But his voice
was still cautious; stopping a few feet short of me, he said,

"I was hoping you'd show up before it snowed, Palmer. Walking through snow would be difficult."

I stared at him, trying to think of an equally civil but distant reply, but before I got anything out, he motioned to the house. "Hortense isn't up yet, but I was fixing myself something to eat. Care to join me?"

I followed him into his house, going through the front door as if it was the most natural thing in the world to do. That Sarouk carpet in the front hallway could've been a red carpet laid out for me alone. I followed him into that spotless white kitchen as if I were his natural son, and not his bastard. But some of the resolve that had helped me get home vanished in his presence; if he'd been a less civil and decent man, I would have had no qualms about demanding a slice of the Holiday pie.

But doing such a thing to Wilbur Holiday would've been beneath me, made me a worse person that I already was. He'd never been cruel to me. Always welcomed me into his store, offered me free bottles of 7-Up or a pickle out of the barrel or a stick or two of Wrigley's. He never embarrassed me by only offering free things to me alone; he did the same for Winston and Dead Fred. After the kindness the man had shown me, I felt guilty over wanting to twist his arm until money clinked down from his open palm. It wasn't his fault that I didn't inherit our Ma's brown eyes along with her wavy brown hair. Wilbur couldn't help what color eyes he had. It was too bad I got mine from him, but that was the draw of the cards. His blond hair would've been a more obvious inheritance, since both our Ma and the old man had dark hair. Coloring my hair would've been *degrading*.

A pan of eggs was frying on the front burner of the Stewart range; Wilbur transferred it to the warming shelf and took down another skillet from its nail over the stove. After getting some fresh eggs out of the refrigerator, along with some butter, he said over his shoulder, "Be a while before the eggs are ready. My bathroom is down the hall, third door to the left. No need to worry about Hortense coming in there, hers is on the third floor. Hers is off-limits to me, and mine is to her. Claims I dribbled on *her* linoleum when I shook off . . . *you're* free to go on the floor if you've a mind to." What was so painful about his speech was that there was no rancor in his tone, only resignation. As if the situation were old hat.

No matter how much our Ma and the old man fought, she

never made him use a separate bathroom exclusively. She knew that men drip, no matter how careful we are. Of course, I doubt that the old man would've stood for being religated to going into a different bathroom in his own house, as if he were a hired man not to be trusted in our Ma's toilet. But I suspected that Wilbur was used to putting up with a lot of things most men would've decked their wives over.

Moist steam hit me in the face like a soggy towel as I opened the bathroom door. Everything was foggy from the billows of steam rising from the freshly filled tub. Extra towels were laid out on the toilet tank, topped with a new bar of Cashmere Bouquet soap. And fresh clothing Wilbur hadn't worn since I played with Tinkertoys was folded neatly under the towels. Even socks and underwear. No shoes, but that didn't matter.

I was touched—and heartsick. I wondered how many times he'd filled that tub, let the water grow cold, then drained it, to begin the cycle again come morning. As if he was sure I'd pass his house on the way home.

The blind faithfulness of his gesture made me want to cry, and I realized that trying to make him take care of me was wrong. I doubted that the old man had filled the old zinc tub in the basement for me.

My bum leg pained me getting into the tub (the swelling and mottled colors were gone, but my kneecap rested crooked under the skin), but after soaking awhile, I felt like a human being again. The incised letters in the bar of soap were gone by the time I was through with it, but at least I didn't leave dark streaks on the towels.

Toweling off my hair until it was dry, I saw that he'd even left a pair of hair-cutting scissors on the sink. When I was done fixing myself up, I almost looked like I did when I left town in May. My hair was raggedly cut short, my skin was clean and spotless, and my clothes were old but laundered.

But when I wiped a clear spot on that foggy mirror with my forearm, to stare at my reflection before the glass clouded up again, I realized my eyes would never be the same. My gaze was startled, haunted, as if what I'd seen had curdled my eyes from within. I hoped Wilbur wouldn't serve up a lot of questions with his meal. True, he'd paid for the right to ask, but I doubted that he wanted to hear what *really* happened.

He must've heard me getting out of the tub, or maybe he

waited for the churgling glug of water going down the drain.
Either way, Wilbur had two steaming plates set on the table;
eggs, toast, bacon, and sliced tomatoes on petal-patterned
Marjolica, with a coffeepot on the table between our cups.
Wilbur was already seated, but wasn't eating. He almost
smiled when he saw me, before changing the upturn of his
lips into a question.

"Scrambled all right? I forgot to ask. There's orange juice
in the refrigerator, if you'd care for some."

It was as if I were a stranger at a depot, and he was asking
for directions. I wanted to thank him for what he did that
morning, but the moment came and went. I shook my head,
saying, "Thanks, coffee's fine with me." Thinking back on
it, it was all so *absurd*. We were *father* and *son*, for Christ-
all-Friday, yet there we were, ultra-polite, asking to please
pass the salt. All the while, I thought he had to break sometime; forget himself and at least smile at me. Anything to
show he cared. He had to feel something, the way he readied
the bathroom for me. But to look at him, you'd think he'd
just met me and invited me in because it was the charitable
thing to do. I suppose the sleeping presence of Hortense a
couple of floors above us inspired his perfect decorum. She
may have been pretending to sleep, straining her ears to catch
any new voice, any foreign sound.

That may have explained his lack of communication, but I
doubted it.

I just don't think the man knew what to say or do, beyond
the kindnesses he had silently expressed. He knew I knew
about him and our Ma, just as he was aware that he'd done
nothing to prevent her death. Or to stop the weekly beatings
that discolored her face no matter how much loose powder
she patted on her cheeks. And the whole town had seen, or .
heard about the beatings through a third party, yet no one
turned in the old man, no one came forward saying, "Enoch,
good or bad, she's your *wife*, not a battering ram." *Including*
the man who sat across from me, who ate slowly and took
furtive glances my way when I wasn't supposed to notice. No
wonder he didn't speak; after all that happened to me and my
mother, what *could* he say that would change anything?

Scraping up the last of my eggs with a piece of toast (Wilbur ate his toast the fancy way people in the movies did,
breaking off pieces and eating those instead of biting the entire slice of bread . . . that morning, I did likewise), I real-

ized that nothing could be changed between myself and Wilbur. I'd go on being the old man's bastard, living in a dank *hole* under the house, and Wilbur, living up in his fine house, would give me an occasional soda or candy bar, our lives crossing no more for the rest of our lives. I knew I deserved more, but I wasn't about to get it. There was no way Wilbur could come forward to claim me, or even help me out.

When we finished eating, and sipped our coffee, Wilbur asked, "Mind if I turn on the radio?" indicating the mirror-fronted Spartan on the counter behind him. I shrugged, smiling. He got up and turned on some big band music. Benny Goodman, I think. Lots of woodwinds. Sitting down again, Wilbur took a small cloth bag from his shirt pocket, as well as some cigarette rolling papers. He usually smoked pre-made cigarettes when he smoked at all, so the sight of the papers piqued my interest. Not trying to seem obvious, I asked, "Did you switch during the summer?" pointing at the bag of tobacco—which didn't look properly cured. It was still greenish.

Shaking out a thin line of it onto his paper, he replied, "I still smoke cigarettes. This is something else. I'd offer you some, but—" he licked the paper shut, twisting it slightly "—this isn't tobacco. Your father wouldn't approve, I'm sure." I caught his tacit drift— Don't tell Enoch about this.

It wasn't until he lit up and inhaled without exhaling for a *long* time that I realized what he was doing. All the while, he looked at my frankly, eyes red-veined and candid. I recalled that trio of movies the City Council had shown to us young folk, *Sex Madness*, and *Reefer Madness*, plus the cocaine film. After smoking a funny cigarette, the people in the reefer movie acted bubbly, crazy, before turning manic and homicidal. But all Wilbur did was *sit*, eyes glassy, mouth sliding into a frown, brow wrinkling, as the kitchen filled with the harsh burning smell of it. That it was Wilbur himself who spoke to us kids before and after each movie made it all the more pathetic. If the City Council had wanted to scare us from drugs, they should've had each of us sit in Wilbur's kitchen that morning. None of us would've wanted to *bother* after seeing him, for fear of getting depressed, too.

When he was done, he took the butt end of it and wrapped it in an old piece of newspaper, then stuffed it in the garbage bag near the sink. He didn't apologize. It was his house, his life. *I* wasn't a part of it. If Hortense didn't know or care, that was her problem. I wasn't *offended*, nor did I feel disgust toward him. At least he didn't act silly, like the Winstons, or just plain mean, like the old man.

He poured himself another cup of coffee and sat down. I looked at him blankly, then stared at the luminous whorls of oil on the surface of my coffee.

He asked, "How did you hurt your leg? I noticed you limping." I assured him it was a cramp, but he added, "If it troubles you later on, tell Enoch to take you to the hospital. Tell him *I* said so." That was the first show of emotion I'd heard from him that morning. I just nodded, telling him I'd do that.

I felt the need to say something more, or get up and beg him to please do *something, anything,* but pride held me back. He'd been the one to create me, not the other way around. I was approaching manhood, but was still a child in the eyes of the law, until I turned twenty-one. My old anger at our Ma flared up again; she should've *known* better. Even if Wilbur was richer and smarter than her husband, kinder, too. Lots of women made bad matches, but they learned to live with them. And Wilbur was ten years older than our Ma, so *he* should've known better. He wasn't some *kid*. He had a wife, two daughters, too.

As he sat, silent and brooding, for some odd reason I thought of the sampler his wife had made for me when I was born, the twin of the one Winston received later, in honor of *his* birth. Our Ma told me that "Mr. Holiday" made the frame himself, fashioning it out of birch from the tree in his backyard. I tried to picture him crafting that small frame—those small *frames*. I was curious if his hands shook the way they did now, as I wondered what went through his mind as he cut and nailed the wood. Surely, he *knew*. Did he wish he was my father in name, too, or was he glad to be free of any responsibility for me?

Then the disc jockey made a silly but funny slip of the tongue. I chortled, but Wilbur laughed, then kept on laughing and grinning, the first time I'd seen him do that. After a second, I saw why he made an effort not to smile. He had crooked teeth, not crooked-*crooked*, but set oddly in his gums. His teeth were pushed in too deep on one side . . . like Winston's teeth were. Only Winston allowed himself to smile once in a while.

The realization didn't change my opinion of either Winston or his mother, but it did explain why Gayleen had had no more children. At least Winston was lucky enough to have his mother's deep blue eyes *and* dark hair. Teeth can be hidden if you're purposefully dour. I wondered if Winston even *realized* the truth of his parentage—knowing how trusting he was, I doubted it. Winston was so smart he was downright stupid.

Wilbur saw me staring at his teeth, for he buried his mouth in the cupped palm of his hand, elbow resting on the table. I wanted to tell him I was glad to be Winston's half brother, but Wilbur was looking past me, out the window, where the last soft smears of color were visible against the growing blue of the sky.

"Palmer, did you see that sunrise?" I nodded, turning to face him. Wilbur incised a lazy circle on the oilcloth with the handle of his fork, adding, "I saw a sunrise like this one in 1913. By late afternoon, the Big Blow came. Two, three hundred people died. Damnest snowstorm I ever saw. Wouldn't be surprised if it happened again. Things have a way of coming around," he finished in a tired voice. The circle on the oilcloth was deeply etched. I doubted it would fade away, but he could easily afford a replacement cloth.

Putting down his fork, lightly tracing the outline of his circle with a manicured forefinger, Wilbur asked, "Would you like a ride home? I can drop you off out of sight of the house. I know how . . . your father feels about me. It's a long-standing disagreement. From the 'teens.'" Wilbur sounded so flat-out beaten and *sorry* I longed to get up and hug him, or put an arm around his shoulder, but I *couldn't*. I liked him, but I couldn't forgive him.

Finally, I blurted out, "I've come this far . . . I can walk a bit longer. Three miles isn't bad." As I got to my feet, my right leg splayed out stiffly; I forgot myself when he quietly asked, "Cramp any better?" for I said without thinking, "I haven't a—" Catching myself, I looked away as I shouldered my knapsack.

Getting up, he said, "Whatever happened to your leg, do let a doctor see it. It doesn't look normal—"

Quickly I said, "I left my old things in the bathroom. I don't want any of it." Pulling the shirt away from my chest, I added, eyes downcast, "Thanks for these. Do you want them back later on?" He shook his head; some of his hair slid down over his forehead, intensifying his resemblance to Winston. Funny, I'd never noticed before.

Limping to the kitchen door, I was halfway out when Wilbur asked, "Are you sure I can't drive you? I'll make sure your father doesn't—"

—*your father*—

The way he kept repeating those two words grated; couldn't he at least slip in a "son" while talking to me? Wilbur *had* to realize how much his calling the old man my *father* hurt me. Caught between liking the man and hating him, I said in as nice a voice as I could muster, "No, sir, you've done so *much* for me already—" and detested myself for what I'd said as soon as my words were uttered. But I couldn't apologize, either. That badness in me, that fresh well of bitter bile, flowed unchecked, to taint every thought and word of mine.

Oh, I did turn around midway down the backyard, to wave; sure enough, Wilbur stood in the half-open doorway, eyes lost and vacant. He returned my wave, then backed into his house and shut the door. Spitefully, I hoped that he'd have a good cry after closing that door—while *I* walked with hot moisture trickling down my face, eyes nearly shut against the rising pale glare of the sun.

The grass had been cut all summer. And what leaves had fallen were being raked. Vern was bent over the splinter-handled rake, work gloves on his hands, back to me as I dragged myself up to the edge of the front lawn. Hearing my splay-legged shuffle on the gravel road, he turned around to face me, incomprehension etched in his wide face. It took a few seconds to register that the whip-thin, scraggly haired creature before him was me, until he whined, "I hadda cut grass all summer . . . rake the clippings, too. Now the leaves. Old man's gonna kill you if you set foot in his barn . . . house, too." I limped past him, not uttering a word.

Up at the house, I let myself in through the kitchen door (the window was out of the question now), and clumped down to the basement. The younger kids were still asleep, three dark heads on the pillows. I took the Shirley Temple doll, bedraggled but still intact despite my tumble off that train, and laid it next to Effie. I shook off my knapsack, hid it in a bottom drawer. I was mildly surprised that Vern hadn't confiscated all my clothing, although my best long-sleeved shirt was gone. Luckily Vernilla wasn't sulking around, so I didn't have to listen to *her* berate me for whatever chores of mine she'd performed in my absence. Perversely, I hoped that she'd had to muck out the barn.

Vern's "Old man's gonna kill you—" echoed in my ears, so I decided, why wait any longer. I had nothing here, or over on Roberts Street . . . or anywhere. At least I'd be with our Ma. After all that had happened that summer—

—*oh, please, please don't tell, and those eyes tearing behind the glass*—

—I sure didn't deserve to keep on living. Even if the old man didn't kill me, he no doubt longed to pound his fists into my eye sockets, knock out a tooth or two, before breaking my jaw or a couple of ribs. I just couldn't run away from the old man—I'd traveled hundreds of miles from him, yet it was as if I hadn't moved a *foot* from him. As Wilbur said, things come around.

So I went back up those stairs, hanging onto the rail as if learning to climb all over again, then lurched across the yard, toward the barn. Out of the corner of my eye, I saw Vern watching, all tense with anticipation of my imminent bloodletting.

I heard the old man in the barn, the scrape of a shovel against cement. Before the Crash, he'd laid in the modern concrete floor. Perfect for slamming errant bastard son's heads against until the skull under the skin cracked and splintered. . . .

The door stood open. Without hesitation I placed myself in the old man's view. He looked up, fleshy mouth curled in a funny sneer—half grimace, half smile—eyes narrowed against the glare of the sun behind my back.

I tensed, in anticipation of a horrible beating. Behind me, Vern's feet slithered through the grass, as he came closer to watch. Maybe it was Vern standing behind me that changed the old man's mind, or perhaps he realized that I could beat myself worse than he could ever hope to hurt me. All he did was point behind his shoulder. "Left your jacket."

I'd all but forgotten the jacket I'd shucked off in that stall, stuck halfway into the dung and straw. Limping past the old man, feeling his eyes bore into me, I entered that stall. My jacket hung on a bent nail, the back and arms greenish brown encrusted, embedded with broken tufts of yellow-gray straw. For a second, I was transported to that narrow, reeking horse trailer, to stand in gagging awe at the geek costume hanging there. The old man didn't *need* to lay a hand on me to beat me.

Knowing full well that I was being watched, silently laughed at, too, I reached up to take down that jacket. And put it on . . . for I *didn't* deserve better than I'd been dealt.

By noon, the temperature dropped from the high fifties to below freezing; by nightfall there was nearly two feet of drifting snow on the ground.

Things had a way of coming around, all right.

SEVENTY-ONE

The glow from the light fixture in Brent's room was soon augmented by the jaundiced shine of sunlight through his window. Beyond need of rest, Brent skimmed over a couple of double-sided pages of events chronicled with obsessive completeness. The reunion of the two Palmers, his uncle's continued family troubles, including a "dilly" of a fight between "the old man" and Vernilla over his discovery that "she was screwing Palmer Winston in back of the Co-op, and the old man swore he'd get even with her, claiming she was 'just like' our Ma, which made Vernilla cry—but I'm not sure if it was over being caught, or over being compared to our Ma."

Brent slowed down only when he came across a passage concerning what happened to Palmer after he fell down the basement stairs and reinjured his knee. . . .

From Palmer Nemmitz's journal—
—hurting so bad I didn't care if the twins and the girls and Shirl saw me crying. When Vern grabbed me under the armpits to hoist me up, I screamed when I put weight on the leg. Shirl ran for the old man. By the time he came, Vern helped me sit down, and Vernilla cut and tore away my pants leg while water boiled for compresses. Even the old man admitted it didn't look good. I was crazy, in such agony—even worse than August, and this time I had an audience—that I repeated what Wilbur said about me seeing a doctor.

While Vernilla wrapped hot cloths around my knee, making me scream more, the old man went upstairs. Between yelps I heard him on the phone, quiet at first, then yelling and swearing to beat the band. I knew he'd called Wilbur, for he barked, " 'Private room' my ass! You want one, *you* pay the fucking bill—well, don't listen in and you won't hear me say that, Operator—you still on the line? Good. You played, so you better pay his bill . . . if you're 'just *concerned*' you come take him to the hospital. Sign him in, too, if you *dare*."

When the old man clomped downstairs, I passed out rather than listen to a blow-by-blow of his conversation. Next thing I knew, the old man and Wilbur were shouting at each other while the rest of the kids made themselves scarce. Wilbur slapped the kitchen table with his hat, beating it all out of shape as he said in a trembling voice, "You've no business *living* like this, Enoch, *none at all*. Not with that big house upstairs going empty—"

"It's my house and my business, you—"

"How do you plan to get Palmer out of here? He can't walk and it's too steep to carry him. Living down here is *idiotic*—"

"Seems to me we all do something 'idiotic' at least once in our lives, *don't* we, Wilbur?" Wilbur's face went all funny, as if he'd been forced to bite down on something alive and swallow it hot and wiggling. Coaxing his hat back into shape, he changed his tone of voice, "If you can get him up the stairs, I'll drive him to the hospital. But you'll have to sign him in . . . I can't," he admitted in a tone that suggested that he sorely regretted the fact.

"And then . . . ?"

"And then I'll pay his bill. Provided you ask for a private room."

It numbed me how Wilbur had knuckled under to the old man. I felt ashamed as well as grateful, a strange combination of emotions. Everything became vague after the old man half dragged me upstairs and helped me into Wilbur's new Packard. I hurt so much I passed out before we reached the hospital across the river. I don't remember being helped into the lobby by the old man and Wilbur. Years later, I found out that Wilbur left in disgust before I was signed in. I did get that private room, though.

I awoke cotton-headed, encased in plaster and bandages from what felt like my hip to my ankle, unable to move, and too groggy to *want* to move. From bits and snatches of talk I heard before the nurse gave me another shot of whatever it was that made me dough-brained and sleepy, I learned that my kneecap had been broken, and the ligaments and whatnot all torn to hell. While I was out, I couldn't feel the searing itch of bone knitting, or torn muscles healing. My groin seemed to be swollen, but I didn't see it, or feel it with my hands. Just a vague sensation. I did wonder why my testicles ached, but guessed that the ripped tendons had extended up that far, so I gave it little thought.

It seemed as if I were out for weeks, months, but when the nurse quit jabbing me in the arm with that needle, and my head cleared, I saw by the calendar on the wall that it was still December.

When I could have visitors, the old man—I didn't figure out the smirk on his face until *later*—told me I was out for eight days, but wouldn't elaborate why except to say, "They wanted you real quiet." As if they didn't think I had sense enough to lie still when told to do so.

Young children couldn't visit, and the twins didn't want to, but Dead Fred and Winston showed up. Dead Fred all but hung over me like a vulture waiting for the carrion to ripen, and Winston stood near the window he'd somehow managed to pry open, blowing smoke out the crack, and tapping his ashes under the rug by my bed, then flopping it over them.

Dead Fred announced he was joining the Marines; between puffs Winston drawled, "Barber won't have much to do when it's your turn in the chair." The asshole took that as a compliment. When we finally entered that mess in Europe and the Pacific, I expected Dead Fred to make Grade-A cannon fodder. From the twinkle in his eyes, I knew Winston agreed with me.

Winston *said* little that day; with Dead Fred flapping his jaws, it was hard to get a word in sideways, edgewise, or under the door. But before they left, Winston hung back; with a look of concern, he asked, "Do you remember me visiting you when you were doped up?"

I told him he'd answered his own question, adding, "I didn't remember my name, let alone a visitor." I was peeved; if he *had* been around, the least he could've done was wake me.

Sitting on my bed, he said softly, "You were awfully swollen around the water-works. One of my cousins broke *his* kneecap, and it didn't swell up *high*. Sure you didn't bust your pelvis?''

I pushed him off the bed. ''Everyone's different, Winston. Some swell, some don't. 'Sides, what's it to *you*? I don't see you in bed with a pitcher under the blankets. Were *you* looking under my covers? Like a four-letter—''

''Dead Fred did. I told him not to, but you know *him*.''

(From the hallway, Dead Fred bellowed, ''Win, you comin' or not?'')

''Enjoy yourself?'' I snapped, crossing my arms.

Winston looked like someone had caught him in the face with a fishing line bristling with hooks and torn both his cheeks off. ''*No*. I just wondered what they *did* to you. Didn't make sense, you being swollen—oh, the heck with you. I don't care if they tore your liver out through your nose. I try to look out for you and I get my ass chewed off. Good-bye,'' he sniffed.

After Winston was gone, I was tempted to lift the covers and do an inventory of the goods at hand, but that would've been giving in to Winston's heebie-jeebies. *I'm fine, I'm fine,* I told myself . . . and when the doctor insisted on putting me under when my knee stitches were removed a few days later, I told myself that was normal. All the while knowing in my heart that it wasn't. But there was nothing I could *do* about it.

The old man actually *smiled* at me when he came to take me home.

That's when I knew he'd bested me, in a way I'd yet to discover.

With my leg treated properly, the healing went fast. By mid-January I was walking with crutches and a light cast. The old man let me accept Winston's parents' invitation to stay with them for a couple of weeks. I slept in their back parlor, on the daybed, which saved me from climbing up and down stairs to get around.

Winston set up a cot for himself in the parlor; come nighttime, he told me of the weeks he spent looking for me. I felt as if I'd fallen off the end of the world, when I learned how close he'd been to where I was that night. The night of Maeve, and Mae. I volunteered little; I'd tired of the carny and left, period. Took me a long time to get back. And no, I saw little of interest on the way down, or on the way home. For some reason he wanted to know what I thought of things like "Burma-Shave" signs, storefronts in sleepy towns, and odd trees by the roadsides. Figuring those were safe topics, I stuck to them, thankful that he didn't want to know much about the carny. "It wasn't White City" seemed to satisfy him.

While Winston was in school, his parents were distant but dopily friendly; Gayleen jangled her bracelets at me, goggling her eyes, but she didn't try to convert me, or pester me about not going to church. Maybe she realized she had no room to throw stones off that glass porch of hers. Porter was gone most of the day, and some nights after supper. I didn't trust the man as far as I could fling him with a broken fingernail, but he left me alone, as if thankful that *I* was Winston's best friend, instead of Dead Fred.

A couple of days into my stay, Winston came home from school shortly before noon. "Pipes froze up. No school today or tomorrow." That was Thursday. He and I had read in his parents' *St. Paul Pioneer Press* about the upcoming Winter Carnival in St. Paul's Como Park, and the big Ice Palace the WPA built.

Winter in Ewerton meant snowmen and maybe an igloo in front of the public library. Winston and I were dying to see that Ice Palace. The paper promised it had colored lights *inside* the thick ice walls; the palace was to be lit up at night. I didn't bother to call the old man to say I was leaving.

We made Minnesota in two hours flat, with Dead Fred along for the ride. The Woody bounced and slid on the road, past a flat landscape dotted with bare trees, strands of evergreens, and telephone poles. The Mississippi was a gray silken ribbon below us, the snow broken in enough places to show black water below, depthless and starry-night cold.

By the time we found Como Park, it was dusk. When they lit up the palace, it was truly a sight. A dozen frozen rainbows, capturing shimmer and fire in squares of purest crystal. Waves of cold came off the palace: all the spectators' eyes danced, liquid points of compressed color, as if their faces were masks hiding fiery, fluid pools of molten lava and gushing water.

Shifting on my crutches, I whispered to Winston, "This is worth bringing *him* along, isn't it?" He replied, "I don't think fucking Greta Garbo, Bette Davis and Carole Lombard at once would be worth having *him* along . . . but this *is* pretty." Meanwhile, Dead Fred was busy making an ass of himself; asking every girl, "Are *you* Queen of the snows? No? Aw, you *should* be." It was too bad no girl rubbed snow in his yammering face. After Dead Fred flapped his yap, the sparkle went out of the moment, and we left the park, in search of the YMCA.

The next day, we roamed downtown St. Paul, then crossed over to Minneapolis, all the while either driving or walking around (Winston let me lean on him so I only had to use one crutch). Winston and I got even with Dead Fred by losing him in a Woolworth. Knowing Fred was notorious for not wanting to ask people directions, we figured he'd be safe in there while we wandered about on our own. We both had an excellent sense of direction. Casually, Winston suggested that we drive over to the other side of town, claiming to "know" someone there. Not suspecting anything, I got into the Woody and he took off.

When Winston stopped in front of the University Hospital, I gritted my teeth, snapping, "It's none of your business *what* happened to me in the hospital. And I don't appreciate your concern." I sat with my arms crossed in front of my chest, as Winston went through half a pack of cigarettes, explaining that what he'd seen worried him, so he'd made an appointment for me before coming home Thursday.

"Dad really does know this doctor, or his brother, at least. He's not a horse doctor, like in Ewerton. *Please,* go up and see him. I've . . . been *worried.* Suppose they messed you up inside? C'mon, you don't even have to pay—it's on me. My folks don't know about this, Dead Fred either." Checking his watch, he reached over and opened the door on my side. "You're going up there if I have to drag you into the elevator with my *teeth.*"

Uncrossing my arms, I said, "I'd like to see you do that."

Winston waited in the Woody after I checked in—I insisted he go out there, since I didn't want him listening at the door while the doctor examined me. The doctor—a short, colorless man with expressionless gray eyes and an impersonal manner—*was* on the ball, not some local witch doctor. That he was a stranger made the whole exam less embarrassing, but I still looked the other way. He said little beyond asking me about my operation and long hospital stay, then told me to dress. He said we'd talk, after he made a call to the hospital in Ewerton, and assured me he'd have some answers soon.

I waited in his office (dominated by a messy-topped desk, which I found comforting) for what seemed like an eternity before he walked in and sat down behind his desk. Without preamble, he said, "Before I tell you what your doctor said, I need to know one thing, young man. Did you and your older sister ever engage in sexual inter—"

"*What?*" I yelped. That was enough; the doctor's face turned ashen. "I figured that was a subterfuge . . . now, Palmer, tell me—no lies—is your sister perchance having relations with your friend, Palmer *Winston*? I'm not making a judgment about your sister's morals, I simply need to *know*. Is she?"

Nodding, I answered, "What . . . does this have to do with my operation?" but my mind had already fit the pieces together—and I didn't like the picture that emerged.

Rubbing the skin between his eyes, he continued, "I take it you and your father aren't on the best of terms. I hate to be the bearer of bad news, but your doctor explained that your father told him that you and your sister—no, let me quote—your sister 'and Palmer' were having sex. As a preventative, he requested, exercising his legal parental rights over a minor child, that you be rendered . . . unable to impregnate your sister. Your doctor reluctantly agreed. But he's since had second—"

"*He did what?*" I screeched. Eyes watering, I stammered, "Bu-but I've *seen* castrations"—the word almost cut my throat—"and my ba—my . . . are still—*They can't* do *that!*"

Pushing me back into my chair, the doctor explained how the procedure was done from underneath my testicles, just the cutting of a couple of *tubes*, but the effect was the same as deballing me. And the operation couldn't be reversed. I'd be . . . functional, but I'd never father children.

I started bawling then, hitching and gagging until I could barely breathe. The doctor kept saying how *sorry* he was, and suggested that I seek clerical or legal aid, in case I wanted to sue when I reached my majority, "But I'm afraid it's your word against his, unless your sister backs you up. I've never come across such a situation—the only involuntary sterilizations I've heard of have involved mentally incapacitated persons—please, take a tissue. I'm *so sorry*, believe me. Your father . . . a *monster*—''

He was right, but he was wrong. My *father* was misguided, tricked into paying for something unthinkable, unconscionable. Never would my *father* have done this to me. But the old man, *thinking* Wilbur had no other son, was monster enough to do this to me. A perfect dual revenge. *What goes around, comes around.*

Gradually, I heard the doctor say, "—don't blame your friend or your sister . . . it's not their fault, not directly. I can't help you when it comes to your father, that's up to you. Palmer told me you're staying with his family. Stay with them as long as you can, promise?"

As he led me out of his office, arm around my shoulders, he kept repeating how sorry he was, then admonished me not to let this get me down, life had plenty to offer—all that bushwah. I wished I had swiped one of his scalpels, so I could slit the old man's throat with it, but by the time I reached the ground floor, I realized that would only prove the old man right—I *was* a worthless bastard, good only for killing. But I vowed to get even.

No matter how long it took. No matter what it cost me *inside*.

The old man *would not* get away with this.

Winston fell asleep waiting for me; his cigarette almost set his gloves on fire by the time I tapped on the car window to wake him up. I fought the urge to let the smoke burn him and his car to smoldering ashes. *Damn you and my slut of a sister,* I thought, before he woke up and I mouthed, "Open up!" In the car, I fed him the line I'd rehearsed in the elevator. Something about an inflamed muscle. Winston was so relieved I fought the urge to knock his lopsided teeth down his throat with my crutch tip. But I kept my silence while he drove back to the Woolworth to pick up Dead Fred (who sat nursing a Cherry coke at the soda fountain), during the parade, and even while we drove home. I mentioned nothing of what the doctor had said, to either of them.

In a roundabout way, it was Winston's and Dead Fred's fault, or partly their fault. Someday, they'd pay, too . . . *how*

I didn't know, or *when*, but someday I'd find the soft spot in each of them. And the bad place inside me swelled and puffed with new importance, happy to be so richly fed with ragged bits of my heart, my soul . . . and my humanity.

When we returned to Ewerton, the rotted spot inside me could've swallowed a dozen men, and it wasn't done *growing*.

SEVENTY-TWO

For months, I took that doctor's advice. I shied away from the old man, sticking close to saner people. My rage cooled, but that sense of *wanting* never left me, either. Then, it was as if a sign appeared before me . . . an omen of badness all around, not just in, me.

What happened on December 7, 1941, took no one in town by surprise. Dead Fred had already shipped off that summer for Marine basic training.

War was coming, all right, and the more Winston heard about it on that Majestic "Charlie McCarthy" radio of his, the more excited he became. He was already ROTC student commander; if he hadn't been my only friend, I would've been tempted to punch his teeth down his gullet after how he carried on the night of Pearl Harbor. Acting as if God sent those Jap bombers just so Winston would be drafted and sent as far away from Ewerton as possible.

I couldn't figure out why he was so damned excited over the prospect of getting his ass blown to bits; he had everything one could want right in town. After his third or fourth beer, I told Winston he was crazy, acting happy because the country was at war.

On the twentieth of December, 1941, the Draft Act went into effect; all male Americans between the ages of eighteen and sixty-five had to register, with those men from ages twenty to forty-four being liable for active duty. Winston and I were seventeen, but Vern was the right age, while the old man was a year older than the cutoff date for active duty. But he had to register, along with all the old men, even the duffers on their bench uptown.

Before his nineteenth birthday in January, Vern decided to join the Army; he couldn't wait to be called up. The old man ranted and raved, since *I* was of little or no help due to my "bum" knee, but Vern was adamant. He was old enough, and he was going.

Listening to them shout, I realized that as much as I disliked Vern, I didn't want him to go. Without him, the old man and I would see a *lot* more of each other. But before Vern went for his physical, he said something which made me wish he was gone and in Europe right then—"When I'm gone you're gonna feel how it is to do the work of two." After that, I wished I'd *never* see him again, even if it meant doing double chores for eternity. Vernilla cried and carried on when Vern took the train out of town, to the induction center downstate. I thought perversely, *The old man had the wrong one fixed . . . those two were always awfully* chummy.

As it turned out, there weren't many chores to be done; the old man sold the cows to some Mennonites south of town. It was all we could do to tend to our Victory Garden. But soon we had an extra pair of hands—the old man yanked Effie out of school too, so four of us tended the farm, such as it was. With the girls home, the old man and I could keep our distance.

Winston graduated class valedictorian, to the surprise of no one. I went to the ceremony, at his insistence. And it hurt to see Wilbur Holiday passing out diplomas (Wilbur was on the school board that year). It wasn't fair, *I* should've been there right after Winston as salutatorian of the class.

Winston was voted Most Popular, Best Dressed, Most Intelligent, Most Likely to Succeed, Most Collegiate, and Wittiest; despite all the hoopla, I still liked him. *Why* I was no longer sure, maybe it was because he was so anxious to chuck everything that was awaiting him.

Winston looked forward to his October eighteenth birthday with such glee I told him to just go on and lie about his age so he could enlist already, but then he became vague and mumbled something about having to "see" about that. Winston didn't go off to college, but stalled by saying he'd register first, then sign up for the winter term at one of the UW schools. Majoring in education, the course of study he'd leaned toward since birth.

"College will be a snap—if you taught a lunk-head like me, doing it for real will be a cakewalk," I told him not long after my birthday, but a couple of days before his. We sat on the steps of Holiday's Grocery Store, me with my leg jutting straight out because cold weather made it ache when I bent it, and ticked off the names of local boys who'd been called up for active duty.

Tom Calder, Clive's kid brother, had been drafted that spring. But before he shipped out with the Navy, he married Beatrice Sawyer (Una's cousin). Bitsy was Tom's age, a plump no-necked girl who lacked her cousin's sharp tounge and open legs. Bitsy was no innocent, but she was pleasant to be around. During the times when Winston and Una were "on" as a couple, occasionally the four of us went for a soda together.

By 1941, Bitsy and Tom became an "item;" I never touched Bitsy except when she'd let me, so I wasn't heartbroken when she and Tom got hitched. Actually, I was relieved; she talked of nothing but *babies*. Not much to look at (she had mousy hair and a moon face even then) but she had "Mother" written all over her, and in our town, that's all that mattered.

Winston's Una was another sort, all bones, angles and hips so narrow it was a wonder she could pee, let alone accomodate her rotating boyfriends. Face put a pickle to shame for sourness. But she *was* legendary as the best screw in Dean county.

Sitting on the steps of the store, hands tucked in our jacket pockets (Winston's was a horsehide cossak with a zipper up the front which he kept unzipped, despite the nip in the air), we counted off the rest of our classmates who'd already gone. Ernest Reish had enlisted, as had Mitch Weiss, Gilbert Andersen, Gilbert Doyle, Manly Thorn, Floyd Wilkes, Eddie Dickerson and Lyle Cooper were already in training, some in the Army, some in the Air Corps, and the rest in the Navy. Dead Fred was Ewerton's lone Marine.

Winston and I both hoped that the Marines forgave the town for siccing Dead Fred on them. He didn't make it to Iceland; according to Mona Ferger, he was "over there," in Europe. Winston and I agreed that Nazi occupation couldn't be much worse than putting up with Dead Fred on a long-term basis.

Resting his back against the closed door of the store (Wilbur was out to lunch, according to the sign hung behind the glass), Winston sighed, "Once I'm registered, I'm *off*. Mother and Father say I'm not going, but who are they to talk? Uncle Sam wants me, and he's getting me come the end of the month. They said I can't go because I'm their only son and heir, but that's not patriotic. I don't believe they can keep me out, not after I turn twenty-one. They can't turn away guys who want to go—''

"There's not supposed to be a black market, but I see some women walking around in five dollar nylons every day—'' I referred to Gayleen, who never needed to paint any brown stripes down the backs of her calves. For Valadictorian, Winston was so *dumb*.

"Extra nylons or gas is one thing, but keeping me out of the draft is another thing *entirely*. They can't *do* it.''

I chose not to reply. Instead, I rested my head against the sun-warmed door of our father's store, not wanting to shatter Winston's previous illusions any further than they were bound to be shattered once his deferment came through. Gayleen and Porter did have friends.

When the two of us went down to Eau Claire to register, the Doc who gave the simple physical (eyes, ears, and the like) said "Uh-oh" when I showed him the web of scars on my right knee. I knew what "Uh-oh" meant. Uncle Sam was going to have to win this war without my help. But Winston was going to take his deferment *hard*.

On the day we were handed our draft notices, I could've saved myself the trouble of opening it. "4-F," just as sure as doctors go "Uh-oh." I was glad to know I wasn't going to die in a foxhole full of mud and splattered bodies, but I did my best to look sad when I read over that slip of paper. It *was* 1942, after all.

Winston fussed and fumed so much I thought the after-shocks of his screeching would shake the paint off that big WPA mural. He barely made it down the post-office steps; I took his arm so he wouldn't walk off into empty air. It amused me in a sour sort of way to see him vent his fury at his folks for getting him deferred. I wanted to say, "Winston, suppose your father, who really isn't your father, but that's *another* story, put you in the hospital and told the doctor—'' but I didn't rub salt into his wounds *yet*.

Winston offered to drive me home, but I only wanted to go uptown. Dropping me off in front of Holiday's store, he took off like a bullet for home. No sooner had his car left than the old man came out of Holiday's store, which was packed with women bearing booklets of blue and red stamps. By this time, the old man had decided that he and the girls could handle the farm just *fine*; after Vern's hitch was up and he came home (the old man was confident that "Jerry" couldn't whup *his* Vern), I'd be "over there" myself, cannon fodder on the front line. That my leg was too bad for me to even do most farm chores didn't phase him. As long as I could shoot a gun, Uncle Sam *had* to want me.

When the old man stood before me, I told him loud enough for those uptown to hear even if they stood by the depot, "I'm Four-eff. I guess you'll have help on the farm after all, *Dad*."

The old man's face purpled up, like he'd taken swipes at himself with his fists. He bawled, "Four-*eff*? My kid's *unfit*? Useless? No goddamn Nemmitz is sitting out the war, you hear? They'll *take* you, or else I'll—"

I hated to interrupt his shouting—especially after he actually called *me* his "kid," a first in my lifetime—but we were surrounded by a tight crowd of people, mostly women. Wilbur stepped outside to listen, too, and I knew *now* was my chance.

Waiting for a lull in his sputtering harangue, I said softly, so people had to lean in and listen closely, "Why don't you enlist, *Dad*? They're taking men even older than you are. It would be *very* patriotic, *Father*. I can handle the farm by myself. Weed the Victory Garden, save fat in the kitchen. Collect tin and rubber, too. *Useful* things like that."

I made out individual breathing patterns in the hush that followed. When I looked past the old man's white-lipped face, over at Wilbur framed in the door of his store, he gave me a quick "V for Victory" sign with his right hand, then stepped forward.

"That would be wonderful, Enoch. Maybe you and Vern will be stationed together. The first father-son soldier team in the country. Probably worth a write-up in the *Herald* or the *Milwaukee Journal*."

That set the crowd abuzz; before the week was out, the old man presented himself to the recruiters, who found him fit and hale for forty-six. An *A-1* specimen. When I learned that, it was as if a great stone were lifted off my back . . . a slimy one, at that.

But with that lifting came the realization that there were unpleasant things squirming about under that immense weight. With the old man soon to be gone, I understood that

I had to stop blaming this or that on *him*, on the way he'd treated me like dirt over the years. *I'd* be in charge from now on . . . so that any of my meanness, my newly doused well of badness, would come back at *me*. Unless I was very careful, very subtle.

During the weeks before the old man was to go down to Alabama for basics, I tried to prepare myself to take over the management of the household in his absence. Vernilla vowed she'd rather join the WACs or go to Milwaukee and be a *welder* than stick around with me. I thought often of what I'd done, shaming the old man into enlisting, thus leaving me everything he had in this world; his land, his farm, and his house. As much as I had reason to hate him, I knew at heart he was my father in *name*; he'd fed, clothed, and sheltered me for eighteen years. I did understand that much. He could've kicked me and our Ma out on our behinds when he figured out who my real father was, but he didn't.

But I'd also reached a point where *realizations* didn't cut ice anymore. Something in me cried out for *more*, it demanded repayment for what he'd done, for what he *planned* to do to me.

On the night before he took the train south, the old man suddenly began speaking to me, in the darkness, waking me and all the rest of us out of a sound sleep. "I didn't have the time to do it yet, but when I come home, you're written *out*, hear? Out of the farm, out of my will. *Out*. Enjoy it while I'm gone, 'cause as soon as Vern and I are back, you're out on your gimpy ass. And don't forget it."

I couldn't do anything about the old man, or the farm, or his will. With luck I'd get a job; men were in demand in the factories. *That* aspect I didn't worry about. But I had plenty to meditate over that *did* concern me . . . and what else I was planning, for later on.

After hearing the old man's threat, I began to wonder if *all* of us, every man, woman, and child, had that bad place inside, where the rotten things we think become real. I decided, there in the damp darkness of our basement, that it didn't matter *how* small a seed of badness any of us had waiting inside—given water, and enough cancerous sunlight, even the tiniest seed could sprout and thrive.

The way I figured it was, there had to be a mircoscopic nubbin of ugly, of pure *mean* in all of us, like a tiny wart you might have in a place where you don't normally look, or can't see even if you try looking. If you're *lucky*, you can find it, or feel the first stirrings of it *before* it makes you do or say wrong, no matter how much the situation *calls* for a bad thing or word to be done or said. Before it gets to *paining* you. But if you aren't so lucky, it gets so big it finds *you*—and, cancer-like, takes you over.

As it took me over. And the rub was, once I realized that something was wrong inside, I didn't care enough to try to change. Ever since returning from the South, it was as if part of me had shriveled, become stunted, in order to let the badness expand—and the dwarfed part happened to be the portion that should've allowed me to become a grown man and a responsible adult. Thus, I was in limbo. My body was adult, but my mind was small, that of a spiteful child. Just the way the badness in me *wanted* it.

And I wasn't the only boy-man running around Ewerton; Mr. Most-Likely-to-Succeed was in limbo, too—no job yet, no college, and now no Army. When not sitting behind the depot at night, downing beer after beer and pissing it out onto the high grass near the tracks, Winston was sitting on the steps of Holiday's store or playing chess inside with Wilbur. It was a blessing neither of them was in the habit of smiling much.

Neither of us could get into gear; all around us the other kids had matured, become adults. (Bitsy Calder was showing, and babbled that she couldn't wait to send "Tommy" a snapshot of the baby once it was born), while Winston and I sat around in his room, listening to Captain Marvel on his Charlie McCarthy radio as if our lives depended on it. Not to mention the Green Hornet and the Lone Ranger.

Those thoughts and more lulled me to sleep before the old man had to leave. Come morning, I was so keyed up I couldn't eat, so I watched the old man gulp down his runny eggs and salted oatmeal. Idly I wondered if I'd ever listen to him smack and slurp his way through another meal again. The other kids were all a-babble, telling him this or that before he left, but all I did was sit there, staring at him, a half smile on my lips and what I hoped was indifference in my eyes, as I stirred that horrid slop Vernilla called coffee. Not her fault, though, what with those posters uptown of Java-sipping soldiers under the legend, "Do with less so they'll have enough." Pretty soon the old man would have all the real coffee he wanted.

Then it was time to go to the station. Twenty other younger

men were leaving too that morning; while mothers and girl-friends cried, and children milled around looking lost, the old man hugged each of his kids, but only offered me his hand to shake. I left it hanging in midair a few seconds before taking it. Squeezing my fingers like a cut lemon above a pitcher, he whispered, "Remember, when we come home, you are O-U-T." I pumped his hand in return, whispering, "If we're all lucky we'll all have farms come war's end. Even if some of us have to buy 'em."

I never spoke to him again. Standing there in the noise and confusion of the depot, the engine hooting and leaving off great gritty billows of dark-tinged steam into the frosty morning air, the old man knew that that was it between us. I don't think he appreciated that revelation . . . but I did.

As the train pulled away from the depot, its windows filled with waving arms and faces mouthing last good-byes, I darted into the depot itself and thumbed a dime into the pay phone.

" 'Lo?" Winston's voice was pure gravel after his nightly ritual; six beers and a bout of upchucking afterward.

I wasted no time in telling him my plan; once I was through he said, "Meet you at your house. Soon as I get my head reattached."

He was waiting on our front porch when we arrived home and he'd brought help. Bitsy's brother Buddy, who hadn't been called up yet, plus Una, her brother Irving, and, of all people, Porter Winston. Porter looked worse than usual; I doubted he'd be of much help, but besides being a crack shot, the old guy (at forty-eight, Porter was an *old* man) was able to shoulder a heavy piece of furniture with the best of them.

Vernilla had a fit when she saw Una, and took off in the car. We didn't need her; even Shirl was big enough to help. I was in charge of directing traffic—the most I trusted myself to carry up was the bedding and pillows.

By four-thirty that afternoon, everything was back in place upstairs. And the basement was just a basement again—albeit with a toilet and sink. While the others were upstairs fixing themselves a meal, I went over to the wall which had been part of Vern's "bedroom" and gently removed his "wall dictionary of segmented Hershey bar wrappers. I placed them in an envelope, then slipped them into that knapsack of mine . . . feeling the outline of Mae's mask as I shoved the envelope inside. I'd hidden the knapsack in one of the old trunks that stayed put downstairs; Una was a nosy thing, and I couldn't bring myself to explain the contents of that knapsack to anyone just yet. Touching Mae's mask, and the thin chain of pearls, almost brought *everything* back, but I chanted the Roosevelt jingle under my breath, "Row, Row, Row with Roosevelt—" until the lightning-blasted images faded.

That night, after the last of my helpers went home (Vernilla hung around outside until the Sawyers left with the Winstons *pere* and nominally *fils*; her first words upon entering our newly restored home were, "Don't expect me to clean this mess!"), I limped *upstairs* to my room, to sink gratefully into my bed. Above me hung my "Thursday's Child" sampler, and for the first time in many a year, I slept like a baby.

After what remained of the family moved back upstairs, things moved quickly—not only our lives, but *everything*. Vernilla couldn't stand living in "her" (our Ma's) house. She joined the WACs and shipped out to Italy, while I was still farming, and hating it. Plus tending the Victory Garden. The house was paid for, so I didn't have mortgage worries, and I'd found a wooden bucket of coins the old man had buried out under the mail box post and then forgotten (lots of farmers did that during the Depression—the money-burying part, not the forgetting)—over forty dollars in Indian Head pennies, buffalo nickels, plus Liberty and Barber dimes. Needless to say, I cashed in the change—most of it near mint—for more than face value in the Cities. I bought War Bonds with the proceeds, one each for the younger kids, and two for myself.

But I was still nagged by the thought that folks considered me a layabout, on account of me being 4-F and there being three blue stars in the front window of the farmhouse. Collecting newspaper, fat, tin foil from cigarette packs, and rubber was well and good, but that Poster Wilbur put up in his store window said it all—"Are You Doing All You Can?" Maybe it was the fact that Wilbur had joined Civil Defense (he watched for planes from his attic roof) that made me do what I did next, but I went and asked the county agricultural agent what crops Uncle Sam was in dire need of. What he said made me laugh out loud, before I told him to order me up some seed.

Hemp has this way of growing just *fine* with a minimum

of care; since I'd re-enrolled Effie in school, she and the other kids were able to help me tend to the bright green fields of marijuana after school let out each day. Uncle Sam *needed* it for rope, but aside from that, it tickled me to think I was doing something right out in the open that Wilbur did on the sly, in the privacy of his home. Just a little tid-bit for the gnawing badness in me.

What with the corn, the reefer (hemp sounded much too *mundane*), and the Victory Garden, the four of us lived quite comfortably. We took to walking more, to save on rationed gasoline, but the shortage of sneakers was hard on the kids. But we made do, we had to.

I think that it was around that time I began seeing *gold* stars in the living-room window; days when I saw the shimmer of gold out of the corner of my eye as I stepped across the porch and went up to the front door.

I think it started as a mental *game*; fool my eyes into seeing what my brain wanted so desperately . . . until my eyes registered two gold stars and a blue one even when I wasn't wishing the old man and Vern would arrive home in flag-draped boxes. I got the heebie-jeebies over that window; I had to purposely *not* look at it . . . *for those gold stars wouldn't go away, or turn back to their rightful blue*. Luckily, the kids didn't notice I was acting strange, or mention the stars, be they blue or gold.

Winston broke down and got himself a job at the sash and door, which now manufactured "parts" for Army shelters. He was off weekends; he did nothing but chain-smoke black market Lucky Strikes (most everyone else I knew rolled their own or switched to pipes) and slop down Leinenkugels by the overflowing glassful, cursing his folks between every sip and puff.

In 1943 he was deferred again; I told him he could join Civil Defense, like Wilbur had, but there was no reasoning with him. Once, he flung his pack of Lucky Strikes at me, snapping, "*Look*. 'Lucky Strikes Green Goes to War'—*I* can't go, but my damned *cigarettes* got drafted!" I held onto the red-bulls-eye decorated white pack until he got over his funk—often he'd become so angry he crushed his pack and the un-smoked cigarettes inside.

June of 1943 brought about a big change in my life, one that came up so quickly I hadn't anticipated it. Bitsy—Tom's baby girl on her hip—put a gold star in her window. And I began paying attention to her, brought her flowers from our garden, food, and gas ration cards. I liked Bitsy; she was a good egg, if not the brightest gal in Ewerton. Best of all, I didn't have to worry about giving her a baby.

I was going on nineteen to her twenty-one, but men were scarce, I had a house (for the time being), war bonds, postal savings bonds, and I swore not to beat her. I didn't care about the baby keeping Tom's name, but I winced when she said, "We'll have plenty more in *your* name."

I should've told her then, but the moment came and went. As it was, Bitsy's doctor (the same yahoo who messed with my cujones) told her he wouldn't "advise" her to have another baby. Bitsy took it well; after a few months of no sleep, plus taking care of my siblings, she wasn't in the mood for more children. I guess she considered herself lucky to get herself a home and a husband to support her baby. Bitsy *was* a lot more fun than Una, so we got on all right.

Angie and I came to an understanding; I was "Palmer" and she was "Angie." It may've been cruel on my part, but from the time that kid could aim her food at me when she spit it out over the high chair tray, I made it plain that I was Mommy's *husband*, period.

I'd already soured inside to the point where, if I couldn't father my own child, I wouldn't open my heart to some other guy's child.

Still, Angie hung around my ankles when she was in creepers, following me like a small shadow; she was playing with my shoelaces that October day in 1944 when the letters from Uncle Sam arrived. My laugh was a bitter thing that tore at my throat until I finally cried the tears I was supposed to shed at that time. The old man, Vern and I, we were all farmers now. Only I didn't have to buy mine.

And the funny part was, I no longer needed to avert my eyes from the small gold starred flags in the window . . . for they became real. And I never did ask Bitsy if she was the one who changed them. . . .

Re-reading the letters for Bitsy and the kids, I learned that the old man was a sergeant, and Vern a PFC. They'd bought it in separate battles in Germany. I didn't request that the bodies be brought home. Months later, I got word they'd been interred in France. Even later than that their effects were shipped home, along with a few charming items they'd laid their hands on. Nazi armbands and deaths-head lapel pins.

Months went by; Vernilla was stationed in Italy, close to an air base, as a clerk-typist. She wrote to the other kids regularly.

Not long after I turned twenty, I got a letter addressed in a neat Palmer-style script I knew all too well, with an Alabama postmark. Government stationery. It was a good thing that Bitsy was gone, taking Angie to visit Tom's parents. I cried like a baby when I read Winston's letter; he'd joined the Army on his birthday, somehow bypassing his deferment. He'd already started basics, and had elected *me* to give the news to his parents. *They* thought he was visiting some maiden aunt.

But the Winstons took the news with bleary aplomb; I could've told them that he went to Germany and joined the SS and Gayleen would have thanked me for passing on the news. Hanging up the phone, I no longer blamed Winston for what he'd gone and done.

Not long afterward, January or so, I heard from Winston again; he'd broken his leg in November (a Willis jeep he was riding tipped and pinned him); the break was bad enough to keep him in the base hospital for a few months, but not bad enough to cause him to be shipped home. Almost as an afterthought, he revealed that he was in officer's training (class phase) and was a corporal. Something to do with his IQ scores and his ROTC. Yet, he seemed ashamed of his rank. Knowing Winston, he'd bitch when they made him General. Trouble was, he *looked* like officer material. His smarts and training were icing on the eclair. General MacArthur wouldn't have made it if he'd been a stumpy little twerp with buck teeth and pock-marks.

Winston was movie-star good-looking; it was easy to imagine a whole squadron of privates saluting him on the way to the latrine every morning.

He and I exchanged letters during his hospital stay; something he wrote in March set me to seeing things, again: "It's too bad about your father and Vernon. I'm glad I'll be gone while you and Vernilla duke it out over the farm. Remember, *she's* the eldest now."

That was when my eyes started playing tricks on me again. Glancing fast at the window (even *not* so fast), I saw three gold stars hanging there. Try as I might, to the point of closing one eye when I passed, I saw three golden stars. Not a healthy sight, considering what happened the last time, but the badness in me *did* enjoy the view. . . .

When the envelope from the government came, I was almost too scared to open it, almost too frightened to check the little stars in the window. But I must admit, I was put out to read that Vernilla was merely *injured* during the bombing of her unit's barracks. True, her injuries were grave, but the government flunky who wrote the letter assured my family that she was in little danger of death. Shrapnel had sunk into her brain. The letter said she'd be shipped to a VA hospital in the States . . . but the letter I received the next day more or less advised my family to disregard the previous letter. And I breathed easier when I saw that trio of golden stars each morning.

After that, it was a matter of making my ownership of the farm legal. The old man wrote out a will when I was two, shortly before Effie was born. Handwritten when we were all sick with the grippe one winter. the old man carried on as if it were the Black Plague, until our Ma handed him some paper and told him to write a will or shut up. Something along those lines; I was only two, but the situation stuck with me.

Being the old man's *only* will, witnessed by two farmhands, it was valid. And it plainly said, "I, Enoch Nemmitz, leave my house, farm, and property to my wife, Treeva Horak Nemmitz. If she dies first I leave everything jointly to my eldest children, Vernon and Vernilla Nemmitz. If this grippe gets them, too, my other child Palmer Nemmitz inherits everything." Since the rest of the kids were underage, and not mentioned or even referred to as "future offspring, if any," I was sole owner of the farm, and could do with it what I pleased.

And it pleased me to sell off ten acres to Harmon Dickinson; I used the money to buy a $100 War Bond. I was doing pretty good; Uncle Sam still needed hemp, I raised chickens and sold the excess to Wilbur Holiday, and Bitsy had Tom's pension. All in all, I was doing fine.

Not long after Vernilla died, I was sitting in the back parlor, figuring out how much money I'd make during the coming months, when Bitsy knocked at the door.

"Palmer, you've a visitor." I waited for her to tell me who it was, but there was nothing but silence on the other side of the door. Bitsy was already driving me crazy, keeping me *hanging*. Finally, I yelled, "Well who *is* it, for Christ-all—"

In answer, the door opened and Wilbur stepped in. He was all dressed up like it was Thanksgiving and he was headed for church. Not his usual grocery store white coat over a striped shirt.

Wilbur stared at me for a few minutes, as if what he saw didn't register. I felt like I needed to wipe my nose or something. Finally he said, "Seems strange to see you with your own family, running the farm. Heard you're doing quite well."

Wilbur was acting as if he were paying homage to me; despite my discomfort, I remembered my manners and invited him to sit down by the desk. He could see my worksheets; I made no effort to hide them. He knew full well what I was and wasn't worth. I wasn't the one wearing the three-piece suit and new hat.

We made small talk, about Angie, the gold stars in the window, and my recent sale of land to Harmon Dickinson, which brought Wilbur to his pitch. Clearing his throat, he hawked phlegm into a handkerchief, which he hastily stuffed into his pants pocket, as if afraid to let me see that he spit like any other man. Quickly, he got to the point.

"Palmer, I've been thinking about speculating in land . . . not real estate, but farmland. I was wondering . . . since you've already started selling off the farm, if you'd care to sell me some of your acreage. I'll top what the other farmers can pay. I don't know much about land yet, but while I learn I thought I'd let you manage it for me. I just . . . want to deal with someone I trust. And since you're already selling—"

He kept talking, but I didn't have to do much listening. I knew what he was up to; a five-year-old could've figured it out. Now that the old man was dead, Wilbur finally decided to fulfill his parental obligations. My ears did perk up when he said he'd be willing to pay $225 *an acre* for land that wasn't worth a fraction of that. Wilbur was going to pay me *$20,250.00 for ninety acres of land*. Almost a thousand a year for every miserable year of my life. I knew then that I was worth something to someone . . . but even at that monstrously inflated rate of pay, deep inside I knew that no sum could ever be enough to pay back what that man owed me.

My jaw dropped when he quoted his price for the land; almost apologetically he added, "Sorry, Palmer, I meant two hundred seventy-five dollars an acre. As I said, I'm new at this—''

An *embryo* couldn't have been that new at anything. Hearing him bandy about such figures, I grew dizzy. Over *twenty-four thousand dollars* . . . at 1945 rates, no less. That was an *awful* lot of cash. If I invested in bonds, none of us would want for *anything* . . . and I'd never have to do another day's work, either.

I found my voice, assured him that $275 an acre was a fine, fair (!) sum. We both knew it was *insane*, but I knew that acreage wasn't the only thing being bought that day. If that made me a whore, well, spread my cheeks and put a red light in the window. I'd paid in blood and more for that money; Wilbur Holiday knew it.

He'd planned out everything; the papers were all drawn up, legal and proper, with his lawyer's signature in all the right places. Only our signatures and those of witnesses were needed. All went smoothly; the cash was mine before suppertime.

I wasn't only the son of a rich man—*I* was a rich man.

Wilbur drove me home from the bank; before I got out of the car, I finally said the words that had hovered just behind my teeth ever since that morning. Knowing the money was safe in my account, I turned to him, hand on the car door, and said, ''Feeling any less guilty now, *Mr.* Holiday?''

For a long time, he said nothing. In the gathering darkness, I saw his face crumple, and caught the clear shimmer of a tear sliding down one cheek. But evenly, he said, ''Palmer, you are the meanest, most unforgiving man I've ever met. I've done what I could for you, when I could. For some *men*, that would be enough. I'm sorry it was too little for you . . . under the circumstances, I doubt *anything* would be enough for you.''

There was nothing I could say to that, nothing I wanted to say. To answer him would have been to admit I was in the wrong, and for me such an admission was impossible.

The next day, I spread the money out among several bank accounts in Dean County, and converted enough into bonds to make me rich when they came due.

I'd received a ''present'' from the Government the Christmas before, but hid it because I didn't want the season spoiled any more than it was already, on account of the old man and Vern dying. I secreted their medals and certificates which told of their valor in battle; Shirl and the girls were upset enough when their uniforms came back. I couldn't help it if I'd forgotten about the medals until they sent Vernilla's Purple Heart in the summer of '45.

All told, there were three Purple Hearts, a Medal of Valor, three Achievement Medals, two Bronze Stars and Vern's Silver Star, all hung on pretty ribbons, looking for all the world like expensive Christmas tree ornaments. I merely glanced at the certificates: Both Vern and the old man saved the lives of their fellow troops, and Vern did something valorous, but I forget what it was.

Them being dead, there wasn't much use in me going over the circumstances leading to their condition. Cowards who hid in foxholes with shit in their shorts got shot just as dead as the heroes.

So the medals rested in my desk drawer, under some old papers.

The war dragged on despite the loss of the heroes Nemmitz. Winston's leg *still* hadn't healed right come VE Day in May, but he'd been promoted again in the mean-time, to second lieutenant. For *what* I had no idea, maybe for having the best head of wavy officer-type hair. Even Winston didn't know. He was already sick of all the operations on his thigh, *and* of all the promotions. I suppose the silver platter wasn't shined enough.

I guessed that he was crabby because the war was ending without him, first VE Day May 8, with victory in Japan no doubt close behind. But Winston managed to ship out in time to see that big mushroom cloud over Japan, and feel a few after shocks. By the time the Regular Army became the Occupation Army, he was promoted to first lieutenant.

After the war ended in Europe, Dead Fred came marching home. I was the first person in town to see him; he made a beeline past his home and *walked* all the way out to my place. For him to do something like *that*—when I saw Dead Fred bobbing down the road, I realized that he had to have a damn good reason to come so far on foot. Just what it was I don't know, but I would soon find out.

No sooner did Fred (dead-pasty as ever, despite his uniform and trimmer figure) step onto the porch than he asked in a desperate whisper, "Anyone else at home?" Bitsy had driven the kids uptown for a soda and shopping spree, so I

was stuck with Angie, but Dead Fred said she didn't matter—
he was worried about folks who could *talk*.

Something potentially *interesting* was afoot. Once Dead
Fred got through playing with Angie, telling her a "little
rhyme" he'd learned in basics that went:

"This is my *rifle*,
This is my *gun*,
This is for *shooting*,
This is for *fun*"

He gave her his hat to play with, and he and I went into my
back parlor. *Then* he spilled his guts.

While overseas in France, he'd regaled his parents with
tales of his derring-do, hinting that he'd walk through the
front door dripping with medals. But he'd seen no action. He
was a file clerk, working far from every battle ever fought in
Europe. Hadn't so much as smelled gunpowder or felt a bullet whiz past his cheek. His co-workers were *women Marines*,
he added with a shudder. He'd heard at the depot about the
Nemmitz clan buying the farm, and figured it had to be worth
a Purple Heart or two. . . .

All the while he spoke to me, I wondered if Dead Fred
remembered the snipe hunt . . . or realized I was still riled
at him. Watching him grovel, all but getting down on one
knee to beg me to please sell him those medals, I recalled
something the old man once said, "Be kind to dumb animals,
pat 'em on the head. *Then* reach around and slit their throats
from behind."

I got out the boxes of medals. His eyes goggled and his
cheeks went paler than usual as I hung those medals on my
fingers, let them dangle and bump one another just out of his
reach.

Ignoring his query about the price of the medals, I wiggled
my fingers; the swinging metal ends clanged softly. Dead
Fred's colorless tongue slid over peeling fleshy lips. I smiled
and kept jangling those medals until I came up with the perfect question for *him*.

"You still cherry? See *any* action?" I'll give it to Fred, he
tried, but I was married, sharing a bed with a woman and
occasionally getting a little. I saw through his bluff, called,
and raised him. Poor Dead Fred, in his mid-twenties and still
cherry. After he'd spent so much time spying on Winston,

too. "Aw Dead Fred, you should've learned something after watching Winston screw Bettie Byrne when they didn't know you were looking. Shame, *shame*—"

"Palmer, don't call me that—"

"*Poor* Dead Fred. *No* action at *all*. Girls not pretty enough? Or too choosy?"

Dead Fred looked like a fish flopping in midair from the end of a hook. I finally let up; he and I were even—he'd ruined my life in '40, and now I had the power to ruin his reputation . . . for good. He didn't flinch when I asked for $50.00 per medal (and since he was too dense to realize that most of them were Army medals, I wasn't about to re-educate him), but after I let him snatch them off my hand, he did notice that a few of them were duplicates.

Trying to hand back the extra Purple Hearts, Achievement Medals and Bronze Star, he anxiously stared at the wad of bills which had clearly disappeared in my trouser pocket, whining, "I couldn't have earned all of these, gimmie some of that back. Aw, be a swell guy, Palmer." I leaned back in my chair, hands in pockets, and replied, "There's bound to be another war. They'll need file clerks, I'm sure."

Dead Fred was so brow-beaten I reached into my drawer and pulled out the old man's sergeant's stripes, the ones I'd taken off his uniform. I tossed them to Dead Fred. "Go promote yourself, your folks should get a kick out of *that*. If they don't notice they're for the wrong branch of the service." I was laughing so hard I didn't notice Dead Fred had left, grabbing his hat from Angie's wet little fingers, until she wailed that her new "toy" was gone.

Inside me, the pit of badness almost sucked me in whole— I *enjoyed* what I'd done to Dead Fred. Especially the promise I made him make *before* I handed over the medals. I hoped he found them to be worth the shame hanging over his head.

I know my bad place found the whole transaction quite fulfilling.

SEVENTY-THREE

Reaching that point in his uncle's tale, Brent had to stop reading; it was difficult to imagine his uncle *doing* something that evil to Dead Fred, for being little more than a snitch. Yet, Bitsy *had* said Palmer had "something over" Dead Fred. . . .

Brent felt betrayed; he loved his uncle, but after reading of such wilful human demolition, Brent wondered if a demon lived inside the old man. Turning the page, eyes burning from reading charcoal gray type that ashed into palest smoke against grainy white paper, Brent found something that confirmed his impression of either great evil or terrible inner sickness in the man. . . .

From Palmer Nemmitz's journal
I still have the picture of Dead Fred that appeared in the *Herald* the week after his homecoming; him in his uniform, medals hanging from his chest like misplaced droopy cujones. Funny thing that no one noticed he was wearing Army medals. I thought the VFW would've caught on, if not the civilians. The account of his war exploits took up three columns. If Dead Fred had had any acting ability, John Wayne's days as the man who kept the nation safe on celluloid would've been numbered. As it happened, Dead Fred was Ewerton's most decorated combat veteran. He was also one of the few boys who came home, never mind in what condition.

The week they printed the names of all the fellows who'd bought European and Asian farms, it took up half the front page (this was county-wide losses). All but a handful of the boys my age were dead. Most of the class of '42, a few girls, too. It was frightening; boys I'd schooled with, lived with, seen roaming around town nearly every day of my life—boys I'd counted on seeing reach pauchy middle age along with me were *gone*. And it was scarier to know that deep down inside, I didn't give a tinker's fuck about the lot of them.

I was supposed to be a man by then; I looked like a man, I shaved regularly, I was married, I had a house and a car, and I had a pile of war bonds and seven savings accounts. By

Ewerton's standards, I *was* a man, self-made at that. I'd turned the farm into a gold mine, and the people living under my roof had plenty to wear and enough to eat.

But something was wrong, *missing* inside me. The person who glared at me from the mirror was more a strange, gradually aging man whose skin covered a boy. A hostile, angry little *snot*.

I'd become a form of half and half. While Daisy-Denny had his "differences" hanging out in the open, mine festered inside, stewing in bitter bile.

Winston and I still corresponded; he seemed preoccupied with the Japanese villagers who lived near his base. He admired their dignity, their charm, and reading between the lines, I realized he wasn't talking about their fine grasp of etiquette. He was too busy working through his delayed adolescence to notice *my* retarded development. Always marveling about how "tiny" the people were—meaning, of course, the ladies—and, as I said, he'd been promoted to first lieutenant, soon to become Captain. All that after a short stint in the Army. Man *sure* looked like an officer.

So his recent promotion made his phone call all the more surprising when it came that Saturday afternoon in early October. I was listening to the radio in the living room, reading the latest *Reader's Digest*, and Shirl was on the floor, reading a Captain Marvel comic book. Bitsy and the girls, even Angie, were at the beauty parlor. When the phone rang, I said to Shirl, "Probably for the girls." Effie and Merle were attached to the telephone by their navels. Shirl just shrugged and didn't bother answering me.

When I put the receiver to my ear, an operator asked if I'd accept a call from *Mr.* Palmer Winston—which puzzled me so much I didn't catch where the call was coming from. I said, "Yes, I'll—" and the next thing, Winston's voice came on the line. From word one I knew he was calling from a place where there was liquor handy. Lots of it.

"Paaamer? Tha' *you*?" Make that an endless supply of liquor. I heard scratchy bar sounds, women laughing, and the sharp tinkle of glasses. I wondered which USO he'd ferreted out in Japan, and speculated on what sort of a tab I was picking up. Quickly, I asked, "Win, are you calling from *Japan*?"

"Oh, *nonono* . . . I'm in *Seee*attle," he said, then added, as if I couldn't tell, "inna bar. In the States. Hear?" He held the receiver away from his ear, so I could pay for the privilege of hearing people in a bar nearly three thousand miles away. I yelled, "Winston? I don't *care* about the bar! Why are you in the States? Didn't you sign up for a long hitch?"

A pause, then, " 'Nuther eighteen months, but no more, no more—" I cut him off in mid-singsong. "What happened? Army move your squadron?"

More bar noise, then the slurp of something liquid close to the receiver. Winston blurted out, "No, I'm *outta* the Army. Been dis-dis*charged*. Shipped out yesterday. Got here hours ago. Gonna come home next week . . . maybe." His voice grew high, tight, sounding as it did when it first started to break in puberty. "I'm an A-okay guy, right, Paaamer? *Right?* Ev-even if I'm not in the Army, right? Tell me I am, Paaamer." He was past drunk now, swallowing down tears.

I slowly said, "Jack Armstrong himself couldn't be more A-okay, that satisfy you? C'mon, what happened?"

Between moist hitches, Winston rambled about "this bastid head shrinker" who tried to "scare" him into a Section Eight, only he was "jus' jealous of me, on 'count of my p'motions." After edging in a couple of questions, I learned that he'd been hauled in by the MPs after some "trouble." Between every dragged-out admission, he begged me, "Tell me I'm okay, Paaamer."

After the third or fourth time he said that, the nasty, festering part of me got all excited; even as I reassured him that he was the "A-okay" guy he wanted to be, I motioned to Shirl to go to the Dickinsons' farmhouse and tell them to pick up their phone. Shirl nodded his short-cropped head and ran for the bike. I calculated that he'd be at their farm in five or six minutes. I stalled Winston until I heard a faint *click* on the line, *then* asked, " 'Did you get an honorable discharge?"

"Somethin' like tha' . . . woudda been 'less than honorable' on count I was an offissa, but my C.O. worked it out. . . . Either that or the brig. Didden wanna go *there*—"

Another *click*. Winston backtracked, telling me and whoever else was on the line by now, that he'd been "married" to maybe "six, seven, *somethin*' like that" Japanese girls, in Shinto ceremonies. And he'd given his new "brides" a parting gift, as in a little clap here and there. Finally, charges were brought against him, enough to court martial him and limiting his future to either Army prison or a Section Eight.

By then, my comments were limited to a few "Oh?" 's—

it *was* my dime, and I intended to let Winston make as big a fool of himself as I could afford.

As he talked and wept, becoming more incoherent and unintelligible, he kept *pleading*, ''Tell me it wasn't that bad . . . *please* tell me I'm not a bad egg, am I? Tell me he didden mean what he wrote about me. *Please*, Paaamer, I didden do it for the reason they thought I did . . . I'm *not* what he wrote, I'm *not*.'' And the black sucking void that passed for my conscience said, *He's paid in full for '40 . . . wonder if he'll be elected mayor after this?*

Then Winston rambled on about another *girl*, not Japanese, but like an Oriental maiden in one crucial aspect: ''She was *small*, Paaamer, real small, an' for a sec-second I thought she was all *blood* down there, *legs* an' everythin' an' she had the funniest *eyes*, Paaamer, should've seen 'em . . . an' her *car*—all white an' the road was real messy but the car was *clean* an' it'd been rainin' and I couldden *find* you, but I found *her* an' she was so . . . I never *felt* like . . . oh, Paaamer, her eyes were so *strange*—two colors, Paaamer, two colors—''

My heart thumped arrhythmically as Winston sniffed back tears. ''Oh, Jeeze, this is costin' you an arm anna leg. I bedder hang up—''

But before he dropped the receiver, I said, after hearing a volley of clicks as his audience tuned out, ''No, it only cost me something a lot dearer than money, *Lieutenant*—or is it 'mister' now?'' Faintly, I heard Winston's anguished ''Paaamer!'' before I hung up.

As I rubbed my sore ear, the cold core of badness in me grew warm with the tingle of excitement even while part of me cringed over what I'd done to Winston.

He'd been with the twins. His description of Maeve was unmistakable. And he'd been in Georgia when it happened. I found myself itching my right arm, until the first trickle of blood came. Only, when I glanced down at the skin I'd been scratching, I saw blood pooling in the faint crescents of Mae's teeth marks.

I got up and hurried to my bedroom, biting the insides of my cheeks in panic. Striding down that upstairs hallway, I thought, *It's her—them—making us act this way. Doing and saying pure craziness and meanness.* Ducking into Bitsy's bathroom, I poured half a bottle of iodine on my arm, dark-staining her sink. My arm felt like I'd stuck a hot poker in an' twirled it around . . . but the sensation of Mae's *teeth* in there still remained.

Heartsick, I made my way to the bed. I flopped down, but the guilt and exultation over what I'd done to Winston wouldn't let me sleep. I'd let something not of myself ruin my life . . . and I was helpless against it.

Restless, disgusted, I got up and paced the room, and spotted a section of wallpaper that was loose near the ceiling. Bitsy had been after me to rip down the paper, but I'd put her off, mainly because the hardward store downtown didn't stock such paper anymore. Pretty paper, with blue cornflowers, vines and trellis' on a pale azure background. Not the pebbly no-pattern wallpaper Bitsy drooled over in the Coast-to-Coast basement.

I stood on her vanity bench and grabbed hold of the floppy corner of the wallpaper, yanking it down with a quick motion that almost sent me crashing backward off the bench and onto the floor.

Nearly the whole sheet came down intact, along with shreds of the backing paper. But this wallpaper hadn't been pasted to a bare wall; whoever papered it covered the wall with old newspapers, most likely to even out a bad plastering job. And in among the yellowing fragments of newsprint, I saw something that confirmed that if there *was* a God, He had nothing good in store for me.

Part of it was gone, torn apart and adhering to the back of the wallpaper I held in my hand, but there was enough left to see . . . to make me shake at the knees, and go dry in the mouth.

A Madison's High Quality and Tested Seed poster, the twin of the one that hung on the wall of the Blue Tulip Cafe was plastered to the wallboard of my room. The little Dutch girl and boy still smiled, as they appeared to walk toward me. Like the Tarot Fool stepping into oblivion.

It hit me; I'd traveled hundreds of miles, yet I could've stayed home and seen the same poster.

There would be no escape for me . . . none at all. The reminders of that summer six years before would be with me always—even if my mind managed to forget it, there would always be fragments of what I'd seen, smelled or felt, *waiting* for me. Ready to catch me unawares . . . taking me back to that hideous rain-drenched night. Through my opened window, I smelled the last faint reminders of the wild roses which grew under my bedroom in the flower garden below. Obligingly, my nose added jasmine, the missing component of *her* scent. But . . . when I leaned out the window, I didn't see a single fushia rose petal left on the thorn-spiked bush far below me. Even as the scent of her perfume lingered in my nostrils.

When Bitsy and the girls came home, I'd already glued up the torn piece of wallpaper. That evening I took Bitsy to the hardware store and let her pick out a new pattern. Pebbly beige ugly stuff. I put it up myself—*over* the old paper.

SEVENTY-FOUR

JULY 19

Brent rolled off his bed, and went into the hallway. After flushing the antique pearlescent toilet in Bitsy's bathroom, he washed his hands (wondering if Palmer had been so eager to change sinks because the old one reminded him of the iodine he'd spilled over a *fresh* six-year-old bite), then walked to his uncle's bedroom.

The old man had gone downstairs, after dutifully making up his bed and hanging his night-clothes over the back of his desk chair. The "pebbly beige ugly stuff" was still on the walls, albeit darker than when Palmer slapped it up in guilty haste to cover the ripped-down section. Brent wasn't sure which corner his uncle had yanked down, and was afraid of peeling back corners at random. But the window was open; the cloying scent of roses and jasmine filled the room, obscuring the manly odors of Old Spice, shoe polish and leather. As he walked to the window, Brent breathed deeply—only to back away, covering his nose with a handkerchief, when he saw that the old wild rose bush was a uniform sun-withered green-gray, with blackened protruding naked hips. And jasmine didn't grow this far north.

Back in his room, comforted by the sweaty-stale smell of his clothes and rumpled bed, Brent picked up the closely typed manuscript, noticing that he had only a few pages left. As if he could put it off no longer, Palmer skimmed briefly over the remainder of the forties, noting only that Merle died of smallpox in November of 1946, while Effie succumbed to polio a few years later. Fearful of his safety, Palmer sent Shirl to a prep boarding school in Minnesota.

Palmer and Bitsy drifted apart, literally and figuratively; Angie resented Palmer for not adopting her—she was teased about being illegitimate because her last name differed from Bitsy's.

Brent sensed that Palmer only paid lip service to the fifties, sixties, and seventies because *she* chose not to manifest herself in any way . . . but, reading between the lines, Brent intuited that Palmer never stopped *waiting* for something to happen, to *give*. Then, he read his own name, and that of Zoe—

From Palmer Nemmitz's journal—

—saw that picture Brent and Zoe sent, two things happened. I itched my arm, felt the warm wetness of blood under my shirt, then I half heard her, pleading, *Oh, please, please don't tell.*

There was no reason on God's green earth why that Zoe should look like *her* . . . like Maeve. And Mae. I'd heard about Zoe's folks, they looked nothing like *that*. But Brent had found *her*, and he didn't live in Ewerton. Brent, the one I thought might be safe, free of all I'd done.

For I was—*am*—certain that my badness killed the old man, Vern and Vernilla, and poor Effie and Merle, too. And I half suspect it snaked into Minnesota and killed Shirl and Joan on that highway. A load of guilt has changed my way of thinking—and believing.

I had the opportunity to meet Zoe, but I didn't go. Partly out of fear that she *wouldn't* be like Maeve at all, and half for fear she *would* be.

Because . . . as much as I dread the memories, I also welcome them, at least the pleasant ones. Maeve appealed to the boy in me; the scared, confused, goofy-romantic kid who just longed to walk hand in hand with a *nice* girl, take her to a movie, and then treat her to a soda. Or a Stardust Bar.

I couldn't have walked hand in hand with Maeve as she was, doing bread and butters when someone or something came between us—even if I'd overcome my fear of what she was, it would've been impossible to explain her to other people. Yet, I kick myself for not *trying*.

But I didn't, so I'm condemned to think of her with the

coming of roses in the spring, and the memories of southern jasmine summers, the taffy-brown-golden turning of the leaves come fall, and the spotless whiteness of winter snows, unmarred by mud or the fall of dusty chimney ash.

And so the darkness within me was still hidden, unsuspected.

Oh, I think Wilbur knew what I was. After he sold me back my land for a dollar after another fit of parental guilt, we didn't talk for years.

I didn't go to Wilbur's funeral, but I cried. I didn't cry for my younger siblings when they passed on.

And then Brent sent me that picture . . . and I knew, in some way I understood no more than I could understand how a wound many decades old could open and close as gently and as perfectly as the opening and closing of a baby's hand, or the budding of flowers followed by the dying—and rebirth—of the blossom. I just . . . *felt* that Maeve would be back. For *me*. But for what purpose I couldn't comprehend.

A week after the photograph arrived in the mail, Una Winston died. I cannot believe Una died from a stroke. But listening to Lenny, I wondered why the twins picked old *Una* to torture . . . Bitsy would've been an easier target, but I supposed that ghosts don't follow normal human logic—if ghosts they were.

Yet . . . Zoe is alive, which only confuses me all the more. And I pray that it is merely a coincidence that Zoe so closely resembles Maeve and Mae. There is still room to hope that it is all a mistake, a trick of the camera, or of my eyes.

Anyway . . . I got to remembering Maeve, and Mae: what they were, both in reality and to me as a person. I recalled what Maeve said about that *Freaks* movie. The more I thought it over, the more I realized I needed to see that movie. Lenny got me a tape of it, the kind with no label on it.

The film was in black and white, which made it somehow worse. The *plot* was simple, as all subsequently complex things usually are. It concerned a one-ring circus, and the freaks Tod Browning had found: a limbless torso, and a half man with no hips or legs hopping on gloved hands like a smooth-skinned, good-looking frog; the pinheads Harold longed for, and a true half and half; a bearded lady; an armless girl; the too short, and the too thin. And the hobbling Hilton sisters, one blonde, one brunette. Both pretty.

But their dignity, their sad but proud resignation, was totally unlike what I had seen on the faces of the so-called freaks I'd worked with that summer. Maeve was right. The South-State Enterprises Carnival was a fake, a sham.

A lady trapeze artist smelled money on one of the midgets, married him, tried to do away with him, and was punished by the freaks.

When the last reel began, and the freaks moved in the mud and rain-drenched darkness in ways God truly didn't *mean* for people to move in a *rainstorm*—well, I sat there, not blinking, not moaning when the strongman kicked open the seal trainer's wooden wagon door, just before the freaks got him.

Those freaks moving in on that woman and her strongman lover were part of a nightmare, only no one would wake up whole and sound when the night was over. There was no denying that the justice they meted out wasn't *fair* . . . or vengeful. After the darkness and the rain went away, it was revealed that the trapeze artist was now a stumpy, feathered mound of flesh that wore the memory of her once-beautiful face. The freaks had avenged the betrayal and near-death of one of their own . . . by creating one of their own. Tit for tat, touche, revenge is sweet . . . and so on to infinity, a mirror facing a mirror, creating a tunnel of diminishing mirrors winding off into nothingness.

And something the friends of the midget groom had said to his new bride rang in my ears, "We accept you, we accept you," only the picture behind my tightly closed eyelids was of Maeve, so pitifully eager to sit and talk to me as we sipped 7-Up under that big tree. She had accepted me, more so than anyone else in my life . . . as the freaks in the movie had accepted that woman. Only to have her turn on them, as I turned on Maeve.

The hiss of the tape in the VCR became the sizzle of rain hitting metal, the surface of the Airstream trailer . . . then turned to the steady drip of raindrops on water-laden tree limbs and soft drenched ground. Opening my eyes, I saw Larry crouched next to me, concern and curiosity playing on his broad face. "What happened, huh? Why'd she bite you?"

Finally . . . I answered his questions, stuttering because of the coldness of the rain, and the growing coldness *inside* me, independent of the wet and fear. "Sh—she's tuh-too m-much for me . . . said sh-she nuh-needed a ruh-real m-man . . . she left her door open. S-she's waiting fuh-for someone to

. . . c-come tend to her n-needs. Buh-be careful, sh-she's a wild one.''

Larry's eyes lit up, and his big toothed grin nearly split his face in two. "She *woman* 'nough f' a couple a fellahs? Think she can open up *wide* 'nough?'' And he laughed, as he took off, only he didn't head for the camper, and he didn't head for Maeve's trailer, either. He went for the geek.

I waited around only long enough to see him leading that bowlegged, hunched-over thing across the muddy ground—straight for the Airstream. With the broken lock on the door. Only then did I realize what I'd *really* done, what would happen to *both* of them. And I prayed and hoped that Larry would stop himself after the sex part. A bite wouldn't be enough to make Larry back off. Not *him*. Not the man who bought crates of live chickens to feed a geek, and dreamed of a two-geek show in that stinking bristling pen of his.

As I've said and hoped and prayed, I do wish that Maeve and Mae are dead. That they died before the worst came, perhaps killed themselves before Larry and his stinking, shuffling *friend* violated their trailer. But Maeve was expecting me to come back, to listen and maybe understand . . . my only desire is that *her* hopes didn't rise for one endless second when the door began to open. . . .

Rubbing away the rain-blighted images from my youth with the bent and puff-knuckled fingers of age, I told myself that Tod Browning didn't find the *best* assortment of freaks for his film. The one Tod Browning missed was sitting in my chair, not able to bring himself to take the damned tape out of the machine. Maeve was right when she said our carny's freaks weren't genuine because they didn't care for each other. I know *this* freak didn't do right by one of his own.

Getting up to press the Eject button, I saw the red ring of moisture on my sleeve. I knew there and then that be they ghosts, or something worse, the twins had not forgotten—or forgiven—me. Out of rage over something that had snowballed beyond all reason or sanity I'd blindly struck out at someone who . . . who I very well might've loved, if I didn't already.

What I'd done had been the death of all three of us—four, if I included what I did to Winston in '46. And what the hell, toss in Dead Fred, too. Dead, all of us . . . only we forgot to lie down and rot.

Winston and Una dragged each other down, until she died

and left him a diddling old wreck. He never became Mayor. The former students who professed to admire him laughed behind his back. As they no doubt laugh at me, too. Winston and I were two old fucks with lined faces, twisted fingers and saggy britches. Dead Fred used to make three. The rest of our generation are long dead, cold names on a bronze plaque in Ewert Park by the river, readable if you scrape off the birdshit with a thumbnail.

And all of this might've stayed to fester in me, except . . .

Dead Fred's body was found last year, summer of '87. Swarming mounded thing of shifting crawling flies, winged bodies blue-green-black in the faint shifting light of the Ewert Woods. When the flies lifted, he squirmed with new, grubby life, the flesh all but eaten to the separating bone. The autopsy suggested a heart attack . . . kind of thing that happens to the tired—or the scared. I wonder what he might've seen in those woods, or elsewhere.

It may be silliness on my part, but I can't stop *anticipating*; I keep expecting the day when Winston leaves me for good— that liver of his isn't cast iron. It may be craziness, but *everything* seems to come around, what goes around. . . .

For my nephew, sole survivor of the Nemmitz clan, has married a woman who looks enough like Maeve to knock the breath—and reason—out of me. And the wondering and the *fearing* in me never cease.

And . . . the cold, dark heart of me is an endless, devouring thing, a summer shadow spread cold and black across green glowing grass, still stunting me, still leaving me with the anger and hopeless *wanting* of an almost-sixteen year old. While my body withers around me, a dried hull trapping the tender seed within. When I die, my tombstone should read: "Palmer Edmund Nemmitz, 1924–1940 He Lived a Spell Afterwards, But it Didn't Count."

So . . . here I sit, getting it all down on paper, to see if the *telling* of it will make the *living* of it make any more sense. To get the memory of Maeve and Mae out of me, and purge myself one last time. Before I die and kill the memory with my passing. For . . . we almost had something worth reliving through these reminiscences, almost as if the remembering and wishing and *loving* can make her real once more. That, perhaps, is the highest tribute I can give her. For a freak, she had me fooled; to me, for a time, she *was* "normal."

If there was anything I could write to change it all, to go back and do it better, or *different* at least, I'd sit behind this typewriter for all eternity. But the life of the *old* me beckons. And the remaining old gossip, old Winston, he's waiting for me, no doubt wondering where I'm off to. *Waiting* for me.

On the old woman's bench, uptown.

THE END

Downstairs, Brent heard his uncle puttering around in the kitchen. The aroma of brewing coffee and eggs frying in butter wafted up, but Brent was beyond hunger. Closing the flimsy blue plastic cover of the manuscript as if it were the lid of his uncle's coffin, Brent told himself that he and Zoe *never* should've come back to Ewerton. The battle between Palmer and Maeve wasn't theirs, but Zoe ended up buying a farm, too. *Oh, Zoe, you shouldn't have done* that, *not after just reading—*

Brent sat up in bed, mouth hanging open in dumb amazement. It had taken him two eye-burning days to wade through Palmer's cramped pages of type. And Zoe hadn't been *in* Palmer's bedroom, let alone had time to look through his things, before Brent and his aunt and uncle left for the DQ and the Midnite Mayhem sale. Yet she was stiff when Brent returned a few hours later. Dead women don't lie in bed, reading the long ramblings of an old man.

Pulling the now bent photograph of Zoe's chest from his pocket, Brent studied the lines, deciding that if his uncle wasn't going to follow that blue road, *he* would. If it didn't lead him to Zoe, it might lead him to her killers. And if he reached the twins, maybe he'd stop them before anyone *else* turned up missing, or dead.

His uncle let himself be turned into something other than human that night; perhaps his current state of being was deserved. But damn, the old man had *already* punished himself for his wrongdoing. Brent doubted that Palmer needed goading toward even *worse* behavior.

Changing his rumpled clothes, Brent decided that since he'd ruined whatever the twin/twins had planned for Palmer, it was up to *him* to finish what the freakish women had started. Follow the "map" they left, in case it led him to an answer. Even if it wasn't an answer to the questions *he'd* be asking.

But first, Brent had to steel himself to do something "beyond wrong" himself . . . to determine if, indeed, his wife was *really* dead after all. And if not, to find her.

SEVENTY-FIVE

Sick. For Winston, *sick* took on new shades of meaning that morning. He couldn't remember ever feeling this bone-deep awful . . . save for his stint in Japan.

"What a time .. what a *time*," he whispered through lips shingled with peeling flakes of dead skin, leaning back to rest his pounding head against the wall behind his bench. It had been the time of his life . . . the *worst*.

It hadn't been enough for Winston to merely sneak surplus saccharin and powdered eggs off the abandoned Japanese air base that served as his unit's barracks. The same poster he'd seen at home, "Do With Less So They'll Have More" was posted in the mess hall, and Winston figured the slogan served the newly fallen enemy, too. Some of the patient villagers who waited around the confines of the base were children. Kids certainly didn't bomb Pearl Harbor. Besides, he'd learned to like the people he'd met, even if most of them spoke only Pigeon-English. Winston never could twist his tongue around those slippery Japanese syllables, but the villagers were so willing to pick up a smattering of pseudo-English that he never did learn any Japanese. He couldn't even pronounce the name of the island he was stationed on.

He really liked the young women; small-boned, slightly flat-faced girls of sixteen to twenty or so, with their smooth pale skin and eyes like small dark stones under gentle folds of smooth clay. When they offered themselves, it would've been insulting to refuse, especially with their *papa-sans* urging him to partake of the girls' favors. Gradually, Winston came to the conclusion that the villagers thought he could offer a few of them *more* than the surplus material from the base—as in a ticket to a better life in the States.

When he found himself—sake-fueled, slightly flushed—the center of attention in what he ultimately realized was a marriage ceremony unlike anything he'd seen in Ewerton, he partook in the proceedings with good grace. He doubted the weddings were binding; he was, after all, a Christian. His "brides" were not. But he'd cheerfully consummated each union, and the brides didn't seem to mind when he took off for the base afterward.

True, he experienced great pain when he urinated, and soon the weddings were coming so fast he wasn't able to shake off the hangover from the *previous* night's union, let alone make it back to the base. . . . Nor was he aware that his demure brides began showing up at the base hospital, suffering from difficulties similar to those endured by their common mate. And when the base Doc—a good man, Japanese but American-trained (once Winston saw the man sew on a finger for a base mechanic; using only a common surgical needle and no magnification—within a month the finger *worked*) finally pried the husband's name from the clap-riddled brides, MPs were dispatched to go find Winston.

Find him they did, in mid-wedding. Dragging him out of a bomb-blasted temple, they threw him bodily into the back of a jeep. Before he passed out, Winston remembered how one of them sneered, "Jap-lover." The next thing Winston knew, he was handcuffed to a bed in the base hospital, isolated in a small room—with two MPs stationed outside.

The d.t.'s he went through while being dried out, cold turkey, were awful; bleeding pale trees and spongy pink ground that sucked his shoes with every step.

The injections of sulfathiazole and neoarsphenamine—Winston was allergic to penicillin—plus enough water to float two battleships finally cured his double dose of gonorrhea and syphilis. The Japanese doctor warned him that he *might* be sterile, since his sperm ducts were scarred from within by the severity of his combined illnesses.

When coherent again, Winston was subjected to IQ *and* personality tests by the dozen, by a dour Army shrink with the melodious name of Major Herman Taub. He and Calvin Coolidge were weaned on the same pickle. All the while he kept thinking, *If anyone at home finds out about this, I'm worse than dead.*

The tests completed, Taub retreated for a few days to study the results, and Winston's C.O. visited him. The captain, a pleasant, avuncular man named Sonders, decided that Winston was "too good a soldier to lose . . . and it's not like them girls aren't willing, eh, Lieutenant?'' Captain Sonders was anxious for Winston to return to duty, after a minor punishment of short duration, everything forgiven and forgotten . . . but the rest of the Occupation Army didn't take Winston's "activities" so lightly. Especially Major Taub. . . .

Digging his fingers into his temples, he thought of a later time, after he'd arrived in Washington state. The bar he'd found there, in Seattle. He'd sat for hours, listening to the jukebox, unable to turn around, away from the safety of the bar. It took him six beers to get up the nerve to call Palmer; he'd shored himself up with the hope that a talk with him would erase the shame and pain that still wracked him after his prolonged "chat" with Taub. Winston needed to hear someone he trusted tell him that he *was* a good guy. Not the *monster* Taub implied he was.

After a few more bottles, he'd entered the little phone booth near the back of the bar. But once he got through, heard Palmer's faint voice crackle in his ear, and started babbling into that black mouthpiece, Winston realized that he *still* couldn't say all that he needed to say, to expunge what was killing him from the inside. That slither-sounding bad thing from *"Lights Out,"* the gutting entity that turned him inside-out even as he sat on the narrow ledge in the booth. Winston expected blood to dribble down his chin as the pain-being wormed its way up his body and out his mouth, but the lacination remained in the core of him, knifing the soft parts until tears welled up behind the dark fringes of his lashes, to spill scalding down his cheeks.

And Palmer pumped him, asked the damnedest things, while the phone line clicked and popped, confusing Winston to the point of saying *private* things; finally, he hung up, his pain undiminished.

When he came home, he found out, by overhearing bits and snatches of street talk, that he'd put on *quite* a show for a very appreciative—if shocked—audience of uncertain size. Winston was tempted to write Palmer off altogether, but he'd already proposed to Una. After doing *that* he needed a shoulder to lean on during the double ceremony, so he talked Palmer into going in for a double wedding/reaffirmation.

Sadly, that much-needed talk with Palmer never came about. Palmer was too mean to approach unguarded anymore, yet he carried on like a child when hurt. Winston acquired a veneer of not caring, of not allowing himself to *feel*

anymore . . . even as he longed in near sleep for that unattainable—and spurned—child-woman of his youth.

Eventually, they spent time together almost daily, and the
need to talk certain things over with Palmer grew unimportant. . . .

*But things could've been different . . . if only Palmer hadn't
taken off like a scared rabbit that summer,* he thought, until
a wave of nausea doubled him over. As he stared at his scuffed
shoe tips hovering over the scintillating sidewalk below, he
remembered reading something Palmer wrote about that call
from Seattle. Only Palmer had thought everything was *Winston's* fault. Not quite certain where or when he'd read that,
yet certain that it was indeed true, Winston morosely told
himself, *My fault or his, he still could've listened to me . . .
might've asked why I was crying . . . man has a selfish streak
a mile wide and ten deep, he does—oh, shit, I must be alive.
Nobody already dead feels* this *horrible—*

SEVENTY-SIX

When Brent stepped into the kitchen, all Palmer asked was,
"Finish it?" as if uninterested in Brent's reply. But his back
tensed under his thin plaid shirt when Brent said, "Yes,"
without adding an opinion to his answer.

They ate in silence, the stillness of the room unbroken save
for the humming gurgle of the refrigerator motor. Ultimately,
Brent pushed his nearly untouched plate to the center of the
table. Leaning back in his chair, arms crossed, Brent waited
until his uncle finished swallowing before he asked, "Was
she, I mean *them*, were they like . . . Zoe?"

As he, too, pushed his plate toward the middle of the oilcloth, Palmer replied, "Like sisters. Sounded alike, too. Yes
. . . she's found me, or maybe never let go. Don't know
which. *I* don't think she's *alive*-alive. Makes a difference.
After what . . . happened, dead is all she can be. Brent"
—Palmer eyed his nephew anxiously—"did what you read
affect how you think of me? If Bitsy knew, she'd have never
married me, I'm sure—"

Leaning over, wrapping his big hand over Palmer's smaller,
fragile one, Brent replied slowly, "I have to admit, it was

. . . *inhumane* what you did. I'd hate to be in your shoes, but . . . I don't know if I'd have acted differently. Under those circumstances. Like with Zoe . . . sometimes it was as if she hurt so much the only way I could cope with it was to back away—if I tried to get her to share it with me, I'd be consumed, burned up. But confronting *them*, considering when you met them . . . you said it yourself. People weren't as understanding then.''

Under Brent's hand, Palmers fingers curled into a tight ball. Licking his lips, Palmer said, ''Once, I checked a book out of the library. About 'special people.' Maeve and Mae were Siamese twins, only the book called their kind 'conjoined.' Showed pictures of some. Betty Lou Williams was one. Trunk and limbs poking out of her body, but no head. And one foreign fellow, he had all *but* the head hanging out of his chest. Little doll body. But backward. Book told how they X-rayed him, found a tiny head *in* his belly. Sure hope that head was dumb. Can you imagine *seeing*, *knowing*, and being *stuck* in someone? With no way to cry out for help?''

''As bad as being stuck half-way out, and knowing you can't escape?'' Brent asked without thinking. He made a *moue*, but Palmer didn't notice his *faux pas*; pulling his hand away from Brent, he continued in a dreamy tone, ''Book said that when the man put on a cape, no one saw what was under it . . . people looking at him thought he was normal. Like Maeve's sling. Clever girl . . . wonder what she did when she was little? Pretend Mae was a doll? Kid can't have a broken arm forever. I . . . keep speculating on what it was like, being stuck with someone under your skin. Someone nasty.''

Brent remembered how Mae called Palmer a ''little runt.'' An offensive maneuver on her part, with a touch of irony thrown in for spite. Brent was curious if Mae was disagreeable because she was what she was, or because she chose to be that way. But Brent feared finding out; what the Wanderer had said and done before Palmer indicated that he *had* met Maeve, and wherever Maeve went, Mae tagged along. That symbolic slit on Zoe's side might be an indication of Maeve and Mae's continued state. Not as dramatic as inserting something alien, like a doll, in Zoe, but the point was made—

''You listening, kiddo?'' Brent mumbled an apology, adding that he'd slept little. He declined to tell Palmer that he doubted that Zoe had read the manuscript; if Palmer needed to believe that she had, Brent wasn't willing to shatter his belief. Palmer wasn't about to seek out the twins anyway.

Remembering the map/photo, Brent pulled it out of his pocket, and placed in on the oilcloth. "Does this look like any of the roads in Georgia, or anywhere the carny passed through? If the twins *are* alive, they might be there—"

Peering at the snapshot, Palmer shook his head. "Never drove on one like that. Doesn't go anywhere, see how it forms a ragged triangle? Man could drive in circles—oh, sorry, I see lines going out, but maybe they don't go anywhere either. Just *in*."

"How about a road here?"

"Nah . . . I've driven here for years. No road in Dean County looks anything like that. Not even the snowmobile trails. Sorry, I think they just left a calling card."

Unable to stand a renewed silence as Palmer rocked back and forth in his chair, Brent got up and switched on the radio. A country song faded off, to be replaced by the cheerful adenoidal bleat of the disc jockey, "Looks like it gonna start out hot and *stay* that way for the rest of the day. Yessir, looks like another *beautiful* day in the northlands, if we're lucky, this weather should hold until *next* weekend."

There was a moment of hissing dead air, then a prerecorded announcement came on—and Brent stood slack-jawed, hand mechanically rubbing his cheek, as Gordy Gray droned:

"—Gray, this year's Water Carnival Chairman. I want to invite everyone to come on up for this year's festivities. Despite the vandalism of Ewerton's rides and equipment, the Carnival *is* on for this July twenty-eighth, twenty-ninth, and thirtieth—and what a time we have planned for *you*! This year's entertainment will be provided by South-State Amusements, and the show promises to be even bigger and better than—"

Slowly, Brent wheeled around—only to see grave finality on his uncle's face. "You *know* who trashed that equipment, don't you?"

Palmer shrugged, then laced his bulbous-knuckled fingers and rested his chin on them. "I'm not sure if *they* did it, but it was one way of getting back into town."

Brent sat down again and blurted, "I still don't understand something. Why Zoe?"

"You said Zoe acted as if she *needed* to come back . . . maybe they needed *her*, to remind me of that summer—as if

I were about to *forget*." Palmer snorted ruefully, then, form-ing his words slowly and cautiously, asked, "Do you believe she's *really* dead? Despite what we saw?"

"Who?" An equally cautious reply.

"Your wife. Her cremation . . . none of it smelled right to me. And there's been some . . . talk, uptown. People don't think she—"

The ringing phone was harsh, strident against the blatty voice of the WERT announcer. After exchanging glances, Palmer told Brent, "I'll get it," and shuffled to the phone. Brusquely he snapped, " 'Lo?" Then: "No, he's not, Stu . . . what is it? Don't patronize me, Stu, I'm not Bitsy—

"Yes, *I* handled it, spoke to him my—

"Oh, you *did* . . ." Palmer motioned for Brent to *quietly* come to the phone. Leaning in close, ear to the receiver, Brent heard Stu Sawyer's faint, "—them yesterday, and they never *heard* of your nephew's wife, let alone cremated her. What the fuck's going *on*, Palmer? If this is a goddamn in-surance scam, don't go thinking I won't report you just 'cause you're married to my cousin—"

Head reeling, Brent backed away from the phone, making tracks for the back door (Palmer mouthed, *Don't slam it!*). After softly shutting the screen door, Brent ran to the back of the house, to the circular arrangement of pretty stones—

—whose arrangement was no longer circular, or particu-larly pretty anymore.

Getting down to his knees, Brent dug at the random scattering of stones with his bare hands, sending dirt and rocks flying behind him, like a bone-crazy hound. He found the metal box first, but instinct made him toss that aside, too. The condition of Duffy's box, half seen through the loose dirt, was important, urgent . . . for the tape that had secured the lid was peeled back, bits of cardboard fuzzing the sticky side.

Breathing through his mouth in anticipation of the stink of decomposition, Brent lifted the flaps . . . only to let out his breath in an anguished rush. The box was empty, save for a few shed gray hairs clinging to Zoe's sweater. No Duffy.

Brent yanked the cardboard box out of the earth, hoping against hope that the cat's body had somehow fallen *through* the bottom of the intact box. As he shoved the box aside, a keening wail erupted from his throat. Nothing but a loose rectangular depression remained.

Brent picked up the tin; it made a soft rustling, muted *rattling* sound when he shook it. What he'd first taken for the sound of bone chips hitting the sides. Gently shaking the tin near his ear, Brent realized ordinary ashes shouldn't produce such a sound . . . real cremains had the remaining bone chips pounded to ashy-fineness.

Brent broke one of his short fingernails trying to pry open the tin, until something warned him that he'd best not look, best not *know* the source of that autumnal rustling.

Behind him, Palmer's shoes slithered softly on the long, dewy grass. "Stu . . . called down to Eau Claire, Wausau, all over. Wants to know what we did with Zoe. He doesn't believe she's dead, either—claims he saw her. Driving a white Pierce-Arrow. With a *peach* on the license plate. Even if it wasn't Zoe, we're both stuck up the creek with broken arms and no paddles. Stu's checking you out. Asked for names, addresses of your friends in the Cities. Already checked the cops *there*, no dice. Only thing going for us is that he's too busy to stop by . . . 'sides, *legally* he can't. No body, no autopsy record, and Lenny's reluctant to stand behind that death certificate now. Once the Carnival's over, he's gonna dig deeper. Thinks something sick's going on . . . trouble is, he doesn't know *how* sick—oh, Jeezus, they took the damned *cat*, too?"

Brent began to cry.

SEVENTY-SEVEN

Ewerton lay like a panting sick thing under the curdled glare of the sun, barely able to lift its head to beg for water or crawl off in search of shade.

Like shining poisonous mushrooms, realtor's signs dotted more and more lawns in Ewerton, some as far north as Willow Hill. No one witnessed the pounding of signs into burnt lawns, just as no one recalled seeing the occupants leave. There simply was no more late-night slam of car doors, no more curtain-filtered light spilling out into the darkness of the insect night.

But the dazzling heat precluded serious speculation about the slow emptying of Ewerton. Instead, with a wipe of a greasy brow over a cold beer, bar sitters spoke of the lean white car gliding through town, and the mad flights of old man Winston and Clive Calder. ("Took off with that student of his, one *you* said killed herself. Went *nuts* is what happened. You seen 'er, one in the collector car without the collector plates—course I mean the one with the fruit plates, there another in town?" "Heard the Doc botched the autopsy on some bigwig's kin, so there was hell to pay. . . .")

And in his car, bare sweaty legs sliding around on the hot vinyl upholstery, Brent glanced from the heat-mirrored road to the photo he'd clipped to his sunscreen, then at the road again. He'd tried attaching the map of Ewerton torn from the phone book up there, too, but the tiny tangle of lines was too difficult to read unless he held the flimsy yellow page under his nose.

Driving up and down and around in every configuration possible, down every street, back alley, private drive, and random dirt road in town, Brent feared that he was on a wild goose chase—even if he did happan upon the "right" road, how would he *know* he'd found it? He told himself that a big sign might be helpful . . . "This is the Place, Sidewalks Rolled Up at 8:00 Sharp!" . . . something as *insane* as this whole situation Brent found himself caught up in.

SEVENTY-EIGHT

JULY 21

Lenny Wilkes hated hot days. First, because a man his size couldn't wear shorts to work (unlike the beanpole kids who worked the bowling alley), unless he wanted to flaunt colorless quivering thighs to an unappreciative world. Second, because every last punk in town was jammed around the video games, tilting or hitting the machines to get better scores, trying to impress the tube-topped and bronze-legged twits who hung around watching the boys feed quarters into noisy machines which impishly refused to give the boys scores *worthy* of the twit's attention.

Third because all the films he could've been renting out were either at home under his TV stand, or out in the back of someone's car, not to be returned until four sharp—and the tape was bound to be a parboiled mess after baking in the sunhatch. And forth—because the phone had a perverse way of ringing just when he was making change for someone whose car was idling outside, keys dangling in the ignition, while his employees were off trying to score with the tube-topped twits and couldn't be bothered with the *phone*. Not when Lenny was within an arm's reach of it.

Lenny was counting out change for a kid who used an Andrew Jackson to pay for a small bag of Cool Ranch Doritos when the phone started in again. It broke his concentration; he gave out an extra dollar in change before he was able to lean over and lift the receiver off the wall. The punk noticed the extra buck before Lenny did, hightailing it before Lenny could yelp, ''GETBACKHERE!'' at the boy's retreating bare back . . . for Lenny's voice was stilled by tense words from the tiny receiver holes—''Ewert Woods. Meetcha there.'' He recognized the sheriff's strangely muted voice. When Stu wasn't barking, he was upset, which meant—

Lenny wiggled out from behind the counter, bawling for someone to come man the register, then left before his skinny tanned assistants could ask what was wrong.

Within two minutes he was whizzing past stop signs, portable flasher mounted on his dashboard. As he speeded, Lenny recalled that night at the Nemmitz farmhouse; people were saying *rotten* things behind his back now. He was unfit to be coroner, writing out ''false'' death certificates. He made a deal with a body seller. All sorts of trash that made Millie puddle up over supper.

He was glad *Stu* called the crematorium, made a fool of *him*self. For Lenny had been too scared to call down there himself . . . just in case that redheaded young man had answered.

Most people knew enough to pull over and let Lenny pass when they saw the flashing red light in his car—*then* turned around to follow at a discreet distance. Brent was heading down Lumbermill Drive, toward the river, when he saw Lenny whiz past, puffy face drawn behind his tinted windshield. Brent cut in front of the convoy of cars trailing the coroner.

A bizarre thought crossed Brent's mind—*Snipe must've got*

'em . . . even though he wasn't sure *who* the mythical beast had mauled.

When Lenny reached the end of the woods, the convoy fanned out on the rough long grass, parked at crazy angles like a dumped-out box of matchbox cars. Thankful that his uncle's Rambler wasn't among the cars disgorging sunburned occupants, Brent drove as close to the parked squad cars as possible before getting out of the Pacer and darting into the woods.

Curiously, the milling crowd was reticent to enter the woods, as if the lack of Stu Sawyer's bullhorned warnings to stay away left them dispirited. Only a small girl, dressed in a pink ruffled halter top and saggy elastic-waist shorts voiced the question of the crowd—"There a deader in there?"

Over his huffing breath, he heard the low rumble of voices deep in the forest . . . followed by a hitching, gutturally moist noise of vomiting. Lenny Wilkes had beat him to the body.

Suddenly Brent hoped it wasn't old man Winston lying dead in there.

SEVENTY-NINE

JULY 23

The autopsy of Clive Calder, performed down in Madison just to make sure that another Zoe Nimitz screwup didn't occur, was brief (due to the decomposition of the remains) but thorough. The ruptured blood vessels in the brain were unmistakable. Doctor Calder died of a brain hemorrhage. Stroke. Case closed.

He was shipped home just in time for the noon funeral on the twenty-third; Craig Reish was grateful. Embalming the remains was impossible. A black body bag would have to suffice.

The mood of the citizens of Ewerton was summed up by one brave—and slightly intoxicated—soul who saw fit to bring up the subject on WERT's *Speak Your Piece* show. "Satchel Ass Sawyer's an' Bib Stanley should be fired for not findin' the Doc sooner." Judging from the subsequent call-ins after the inebriated gentleman hung up, the consensus in Ewerton was, ''You bet your sweet fanny they should!''

In self-defense, Stu and Bib each made recorded messages, absolving each other of all blame in the situation. Each tape ended, ''According to the law, no adult can be declared missing until twenty-four hours have passed.''

''Like locking the barn door after the horses have run out,'' Palmer groused on the morning of the funeral, while he and Brent waited for Bitsy to get dressed. Clive's death had brought about a truce between the old couple; Bitsy came home Thursday night (''Poor Angie, Clive was only a few *blocks* away . . . almost in her backyard!'').

Brent assumed that she and Palmer would sit together at the funeral, which suited him fine. He intended to make an appearance at the church, go to the cemetery, then resume his search for that elusive road to nowhere.

Clive Calder's funeral was subdued, and brief, save for Angie's loud sobbing in the front row. Brent nearly gagged when the minister solemnly proclaimed, ''Clive's playing ball on the Lord's team now . . . we'll all miss Clive, especially the Little Leaguers. Clive bought fundraiser candy bars from each team member, just so they could buy new uniforms.''

While Brent listened to the minister—whose straight face made his remarks all the more inane—he wondered if he'd be able to make it through the graveside service without cracking up. Deciding that hick towns not only got idiot doctors like Clive Calder, but bottom-of-the-barrel ministers, too, Brent wondered if he could worm his way out of going to the cemetery with his aunt and uncle.

But as he glanced at the old couple, both of them slumped and wrinkled in their dark clothes, Brent realized that he had to make sure they were all right at the grave site. If the minister brought up baseball again, though, Brent knew he'd have to restrain himself from drop-kicking the guy into the astroturf-boardered hole . . . and kicking dirt in after him. *Then* let the good reverend come up with a dugout quip to cap off the eulogy. . . .

The minister kept his graveside words brief and properly biblical. While he politely sat during the prayers and lamentations, Brent's eyes darted around behind his mirrored sunglasses. There were paths among the graves; more than a few of them were strangely angled. And that tall monument and vault, the one Palmer said was old man Holiday's—that was interesting in itself. His uncle had mentioned something about a "funny inscription" on the stone, but Brent had other things, other roads to check out, before he could take the time to check out his uncle's father's tombstone.

Surreptitiously inching his hand down to his left shoe sole, Brent flicked off a piece of semisoft tar with a thumbnail. The roads all over town were cracked, some deeply enough to require a drizzle of tar over the cracks to seal them . . . and for the first time, Brent had noticed how some of the lines formed odd, softly geometric configurations.

Including soft triangles.

EIGHTY

As Sarah Andersen rinsed off Li'l Scoot's dish, placing it on the already full rack to drain, she thought about Brent Nimitz, in the launderette, when he'd said that he couldn't figure out why Zoe had wanted to come back to Ewerton.

Glancing out her kitchen window, Sarah saw a familiar sight. Brent's Pacer, cruising slowly down her street. Watching the Pacer roll slowly down Hemlock Street, Sarah remembered that bottle of Bold 3 she'd picked up that day in the Super Suds, before they all drove out to the fairgrounds. She reached under the sink for the bottle. If she was lucky, he'd tell her to just keep it.

Taking a last look out the window, Sarah saw the low tail end of the car crawl past the fire hydrant near the curb. She flip-flopped in her thongs out the door, down the driveway, and across the lawn, bottle in hand. She heard the low snick of the Pacer's tires on the pavement as she reached the curb, eyes downcast so she wouldn't step on any grass-hidden kiddie toys, but when she looked up, the car was *gone*.

Which made no sense—if he kept going the way he was headed, Brent should be crossing the bridge by now. If he turned the corner, she'd be able to see him through the sparsely situated homes around her. *The Pacer was not there.*

Squinting her eyes didn't help either. The Pacer *had* vanished.

Turning toward the bridge, she looked for the squat outline of the car across the river, but saw few cars . . . and *no* Pacer.

Hugging the Bold 3 bottle against her boney chest (*I saw him, I did, he was going past the house, I* saw *the bumper next to the—*) Sarah tried her damndest not to shiver . . . but shivered nonetheless, under a baking sun.

PART FOUR

Death and Forever

somewhere i have never travelled, gladly beyond
any experience, your eyes have their silence;
in your most frail gesture are things which enclose me,
or which i cannot touch because they are too near

your slightest look will easily unclose me
though i have closed myself as fingers
you open always petal by petal myself as Spring opens
(touching skilfully, mysteriously) her first rose

or if your wish be to close me, i and
my life will shut very beautifully, suddenly,
as when the heart of this flower imagines
the snow carefully everywhere descending;

nothing which we are to perceive in this world equals
the power of your intense fragility: whose texture
compels me with the colour of its countries
rendering death and forever with each breathing

(i do not know what it is about you that closes
and opens; only something in me understands

the voice of your eyes is deeper than all roses)
nobody, not even the rain, has such small hands

—e. e. cummings

"I think, therefore I am."

—Rene Descartes

EIGHTY-ONE

Winston was over the worst of his sickness; the gut-roiling sensation was abating when he awoke. Hanging on to the curved armrest of the bench, he got to his feet. According to the reflection in the hardware store window, no matter how much better he felt, he might as well be dead. He looked it. No dead man could ache as he'd ached; if he was stuck with life, he might as well make himself presentable.

He gingerly crossed the street to the barbershop door affixed with a jangling bell. For a breathless second he stood in the half-opened doorway, expecting someone to tromp downstairs to wait on him. When no one showed up, white sheet and razor in hand, to tackle his beard stubble and unkempt hair, Winston let out a shaky sigh before walking to the nearest mirror.

His eyes weren't too bloodshot, but the faint bruise-dark circles under them indicated that he needed sleep . . . plenty of it, on a regular *bed.*

With only slightly shaking hands, he shaved, then washed his hair, leaning forward unsteadily into the sink. Touching the raw spot on his cheek where he'd just nicked himself, he remembered that Mr. Haskins the barber used to live above his shop. Did his own cooking; sometimes, years ago, Winston used to smell meat roasting while getting his hair cut.

Winston's legs were still cramped, but he climbed the stairs two at a time. When he reached the landing, he closed his eyes in relief. There was a bedroom just off the living room, and a kitchen beyond the bedroom. Raking shaky fingers through his damp hair, he vacillated between eating and sleeping, then entered the dazzling white kitchen.

But he'd only taken a sip of orange juice from the earthenware pitcher in the Frigidaire before he felt his whole body go slack. He barely made it into the bedroom before flopping down, clothes and shoes still on, and cradled his head in the crochet-trimmed pillow. As he drifted off to sleep, a soon-to-be-forgotten whisper echoed in his ear, *Stay off the street . . . he might see you. . . .*

•   •   •

Brent rubbed his eyes as he made the turn down Spruce Avenue and headed for the Mill bridge; he'd crossed it so many times in the past few days he could do it blindfolded. Taking his fingers out from under his sunglasses, he stared blearily at the paper mill. Lunchtime must've been extra long today; no cars were parked in the lot.

The heat was worse; twisting streamers rose high from the pavement, making everything outside the car waver and sway in the postnoon glare, and totally putting paid to his notion of following the soft squiggles of tar on the cracked streets, for even *those* were rendered invisible. Flipping down the sun flaps, Brent squinted behind his smudged lenses, but the heat shimmer grew *worse*, which made no sense at all. His $100 black sunglasses were *supposedly* glare resistant. . . .

Tooling down county trunk QV, Brent shook his head, poking at his eye with a blunt fingertip, wondering if he had an eyelash stuck in there . . . until he saw the *sign*, in the rearview mirror—

Brent braked so hard Pathfinder flopped over on one black-winged side. As he made a U-turn, Brent tried to recall how the "Ewerton Welcomes You!" sign looked on the day he drove Zoe into this wretched burg. Closing his eyes for a second, he focused on the memory.

A corners-rounded black wood sign with raised yellow script lettering, surrounded by six tiny round signs for the Jaycees, Kiwanis, American Legion, Lions, Chamber of Commerce, and "Home of the Ewerton Rams." He remembered *that* sign because Zoe snapped out of her semi-catatonic doze to mumble, "Opposing teams call'em the Ewerton Sheepfuckers."

Approaching the sign face-forward now, Brent panicked. *Someone made off with the Sheepfuckers . . . all the rest of 'em, too.* The sign before him, which gained in size as he approached, was not the same sign he'd seen in June. The shape was wrong, and it was painted—not covered with raised wooden lettering. Flowing *cream* script read:

Welcome to Ewerton!
Population 3,251 and Growing Every Day!

Under that was a smaller line of script, unreadable at a distance of ten feet.

Not wanting to drive any closer, Brent stopped the car, and sat inside, screwing up his courage. To get out, check the sign, maybe touch it, prove to himself it was just a mirage. Too much time spent driving, too little time spend sleeping.

Whatever it was, it wasn't heatstroke. He was sure as he got out of the Pacer and walked to the five-foot-wide wooden sign. Praying that the false image would dissolve when he touched the warm surface, Brent stood near enough to read the delicately painted line of script aloud . . . through lips wooden as the surface on which the words appeared:

Sidewalks Rolled Up—8:00 P.M. Sharp!

Forcing himself to step forward, so he could brush his fingertips against the warm skin of paint, Brent mumbled, "Let it be heatstroke, anything—" until his fingers made contact.

The sign was solid, thickly painted; the swirl of the "S" rose above the surrounding midnight-blue background. Up close, Brent saw the creamy lettering *float* above the dark surface below—then everything hazed up wiggling ebony-magenta as he fell forward, onto the soft shoulder.

EIGHTY-TWO

Winston awoke under the spinning blur of a ceiling fan hanging five feet above him; it cast dark, lopping shadows on the wall opposite the room's small window. He felt relatively comfortable for the first time since . . . he didn't know when.

Winston sat at the edge of the bed, staring up at the quietly snicking fan *(Did I pull the chain, start that up?)*. Rubbing his hands on his thighs, he realized that he needed something new to wear—his uniform was awful.

But there were no clothes in the small wardrobe, nor in the drawers of the bureau across from the bed. Winston remembered seeing a haberdashery down the street, on the same side as the barbershop. Surely, they had to have something in his size.

It wasn't until he left the shop, and was on the street, that the voice whispered, *Plenty of clothes waiting for you at home . . . on Winston Street. It all fits you—*

Betrayed by his own brain, Winston carefully said out loud, his voice echoing flat, overemphasized in the silent street, "That *house* is empty. It is not *mine* anymore. It was *sold*. Nothing of mine is there. *Nothing.*" He took a few steps forward, until the voice needled, *Your father wants you to live there . . . it would make him so* glad—

The voice droned on in Winston's confused brain; plugging his ears only made the voice clearer, louder—

Deathly afraid that the dreaded d.t.'s were back, he made a run for the haberdashery—and plowed smack into a street lamp. Winston never felt the hard slap of pavement against his body.

As sunset cast deep gold-washed shadows across Brent's and Winston's still, sleeping forms, the fallen men shared more than *unconsciousness*, more than a mere *dream*. . . .

. . . she awakened to the glare of sunlight through closed eyelids; instinctively, she shielded her eyes against that blood-infused glare with her hands—

Suddenly, Maeve opened her eyes, to stare in awestruck rapture and dread at her two *perfect hands. Equal-sized hands, small palms deeply lined, short fingers curled protectively against the harsh no-color glare of the sun.*

Stunned, unable to consider other, more obvious questions, she lifted her pair of perfect hands and arms . . . to do something she'd longed to do from childhood. Something silly, yet healing.

Eyes squinted half-shut, she pressed forefinger to opposite thumb, each hand joined and unjoined in turn, as the Itsy-Bitsy spider climbed up the spout. . . .

". . . and down came the rain, and washed the spider out!" until she got tired of seeing the "spider" climb up and down in the clear stillness of the warm air and pale sky above. Pressing whole palm against whole palm, fingers arched skyward, she moved her hands in time with her softly chanted words, "This is the church, *this is the* steeple, *o-pen the* doors *and out come the* people!"

As Maeve's wondrous, rose-petal fingers endlessly rebuilt

and emptied the church above her prone body, her mind labored deep below the level of conscious thought; memories tried to surface, only to be washed down like the Itsy-Bitsy spider in his water spout . . . stabbing, frantic memories, recent, but seeming as if they'd happened a lifetime ago. . . .

Palmer. Mae, shouting. Open door. Panic, rain-drenched pain. Then, clean rain, washing the filth, the red agony. Spurting, gaping—

She forced the horror to another part of her brain, the part not enjoying the simple, joyous fingerplay above her head—

"Is that all you plan to do?" Hearing Mae's voice drift down to where she lay in a shallow ditch, Maeve rolled onto her left side. Only then did it sink in that something was missing—someone so familiar to her that her loss was all the more startling. Maeve was lying on her left side—and not crushing Mae.

Peering up, Maeve saw Mae standing at the lip of the ditch, wearing one of Maeve's dresses. The dark blue flowered one Palmer had stared at with his bright green eyes.

Feeling stones press into her nearly naked body, Maeve realized that Mae was normal-sized. Quickly probing her left side, she felt for the gap in her ribs under the maroon-stained tatters of her slip, but all she found was a curved cage of ribs around her lungs. Nothing to mark the spot where Mae had resided within her for sixteen years.

(She remembered the liquid glints of black blood and stunted bone, before Larry threw Mae free—)

Pulling the remains of her slip over her exposed breasts, Maeve shook the hair out of her face and asked, "Are they . . . still here? Is the car—"

(A memory too cruel to voice, the spiteful hiss of a ruined tire.)

Mae crossed her arms (Maeve almost felt elbows jab into her chest). "Only fools stick around at a murder site . . . but they aren't what we are." The implication of her words was plain to Maeve. She got to her feet, and Mae helped her out of the ditch.

Having come alive in an altered form, Maeve wasn't surprised to see that their trailer had been righted, that the flat tire had been fixed, but she was shocked to see that their trailer and car weren't the only vehicles parked in the clearing that almost looked like the place where the carny had been encamped yesterday. She thought that the kootchie girls

(How *could* Palmer have slept with—) *were still here, until she saw that the curtains were all wrong, paisley instead of dotted . . . Maeve felt a dizzying twinge, as if she'd seen this bus long ago, before her birth.*

At her right, Mae snapped, "You are going to put on some clothes before seeing Mr. Quigley, aren't you? He's the religious sort . . . after he's come this far, it wouldn't do to offend him."

Maeve mouthed Quigley? *but Mae steered her toward the Airstream. "Be quick about it, he says we haven't much time . . . we've things to accomplish." Neither twin spoke of what had happened to them—either jointly or separately—during that bloody night, but they shared a impulse.*

The dream was horrible, yet so sharp and *real*, that Brent awoke with a quivering whimper, brain reverberating with an urge for *revenge*.

He was unable to focus on the rich gold of the street lamps that trailed off like ropes of carnival lights bobbing in the darkness. The globes were funny-shaped. Around him, all was greenish darkness; the "Welcome to Ewerton!" sign was a depthless oblong of black above his head.

Far off, he heard a harsh grating, a stone-on-stone *rubbing*, like a rock shoved through a ring of concrete. Getting up, his whole body tender, Brent pushed a button on his watch, to faintly illuminate the dial: 8:01.

Understanding the screeing stone-on-stone noise, Brent climbed into the Pacer and rolled up the windows. The sidewalks were rolling up on time—at first the thought was hysterical, then purely abhorrent.

Even as the interior of the Pacer grew warmer from his shed body heat, Brent shivered in the darkness. Tightly, he shut his eyes, until they pulsed and sparkled from within, a head-show of lime green, pulsing red and wavering blue . . . culminating in a crawling nest of purest, deepest black.

The rolling sidewalk dumped Winston into the street; he came to in time to see the retreating slab of formerly flat concrete and rounded curb slide away from him, curling up against the buildings like a huge stale jelly roll. The street lamps remained, exposed bases moored in loose dirt and rusted chicken wire. All the benches had tipped over onto the dirt and stones, toppled by the snail-wound pavement.

"Sidewalks can't *do* that," he whispered in a small-child hush. He winced as he cautiously probed the lump on his forehead. The avenue had been rendered unwalkable for the night, the uneven surface defying anyone foolish enough to be out and about in the darkness to use them. Marveling at the impossible made possible, wondering how the stiff and unyielding surface became so pliant, so easily *rolled* with nary a crack or crumble, Winston felt the return of an old fear. *Terror.*

His *refreshing* nap had been a subterfuge, a time of regrouping for his physical and mental punishment. The d.t.'s were back, in spades. His mind was addled, his body tortured, and now the damned sidewalks were gone. . . .

"No *fair*," he moaned. Sickened that his progress was illusionary, he felt defeated, for his punishment would *never* end. As if to double, no, triple his misery, he heard Una coo his name again.

Rising so quickly he almost fell down again, Winston tried to scream, to drown out the echoing repetition of his name, but all he produced was a gurgling squeak. His eye fell on the Case Model X sedan parked by Holiday's store. He could roll the windows up, shut out Una's voice, then curl up on the backseat.

Winston didn't think it strange that the doors were conveniently open; he scrambled into the front seat, rolled up both windows, then climbed in back and shut both those windows . . . but forgot to shut the driver's side door in his confusion. Seconds after crawling onto the wide backseat, he fell asleep.

And didn't hear the metalic *whump* of the door closing, before the car began to move down the avenue. . . .

EIGHTY-THREE

As Brent awoke in the cramped, stale confines of the Pacer, a last wisp of morning dream faded from his mind and he focused on his curled right arm, which he'd tucked under his head as he slept.

Stuck to his skin were hairs not his own—long, whisper-thin smoky-gray animal hairs, which fluttered with each breath he took. In his mind's eye, Brent saw Duffy, mop-paws extended, stretched up against his leg . . . then Duffy, perfectly posed, on Zoe's old sweater, before Brent tucked the sleeves over him . . . then the same sleeves, empty. Sitting up, rubbing his burning eyes with his knuckles, Brent protested, "But I had the windows rolled up."

Too late, Brent remembered the long hairs on his arm, but they had already fallen off, to mingle with the dusty, lint-and-fur matted interior of the car.

He refused to acknowledge the strange "Welcome" sign while putting the car in gear. *Had* to be a joke. Voice cracking in the dry stillness of the car, he muttered, "None of this is *funny* anymore, hear?"

Winston awoke abruptly; sunlight shone hot and bright into his aching eyes. He prided himself for remembering that he did, indeed, climb into *this* car on his own . . . but raising his head above the solid half of the car door, he was positive that the car hadn't been parked outside the Holiday *house* last night. The store, yes, but the house . . . most certainly *not*.

But this *was* Roberts Street; sparkling, shooting off hair-thin bands of colorful light even as he stared at the house from the protection of the sedan. The Holiday house hovered above him, fine faux woodgrain patterened siding twisting like a moire ribbon. As if *breathing* in the clear light.

Winston longed to enter the house, but instead turned around in the car, head below the window. He opened the rear door farthest away from the house and slid out into the street, shutting the door behind him.

Crawling along the hot pavement for a few feet, he then rose to run, bent low at the waist, until he reached Share Avenue. Not once did he look back—just in *case*.

The Pacer lapped up pavement, entering town sooner than Brent anticipated, but he still chose to believe that the sign was a prank. Kids from Lumbe, or Hunterstown, too chicken to scrawl "Ewerton Sheepfuckers" on the sign did the next best thing—replaced the *whole* sign. Less trouble if they got caught. Stu Sawyer would blow his graying crewcut when he saw it.

Despite the humor of that image, his eyes sobered him with a knowledge his brain refused to accept . . . *nothing* was right, anywhere.

The *not-rightness* wasn't too obvious at first; houses lined the streets; trees, telephone poles, and street signs stood in front of the homes, and as the Pacer lopped past, Brent was dimly aware that he passed parked cars. But things were . . . *strange*, nonetheless.

Everything *lunged* at him, the way a moving train seemed to bow out at him, then pull back into a straight line. Even the trees did that, each leaf looming out large and distinct, before receding into the mass of foliage covering each branch. His whole view, block after block of it, reminded Brent of something. . . .

Before he reached the business section, it came to him. Curvilinear perspective. A false roundness, tricking the eye into dismissing the realities of a flat canvas.

Brent was midway up Ewert Avenue, close to the beginning of the business district, when he braked hard and cut down First Avenue East, not stopping until he reached Dean Avenue, turned onto Byrne Avenue, then drove up Winston Avenue to the top of Ewert Hill.

Not only did the sudden rise in altitude make Brent feel dizzy—he just never felt so disoriented in his life. For he was in a town he'd been living in for close to a month . . . but he wasn't in the Ewerton *he* knew.

Parking in the driveway of the Winston house, setting the emergency brake, he opened the door and sat half in, half out of the Pacer, feet resting on the gravel driveway.

Shaking his head, rubbing his eyes, Brent remembered— the "For Sale" signs. *Gone.* Staring down at the town, Brent's worst fears were confirmed. No realtor's signs, no snaking wind socks, no plastic turtle wading pools, no bagged piles of trash resting on curbs. No clunker Pintos or subcompacts, only big, boxy *rounded* autos, with thin license plates.

No Woodlawn Development; just an uninterrupted expanse of grassy plain and trees beyond the river. No TV antennas or satellite dishes. The Seventh Avenue bridge wasn't there either . . . the same bridge that welfare woman missed before her plunge into the river.

Brent couldn't see if the farmhouse was there—too many trees, too much distance between himself and the Nemmitz land. Strange, hadn't his uncle mentioned how he and Winston signaled each other via lights in their windows? Brent supposed the view from the upstairs windows might be better—but he wasn't about to enter the house to check *that* out yet. The whereabouts of the farmhouse were important . . . for Brent had realized what *else* was missing below. . . .

No movement, save for the random gentle dip and sway of tree branches, and the twinkle of sun-catching leaves. Clumsily, Brent climbed onto the roof of his car, to get a better look at the town.

Soul sick yet curiously euphoric, Brent tapped off the missing . . . *items* of the town on his bare thigh, but he saw some good things, too, things missing in the real Ewerton. Clean, debris-free streets, trees unmutilated by power company saws in an effort to free power lines from stray branches, and as for the business district—

From his king-of-the-hill position, Brent recalled when, sitting on this very spot, he'd told Palmer how he wished he could've seen Ewerton as it was decades ago. . . . *Looks like I got my wish.*

Getting off the hood, he remembered the snapshots Bitsy had shown him. Below were the *same* buildings that served as a background for those photographs—unchanged, needing only people stiffly posed in period clothing to complete the illusion.

Filled with queasy exhilaration, Brent realized that he'd *done* it. *How,* he had no idea, but he'd *done* it. Left Ewerton, and found this *place*, where the twins were most likely hidden, and where he prayed Zoe was, too. Perhaps in one of the houses . . . but there was so *many* houses.

His elation dampened, Brent walked around the Winston house. He peered into windows, but the sun acted in strange ways on the glass; his reflection was mirrorlike.

Returning to his car, Brent drove down Ewert Avenue, until a rich, buttery aroma wafted into the car.

He hadn't eaten in over twenty-four hours. And popcorn *was* his favorite pig-out food . . . fluffy white kernels smothered in greasy butter, the box already translucent in spots when the woman behind the concessions counter handed it to him.

Instinctively, Brent slowed down the car, nose extended like a hunting dog tracking fallen game, searching for the source of that mouth-watering, nostalgic odor.

He braked when he saw the sign on the sidewalk, and the

twin opened doors beyond. "Dripping" ice-blue lettering on the self-standing sandwich boards boasted, "IT'S COOL IN-SIDE!"

Indeed, the air rolling out of that open doorway was like the first Popsicle of summer, the chill of pond water under a smacking belly flop, or the sweet kiss of fat raindrops on sunburnt flesh. All he had to do was put his hand and arm out of the open window and scoop up a handful of *cool*. . . . But the rest of him wanted in on that ice-box frostiness, too.

On the marquee, the film *Mad Love* was advertised. But the more Brent looked at this theatre, the less he recalled of the closed movie house of his boyhood summers in Ewerton. It was as if the building had *never* closed, never had its windows papered, never had its twin doors padlocked shut. But the Ewerton Theatre closed down when his *uncle* was a little boy. Brent had never been inside, yet he knew—he just *knew*—that the concession stand was just inside the door, to his left. The steps leading down to the screening room fanned out to his right, with the balcony stairs winding up and over his head.

"Silly," he grumbled; *every* old movie house in America was laid out something like that . . . but certainties about *this* theater came to him, unbidden yet not unwelcome: The popcorn machine was blue, gold gilt trimmed, and the candy counter had all the *good* stuff on display, Baby Ruths, Hersheys, Tootsie Rolls (*and Pops, Maeve likes the Pops*), Milk Duds, Goobers, and those Stardust Bars. The ones the Happy Wanderer gave to Palmer.

The Wanderer *had* been here, Brent sensed it. . . .

Too excited to be afraid, yet vaguely aware that he had reason to fear *something*, Brent left his car and headed into the butter-scented coolness of the movie house, his body washed and numbed by waves of chilled air, his mind benumbed and dazed.

Once he reentered the barbershop, Winston felt better. Sitting on one of the leather-covered chairs, feet resting on the sink set into the counter, he adjusted the wet towel draped over his eyes, as he tried to figure out why his d.t.'s had returned without warning. It didn't seem *right*—his body felt fine and his head—apart from the walnut-sized lump over his left temple—was clear.

Opening his eyes under the cloth, his field of vision now a nubby, gently illuminated white patch, Winston was rudely jolted by the return of his unwelcome companion, the soft, clear voice. *What makes you think you're the only one who's real in this place? Think you deserve a whole town of your own?*

Winston yanked the wet cloth off his eyes, tossed it in the sink, and got off the chair. Wandering about the weirdly glinting room, running his hands over the two chairs, the Atwater Kent radio, and the pile of magazines resting on a paint-splattered table—*St. Nicholas, Saturday Evening Post, Reader's Digest*—all dating from 1923 or earlier. The year niggled his mind, but Winston was born in 1924. Bothersome or not, he didn't think that 1923 *concerned* him.

Sighing, he trudged up the stairway, bypassed the kitchen, and reentered the bedroom. There he looked out the window, elbows propped on the sill, chin resting on laced fingers. Tranquilized by the lack of movement on the street below, and by the thick heat surrounding him, Winston dozed, wide blue eyes half open even as he slept.

EIGHTY-FOUR

Brent stood in the center of the lobby. Air-conditioning swirled around his hot, aching body, as he deeply inhaled oily-sweet air. His eyes were closed, adjusting from the brassy light without to the dim illumination within. When he opened his eyes, everything *was* as he'd thought (*knew*) it would be— blue and gold popcorn machine merrily popping and tossing snow-fuffs of heated corn behind fogged glass; bars and boxes of crinkly and shiny-wrapped candy behind the glass wall of the showcase; soft drinks bubbling in glass-topped containers . . . while to his right, the velvet-roped marble staircase to the screening room receded into lush blackness.

There was no one in the ticket booth, no one operated the popcorn maker, nor did anyone stand behind the concessions counter. Yet, everything smelled *fresh*. No tell-tale coat of dust on the candy bar wrappers. The chess-board tile floor was waxed, its marbelized black and gray squares free of ground-down popcorn hulls and frazzled cigarette butts . . .

swept, polished and dusted, all to please the lone customer who stood in the lobby, stomach grumbling, and mouth watering as he watched the fat kernels of popped corn dance in the confines of the popper.

It would be an *insult* not to partake of what was so tastefully offered. Brent visited the ticket booth, said "One, please," and snaked his hand through the arched opening to rip off a perforated yellow ticket from the wide roll within. Digging around in his pocket, he found a couple of pennies and a nickel. Pushing the coins into the booth, he nodded thanks to the non-existent ticket-taker.

He helped himself to popcorn, filled a waxed paper cup with orange soda, and picked out some candy bars, including a nut roll dubbed a "Chicken Dinner." Then, realizing that there was no place to sit, Brent reluctantly went down to the screening room. Eating in his car didn't seem . . . *right*; silly notion or not, Brent believed that the only place to eat movie-food was *in* the theater.

Beyond the marble steps, the incline leading to the theater was carpeted; his shoes *shoof-shoofed* as he padded close to the screen. Everything was so still, so velvet-and-damask *quiet*, that even the *shoofing* of his steps was absurdly loud. Half-expecting someone to "Shush!" him, Brent went to the third row from the screen, middle of the row—his favorite seat in *any* movie house.

The screen was a luminous rectangle, smaller by half than the screens he was used to . . . yet, as he crammed popcorn into his mouth, savoring the oily richness overlaying the dryness of the corn itself, the idea of a bigger screen was *absurd*, a waste of space, really.

He'd taken his first sip of soda when darkness enveloped him. *Total* blackness; until a shifting cone of white light spilled out of the projection booth.

The screen flicked; in scratchy gray-white-blackness the titles for Karl Freund's *Mad Love* began.

At least he enjoyed the movie; Peter Lorre had never been better as the psychotic Dr. Gogol, mooning over the wax dummy of the actress of his frustrated obsessive love. Brent realized that *this* choice of a film was deliberate . . . and quite in keeping with the as-yet unseen but inevitable inhabitants of this alter-Ewerton. Apparently, his intrusion in this place wasn't unwelcome or *unexpected*.

Mistaking the real Mrs. Orlac for her costumed dummy,

Dr. Gogol began to strangle her—only to be killed by a hurled knife. Over the *snick* of the knife, Brent heard a new sound. Not the flutter of the film, but a soft, *sliding* noise. Smooth shoe soles making brief contact with the carpet, the sound coming closer, closer.

Brent didn't dare breathe, lest he obscure that faint whispering slide, or the almost imperceptible susurration of *something* passing against the upraised plush seats in the row behind him. The strangely *erotic* sound of velvet rubbing against ribbed or nubbed fabric was accompanied by the thin *scree* of a seat being lowered behind him. The hair-lifting-on-his-arms sound of soft materials brushing close against each other came from *directly* behind him. A seat back gave slightly as something leaned against it. Then, nothing, but as the movie ended, the screen was overtaken by shadows, and in that void of silence, Brent realized that he heard *breathing*.

Soft breath, an almost inaudible taking in and letting out of air through a small nose. Oh, he imagined it to be small and *(oh, please, God, please?)* human, not some *monster*, a thing that baited and trapped him here, perhaps to die . . . or *worse*.

Someone swallowed; Brent heard the delicate sound of a tongue running along dry lips. Spinning in its grooves, his mind repeated the same thought, *Please be Zoe, please be her, oh, please—*

"Your coming here won't change anything . . . you *do* know that." The voice was—*like* Zoe's, but not hers. Sinking down in his seat, Brent was reminded of how Bette Davis and Katharine Hepburn used to talk on those Late, Late Show movies on Channel 5 out of Minneapolis. Each word crisply inflected, almost to the point of caricature, yet not *forced*— the speaker talked that way, period. A lovely, if slightly monotone, voice, well suited to giving imperious orders—

The screen cast chiaroscuro shadings on Brent's upper body, and on the rounded seats near him. Brent told himself, *Easy . . . turn slow, as if you wanted to anyhow*—Heart fluttering, he turned his head, twisted his upper body, until he saw—

—for a moment of exquisite agony, his mind insisted *Zoe*, until reason stepped in. *Look at the nose, her neck.* After he stared longer than etiquette permitted without saying *something*, he turned around, closing his eyes to seal that deeply shadowed image in his sight forever.

As Palmer had said, *close*, but not identical. Not Zoe, but oh-my-God, so, *so* close. Same carmel-gold hair, dipping close to the left eye, the pale skin, the smudged dot of a beauty mark on her chin, and her *hands* steepled in her lap. True to Palmer's closely typed words, she could've been anywhere from her teens to her thirties in age.

But she was sixteen almost fifty years ago. If Brent were seated in front of a living woman, she would've looked the way Bitsy did; crepe skin over pads of fat, three drooping chins merging in a turkey wattle neck, with hair either dirty gray or peroxide white, not flowing softly over the shoulders of her black suit. Her jet buttons and circle pin (a row of diamonds around a ring of ebony metal) cast rainbow dots onto her smooth neck and the underside of her firm chin.

And she had two perfect, small hands. That hit Brent hard, until he reasoned that if she could appear young, she could manage to appear whole . . . she hadn't *used* that hand yet—

His shoulder suddenly stung where she'd tapped it—with her *left* hand, as if to quell Brent's unvoiced speculations. It felt like a swarm of bees had each in turn jabbed him, not enough to leave lasting pain, but enough to make the skin under his shirt jangle for a few miserable seconds.

Her perfume was cloying and heady in his nostrils, that intense, feminine roses and jasmine blend. Maeve leaned forward, asking, "Care to stay for the second feature?"

There was a slight *curl* to her voice, a verbal twisting of the lips into a half grimace . . . but Brent was so wrapped up in the electric essence of the being behind him that he paid scant attention to the tone of her voice. All she'd done was touch his shoulder (briefly, carefully), and spoken to him twice, yet she exuded something *more*. . . . An aura of *fe*-*male*ness, and . . . something deeper, almost dangerous (*she bites . . . or her sister does*). Brent was calm, not terrified or frightened, but definitely wary. Forcing himself to sound casual, he said, "I wouldn't mind seeing something from the forties . . . you know that year quite well, don't you?"

He'd expected a slap, or a haughty retreat into icy darkness, but her laughter caught him off guard. Soft, yet throaty, coming from deep within a well tinged with bitterness, too. When her mirth died down unself-consciously, she said, "I trust your uncle mentioned me to you."

Sensing that silence was the best way to coax more from her, Brent turned his attention to the blank screen. Watching the unwavering patch of cold white with rapt enthusiasm, as if already enjoying the feature, he heard her shift this way and that in her seat. The silky susseration of velvet and gaberdine was tense, sensual in the chilly cavernous room.

Part of him, that which mourned in the most basic way for Zoe, stirred; Brent placed his cold cup of soda there, biting his cheek in exquisite agony.

Then, in a harshly contrite voice, "I hope you like the next feature, Mr. Nimitz. You're not the first man—or the last—to seek something lost *and* unreplaceable. I . . . *was* hoping that Palmer had come, but that's only a matter of time, isn't it?" Brent remained silent as the screen went dark, save for a small window of light in the distance. . . .

Winston was almost fully asleep when movement down on Ewert Avenue caught his eye. He got up and bolted down the stairs before his mind had time to register anything so basic as the sex of or *type* of being he saw. It was enough to see *something* move around.

The Happy Wanderer bobbed down the street, oblivious to Winston's plea—*"Stop, oh, please, stop!"*—intent on entering the twin doors of the movie house. The Wanderer had a head start of perhaps thirty feet. Pausing to catch his breath outside the theater, Winston failed to notice the lone *different* car parked by the curb.

Steadily, tunelessly, the Wanderer hummed; he didn't notice—or care—that he had company.

Head hanging, leaning on the candy counter with both hands, Winston watched the Wanderer's none-too-clean fingers feel each bar. *He* must *see me . . . stupid he is, blind he isn't.*

Desperate to prove that he *wasn't* insane, Winston reached over and grabbed a greasy handful of the Wanderer's jacket, rubbing his fingers over the rough fabric as if it were the finest grade of silk. The Wanderer remained nonplussed, pawing over the candy in the case, as Winston cried out, "Oh, Cooper, you *are* real . . . Cooper, I *know* you can talk, please, speak to me. You don't know how I've needed to hear a voice—a *human* voice, besides mine. Cooper, never mind how *you* got here— *just get me out of here*!"

Tugging at the Wanderer's beefy arm, Winston sobbed . . . until Happy, his pockets full of candy bars, looked curiously at Winston, as if the latter's clutching fingers were flies light-ing on his sleeve, searching out smeared-on food. His stare was vacuous, uncomprehending. Winston leaned across the counter, saying with childish eagerness, "Cooper, remember me? Palmer Winston? Taught you in school. Remember? I—I know I look different, but *think*, Cooper! *Palm*-er *Win*-ston. *High* School. Please, *think*! I knew your aunt, Betty, I taught your nephew, Craig—"

A moue of distaste puckered the Wanderer's lips; Winston all but jumped onto the counter with joy over the show of recognition.

"*Yes!* Please, take me *out* of here, I can't *stand* this any—"

Happy shook off Winston's grasping fingers. In a voice shrill from dis-use, he said, "Don' *like* Pa'mer Win'on . . . he—" With chocolate-smeared fingers, the Wanderer mimed explicit, detailed motions. The Wanderer concluded, "—*that!*"

Shaken by the pointed—and accurate—assessment of his previous behavior, Winston stumbled out of the lobby. Waves of heat hit him with the stinging force of a well-aimed slap. Again, he missed the Pacer as he staggered down the avenue, psyche rattled by the realization that even if he could go "home" he didn't *want* to anymore. Not if he was only thought of as a skirt-lifting old pervert.

Disgusted, wishing he were dead, rotting, and worm-riddled out in some ditch, Winston threw himself onto the bed above the barbershop and lay there, staring up at the stamped tin ceil-ing and the still fan. Tears spilled out of the corners of his eyes. He let the salty burn run unwiped down and over his face, pun-ishing himself for decades of obscene behavior with the first of many a scalding cry.

EIGHTY-FIVE

Huge hair-rimmed lips formed a single, resonating word—"Rosebud!"—then the hand holding the glass ball relaxed. The snow-scene fell, bounced down the carpeted steps, onto a marble floor—and shattered in a spray of sparkling shards.

Letting out his breath in a shaky gust, Brent asked, "Are you my uncle's 'Rosebud'?"

Shivery laughter, wind coursing through stiff, ice-laden branches. "Do *you* think so?"

Not taking his eyes from the chiaroscuro flutter of the newsreel on the screen, he slowly replied, "I . . . not sure. You *are* Maeve, aren't you?"

"Do you want me to be?" He felt her shift forward, her breath even and neutral on his exposed neck. Squashing his half-empty popcorn bag with his fist, Brent said, "To be truthful, I want my *wife* back . . . my cat, too. I know they're both here—"

"Do you? You're sure?"

Brent wondered if she'd toyed with Clive Calder like that. His voice level, Brent replied, "Yes, to both questions. I'm her husband, and to be frank, I don't think you had the right to . . . *do* what you did to her. The . . . *difficulty* you had with my uncle wasn't any of her business. I just want her back. And our cat. I found the empty box . . . I was supposed to, wasn't I?" He added it with leaden certainty. He barely heard her "Uhm . . . uh-huh."

He started to ask, "Where *is* my wi—" when he heard her seat spring back into place. As she stood, her suit skirt rubbed against the velvet.

"If you are very lucky, Mr. Nimitz, perhaps you will . . . someday understand"— he turned in time to see her wave a luminous white hand in a circle in the air—"all of *this*, and know that it never concerned you in the same way as it does the *rest* of us. Which makes you far luckier than you can imagine." Then she was gone, footsteps all but swallowed in the darkness and humming coolness. Too proud to go running after her—as if she'd actually *wait* for him next to the popcorn machine—Brent turned his attention to the flickering screen, as Charles Foster Kane said to Susan Alexander, "—I too know many people. Obviously, we're both lonely—" Stomach knotting, Brent thought, *The film shouldn't* be *at this point yet*—

—until Orson Welles broke character, looking down at *him* from the screen, adding, "Oh, by the way, I'm *terribly* sorry about your grandmother—the Mercury Theatre extends it's regrets—"

—and Brent dropped his wrappers and cup of soda on the floor, as he ran, hyperventilating, up the carpeted aisle. . . .

•   •   •

Still shattered by his meeting with the Wanderer, Winston watched the fan revolve lazily above his head (he'd interrupted his self-induced agonies long enough to stand on the bed and yank the chain, then shucked off his coat and shirt). The blades cast writhing blue-gray shadows on the ceiling's stamped flowers, and on the rose-patterned wall opposite the window. The blur of the moving blades, coupled with the fluttering shadows, made him slightly dizzy, yet he couldn't stop watching, for the sicker he felt, the better he felt, for reasons he didn't care to define.

Watching the blades lop around the fan's hub, Winston thought, *They must've made billions of those fans*. The one in his base hospital room had looked like this one, only it was gray. *Like that damn mound of cement outside my window.* Back home, the USA had been dying for cement, yet the Army had a mound—a dusty dry *train*-load, a *mountain* of the crap—dumped out in a heap next to the base hospital. Instead of parceling it out to the villagers the Occupation Army was supposed to be helping (some mission, giving our former enemies *democracy*, but one could *eat* it, or *sleep* under it), they'd left the cement out there, uncovered. When it rained, the mound turned into a *real* mountain.

Winston remembered how the kids played on it while he was busy slipping their folks surplus sugar substitutes. Typical Army know-how—there were no diabetics in his outfit, so the base got *cases* of it. Which they were ordered to junk, which made as much sense as Mount Concrete on that abandoned Jap airbase.

He'd been helpless to prevent the rain-soaked concrete, but the surplus saccharin—he wished that Captain Sonders, hell, that shrink Taub, could've seen how those people bowed as if Winston had just given them the moon. And it wasn't as if they had *their* hands out, gimmie, gimmie. They had diddley, but brought him little carved doodads, netsuke, or half bottles of their beer or sake—it tasted like kerosene to him, but he would've given both arms and his dick for a sip of it while on the base hospital. Lord, was he *sick*. . . .

And every evening, when the sun set, it went behind that big mound of lumpy concrete, its shadow big and purple, like the bruises Palmer's mother used to have. Gayleen tried to get Treeva to go to the police, but Gayleen didn't *understand* Enoch Nemmitz. And it was bad, damn *bad*, when

Treeva died like that. And Palmer couldn't cry; Winston had cried more than his best friend did. . . .

Above him, chopping shadows darkened the ceiling; stamped blossoms moved, blown by an invisible breeze before they sank into the smoothness of the ceiling . . . as a larger, deeper shadow, plum-purple, slid across the room.

Watching the fan's motion through heavy-lidded eyes, Winston remembered how he'd cried plenty in that hospital. Terrible pain. He didn't know if his parents had been told, and for once he cared little what they might think. He'd never *hurt* so much,—save for that time in Georgia, with the child-woman. Lying handcuffed and strapped down, he'd realized that *she* was what he'd been searching for. That wonderful pleasure-pain-release he'd felt with her. Only this time, the smallness of his partners didn't *work*, didn't bring the whole experience back to him. He couldn't make anyone understand that he'd only been searching for *her* . . . those village girls *were* so delicate. But the MPs sneered, "Lieutenant likes 'em small and brown, like—" and Winston couldn't explain what he couldn't *quite* understand himself.

All *they* cared was that he'd been in a rut, and smashed the whole time. Then Major Taub came; before, Winston thought he knew what bleeding was all about. But Taub was a *brain* vampire, leaving Winston all dry and hollow and sighing inside, like blowing across an empty bottle until the moaning was enough to make a person cry.

The purple shadow crossed his face, cooling his skin. Peering through the capri-shell filter of his lowered eyelashes, Winston remembered his hospital room. He'd had nothing to do in there all day but rub his wrists where the straps and handcuffs had chafed him badly while he'd thrashed and screamed earlier. The only furnishings in his room were the bed, a basin-topped table, and a small chair—and he'd tired of *those* as soon as his eyes focused clearly again. But the fan . . . it *whirred* endlessly, shadows going around like a roulette wheel with no bobbing ball, just the flick-flick of light-dark-light, until the big concrete shadow overtook it each night. With every spin of the blades, he had felt worse and worse about himself, even as his body healed.

The situation was a hundred times worse then when he broke his leg in basic.

Only Captain Sonders visited, slapping his robed back and saying, "So you sowed some wild brown oats, happens to most every Joe one time or 'nother. Might've been worse, could've laid a coon, eh?'' Winston didn't find the cultural bias comforting, but nodded when Sonders mentioned a promotion ''once all this hoo-haa blows over.'' With his string of Outstanding ratings, a promotion *was* all but his. Should've been his, if not for Major Taub's report—

Fresh tears slid out of Winston's eyes. Sobbing, he went to rub his eyes with his bare forearm, but the rough fabric of his sleeve burned his sore eyes—*Wait a damn second!*

His shirt and jacket were across the chair by the door, so his arm should be *bare*—heart thudding, Winston pressed his arm across his eyes, but he *still* saw light around the outline of his arm. *It's evening,* he insisted, but his eyes told a different tale. The cloth of his sleeve was coarse, familiar . . . he'd lived for weeks in Army-issue nightwear, in 1946—

Winston took his arm off his eyes and sat up in one fluid motion—then slumped down on his lumpy Army bed, in his base hospital room. *Bump on my head's worse than I thought,* and he reached up to feel the tender knot on his brow—which wasn't there anymore. Rubbing his eyes again, he stifled a rising sob as he heard:

''Lt. *Win*ston, would you please come with us?'' The distaste and distain in the MPs voice wasn't lost on Winston; for he'd heard those words before.

Too scared and helpless to protest, he meekly climbed out of bed, scuffed his feet into slippers, then pulled on his thin blue terry cloth robe. Passing his window, he saw the huge humped mound of solidified concrete . . . *and* the distant mountains of Japan, which stood gently rounded and tall, miles from the abandoned airbase.

Flanked by the two armed MPs, Lt. Winston swallowed down rising nausea and bent his head as he walked out of the room.

EIGHTY-SIX

Ewerton's six bars did only fair to middling business on Sunday nights; Wisconsin law stipulated that all bars had to be closed by 2:00 A.M., but most Ewerton taverns closed early on Sunday night by choice. Said fact did not please the last patrons of Pearl 'n' Earle's; Betty the fill-in bartender had to all but kick out the four young men, then lock the door.

"C'mon, Betty, open up!" Dusty Parks banged on the warped wooden door, until Jeff Wilkes and Bobby Gray pulled him away and tossed him into the back of Gray's mufflerless wagon. Scooter Andersen hawked a blob of phlegm, beer, and bits of macerated pizza stick at the door.

"One o' these days, Betty . . . Pow! Right in the kisser." Betty still didn't open up. Scooter sighed, burped loudly, flexing his diaphragm to make the most of it, then leaned down to shake Dusty's greasy shoulder. "Fuck 'er. We'll buy a six-pack at the Igeeayy, hokay? You an' me an' Bobby an' Jeff . . . like when we were at EHS . . . *c'mon*." As Scooter smacked Dusty upside the lolling head, he slipped and almost fell into the gutter outside the bar, grabbing the street lamp at the last second.

His three companions for the evening agreed. To the *good* old days of high school, and no responsibilities. The days when they were all willing to be *seen* with each other in broad daylight. Jeff and Scooter and Bobby each got behind the wheels of their cars. With Dusty backseat driving, the trio burnt rubber pulling away from the curb, heading for the open-all-night IGA liquor department.

The occupants of the three cars had come singly to the bar that afternoon, still separated by jobs, differences in social strata, and personal tastes. But six rounds of drinks propelled them backward in time, to the days of their mutual buddy-buddy-hood.

Being the most visibly sober member of the renewed clique, Jeff bought the beer. Afterward, the trio of cars drove nearly abreast up and down the wider streets of Ewerton; the two

wagons side by side, with Jeff's Duster tagging close behind.
The four men shouted to each other through open windows
as the wind whipped away stray words in loud tatters.

"—trashing old man Holiday's pumpkins? Thought he'd
freak—"

"—hubcaps an' put 'em on the War Memorial, like a couple of—"

"—petals off Pearl Vincent's garden daisy? She took
out—"

"—can't *stand* them bend-over things—"

"—of you in that group that went to the cemetery, oh,
'leven, twelve years back? Friggen Earth Day clean-up? Old
man Winston an'—"

"Y'mean Diddler?" Scooter slowed down his car a bit.

"Shaddup. Old man Winston and Una-Pruna was in charge
of cleanin' off the graves, Una was yellin' for us to throw
away all the wreaths an' shit—"

"Hey, Dusty, don't they take the frames and reuse 'em?"
Jeff asked, but Scooter cut in, "Nah, they only done that in
that zombie movie—out here they're too fuckin' *dumb*—"

"—'cause old Una-Pruna said the wreaths an' shit was
'cluttering up the *graves*' an' I thought it wasn't *right*, an'
that people shoulda put real deep stakes on the bottoms, so's
we couldn't pull their crap off—"

When Dusty said that, the quartet of EHS Class of '78
members quickly made a delirious, crazy decision. Suppress-
ing whoops and giggles, they drove onto curbs and sidewalks,
arms dangling out of windows, to grab-snatch whatever
schlock was within reach; knocking over the occasional garbage can, and squashing three plastic tricycles, one wiffle
ball, and seven blue driveway directional markers.

By a little past midnight, they'd appropriated bend-overs,
daisy spinners, a metal jockey, mushrooms, owls, flamingos,
a tiny wishing well, the wooden Dutch girl and Dutch boy
silhouettes from Old Dutch Distributor Wayne Mesabi's lawn,
and a wind sock shaped like a pencil.

Buoyed by the sheer insanity of their mission, the trio of
cars sped down the county trunk QV, as the pencil wind sock
dangling out of Jeff's car bobbed and scribbed on the dark
parchment of night air.

The cemetery gates were locked, but Bobby had a pair of
wirecutters in the mass of junk and mashed cans in his trunk.
The four men's shadows loomed long, wavering among the

flat headstones and humped markers; when viewed in sloping
shadow, their burdens took on grotesque shapes.

In parody of the Earth-Day denuding years before, each
grave within sight of the headlights sprouted pagan memori-
als: bunnies rested on engraved baby headstones, bend-overs
stradded double monuments, and a wishing well perched on
a slab of granite. Scooter saved a couple of deer for Una
Winston's grave—hoping their sharp hooves would rip through
the turf—and her casket.

Dusty circled his head with the wind sock like a lasso,
shouting, "Where's the highest spot? I wanna see this sucker
blow." In the distance, faint but discernible, stood a marker
far taller than any other . . . a granite obelisk with a marble
eyelike inset that shone faintly in the distance.

Everyone piled into their cars, racing between the rows
("Goddamn broke my headlight—hope you died real *bad*,
prick!"); they couldn't *walk* to the towering headstone . . .
not at halfpast *midnight*.

Despite his beer-induced stupor, Dusty covered his greasy
head with his arms when Bobby missed Wilbur W. Holiday's
marker on the first run-through, swerved around—and plowed
into the back of the monument. Bobby almost flew through
the windshield—a huge spiderweb crack appeared on the
tinted glass—but stopped short of going through.

The others jumped out of their cars and ran to Holiday's
grave before their engines stopped humming. In the crazy
overlapping headlights, the crack in Holiday's aboveground
vault was a deep black fissure, only slightly overshadowed by
the tilted-forward granite marker. Scooter yelled, "Hope it
didn't break the coffin—be a stinker if it did." Dusty and
Bobby Gray—stumbling like a second-string extra in a living
dead film, oblivious to the ribbons of blood twisting down
his forehead—were no strangers to things which smelled bad,
so they lumbered over to the cracked vault. Dusty asked,
"Guys got a light? I wanna see—"

"You don't wanna see *that*," Jeff mumbled from behind
his hand. Scooter scrambled to his battered car, fumbled in
the glove compartment, then shined his flashlight under his
chin, saying in a basso rumble, "Heeeeey, Jefffff—"

Jeff took one look and almost upchucked on his shoes, just
as his father had done when he saw Clive Calder's fly-
squirming remains.

"Lookit, Wilkes is pukin'!" Dusty was about to wander

over to investigate when Bobby pulled him aside. Blood formed black glistening cracks across the greasy oval of his face as he said, "You seen barf before. C'mon, this'll be *good*. Bones an' shit. Stink, too." Leaving Jeff to heave in private, Dusty joined the other two men who stood alongside the toppled stone and ruined vault, noses quivering in anticipation.

The beam of Scooter's flashlight was aimed at the interior of the rudely violated vault; there was a blinding glint when the light hit a brass handle, and then a bit of torn blue silk, then all three hunkered down—until Scooter made soggy gagging noises and got to his feet, followed closely by Bobby and Dusty, who slid along the wet grass in their dirty tennis shoes. Dusty's shoes were soon hot and wet, the vomit soaking through the canvas and suede tops.

As the men ridded their bodies of bile-laced beer, the flashlight Scooter had shoved partway into the coffin wobbled, then fell into that blue satin-lined box, to light it from within, long after the four men climbed into the cars and gunned out of the cemetery.

And the faint golden glow coming from within Wilbur Holiday's coffin was a false ground-based dawn, anticipating the real dawn hours away. . . .

"—instances of vandalism reported at area residences. Garbage cans were overturned, and many residents reported lawn decorations missing—"

Palmer Nemmitz sighed, and leaned over the counter to turn down the babble of WERT. Ordinarily, he'd have a good laugh over stolen lawn junk, but today he was more worried about Brent. For all he cared, they could take a wrecking ball to the whole town, and put a match to the rubble which remained.

He'd last seen Brent at Clive's funeral—one second the stocky young man was there, hands stuffed in his suit pockets, face drawn behind mirrored sunglasses, and the next both Brent and his car were gone—Palmer saw neither the Pacer nor his nephew since.

Bitsy fussed and fumed when Palmer mentioned he was worried about Brent; she up and left the farmhouse, blubbering, "You're so *cruel*—poor Clive's dead and you're worried about a man who can take care of himself!" Palmer wasn't sorry to see Bitsy leave for a second time that month. "I'm not gonna starve without her, am I?" he asked the dirty dishes in the kitchen sink. Some feast; a cup from coffee and the plate from the toast he'd torn to pieces and tossed out the back door for the birds to peck at.

The longer Brent was gone, the more guilty Palmer felt. If he'd found the "place" they'd been discussing, why hadn't the young man returned, as the Happy Wanderer always did? He hoped all this had nothing to do with his bad dreams; frantic, speeded-up things, like movies run through a VCR too fast.

Horrible, yet real-seeming nightmares of the twins, and of Winston being marched about by two bullet-faced men toting guns. That morning, he woke up from a dream of Duffy. Thinking about the cat reminded Palmer of the empty, caved-in box in the backyard . . . and of the metal tin of *something* that rustled and shifted when shook. There was nothing Palmer could do for Duffy, but he *could* take a peek in that tin.

But once he took the tin out of Brent's room, and carried it into his own, Palmer simply put it on the dresser, unopened. The thought of someone *taking* Zoe, be she dead *or* alive, for purposes utterly unfathomable, filled Palmer with a numbing anger. He stood there, finger lightly tapping the tin's lid, muttering, "What are we going to do? Go off on a wild goose chase? Hole up like a hunted fox?"

"Sorry, Bitsy, Stu's out . . . no, I can't reach him on the scanner, haven't you heard? Lots of shi-stuff swiped around town. Him and Bib got their hands full. Want to leave a message?" Deputy Terry Von Kemp stifled a yawn; Mrs. Nemmitz made his ass tired in *person*; over the phone she was a wheedling, disembodied *voice* that *wouldn't shut up*. Terry was tempted to say, "Look, *Bitsy*, some nut-case drove through town last night scooping up every bit of lawn crap he could get his paws on, trucked it out to the cemetery, and turned the place into a goofy golf course. Then puked to celebrate. Stu don't want you to know he probably plowed over old Doc Calder's grave. *Satisfied?*"

Instead, Terry said, "Okay . . . 'Call Palmer and talk some sense into him' . . . that all? I'll relay the message as soon as he gets back. Yes, it is too bad about Clive—sorry, there's a call on the other line—yes, I'll *give* him the message. *Bye*, Bitsy.'' He slammed down the receiver.

Terry dropped the slip of paper bearing Bitsy's message into the shredder. Stu had enough trouble already. Let the old bat ''talk some sense'' into her old man herself. . . .

''—know what this town is *comin'* to,'' wailed the sexton, a short, hyperthyroidal man named Elmer Ritter. He led Stu past bizarrely embellished rows of graves, tire-marked and tipped-over headstones, and the first of four puddles of dried vomit.

Voice quivering, he complained, ''Weren't satisfied with stealin' stuff. Just glad *I* found it, not some mourner. 'Course, I checked Clive's spot first—bastids missed *him*—but those—*pigs* puked all over—''

''More than one pig or one real sick pig?'' Stu asked, nearly tripping over a toppled marker as he followed Ritter to the place where the Holiday marker used to be the tallest thing on the horizon. For a second, Stu's mind supplied the missing spire, then denied that it *ever* stood there. Dizzy, confused, he swerved sharply to avoid a puddle of yellowish vomit.

His on-belt beeper sounded. With an apologetic wave of both hands, he said, ''Sorry, Elmer, but I told Terry to page me if something came up. Somebody probably noticed their lawn frog is missing. Be back 'fore you know it. Keep them gates closed and don't let the families see anything. Get busy and pluck them things off—aw, Elmer, don't *gibber*,'' he yelled over his shoulder as Elmer wordlessly pointed at the fallen stone, then was off, belly jiggling, striding to his squad car. After a second's wait, Ritter made for the farthest row of ornamented graves—he couldn't face that opened vault, or the strange faint light that shone within.

EIGHTY-SEVEN

"Scooter, I don't care if you have five hangovers, I want the *garage key*. It's too hot to walk to the IGA and back with the kids tagging along. Scooter, are you *alive*?"

Sarah jabbed at the sheet-covered mound on the bed, until her husband growled, "Leave me the fuck *alone*!" Sarah felt shaky herself, overtired after trying to wait up for Scooter. *When* he slid into bed she wasn't sure, but he was there come morning, smelling like a Breath Blasters doll.

This summer had been *too much* for her—and now Scooter was playing hide-and-go-seek with the garage keys.

Taking off her hair clip, Sarah gently felt around on the bed. A second later, Scooter sat up with a yelp, pulling off and tossing the plastic clip against the wall. "You *bitch*, can't you lemme sleep it off in *peace*? Bug *off*." Sarah yanked off his covers, saying, "Gimmie those keys or I *will* 'bug off'—right out of *town*. Scott, listen. There's nothing for us here, can't you see that? You got laid off, this place is *dead*"—Scooter laughed at *that*—"Mrs. Potter next door says someone opened some *graves* last night—is that sick or *what*?"

Scooter chose not to reply; instead he got out of bed, stomped past Sarah into the bathroom, and slammed the door. Flip-flopping over to the closed door, she shouted, "Hear me, Scott? You *want* our kids growing up here, in this environment?"

Over the running shower, he replied, "After the reunion. I'm not leaving, then coming back for it later—*'sides*, it's only a week. Less. I got unemployment coming."

Scooter and his precious *reunion*. Everything came back to that reunion. Walking into her kitchen, loose hair hanging in her face, Sarah wondered if she'd see Zoe there . . . for earlier that morning, while fixing breakfast, she'd seen the tail end of that white, classic car again as it glided past her house.

The phone rang over twenty times before Palmer Nemmitz shuffled down the carpeted stairs in his stockinged feet. With each jangling ring, he hoped whoever was calling would give up, let him be. "'*Lo*, Palmer, how's the old buck been doing lately?"

Wishing he could strangle Mesabi through the wire, he said curtly, "The 'old buck' was taking a nap, until the young *fuck* woke him up."

Chortling like a chin-chucked baby, Mesabi warned, "Now, now, Palmer, mind your language. You heard abo—"

"If you called to tell me about the vandalism, I heard the radio, I din't do it, if that's what you're implying—"

"Oh, no, no, *no*, Palmer—didn't say you *did*—calm down, old—"

"I'm hanging *up*, Mesabi—"

"Palmer! Lissen—'member the fairgrounds break-in—"

"I was *there*. Wasn't responsible for that, either—"

"Palmer, you old scamp. I'm just asking if you remember those booklets we pass out every year, for a free-will donation—"

"Bullshit. They say 25 cents right on the cover. I've seen enough of 'em tossed in the gutters come August to choke a horse. Quit yammering and get on with it." Palmer wrapped the curled cord around his fist.

"Well, uh, me and the rest of the committee, we were cleaning out the building—on 'count of the other amusements coming into town—"

(Palmer's eyelids fluttered, and his face sagged as Mesabi rambled on—)

"—found that whoever bust up the stuff in there went and wrecked the box of booklets from last year. We *were* gonna update the middles of those and use 'em this year. 'Course, if that friend Winston of yours hadn't of left town, I'd ask him to do this, but since you and him were—"

"Wayne, I am an old man. I need rest in this century—"

"*Hokay*. Whoever busted the equipment ruined the booklet master sheets, too. Can't run off extras like before. So, we got to thinking maybe it's time for a new booklet—"

"To clog the gutters for at least *three* months—"

"Aw, we sweep 'em up in a week or two. Anyway, the old booklets were getting stale, time for something new. Considering Winston can't do it, *you'd* be the perfect one to write it, you know so much about this town—"

As Mesabi piled it on higher and deeper, Palmer wished Winston was here; he was good at deflating Mesabi at the Rusty Hinge. . . .

"—thought you'd give the booklet a different slant—"

Want a "different slant," do you? Palmer mused, as he agreed to write up a few pages worth of information about the town, "any sort of interesting odds and ends, just make sure we can photocopy it. Single-spaced's fine. Just have it ready by Wednesday. This new machine at the courthouse, feeds the pages in, spits 'em out in bundles by itself. Oughtta see it. Best toy the city ever bought. Uh-go, gotta deliver the chips. Thanks, old guy."

Feeling too bone-tired and heat-sapped to start work on the booklet that afternoon—not that what he had to say would take him all *that* long—Palmer trudged upstairs. As he itched his forearm, his annoyance over Mesabi's call was replaced by another emotion.

The first stirrings of jealousy, as a part of him hated Brent for having found Maeve's hideaway, when he himself lacked the courage to go to her.

EIGHTY-EIGHT

On the morning of what Brent thought was the twenty-fifth, the Pacer's gas indicator needle slid into Empty. No amount of wishful thinking (*shit, it worked with the stupid* sidewalks) made the Pacer go again once it shuddered to a stop midway down Evans Street.

True, there were a couple of gas stations, but none carried unleaded. Brent reluctantly began to search the town on foot.

In retrospect, he realized he'd been foolish to burn precious fuel tooling up and down the same-named but *changed* streets. But the heat was so oppressive—and his candy, popcorn and soda diet easily converted into the shakes if he moved too much. Besides, being *in* the car gave him an excuse not to *have* to go up and knock on the front door of every opaque-windowed house. . . .

And, as much as Brent hated to admit it, he simply felt *safer* in his car. He slept in it; rolled the windows and locked the doors, for he feared waking up to find Maeve in his car, tiny fingers working in endless fingerplays, oddly canted eyes appraising him coolly.

Brent hadn't seen the girl of Palmer's nightmares since the

afternoon in the theater. After *that*, he was careful not to go beyond the popcorn machine. Brent tried not to think of how the candy replenished itself, or the way the level of popcorn in the machine never bottomed out—no matter how many boxes of the stuff he carried out to his car.

Nor did he question how the theater doors closed at night, locking in the cool rippling air and golden lights around the candy counter, before the sidewalks came to grating life, pulling in, in . . . for they were mysteriously open come morning. He preferred *not* to know . . . in fact, after grabbing what food he could carry in one trip, he took off for a residential area, and ate in the stifling warmth of the Pacer.

Walking back to the theater on Monday morning, after his car expired, Brent worried over smeared prints he'd found on the outside of his car windows that morning. Small, shapeless smudges dotted all the windows all around the car, even the windshield. Which meant that whatever had tried to get in was small enough to crawl around on the hood of the car without denting or scratching it.

If it *was* Duffy, Brent didn't understand why he didn't stay curled up on the hood of the car—Duffy used to love to sleep on the sun-warmed Pacer. But if it *wasn't* Duffy, Brent didn't want *it* in his car.

The sensible thing to do (to have done, since the car was dead) would be (would've *been*) to get over his funk and search every building, picking a "safe" house as a hideout during the evening. Just what he should look for wasn't clear, though—signs that someone was living in a house might elude him. He'd been too spooked to break into any house to find out, but he doubted that he'd open a door and find the twins or old man Winston or (yet he *wished*) Zoe sitting in a parlor, reading a newspaper and listening to *The Shadow* on a table-top Zenith.

No, any sort of *being* who could survive as the twins did could protect themselves *very* well. The full import of Maeve's words about his coming not making a difference hit home—he'd found her "place," but all it got him was a bone-dry car and a bad case of hypoglycemia.

Entering the business section of Ewert Avenue, Brent saw the Holiday's Grocery sign just away from the store. Brent couldn't *face* another candy bar . . . or kernel of popcorn. With or without butter.

Pressing his face against the glass, Brent made out stocked

shelves inside. Assuring himself that the edibles within *had* to be as substantial as those he'd found in the theater, Brent supposed he'd have to jimmie the door open—but saw that it was unlocked. A pane of glass in the multi-paned door was broken out. Shattered bits of glass twinkled at his feet. . . .

Sandwiched between stone-faced MPs, Winston had no option but to march forward, legs moving in time with theirs, face turned forward, eyes downcast. . . . At first, panic and halfhearted reason warred in him (*I'm just* remembering *this, that's all*), but as hallways turned to *more* hallways, fear and reassurance gave way to shreds of memory, disjointed yet *too clear*, like water-magnified snow in a paperweight. . . .

As he drove Palmer and Dead Fred home from the St. Paul Winter Carnival, Fred snored in the back seat of the Woody, while Palmer cried and moaned in his sleep. The sun set colorlessly; the sky was a dove gray expanse that gradually faded to cloud-wrapped and moon-illuminated darkness that merged with the moon-touched snow below. The road was straight, flat, and the trees were thin, branching upwards, to almost meet the low-hanging sky.

No matter how far he drove, Winston detected no *change* in his landscape—as if he were driving inside a pearl, or the interior of an eyeball. He wondered if, driving on, he'd meet himself. . . .

Winston marched down hallways with no end, his mind a revolving pearl, unable to find a steadying surface . . . until the MPs flanking him stopped, and he saw a door. Which opened soundlessly, revealing a frowning man sitting behind a makeshift desk, an empty chair waiting before him.

As he'd done before, Winston obeyed the orders of the MPs, went into the room and sat down, to face Major Herman Taub, Doctor of Psychiatry. Trapped in the pearl of his mind, he once again accepted a cigarette from the major, who regarded him with a disdain normally reserved for floor-crawling vermin, prior to swatting said vermin with something heavy and deadly, wielded with great speed and malice. Just as Taub did the *last* time.

Winston sat stiffly, mechanically tapping ashes, as Taub went through the test results, but there was something *new* going on. His mind protested, *It wasn't like this before*—only to be rebuked by the inner voice, *Perhaps you weren't* listening *the other time*.

He tried not to flinch when Taub, his eyes *not* as cruel as Winston's memory had colored them, mouthed the terms "sexual dysfunction" and "chronic substance abuse." Once again, Winston's eyes were drawn to a term on Taub's upside-down report. A long word of Greek origin whose meaning Winston all too easily inferred, its meaning spreading like poison through his veins. Winston listened—*really* listened—to Taub berate him, saying words Winston had tried to drink away for the last forty-two years:

"—GIs are content with the Yoshiwara district in Tokyo, the *mizushobai* is good enough for *them*. But not *you*. Standard "Water trade" wasn't *stimulating* enough . . . you needed the *jogakusei*, the little virginal *schoolgirls*.

"Know what those sweet young brown *animals* and their kin call us *gaijin*, us Americans? *Mongrels*. And you had the nerve to tell me, 'I only wanted to *help* those people!' Did they think about helping us at Pearl Harbor? Did they want to help our boys when they tortured *your fellow soldiers* in hell camps? Bad enough we're taking these Japs under our wing, spreading 'democracy' among the slant-eyes. Your orders were to help establish that 'democracy'—not play Santa Claus with Army material. No one *ordered* you to do that, and no one *ordered* you to spread clap among the heathens. *Some*thing to write home about.

"Now I'm not staying in this man's Army, but while I'm in, I have to put aside my . . . *distaste* for our forgive-and-forget policy, because *those are my orders*. If the Army wills it, these people get their 'democracy' whether they want it or not. But I don't have to *like* it, just as I don't have to pander to the wishes of Captain Sonders and pull strings to get your charges dropped.

"The Army got along very well before *you* enlisted, and it will persevere without the likes of you. And a court-martial is the *least* of what's coming to you, *Lieutenant*—"

As Taub vented his spleen, dredging up his own dissatisfactions, Winston blinked back tears, eyes riveted to the spiky word that filled him with loathing and revulsion, underscored by a stunning revelation—

For all their hate and prejudice, Taub's words were underscored with real *pity* . . . the very thing Winston had fought to forget.

EIGHTY-NINE

As Brent pulled food from the shelves of the store, prior to adding it to the pile at his feet, he realized that the store was growing colder by the second . . . and there was no air conditioner, no ceiling fan, to circulate the formerly warm and sluggish air.

Assuring himself that there *must* be a refrigeration unit for meat in the back room, Brent glanced at the signs tacked in the window (''Bread—9¢ a Loaf''), but saw no meat prices posted. Shrugging, Brent noticed the pickle barrel; a pickle was as good a breakfast as any. He removed the round wooden lid, then stuck his hand into the spicy-smelling barrel. Thinking, *Suppose something yanks your hand down?* he blindly grabbed the first knobby shape under his damp fingers.

Just a good old dill pickle; it dripped on the floor and onto his shirt as he ate it. After nothing but sickly sweet foods to eat, it was ambrosia. In the middle of his second bite, he became aware of a faint, subaudible *sound*; cast-off vibrations of what *should* have been a loud noise. All Brent felt/heard was a *thrum* throughout his body, like a Civil Defense radio test. A buzzing nonsound that rang in the ears long after the music came back on the air.

Then . . . came ghosts of voices, distinct sounds, yet too soft to make out plainly. The air was thick with vibrations; his skin tingled as his ears strained for the first true word.

In the rapidly cooling store, everything came into what used to be normal focus for Brent. The sounds became louder, near distinct. Moans and screams, teeth-gritting pain that soon subsided into incoherent moans, keening breaths.

The subsounds came from the direction of the counter. Brent stepped closer, not wanting, but *needing* to. One voice was male—sharp, angry, upset; the other female, a droning gibber of denial, or refusal. But . . . the store was empty, save for Brent. Passing the sawdust-spread place behind the counter before entering the back room, Brent *felt* sound-vibrations . . . and more.

Movement. A sense of motion in the empty air; a disorienting, skin-crawling sensation of something moving in *his* space, displacing *his* air. In his search for the source of the hideous *crawling* feeling, Brent jerked his head upward; his eyes drawn to crudely painted words on the low ceiling . . . "Whore of Babylon," and many, many more—

Outside, the commotion grew louder, plainer. Brent felt a rush of air pass him, and *almost* felt something brush against his bare leg. He followed the source of the invisible movement out to behind the counter, and saw—

Bedlam. A shelf near the doorway overturned, a splintered mess of shattered glass and wrecked shelving. The overhead bulb was sickly yellow-white, pus-murky, and on the sawdust at his feet—a seeping red stain *grew*, spreading in subterranean rivulets, as the sawdust *shifted*—

A woman's voice broke through the subsound distortion— *"No!"* A sack of flour fell . . . before it arrested in midfall, writhing and jerking in midair. Then came a whispered plea Brent was unable to understand, as the cloth sack burst apart in an explosion of puffing white. Flour rose, then fell, descending in a thick white-gray rain upon the red-soaked sawdust below. The tang of hot iron burned the inside of Brent's nose. And as the flour settled, it took strange form, hovering over an unseen but quickly defined shape—

Brent could look no more. He held his face in hands that still smelled of dill pickles, and plugged his ears with his thumbs when the woman shrieked, "You *fool*, *look at that*, how will—" but her words were drowned out by a keening wail, *two* distinct infantile yowlings. . . .

Brent's skin grew cold. Through the cracks in his fingers, he saw *snow* beyond the window, the clean bright glare of the sun on *snow*, as the woman's voice rang out clear and angry, "Maybe God will forgive you for it, but Jee-*sus* H. *Christ*, how will *that* down there ever forgive us?"

He had lost it. His sanity, his mind. Brent closed his eyes; the red-veined shade of his eyelids was bright, and *(blood, I still smell—)* abstract before him . . . until everything *stopped*.

The cold, the smells, the sounds . . . his ears rang hollowly with the total silence of his surroundings. Thinking he was safe *(sane)* once more, he opened his eyes. Plain, unmarred sawdust at his feet. No fallen shelves. Bare, dry sidewalks outside the window . . . then he noticed he wasn't alone.

She stood near the pickle barrel window, dark dress blended

into a corner shadow, collar white under the pale oval of her face. And that caramel-apple hair.

When their eyes met, she smiled; a crooked grimace that narrowed her bicolor eyes. Hands on hips, a challenge-me stance, she said in a teasing sneer both familiar and strangely inflected to Brent's ears, "I thought my sister warned you to get out . . . hope you liked the *show*." Brent felt gutted by her tone, his psyche scraped raw and vulnerable. Then Mae turned on her heel and walked out the door . . . whose windowpanes were whole, unbroken.

Slumped against the counter, glad for its reassuring bulk, Brent knew that if she'd been able, she would've eaten him alive . . . and with those legs of hers, stomp all over his remains.

His anger at Mae snapped him out of his daze—if she wanted a confrontation, he'd *give* her a reason to attack. Running to the door, Brent opened it and looked around . . . but there was no one in the street.

Through unshed tears, Winston kept reading and reading the word "satyriasis" on Taub's report—underlined, for emphasis or spite, or both. While Taub had yet to use that specific word in his verbal attack on the young lieutenant, Winston knew what it meant.

Him, as in a guy who didn't just search for a small, *special* girl, but the kind of guy who looked anywhere for any female—not letting go until he was finished with her, his lust expended for the moment only, until his erect organ pointed out the next female, and the *next*—

Definitely *not* "officer material." And that was the least of the negative implications—

Taub had hit his stride; with lip-licking relish he barked, "*Look* at me when I'm speaking, *Lieutenant*. Now I'm aware that everything I've said so far has rolled off your oily little back—croc tears *never* fool me, mister—just as what I'm going to say *now* won't get through, but I'm going to tell you because *I* want to hear it said, at least once, to a kid who *deserves* to hear the straight truth told to him. And you aren't going to pass it off as Tough Shit, because *this* time your C.O. can't come to your rescue, pat you on the back and hand you another achievement medal like a good-boy sucker at the doctor's office. Don't give me that sick-dog look, and don't fill out a T.S. slip and mail it to the chaplain, *'cause it won't wash.*

"I know you better than you do yourself. You laid yourself bare when we talked, no matter how you tried to cover up with your fancy set of smarts. I've only made major because I'm an old fuck who got caught up in this stinking confrontation, but long before I had *these* on my shoulders, I had a shingle in front of a stateside office.

"Believe me, kid, I've seen 'em *all*. Want to know what *you* are, *Lieutenant*?" Taub paused to light a cigarette; exhaling, he said, "Tell you for free. No fee like I'd charge before kicking your *ass* out of my office in Ohio. Don't *wimper*, I'm telling you *why* the sight of you sickens me so, why I'm doing this to you—and it isn't your rank. No matter how it *galls* me, the Army would've been insane *not* to promote you.

"Surprised? I'm a jealous old prick, but I'm not *dumb*. Under different circumstances, you'd make an excellent officer. Sonder's gunning for you attests to the fact. If you were a halfway decent individual, I'd share his opinion." Taub ground out his smoke methodically, light blue eyes locked on Winston's moist dark ones.

"But I won't give in to him, I can't give in to the Army, and I'll never let you off with a slap on the wrist. The Army doesn't need someone as *sick* as you are, young man."

Winston stopped putting his cigarette—his fifth since Taub began speaking to him—to his lips; only when he felt the dot of hot pain on his fingers did he look down to see his flesh burning.

Taub reached over and briskly plucked the butt out of Winston's grasp, leaving him to stare uncomprehendingly at his pink, seared flesh. Winston tried to focus on his wound, not on Taub's stinging flood of words, but *this* time, his hearing was acute. Every word cut into him, made his blood burn and sting inside him—for Taub spoke the truth in that dank office:

"—no one else will ever *dare* to do so. You're a fair-haired boy, oh, *sorry*, Lieutenant, make that *dark-haired* boy, from a good if perhaps *undeservedly* well-to-do family, born and raised in one of those 'good' little Midwest towns that wouldn't know *goodness* if it landed on their roofs and shit down the chimney. A boy who gets away with murder because he's lucky enough to be born into the 'right' family.

And once you get your ass back in that *dear* little town, no matter what *hole* you get yourself stuck in, all will be forgiven, no charges filed, because *you* have the good life *coming* to you. It's your *birthright*.

"And another thing . . . the *sickness* you have won't improve on its own, any more than the syph and drip you have would've healed without treatment. But because *this* illness won't make you scream bloody murder when you piss, or corkscrew through your nervous system demolishing your motor reflexes, you'll ignore it.

"But it'll *just get worse*. I'm not saying this because I like you, or even because I think I can help you—if you'd let me. Your sickness *can* be treated, with therapy, although once you're discharged or tossed in the brig or *whatever* happens, you'll wind up home, where you won't ask for anyone's help. Because the *good* little boy from the *decent* little town can't be *sick*. Look at him. Tall, handsome, smart, well off . . . *he* can't be a *pervert*. Not Lt. *Winston*. No one as perfect-looking, -sounding and -acting as *you* ever needs *help*. Especially not for a *mental* problem . . . a sexual *dysfunction*. Not *lack* of function, but a dysfunction nonetheless."

Taub let out a shuddering breath that smelled of stale cigarettes and bitterness. Leaning back in his chair, he smiled tightly as the tears rolled unwiped down Winston's cheeks.

"I know what you're thinking. 'This old goat hates me like nobody's business.' An intelligent surmise on your part. True, I'm not fond of you—but I don't hate you. I hate what you've *done* to yourself, to your uniform. I hate to see you drink your brain to mashed bananas—you've a *very* addictive personality—but I'd be a worse man than I no doubt am to *hate* you."

Taub leaned forward, watery eyes glittering, and said quietly. "I *pity* you, Lieutenant Winston. And I'm glad I'll never see you again after you're escorted from this office, because I *know* that once you're stateside, no matter how respected an individual you'll become in your hometown, your life will be a *mess*.

"Your illness won't pain you, won't show, but it will consume you. Since you'll never seek professional help, my advice to you is that you find a girl as sex-crazed and *sick* as you are and marry her. Maybe if you get enough at home, you won't go spreading yourself too thin among your neighbor's wives . . . and their little girls."

At that point, Winston let his head hang down, tears falling straight down to blossom on the dry fabric of his bathrobe, and he told himself, *That's the worst of it . . . I don't remember any more*—but this time Winston heard what his sobs had drowned out the first time, looking up as Taub said, with genuine sorrow, "According to both sets of IQ tests you took, you're one of the smartest officers in this man's Army. An IQ of one fifty-six. It's a shame you'll fuck your brains out by the time you're fifty."

NINETY

Wrapped in a smothering cocoon of muggy air, Brent remained chilled by his experience in Holiday's store. His back supported by the curved slats of a bench, Brent's head lolled back as he collected his sluggish thoughts.

Maeve and Mae had to be that flour-covered *thing* wiggling on the floor in there. He'd heard the cries of *two* babies. And the woman's voice implied that the babies were *wrong*.

So the twins were born in Ewerton . . . but to whom? No one mentioned a freak birth, but Uncle Palmer did mention—

Another couple, who left town in the twenties, right before the Palmers were born, when Dead Fred was young—

Something clicked in Brent's mind. His foot beating an excited tattoo in the humid air, Brent thought, *It fits. Maeve and Mae were rich. They were at least a few months older than Palmer, so maybe they were born in the* winter *of '24. And the Ewerts had money.*

"Hey, *girls,* I'm *on* to you!" he shouted down the empty avenue. Immediately Brent felt foolish, yet was strangely comforted, bursting to tell this strange doppelganger town that he'd discovered at least a small part of the twins' secret.

Then it hit him. *Holiday's* store. A man coming out from behind the counter, and a woman following—Brent wasn't positive, but the man's voice seemed familiar . . . Wilbur and the woman must have been in the back room making out when Mrs. Ewert broke one of the panes of glass in the door—

The image of the bloody women's clothing in the trunk came back to him; helplessly, Brent giggled as he ticked off months on his fingers. October, September, August . . .

March . . . January. As in snow and biting cold. And Maeve's necklace had sixteen pearls on it, months before Palmer turned sixteen himself.

Brent still couldn't understand how Zoe fit in, other than being born with a face so like theirs— "But I know enough to warn my uncle away from you two," he shouted to the empty, echoing street. It mocked him with rainbow-tinged perfection, the buildings leaning out at him in silent rebuke.

Undaunted, Brent started for the nearest car, a shining '23 Auburn. If he got into this place, he could get out. Gas up one of these old cars, hot-wire it, and drive out to warn Palmer. Get his own ass back where it belonged, Zoe or no Zoe.

Neither option was to be forthcoming . . . for he heard the slap of hard leather shoe soles hitting the pavement.

Someone was walking toward him.

When the guards showed up to take Winston away, he went willingly. Then, all was a blur, a whirling centrifuge of words, options, decisions: accept a court-martial, duck under an insanity plea, or . . . sign a document allowing him something better than the less-than-honorable discharge. By acknowledging that he had not fulfilled his military options and duties, he'd be discharged honorably, without punishment—*if* he swore never to join any branch of the military. A face-saving, if not wholly pleasing, solution to his problem.

In the tornado swirl of words, faces, sights, one thing now stood out: Captain Sonders said that Major *Taub* had recommended this particular alternative.

Déjà vu washed over Brent, as if he'd slid off into a different, tilted plane, a place where *everything* was bigger, and he was small, vulnerable again. He caught himself swaying, unable to believe what—*who*—he saw strolling down the street.

The sun made the man's hair a blaze of palest gold-blond, and his eyes squinted pale green against the brassy morning light. When Brent last saw him, the man was ancient, wild-eyed—but the man before him was *young*. Mid-forties or so, face still well defined over strong bones, his walk firm, bouncy.

Holiday came to a stop four feet from Brent; he *looked*

very much alive, and unthawed. He had nicked himself *shaving*. A faint, one-sided smile played about his thin lips; his eyes had the same twinkle his son Palmer's had had when the latter found those cast-off bathroom fixtures.

Holiday's clothes were exquisite. Shirt perfectly tailored, delicate pale peach and apple-green stripes, with a white collar. Peach tie. White flannel trousers. Brent last saw clothing like that when he and Zoe rented *The Great Gatsby* in the Cities.

Holiday spoke, his voice dry, cynical, and slightly ironic. "Are *you* the fellow responsible for those *sidewalks* lately?"

Brent swallowed. *This place* feeds *off people . . . our wants, our needs . . . our mental jokes. But I wasn't here when I thought that about the sidewalks rolling up at eight. If this place read my thoughts before I arrived—*

Not wanting to seem the same doltish, scared kid he was in the early sixties, Brent forced himself to ask, "If I'm the one who made it happen, how can I stop it? The sound drives me nuts—"

Smiling, Holiday added, "Likewise. It didn't stop because *you* weren't sure you could stop it. You'll learn how this place works. Come with me, you'll see how easy it is."

Without letting Brent ask what "it" was, Wilbur took off at a fast trot for Roberts Street while Brent chuffed after him. *Maybe I should've walked more . . . I can't keep up with a a century-old* dead *man. . . .*

When Brent caught up with Holiday, Wilbur sat behind the wheel of a rich blue classic car, a long, lean one whose make Brent couldn't immediately place. "Hop in, it's too hot to walk out there."

They drove out to the Ewerton "Welcome" sign in silence; Brent was acutely aware that he *had* to smell worse than a dog who'd rolled in something irresistibly *awful*, but Holiday was tactful enough not to mention it.

To Brent's relief, the welcome sign no longer bore its daintily scripted admonition about the sidewalks. When Brent got back into Holiday's car—the seats were real leather, warm but *natural* against his bare thighs—Holiday said, turning the key in the ignition, "Think of it as a . . . *welcome* to this place. Well intentioned, but . . . clichéd, no?"

Despite his uneasiness (*I'm riding in a car driven by a* corpse—) Brent laughed, prompting Holiday to add, "I think

I can offer you a better welcome . . . please stay with me, in my house. I've plenty of room, and no company. . . . Well, we nearly have the whole town to ourselves. I wish I'd found you sooner, but I seldom venture out in *this* weather—'' His tone implied that he actually had a choice of climates.

Taking one hand off the wheel to shift gears, he accidentally brushed his hand against Brent's bare leg.

It *tingled*, like Maeve's tapping finger. Reflexively, Brent inched away before he remembered to be tactful. Holiday smiled apologetically. ''Takes some time to get used to. Imagine how it feels when I have to use the bathroom. . . . '' There was no bitterness in his voice, just matter-of-fact acceptance.

Leaning back against the leather seat, Brent half closed his eyes, thinking, *I should be scared shitless, going into his house after what happened to my grandmother . . . but that was another time, another place . . . I hope.*

NINETY-ONE

When the sexton realized that Stu wasn't coming back to the cemetery, at least not right off, Ritter flung a tarp over the ruptured Holiday vault, posted the ''Grounds Closed'' sign on the freshly padlocked gates . . . and got the hell out of the cemetery. After a few antsy hours of waiting, Elmer called Stu's office.

Sawyer hemmed and hawed, giving Ritter the strong impression that the beefy Korean War vet was *scared* to return to the scene of last night's vandalism.

By the time Stu agreed to come back to check out the tarpaulined vault, the batteries in the flashlight that had slipped into the coffin had all but given out. It emitted only an anemic glow that gave one edge of the tarp a slight phosphorescence, like rotted fish come nighttime.

Breathing through his mouth just in *case*, Stu prodded the edges of the tarp with a wing-tipped shoe, asking, ''That been shining since morning?''

"Yeah, only real bright before. I thought his . . . went all lardy and glowing. Does that. When that happens,—"

Stu's breakfast shifted unwholesomely in his stomach. " 'Nough, Elmer. I know what happens when a body rots and Wilbur wasn't embalmed—"

Stu backed away, still unable to lift up the protective tarp. Tentatively, he poked the tarp, ran a toe along the lumpy hem. "Y'know, Lenny oughtta be here. His job and all. I'll call from the car—"

"I'll help." Elmer tagged along, until Stu turned around and reminded him, "Only takes one to work the radio, Elmer. Why don't you keep old Wilbur company?" Stu waited by the squad car until Lenny drove up.

Lenny Wilkes sat back on his heels, brown eyes puzzled, and asked, "You two *sure* the casket broke? I don't smell nothing. *I* think we should get the marker off the vault so we can see what's in there. I don't think it broke, top may be cracked, but—"

Stu began to pull off the tarp when Ritter screeched, "Where do you think that *light* was coming from?"

"Lenny's right, Elmer. We got to get the stone up."

The marker was undamaged, except for a crack in its base. After much sweating and grunting the three men managed to pull the huge stone off onto the grass parallel to the grave. The crack in the vault was hidden in a crescent of shadow.

In anticipation of the odor, Lenny covered his nose with a clean handkerchief before hunkering down, Stu's flashlight in hand, to peer into the crack in the vault. He said something that was muffled by the hankie before he backed away, face gone the color of month-old cottage cheese. He had the foresight not to drop another flashlight into the ruined coffin—he handed it to Stu before ducking behind one of the neighboring tombstones.

For once, Lenny's famous "I ain't never seen nothing like it" line hadn't been necessary . . . for Stu's flashlight picked up only the dead flashlight lying in the empty coffin.

NINETY-TWO

Wilbur Holiday played the good host; he urged Brent to set himself up in a spare bedroom, bathe and change his clothes, then share a meal with him. Noting the difference in their sizes (they were the same height, but Wilbur was close to whip-thin, while Brent's junk-food diet had done little to improve his figure), Holiday urged Brent to rummage through his closet.

Remembering the account of Palmer's homecoming, Brent wasn't surprised to find a pair of lightweight trousers that fit, plus a polo shirt of margarine yellow.

Brent glanced at the contents of the bedroom. A huge, ornately carved cherry dresser and nightstand like something out of a Korvel book; a brass bed, a moon watch and old change, mostly buffalo nickles, Liberty and Mercury dimes, and wheat pennies, plus keys, in a metal and glass tray; a hair brush set with golden hairs wound in the bristles, and bay rum and other beautifully bottled men's colognes Brent didn't recognize. On impulse, Brent pocketed a couple of Liberty dimes and buffalo nickels. Small proof of this house, of this *place*. Just in *case*.

But there were no hairpins, no marcellers, or flowered china powder boxes around. The closets only held suit after exquisitely tailored suit. Unless the essence of Holiday's wife used another bedroom, the man wasn't lying when he said he lacked for company. And no one came downstairs to join them as they ate, answering at least one of Brent's questions. When Holiday served coffee, he didn't roll himself a cigarette of any sort, legal or illegal. Brent noticed that his host wore a moon watch, different from the one upstairs. *This* one was a genuine Patek Philippe. Sipping his coffee, Brent reflected, *Watch like that costs as much as a BMW.* More. *Glad the old guy found a way to take it with him, but couldn't he have left a little for his son . . . make that* sons. Brent remembered Winston's hovel . . . with the unplugged phone jacks.

Wilbur watched Brent with a fascination akin to a starving child eyeing a moldy slice of bread. When Brent began to squirm, Holiday graciously explained, "Oh, excuse me . . .

it's just that there's a lot of your father and your grandmother in your face. I was sorry to hear about your parents. Palmer put a notice in the paper. It was rude of me not to forward my condolences. . . ."

Brent mumbled, "No offense taken, Mr. Holiday." His host urged, "Wilbur, please. I may be . . . *ancient*, but you've no need to be formal. You're Palmer's nephew, that's almost family to me," he added, without having to ask if Brent knew of Wilbur's blood ties to his uncle. Brent didn't miss the implication—*I'm putting up with you for* Palmer's *sake*. Not a hostile inference . . . but distancing, nonetheless.

Glancing at his Patek Philippe watch, Holiday said, "Mind if I change clothes? I prefer to wear something more comfortable when we talk in the library . . . you *do* wish to talk to me, do you not?"

Brent replied, "If it doesn't trouble you." *Now I'm talking like him. This place* is *getting to me. Or getting* in *me.*

Wilbur laughed, showing oddly crooked teeth. Getting up, he said, "Meet you in the library in a few minutes. It's down the hallway, two doors down on the right."

Eight-foot-high walnut shelves, volumes jammed in on the horizontal in the narrow spaces between the tops of the books and the bottom of the next shelf up. Not the usual paperbacks available at Ewerton garage sales, but *books*. Leather-covered, hub-spined, gilt-edged *books*, with weight, texture, and that special, sharp musty odor that wafted up when you opened the marbleized front piece.

Volumes gently worn from frequent readings, the top of each spine slightly frayed. Dozens of writers: Hesse, Poe, Lawrence, James (both Henry and M.R.), Hawthorne, Dickens, Twain, Wolfe, Joyce, and others.

Encyclopedias, gold stamping on the spines worn to a deep green-bronze.

Small, issue-perfect quatro volumes from the mid 19th century, covers glowing in crimson, darkest blue and soft wheat shades. Mrs. Brownings' poems, cream spine traced with delicate vines of soft gold. And a set of books published by Kegal, Paul, Trench and Trubner & Co., Ltd., London, 1901, entitled *Books on Egypt and Chaldea*—Brent discovered the date of publication by pulling down the most worn volume. Number II, "Egyptian Magic," by a man named E. A. Wallis Budge. The book fell open to a frequently read page, where someone (Holiday?) had underlined with faded sepia ink:

> —would live for all eternity in the company of the spirits and soul of the righteous in a kingdom ruled by a being who was of divine origin, but who had lived on earth, and had risen from the dead, and had become the God king of the world which is beyond the grave. . . .

Brent quickly put the book back on the shelf, before another volume caught his eye.

Magick in Theory and Practice, by Aleister Crowley, the lettering rubbing to colorless outlines against the worn cover of the book, which was pointedly shelved between a Gideon-plain Bible and a newish copy of the lost books of the Bible. The Crowley was a first edition, published in London in 1929.

Paging through the arcane tome, Brent saw that someone had found Crowley's egotistical rantings important enough to underline in sepia:

> . . . every human being is intrinsically an independent individual, with his own proper character and motivations.

The last was heavily underscored with wavy lines; other isolated ideas were also unified in the underliner's view:

> . . . Every man and woman has a course, depending partly on the self, and partly on the environment which is natural and necessary for each. Anyone who is forced from his own course . . . comes in conflict with the orders of the Universe and suffers accordingly. . . .

> . . . Every force in the universe is capable of being transformed into any other kind of force by using suitable means. . . .

Before Brent read the next sepia-scrubbed passage, he heard Holiday's voice. "Found the 'Wickedest Man in the World,' I see. The only truly comprehensible part of the book is the introduction, is it not?"

Brent wondered how Wilbur knew which book he had been

reading—Brent's broad back effectively hid both the book he held *and* the empty space on the shelf.

Ignoring the implication of Wilbur's observation, Brent turned around to face Holiday, who sat in the wing chair closest to the cold fireplace, hands laced together in his lap, a worn smile on his face. Brent sat down in the wing chair that faced Wilbur's.

Wilbur poured each of them a couple of finger's worth of brandy, saying as he did so, "I'm . . . doing this more for you than for myself. Above all, do keep that in mind."

But Brent, sensing that he was close to learning the so far unattainable "Why?" behind the events of the past few weeks, overlooked the remark as mere stalling on the part of his host. He failed to consider the true implication of Holiday's comment.

NINETY-THREE

Palmer Nemmitz came home from the library with little more than a headache and a few scribbled notes on the back of a checking account deposit slip.

When he'd asked the librarian for the earliest copies of the *Herald*, the ones published in 1913 and before (since the cornerstone of the newspaper office read 1913, before they slapped siding over it), she'd patiently explained, "If there were copies of the *Herald* before 1914, they'd *be* in the file. If they aren't, then there *weren't* any before 1914, right?"

Upon entering the empty house, Palmer headed upstairs, feeling defeated, but when he stepped into his room, what he saw made the tiredness snap out of his bones like the wet smack of a towel across his backside.

Years of humidity had finally done a number on the wallpaper; the beige layer fell completely away in places where it wasn't attached by nail-held pictures. In a few spots, even the blue-flowered paper rippled or curled down, too, exposing the smiling faces of the Dutch boy and girl on that old seed poster, as well as the crumbling pulp of yellowed newsprint. Papers printed *before* 1914, some as long as ten years prior to 1914. When the paper was known as *The Robertsville Gazette*, before Ewerton *was* Ewerton. . . .

Gradually, Maeve's scent of mingled roses and jasmine filled the room, but the musty odor of old wallpaper paste soon overcame the sweet perfume, as Palmer busied himself. Soon the floor was littered with ragged curls of yellow-backed paper—as Palmer moved from wall to wall, tugging and ripping, mindful of the fragile newsprint below—until he was surrounded by four walls covered with dozens of old issues of the *Gazette*. Some sheets were pasted on front side up, others backward, showing local columns that told who did what where, and with whom.

Wayne Mesabi *had* asked for a new slant on the history of Ewerton . . . but there had *been* no "Ewerton" before 1914. Just a place called *Robertsville*.

Named for a man named Zachary Roberts, or so said the papers that Palmer dared not peel from the walls, for fear of shredding them into unreadable ribbons and tatters.

Leaning in close to the north wall of his room, Palmer read, learning, how Mr. Z. S. Roberts had been the tiny village's most influential citizen, a combination Andrew Carnegie and saint, sawbucks and goodness incarnate. But when Palmer scanned the pages for items about *his* own family, and those of the other cream couples, he realized that things weren't what he'd been led to believe.

Holiday took a sip of brandy before asking Brent, "How much do you know of the history of the real Ewerton?" He leaned back, waiting, circling the rim of his glass with one finger, while Brent told the little he knew, finishing within five minutes. He sipped some brandy while Holiday sat watching him, a half smile playing on his lips.

"So . . . that is what you know of *Ewerton*. Nothing much happening before the twenties . . . doesn't surprise me. Not in the least. Not . . . after Otis Ewert remolded Robertsville in his own image—"

"Roberts—"

"Yes, *Robertsville*, Wisconsin, formerly Crescent Corners, formerly a few miles of woodland in the northland exploited by lumbermen . . . but a *decent* exploitation. Not Otis Ewert's brand of rape.

"But I'm getting ahead of myself. Zach Roberts had been a stockbroker, from New York City. Made his money cleanly and got out before the temptation to make even more money less cleanly corrupted him. He and some friends vacationed here, Zach liked what he saw, and stayed on after his companions returned to New York. *This* is secondhand even to me; my wife and her parents told me of Zach's arrival here.

"As fate would have it, he came just when the lumber industry was beginning to sour. But as one form of luck left the area, Zack brought in his own luck, made it work here—"

When it grew too dark to read comfortably, Palmer switched on the overhead light, which threw warm light and slanting shadows across the fragile newsprint. The story of Robertsville, told in inexpertly set type across glue-stained pages, surrounded him:

Z. S. ROBERTS SAVES CRESCENT CORNERS
FROM BANKRUPTCY
VILLAGE TO BE RENAMED

ROBERTSVILLE TO BE INCORPORATED
TOWN COUNCIL ELECTION APRIL 6

NEGOTIATIONS FOR SOO SPUR BEGIN
ZACH ROBERTS SPEAKS TO OWNERS

SASH AND DOOR TO OPEN HERE MONDAY!

Grainy engraved drawings and crudely reproduced photographs attested to the growth of the town; here a hospital ground-breaking, there a new bridge by the paper mill. The number of children graduating from the grade school doubled in a year, or so the June 1908 paper on the west wall indicated.

Robertsville became a real town, but as Palmer inched along his walls, scanning the rotting pulp papers, something nagged at him. Things weren't *right*. . . . Of all the families he'd been taught were important to the town *years* ago, only Horton Crescent was infrequently mentioned by name in any of the articles. Crescent had been one of the principal investors in the lumbering before the trees became blighted, but he alone came through the lumber decline with money, and built himself a fine new house in 1903, but Horton's political

clout had been *nowhere* what it was when Palmer was growing up.

But after the coming of Zach Roberts, Horton's name did
crop up more and more often, usually in conjunction with
that of the former stockbroker. . . .

Holiday splashed more brandy into his glass before continuing, "Zach Roberts was a benevolent despot who would've
given the skin off his bones to make someone else happy.
Missed his calling as Santa Claus. From what *I* knew of the
man, he simply wanted to make a better life for himself and
for the people who ultimately worshiped the stones his shoes
kicked. Oh, power *was* a motivating factor in his decision to
plow much of his money into this town, but Zach gave as
much as he took. Coming of the factories was his doing,
along with the Soo depot. Crescent Corners escaped the fate
of Dunnsville and Appolonia, and tripled in size—a fine return on his investment. I can think of worse abuses of power.

"My father-in-law took pains to latch on to Zach's coat-
tails—not that *he* was hurting—both the Holidays and the
Crescents came to this country with money and made more
once they arrived. My father was a pharmacist, while Horton's parents were big on investing. Which made Zach Roberts irresistible.

"Trouble was, Zach liked *everybody*. A good dose of basic
mistrust might've saved Zach. Then again, perhaps it all was
fated. . . . God help him, the man even liked Otis Ewert,
and *he* was a man *no one* could love—or so I'd thought upon
meeting him."

As Palmer sat, cramp-legged but enthralled, on the floor near
his closet and tried to read a tightly printed column of social
events, he discovered that none of the soon-to-be important
families interacted at any level yet. The Winstons had been
chicken farmers and ne'er-do-wells, the Fergers mill workers, and the Niemiec clan farmed. The Winstons were Lu-
therans, the Fergers Congregational, the Niemiec clan avoided
church, and the Crescents were pillars of the Methodist
church. None of them so much as ate at each other's houses,
according to Palmer's limited source of papers.

Curiosity turned to apprehension when he asked himself

which families the *wives* came from. No matter which families the wives belonged to, *their* families apparently didn't socialize with the kin of their future husbands. Which made no sense; small-town life was castelike, segmented, chains of familial/social ties were formed; dividing lines such as those were long-standing. Yet six couples were crossed-fingers close by 1923.

It didn't jell for Palmer, until he remembered the children . . . the young people had to be friends. But a check of the social columns methodically quelled *that*.

Scooting around on his fleshless behind, Palmer searched the walls, but the facts he'd been hoping to disprove kept coming back at him. Six couples who were so shortly to become *inseparable* didn't have a *single thing* in common a mere ten years before 1923. The papers, which dated up to 1913, said so.

But his selection of papers *was* incomplete—Palmer's room was thirteen by fifteen feet, with ten-foot-high ceilings. He stood on a chair to read some pages, but none of them revealed that vital, first link between all the couples. Then he remembered that his closet was once part of the room's regular walls and there was still blue-flowered paper in there.

Soon his bed was heaped high with mothball-scented suits, old raincoats, and moldy shoes. Palmer unplugged his desk lamp, replugging it close to the closet. In half an hour, he carefully peeled away most of the blue paper—and discovered the first links between the couples.

Young Porter Winston, Fred Ferger, and Enoch Niemiec's names had been absent from the gossip columns, but close by the floor, near the corner by the closet door, Palmer saw a notice of legal and court news. Midway down the list of arrests and lines he found:

Fredric Ferger, the 18-year-old son of Burton Ferger, was discovered in the act of stealing the sum of ten dollars from a cash box belonging to the elder Ferger. When his son refused to return the money, Sheriff Alfred Sawyer arrested the youth. He was held in the Dean County jail for a period of six days, until Mr. Ferger requested the boy's freedom in order for him to reroof the house and stable.

The item was undated, but occurred in June or July, the time of the next incident reported:

July 19th, Enoch Niemiec, 17, stole Eric Byrne's 1912 Harley Davidson motorcycle from outside the Bakery, where young Eric, son of Funeral Home Director Etan Byrne, had parked the vehicle. Niemiec drove the motorcycle across the bridge, prior to pushing it into the river, where it sank. This act was witnessed by several persons on the bank of the river. Niemiec fled the scene on foot. Sheriff Sawyer gave chase and captured the thief. Being unable to pay his fine of $25.00, and since his family was unwilling to do so, Niemiec spent two weeks in the Dean County jail.

And, directly below *that*:

Twelve windows of the Vernon Doyle home were shot with bird pellets by Porter Winston, 19-year-old son of Mr. Peter Winston of Share Avenue. Young Winston gave no explanation for his actions on the evening of the 20th, but did seem to be intoxicated, when he was found, gun in hand, lying under the big elm in the Doyle front yard. Sheriff Sawyer escorted the young man to jail. He pled "No Contest" and was ordered to spend one week in the. . . .

Three youths, jailed for close to a week together (or so Palmer supposed), all no doubt *known* to each other, but not friends—yet. Jail can make friends of the most unlikely strangers.

And a notice near the ceiling provided Palmer with more names—the Crescents of Robertsville and the Warren Holidays of Edina, Minnesota, were proud to announce the marriage of Hortense Crescent and Wilbur W. Holiday, in February of 1913. The next issue of the *Gazette*, dated mid-April, provided half of the final couple.

A "Mr. Otis Ewert, retired stockbroker from Milwaukee, was a dinner guest at the home of Mr. and Mrs. Z. S. Roberts of Myrtle Street." Sitting back on his heels in the stuffy, mothball-nauseous closet, Palmer said aloud, " 'Retired stockbroker'? Ewert 'retired' in his early *twenties*?"

That he hadn't seen the announcement about Zachary Roberts' marriage didn't bother Palmer; he assumed the identity of Roberts' wife was of little importance in the sceme of things. For by the next available column, the Robertses and the ever-stag Mr. Ewert were dinner guests at the Horace Crescent home, which also housed his daughter and son-in-law.

Ewert bought up property, including the tract of trees beyond Willow Hill, stating in a small sidebar article in the last July issue of that year:

> By fall, I hope to establish a Hunting Club, for the young gentlemen of Robertsville, whose aims would be the pursuit of good sportsmanship, proper handling of firearms, and the building-up of respect for other hunters and for the woods themselves.

There was more, but Palmer had read enough; besides being a filthy rich young buck, Mr. Otis Ewert had fancied himself a great white hunter. And he wasn't alone. . . .

Porter Winston could shoot the squaw off a Leinenkugels beer can after downing half a case. In '43, when a crow impaled itself on the Fergers' lightning rod, Fredric, Sr., shot the bird clean off. And Palmer *knew* how Enoch could shoot.

Sloshing the remaining brandy in his sifter as he spoke, Holiday continued, "Even after all these years, it still isn't easy for me to think of Otis Ewert. He was unconditionally *sane*. Never did rash or impulsive things for the sake of *doing* them—he was a most logical, methodical man. He seldom said much, didn't arouse the suspicions of most people. Except me, and I was only Hortense's *husband*, so my opinion counted for naught.

"And Otis never *said* where his capital came from; even when asked. If he'd said, 'Good investments,' I wouldn't have thought to ask twice about it, but his evasiveness *grated*. The most he ever said was, 'I've dealt in stocks.' Period. He was so *cold* when he told me that. . . .'' Holiday shuddered, and began circling the rim of his glass with a damp finger, producing an irritating *squeegee* noise. Eyes focused somewhere past Brent, he went on, "Initially, all he wanted was power, so he latched on to the only other truly powerful man in town.

"Zack Roberts was *loved*, which Horton and Otis weren't.

Oh, once Otis bought into things, he was *respected*, but liked . . . never.

"Not that it bothered Otis in the beginning. You could just sense that being loved wasn't a necessity for him. Then . . . something happened. He became all nervous, agitated, almost another Otis entirely. It was September, maybe late August, that he underwent this transformation. Around that time he came up with the idea for his Hunting Club.

"His boys, his Hunting Club regulars—your grandfather, Porter, Fred, Sr., even my father-in-law—were all cut from the same cloth. Not as bad as Otis individually, but together. . . . Hortense and Horton urged me to join, too, but I could buy my own drinks—"

"I don't know if Otis hunted before 1913. It was something in his present that made him do things he wouldn't have considered earlier that year . . . something he didn't count on, I'm sure. Otis fell in love. I neglected to mention this before, but earlier in '13, Zach Roberts did a most foolish thing, a thing many a man does when gray hairs come in before *heirs* do. He married a local *girl*, Abigail Andersen. Abigail wasn't yet seventeen when she married Zachary. They were already married when I arrived in town.

"If Zach hadn't been Zach, people would've been scandalized. Abby was young enough to be his granddaughter. Big hips on her. Zach was anxious for children. Said so *constantly*. After a while it was *embarrassing*.

"Lord, Abby *was* something else—look at her once, you'd think her plain, look again and your organ did a jig in your long johns. She . . . was unlike any other woman in town. Seemed . . . younger and older than seventeen. Doll-like hands on her, smaller than her face. Made me think of a bisque doll. Never saw such dainty hands on a grown woman. And her voice was . . . *filtered*, but harsh if she wanted it to be.

"And Otis fell in love with her. Not long afterward, he instituted his Hunting Club."

NINETY-FOUR

Craning his neck until it ached dully into his jaw, Palmer saw that the still-stag Otis Ewert was now a frequent guest at the Roberts, Crescent, Ferger, Winston, *and* Nemmitz homes. Palmer's room resembled a bombed-out hovel, with the furniture protectively huddled near the center. And he didn't dare rip down the rest of the wallpaper in the upstairs bedrooms.

Yet he was still nagged by a question that gnawed like a rat trapped in a lidded garbage can. How had Mr. Ewert come to rule his little kingdom by the river? *Something* happened in Robertsville, something catastrophic enough to make Roberts leave the town he loved.

Frustrated by the lack of answers, Palmer felt such rage over the whole ruined mess of his life that he was caught up by an impulse to make the destruction complete. With a single swipe of his forearm, he cleared his dresser of knick-knacks, coins, combs, brushes—and the cremains tin.

Covering his eyes with both hands, Palmer imagined a cloud of gray dust settling down over the ruins of his room. *Zoe or not, I can't scoop up that with my bare hands*—but when he opened his eyes, he saw only a yellowed spill of *more* newspaper.

Bending down on popping knees, Palmer picked up the pieces of paper. Sitting at his desk, he looked at them in shocked wonder. The scraps of paper were whole articles, carefully snipped from newspapers, then rolled up so as to fit, cigarette-style, into the heavy tin.

Not wanting to ruin the fragile newsprint, yet heart-thumpingly eager to read them all, very quickly, Palmer made himself slowly unroll the first clipping that came to hand. Uncurled, it was dated along the top in faded sepia ink "November 25, 1913," in a hand too cramped and blurred to make out clearly, let alone identify. But the headline across the top of the story was quite explicit:

GREAT TRAGEDY! MORTAL ACCIDENT IN
EWERT WOODS! TOWN MOURNS LOSS!

Bent low over the brittle fragments of newsprint, Palmer's head cast a looming shadow over its yellowed surface as he read:

A terrible accident occurred November 21, in Ewert Woods. According to the members of the newly formed Robertsville Hunting Club, it was a most horrendous and tragic—whilst completely unavoidable—occurrence. . . .

Wilbur continued to rub his finger around the rim of the glass; the noise set Brent's teeth on edge. His host went on, "By November, Ewert's so-called Hunting Club had attracted a large membership, although it seemed to me that any organization that spent most of its meeting time ensconced in the Rusty Hinge Saloon wasn't terribly interested in hunting, per se. But Hortense kept after me, hinting that her *daddy* found me to be less than manly for my abstention from the club. To keep peace, I agreed to join the charter members of the Club and go deer hunting on a Friday morning . . . twenty-first of November.

"I wasn't proficient with firearms. If I could hit a barn I was unusually lucky—provided it stayed put and the wind died down." As Holiday laughed softly over his ineptitude, his eyes were bilious pools of pure misery.

Brent sat mesmerized as his host went on softly, "Horton *assured* me that marksmanship wasn't everything, so, very early, well before daybreak, he and I got into his Pungs-Finch—a two-passenger roadster—and headed for the woods. *Ewert's* woods, north of Willow Hill. They've cut down much of the woods in Ewerton, but in '13 they extended *miles* deep in places . . . so dense the branches of the evergreens intertwined like huge meshing fingers.

"Horton and I had little to say to each other during the drive—we were distant cousins, but we could've been from warring tribes in Africa considering how we got on. I do remember him saying, just as we pulled up alongside the other cars in the clearing before the woods, 'Wilbur, this is going to be a *very* good hunt. Lots of horns among the trees . . . Lots of nice, *big* horns.

"Without thinking, *I* said, 'Antlers, Horton, they're called antlers,' but he just *smiled* at me—a rare action on his part—before he got out of the roadster and said, 'You're the scholar, Wilbur . . . sure look like *horns* to me.'

"I hadn't the chance to think of what he'd said, for the

others were out of their cars, rifles tucked under their arms—Enoch, Porter, Fred, Otis, plus Zachary Roberts stood there, stamping their feet in the cold predawn darkness. Only Zach and I were hunting neophytes. Even my rifle wasn't my own.

"On Otis' order, we waited until the sun rose, and when I saw those clouds, every beautiful color imaginable, lit from behind with pure gold-white light, I didn't want to leave that marvelous sight until every last bit of glorious color was gone from the sky. Glancing at Zachary, I saw his gray hair aflame from that beautiful sunrise. . . .

"But Otis kept rubbing those smooth-gloved hands of his, blowing foggy breath into the air, and urging us to 'get in there.' The *way* he said it, I had to muster all my Dutch courage just to step into those woods after him. Every cell in my body told me to *run*, to jump into that Pungs-Finch roadster and take off—"

. . . When darkness outside her window was nearly complete, they came for her. Pulled her out of the safety of the bed, stood her up on feet that pin-prickled along the soles, and dressed her. That accomplished—with little cooperation from her—she was walked out of the room, past the oval rose window that shone like a ravaged ruby in midair, down the stairs and out of the house. During the ride in their white car, she sat on the backseat, eyes closed, mind sluggishly working. A single thought surfaced from the stagnant muck—I must . . . kill myself. Before I see—but she did not act upon the thought. She could not . . . for she was afraid—

Of them, *in the front seat. One driving, one turned around sideways, watching her. Unseen, but* felt. *Watching, making sure . . . of what? She was being driven somewhere far from the safety of her bed.*

Otis, *help* me, *her mind cried, but there was no Otis, only* them, *sitting up there on that pink upholstery. Another thought broke free of the fear-slush of her mind:* The girls so love the car Otis bought for them. Only one like it . . . special order seats. Pink. Pink for his little girls—*even if Maeve was the only one who could drive.*

But she knew, without looking, that Mae *was driving the car.*

In her rigid silence, she felt the wheels of the car move

forward, forward, through her newly shod feet which rested flat on the floor of the Pierce-Arrow. As the car sped through the deserted streets, its vibrations hummed through her, giving her strength, making her less afraid.

But her newfound courage all but failed her when she heard/felt the car pull onto a different surface . . . an unpaved, packed-dirt place. She'd felt those same vibrations when Otis drove the Daniels across the fairground—

No!!! her brain screamed, and she opened her eyes. Only to meet the calm, slightly cold eyes of the girls . . . the eyes that looked so much like her own. Those four eyes warned, Don't fight us.

They all but carried her into the place, past the oddly canted smile of the red-haired man at the door . . . the unctuous, dark-suited man whose face she'd hoped never to see again. Broke my watch, *she thought. She remembered his name—Hypnotique, the mentalist. Only the newspaper said he was named Quigley, Jonathan Quigley, said he—he—died.* But he's here, alive—

Behind the dead man, who smiled and helped bring her inside, was glimmering, depthless, all-colors of wonder, and time, and memory. When she passed the man-thing in the box, something about his rubbery face quickened old memories, but when she started to utter a name, she was whisked away, unable to protest, or question. She did come to a halt before a green-lit tank, her face pressed mere inches from a moon-faced bloated bobbing thing, but it was three against one, and she was pulled faster, faster, her feet unable to stumble along, so she dragged them toes downward.

Her head bobbed unsteadily as she passed garish booths and a spinning Tarot-carded wheel (Madam Zola said Death was in my future). In a fun-house mirror, her face became a twisted, elongated monstrosity. Passing the stuffed and mummified creature that squatted, overalls encrusted with dried dung and straw, in a blanket-screened pen, she tried to cry out, break free . . . but was pulled forward.

To the tall, upright thing with the crank on one side and eyepieces affixed to the front—a nickelodeon, something comforting in this place of strange sights and pulsing, brilliant colors. Gratefully, she pressed her face against the small eyepiece—until she saw, *and reared away in fright. The fluttering images within were in* color—*and needed no cranking on her part to continue their movement. She was pushed back to the*

machine, to view the scene within, as one of her girls said,
"Look what *you* wrought."

Brittle newsprint split under Palmer's fingers, but the words
remained legible . . . and curiously indifferent, considering
the subject of the article:

> . . . result being that our town's most esteemed citizen,
> Zachary Robert's, now lies dead in the Reish-Byrne Fu-
> neral Home. Due to the most unfortunate circumstances
> of the first real outing of the Robertsville Hunting Club,
> founder Otis Ewert has taken it upon himself to dissolve
> and disband the organization. . . .

In the darkness of the library, Holiday's eyes were empty caves
above his barely working mouth as he continued, "Once we were
in among the trees, Otis did a strange thing. Common sense told
even *me* that making lots of noise was the *last* thing a hunter
would want to do—but he gave us *orders*. Told us all where to
stand, how to advance through the trees. By that time, we'd gone
in so deep—and the mixed pines and hardwoods were so dense—
I *knew* I'd get lost if I left the group.

"When Otis blustered up behind me, I was so rattled I all
but jumped out of my boots. He said I was to walk into the
woods at the head of a diagonal line, on a north-northeasterly
slant. Noticing my nervous state, Zach piped up, 'You'd best
listen to Otis, son, he's quite the huntsman. Claims he's
bagged many a doe this way.' Before I could tell him that
shooting *does* wasn't sporting, Otis separated us, ordering
Zachary to stand farther down the line. I . . . never spoke to
Zach Roberts again.

"Soon we were all *arranged* to Otis' satisfaction, in a line
that slanted from the northwest to the southeast. Me at the
top, then Ferger, Porter, Zach, my father-in-law, Otis, and
your grandfather at the opposite end from me. We resembled
a marching band, ready to high-step down a street. . . . We
set off in that bizarre formation, stalking slowly, each of us
perhaps five yards apart. The trees were so compressed it was
impossible for me to see Ferger to my right.

"We were to keep going until one of us spotted a deer, or
we exited the woods, whichever came first. It sounded . . .
wrong, but we were in Ewert's private woods, stalking his

deer. Only . . . I saw no deer. No tracks or droppings on the barely snow-dusted ground. But it was Otis' show—he said 'stalk,' so I *stalked*. . . .''

. . . The scene moving, uncranked, through her eyepiece was faint, but clear, as if seen through a lens of memory. Distant, yet painfully vivid memory. The point of view changed fluidly, with a grace and ease no camera of her youth could approach. The delicate hues of the misty trees and rough brown hunting clothes were overshadowed by the remains of a glorious sunrise beyond—then the viewpoint shifted. Trees slapped the lens of the camera that couldn't-be-a-camera, as the seven men entered the woods. Their breath plumed out diffuse white against the dark trees, the needle-strewn ground. She longed to hear Otis' voice as he ordered the others about, toy soldiers on a field of play. Soon, the men were in line, advancing . . . first in a straight line in her bird's-eyeview, then she saw the men only as dark splotches through the trees. Then . . . she noticed something odd. While the northernmost hunter pursued a forward course, rifle at the ready—

Most of his companions did not. . . .

NINETY-FIVE

''I'd been assigned the densest section of the woods,'' Holiday said in a near whisper, his words almost drowned out by his relentless circling of his snifter rim with a moist fingertip. ''It was all I could do to move forward. There were interlaced branches, and raised, gnarled roots ahead of my every step. Tracking anything was impossible. But I'd so tired of my wife's parents remarks about my 'unmanly' pursuits—as if chess and Freud were *feminine* interests—that I kept trudging along, unable to make out any of the others behind me. That I was *alone* in my part of the woods didn't sink in until I stopped to use the nearest tree as a comfort station. As I buttoned my trousers, it dawned on me that the *silence* around me was nearly total. No one can walk through the woods without stepping on a branch, *something*. But being the least experienced member of the hunting party, I didn't *know* these woods. I looked behind me, expecting to see Férger, but I was really *alone*.

"Not wanting to be taken for a buffoon, I kept going, praying that this all wasn't a joke at my expense. I simply couldn't lose face. So, like the fool who approaches the edge of a cliff with a smile on his face and not a care in his heart, I pressed on."

. . . not wanting to see more, but unable to leave the nickelodeon, for they stood behind her, forcing her to watch, she saw the six remaining hunters make a curious formation. The man in the middle (him she remembered with a twist of her stomach and a flutter of her heart—not to mention the guilty flush of her cheeks) advanced slowly, as befitted his years, while the remaining hunters circled around him, carefully staying out of the gray-haired man's line of sight.

Unable to stare at the doomed man and his hunters, she looked in vain for deer in those dense woods, but saw none. And the lone hunter to the north kept advancing. . . .

"When I stalked *out* of the woods, into a clearing, I was shocked. Especially after I waited a few minutes for the others. It was so *eerie*, Brent—just the faint sound of the breeze as it blew through denuded oaks and heavily boughed evergreens, that special tangy smell of decay, and me, alone in that rough clearing. No gunfire, no voices, nothing but the wind and my labored breathing.

"Presently, I realized that I'd been played for a fool, yet I was torn—go back into the woods, or press on for the next swath of trees, perhaps an acre away? Then something struck me funny—if the others were as unlucky as I, seeing no deer, why hadn't they emerged from the woods yet? I stood there trying to make up my mind, when the answer came.

"A shot shook the stillness, but there was something *wrong*. I knew little about firearms, but I did know how loud a single rifle shot *should* be. What I'd heard sounded like a *cannon*. At the time I thought that more than one of them had sighted on a single deer, shooting simultaneously. So . . . I decided to run back into the woods, in case I could be of some help—"

• • •

. . . Her view shifted from an impossible height to swiftly descend, as the focus tightened on the middle man, whom she so casually betrayed to Otis, as Zach kneeled down to tie a bootlace. Then, the view spread out, to include the five circling men, each of whom stopped, and took steady aim at their half-seen target. When Otis gave a low whistle—the signal to fire—she pressed small palms over her ears. For she heard the soft shrill noise come from those soft puckered lips (Otis, you said you'd do it, make it look like an accident—not a slaughter), but instead of masking out the sound, her cupped palms intensified the noise. She heard the five simultaneous clicks of five triggers pulled in unison—the resulting blast echoed, thundering, in the tortured confines of her shuddering psyche.

As she watched, helpless to prevent the massacre, something went wrong—just as the men fired, the target moved, looked up in time to see one of his assassins, before jerking aside. With a sputter of movement, the scene changed to the lone hunter waiting outside the woods—his body stiffened when he heard the shot (oh, please, not that sound!), then relaxed for a second before he ran—straight into the massacre.

And the scene changed yet again, a blood-spurting close-up of Zach's shoulder . . . from which his left arm hung by a few soggy threads of flesh and sinew.

She rubbed her nose, trying to wipe away the cloying blood reek, but the smell filled her nose, her lungs. The air was impregnated with the lingering redolence. Helplessly, she watched as Zach stumbled with frenzied swiftness to the north.

And all the while, the twins watched her, expressions of feigned indifference at her plight frozen in their eyes.

"—what a foolhardy thing I was doing until I was into the woods, running *toward* the aftershock of that huge blast. Then I saw . . . instinctively, I hunkered down behind the fullest pine I could find. I feared to go any farther, for . . . I saw him. Ewert. Running toward me, but backward, only looking around once in a while to get his bearings.

"He had his gun on his shoulder, aimed at something still in the woods. To Otis' right I saw Porter Winston, to Otis' left I saw Horton. Both ran forward, but with their torsos twisted to face each other, aimed at a central target, or each other. I couldn't tell from where I was crouched.

"Otis was fifteen feet from where I'd hidden myself. He sighted *in* on something that emerged from the woods, wheezing, *sobbing*. A low, moist sound I can still hear to this day. Like ragged breathing after a drop-dead run, only so *desperate* . . . loud, too, as if he were twenty inches away, and not twenty feet.

"Knowing it was sheer folly, I peered out from behind that tree. I saw your grandfather and Ferger bring up the rear of that *circle* around . . . the bloody thing. Only . . . it wasn't a wounded deer, but Zach Roberts. One arm . . . *hung*. He wore this expression of pain and fear and *betrayal* in his glazed eyes."

Holiday's voice quivered. His chest rose and fell with noticeable and obviously painful shudders, and his eyes stared unseeing past Brent, as he went on, "Then he stumbled—Zach—and the rest of them, they were like a well-oiled *machine*, a killing creation. They sighted as one, drew a bead on him, Otis shouted 'Fire!' and then . . . Zach just seemed to—"

. . . Explode. A fine mist of pink-red-white matter covered her field of vision. She pawed at her eyes, to wipe away the spray of blood and bone; when she opened them (Oh, Otis, not like *that* . . . oh, *why*, why?), *she saw the hunters lower their rifles as the lone witness behind the tree stood with trembling legs and tried to run away. . . .*

"—insane to run, but after what I saw, my only chance was to escape those woods. Then I heard Horton call my name, order me back. I considered putting the end of my rifle in my mouth, pulling the trigger, but I had a half-assed notion of them turning themselves in. After all this time, I'm still not sure *why* I turned around. I just *did*, even though none of them were running after me, rifles shouldered, ready to fire. I do recall thinking the sheriff wouldn't go hard on them, no matter what *I* had to say, and then . . . I was back where they all stood, still *circling* poor torn-up Zach, as if he were going to up and run off again—"

Holiday reached over to slosh the dregs of the brandy into his snifter. He swallowed it with one gulp before continuing in a hoarse whisper, "When I came near enough to see him clearly, he . . . *was still breathing*. I *heard* him—a bubbling, sighing noise, like filthy water being sucked down a half-clogged pipe. But it was so *crazy*. . . . You see a chunk of his head was gone. Just *gone*, the way you'd lop the top off a soft-boiled egg. Blood all over, *red*, surging out, out. He was shiny, *reeking* from it, but . . . he still had both eyes.

"He was *looking* at me, mouth jerking, as blood foamed through his teeth. *Red* striped his face . . . and . . . *I don't know how*, but he managed to keep himself upright, swaying as he half sat, half stood, but *upright*. His . . . brain was all soft, pulpy pale, *showing*—

"Otis turned to stare at me, with that thick-lipped *smile*, and then . . . he said, as if nothing was amiss, nothing at *all*, 'The *buck* isn't quite done in, and our guest hasn't had a chance to shoot yet. Let's let *him* do the honors—' "

Brent's mouth fell open, tongue and teeth dust-dry as Wilbur droned on, "So . . . after they all drew a bead on *me*, your grandfather and all the rest, I . . . raised and shouldered my rifle. I considered spraying as many of them as I could, but . . . as I took aim, I told myself, 'Only putting him out of his misery, only—' and then . . . I . . . I squeezed the trigger. I couldn't take my eyes off that rounded pool of . . . *brains* . . . for then, after . . . *after* . . . his body fell still—"

. . . not caring anymore, unable to keep watching and listening and smelling and knowing, she whirled away from the whirring nickelodeon. She broke into a run across the reverberating floorboards, footfalls pounding hollow and loud, screaming as she ran, "I am so *sorry*, Zachary . . . no more, no more, please, let me go, I want to die again . . . I AM SORRY!!! *Hear?*"

She pounded on the locked door of the building, dimly aware that she was being followed, the steps slow and cautious, as she cried, "What more do you *want* from me? I died once for you, must I die for—" *and as the realization hit her, she fell sobbing to the floor. They stood over her, watching, as Abigail Roberts Ewert left them once again. Then stood ready as the body at their feet stirred, then feebly asked,* "Brent, where are you?"

• • •

In an anguished monotone, Holiday finished relating the events of November 21, 1913. His father-in-law and the others all but *scraped* what was left of Roberts into a blanket ("—bought at my store, wouldn't you know?"), and slung the cigar-shaped bundle into the back of the Roberts car. Which *Otis* then drove back into town. Horton pulled Wilbur aside, told him it was all an *accident* . . . with no one to blame except Zachary himself, "for getting in the line of *fire*."

With downcast eyes, Holiday related how he and Horton got into the roadster and took off for town. Horton drove, while Wilbur stared through the roadside trees at the quiet town across the river.

"I thought, 'This town may not know it yet, but it's *dead* . . . no place can exist without honor.' And to this day, I'm not certain if what happened next was a trick of the sun coming through the gathering cloud cover, or if it *was* something real, quite strange, but the whole town *dimmed*. Everything looked . . . less *alive*. As if its very *soul* had up and gone, leaving husks behind. Form, without *substance* . . . but the altered appearance of the town didn't change when the clouds shifted above us. . . .

"Finally, Horton spoke. He acted as if I'd merely bagged a deer, a *horned* buck, that Otis had the honor of driving into town. He turned to me, asking, 'Come spring, you and Hortense will be looking over house plans, no?'

"I mulled *that* over for a while, figured out what the old so-and-so was driving at, and realized I'd better go along with him—after all, Zach had *my* bullet in him, too. So . . . speaking very slowly, very clearly—I couldn't count on being civil to him if I had to repeat myself—I told Horton that I wanted the *biggest*, most *e*xpensive house in town, 'better than yours, or that of any member of Otis' goddamn *Hunting Club*.' And I told him I hoped Otis paid Horton very well for his 'services' for *I* wasn't paying one bloodred cent for my house.

"And I didn't . . . but I do know that every last *dime* in my bank account and stock certificates was generated by *me*. The others made themselves into wealthy, respected men in *Ewerton*, thanks to Otis' little . . . *paychecks*."

In the darkness, Wilbur leaned back in his chair, his breath slow and deep. While his host composed himself, Brent knew he should hate Holiday for what he had done, but yet, he couldn't *blame* him. Roberts was dying; Wilbur had had nothing to do with *that*. He was probably only brought along as a cover.

"Otis paid all of them off, and still had plenty for himself. And I . . . I was sucked into it all, my silence housing me, my lot thrown in with theirs by the memory of five rifle barrels aimed at my head.

"Funny, I used to think that if there had been no Abby Andersen, there would've been no Ewerton. *She* was the spark that lit Ewert's blood lust, which was worse than power and money lust combined. Today, their affair would've ended in her divorcing Roberts, or vice versa, but then . . . small-town people didn't do that."

Brent tried to remember Abby Ewert's face from the photo Bitsy showed him, but all he came up with was a vague teasing smile under a drooping hat brim. But Wilbur had a photo album, too . . . flipping through it, Brent asked, "Got a picture of Abby?"

"Here, I'll find it." Wilbur reached for the black-bound photo album. Paging through the stiff black leaves, Holiday quickly located the picture. Brent would've recognized that face *anywhere*. Wanting to wimper, Brent forced the sound back down his throat. *Zoe*. Or the *twin* of his wife, dressed in a long sweeping shirtwaist with puffed sleeves from the early 1900s, hair puffed out around her face, one eye turning out slightly. Her resemblance to Maeve and Mae *was* strong . . . like mother and daughter.

Helplessly, Brent cupped a hand over his lips, to stifle a rising scream—a gesture which Wilbur mistook for sleepiness. Closing the album, he suggested, "It's quite late. We can talk in the morning." Glancing at his moon watch, he added, more for himself than for Brent, "Midnight already . . . seemed like *minutes*. . . . "

Pushing aside the curls of newsprint, Palmer rested his chin on his folded arms. Seconds later he was asleep, sliding deeper into internal darkness, ears deaf to the crunch of tires below his room, as well as the muffled metallic thump of a car door opening and closing. And the scuff of a *single* pair of shoes on gravel. . . .

NINETY-SIX

JULY 26, 1988

Out of the darkness of summer shadows, morning established itself in the hazy glow of gold . . .

. . . as Brent Nimitz slept uneasily in Wilbur Holiday's house—

—as Palmer Winston (formerly Lt. Winston, U.S. Occupation Army) dozed, head pillowed on his duffel bag, as he waited for a State-bound plane—

—and as Palmer Nemmitz leaned face-forward in sleep crossed arms in his farmhouse bedroom—

The three men shared a strange dream of the most *real* sort. . . .

It wasn't *fair* that Bitsy and Buddy, Irving and Una, all had to crowd into Uncle Ross' old junker just 'cause Mommy and Daddy and Una's aunt and uncle wanted to see *their* friends down-state—'specially when Una and Irving could've stayed overnight at Palmer Winston's house.

But *they* said only *Irving* could. It wasn't *nice* for little girls to stay with little boys overnight. Even if *his* Mommy and Daddy said it was okay, so Una stomped her feet and dragged the toes of her ugly shoes along the sidewalk until she wore holes in the scruffed tips, *then* bit Irving's ear.

After that, Daddy said she and Irving *both* had to go, 'cause he couldn't take his eyes off either one of them for two minutes.

Una thought the ride was bumpy. She had to pee all the time, and looking out the window for out-of-state license plates wasn't *fun*. That was okay for Buddy-Duddy, Bitsy-Brains and Irv-Thing to do. . . .

Una sat, arms crossed, lips downturned, eyes scrunched up, all the way to Madison. She wouldn't take food or soda pop from Aunt Fern or Uncle Ross, which made Daddy mad. "Una, you're eight years old, not eight months!" Una pushed out her tongue, drumming her heels against the backseat.

When they got to Madison, Una didn't like it. The buildings were dark and funny-looking. And the houses were real old, like on Roberts Street back home. Una hated them.

She stuck out her tongue at Mommy and Daddy's friends the Hansens. They said, "My, how *precocious* Una is," but it didn't sound like a compliment. She only stayed *in* the Hansens' ugly house for a couple of hours, before the grown-ups shooed all the kids out to play in the yard (Una ripped the heads off Mrs. Hansen's flowers just *because*). After that, the grown-ups came out saying it was time to go home.

They all got back in the Ford but hadn't driven very far before Mommy got all excited, telling Uncle Ross, "Go down that street—isn't that Otis and Abby? Honk before we miss them!" Uncle Ross honked, and a Haynes roadster slowed down.

Una opened her eyes a little, just to see who the people were. The man was big and jowly, with liver lips and little veins all over his nose. The lady was real pale with a short veil over her face and an ugly orange dress with dots on it. The couple *did* know the grown-ups, so cars squeezed past the two cars parked side by side in the middle of the street until the grown-ups agreed to meet at the couple's house.

It was *real* big, brick-covered, two stories and an attic with windows in the roof. Una said it was ugly. Irving stomped on her feet for that. The veiled lady said "How *dreadful*," to no one at all. Inside the house was lots of fancy furniture like the Holidays had in their big ugly house.

After Una knocked a saucer to the floor, grinding the remains into the oriental rug, Mommy said they should all go play outside. They did, but it wasn't fun 'cause Buddy wouldn't play doctor so she snuck into the house and up the stairs that went around the back of the house.

It was *real* quiet and cool in the hallway. Una was looking for the bathroom when she tripped on something small on the floor.

A *doll* shoe. White kid, with ribbon ties, big enough for a Tickle Toes doll, the one Daddy promised Una if she was a good girl, but Una wasn't getting the doll even if she *was* good 'cause Una and Irving found all the Christmas presents in the hall closet. And there was only an ugly Minerva-head doll and stuffed Tabby cat for her.

Turning the doll shoe over and over in her hands, Una got *real* mad, 'cause the couple didn't say anything about having a little girl. Shoe in hand, Una tiptoed in her scruffy and holey-toed shoes, looking in rooms . . . until she found the little girl's room. They *had* lied. It was like a Wish Book page, all flirty eyes and sleepy eyes and Teddy bear eyes *staring* at Una.

There were *three* dollhouses. The cream bungalow and the brick-patterned house plus a *wooden* dollhouse with *real doors*. And *two* doll buggies, the biggest size in silver and blue reed, and the other two-tone green with pale green stripe wheels, the one Bitsy had *her* heart set on for Christmas and there were dolls in the buggies . . . a *big* "Baby Sunshine" in a pink dress, and a doll with "Baby Dimples" embroidered on her white organdy dress and bonnet trimmed in flutters of squished-up lace.

Una couldn't believe it. Piled on the white enameled brass bed with the flouncy white and pink cover were Perfect Beauty, with a human hair wig and rosettes of lace and organza on her organdy gown, "Billy Boy" in black velveteen, an "Aunt Jemima," plus the clown bear Una wanted last year, its pink, white and blue fur lustrous, its clown hat and ruffled collar *perfect*.

And a Kewpie doll, the special "Fairy Princess" with teeth and a *tongue*, plus a great *big* "Flossie Flirt" doll, the one the catalogue said *walked*. She went and moved the doll. As the eyes rolled, it said "Maaa-maaa."

Sitting in a Doll Crib De Luxe was a Tickle Toes doll, the biggest Una had *ever* seen. The thumb was stuck in its open mouth, its flirty eyes stared right *at* Una. And it wore the most *expensive* outfit, the hand-crocheted sweater and cap.

Tickle Toes was prettier in the *catalogue*. Una squeezed one of the soft rubber legs ("Just like a real baby," the Wish Book said), heard a cry, then tried the other leg to get a different cry.

Pulling the soft rubber thumb out of its mouth, she put the ribboned pacifier in its place. *This* doll had both shoes on. So Una looked until she found *another* "Tickle Toes." A smaller one, sitting on the green and ivory fancy doll dresser in the corner, near the *real* fur Spitz dog, the white *Angora* cat, and the brown Mohair bear. *This* doll had a shoe missing. Una put it on, then tweaked both legs. Just *because*.

And in *another* corner was "Baby Sunshine," and "Dolly Sunshine," and a "Toddle Tot." Una hunkered down, Buster Brown bangs in her eyes, and peered into the doll houses.

Complete sets of Tootsie Toy furniture, Daisy furniture with the pink metal bedroom Bitsy wanted, and in the *big* house, the *wood* one, was Really Truly *walnut* and *mahogany* furniture. The *good* stuff, nailed and glued, like the Wish Book said.

Una played with the dollhouses, only she got mad 'cause *she* didn't have a dollhouse, only a shoe box Uncle Ross made and furnished with spools and matchboxes. Sitting cross-legged on the floor, Una got madder and *madder*. Metal chairs and beds and tables hit flowered pink wallpaper with muted *pocks*. Una kicked over the bungalow just *because*, then picked up the Angora cat and hit it.

"Wanta hear a story, kitty?" she said real soft, so the grown-ups wouldn't hear. "Uncle Ross got mad at his cat, so he took it and threw it in the leaf fire, only the next morning, there it was, wanting milk. So he took the cat and threw it in the *river*, but the next day it came back, all wet and hungry." Una pulled tufts of fur off the toy cat.

"So Uncle Ross got *real* mad and shot the cat, and when it *still* came back, he sawed it in *half*, but next morning it was back. Uncle Ross got real *tired* of it then, so he took his ax and cut off its head, and the next day it came to the back door, with its head in its mouth, only it didn't eat 'cause when it opened its mouth it lost its head and—I don't *like* you, kitty." Una tore off the cat's head, and threw the body on the ruffled bed. Una thought she hit a "maa-maa" doll, but the muffled *"Mine!"* didn't come from any *doll*.

There was a wardrobe in the room, big and wooden and flower-carved with gold handles. One door wasn't all the way shut. Una heard a soft "Shush!" then the same sound Irving made when Una stuffed his shirttail down his throat, just *because*.

That was why there were so many dolls. The mean people had two little girls. *Neither* wanted to play with Una. She was mad, real *mad*. Clomping to the wardrobe in her ruined shoes with the thick soles that were supposed to *last*, Una yanked open the door.

All Una saw were *dresses*. Wool jersey, embroidered velveteens, wool challis, the kind Una *never* wore. Poking the dresses, she saw one of the many pairs of shoes had *legs* and *stockings* in them. Una heard *two* little girls, so she opened the other door, but *doll* clothes hung there, so Una poked the big dresses . . . until her hand hit something real *funny*—

A girl came out from behind the dresses, with a soft, *slithery* cloth sound that made Una pee her pants—

The girl was six or so, but . . . Una didn't want to *think* about how her heads and arms were all different sizes. All four of her eyes were funny-looking, the left ones wall-eyed. Real *horrible*. Una tried to run, but *couldn't*. Her legs were sticky hot where the tinkle ran down.

The *little* head said, "Go 'way, ugly," and the *big* head said, "Get out—and don't *tell*!" The wall-eyed *monster* came closer, closer, hand *out* for—

"Una? *Uuuuuna?* Where *are* you? You're in *biiiiiig* trouble. If you don't come we'll all get whupped. Una? *Uuuuuuna*, where *are*—"

Una spit at the monster before she left, hitting the small head in the cheek. Then Una *ran*.

She told Bitsy she couldn't hold it and had to go. All the way home Irving called Una Tinkle-Pot, makes it nice and hot, only Una was too scared to beat him up . . . just *because*.

NINETY-SEVEN

Nemmitz woke with a start; the back of his neck cracked as his head jerked with residual fear. The more-than-a-dream faded before he opened his eyes, but one thought remained— Palmer was *glad* Una Winston died the way she did. The *hurt* the twins must've felt, knowing they could never play with normal children—despite a whole Wish Book full of dolls, buggies, and dollhouses—made him feel weak, sapped inside.

And you only compounded that agony, he reminded himself, not wanting to open his eyes again—ever. But he heard the early-morning chirp of birds, and smelled the odor of grass, and the sour tang of sun hitting acidic earth and drying cornstalks. Praying for daylight, and sanity, he sat up.

But when he opened his eyes, the first thing that came to his mind was, *Did I dream everything last night?* The hours he'd spent reading the newsprinted walls *had* to have been heat-madness. Then he remembered his wallpaper had never been *pink*-flowered. And as perfect as the rest of the room looked, it had all been *changed*, just as surely as *he'd* been moved—desk, chair, and all—from the center of the room to the west wall.

Clean, dustless, neat. Pink rosed walls cheerful in the bright sunlight. Bed smoothly made, covered with a flouncy ruffled white and pink comforter, not the tossed contents of his closet. His stack of unread sporting and hunting magazines was gone, but the "Thurdsay's Child" sampler still hung above his bed. As for the dresser . . . if Palmer didn't half-remember the way it *had* been only last night, he might have sworn his dresser had *always* looked this way. For a dizzying second, he asked himself, Was *it this way all along*?

A silver-backed comb and brush set was neatly arranged on the white lace dresser scarf, next to his wood and tortoise-shell set. Gold-brown hairs intertwined in the pale bristles of the silvery brush. Next to his tray of small change (which included Mercury dimes and wheat pennies) lay a rose-topped enameled compact, near a half-full bottle of La Rose Jacqueminot perfume.

With shaking fingers, Palmer lifted the glass stopper from the delicate flask. *Her* odor lingered, like a soft touch on his cheek.

There were scattered hairpins, tortoiseshell hair combs, and pearls on a thin gold chain among his few remaining belongings, plus a calfskin-covered Bible, with a golden-lettered name stamped on the cover . . . MAEVE MAE EWERT. And . . . hanging from the mirror, Mae's puppet mask.

Palmer picked up the New Testament, tracing the golf-leaf letters with a trembling fingertip. Seeing their last name, as in Ewert . . . as in *Otis*, something exploded inside him like a swift-blooming flower. Gently, he replaced the Bible among *their* belongings.

Palmer's clothes were hung up once again in the closet . . . but hanging *next* to them were silky, musky-sweet smelling dresses, on quilted mauve hangers—grabbing a shirt and a pair of trousers, he shut the door quickly.

Across the hall, he rummaged through Brent's abandoned belongings, until he found the half-finished drawing of Zoe and her cat. Zoe's likeness wasn't *quite* like that of the twins— but he doubted that the Happy Wanderer would know the difference.

• • •

Brent sat up in his brass bed, looking stuporously at the scattering of soft gray animal hair clinging to the depression in his bedding. Even the *chance* that Duffy had come here, had *been* with Brent as he slept, gave the young man hope.

Breakfast was oatmeal—not Brent's favorite, but it smelled good. Sprinkling a tablespoon of sugar in his bowl, Holiday said, "I'll answer whatever questions you have—after we eat."

Brent decided to hold off asking about Zoe and Mrs. Ewert until he heard what Holiday had to say about other things. He didn't want to scare him into silence, or self-serving lies . . . in case Holiday had done even *worse* things than killing a half-dead man.

Winston woke with a stiff neck and a dull headache behind his eyes. His entire *body* was stiff, aching; when he opened his eyes, and saw the ticket booth of the Ewerton depot, he whispered to the echoing wood and linoleum and plaster, "I *was* in here all along, I was, I *was* . . . oh, *let* me have been here all along."

NINETY-EIGHT

Stewing over the possibility that he had a case of body-snatching on his hands, Stu Sawyer was sorely tempted to tell the operator who asked him if he'd accept a long-distance call from Beatrice Nimmitz, in *Minong*, of all places, "No way!" But resignedly, he replied, "Yes, Operator, put her—"

"Stuart? This is your cousin Bitsy. I'm with Angela and Dick, in *Minong*—"

"The nice lady told me already. Bitsy, this *is* the official line—"

"Stuart, did you talk to Palmer yet?"

"Bitsy, I was elected *sheriff*, not baby-sitter for an old *coot*."

"—tried to call him all morning. There's been no answer, so I figured you could—"

" 'Could' *what*, Bitsy? Send out *bloodhounds*? I've enough problems—" Lenny Wilkes stood outside the door, pearls of sweat beading his crew cut, a look of uncertainty on his shiny face. Anxiously, Stu waved him in. "Just quit worrying, okay? He's a big boy. Good-*bye*, Beatrice." Bitsy's "*Well*, Stuart!" was a faint squawk as he dropped the receiver. Giving Lenny a smile he didn't feel, Stu asked, "Well? *Was* he in—"

Lenny settled down in the office's other chair. "I looked over the coffin. Ritter and his boys removed it from the vault, so I could—"

Stu winced, holding his nose, but Lenny protested with a shake of his head, "Nope. No seeping, no decomposition. Not a hair on the satin pillow. Showroom fresh. *Nothing* rotted in that coffin. Old bastard was *dead*—"

Stu brought his fisted hands down hard on the desk. "Yeah, and *you* said that about Zoe Nimitz, too! And I don't know where the fuck *she* is, either!"

When Holiday pulled on a beige flannel jacket over his long-sleeved shirt, prior to their walk into town, Brent was puzzled. And misgiving turned to distinct uneasiness when Wilbur asked casually, "Think that shirt will be warm enough?" He handed Brent a pale gray felt hat with a wide brim, then put on his own camel-colored fedora. When Holiday opened the front door, a gentle breeze blew in a rattling of curled, dried *fall* leaves. Willingly, Brent put on the corduroy jacket his host found in the downstairs closet.

The tree leaves were opalescent, pulsating in bright colors against the deep blue autumnal sky. Holiday scuffed through piles of fallen leaves along each street, craggy features lit up with a childish smile. "My favorite part of fall," he admitted sheepishly, as crackling leaves spiraled with each upward kick of his shoes. Brent nodded numbly, nose full of the special fall odor of crumbled leaves, drying grass and woodsmoke . . . even though the intense sapphire sky was devoid of smoke.

Reaching up to touch the branch of a low-hanging maple, Brent rubbed a red-orange leaf between his fingers. It left the branch . . . as easily as a leaf ready to fall naturally. Beside him, Holiday stopped in mid-shuffle.

"Same principle as the sidewalks . . . I always thought autumn was the time for long walks and talks. Don't you agree?"

Placing a bright leaf in his trouser pocket, Brent said, "Beats the heat . . . wish I'd known about this before." To show how accepting he was (and how willing he'd be to listen to *whatever* Wilbur might tell him), Brent shuffled through the crisp scattering of leaves for a few feet.

When they reached the south end of Roberts Street, Brent cautiously asked, "How did you come to find yourself here after you, uh . . ."

"Died?" Holiday's smile looked genuine, but his eyes were shadowed by his hat brim, and the clear deep blue of autumn shadow. Brent listened carefully over the crackle of leaves, to detect any evasiveness in his host's story.

"I really don't know. One minute I was lying on a floor upstairs. I felt my blood slow . . . every second I grew colder, stiffer. Then I was waking slow, *very* slowly. When I was warm enough to *feel*, I realized I was in my own bed."

He steered Brent down Crescent Street, as he went on, "When I reached the point where my body and soul were *used* to each other again, my flesh started to . . . *pull*. As the sensation washed over me, I simply rested on my bed, unable to fight it. I had *opted* for the unknown, therefore I had to endure it."

Having reached the intersection, they strolled to Ewert Avenue. Brent asked, "Are you sure this *is* your old body . . . or is it another mind trick this place likes to play?"

"I'm not sure. Everything I've encountered here *seems* to be real—even when *I* don't wish it to be—yet the mutability of the place gives one reason to *doubt* at times. I *think* I'm alive. I need food, warmth, companionship . . . I sleep, I dream, I think, I *want*. . . .

"My need to sustain myself has been taken into consideration. When I open my refrigerator, there's food inside. If I were still *dead* my pantry should be empty, since I wouldn't *care* about eating. And *you* managed to find food, so apparently whatever runs this show wants us to live."

Brent stopped in the middle of a pile of windblown leaves, asking, "But what about the twins? Are they real, or ghosts, or what?"

Holiday pulled his coat collar close to his neck, adding, "By an odd quirk of fate, Otis and Abby remained childless for nearly *ten years*, but in 1923, Abby found herself in a delicate condition—"

North of the walking men, one thin and blond, the other dark and stocky, far enough away so as not to be seen by them,

Winston circled the depot, discharge papers and duffel bag in hand, trying to figure out what in the hell *happened*. He *should* be in Seattle, calling Palmer, not *here* yet. But the small voice crooned, *It's all right, it's fall, isn't it? You came home in the fall, so it's all right.*

NINETY-NINE

Arnie the bartender was watching a syndicated game show when Palmer walked into the Rusty Hinge that afternoon. He'd spent the better part of the morning looking for the Wanderer. Dry-mouthed from the heat, he sat—drinkless—at the bar for five minutes, until a commercial came on, and Arnie finally noticed him.

Glancing up at the wall-mounted set, where a spot extolling the remarkable staying power of a toilet bowl freshener aired, Palmer snapped, "Thank the Lord for singing toilet bowls—otherwise I'd have died of thirst. You *know* game shows are fixed, don't you? Folks don't win 'less they swear to jump five, *ten* feet in the air when the girl in front of Curtain Number Three shows her cleavage—"

Arnie ignored Palmer's jibes with cheerful aplomb—Nemmitz had been a customer at the Rusty Hinge longer than game shows had been on TV. Sliding a can of beer and a glass across the worn imitation wood counter, he remarked, "Been hoping you'd stop by my shift—I got something I want for you to see."

A game show came on the TV; with one eye keeping track of the action on the screen above, Arnie opened the cash register and lifted up the change tray. Taking out something wrapped in a paper-clipped napkin and handing it to Palmer, Arnie watched the screaming woman in the polyester pants suit and six necklaces jump up and down over her prize—a whirlpool and six sets of designer bath towels.

"Arnie, where did this *come* from?" Palmer held the unfolded dollar bill in a liver-spotted hand, his eyes unable to focus on its printed surface. When Arnie glanced in his direction, he asked, "You gonna be sick? If you are, you know where the gent's is—don't puke on *that*, whatever you do."

He reached for the 1923 goldback dollar, but Palmer hugged

it against himself with a back-off glint in his green eyes. Arnie withdrew his hand. "Women left it in here, oh, lemme see, the last time you and Winston"—Arnie crossed himself with an odd look in his eyes—"were in here. Was sitting in a back booth. Far back, so I couldn't see her plain. Had on dark clothes. Didn't say much. Had a 7-Up and left this as a tip. Pretty hair. Color of a taffy—hey! Palmer! I only wanted for you to *see* that! Come back you son of a . . . oh, *shit*," Arnie finished as Palmer got into his Rambler and drove off, burning rubber like a sixteen-year-old whose license just arrived in the mail.

Sighing, Arnie wrote "P. Nimmitz, 1 beer, 7-26-88" on a slip of paper, stuffed it in the cash register, thought it over, then added, "Took my tip—$1.00!" before returning his attention to the game show.

Winston hid in the depot's antiquated restroom, slumped on the floor near the gushing urinals. He tried to fight the voice which gently urged him to go home, see his parents—for he was half-certain that Porter and Gayleen were dead and buried.

But the maddening thing was that he wasn't *sure* anymore—not only of his parent's living-or-dead status, but not *sure* of *anything* any more. As in what *year* it was, what month, how old he was—he could've been *born* in this ammonia-tinged room, for all *he* knew.

Feeling his face with spastic fingers, Winston couldn't even remember what he *looked* like. In frustration, he banged his head on the graffiti-incised wooden walls ("Mary Swaine Fuks Good"), but was rewarded with a bigger headache. Yet, the more panic-riddled his thinking became, the more gentle and comforting the tiny voice became. . . .

ONE HUNDRED

Brent and Wilbur reached the grocery store. Holiday chose to lean against the door, hat pushed down low over his green eyes.

Wilbur told him about a carny Tarot reading gone *very* wrong: One by one, those who had their cards read by Madam Zola heard nothing but the *truth* told about themselves, both past *and* present. While nothing *specific* about Zach Roberts' death was revealed, after Death came up for Abby Ewert, the reading ended. Holiday mused that the card reader's gender most likely saved her life, before he related the unfortunate events that transpired in the mentalist's tent—

"—enough to make Abby faint dead away. *I* felt slightly sick. It was so *obvious*, that was the worst of it. Her being in a delicate state and all. Otis ordered me to drive her to their house.

"Hortense and I placed Abby on the divan. When she came to, she began *punching* her midsection, screaming for us to cut out the baby . . . *then* I supposed it was just her reaction to the mentalist and the Tarot reading—"

"Bitsy said Stu found a postcard in your hand—it was a Tarot card, wasn't it?"

"From the very deck used in '23. It's in the library . . . uhm, your aunt didn't say where the 'postcard' went to, did she?" Wilbur smiled, a tight lips-sealed upturn of his mouth that Brent found slightly condescending.

"She claimed Stu couldn't find it . . . it's with the rest of the deck, isn't it? The Lovers?" Pushing aside his jacket, Brent's host shoved his hands into his pockets, as his smile went sour.

"A final self-deprecating joke. Too bad Stu didn't take the card with him. Perhaps it might've assuaged some of my guilt—"

Holiday stared down at his shoes. "But it's over." He lifted his head, resting it against the door. "Hortense got some sherry into Abby, then we helped her upstairs. I'll never forget, there was a rose-patterned window set into the stairway landing, and the street lamp outside cast a red splotch onto Abby's midsection. Turned her blue dress *black* there. . . .

"Once Abby was in bed, my wife and I went downstairs, to wait for Otis. Things were strained between us—but Hortense was so shaken she forgot she couldn't stand me, and babbled about what we'd witnessed in that tent.

"For once, she was most astute, asking if the mentalist meant a *farmer* when he spoke of seeing that 'man-thing' of mud and wood. Either a farmer, or someone connected with those things. But the first thing *I* thought of was of the sawdust sprinkled on the floor behind my counter . . . tan and crumbling, like the soil in that man's vision. I had good reason to think of my store in connection with such an obviously sexual vision.

"Anyhow, the mentalist was found dead the next day—
Coroner Wilkes said it was 'natural causes.' With the remains
of the Robertsville Hunting Club on hand, I had no doubt of
what had happened. Still, more than one person who was in that
tent breathed easier after reading of his death in the *Herald*.

"So. Things went on as they had before Otis brought the
carny to town. Abby got bigger, Mona Ferger kept on screwing Otis so her husband Fred could keep his job—yes, Dead
Fred *was* Otis', but that's a moot point now—and I . . . I kept
on with my storeroom assignations with your grandmother.

"Don't take it as an insult. I *wanted* to leave Hortense to
marry Treeva. But I was over a barrel—leave Hortense, and
Horton could make things . . . difficult for me. There's no
statute of limitations for murder—

"I *know* he was dying, but after *I* shot him he was *dead*.
And Treeva didn't know. None of the wives did. Suspected,
maybe. But none of them *knew*. And . . . I didn't think Treeva
would want to marry a murderer." Holiday paused to lick
dry lips, before going on in a rush, "She and I were . . .
lovers for three years, staring in 1920, friends for longer than
that. She used to visit my store when she was a girl, and new
in town. She came in one July day, eyes all wide, and said,
'Are *you* the gentleman with the marvelous house? I've never
seen anything so grand. Do you decorate for *all* the holidays?'

"It started like that. After Treeva came in all giddy over a
little bunting draped over my porch, I made it a point to
decorate the house to the hilt for every holiday . . . she loved
it so. Even after she was . . . gone, I never stopped decorat-
ing my house for her. . . .

"I loved her long before she married Enoch, but I was
chained to Hortense. People didn't *do* that—divorce—so
readily in those days. The options for 'respectible' people in
the Midwest were *different*. And it wasn't Horton's money
that kept me with Hortense. Or even the figurative gun pressed
to my temple. People just didn't *do* those things. Not *then*.
Divorce was something tainted, illicit. Only people of the
'wrong' sort did that, and there *was* Hortense to think of. I
hated her by then, as much as the relatives who'd arranged
our union, but she *was* the mother of my daughters. God help
me, I didn't love them either . . . but I couldn't disgrace them.

"I know what Treeva and I were doing was wrong—the
Bible said so, and I knew the Good Book as well as any man,
but yet . . . neither of us had a *real* marriage. We were both

lonely; what we had *mentally*, *spirtually*, was more binding to us than our legal unions to others.

"There came a time when friendship progressed. We tried not to succumb, but . . . we both knew that we were doing wrong, but we went ahead anyhow. Enoch was beating Treeva long before we became intimate, so she had a damned-if-I-do, damned-if-I-don't attitude. Maybe it hurt her less to be beat for what she *did* instead of being pounded for what she *hadn't* done. I wish she hadn't married him, but he *needed* a wife. Appearances sake. Despite all the money Otis gave him, Enoch remained the eternal lout. Bastard . . . but he was a bastard with money, and a farm, so her people thought him a good man. You see, while Treeva was lovely to *me*, others . . . thought her plain.

"She and I, we spoke of running off, but after her twins—"

If the twins were Wilbur's, and Winston *was screwing Vernilla*—but as if he'd anticipated Brent's question, Holiday added, "The twins weren't mine. If I'd suspected Vernilla was mine, I'd have warned Winston away from her. It's too bad what Enoch had done to Palmer. I learned of it from the doctor who . . . did it. The good doctor couldn't eat solid food for a week, and I couldn't use my right hand for longer than that . . . but he billed me anyway. That was the lowest blow on Enoch's part. Where was I?

"My time with Treeva reached its peak in January of 1924. By then, we knew that Hortense *knew*. Not who the woman was, thank God, but my wife *knew*. We knew we had to break it off . . . but it was so damned *hard*."

In the chill wind, Holiday's eyes watered, and he rubbed them self-consciously. "I *loved* Treeva. She was . . . *good*. What we had hadn't tainted her. . . . That day, January third, was out last 'time' together. We hadn't planned it that way, but after Abby broke into the store—" Holiday stepped aside, his left hand snaking out of his pocket to encircle the doorknob next to the broken pane of glass, as he said, "I can explain much better in here . . . if you're up to it." With only the slightest trepidation, Brent followed him into the store. The remainder of the broken glass in the pane dropped to the sidewalk with the most delicate sound, softer than a snowfall, but sharper than the splinter of thin ice.

ONE HUNDRED ONE

On Wilkerson Avenue, not far from Mill Road and the Mill Bridge, Palmer not only found the Happy Wanderer, but easily coaxed him into the Rambler. Parking under the shade of a big lawn-growing elm, Palmer asked, "See anyone who looks familiar on these pages? Familiar to *you*?" he amended himself, as he held open the black-paged photo album where he'd fitted the folded-down drawing of Zoe.

Staring at the exposed pages, the Wanderer nodded; using a black-rimmed forefinger, he indicated Zoe's face. Palmer *warned* himself not to get all excited until he was *sure*.

"She the only person you've seen . . . there, who looks like that?"

Eyes sparkling, the Wanderer held up three fingers, smiling in reply to Palmer's whispered, "You've seen them *all*?"

Stunned, glad, and scared, Palmer didn't notice that his passenger was pawing through the album, occasionally rubbing the white-edged images with a grimy forefinger, as if trying to scratch the people out of the pictures. Then he lifted the album and shoved it under Palmer's nose, tapping a photograph.

One of the double wedding pictures, of the two Palmers and the two Sawyer cousins. As Palmer asked, "What, what is it?" the man deliberately pointed out first Una, then Winston, nodding when Palmer asked, "You've *seen* them?"

Matted hair shook as the Wanderer added in his reedy voice, "Like *this*," tapping Winston's uniform-suited chest, then circled the youthful face in the photograph.

Under the bandage on his arm, Palmer felt the renewed flow of fresh blood.

. . . *Winston ran from mirror to mirror in the rest room. Every mirror showed a different face, the years melting away like hot soft wax, dripping away all character and definition, until there was nothing left to be seen in the last mirror but two dark disks under slightly formed skin, the veins visible,*

*beating faint under translucent unborn skin, like tiny map
lines of red and blue—*

Winston shifted in his sleep, head close to the gushing
urinal, and then . . . *he was home, discharge papers in hand
like a bad report card, only the steps leading up to his house
were* endless, *and he couldn' count them, couldn't remember
the rhyme Daddy taught him for climbing up to the top. . . .*

Brent leaned over the store counter, head buried in his hands.
Numbing cold made his ears ache, as Holiday finished, self-
consciously, "When I *saw* them, the first time, I knew I
couldn't let them die. Them *dying* didn't fit in with what the
mentalist said he saw. And then . . . Treeva, God help her,
tried to smother them with a sack of flour. She was a mother,
maybe she knew better—but I stopped her. And in doing
so, *another* part of that poor devil's vision came to pass.
Flour rained down like grayish ash when the bag broke. That
cinched it for me.

"Somehow, Quigley had *experienced* something *meant* to
be. Coupled with the readings from the fortune teller . . . it
all *had* to be real. And it started in my store—at least the
visible part did."

Tapping him on the shoulder, Holiday motioned for Brent
to follow him out of the store. Gratefully, Brent left the horrid
ripe smells and seeping redness behind, to join Wilbur on the
bench outside the hardware store, where Holiday patted the
empty spot beside him.

As Brent sat down, Holiday took a pack of Lucky Strikes
from his jacket pocket—the package was green, with a red
bull's eye. Brent accepted one thankfully. After blowing the
first puff out through his nose, Holiday went on, voice gaining momentum as he spoke.

"While we cleaned up Abby . . . and the twins . . . I heard
pounding on the door frame. Gayleen Winston. Abby had
visited her earlier, and she was worried about Abby being out
so late in her term. When I first heard Gayleen banging—
thank God she was too tipsy to just let herself *in*—I told
Treeva to carry the babies into the back room. Stifle their
cries if she could. The look on her face when she picked
them up was the end of any further intimacy on our part. She
returned from the back room rubbing her arms as if they were

covered with slime. I don't know how she'd quieted them. . . .

"Gayleen never realized the babies were alive. One thing, she stopped Abby's bleeding. Shoved her gloves up in her. I managed to get someone from the hospital to come, as I thought of what else Quigley had said. About the 'man' born of earth and wood. Treeva was a farmer's wife, and we'd been lying on sawdust. On a blanket *over* sawdust.

"But the mentalist hadn't said anything about *two* babies—almost two, at any rate—until I recalled him shouting that 'the skinned birch is *cleft.*' In retrospect, it was a crazy notion on my part, but some *alien* part of me said, ' *two need* two.'

"Gayleen had been after me for years. Pitiful. She wanted a baby in the worst way . . . so, I asked her to return to the store later on. I told the ambulance attendants that I'd take the baby's body to the funeral home—then I called Otis. The look on his face when he saw his offspring . . . and, after Otis took them away, Gayleen returned. . . .

"Come October, I had two sons, albeit illegitimate. Strange, how both their mothers remembered how I'd said my favorite dining spot in Chicago was the Palmer House. . . .

"So there I was, with two fine sons I couldn't acknowledge. And the worst hadn't happened to me yet. . . .' "

Stubbing out his cigarette, Holiday went on, "Come December, later in '24, I had odd flashes of images, when I was on the rim of sleep. They were garbled with just the *hint* of meaning. Enough to make me remember just a *little* of each vision come dawn.

"I saw the birth of a . . . *place*. Land, hills, trees, a river, all taking on forms I recognized. Like live things, buildings took shape . . . *Ewerton* homes, businesses. . . . I saw my town *reborn*, everything shining in the sunlight with a faint rainbow tinge . . . and the voice grew intelligible, first thing I understood was *soul means memory means imagination means reality*, over and over.

"Remembering the day of Zach Roberts' *death* and the big snowstorm later that afternoon, I wondered if the *sapping* of the town I'd witnessed had been something real. In my visions *certain* things were almost like *my* town. Trees were in the same places, most of the buildings were duplicated. Up until the late thirties, this place was almost a mirror image of my town . . . with differences. No people, no animals. . . . Fireflies, there were fireflies from the start. Don't know *why*."

A small whirlwind sent up a swirl of claw-curled leaves that spiraled down the avenue. Letting out a blue-gray cloud of smoke, Wilbur continued, "I experienced the *growth* of this place, but I told no one what I saw each night. During the day, I saw my sons grow up from afar, and what I saw hurt me something terrible—"

Unable to stop himself, Brent cut in, "There's something I need to know—was it true that your wife . . . killed my grandmother?"

"Treeva dragged herself over three miles to my house. She arrived early in the morning. Enoch had beat her worse than ever. She was . . . bleeding. From her ears, her nose. Not coherent enough to just *call* me, or think it all through.

"You see, when the Depression hit, Enoch lost all his margin stocks. Treeva did cleaning for people in town, including my wife. Hortense gave Treeva a key for the back door, for cleaning when I went to the store and she slept in late. Later, I found . . . blood, on the stoop.

"Hortense was awake that morning—any *other* damned time, she'd snore to beat the band until *noon*. That Welles broadcast scared her.

"She heard Treeva. . . . Treeva was incoherent. She told Hortense she didn't *care* anymore, that she loved me and that we were going to leave . . . or so Hortense told me time and again, afterward. I didn't hear . . . I was asleep. . . .

"Somehow, Treeva made it up the stairs, past Hortense, and *then* I heard them, only . . . it was like a *dream*, all foggy and indistinct. Hortense shouted, 'Slut, whore, bitch!' and Treeva screamed. . . .

"When I got out of bed and opened the door, all I saw was a blur of brown . . . her coat. After Hortense *pushed* her. I . . . heard bones grate. . . . Fell down two flights of stairs. . . .

"I shoved Hortense out of the way, took a look down there . . . it was worse than Abby Ewert and the *birth*. Smears of blood all over the stairs, each step dotted . . . she was all jumbled, like a rag doll thrown by a willful child. A suitcase fell with her, opening. . . . One of her panties was lying on a step, as if she'd just shucked it off. . . ."

Wilbur's pale face darkened with disgust. "She . . . *we* picked up all the things from Treeva's suitcase, the valise, too. Hortense burned it all in the furnace. Then I called the police, told them Hortense had scared Treeva as she climbed the stairs to start work.

"For the next two years, I was sickened by the way my boys were treated, but was helpless to stop it. My marriage was a sham, I was depressed to the point of dying. Then something happened. I was able to tap into *this* place during waking hours. And it was all mine to explore at will—if I desired to see something, I saw it. The town seemed *eager* for me to inspect it, and I was willing to do so from the comfort of my library."

"As this place . . . *matured*, I sensed that it was *waiting* for something, a missing component that would make it 'really real.' Through the years, I saw the *real* town I was trapped in become leeched out, sucked dry until it was a sterile, drab place. But the other town was a different story. A fairyland, almost. By 1940, it stopped growing, as if it didn't *need* any more. It *was* complete, a tiny gem of a town, lovingly kept up. Grass never grew too long. Autumn leaves vanished before the first snow. Paint never peeled, shingles didn't blow away, and the sidewalks didn't crack. I supposed that the more soul, the more memory the other town took away, the stronger it became.

"By early 1940, I learned what it lacked. Its *need* was a palatable thing; cutting through the necessity for words or symbols between this place and myself. And it was so basic, so simple . . . so like my own reason for staying in Ewerton.

"*This place wanted its children.* What should've been plain from the day I heard Quigley relate his vision finally came clear for me. The twins, the Ewert babies . . . weren't wholly the offspring of Otis and Abby. I *know* it sounds insane, but it was all *there*. It all fit. There was a big twin, almost fully formed—just slightly lacking one normal arm—and there was a small, identical twin growing *from* her sister. *Just like the two towns*.

"It *was* because of Abby that the town divided. Perhaps the split-off soul, or what-*have*-you, realized in some primitive way that this was not a normal situation, so it turned the babies into a punishment and calling card, all in one. 'We're split yet not separate, real but not natural—'

"Regardless of *how* it generated those children, this place then told me in a small neutral voice that its 'children' would return by year's end . . . it sensed that they'd *need* to come

home, 'until.' That was what it said. 'Until.' And then I—
I'm not sure what else happened. But I saw enough to make
me afraid. For if the town's 'children' *were* out there, would
the other town become really *real* when they returned home?
Once *that* happened, what of the Ewerton *I* knew? I didn't
know . . . and I was loathe to find out.

"But I really worried when I saw Palmer fixing to leave
town that May morning in '40. It was as if the small voice
was *laughing* at me, *daring* me to stop the boy from going. I
did my best to keep him from going, for I knew he was
doomed. I *knew* he'd meet up with those twins . . . there was
no escaping *that*. And I didn't know how he'd face them
without losing his sanity. . . .

"A few days later, I got the idea that if *anyone* could find
Palmer, it was my other son. But Winston wasn't able to
break free for almost a month. After he left, I felt only a sick
certainty that he wouldn't find his brother—but that he *would*
find . . . something.

"Then, the images I received were *more* real, more frag-
mented—odd sights even this place couldn't understand. A
hand, lying bloodless on a bed. A *face*, disembodied, on the
bottom of something wet and dark. And . . . I felt *fear* from
this place, a protective drawing-in of itself after something
went terribly *wrong*. After that, I couldn't reach it, couldn't
communicate with it.

"I jotted down the date in my almanac. July twenty-sixth.
A Friday. Then, nothing. The town spoke to me no more.

"Winston came home alone, strangely silent about his trav-
els. He'd experienced . . . something terrible, by his silence
I sensed he'd seen *too* much.

"When Palmer came home—the day of the Big Blow, the
storm that was twin to the one back in '13, when I . . . *killed*
Roberts—he had even less to say than his brother did. But I
saw the change in his eyes. He, too, had *seen*. Lord, he was
so different afterward. I almost didn't know him, or want to
know him.

"Years slid by. By 1950 or so, I thought the whole soul-
mind town business was something I'd dreamed up to deal
with my guilt. Then, I got to thinking, 'Suppose it isn't dead,
but *hurt*?'

"That's when it made contact again, only not like before.''
Holiday whispered, "It sent me Treeva. *Not* a ghost, or a
vision, but *Treeva*. I thought her a ghost, but she spoke to

me, smiling afterward in her coy way, like that first time she'd complimented me on my house.''

Holiday bent his head to puff on his cigarette until the match flame took hold at the end of his Lucky Strike, frowning slightly, waving the match in the air, fanning out the flame. ''She was whole, not bruised and shattered as I remembered her. She was *all right*. In every sense. Happier than I ever saw her before. And she said Enoch was nowhere *near* where she was living—

''You see, I was alone, Hortense was off visiting friends and . . . I was passing this little room under the stairs when. . . .

''She called my name. When I turned around, my mind shouted, 'You're *insane*, it's a dream, a nightmare—' but there she was. So pretty. And *alive*, in there . . . when she came forward and touched my hand, all I did was cry. She whispered that she was from a place so like Ewerton that I might not believe it. Only of *course* I did—''

''And you went there with her,'' Brent said, confident of the answer.

Holiday said simply, ''Yes. Just once. It was so simple how we crossed over. We stepped in that little room under the stairs, and she shut the door. When she opened it again, we were in *another* Holiday house. Unfinished, except for that room. No . . . not unfinished, but *unformed*.

''But I didn't care about *that*. I had my Treeva. She and I left that doppelgänger house and went into town itself.

''As we walked about, much as you and I have done today, shuffling through fallen leaves like children, she explained that there were other crossing places—'links,' she called them— all over town, in odd places. Just *where* they were she either couldn't or wouldn't say. I wasn't about to question her too closely, for fear I'd wake up to find myself hugging empty air.

''In those hours I spent with her, *nothing* mattered, except that she was *all right*. My Treeva was fine, and that alone made me grateful. Even though I had to leave before Hortense returned.

''Yet, I was uneasy, too . . . for as beautiful as the place was—as it is now—there was something not *right* about it. What I'd taken for goodwill was gone. The place had gone malignant, like an opalesque cancerous tumor growing deep in someone's body, glistening and gleaming when exposed to the light . . . *very* bad.''

With a barely suppressed shudder, Wilbur went on, ''For

a while I sensed life in this town before I entered it, the place wasn't *just* alive, spirited. Something cold and angry and full of pain was at the center of it, a thing that threatened to turn this version of Ewerton as sour as its twin.''

Taking another cigarette, Brent asked, ''The Ewert twins were there by then, weren't they?''

''I think so . . . perchance they accounted for the warped feel of the place. It was as if this town finally had a *focus*, a purpose I realized it lacked before. It was as if the twins' coming here made the difference; their loneliness and bitterness leached into the fabric of this place, along with their desire for revenge. And now, the twins have the perfect weapon to use against Palmer—isolation. . . .''

ONE HUNDRED TWO

Brent and Wilbur walked back to the Holiday house; after a fast meal of soup and bread, they got into Wilbur's car, which Holiday drove aimlessly.

''I meant to ask you . . . did your uncle send you after the twins?''

''Ah . . . sort of. Actually, I'm trying to find my wife. I thought she died, but—''

''You mean she disappeared and you thought she was—''

''Oh, no, I found her—body. On Palmer's bed. Her arm and her left side were . . . slit. She'd wanted to be cremated, so she ended up not being autopsied, either. Then I learned she wasn't delivered to the crematorium. So I don't *think* she's dead. Not *really*. Now that I see *you're* alive, and you said my grand—hey, where *is* Treeva?''

Holiday snapped, ''Never mind Treeva. She's *fine*.'' In a softer tone, he added, ''Why did you think your wife was *here*? How did you—''

Holiday had to brake hard or else he would've crashed head-on into a street lamp when Brent shoved the two photographs of Zoe under his nose—a wallet-sized snap, and the photo-map of her chest.

''You realize who she—'' Holiday began, after parking the car on Lakeview Road, near the leaf-bloated rippling lake.

Taking back the pictures, Brent said, ''I saw, last night. I just didn't trust you enough to tell you. I wasn't sure if you were on her—*their* side—''

Holiday's fingers drummed the steering wheel as he asked, "Was your wife born here? Related to anyone from this area?"

Brent thought it over. "I don't think she was born here, her folks vacationed here on and off for years, camping and—"

Holiday placed both hands on Brent's shoulders; Brent wiggled under the tingling pressure as Wilbur asked urgently, *"Was she conceived in Ewerton?"*

"I . . . her folks used to camp—"

"In the *woods*? Ewert's woods, perhaps?"

"She never said where they camped, and neither did—oh, *shit*." Rubbing Zoe's photographs between thumb and forefinger, the smooth, colored surfaces sliding against each other, he asked in a subdued voice, "Could this . . . *place* have—"

"I don't know," Holiday replied as he started up the engine. "But if it did, Maeve was wrong when she told you that all of this didn't concern you. Just maybe through Zoe— your wife," Holiday corrected himself. Brent had never mentioned his wife's name.

ONE HUNDRED THREE

Outside the rectangle of Palmer's window, the sky darkened to a rich, three-shade field of blue, lightly sprinkled with stars in the deepest part. Nemmitz found himself staring at the stars, unable to look around his room—*their* room, now, by the looks of it. The dainty dresser arrangement was untouched, and the walls shone delicately pink and flowered.

Palmer sat, fingers drumming the surface of his desk, and the paper that he'd pulled from his thirty-six-year-old typewriter—not the beginning of the promised Water Carnival booklet insert, but something more important. He read over what he wrote after consulting the experts in town:

SOLD—by me, Palmer Edmund Nemmitz, for the sum of $1.00 (one dollar), my house, and the surrounding properties, and all items contained within said property, to Maeve Mae Ewert. July 26, 1988.

He was certain he'd used the correct legalese; when Wilbur sold him back all the farmland surrounding the house, all Holiday had charged Palmer was a dollar. While he couldn't remember the whereabouts of the document, he *thought* the one Wilbur had had drawn up for him to sign looked like this.

Palmer put his signature on the bottom of the page, over the place where he'd typed it in. With a trembling hand, he made a large X over the spot where Maeve's name was typed. He prayed that simple mark would be enough. Then, using one of those plastic-coated paper clips Bitsy bought last fall—a pink one—Palmer attached the goldback bill to the document.

The Register of Deeds claimed she could file it unauthorized; she said many parents did that to avoid inheritance taxes. The casual way most legal affairs were handled in Ewerton made Palmer confident that his plan would work. After all, it *was* Maeve's dollar bill. *Had* to be.

As he prepared for bed, Palmer told himself that he'd done the right thing. Maeve (not so much Mae, he hoped) already had the run of his house, so he might as well make it legal. Besides, after the Water Carnival, Palmer felt that there would be no stopping Maeve from taking over his entire life.

Lying down on the strange ruffled comforter, Palmer doubted that Bitsy would want any part of the house once he was gone . . . or dead.

Brent and Wilbur sat at the outskirts of the Ewert Woods, waiting for full darkness to fall.

Finally, Holiday said, "Brent, once you *see*, you'll understand that if your wife *was* conceived in there, you might *not* want her if you do find her. If I am right, she won't *be* what she was before. If she ever was.

"You see, Abby Ewert was a strong woman in her own right, and the men who loved her spent time in these woods . . . thinking of Abby, wanting her, *dying* for her."

Numbed, Brent sat silent, until something cold and hard poked him in the side. A flashlight.

Solemnly, Wilbur said, "Use this on the way in. I can't

hear it tonight, so you might sneak up on it unawares. Just go in and walk until you hit the small clearing and *see*."

Before Brent could ask " 'See' *what*?" Wilbur leaned over and opened Brent's door, gently pushing him out of the car. The door shut with a decisive metallic *whump*. Thumbing on the flashlight, Brent reluctantly entered the woods . . . alone.

The golden circle of light turned the leaves and approaching needles on the lowest branches into gold-green-red scintillating bursts of color. As Brent moved deeper into the woods, he remembered with rising revulsion his *last* foray into the Ewert Woods. The day Clive was—

Fallen needles, leaves, moss, and loose soil shifted slightly under his shoes, sagging flesh sliding over root bones. When he nearly tripped over an exposed root, his flashlight caught a faint cloud of dust as it rose from the disturbed ground. Dead Fred had sat *most of the night* in these woods, alone with the creak of wood shifting, the needles-on-needles rubbing—and, worst, the sound of his own breathing, distorted, overloud . . . just as Brent's was now.

And the *smell* . . . decay and growth, musty rotten and tangy fresh, overlaid with the saturating, sappy perfume of pine and spruce and whatever else grew there. But now, very faint, almost a lingering trace of something long gone, was another odor . . . the smell of *rut*, of rumpled sheets and cramped car backseats—

Then Brent heard *sounds*; moist, breathy noises, a soft tearing, a rending of flesh, and a *plashing* sound more felt than heard. Following the sound and the scent, doglike in his quest, Brent dived deeper into the woods. When the fulsome odor was strong, a near *taste* in his mouth and throat, he aimed his flashlight at its source . . . and saw the dark power of the woods fully revealed.

As Winston had before him, Brent stood transfixed, unable to avert his eyes from the spectacle, praying to be struck blind . . .

In a slight clearing not ten feet away, he saw Una Sawyer Winston, much older, more wrinkled than when he'd seen her last. The wilderness previously hinted at in her wild eyes had erupted over her bloated, twisted visage. Worse yet, her face was contorted not with fear, but with *pleasure*.

The *source* of her rapture had her pinned against a tree. Sharp hooves and antlers ripped her sagging, luminescent naked flesh, its black hide sparkling with an olegraphic sheen of muddy color against its rippling skin. Una moaned and writhed. The upturned curve of her mouth spread and smeared, the open space within deep, colorless black.

The thing ripped open her pendulous flap of a belly, winding her intestines around the enormous spread of cruel and jagged points. And *still* she smiled in delectation. . . .

Musk reeking, the stupendous beast jerked and danced away from her, pulling pulsing loop after glistening loop of intestine away with it. Una's twitching body followed, bare feet lightly skipping along the dirt in an intricate death dance . . . but soon the eviscerated Una-thing and the blood-scented creature died a death of a different sort, hitching and bobbing in time, as the private odor grew more intense—

Brent snapped off the flashlight and *ran*. Behind him, unmuffled by the interlaced branches, came a screaming moan of ecstasy.

His feet slipped on the scatterings of slick needles and damp leaves. Sharp, pungent turpentine odors cleansed his nose and head as Brent remembered the worst thing of all— the red glow in the eyes of the thing was matched by the sparkle of *anticipation* in Una's eyes. With sick certainty, Brent now knew what sight had caused Clive Calder's fatal stroke. . . .

As Brent saw the headlights of Wilbur's car, Holiday grabbed him by the arm. "It's over . . . *over*, Brent. It . . . won't hurt *you*."

ONE HUNDRED FOUR

. . . faint screams broke her slumber; in the cocooning warmth of the bedclothes she lay quiet, waiting for more screams, proof that she heard again, was once more alive and real. Dimly she remembered the razor blade, rending soft skin. Then, coldness, darkness . . . and a memory vaguely observed, as if from a depth of barely animate flesh. A window, bleeding rose-red tears of translucent color, a long building of strange sights, and . . . Otis, the name Otis had seemed so important, so urgent for reasons unknown to her now. Whoever had possessed her had departed from her

in that strange bright place . . . driven away by the ones who made her wait here, until her time to return. . . .

And when the pleasure screams came no more, she turned over to fall asleep, as a man's name escaped her lips, uttered in a rush of sleep-expelled air, followed by a desperate—

"Brent . . . help. . . ."

ONE HUNDRED FIVE

JULY 26

The blowing train whistle had woken Winston up; groggily, he'd stared down at his duffle bag, with his discharge papers inside. Hearing the release of steam from the thrumming engine outside the depot, he'd left the depot, stepping into warm sunlight that almost dispelled the nip in the air as he headed up the hill for home, walking past houses, trees, cars that no longer scintillated, no longer burned with chilly hell-fire.

Climbing the last steep stretch of Winston Street, toward his hill-perched home, Winston smelled real meat cooking, and thought, *I'd be just as happy with Spam, for a treat she could've cooked it, but at least the war's over and I'm out of the damned service*—until the voice chimed in, *And you can't reenlist, even if you* need *to.*

In a low, firm voice, he said, "Shut up, shut *up*. . . ."

When he reached the bottom of the nearly vertical front lawn, banded by rock-studded mossy concrete and inset with steps that led up to the front porch, Winston recalled a childish game he and his father (*Are you certain?* niggled the voice) used to play, when Winston was small enough to be scared of the *long* climb up to his house.

Daddy would take his hand, and starting with the right foot on the bottom step, they'd chant together, "One, two, buckle my *shoe*." On the third step they'd continue, "Three, four, shut the *door*," and went on through picking up sticks, laying them straight, and all the rest, until the thirteenth step, when they started again. Winston was *scared* of the thirteenth step; he sucked in his breath and whispered, "One, two," in a tiny voice, face pale under his Buster Brown bangs.

By the time he and Daddy reached "Seven, eight, lay them straight" again, they were at the porch.

From the curved brick safety of the porch, Winston would look down at *all* those steps, each rock-embedded tread farther away than the last . . . until the day when Winston ran up the steps without having to count them two by laborious two. Soon after that the steps were never too big or all that steep any more.

And be he at the top or bottom of the stairs, Winston never thought of them as an *obstacle* again—until now. It was as if the lawn and stairs had grown, or he'd regressed in size, the stairs were a lumpy snake slithering up to his boyhood home. Winston wished he was holding onto his Daddy's hand (the Daddy of the days *before* "sick calls" every Monday morning to school), and hearing Daddy count off the steps with him. He felt the weight of the duffle bag on his shoulder; his left hand ached as he held the strap . . . and his right hand grasped the imaginary hand of his long-gone "Daddy". . . .

Closing his eyes until he saw little more than his black shoe-tips, Winston whispered, "One, two, buckle my shoe, three, four. . . ." and with each step he told himself that he was glad he'd forgotten to call and tell his parents he was coming home so early. They'd be so surprised, so happy to see their only son. (*Really?* came the voice.)

When he reached the last step, and touching the rough brick porch with his free hand, Winston decided not to knock. The key was under the rush mat, as it always was. Noiselessly, Winston put the key in the lock, leaning against the door so that it made no sound when opening. As the warm odor of roasting beef filled his nose, Winston was chilled by the voice in his mind as it asked, *Home safe, soldier boy?*

When he saw the banner strung across the end of the hallway—"Welcome Home, Son!" in bright blue letters, like the star-embellished flag hung in the front parlor window—Winston let his duffel bag down with a muted *whump* on the polished hardwood floor. He whispered, "It *will* be . . . it *has* to be. I've nowhere else to go."

Far down the hallway, in the back parlor, he heard voices . . . two voices, speaking loud and fast. Quietly sliding his feet along the slippery floor so as not to scare the speakers into silence, Winston went down the hallway, to where his mother and father were talking.

About *him*.

* * *

In the parlor of the Holiday house, Brent and Wilbur compared photographs of Zoe and Abby Ewert. Looking from one to the other, Holiday mused, "Coloring, hair . . . identical."

Brent took the two pictures from his host and replied, "Zoe and Mrs. Ewert . . . exchange the clothes and the hairdos, and it's the same person. Carbon cop—no, like two originals—"

"Not two originals. But the copy is flawless, nonetheless," Wilbur said, then added as he glanced at the photographs in Brent's hand, "I'm sorry about what happened to Zoe. I do hope you find her. If she remains here, the town might use her for any sort of purpose. . . ."

While Holiday stared off into space, Brent thought of his still-unanswered question about Treeva. "You promised to tell me earlier . . . where *is* my grandmother? Years ago you said she was still fine—"

"I *hope* she is," Wilbur replied in a far-off voice, his eyes still fixed on a point unseen by Brent, "but I'm not *sure* now. When I decided to end it all, I shut off my heat, picked the coldest day of the winter to lie on that floor, card in hand, waiting for Treeva to come for me, as she had for everything *around* me.

"Not long after Hortense died of a heart attack in the early seventies, I kept wishing, begging for Treeva to come back to me. She never came, but things began to . . . not *be* there. A knife, a book, a favorite sweater of mine. *Gone*.

"It was as if everything that had mattered to me was draining away, leaving me in little more than a shell of a house, with nothing to keep me company or sustain me. On the last day, I woke up on the floor, my bed vanished from under me, with nothing left in the house but an old deck of Tarot cards and a change of clothes. . . .

"No food, no furniture. Just a dead cook stove and sink in the kitchen, and a half-forgotten scrap of mistletoe over the cellar door. As if to say, 'It's *time*, my love. . . .' So I entered that little room, for I *wanted* to join her. I thought that she and I would spend eternity together, the two of us in our own dream town with no one to hurt us anymore.

"By the time I died, I was totally alone. Just an old man with a Tarot card in his hand. Two naked people under a threatening cloud . . . my belated confession of adultery. I didn't realize how prophetic it was to be. . . .

"When I could finally move about here, I looked for Treeva, shouted her name, then tried every house. Most of them are useless shells, nothing more. Then I thought, 'Silly fool, she's at the farmhouse.'

"Naturally, I hopped in my car and tried to drive there. But the road that should've been straight and treeless became twisted, tree-looming, and the branches finally closed in on the windshield, covering it. And the *leaves*—they didn't feel right, not at *all*—pressed like palms against the glass, smearing it. Walking was no good, grass grew high and the trees pressed in. The hardest part is, I *know* she's out there, in that farmhouse.

"As she knows I'm *here*, knocking about town, thinking of her, going half crazy . . . I tell myself that Treeva is there, sane, waiting for me.

"Likewise"—Wilbur's face was ashen, his mouth a quivering white-edged line—"I pray she has no unwelcome company."

Shaken by the depths of the older man's sorrow, Brent changed the subject. "My wife and I came to Ewerton about a month ago—"

"Please start from the day you two decided to come back here—and don't leave *anything* out—"

ONE HUNDRED SIX

As Stu Sawyer drove back into town after another visit to the cemetery, his eye was caught by the proliferation of "For Sale" signs (more than one hand-painted and nailed to trees near piles of left-behind garbage), the number of outgoing cars dragging U-Hauls behind them, as well as every punk brat who openly gave him the finger as the squad car rolled past.

Nobody *cared* anymore, either about the town or each other. When he passed his third "Moving Sale" sign tacked to a telephone pole, Stu bit his lip and turned on the radio. Good old WERT. He hoped to catch the tail end of "Polkas on Parade," the half hour polka-fest sponsored by the Super

Suds Launderette as a lure to haul in more duffers, but instead
he tuned in just in time to hear the blatty whine of a female
caller on *Speak Your Piece*.

"—from my boyfriend that there's a body missin' from a
grave in the cemetery, an' my *boyfriend* says that they buried
the coffin empty, just to cover up 'bout the body bein' *gone*
an' what I wanna know is, where'd the body *go*?"

The announcer hemmed and hawed, "Well, uhm, ma'am,
there's, ah . . . nothing in the *reports* here that would suggest—"

"Aw *c'mon*, you know they don't tell us *nothin'* around
here!"

Stu switched off the radio.

And when Stu returned to his office, he carefully ripped up
the few notes he'd taken at the cemetery that week, and fed
the pieces to the shredder. As he sat in his hot, quiet office,
with his feet propped up on the desk, Stu thought that he'd
hit rock bottom. But as he stared out his window, he *saw* it,
again. A lean white car. The driver *waved* at him. Fumbling
with the blinds stick, shutting out all that was illuminated by
the harsh July sun outside his window, Stu muttered, "If this
shit keeps up, I'll be seeing Wilbur Holiday and Palmer
Winston playing fucking *chess* in Holiday's store. . . ."

Listening with sick fascination, Winston crouched on the
hallway floor as his parents fought in the parlor a few feet
away. Wincing as his parents traded insults, he hugged the
duffel bag closer to his shaking body. He'd never realized just
how *much* his parents hated each other; how that hate festered
within them.

Winston sank to the floor, trying to melt into it and disappear. Any fate was preferable to listening to the two most
important people of his childhood demolish each other, slicing the facade of their married life into bloody frayed ribbons
of flesh. . . .

"—*enjoyed* marrying a *sot*? **Town** *dipso* at the tender age
of *nineteen*?" Gayleen shrieked, as a shadow whirled across
her son's face, but whether it was hers or that of Porter, Winston couldn't be sure.

"Your father was plenty eager to get rid of *you*! Whassa
matter, Gayleen, couldn't get some oaf to put a bun in the
oven, like your sister Eileen?"

"*You* paid Father plenty when you married me, bun in the oven or—"

"Only because I felt *sorry* for the miserable *clod*—"

"Like you felt 'sorry' for the school board? How much did you pay *them* for your superintendentship? Huh, Mr. Can't-Even-Get-It-Up?"

"Right, *right*, *absolve* me of all blame for *your* son! Goddamn *Jap* lover! Sticking it in *slant-eyes*!"

"At least he's capable!" Winston saw the jerking shadows lurch, as pottery hit the wall with a chalky crunch.

"Shall I put a notice in the *paper*? Tell the few people in town who don't already *know* that *your* son spent his stint in the service sticking his Democratic *dick* into—"

"Why *not*? He's a *man*. Not like *you*, you—you—"

The shadows bent, merged, separated as something heavy hit yielding flesh, then Porter screeched, "Maybe he wouldn't have become a *per*vert if his *mother* hadn't bedded with that son of a bitch down on Roberts Street, like your friend Tre—"

"At least he *could*. It has to go up and *in* before a baby comes—"

There was an ear-ringing dull as the shadows went still.

"Then . . . it's tru— You mean he *isn't* my son?" To Winston, Porter's voice was a grievous mixture of relief and disappointment—as if Porter had only claimed Winston for his own son just to prove that *he* too could father a child of his own.

"You are so *right*—for a change! And for your information, we didn't *do* it on Roberts Street, we did it on the *floor* of his *storeroom*. In the goddamned *sawdust*, and it was a damn sight cleaner than *your* pissed-up—"

"Well, I'm proud y'hear me? PROUD that that oversexed *bastard* isn't my son! I'm so *thrilled* there isn't a God-blessed *drop* of my blood in his—"

"*So am I!* He's lucky enough to have his *father's* brains! Not *your* noggin of soggy mash—"

"Think his *father's* a swell guy, huh . . . ?"

On the hallway wall, Winston saw their shadows slap and dance around each other in a malevolent tango. Terrified as he was, Winston couldn't muster the strength to get up and run away. Deep in his brain, he heard an undertone of dry, ironic laughter, as the voice said, *Welcome home, soldier boy . . . satisfied now?*

According to the grandfather clock standing five feet from

him, the time of Winston's homecoming grew closer and closer—his *first* homecoming, the one he now half remembered from *another* time.

After Brent uttered the last sentence of his story, Holiday sat on the divan, deep in thought for many minutes.

Looking up sharply at Brent, he said, "Whatever this place is planning, I know nothing of it. But I think Maeve and Mae might know. If they're *here*, I think I know where we might find them. Come on, let's go for a drive."

"To the fairgrounds."

ONE HUNDRED SEVEN

As the last reverberation of the chimes on the hallway clock died down, Gayleen said in a dazed voice, "Noon . . . Winston will be home soon. . . . Oh, the *roast*. Must be dried out . . . have to add water—Porter, can you—*will* you *please* attend to the . . . broken things?" Shard by shattered shard, Gayleen's voice rebuilt itself into a semblance of the semi-cultured tones her son was used to.

Porter said, "Won't . . . look right if we're going at it when he walks in . . . must save face, y'know." His miserable attempt at humor made Winston's stomach do a flip-flop.

" 'Face'? Oh, yes, yes . . . if he has *any* chance left at being mayor, he can't *know*. . . . Name's been dragged through the mud as it is—"

Clumsily, Winston got to his feet and barged head-down into the parlor, eyes squeezed shut both from shame and his inability to *look* at them, he shouted in a tear-choked voice, "*Screw* the precious 'Winston' name! Hear—"

—and when he heard the dull *hissing*, followed by a metallic thump of metal hitting metal, he opened his eyes . . . to the sight of a near-empty space, dominated by the windup Victrola on a small table in the middle of the carpeted dining room. There was a record on the turntable, surmounted by two taped-on paper dolls, crude, near-shapeless things, one vaguely male, the other a parody of a woman, their shadows long and parent-shaped. Not needing to go up to the record and read whatever was written on the paper label, knowing full well the name of *this* recording, Winston roughly wiped away his tears, snagging his nose on the ornamental buttons on his cuffs, as he continued in a subdued voice, "I'm no *Winston*. Hear that, wherever you two *really* are? I'm nothing to you and you've *always* been less than nothing to me."

In reply, the cellophane tape holding one of the dolls released, letting the cut-out flutter to the floor. Winston fled the room, the house, leaving behind the dufflebag and the record of the ear-burning fight he'd just heard, emerging from the house into the town that had really never went away, the place of shimmering surfaces, uninhabited emptiness . . . and welcome silence. As Winston ran down the stone-ribbed steps leading away from his boyhood home, the brick and frame house stood empty . . . odorless and silent, its cache of memories and hatreds and weak spirits purged clean.

Driving through the wooded stretch of Wisconsin Street that led to the fairgrounds, Wilbur told Brent, "Often, late at night, I hear sounds from the north . . . from the third story, I've seen flickers of light coming from *inside* the big storage building. Once, I used my binoculars, and . . . I *think* I saw the mentalist I spoke of before. *Alive.* Same red hair, moles on his cheek—" On their third pass around the building, Holiday braked suddenly, for the huge door had opened—

Brent fought the urge to hunker down in the footwell and hide as the doors opened silently, sliding along the building to reveal colored-lights-dotted darkness within. Just inside the slowly self-parting doors stood a tall, thin man, auburn curls plastered down over an oval powdered face, rings of kohl around his darting blue eyes.

Bowing deeply at the waist, black cape sweeping the ground in a graceful arc, he said in a surprisingly resonant, deep voice, "Welcome to the show, gentlemen! None like it *any-where.*"

Then—after Wilbur and Brent cautiously stepped into the building—the doors slid together with a shuddering *crack*.

When he arrived home from his errand at the Register of Deeds, Palmer went directly to his room. Gently shaking the precious curls of paper out of the tin, Palmer sat down and chose one at random, smoothing out the brittle, dry-scented paper with fingers that fluttered like dying moths. As he un-rolled each piece, noting that the faded sepia dates were much, much older than before, he pinned it to his blotter with brightly colored push pins, hating to pierce the paper, but doing so anyway.

Palmer took a perverse pleasure in seeing the history of Mr. Otis Ewert skewered down like a helpless animal caught in the sharp teeth of a trap. As his blotter was overtaken by the spread-eagled articles—each bearing the sepia-underlined name of his quarry—he mumbled, "Okay, Mr. Ewert, let's see *how* you got to be so damned powerful so fast."

Quigley stood guard next to the closed entryway, while Wilbur and Brent explored the vast array of partly disassembled rides, booths, and . . . other *things*. The high ceiling was crisscrossed with colored lights; strung on black cord, which provided shifting, prismatic illumination for the wonders—and abominations—below.

In a glassed-in box, the head and shoulders of a man were visible—a life-size dummy with thick shining slug lips, close-cropped gray hair, and a pseudo-military getup. Affixed to the front of the machine was a tiny patina-covered bronze plaque with "Dead Fred" engraved on it, next to a smaller sign over a narrow vertical slot—"Insert 10¢ Here."

Transfixed, Brent stood before the box; it had to be a sick, *sick* joke. But if it wasn't . . .

Next to Brent, Wilbur gasped, then said in a shaking voice, "If we put in a dime—" Digging around in his pocket, he extracted a Barber dime. The thing in the box came to me-chanical life, glassy eyes rolling from side to side.

Pink glistening lips parted with automated effort, the chin bobbing in time. The interior of the mouth was simply a *maw* surrounded by a few broken teeth that looked *real* . . . from which a scratchy, popping voice issued, in tinny wheezing parody of the old man's original voice:

"This is my *rifle*,
This is my *gun*,
This is for *shooting*,
This is for *fun*. . . ."

The voice dwindled away into a rusty *laugh*, as a glassy eye *winked* at the two men.

Passing the Mystic Tarot Wheel of Fortune, the bottle toss, and the rifle-shoot booths, they stopped for a shuddering second in front of the geek pen. Brent whispered, "Palmer knew him . . . but this guy wasn't the geek before." Holiday only grimaced and went by without a backward glance.

He joined Holiday quite willingly when the older man motioned him over to a row of tall, ornate nickelodeons lined up against one wall. Holiday whispered, "*These* weren't part of the carnival *I* saw in '23."

Brent leaned over to look into the nearest eyepiece—and pulled away when he caught a glimpse of bare, wet flesh. Two young bodies, embracing against damp tile walls—a scene Zoe once described to Brent. She *had* to be in town.

Turning his back on the row of nickelodeons, Brent's attention was caught by a cluster of small glass boxes. Each glass box showed a tiny mechanical scene, the people and props guided within by thin metal rods. Brent moved in closer and Wilbur followed. As they approached a box filled with figures in Edwardian garb, the box came to sudden light and life below them.

Under the observant eye of Quigley, they watched each of the mechanical scene boxes in turn. Helpless, they saw a tiny Otis *kill* people in glassed-in installments: a mechanical horse was spooked by a stone tossed at its flank, dismounting its soon-to-be trampled rider; a tiny Model A failed to stop before a moving train; a house burst into tongues of painted flame, as Otis ran—only the box *itself* became hot, the scene sooted from view; and then, worst of all, they watched the Otis simulacrum grab a metal and paint boy, shoving a white object–filled hand into the minuscule red and white maw of a mouth, while small legs and arms went up and down with clockwork precision . . . until their movement stopped altogether. . . .

After unrolling the fragile clippings, Palmer sat back in his chair, seeking the one with the earliest date. He saw it among the mass of crumbling newsprint—an obituary for a Mr. Hyram Ewert, of the Milwaukee suburb of Birchfield, uncle and guardian of a youth named Otis Ewert, Jr. The elder Ewert passed on in his sleep in 1908, and left Otis and his cousins heir to the entire Ewert family fortune.

Hyram Ewert was preceded in death by his brother Otis, Sr., *his* wife Maeve, as well as Hyram's wife Mae.

Palmer found a follow-up, written in 1910, which bore the headline, "Sorrow for the Birchfield Ewerts," detailing the "cruel blows" Fate had dealt Otis' family. Within two years of the death of Hyram Ewert, all but one of his family had died in "a series of mishaps of the most unforeseen sort, the youngest of Hyram's brood, little Peter, in a "most curious manner":

Master Ewert, according to the household staff, was wont to toss whole sugar cubes into his mouth in sport. But on March 15, one of the cubes so carelessly tossed into his mouth lodged in his windpipe. Before the cube dissolved, the lad ceased breathing, despite the efforts of a butler summoned to the scene. . . .

Grumbling, "Bastard . . . he was only a little *boy* . . . you killed a *baby*, in cold, frigging blood," Palmer was about to look for the next impaled clipping when something about *cold* and *babies* clicked in place in the back of his mind.

The old man had always chided our Ma about how she *happened* to be at Holiday's Grocery Store around *noon*, the time when it was closed for lunch, when Treeva helped Abby Ewert to deliver that January of '24. And Palmer was born in October. "So my life began with her birth . . . *had* to. Like a chain, one link attached to the other . . . and Gayleen, she probably conceived Winston on that day, too. He was *always* late."

Then he noticed a follow-up to an earlier piece he had read, giving Coroner Wilkes' verdict on Roberts—"Death by misadventure; gunshot wounds to the head and left arm." Also included were the names of those club members present that bloody morning.

Palmer was mildly surprised to see his father's name listed. Leaning away from the desk, he thought, *Wilbur and I have some talent for being around Ewerts at the worst times—* before his reverie was shattered by the ringing telephone.

As the last tableau box went dim, Holiday suggested that they search the building. Wordlessly he set off toward the back of the arcade, seeing a glass box filled with prizes, waiting to be scooped up with a clawlike set of motorized pinchers. The machine had a slot near the bottom, surmounted by the instructions: "Deposit 25¢ Here."

Brent almost left the machine, until he noticed how odd some of the prizes within were—a woman's *real* gold watch, a small pearl-handled pistol, and a blood-flecked Teddy bear. Aflame with curiosity, Brent dug in his pocket to find a large greasy coin.

It *was* a quarter, that much Brent saw before dropping it. Swearing, he hunkered down and patted the dark floor, wishing that the colored lights above were just a *little* brighter— when everything went dark, and Brent swore again, only louder this time—

Palmer let out a silent curse when he heard the voice on the other end of the line.

"—in town on the twenty-eighth to pick up my things. I want everything that isn't *yours* so you'd best haul in some boxes. Angie and Dick haven't any to spare, they're moving to the Cities themselves. I *s'pose* because of Clive and all, but I don't know if I'll *like* the Cities—"

Bitsy blathered on, her jumble of words punctuated by Palmer's affirmative grunts. When she hung up, Palmer let the receiver swing from the long curly cord. Faint *beep-beep-beeps* followed him as he hurried upstairs.

He found his bankbooks, checkbooks, CDs, and bonds hidden under his mattress, one of the six sites around the room he chose at random each week, just so Bitsy couldn't go spend his money on the crazy things he *knew* she wanted to.

After putting the booklets and papers into his inner jacket pocket, Palmer paused for a moment near his dresser. Gently, he stroked the curve of her perfume bottle, and saw his small concave reflection smile back at him.

For the first time, his whole room seemed *right*. Why he couldn't explain, but its newfound integrity was enough. Patting the assortment of bank statements against his bony chest, Palmer hurried downstairs.

•   •   •

—after a few groping seconds, Brent felt the metallic round-ness of the quarter. Before he picked it up, though, the floor *shifted* under him—a movement-without-*motion* that made him dizzy.

The lights *still* hadn't come on, so Brent hid his rising terror with a petulant shout, "Wilbur? Quigley? *Anyone?* Get the lights, will you?"

Still crouched down, he saw the *floor* light up. A wedge of pale sunlight from an open door crossed the floor. Brent turned around on his hands and knees—and was rewarded with vague dark shapes against brightness. Shielding his eyes against the glare, he said, "Wilbur, let's get back to the—"

"Let's get back to the *what*, Nimitz?" Stu Sawyer's voice was harsh and mocking.

Quickly Brent got to his feet. When he saw *where* he was, he swayed and fell in a faint.

Voice tight with excitement, Terry Von Kemp said to Stu, "Think he meant the same Wilbur you been—"

"Shut up and drag him out of here."

ONE HUNDRED EIGHT

When Brent came to, Sheriff Sawyer was reading him his rights. Meekly, Brent rode to the law enforcement center, but balked when Stu tried to lead him to a cell. After an irate Brent reminded him that he *was* Bitsy's nephew, Stu resign-edly escorted the young man to his office. Slamming the door shut, he brusquely ordered, "Park your elusive behind there, *Mr.* Nimitz."

Brent sat, arms crossed, right ankle resting on his left knee, while Stu tried to call Palmer, but even Brent heard the busy signal. Snorting, Stu tried another number as Brent asked, "I do think you forgot to tell me what I've been arrested *for*, sir. I didn't hear the charges when you—"

"That's because I didn't *mention* any," he replied, cupping the receiver to his chest, before he hit the square buttons again. Brent sighed and crossed his legs the other way, hitch-ing up the fabric of his trousers to give his knee more room. Eyeing the contents of his pockets, which were scattered across Stu's desk, Brent asked, "Aren't you supposed to give me the traditional *dime*, let me make my own call?"

Giving him a sour stare, Stu replied, "Knowing you Nimitzes, *you'd* call for a frigging pizza. Smart-assed enough to do it, you and your uncle both." Leaning over his desk, midsection squeezed against its pseudo-woodgrain surface, Stu said, "I'm tellin' you this *once*, so get out the earwax and *listen*:

"As of this moment, *you* are the prime suspect for *all* this shit that's been going on around here—what happened at the fairgrounds, the vandalism at the cemetery, and *especially* for what you *done* in the vault. Folks are real upset over what's happened, and since you haven't said word *one* about how you got in a *locked* building, you either better shut up until you got a lawyer or spill everything now and save me the trouble of getting Terry in here to play good cop/bad cop to worm it out of you.

"I *sure* would appreciate a way out of this mess 'fore the fall election comes around. See, I don't draw no paycheck unless the voters give their say-so. And frankly, I'm too damned *old* to start all over again."

Subdued, Brent stared up at the ceiling, wondering if he was dumped here on purpose. *Just* when Stu and Von Kemp happened to be cruising the northern half of the city—*including* the fairgrounds.

Closing his eyes, feeling overwarm in the jacket Holiday had lent him, Brent almost dozed off when Stu startled him. "Hey, Nimitz, uh . . . off the record, where *did* you hole up for all those days?" Stu was eyeing Brent's fall garb—and the crumpled but still supple autumn leaf Brent had taken from his pocket—with wary eyes.

Without giving Stu the satisfaction of seeing him wiggle under his stare, Brent said, *"Well* . . . for the past two days I stayed with a really fascinating guy. Greet cook. Library you wouldn't believe. Name of Wilbur Holi—"

"What did you do with his body?" The sheriff's tone was so shaken Brent *had* to look Stu in the eye. Not knowing *what* Stu was talking about, but vaguely pleased that Stu *was* scared, Brent decided that his best defense was an offense. Crooking both arms behind his head, Brent said, *"Body?* The guy's not *dead.* He's living right in his *house.* We sat in his library and killed a couple of bottles of brandy. And I *never* booze it up with corpses—"

From the way Stu reclined in his chair, not taking his eyes off Brent as he rubbed his stubbled chin, Brent realized that Stu *couldn't* tell if he was being put on or not. Leaning forward, Brent added, "Met the Ewert sisters, too. Lovely girls . . . daughters of the guy this place was named for. They—"

"Bull*shit*! I *know* town history, bub! Otis Ewert left town after his *child* died—one, not two. Besides, that was over sixty years ago."

Behind Brent, the door opened a crack. Terry Von Kemp poked his head in. "Old man Nemmitz is here, wants to bail out his nephew." After the door closed again, Stu got up and circled his desk, saying as he approached Brent, "Better not plan on taking off in the near future, though. We're having a little *talk* once things quiet down—"

It wasn't until Brent had left that Stu realized he'd forgotten to return the young man's change. As he went to scoop the coins and orange leaf into an envelope, the design on one of the dimes caught his eye.

Weird, he thought, as his fingers brushed against the oddly smooth leaf, *I haven't seen a Mercury dime in ages. . . .*

Sitting in the Rambler, elbow poking out the window, Brent asked his uncle, "How'd you know I was in the clink? Stu couldn't reach—"

"Phone was off the hook. Anyway, I was in the bank when some bozo in the line next to mine said something about Stu finding you out at the fairgrounds.

"But never mind that. *Did* you find—" Palmer's voice conveyed an emotion alien to the tones Brent was used to hearing. The obvious *desire* was almost embarrassing.

"I found the place. The twins *are* alive. And . . . I found your dad. He's alive, too. *And* your mother—"

Palmer listened to Brent, careful not to miss *anything* his nephew had to say. Brent finished with, "—shaft of light came in. When I turned around, there was Stu. You've heard the rest."

In answer, Palmer rambled on about what the Happy Wanderer had told him, adding, "So Zoe *was* there. Too bad you never found her." Palmer was disappointed that Brent hadn't seen his half brother, but assured himself that even the smallest facsimile of Ewerton *had* to be large enough for two men to miss each other—or be *forced* to miss each other.

Palmer didn't tell his nephew about his changed room—Brent *had* to see that for himself—nor did he tell the younger man the nature of his bank business. He had withdrawn all but the minimum balance from the joint account, and wiped out the five accounts from various Dean County banks, numerous CDs, and two T-Bills that were his alone.

The packets of money were safely stuffed in his inner jacket pocket, plus his formerly empty money belt.

When Palmer reached the end of his abridged narration, he asked Brent to tell him more about the *other* Ewerton. He was puzzled; Brent seemed predisposed *against* the place. As far as Palmer could tell, it sounded like an *ideal* place in which to live.

ONE HUNDRED NINE

After fleeing his family home on Winston Street, Palmer Winston ran to the safety of the barbershop and dropped exhausted on the bed. As he watched the swirling shadows from the ceiling fan, Winston came to a decision. He would go to the house of his father . . . the Holiday house.

Watching the slow revolutions of the blades above him, Winston made a discovery about himself: For the first time he understood the *why* behind his old sexual frenzy. The sexual *act* had been a prelude, a way of securing a few *seconds* of temporary love and devotion. And since he had been unable—save for that one encounter—to find *her*, the woman-child-imp, he had needed *someone* to fill that void in him, to take *her* place long enough to keep that void from widening and sucking him into the nothingness of spirit he feared more than anything.

Tears pooled in Winstons' eyes as he realized that Major Taub had had it all wrong. It wasn't pure lust, not at all. After he'd *told* Winston how bad he was, how *sick*, Winston had felt so awful about himself that he was willing to believe any rationalization Taub offered him, no matter how painful.

Winston sat up, elated, as if an element of his nature that had been foisted on him had been removed, leaving him more *whole* than before.

With that, the small voice returned, gently coaxing him to

go see his father, *now*. No longer compelled to resist, Winston left the barbershop headed for the Holiday house.

Seated at their usual places at the kitchen table, Palmer and Brent talked during their brief supper of sandwiches. By the time the sun dipped low over the horizon, Palmer wondered out loud why the Happy Wanderer slipped so easily from one Ewerton to the other.

"I . . . never told you this, but the night Clive disappeared, I saw the Wanderer slip through. Bobbing down the road one second, then . . . *gone*. I drove past where *he* went through, but *I* didn't—"

"Y'know, when I was there, I thought it over a lot—not much else *to* do there—and while I was sitting in Stu's office, I realized that whenever I did cross over, I wasn't thinking about it per se. It's more like mental relaxation . . . opening up the mind through inverse concentration."

Palmer swallowed a bite of his sandwich, then said in an offhanded tone, "No wonder the Wanderer can slip through at will, he's a grand champion of 'inverse concentration' . . . ironic, how *he* can find those linking places, yet can't explain it to anyone—"

Brent gulped down the last of his ham and rye unchewed; it rode roughly down his throat as he said, "Who cares if he can explain it—can't he take someone *with* him?"

"Damn!" Palmer slapped the oilcloth with an open palm. "Bless you, Brent. Let's head out to the group home and—"

"You wouldn't want to pop into that place at night," Brent warned, remembering Una's frenzied snipe dance. He suggested that they get some rest first, "until five or so in the morning. The Wanderer starts running around then, doesn't he?"

As they left the kitchen, Brent put his arm around the older man's fragile shoulders. "Besides, we can accomplish more as a team than we can by ourselves."

It was sundown before Winston reached the Holiday house. Climbing the steps without hesitation, he rapped on the door until he heard footfalls approaching the door from within. The light in the house went on, illuminating the silhouette of the man standing on the other side of the glass insert. Then, the door unlocked.

Winston held his breath as the door swung open by itself, revealing his father, who regarded Winston with a mixture of joy and trepidation on his face. Winston cleared his throat, then said, "I'm home, Father."

But as he sobbed against his father's shoulder, Holiday quickly scanned the silent, gold-tinged street, as if searching for someone who *might* be there. He feared that that stranger, his *other* son's nephew, might have found his way back here, to continue his meddling—

Holiday, arm curled protectively around his son's shoulder, led him into the house. Quietly, he shut the door—and double locked it.

ONE HUNDRED TEN

. . . *with Quigley, they journey on the road in* between, *a snaking trail lined with preternatural, leaning trees, until the road merges with one they remember, and the trees do not bow down with their passing* . . . *where they find the carny, still in guilty flight.*

Those with whom they have no quarrel, no strong *reason for revenge, they warn. The redheaded owner, the dancing girl, jointees, ride jocks, and others, all flee in fear—and relief.*

But some feel their wrath, and cannot flee. For, through Quigley, through experience, *the girls have learned who and* what *they are, and try out the powers of their true parentage to aid them in their quest for immediate revenge.*

And after they finish, they take along their living trophies, as Quigley leads them north.

Here, past the road in between, *lies culmination, the peak of their revenge—*

But there is a stop to make before they reach their home. The false brick home they've known since infancy.

Somehow, the man and the women sense their return—and are dying even as the rejoined (in their old *false* world) *twins open the door of their childhood home.*

• • •

The dream was so disturbing, so allegorically *precise*, that Brent tossed and turned in his hot, rumpled bed—until a sudden coolness on his chest woke him up. Reaching for the bedside lamp, Brent switched it on—and saw the delicate matting of long gray hairs on the sheet concentrated in the shape of a curled, sleeping cat.

Brent sat up, heart lopping crazily in his chest. Out of the corner of his eye, he *saw* it . . . the feathery plume of a cat's tail, long dark hair fluffed out from the thin whip of flesh and bone. It rounded the door frame, and disappeared into the hallway. In one fluid motion, Brent was out of bed; his feet smacked the floor as he took off after the now-vanished tail.

"Duffy?" he whispered.

In the almost-dark hallway, he barely saw the feathery tail round the bathroom door and disappear. Panting as he ran, Brent followed the disembodied tail. The cold floor jolted Brent into complete wakefulness when he padded into the bathroom. Enough light came in through the drawn shower curtain for him to see the old-fashioned toilet and sink.

Bending down, he scooped up the cat, and felt pads of fat under the long thick fur, not the skin and bones of advancing illness. But as he stood there, hugging the cat, a troubling thought crept into his consciousness. *Suppose this is a stray that got into the house? Duffy was* never *this fat.*

In near panic, still pressing the purring animal to his chest, Brent reached for the light chain over the sink and yanked it—immediately, he let out a shaking sigh of relief. It *was* Duffy.

Nuzzling the soft fur over the bulge of the cat's inner ear, Brent crooned, "Daddy's boy . . . Duffy's all right now—" until he realized that while the *cat* he held was his, the *bathroom* wasn't the one he knew—

The shower curtain was thick tan *canvas*, not nubby pink plastic, and the walls were all wrong. Pale yellow, instead of warm peach. But before he could search for the things he knew *should* be there, he heard footsteps down the hallway. Then a voice, more than a little fearful—"Who are *you?*"

Turning around, Brent found himself face-to-face with someone both familiar and alien. Familiar from a photo album; alien by virtue of being *alive* . . . and nearly his own age.

His *grandmother*, Treeva Nemmitz.

ONE HUNDRED ELEVEN

JULY 27

Come five sharp, Palmer was awakened by both his own alarm clock and Brent's—but after he shut off his alarm, his nephew's kept buzzing.

When Palmer entered Brent's room, the words, "*You* were the one who said we should—" came out before his eyes registered that the young man wasn't there.

Palmer's annoyance turned to dis-ease when he found the bathroom empty. Ditto for the rest of the house. Reentering Brent's bedroom, Palmer noticed the fuzzy outline on the sheet. Picking up a single gray strand of hair, he realized that if Brent had left the house, he hadn't used the front or back doors.

He could've taken me along, Palmer thought petulantly as he trudged downstairs, feet leaden with resignation. He fixed a breakfast he hardly felt like eating. As he chewed, fragments of last night's dream came back to him. Despite his impression that what the twins and Quigley did to those carnies was *wrong*, there was a certain *rightfulness* about the whole business that secretly pleased him.

He felt a bit closer to the girls, much less disgusted with them . . . even though he'd witnessed their vile deeds with his own dream-sight.

But Palmer had scant time to reflect on his dream, for Gordy Gray or Wayne Mesabi would be coming around today to pick up that damnedable *insert*. As he trudged upstairs, clear roll of tape in his hand, he said aloud, "They want something folks haven't seen before. By gummy they're gonna *get* it."

It was ready by the time Gordy knocked on the front door, the few but important pages held together by the blue plastic binder that had held his *other* manuscript only hours before.

As Palmer watched the younger man pull out of the driveway, he was torn between reproach for doing such a damn-fool thing, and release such as he hadn't felt in years. The bad luck that seemed to stalk those who read his manuscript no longer bothered him—he no longer *cared* what happened to Ewerton. All the people he did care for, or wanted with a desire he hadn't been able to admit to himself before, were over *there*, in that other town. Wherever, *when*ever that was.

Walking back to the house, Palmer was filled with a fresh resolve—somehow, some way, he'd have to go there, too. He decided to have that talk with the Wanderer he'd planned before Brent disappeared again, but before he could leave, the phone rang. . . .

As her lover had done before her, Treeva found Brent some clothes and shoes to wear. As he put them on in the room that occupied the same space as the one he'd left behind, Duffy wound around Brent's feet, plumed tail brushing against his legs.

Following the smell of brewing coffee, Brent came downstairs, with Duffy backtracking and winding around Brent's feet with every step. Downstairs, the house was different, but Brent sensed that the dissimilarity went beyond a change in furnishings and wall decor.

There was a different atmosphere in the house that Brent was hard-pressed to define. When he entered the kitchen, Treeva turned around with a gentle swish of her full-shirted Hooverette. She took off her apron, slipped her head of dark hair out from under the bib, then nervously smoothed out her rickrack-trimmed red dress.

When she smiled at him with a warmth that verged on the tearful, Brent realized where the true difference between the two versions of the house lay—and knew why Wilbur didn't want to give her up.

Motioning for him to sit down to the steaming cup of coffee on the table, Treeva said, "So you're Shirley's little boy. I see your father in you. *His* father, too," she added with a trace of fear that quickly melted into concerned warmth.

Treeva sat down at Brent's right elbow, at an angle to him. Sipping her coffee, she asked, "How in the world did you *get* here?"

Putting down his cup, Brent replied, "Through the bathroom, I guess. Back . . . home, Palmer put in fixtures like the ones in your bathroom. I was so happy to see my cat I didn't notice I was in a different room. . . . Was Duffy in your house, before—''

"Kitty-Kitty? He's been roaming around for a few weeks. He was the first animal I'd *seen* since . . . save for Puss-Puss—''

'' 'Puss-Puss'?'' Brent felt as if he was caught up in a bizzare echo chamber, until Treeva replied, "He's outside somewhere. Skittery thing. Prettiest cat I ever saw until your kitty showed up. Dark gray, and sleek like a seal. Deepest green eyes of any cat I've seen. Just the sweetest—''

Something in his grandmother's description of Puss-Puss made Brent take notice—Sarah Andersen had mentioned that she'd lost a dark grey cat, with a funny name—

"Does the cat resemble an Oriental Shorthair—sorry, it's a new breed,'' he added, seeing the puzzled look on Treeva's face. "Like an all-dark Siamese. May I take a look?''

Treeva got up and put a small pot lid over Brent's coffee cup. The screen door smacked behind him as he stepped outside and softly called "Chewie? Chewie kitty-kitty?'' feeling rather foolish until the long, lean cat loped across the shaggy lawn.

It *had* to be the Andersen's cat—Brent wished he could get the animal back to Sarah just then, to see the expression on her tanned, pinched face. The cat flopped on the grass, arcing its back and rubbing the top of its head along the ground. Brent itched its sleek belly, listening to the soft *churrup* it made when he called the cat by name.

From the kitchen, Treeva said through the screen, "I think he likes you. Did you say his name is 'Chewie'?

Brent got up and dusted off the knees of Enoch's old trousers as he approached the farmhouse. "Belongs to a family back in town. They're Andersens—Scoo-Scott and Sarah. They have kids, whole family misses the cat like something else.'' He let himself in, to sit down to his still-steaming coffee. "They were worried that someone was torturing the poor thing. I'm glad he found you. He seems to be happy.''

Setting down her coffee cup, Treeva affirmed, "He is. I . . . wondered if maybe he slipped through one of the linking places, then couldn't find his way back. Not that he didn't have company in that respect.''

Sipping the last of his coffee, Brent asked, "Has it been . . . bad for you, living here while Wilbur—''

Giving him a wan smile, Treeva shrugged her narrow

shoulders. "Not the most unpleasant existence—not hell, certainly—but loneliness is the worst part. Ever since the last time I saw Wilbur, I've been cut off . . . you said he *is* well?"

"Fine," Brent assured her, patting her hand. He was used to the way her animated flesh felt under his skin; he didn't insult her by flinching. "He misses you too, something terrible. Uh . . . did the twins—"

"Please, let's save talk of them for later . . . *please*? There's so much I'm curious about—what the world is like out there, your life, *everything*. I want to hear all about you—my own grandson and you're a stranger to me. That shouldn't *be*. Not if the situation can be remedied," she added with a sweet smile that made Brent want to cry.

She was so small; the thought of her discarded doll tumble down Holiday's staircase made Brent tremble inside. And Enoch used to pound on her—Brent hoped the *putz* was rotting in Hell.

He sighed, then asked, "There's so *much* new out there—want to know anything in particular?"

Eagerly, Treeva leaned forward. "About *you*, please. And the rest of the family. Wilbur told me Shirl had been sent to school in Minnesota—"

Gently, Brent broke the news about his father's death, as well as the deaths of Treeva's other children. His grandmother was shocked, but stoic; after looking down at her tightly laced fingers for a few minutes, she took a deep breath and said, "No wonder Wilbur didn't mention. . . . I hope they're at peace . . . and not with *him*." There was no need for Brent to ask her which *"him"* she meant, before she went on, "After all I've been through, all the years *alone*, nothing much should shock me anymore . . . please, go on about yourself. I'm *so* interested . . . and curious why you came to be here—"

Feeling like a top-ten single spun endlessly on a turntable, Brent once again launched into his now-familiar account. . . .

ONE HUNDRED TWELVE

True to the word of Wayne Mesabi and Gordy Gray, the new photocopying machine at the court house did an *admirable* job of reproducing and sorting Palmer's carnival insert into many little booklets, enough for all the programs to be sold the next day.

The only thing that the marvelous, expensive new copier *couldn't* do was staple the sets of pages together. So a trio of volunteers Rosemary Gray (wife of Gordy), Susie Reish (Craig's spouse) and Val Sawyer (the Sheriff's wife), put three staples into the spine of each insert. Occasionally they dropped a small stack of papers on the floor, which scattered across the glossy title of the County Clerk's office.

Whenever someone dropped her soon-to-be-stapled booklet, one of them got a chance to read the pages *inside*. Susie was the first to complain out loud.

"I thought the old coot was supposed to write *up* a town history. This is *cut* and *paste*. *Juvenile*. We did better on the EHS yearbook." Stapler in hand, Susie continued, "Too bad Mr. Winston left town. *He* knew how to *write*—"

Winston woke up late. For the first time in his entire life, he felt as if he'd *arrived*, had found a place of comfort and belonging. True, his dreams had been bad—vicious, yet oddly *just*, too. Winston slipped on the pale blue shirt and cream flannel trousers his father had left out for him the night before, and assured himself, *No more nightmares . . . I'm finally awake*.

Downstairs, his father yelled, "Palmer, breakfast!" In the kitchen, the two men exchanged lopsided grins, then sat down to eat in peaceful silence, only occasionally speaking between bites. Each was aware that there were still more questions to be asked and answered, but they were of little importance at the moment.

Morning slipped into early afternoon as father and son finished their late meal.

Palmer's caller was Bitsy; she would be back in town tomorrow, to pick up her things.

Smiling to himself, he replied, "Everything will be waiting for you, dear." He even agreed to pack up her family belongings, so she could take them along with her clothes.

After Bitsy hung up, Palmer found a big cardboard box in the garage, which he set in the middle of the living room. Using old newspaper, he wrapped the few items that Bitsy alone had brought into their life together—the ugly maroon ashtray Buddy and his wife brought from some village in Oklahoma, the Disney World serving tray, and the framed pictures of Bitsy's relatives—plus her books and paint-by-numbers—which left white squares and rectangles on the now cream-colored walls. Palmer figured the place could breathe easier, with all the garbage gone.

After rounding up Bitsy's treasures, down to her refrigerator magnets, Palmer had filled the box halfway when he remembered that he had to lug down her remaining clothing. Palmer opened her bedroom door . . . and saw that someone had beaten him to his self-appointed task.

The room was stripped bare. All of Bitsy's drawers were emptied. The suitcases Palmer had intended to pack sat, stuffed and zipped, on her stripped bed. The mattress shone obscenely under the clear, zippered plastic cover. Her bedclothes were neatly folded and draped over the back of a chair. Palmer rubbed the back of his hand under his chin, thinking, *So neat, so tidy. I'd forgotten how precise you were.*

Brent finally told Treeva all that he knew of the happenings in the Ewerton he'd rather unexpectedly exited that morning; when he was utterly talked out, he sat quietly at the kitchen table, looking expectantly at Treeva. She merely *sat*, hands folded over the slick oilcloth. Her brown eyes spoke of such misery he couldn't begin to comprehend it.

Then he spoke again. "Fair's fair . . . I told you what I know—"

Licking her lips, Treeva replied, "After all this time— Being *alone*, not seeing or hearing—I almost gave up. But now, after what you've said—"

Suddenly she got up and opened the whooshing, dome-topped refrigerator, sending a blast of chilly air Brent's way. He turned around to watch her shift food from one shelf to the other, her shoulders stiff under her cotton print dress.

After a few minutes, Brent asked, "Treeva, what is it that you don't want to tell me. Is it about this place?"

Silence.

"There's something I don't understand: Why did this place revive *you*? To lure Wilbur here?"

She continued to move food from shelf to shelf, back rigid.

"He might've come here on his own . . . he *was* aware of the place, curious. . . . Was it to punish you? Him? Your son? First this place gives you life, lets you see Wilbur, allowed him to visit you—then, once he finally decides to come here for good, you're hidden away like Rapunzel in her tower. And I've *been* in this place before, I *know* it does nothing without *some* purpose. . . .

"Treeva . . . why are they holding you here?"

Shoulders heaving as she spun around, Treeva sobbed, "I'm *sorry*—I wasn't supposed to say *anything*, but you're as trapped here as I am. I *had* to lie, but . . . I didn't think that you'd want to hear the truth. And I *was* so lonely. That much *isn't* a lie. I doubt you'll like what I have to say. There are things people shouldn't have to *admit* to each other."

As her grandson led her to the parlor, Treeva walked like a condemned woman who sees the shadow of her own scaffold against the prison wall.

Wilbur and his son sat talking on the front porch steps, feet resting on fallen leaves. Winston spent the better part of an hour laying bare his deepest doubts and fears without hesitation—or fear of recrimination.

When he was through, he sat drained, hands tightly interlaced between his spread knees. Wilbur dug a green-boxed pack of Lucky Strikes from his jacket pocket, and offered one to Winston. Both lit their cigarettes off a single light.

As he shook out the match, Wilbur said, "That Major *was* right—you did need help, but not the kind he suggested. Only 'help' that ever takes is the help *you* give yourself."

Puffing deeply, Winston exhaled before replying, "Then . . . what's been happening to me was meant to *help*?"

"Taking the cure in the Army didn't work, did it? You weren't ready for it, so it didn't matter if they forced a cure down your throat with a broomstick—be it for drinking or your *other* problem. What a body doesn't want, a body won't keep down. You needed to reach a point in your life where you *wanted* to change yourself.

"Same as trying to use a carrot on a stick to make a mule go where you want it to . . . if that mule isn't *hungry*, he won't budge an inch. . . ."

Palmer knew that the Happy Wanderer usually took one last walk of the day before the group home served dinner. Despite the uncertainty of driving around aimlessly until he spotted the Wanderer, Palmer preferred that to dropping by the home.

As the chimes in the Lutheran church marked five, he caught up with the Wanderer close to the river. Opening the passenger door, he asked, "Need a lift, Cooper? I've some cans of soda." He stopped the car, let the smiling rotund gentleman into the front seat, slammed the door shut, and began to fire off questions: Had anything *changed* "there"? Did the Wanderer see a tall, heavyset young man roaming around? Were the ladies with the pretty hair still "there"? Did he know where the nice ladies *lived*?

Belching as he downed the last of his treat, the Wanderer thought things over for a couple of minutes. In his high-pitched, yet soft voice, he said haltingly, "Been . . . funny there. *Bad* funny . . . don't go no more. Bad—" He tapped both ears, cocking them to imagined sounds. "One house . . . *bad*. Don't go no more—"

Palmer leaned over, touching the Wanderer's shoulder as he asked, "Cooper, is there a house *here* like the '*bad*' one *there*? If I drive you, can you show me the house?" Palmer smiled as the Wanderer nodded emphatically. . . .

ONE HUNDRED THIRTEEN

Slowly at first, Treeva told Brent, "Both you and Wilbur were wrong, about when I came to . . . *be* again. I remember nothing of my death . . . one second I was falling, and the next—I was walking, down a serpentine road that I *thought* was the road leading to my home.

"What made it so hard to get used to being *dead* was that I still *wanted.* Food, water, everything . . . and the house supplied it. Food appeared in the pantry. Water flowed in the taps.

"But what I needed most wasn't supplied—at times I'd have settled for *him,* even if it meant being beaten again. I took to imagining that my family was around me, *anything* for comfort. Came a time when I thought I'd had no other life before this. Just wake up, eat, and wander in and around the house. *Leaving* was impossible. Road wouldn't *let* me.

"Then, in what was maybe 1940, something . . . changed. Like trying to tune in a radio, and picking up bits and snatches of a distant signal—not enough to understand, but audible. I heard this small, soft rustling in my brain, hisses and whispers no louder than a breeze rushing through trees. I doubted my sanity, resisting it at first . . . then, as what I thought was summer wore on, I gave in and *listened.*

"It was the small voice Wilbur spoke to you of. Being a mother, I sensed things in that voice I doubt Wilbur caught. This place *loves* those girls. It *wanted* them, as desperately as I wanted *my* children. The sense that they had sprang up from *this* place, and somehow *entered* Abby, was strong. I wondered if this was my punishment for wanting to kill the twins at birth, but the voice never spoke to me, never recriminated me, as if I was *forgotten.*

"Then, came the night of the twins' . . . *death,* but they *didn't* die. I don't think they could, not being part of *this* place. But something awful happened here that night. At the moment when it *happened,* this place sent a *jolt,* to help them. Gave *them* the strength to live again . . . at a cost.

"You see, what is around us is *not* what this place looks like. It's alien-looking, almost like the moon, or *Mars*," she added with an ironic, bitter smile. "In fact, it's closer to how Quigley described it in his vision.

"The whole place curled *in* on itself to send forth Quigley. I saw him driving in that old orange bus, across the fallow soil. Somehow, Quigley brought them here again, as two whole, adult beings.

"After what . . . happened, this place remained . . . strange. It took years for the girls to be powerful again. Those horrible things they did drained them. They . . . *hid*, for years while the town rebuilt itself around the sleeping beauties."

Treeva slumped against the back of the sofa, spent, as Brent asked gently, "What about that building I saw, the things in there that didn't come from their old carnival?"

Treeva shook her head sadly. "I'm . . . not sure, but I think I know where Abby died. If I'm right, your wife is *not the child of her parents*. Zoe *is* Abby, believe me."

Brent believed . . . for he now suspected that Abigail Andersen Roberts Ewert wasn't a woman who took death lightly—or would be willing to give up all *that* easily once she conquered it.

The early evening buzzed with insect sounds as Palmer and the Happy Wanderer sat in the Rambler, in front of the house the Wanderer finally pointed out. Palmer sat stunned, as he stared at the counterpart of the house where the Wanderer said the "ladies" were the last time he visited the other town . . . for it was his own farmhouse. Not only were the three women all there, but according to the Wanderer, the place was "hurtin'."

As the chimes at the Lutheran church struck seven, Palmer asked his companion, "Can you be here tomorrow, by ten o'clock?"

Sniffing, Treeva went on, "This place *uses*, Brent! It uses memory, it uses people . . . but I think Abby Ewert used *it*. The twins think different, but—"

At the same instant Treeva clamped her hand over her mouth, as if to recapture the words she'd just uttered, Brent sprang to his feet and grabbed her forearm.

"I thought you said no one's *been* here!" Furious, he squeezed her arm, until the terror in her eyes made him relax his grip.

Treeva tried to speak, but she was crying too hard to make herself understood. Sobbing, she curled up on the sofa, her back to him.

Torn between pity and anger, Brent watched her for a few seconds, until a more urgent concern made itself known to him. The dull ache in his bladder was sharp, insistent; without excusing himself, he pounded up the stairs and stomped into the bathroom, not remembering the downstairs bathroom until too late.

He was close to wetting himself as he raised the lid of the pearlescent commode . . . when the urge to urinate suddenly left him. In the otherwise clear water, a long strand of used green dental floss floated . . . and a fast check of the medicine cabinet revealed a modern dispenser of floss, in among personal products the likes of which hadn't been sold in over fifty years. . . .

The return of the pressure on this bladder made him reluctantly relieve himself, but he averted his eyes from the fuzzed-out strand of floss. On his way downstairs, he shouted, "What *else* wasn't I supposed to know?"

Sitting up, legs tucked under the folds of her skirt, Treeva sniffed, "Believe me, Brent, I was afraid to say anything. You don't know what they're like—"

"After all the crap you've endured, I doubt they could've sprung anything *new* on you," Brent snapped, crossing his arms as he stood watching her.

His grandmother glared at him, brown eyes smoldering. Smoothing her skirt against her knees, she replied, "You'd be surprised, Brent. You'd be quite surprised. You've seen them what, once, twice? And you've never seen the Abby Ewert I knew. If you had known her, you'd be more scared than I am. Abby wasn't an *obviously* evil woman, not like Otis, but in her own way she was *worse* than Otis ever *could* be.

"Those scene boxes you saw may well be all that's left of Otis . . . but your wife *is* Abby. I saw her, only a glimpse when the twins brought her here a few days ago, but she *was* the Abby I knew. The face . . . as well as a certain . . . *look* in her eyes.''

Brent knew that *look*—the odd light that came into Zoe's two-color eyes when she spoke of what she'd seen in that shower room in high school, on whenever she found cause to delicately rip into someone she hated. And there was that watery scene in that nickelodeon. . . .

"Brent," his grandmother said softly, "none of us saw this coming when Abby married Zach, either. He was a wonderful man, and they seemed happy. But when Otis came—Abby had an inner resiliency, from putting up with the taunts about her illegitimacy, that none of us *sus-pected*. It made her *hard* inside, while the outside was gentle, unassuming. Otis made that hardness in her *bloom*.''

Reaching over to scoop up Duffy, from where he slept on a nearby footstool, Brent said, "I still don't understand why Zoe was cut like that . . . on her side. You say she's Abby all over again, but to Palmer, Zoe was the second coming of the twins. The cut only reinforced it—"

"Ever hear about killing two birds with one stone? Zoe is the stone, Brent. I think the twins needed her back here for their own ends, and to end their anger at their mother. From what you said, they need Palmer, and Winston, too. Remember, this place used me to get Wilbur—"

Hugging his cat close, Brent said, "This place already had the twins to entice those two old men. It didn't need Zoe—"

"Yes, it did. You see"—Treeva's eyes lowered as she laced and unlaced her fingers in her lap—"the twins never went into your town until Zoe returned with you. They *couldn't*. What they are *here*, in their *home*, isn't what they were out *there*. Here they're two separate people, but over there. . . .''

"They aren't," Brent finished for her.

Silently, Treeva nodded her head of brown curls, rocking back and forth in place, then whispered, "I don't know if you were aware of it, but people in your town have seen the twins driving around in the Pierce-Arrow. Since it's known Zoe was in town, people *assumed* Maeve is Zoe. Zoe gave them mobility . . . when they leave this place, some of their *abilities* remain with them. Not enough to keep them separate, but enough to allow them to *do* certain *things*—''

The fresh pink walls in his uncle's room. That lingering redolence of flowery perfume. A dead body that wasn't a *dead* body—

"—heard them say something else. Something you must know. Whatever they did to Abby, in that fairground building, they believed it made her go away, depart forever from Zoe. Whatever *performance* Abby put on, whatever throes she went through, it *touched* the twins. And this place. I felt . . . *pity*. So now, Zoe has *abilities*, because of it—"

Getting to his feet, Brent asked, "Where is Zoe now?"

"They all left a few hours before you arrived. I don't know where they went. She added, as Brent raced to the kitchen door, "The road outside leads *nowhere*. And the bathroom won't work again, either. You're too conscious of it." Duffy protested as Brent shifted him to a carrying position under his arm. "I can't stand around . . . if I don't at least *try*, I'll go nuts." Brent shook off her hands and headed for the door. He heard Treeva's quick footsteps as she followed him out the back door, into the murky darkness of that path between the house and the barn. Finally, she spoke, "At least take the car . . . the road is horrible enough on foot, in daylight. I don't know *what's* out there in the nighttime. Please, use the car, I'll worry if you don't."

Duffy squirmed in his arms; Brent knew that he couldn't hold onto him for long. Reluctantly, he said, "If you don't mind never seeing the car again. 'Cause when I find Zoe, it's leaving town with us."

In the gloom, he barely made out Treeva's nodded assent, as she said, "It's in there, if you *must* go. There's gas in the tank, keys in the ignition."

Inside the barn—which bore lingering manure and straw scents—the car, a model Brent didn't recognize, was parked just inside the door. When he ran a hand along the fender, his fingers touched something sleekly warm— Chewie, curled up on the car. The cat *churruped*, then jumped down, to rub against Brent's legs. Treeva hung back, silent. Not knowing what else to say to her, he got into the car. He called for Chewie to jump in, too; with both cats curled up on the front seat beside him, he turned the key, shifted the clutch and felt the car purr with life beneath him.

The headlights casting twin cones of shifting light before him, Brent pulled out of the barn and down the drive, the wheel strange-feeling under his fingertips. With a shamed half smile he paused to wave at Treeva, then set off down the road . . . which curved *as* he drove.

In the distance, there was no merry glow of golden street lamps to guide him into town—if there even was a town before him. Then the trees appeared in the darkness; the branches gradually bent close to the car, the tips of the thick green-black leaves softly patting the windshield. . . .

After driving what the odometer said was *ten* miles, Brent pulled over to the side of the road, making sure that all the doors and windows were secure against whatever might wait outside. That done, he said, "Come morning, we drive right into reality."

Far from Brent, the slumbering women dreamed, no longer fearing intrusion or discovery in the renewed security of the old Ewert house. And even as the twins slept, a single hope was shared between them—that tomorrow they wouldn't be failed, as they were in life.

PART FIVE

The Water Carnival
Thursday, July 28, 1988

In visions of the dark night
   I have dreamed of joy departed—
But a waking dream of life and light
   Hath left me broken hearted.

Ah! what is not a dream by day
   To him whose eyes are cast
On things around him with a ray
   Turned back upon the past?

That holy dream—that holy dream,
   While all the world were chiding,
Hath cheered me as a lovely beam
   A lovely spirit guiding.

What thought that light, thro' storm and night,
   So trembled from afar—
What could there be more purely bright
   In Truth's day-star?
              —Edgar Allan Poe
               "A Dream"

ONE HUNDRED FOURTEEN

6:01 A.M.

"—is Thursday, July twenty-*eighth*, the two hundred and *tenth* day of the year. Looks like it's gonna be a *great* day, WERT sign-on temperature is seventy degrees, not a cloud in the sky. The annual Ewerton Water Carnival kicks off today—"

6:13 A.M. Running through town toward the fairgrounds, Tony Wilkes and Adam Doyle assured each other that the South-State people would have a *heck* of a time erecting anything until Tony and Adam showed up. And they'd pay in free tickets, too. But when they reached the site, they realized they were too late.

The riders were set up—merry-go-round, Ferris wheel, tilt-o-whirl—plus booths and concession stands. A big sign outside the storage building read HALL OF WONDERS! in glistening and shimmering red letters. There *was* a long truck parked to the rear of the rides, but Tony whispered to Adam, "No tracks . . . how'd he do that?"

The "he" in question was a redheaded fellow, with three moles on one cheek. Making sure that the "Mystic Tarot Wheel of Fortune" sign hung just *so* over a booth, he turned to face the two boys. In a clear, melodious voice, with just the hint of an accent, he said, "No need to leave. Just don't get in my way, hear?"

Edging closer, they watched the man in silence. He righted the hot-dog stand, lifting the wooden structure as if it were a toilet-tissue carton filled with nothing but air. Tony asked, "Your crew coming later?"

"Ah . . . my *helpers* left early this morning. I need no assistance. Oh, I see. . . ." From his tight black coat, he withdrew a huge roll of tickets. Handing it to Tony, he admonished, "Your friends might want some too."

Backing away from the odd man, Tony whispered, "Th-thanks, mister," before he and Adam *ran*, precious roll of tickets tucked under Tony's arm. Behind them, the man shouted, "Carnival opens at ten sharp! A *wonderful* time to be had by all. . . ." Then, softly, to himself, "A *most* wonderful, time, *indeed*. . . ."

7:08 A.M. Brent woke up both tired and hungry; his legs cramped and his back aching. The cats, also hungry, mewed and pawed at him. Rubbing his stubbly face, Brent mumbled into his hands, "Sorry, guys, didn't think to bring a case of food. . . ."

The Andersen's cat stood on his hind legs, pawing at the glove compartment, his mouth a jagged cavern of stalactite and stalagmite teeth. Stroking the cat's sleek, rounded head, then running a finger down his slightly bumpy nose, Brent watched Chewie try to pull open the little glove compartment door with his pearlescent, sharp-tipped claws—until one needle-tip caught the upper edge of the tiny closure and pulled the door down.

Inside the compartment were two cans of Fancy Feast Chopped Grill cat food, the kind Duffy loved. While the cats pawed his arm, mouths open, Brent ran a finger over each can—they *were* real.

He pulled open the lids, and set the cans on the back seat. The car was filled with moist, jiggly smacks as the cats chowed down. Listening to them, Brent wondered, *Did you girls make a pit stop in the kitchen after changing Palmer's room?*

After the cats licked the cans clean, he started up the car—which he now saw was a black sedan of some sort, and drove slowly down a road that lopped under his wheel. Slapping branches left kisses of moisture on the windshield, obscuring his vision. Not that *seeing* that road helped.

7:39 A.M. As he packed the old knapsack he'd lugged up from downstairs, putting in enough clothes to hide his bundled money and conceal a few items, Palmer felt curiously euphoric over the prospect of leaving everything behind him. Take off into the void, meet his fate after a forty-eight-year wait. If he died, so be it.

Palmer kept glancing at his watch, hoping that the Wanderer would arrive on time.

8:12 A.M. All over Ewerton, members of the EHS class of 1978 prepared for that night's reunion; getting up early to fit in a hair appointment, putting final touches on a new dress, or washing the car for the run out to the moderately swanky Hole-in-One Club.

After shooing the younger kids outside, Heather Thorn Wilkes picked up the modular phone from the cereal-and-banana-peel-littered table, and dialed a number with fingers that shook from excitement. In a much-too-bright voice she chirped, "Hello? Are . . . are you coming tonight? Oh, *good.* I saw you at Clive's funeral, but I didn't get a chance—I keep *meaning* to run up your way, but . . . yeah, it's been a *long* time. But you *are* coming, aren't you? Oh, *great*—"

Across town, Susie Parkinson Reish put down her phone with a funny smile; her husband Craig asked her before he left for the funeral home, "You okay, Susie? Face is as red as a beet—"

Susie shook her head of honey hair; her large breasts moved in time with the motion. "Excited about tonight, that's all. I have to get my hair done . . . I'll pick up your suit from the cleaners on the way home. *Bye,*" she prompted, pushing him out the door.

8:27 A.M. Stu Sawyer took extra care with his dress uniform, going over the pants with that sticky roller Val bought at some house wares party. He wondered when he could gracefully shake loose from the Water Carnival and drop over at the Nemmitz place . . . something told him that Brent had itchy feet.

And something else nagged at Stu, beyond the old coins and crumpled bright leaf Brent had taken from his pockets, something Stu hadn't quite *processed* before. Brent wore clothes like Stu's *dad* used to wear, in the '40's . . . including a light *jacket.* During a heat wave. And Brent wasn't the least bit sweated when Stu helped lift him off the ground after he fainted.

Stu Sawyer decided that he had to check out Brent again, and soon. But as he put away his lint-roller in the catch-all drawer in his dresser, Stu remembered that he had to talk to that goomer from WERT *before* the ribbon-cutting ceremony, officiate at *that*, then he had to . . .

9:01 A.M. All around Ewerton, the carnival booklets with Palmer Nemmitz's curious history of Ewerton shoved inside were placed in bundles of twenty copies each next to a paper-covered soup can with a slit in the lid. A card read "Official Water Carnival Programs—Goodwill Offering, 25¢." Many people took the booklets, but few thumbed a coin into the narrow slot.

Once people paged past the photos of "Beautiful Ewerton," they came across a photocopied little booklet, with the inexpertly typed heading, "Ewerton ** The REAL History by Palmer E. Nemmitz."

And almost everyone who bothered to read it was hooked when the old newspaper articles began, telling of a man named Zach *Roberts*.

9:25 A.M. Sarah Andersen tried to concentrate on her bowl of puffed wheat, telling herself that she was over-worried about the reunion. *That* made her dream of Zoe. But the intensity of the dream refused to leave her, even as the details faded from recall. But Chewie had been in the dream, too. He was the only clear thing she remem-bered—he was sitting, eyes closed, purring, on the top of a high car seat.

A tear slid down Sarah's cheek as Blaine spit puffs of wheat at his sister, Brook wailed and kicked Blaine's feet under the table, while Li'l Scoot poked his fingers into his bowl, sub-merging each puff—and boo-hooed when they bobbed up again.

Sarah wasn't aware of all the noise until Scooter stomped in from the garage—where he'd been spray-painting the car—yelling, "Sarah! I can hear them God-damned brats all the way in the garage! How the fuck can I concentrate, huh?"

"Scott, I'm not going to the reunion." She said it in a rush, not taking her eyes off her bowl of flesh-colored cereal, so she didn't see Scooter stride over—but she felt his open-palmed and stiff hand as it came in contact with her cheek.

The kids blubbered as Scooter barked, "Will you *quit* that shit? *We're going.* I've waited ten years for this and I'm *not* gonna miss it. And shut them *brats* up, will ya?"

While the kids finished their meal in scared silence, Sarah hid her face in her hands, head bent low over her untouched cereal.

9:36 A.M. Under the glare of the sun, the Happy Wanderer ambled toward the Nemmitz farmhouse, hoping to make it before the group-home leaders found him. He'd slipped away before the others had piled into the big yellow van, which was going to take them all to the fairgrounds. But Happy didn't want to watch people go around and around on the rides. It made his head all woozy.

Not owning a watch, the Wanderer wasn't sure if he was late or not, but if he was, he hoped the old man wouldn't yell at him.

9:40 A.M. "Palmer, how *could* you? You—you—*you old fart!* All our *money*—"

"I left in more than *you* ever put in, Beatrice. You can check the passbooks yourself. According to them, you deposited a total of five hundred and fifty *combined* in savings and checking. I left you more than that—"

" 'More than that' my *foot!*" Bitsy threw the bankbooks to the floor, stomping in place. "I won't put up with this! My lawyer in Minong issued a restraining order! I have rights, too, I deserve my share! And quit *laughing* at me!"

When Palmer was unable to stop, she stomped over to one of the end tables and knocked off a lamp. The base shattered into fragments of hobnailed milk glass, as the nubby shade bounced in place on the flowered carpet. Kicking in the TV screen with her thick-soled, very sensible shoes, she chortled, "There! Pay for that out of *your* share!"

Palmer felt as if he were floating *above* it all as he watched her rampage—until Bitsy saw the stuffed knapsack. Coming to his senses, Palmer shouted, "Get your fat hands off that!" Bitsy stood there, a sly smile spreading across her puffy face.

"Oh? What's so special in here?" she asked, reaching in to feel around in the knapsack. Swiftly, when her attention was focused on the contents of his bag, Palmer reached over and picked up one of the old photo albums, which he brought down on top of Bitsy'd permanented halo of gray curls. The rifled knapsack plopped down on the couch a second before Bitsy softly went "Umph!" and sank to the floor, a stack of banded fifties still in hand.

Palmer paused a second to make sure she was still alive, then snatched the money out of her hand, shoved it in the knapsack, and looped it around his arms, his joints popping with the exertion. Without a backward glance, he walked from the house, leaving his car in the garage and Bitsy's rented Audi in the driveway. He couldn't see the Wanderer yet, but figured he'd meet up with him down the road.

9:41 A.M. As Bitsy kicked in the tube of the color console television, the yellow group-home van chuffed to a stop next to the Wanderer when he was half a mile from the farmhouse. "Park your butt in here, Cooper, or I'm calling your nephew and *he'll* deal with you!" The Happy Wanderer made his way to a backseat; he longingly watched out the window as the van did a U-turn and headed back into town.

10:01 A.M. The ringing phone woke Bitsy up; rubbing her head, she gagged on the large foreign objects in her mouth. Spitting them out, she clumsily started to get to her feet when strong arms encircled her, lifting her to her feet. Turning around quite easily in those strong arms, freed from the girth of old age, Bitsy looked into a pair of eyes she hadn't seen for decades—

"Oh, *Tommy*!" she squealed, as the phone rang on and on.

10:02 A.M. Even though the sound of the ringing phone carried exceptionally well that morning, Palmer failed to hear it as he slowly walked away from the white farmhouse. But as he trudged in the oppressive, damp heat, he *did* hear something that made him spin around anxiously—

Vern Nemmitz whined to his younger half brother, "Well, who's gonna cut the *lawn*?" until his voice was drowned out by the blat of a poorly muffled car.

10:03 A.M. Stu let the phone ring thirty times before he hung up. Instead of dialing again, Stu debated whether or not to call the operator and find out if the Nemmitz phone was connected, or just go over there and see if anyone was home. Out in the main lobby, Terry Von Kemp moped at his desk, bemoaning that he'd pulled desk duty during the opening of the Water Carnival. Stu strode out of his office; over his shoulder he told Terry, "You're in charge of the whole shootin' match, make sure nobody runs off with the keys," and was out the door before he could hear Terry's colorful reply.

10:05 A.M. As Stu Sawyer's second-in-command called him a "card-carrying shit-for-brains son-of-a-whore," Palmer watched Tom Calder's Dillinger jalopy race past. Clive Calder was driving, and Tom and his gal Bitsy Sawyer were in the backseat; both were too busy snuggling to notice him as he gasped in astonishment at their passing.

Not daring to look forward at the diminishing roadster and its young occupants, or backward at the farmhouse—what he'd seen when he looked the first time both scared and angered him—Palmer kept walking, feet kicking up dust, thinking, *The old man and Vern . . . they can't do that to me. I don't have to take it. I have money, I can go anywhere just as long as it's away from here.*

Vern's voice grew faint as Palmer walked away from him; *I hope you have to mow the damned lawn morning, noon,* and *night.* In the middle of his mental tirade against Vern, Palmer felt something rush past him at great speed—something big enough to displace air all around him. Then the sensation was gone, and only hot, heavy air pressed down on his skin.

Undeterred, Palmer adjusted the knapsack on his back.

Cat walked over my grave. . . .

The road stretching before him was like a live thing, growing in length with every step, so that things that lay far away *stayed* far away. Spooked, he put one foot before the other, looking downward to avoid the white glare of the sun.

Every time he looked up, the trees on either side of the road were more dense, and overhanging. About that time, his skin began to itch, but as he resolutely marched forward, Palmer only said aloud, "Damn heat rash."

10:10 A.M. Pulling up alongside the Nemmitz mailbox, Stu couldn't explain those two pockets of air (one big, one small) that shook the squad car about a mile from the farmhouse. But when he took a good look at the house, he forgot all about the strange *jolts* in the air, for Palmer's Nash was visible through the uncurtained barn-cum-garage doors, as well as a small tan car parked in the driveway.

Walking over to the rental Audi, Stu saw papers on the front passenger seat. Leaning in through the open window, he read the top sheet. A restraining order, to keep Palmer E. Nemmitz away from any and all assets of Beatrice C. Nemmitz.

Stu mused, "So she's ditching the old fart at last," then looked in the garage for Brent Nimitz's car. The Pacer wasn't there, but it hadn't been at the fairgrounds the other day, either.

But Bitsy was never a walker. Once Stu saw her drive the Rambler from end to end of the same block, rather than walk from a store at the beginning of the block to a store at the opposite end. And the Audi's engine was cool.

So someone was in the house when he was trying to call. Taking a deep breath, resting his hand on the butt of his pistol, he cautiously approached the silent house. . . .

10:21 A.M. While not in actual *pain* (nothing topped falling from that train, or getting Mae-bit), Palmer felt so strange he wandered into a tight grove of trees close to the road, telling himself that he needed a rest anyway—but as soon as he sat down, Palmer felt around in his knapsack for that silver-backed mirror of Maeve's.

Leaning against a thick tree trunk, Palmer closed his eyes, positioned the mirror in front of his face, then slowly opened one eye. Shaken by what he saw, he replaced the mirror in the knapsack. After examining his hands in the green-filtered light—until he could no longer bear to look at the infinitesimal writhing of his skin—he used them to pillow his head as he curled up under the tree. Squeezing his eyes shut, he insisted, *Nothing's wrong with me . . . just tired, that's all . . . eyes playing tricks in the sun . . . just . . . so . . . tired. . . .*

10:32 A.M. When the Water Carnival Committee volunteers came to the fairgrounds a half hour before the festivities began, there was no one from South-State Amusements manning the rides, or the booths—let alone someone to tell them how much this was going to cost the city. But the committee men did their best; they manned the booths, operated the rides, and if any of them wondered how all this stuff *got* into town, no one voiced his concerns aloud.

When Gordy opened the newly christened HALL OF WONDERS!, he did find someone in charge of the clutter inside, a redheaded fellow who insisted on overseeing the "amusements" in there himself—after assuring Gordy that he'd go an honest fifty-fifty on the profits with the committee.

The meager crowd drifted over to the rides and booths, while a loudspeaker blared out polkas and country-western

ditties from the WERT studio and several locals spent the
better part of the morning with their noses stuck in the pro-
gram insert, seduced by the prosaic line:

A long time ago, Ewerton was a different place altogether, name of Robertsville—but that was before the
evil came. . . .

Those old enough to remember a *little* more than most
nodded, saying to themselves, *I heard tell them couples were
no good.*

As she stood next to the merry-go-round, keeping one eye
on her offspring, Sarah Andersen devoured the pages of Mr.
Nemmitz's "History." She shivered despite the muggy heat
as bits of dream/memory floated back into the pool of her
consciousness.

Suddenly, she paged backward, until she found the place
where Palmer had painstakingly described the trucks that carried the disassembled carny from site to site down South. She
glanced at the lone truck parked to the north of the fairgrounds.
The names were too similar to be a coincidence.

As her children circled the carousel, rising and falling
around its mirror-studded core, Sarah wondered if she was
looking at the same truck Palmer Nemmitz had seen over
forty years ago. She *had* to get out of town. Tonight. Before
darkness and the things that hide half seen there came out
into the wavering moonlight. . . .

While people lingered in the HALL OF WONDERS! before the
strange tableau boxes, puzzled by the unusual scenes within,
more than a few of them felt their fast-food breakfasts rise in
their throats.

Despite their elders' reactions, the children present couldn't
get enough of the displays and curiosia in the building. Most
of them clustered around an upright glass box, all but obscuring the mechanical figure within. The kids pressed
around, feeding it change, and those who broke away, satiated, quickly recruited new viewers with the whispered aside,
"Over there . . . *real* neat!"

10:52 A.M. After Stu placed a BOTL on the police band for
both his cousin and her husband, plus Brent Nimitz and his
Pacer, Lenny Wilkes picked it up on his scanner and drove
over to the farmhouse. He explained, "Knowing them Nem-

mitzes, I didn't think it would hurt none to come," as the sheriff stood in the middle of the farmhouse living room, surveying the damage with a puzzled look on his face.

Stu scanned the room again, taking in the exact damage—and the lack of it. There was the broken TV, tossed photographs, shards of broken glass; but no pools of blood, no pulled-out hair, no indications of shots fired or hard blows landed.

Before Lenny arrived, Stu had searched the entire house, alone, gun in hand, but the other rooms were clean. No signs of forced entry or exit. Nothing out of the ordinary—aside from the fussy pink-walled bedroom obviously shared by a couple, despite Bitsy's years-old confession to Val that she and Palmer no longer shared the same bed.

But an old couple deciding to share a room again wasn't a *crime*, so Stu marched back downstairs, in time to hear Lenny banging on the front door. Now, while Lenny yammered over by the broken TV, Stu made a mental note to dust everything in the room for prints—not that it would do much good, without being able to roll the fingers of the Nemmitz/Nimitz clan for comparison prints.

Lenny, trying to be helpful, bent down and picked up a bankbook and checkbook, shoving them into Stu's preoccupied line of sight. "Lookit. Think Palmer dropped 'em?"

Taking them from Lenny with a swipe of his big hand, Stu opened the last page of the bankbook. Looking at the name of the bank that issued it, Stu said, "I *know* Palmer had accounts in other banks in the county. Used to see him making deposits all over . . . but hell, even if he just cashed in this one, he's got over fifteen thousand dollars on him—"

Silently, Lenny shoved other papers under Stu's nose, plastic envelopes and carbons of CDs. Flipping open the other bankbooks, and paging through the flimsy yellow carbons, Stu did some addition. *Old bastard has close to a* million *and he drives a friggin' Nash Rambler. No justice in this world, no way, no how—*

Looking over Stu's shoulder, Lenny did some figuring on his own. "You don't suppose he had it *on* him—"

"I can find out from the banks. Let's check this room again—the fight didn't go beyond here. Just don't *touch* anything, okay?"

Lenny gave Stu a thumbs-up, but while Stu examined the broken lamp for blood or matted hair, Lenny forgot Stu's warning and picked up something from the sofa. Holding it in midair, he said, "Hey, Stu, lookit. This Bitsy's?"

Telling himself, *I cannot kill him, he's the coroner. I'm the sheriff and folks wouldn't like it*, Stu walked over to take a better look at Lenny's find—a woman's tortoiseshell comb, with a long strand of gold-brown hair wound in the teeth— and only when he came within a foot of the sofa did he step on Bitsy's discarded false teeth. *

11:07 A.M. By the time eleven o'clock rolled around, only Winston felt sufficiently awake to go downstairs and find himself something to eat.

His father still wasn't up when Winston finished his toast and coffee, so he wandered around the house and soon he found himself in the library.

Awed with the sheer size and scope of it—the volumes were even more numerous than his last memory of the place— Winston walked from shelf to shelf, hands clasped behind his back like a schoolboy.

Peering at the titles, he marveled at the age and preservation of the volumes—until he saw Crowley's *Magick*, and the other occult volumes, and noted their oft-read condition. Frowning slightly, he kept on looking at books, until he found a big leather-bound, blank-spined volume on a bottom shelf.

The worn top of the spine, ripped from frequent removal from the shelf, made it so inviting, so, curious over the volume's no-name status, Winston felt an irrational urge to pull the book out and page through it, carrying the heavy ledger-style book to the wing chair next to the liquor-bottle-covered table.

The pages were black paper, the edges irregular. *Photo album* flashed through his mind, until he opened the book— and saw all the newspaper clippings fitted into the crescent-shaped slots cut into the black pages.

Settling back in the chair, Winston scanned the brittle, yellowed squares and rectangles of newsprint, as he read of his father's marriage to Hortense Crescent, the opening of Wilbur's store, and other events in *Robertsville*, not Ewerton. On a few pages there were gaps, places where some of the sepia-dated articles had been removed. The fall of 1913 was missing, as well as—

"*There* you are."

Winston peered out from behind the right wing of the chair

to smile at his father—who didn't return his smile. Feeling like a criminal for going through Wilbur's papers, Winston let the album fall shut with a muted *chuff* and placed it on the bottle-strewn table. Wilbur circled around to sit in the chair opposite his.

Before Winston could ask his father why he looked so upset, Wilbur said, "I'm awfully worried about that brother of yours. He's been gone for so long I don't know what to think. Could you take the car, go looking for him? You understand him best, know where he'd most likely be—"

Winston knew it was logical that he go, but had a hunch that something wasn't as it *should* be. Nothing seemed strange about his father's request. Winston could drive, and Wilbur *said* he'd loan him the Woody . . . yet things refused to add up, as if his subconscious was hiding the rest of the facts in the matter—

Affiably, he found himself replying, "Sure, I'll go after him, he can't have gone very far on foot. I just wish I knew why he took off—"

Traces of old guilt nagged at Winston's conscience, but his father was saying, "—not important, now." He reached over and gave his son's shoulder a squeeze. "What's important is that you find Palmer, and bring him home. Tonight," he added, almost as an afterthought.

Dutifully, Winston got up, but the conviction that things were *way* off kilter refused to leave him.

12:56 P.M. Brent had to drive with the windows open only a crack, least the cat jump out and vanish in the glowering tangle of trees that pressed in on the ever-writhing road. There was no question of trying other routes—but Brent kept a lookout for any clearing or path veering off from the snake-in-heat course.

"Hang in there," Brent said, adding to himself, *There* has *to be an out*.

2:15 P.M. It had taken Stu two hours of running around—none of the banks would cooperate over the phone—but he finally got the information he wanted.

Now, as he sat with his Tony Lamas propped up on his desk, Stu sucked in his breath as he rechecked his figures, and let it out in a quavering whistle.

Over three quarters of a million, in twenties, fifties, and

hundreds. Palmer could buy and sell half of Ewerton and Palmer wouldn't so much as buy Bitsy a secondhand Yugo—

Poking his greasy head into Stu's office, Terry Von Kemp said, "I just got a call from the Register of Deeds—said old man Nemmitz sold his house the other day—"

"I don't care if he sold his mother into—*what'd* you say?"

"He sold his house to some woman. For a *buck*—"

Leaning back until the top bristles of his crew cut touched the window behind him, Stu thought, *And I'll just bet she has taffy-brown hair.*

5:03 P.M. The posterboard sign in the Hole-in-One Club lobby read: "Welcome EHS Class of '78—'78 is GREAT!" but Sarah Andersen didn't feel so great as she nervously ran her fingertip along the thickly madeup spot on her cheek where Scooter slapped her that morning.

She couldn't eat the sliced ham and cold chicken at the buffet table, even after Scooter gave her an I've-already-*paid*-for-this glare from across the room.

Pacing the lobby, she glanced at the card table set up next to the posterboard and tempera sign where those name tags not claimed now lay.

The sight of Zoe Lawton's card filled Sarah with dread, even though it was still lying on the table. That a card *had* been made up confirmed Sarah's suspicions that Zoe *couldn't* have died . . . for Susie Reish knew better than to print out a card for a *dead* woman.

6:45 P.M. In the HALL OF WONDERS! there was a commotion over by the Dead Fred machine. Wayne Mesabi reared away from the still-squawking box, babbling, "Dead *Fred* . . . oh, shit, he's *in* there! Outta my way, you goddamn brats, 'fore I—"

Before Wayne made good on his threat, he sank to his feet and passed out before the machine that faintly intoned, "—this is my *gun. One is for fighting*—"

7:07 P.M. Winston couldn't help but notice that the trees that whizzed past the Woody's windows on that curiously empty road were like the ones he'd seen once in Georgia. Yet he couldn't remember *being* in Georgia before.

He hadn't been driving long enough to be *this* far south,

even as road signs proclaiming "Jesus Saves" lopped past, which meant that he *had* to be in the Bible Belt.

7:25 P.M. As Brent drove down the outlet-less road, the rumbling of his stomach reached audible levels. He figured that the buffet-dinner part of the reunion was over . . . Zoe had said something about wanting to attend the dance, which was set to begin at 8:00 P.M.

According to his watch, if Zoe or Abby or *whoever* was going to attend that reunion, she'd be arriving in a little more than half an hour. While the cats mewed and leapt back and forth from front seat to back again, Brent said out loud, "Ironic . . . a few days ago I couldn't wait to cross over to this place, and now I'd do anything to get *back* . . . even risk losing Zoe again, just to stop her—"

As if they understood, both cats began scratching the front passenger door. Glancing at them, Brent asked, "Whatsamatter, Duffer, you miss Momma?—"

Suddenly, *everything* was clear. No matter why the twins had decided to bring Duffy back to life, the words Brent had whispered to the dying cat so many weeks ago came back, hauntingly real. Maybe, just *maybe*—

Stopping the car, leaving the keys to dangle in the ignition, Brent scooped up Duffy and whispered into his tufted ear, "You find Mommy, okay? Make like a doggie, huh? *Find* her."

Brent opened the car door. Warm leaves smacked wetly across his face as he bent low to follow the leaping cats through the tightly packed trees. Brent willingly followed, for there was no other way for him *to* go.

7:52 P.M. Sitting in his library, Wilbur Holiday pressed his fingers into his eyes. *They're both on their way. If sending my sons into the unknown makes me a Judas, so be it. I don't deserve much more. Not after what I've done.*

Rising in the hazy semidarkness of the book-lined room, Wilbur stepped into the equally dark hallway. He found himself climbing the stairs, his hand limp and clammy on the railing. Heading for the little room under the stairs, he thought, *If I was halfway sensible, I'd end it all now. I wish I wasn't a part of this mess . . . hear me, out there? I won't do it again. Isn't it enough I sold out my own flesh and blood—*

Under his fingers, the knob felt cold, a biting chill that

overwhelmed Wilbur, bringing back memories not associated with his death at all, but tied to death nonetheless. He tried to pull his hand from the knob, but it stuck fast.

And when the door opened by itself with an icy *scree*, his eyes were blinded by light reflected off frost, the cool pure light of an early morning sunrise mirrored off a dusting of snow—

When he could lift his hand from the knob again, he pressed it to his lips as he reflexively walked forward. If the door shut itself behind him, he didn't hear it.

Eyes darting in horror, Wilbur saw that he wasn't in the little room under the stairs. Weak sunlight shone through a filter of circling pines and spruces, crisscrossed with stark bare hardwood branches. The radiance brought out the metallic sheen on the barrel of the rifle he now held in his ungloved hands. When he exhaled in panic, his breath hung before him, a misty extension of his fear.

Then came the sound of careless, running feet trampling fallen branches, overlaid with the thin, reedy wheeze of agonized breathing.

Mechanically, Wilbur crouched behind a tree—*again*—hugging the rifle against his rough hunting clothes covered body. Zachary Roberts' blood blazed, liquid rubies running down his body, a pulsing gusher of rich, glittering crimson. Only with difficulty did Wilbur manage to look away from the crushed garnet and pomegranite seed *maw* that had been Roberts' shoulder—and into the dying man's eyes.

Those eyes *begged*, while a clear, small voice Wilbur knew all too well pleaded, *You* can *get off a shot at each of them. You* can. *Easy as targets at a rifle-shoot booth*—

They were all there, running shapes against the deep green and figured black-gray of the woods. Horton, Porter, Enoch, Fred, and Otis, all moving, yet . . . flat, smears of drab color hovering in space—

He pointed his loaded rifle at each of them in turn. The weapon kicked against his shoulder with each shot; he barely remembered reloading as each of the men fell backward, revealing themselves as cutout figures, devoid of substance. When he gunned down Otis, the woods shook with an unheard scream.

Only then did Wilbur step out from behind the tree, to stand face-to-face with Zachary Roberts, who said, in the small, clear, sexless voice of *this* place, "See you *could* have killed them, as they once killed me. Wilbur, I congratulate you, for you know what I am—'' Roberts lifted his shattered left arm to indicate the woods around them, and beyond— "do you not?" Wilbur backed away, shaking his head.

Nonplussed, Roberts continued, "You had so little *proof*, yet you made an educated guess—" here the droning voice grew mocking "—and discovered my true identity. And the young man believed your subterfuge . . . as you yourself chose to half-believe it, even as you co-operated with my children, rather than face up to me. You've beaten *some* of your demons . . . but you've yet to deal with *me*. I realized your choices were few that day, but they were *choices* nonetheless—"

"*No,*" Holiday mumbled, "I've paid. I've *paid* for what I did, my sons have paid. I didn't *want* to kill you, but—"

Defensively, Wilbur raised his rifle, aiming for the living soul of Ewerton—

7:53 P.M. Treeva got up from the sofa where she had sat for what seemed like an eternity. Trudging up the stairs to her bedroom, she thought, *If I hide, climb into bed, pull the quilt over my head, I'll miss it all. I want Wilbur, and I want my son, but I'm* tired, *so tired.* But as she climbed the stairs, they shifted, changing under her feet, as did the railing under her hand—

When she looked up, expecting to see the landing of *her* house, Treeva's eyes came to rest on the smug, grinning face of Hortense Holiday. She stood clothed in her dressing gown, arms folded, staring down at Treeva.

Treeva's hand tightened on the suitcase she was holding—just as it did in 1938. Carried on by an irresistible inertia, Treeva mounted the rest of the stairs, until she was face-to-face with bigger—and angrier—Hortense. But this time Treeva's head didn't feel fit to burst open and drip out brains—she was able to *think*, to *act*—

"*Whore, slut, bitch,*" Hortense seethed. "You can't *have* him, he's *mine*. He's not going off with a farmer's cow of a—"

Dimly, Treeva remembered that *before*, she'd tried to push past Hortense, intent only on reaching Wilbur—but now Treeva saw that Hortense was a closer target, a target balanced just as precariously on the landing as Treeva herself was.

This time, Treeva said nothing, but swung her suitcase as

Hortense reached out for Treeva's shoulders, knocking Hortense off balance . . . and down the stairs, in a tumble of robe, fat arms and legs, and snapping bones, the sound as loud and echoing as a gunshot—

7:58 P.M. —the rifle kicked against Wilbur's shoulder with such force he was knocked out of bed and onto the floor in a heap of twisted bedclothes, suddenly wide awake enough to hear Hortense's "I'll teach you something about 'falling for' another woman's man—" and the *whoosh* of something heavy swinging through the air. To make contact with something equally heavy . . . but *yielding*—

When he reached the doorway, he saw Treeva, suitcase in hand, looking down at the source of the bumping and cracking noise that grew fainter as Hortense's body tumbled down the stairs.

Turning to look at him, eyes tearing, lips drawn back in a shaky smile, Treeva whispered, "I . . . I wasn't going to, but oh, Wilbur, I'm so *glad* now. . . . And I . . . I . . . *oh, hold me already!*" Flinging down her suitcase, she ran into Wilbur's arms.

As he hugged her, lifting her and swinging her around, Wilbur glanced down the staircase . . . where only a valise and scattered clothes lay strewn on the carpeted treads.

Until they, too, dissolved and vanished.

8:02 P.M. Unseen and unnoticed, Zoe Lawton Nimitz—clad in a black suit with a peplum jacket and padded shoulders—emerged in the Hole-In-One Club from a hallway that she had not entered earlier. Walking with an easy grace missing during her tortured days in the halls of EHS, she went up to the bar.

In a quiet voice, she asked, "Rum and cola, please?" Not taking a second look at who ordered the dark concoction, the bartender slopped Coca-Cola Classic and Bacardi into a tall glass and slid it across the already wet and glistening bar to Zoe.

Seating herself on one of the black, padded barstools, Zoe sipped her drink. She noted with satisfaction that nearly all her tormentors were present, and smiled in anticipation. Behind her, some man gibed, "Where's old man Winston? Wear him out?"

Zoe ignored him, intent on the two women chatting at the far end of the bar. Susie Reish and Heather Wilkes—one full-chested so as to almost be a parody of womanhood, the latter carpenter's plane flat, and both visibly excited by the other's presence. Heather whispered, just loud enough for Zoe to hear, "I *told* you Pop Wilkes was lying through his—"

Zoe smiled to herself; how *easy* things would be now. For years, two faces were seared in her brain, faces shame and pride wouldn't let her forget. Not until she found a way to *best* them, shove their hypocrisy in their faces and grind it in until the blood came. An eternity ago, in a strange bedroom, she'd almost let a razor ruin her chance at retribution. . . .

But tonight, both birds were poised within her sight, and picking them off would be easy . . . once they roosted in the same bush. Watching the women out of the corner of her eye, Zoe saw first Susie, then Heather casually leave the bar and saunter down the hallway to the ladies' room.

Zoe finished her drink, and was about to follow the pair into the rest room when a classmate of Zoe's who had moved from Ewerton years ago slid onto the booth next to Zoe's, beginning by rote, "I'm updating my annual—see, everyone's signing next to the place where they signed be—oh, it's *you*, Zoe. They said you wouldn't be coming . . . but I'm *glad* you showed up, *really*."

Nancy Weiss's face flushed under a coat of splotchy Cover Girl and pressed powder, frowsy white-blond hair bobbing with nervous jerks of her head (Nancy always wore too much make-up back at EHS . . . in the days of the accusing circle, and the question capped off with Susie's "We *have* to know, you know. . . .").

With false-nailed hands, pre-colored surfaces twinkling, Nancy placed a 1977 EHS yearbook and pen in Zoe's hands. Nancy twitched when her fingers made contact with Zoe's flesh.

Her smile deteriorated into a squiggle as she prattled on, while Zoe paged through the book she had never been asked to sign at the beginning of her senior year eleven years ago, "Almost everyone else came, I'm so *glad*, y'know, 'cause I couldn't wait to see what we all looked like, 'specially the guys, y'know, and—"

Tuning out Nancy's hitching, terrified prattle, Zoe flipped pages, watching hated faces go past. She paused to scan small groupings of hand-written comments, until she found what she sought. Words she only half-remembered seeing years ago; words she hoped were as devastating in their simplicity as they were over ten years ago. When cheerleader Nancy Yates was bucking for a place on the student-elected homecoming court, she let Zoe *look* at her yearbook . . . not long enough to sign it, but long enough for Zoe to read at least one inscription all the way through.

Words written near a picture of the Pep Club; a few lines, in a rounded, too-perfect handwriting, with lopsided circles over each lower-case "i":

"Thank you Nancy for letting me be part of the group again this year, and for talking to me. Susie P., '78."

The words were as Zoe remembered them, in all their circles-over-the "i"'s irony . . . pretty Susie, steady squeeze of football captain Craig, Miss Pom-Pons and Choir soloist, all around EHS Suckie-Girl had to *beg* the other "in" girls to allow her to be part of their clique. Susie, who then had the gall to treat Zoe as if *she* was the one who had to beg for the slightest shred of dignity or respect. The same "in" school darling who openly accused Zoe of things Zoe never *dreamed* of doing . . . when she herself did those same things with Heather Thorn. . . .

Teeth set behind her perfectly painted lips, Zoe handed the annual back to Nancy unsigned—which Nancy failed to notice. She was too busy twisting her faux-nailed hands in her lap.

Without a word of good-bye, Zoe got up and walked to the ladies' room, thinking that the *girls* should have had enough time to get started.

8:09 P.M. Neither Susie Reish or Heather Wilkes heard the muted *scree* of the bathroom door hinges, or the sharp *tippy-tap* of high heels with new soles slapping against the tile floor. But each flushed and giggling woman found herself reliving the same moment from the past . . . a time when they thought themselves alone in the tile-walled EHS shower room.

But with pleasant remembrance came realization. They *weren't* alone that afternoon. An echoing memory of bare feet on wet tile came back to Susie and Heather; each recalled someone other than themselves *breathing* out of their sight, but not out of sight of *them*.

And another, unrelated recollection returned to both women as they stood face-to-face, bare knee to bare knee, near the cold commode that shared their cramped stall quar-

ters. Only *then* did Susie and Heather hear the tap of footsteps
outside, and pressed closer, this time out of fear.

8:10 P.M. As Palmer slept, the odd trees around him *shifted*,
losing their imposed form, taking the shape of trees from
another time entirely—

When he awoke, in darkness, he lay quiet for a few seconds, eyes closed, wondering why he was sleeping in the
damp woods. The incidents of the day came back, unbidden—his almost contact with Maeve, the fight between Jomel
and Harold Shea, playing cards with Larry, the Fat Lady, and
then . . . and *then*—

Heart racing, Palmer got up in a panic—and felt the splatter
of cold rain on his skin; dripping, drenching *sheets* of it,
along with the *pain*. Instinctively, Palmer grabbed his right
arm, only to recoil in stinging agony.

8:12 P.M. Susie and Heather held on to each other, their
perfumes growing intense, breathing quietly through their
mouths, as the person on the other side of their stall went
about her business. Whoever it was, she took an awfully long
time to do something as simple as go to the bathroom and
wash her hands afterward. Water ran for a full two minutes
while she washed up, and she pulled down towel after towel
with dry snicks.

Then . . . the other sound began. A teeth-jarring squeal, a
fingernails-on-blackboards shrilling that went on and *on*, with
short pauses that only prolonged the aural agony. Heather
tried to look through the narrow crack between the door and
the support where the door was attached, but the mysterious
woman was out of her line of sight.

And when silence returned, it was like a roar of white
noise, followed by the retreat of the unseen tapping shoes.

The women stifled giggles against each other's shoulders;
Susie whispered to Heather, "Where were we, hmmm?"
Soon, soft rustlings and other sounds could be heard, as they
shifted and reshifted position in the close confines of the pink
stall, not caring how loud their delighted cries were.

8:13 P.M. As Winston sped down the back roads identical to
those in Georgia, his car hood still wet from that evening's
downpour, he cursed himself for wasting time with that Jomel. Even if she *did* know of that carny in town, most likely

she wouldn't have told him about it. Not if she wanted to collect that dollar fee later on.

Biting his lip until warm salinity touched his tongue, Winston pressed his foot on the gas pedal.

If I hurry, I can find Palmer before it's too late.

8:16 P.M. After she gave up looking for Zoe, Sarah came to the bar for a free drink. An elongated rectangle of light against the other side of the hallway caught her eye; the door of the ladies' room had been propped open.

It filtered into her already worried mind that quite a few people were making that long golden rectangle waver and fill with shadows. Shades moved in silent laughter before retreating.

Sipping her second Tom Collins, she studied the faces of Scooter's classmates as they came down the hall. Some were disgusted, others openly pleased; while the majority snickered nervously into their hands.

With growing uneasiness, Sarah realized that no one made a sound while standing *in* the doorway—as if not wanting their presence to be known to whoever was within the room. As one group of watchers exited, another knot of them inched forward, to pause and lean in the open doorway before lurching away, doubled over in silent mirth.

By the time Sarah downed a third drink, some of the viewers came back for a second peek. At that point Sarah decided she had to see what was so damned interesting in a plain old *bathroom.*

Gingerly she got off her stool, then tottered down the hallway to the rest rooms in the sling-back pumps she wasn't used to, passing a pair of women who wouldn't look her in the eye as they hurried by. Despite her blurring vision, she noticed the women's cheeks were flushed.

The door was propped open with a small rubber wedge; the hall itself muffled noise from the bar and dance floor, making it difficult to notice that the door had, indeed, been left open.

When Sarah leaned in, holding on to the door frame for support, she heard *sounds*—especially from a voice she knew from many a morning spent glued to the phone—and felt herself getting sick.

At the far end of the bathroom, the moans and soft personal sounds continued, uninhibited and unabated. Ducking down to peer under the stalls, Sarah realized that the women couldn't *know*. . . .

Seeing that she was alone in the hallway, she pointedly walked into the bathroom, stomping like a five-year-old in her uncomfortable shoes as she ran the water. When she went to get a towel, she saw the mirrors—

Sarah forgot about warning the women in the last stall as she ran from the rest room, the door swinging shut behind her. Only after Sarah left did Heather and Susie timidly unbolt the pink door and poke their heads out of the stall, quickly pulled up panty hose catching their slips in lumpy ridges under their skirts, faces aglow with both excitement and growing shame. From where she stood behind Susie, Heather said, "I don't think anyone heard us . . . we could begin again if—"

Susie stepped out of the stall. After looking around to see if anyone was in the room, she turned her head to check her smeared lipstick and mussed hair in the mirror—

—and her scream drowned out the last of Heather's words.

8:20 P.M. Fully alert, Palmer saw lightning illuminate the carny trucks and trailers in the distance. Then, muffled by the boom of thunder, he thought he heard . . . screaming. He remembered passing out after telling Larry that Maeve was waiting for a *real* man, in that unlocked trailer of hers.

Maeve and Mae had company. Getting to his feet, knapsack thumping like a back-slap, he ran past trees, face smacked by dripping branches, as he raced for the carny site, but it grew no closer.

8:20 P.M. Sarah bolted across the dance floor like a hunted thing, despite Scooter's shout for her to come back. She pushed through the glass-paned door, into the stiffling heat of the parking lot, trying to shake the image of what she'd seen etched into that mirror out of her head *(it was smooth, like it was* in *the glass, not* on *it)*, that pathetic handwritten inscription: "Thank you, Nancy, for letting me be part of the group again this year. And for talking to me."

Running for their repainted wagon, shoes tucked under her arm, Sarah didn't see the woman until she bumped into her.

"Oh, sorry, I—oh . . . *no.*" Backing away, Sarah couldn't stop *looking* at Zoe, whose black suit all but blended into the darkness, jet buttons flashing in the light from the street lamp in the far corner of the parking lot. Zoe was the very image of the woman Sarah had read about only that morning.

"Sarah, don't be afraid—''

Letting out a fluttering breath, Sarah forced herself to step forward. It *was* Zoe, alive, well . . . Yet, some facet of her being was changed, off kilter from the Zoe Sarah remembered.

Zoe came closer, her footsteps echoing in the parking lot. Sarah relaxed. Zoe *had* to be real, Sarah could hear her. Then Zoe asked if she'd seen what was in the *room*—

"Do you understand why I did that to them?" Zoe's voice was distant—not physically, but emotionally, spiritually. Sarah only shook her head, as she looked questioningly at Zoe.

As if speaking to a very small, frightened child, Zoe continued softly, her words barely carrying the distance between herself and Sarah, "Those two killed a part of me I . . . needed, to grow as a human being. Because of it, they didn't grow either.'' Zoe's voice grew as fine as the mist that rises from hot pavement after a summer rain, as Sarah listened, entranced by the soft voice she barely understood. "The others enjoyed the show, watching without stopping it.

"But you did something about it. Not that it will change things, but you can consider yourself the better for having done that much.''

Zoe turned and began to walk away; before she all but vanished in the surrounding blackness, Sarah cried out, "Zoe! Don't leave. I know no one cared before, but you've settled your score. Please, Zoe, come back—''

Zoe's face was a tiny oval floating above the rich blackness of her suit; when she spoke, her mouth was a small, working O of blackness.

"Go back inside, see the last of it. I'll be back later.'' Then, so quickly and entirely that Sarah missed her passing in the blink of an eye, Zoe vanished.

Caught up in a surreal fog of uncertainty, Sarah walked back to the club, across the dance floor, and down the hallway to the closed bathroom, telling herself, *I* am *drunk . . . or getting there. I wanted to see Zoe, so I saw Zoe. It can't be that bad in here—*

It was worse. When Sarah opened the door, her eyes were greeted with the wet-white glare of steamy white tiles and the steady *drip-drip-drip* of water from wall-mounted shower heads. In the distance, gleaming pinkish tan against the purity of the room, were Susie and Heather, hair flattened and dripping down their bare backs.

They didn't stop what they were doing, even as Sarah walked into their space of clinging steam and slippery tile, bare feet smacking like openmouth kisses as she approached the girls. They remained oblivious to Sarah, even as she screamed for them to *stop*, just *quit* it, someone might come in and *see*—

All the while she stood there, hair growing limp, clinging damply to her forehead. Sarah felt as if she were in a movie. Only she was alive, and the other girls *weren't*—

(Miles to the north, in the HALL OF WONDERS! Dusty Parks rubbed at the eyepiece of the nickelodeon he was raptly viewing, muttering, "Either take yer dress off or get outta the scene—")

—and the tile walls and floors made *every* sound echo maddeningly, nauseatingly. Sarah whirled around, to find herself staring into the word-etched mirror.

It was thickly steamed, but not fogged enough that Sarah couldn't see the vague reflections of Susie and Heather. They lay on the floor half naked and wet, their reunion dresses sopping from contact with a wetly tiled room—only now Sarah felt *dry* tiles under her feet.

8:26 P.M. Palmer felt as if he'd been running through the woods for two forevers back to back with ten years added for spite. Aside from a *slipping* sensation—not physically, but as if the ground altered under his running feet, to become more real than *real*—the trees grew no thinner, nor did the distant carny increase in size.

But the noises were loud, inhumanly agonized and painful. And Palmer knew *he* was the cause of all he heard; the screams, moans, and yelps of pain, from two female voices.

As he ran, he panted, "Oh, please, let me help. Got to go to her—have to *stop* this—"

The next flash of lightning was so close, so ozone brilliant, that Palmer stood still for a moment, eyes smarting and nose prickling from the scent of resin smoldering in a lightning-struck tree.

When he opened his eyes, he saw that he was *out* of the woods, close by the clearing where the carny was encamped. Lights were on, moving, shifting as some vehicles fled the scene and others remained. Against the crisscrossing lights stood dark, featureless silhouettes, watching.

The only people moving in the rain were Larry and the twins. He was dragging them through the muddy ground by Maeve's dark mane of hair, their bodies nearly naked, their grotesque true form wetly revealed.

When the next pure flash of light came, Palmer saw the helplessness on the twins' faces, then saw that Larry had a knife out, pointed at the place where Mae jutted out of Maeve.

"You don't wanna put out, I'll pull *her* out," he said; the blade flashed like wavering quicksilver before he thrust it at the peeled birch flesh of Maeve's torso.

Screaming, Palmer ran forward—

8:28 P.M. Winston thought he heard screams as he drove, but couldn't locate the direction. The renewed rain and thunder were too noisy, and the branches smacking his windshield only added to his confusion. One minor but meaningful detail stood out—the leaves looked like *leaves* again.

And as he drove, something deep within Winston, an urge almost buried by his inexplicable *need* to be with Palmer, told him without words that his half brother wasn't the only one who desperately needed Winston's help. There was a woman in danger, in terrible trouble who needed *him*—and him alone. Then the feeling found voice, a subtle yet urgent plea, *It's terrible to be small and helpless and hurting in a huge, hurting world*—

Trying to keep from sliding off the road onto the muddy soft shoulder, Winston was night-blinded by a flash of lightning, as the Woody barreled off the road, into the tall grass and taller trees—

8:28 P.M. Mud flew under Palmer's feet as he raced to Larry. Catching sight of him, Larry said, "You didden say nothin' 'bout *this*—" but said no more when he saw the rage in Palmer's eyes.

When Palmer grabbed the knife, plunging it deep into the man's neck, all Larry did was leave out a moist "Umph!" that disintegrated into a bubbling gurgle as Larry swayed in place, then fell in a soggy heap to the ground. On impact, the ground *shifted*, as he began to vanish, becoming a formless mound jutting out of the rain-blistered mud below.

With a strangled cry that slowly died unvoiced in his throat,

Palmer looked at the knife still held in his hand, as its red-beaded edge was washed clean in the rain, until the last trace of Larry's blood was gone, as Larry himself was gone.

Whipping his head around, Palmer saw the remaining carny trucks and trailers shimmer and dissolve in sheets of rain, leaving nothing but rainy darkness around himself . . . and the twins.

Gulping, Palmer faced them, staring at the thin glistening black sap-runnel of blood on the soft swell of Maeve's left hip . . . Shamefacedly he raised his eyes to meet those of the twins.

Fearing that their ire would be fierce, he waited for certain death—but moaned deep in his throat when Maeve reached out and wrapped her right hand around his. Moving the knife *closer* to her flesh, positioning the tip between her body and that of her sister, she said, *"Now,* Palmer, for all of us—"

Trying to back away, he gasped, *"No!* You'll . . . *die* again . . . like before, this all happened *before*—"

"Not the way it was meant *to work!"* Mae screamed above the rumble of close-by thunder. Moving as one, Maeve and Mae pushed the knife in Palmer's hand against their shared flesh. As the glint of silver disappeared into their luminous whiteness, tarry blood flowed. . . . Before Palmer's eyes adjusted to the *change*, everything around him grew murky tan-gray and *dry*, the earth below them arid, crumbly.

His footing uncertain, Palmer fell forward and wrapped his muddy arms around Maeve—*only* Maeve—the stray twigs and tree needles clinging to his skin pressing deep into her flesh. He felt her blood flowing warm and impossibly thick against his skin, sheeting over his torn forearm. He thought, *Please don't die, you can't die, I've come so far to save you. Heal, please, become what I thought you were all along*. He held her tighter . . . until *she* hugged him back. With two arms . . .

And Palmer didn't notice or care where Mae went.

8:30 P.M. Winston's eyes finally grew accustomed to the darkness; when he could finally see again, he realized that he was looking at a white Pierce-Arrow, parked crookedly, close to the side of the road, the back end hidden in the dark trees.

Getting out of his car and looking around for the driver of the lean car, Winston told himself that the girl *should* be somewhere nearby, but it wasn't *raining* that time, as it was now, until the small voice overrode his thought, *She's very small, you'll have to look* very *hard for her, harder than you looked for the Teenie-Weenies when you were a little boy. But she's* out *there. She can't come to you. You'll have to find her this time.* The tree-filtered rain soaked Winston to the skin within seconds as he bent down near the white car, his eyes casting about the long grass.

Then he saw her. She was lying on the ground near the rear wheels, wet hair tangled over her face, her baby hands, as finally Winston saw her for what she was. Fear and wanting warred within him; loathing for what he saw, and the half-dream desire for his fantasy woman-child . . . who now lay before him, alive, and in dire need of *him*.

High above them, the moon shone through a break in the roiling clouds, fully illuminating—

—the bloody terminator where smooth flesh gave way to skinned thinness and cloisonné tracings of exposed, pulsing arteries and veins, trailing off to stick-thin crooked limbs too fragile to support even the smallest of bodies.

Slowly she raised her arms, her eyes pleading; ignoring his revulsion, Winston dropped to his knees and swept her into his arms, holding her stunted body tight, tighter . . . until she was small and fragile no more, and he felt the pressure of her legs resting against his own.

And as his old memories merged with this moment, she once again became alien yet familiar in his arms . . . as the soil under their intertwined bodies grew powdery and ash-soft, as a dim light shone all around, sourceless.

[. . . In a place between memory and reality, Palmer saw how Maeve had changed—her withered arm was full, whole, and real to the touch, a fast-growing branch on a wounded tree. Like the ground and sky surrounding them, Maeve and Palmer saw each other with a sight familiar to this *place, where it occupied the space* between *time.*

[And in their universe within the world they'd known, the swaying treelike woman-figure embraced the rough-formed man-thing, both healing and healed in that melding embrace. . . .]

[. . . Another space between remembrance and substantiality, where the true sights and sounds of the region were the

norm, Winston and Mae united in a restoring union. Bodies merged as surely as their minds, until they reached a point where body and soul leave off. . . .

[Discarding fragile body-shells, the newly webbed and strengthened soul-mind sought out the parent soul-mind. . . .]

[. . . Even as the freshly healed beings who once knew themselves as Maeve and Palmer shed their delicate forms, seeking union with a more powerful force. . . .]

8:31 P.M. Barely able to keep the tireless, running cats in sight, Brent lost track of them more than once. Before him, the cats were little more than upright tails, one sleek and thin, the other a fluffy brush over pumping hind legs. Bent low to avoid clunking his head against a low-hanging branch, Brent panted as the cats gained on him again, loping across short, sunburned grass—

When Brent stood up, no more wet clinging leaves rested against his cheeks . . . for he stood among *houses*, the rundown dwellings of the Roberts Street he knew from that terrible Midnite Mayhem night.

A quavery, phlegmy voice started him with the question, "Awfully hot night, isn't it young man? Oh, what lovely *kitties*!"

The source of the voice was an old woman, hair Q-Tip fluffy around a softly sagging and wrinkled face. She sat in a rocker on her screened-in porch, next to a balding man with gnarled hands folded on a cane propped between his knees. Moths fluttered around the yellow bulb behind them; soon Duffy and Chewie were hanging on the screen by their sharp curved nails.

Their sudden leap elicited a startled "Ohhh *my*!" Brent hurried up to the screen and lifted each cat off in turn.

"Sorry, Ma'am, they saw the moths—"

Leaning forward, the man asked, "You a Nemmitz, perchance? Kin to Enoch? You look familiar—"

As he hefted the squirming cats, Brent replied, "He was my grandfather—"

" 'Was'? My, my, did poor Enoch have an accident?" the elderly woman gasped; her husband interjected, "Man's an s.o.b. Blanche, no use getting worked up—"

Thinking, *I finally escape that place and now I meet up*

with a couple who lives in the Twilight Zone, Brent said, "Yeah, he passed on. But tell me, have you seen my uncle, Palmer Nemmitz? Or—" he played a wild hunch "—Wilbur Holiday or Palmer Winston around?"

The couple shook their heads, but the man did say, "You want to check on Wilbur, try the house right behind you . . . he should be home." Turning around, half-expecting to see the restored Holiday House, Brent sighed when he saw the weathered version. Facing the white-haired couple again, he said, "Looks like he's out . . . could you two do me a *big* favor? I have to get some place in a hurry, and it's kinda rough with these guys—"

"Certainly, we'll watch your kitties," Blanche said, getting up to unlatch the door. After Brent pushed the cats through the opening, she added, "They'll be just fine. . . . Are you perchance planning to attend the carnival? Or that reunion the nice Meals-on-Wheels man spoke of—oh, I was hoping it was the carnival. We *planned* to go, but—"

"Man doesn't care about that, Mother;" tapping the porch floor with his cane, the man continued, "If you get back here 'fore we turn in for the night, let us know what all that commotion was out that way, would you? We saw lights 'way off in the distance,—" he used his cane to indicate the direction of the Hole-in-One Club "—sirens yelped to beat the band. Could've heard it without *this*." He tapped the hearing aid in his right ear with a horny finger nail.

Out of politeness, Brent nodded and smiled, soul sick and utterly crushed.

He was too *late*.

9:15 P.M. The ten-year reunion of the EHS Class of '78 came to a premature end by thirty-one minutes past eight; within ten minutes most of the cars had pulled out of the parking lot. So many, in fact, that the two ambulances and the squad car had a hard time pulling *into* the Hole-in-One Club lot.

Not that the two women were in danger of death. But those who looked into Susie Reish's and Heather Wilkes' eyes, before they were covered and strapped down on gurneys, later agreed that *something* had died within both women.

When Lenny Wilkes stepped into the blighted room, the very tiles and hydrangea-pink walls reeked of something private, personal, something best confined to other places. He saw the broken mirrors, and how the silvery shards littering the floor were still clouded with *steam*. More than one piece of silvered glass was incised with thin, curving lines, like writing.

Sarah and Scooter Andersen were in the wagon, heading for the baby-sitter's house at the junction of Roberts Street and Byrne Avenue.

Sarah kept on saying, "*There*. Had enough *reunion* to last you awhile?" while Scooter maintained his white-knuckled silence, wondering what in the hell had *happened*.

9:32 P.M. Wilbur and Treeva cradled against each other in his big bed, content to merely feel real skin against real skin— not the twitching pseudo-life of before. Then, getting up on one elbow, Treeva whispered, "Feel it? It's happening. Even the air is strange—"

Softly Wilbur brushed his hand across her cheek and lips, shushing her with a quiet, "It'll happen without our help. . . . It's up to them now . . . but we're almost home free, Treeva, almost back where we should be."

9:33 P.M. In that last minute, the last sane moment left, *before—*

Brent made it to the Mill Bridge in time to see the pair of ambulances pull into the hospital parking lot—and sank to his knees in frustration;

Carnival-goers left the rides at the fairgrounds, and headed over to the banks of the Dean River, to watch the Water Parade at ten;

The men of the Water Carnival Committee placed the last of the pontoon-mounted floats in the water;

The members of the Water Carnival Queen Court protested about having to go down in the water when they distinctly heard rumbles of thunder, despite the clear, cloudless indigo sky above;

While Scooter dashed into Mrs. Rice's house to pay her, Sarah tried to comfort the kids as they cried and fussed in the backseat of the station wagon;

Tony Wilkes and Adam Doyle hung around in the deep shadows of the half-lit HALL OF WONDERS! under the indifferent eye of the redheaded man, who seemed more . . . *preoccupied* than before;

Stu Sawyer hunched over his desk, waiting for word on the

three missing people, none of whom he seriously believed he'd ever see alive again;

And the strange thunder in a cloudless sky echoed throughout the town, its source both immeasurably distant and quite, quite near. . . . A wild storm, intense as any the two Palmers and the twins remembered.

A tempest fed and made real by memory, augmented by the decades-old power of the soul and mind of a man named Zachary Roberts, who once, long ago, claimed the real town as his own. The whirlwind built up, floating free *between* the space separating *here* and *there*, until—

—the clear, hot, and still sky over Ewerton *imploded* with a mass of seething, churning clouds, pounding rain, dazzling white-hot forks of lightning, and a nearly deafening clap of thunder that appeared like a fist thrust through a wall of wet black tissue—

—and in that second, the waters of the Dean River arced up in chopping, wind-driven waves, as men dived into the foaming waters, to rescue the screaming girls on the tossing pontoon floats;

From his place by the Mill Bridge, Brent cursed himself for being helpless to stop what*ever* was about to happen;

On the Woodard's front porch, the screen glassy with trapped raindrops, Chewie and Duffy meowed, pawing the wire mesh around them. Puzzled, Blanche and Manther got stiffly to their feet and tottered over to the porch door. When Manther opened it to stick his head out, the cats slipped away through his feet. One ran toward an on-coming station wagon, while the other headed for the Mill Bridge.

Gingerly, the couple made their way down the porch steps, into the ribbons of whipping rain . . . it plastered their sparse hair onto their mottled scalps, yet felt so good;

Scooter braked just in time to avoid hitting the cat which dashed into the twin sparkling cones of his headlights, where the raindrops sparked up like fireworks. Sarah opened the door, calling out in a voice shaking with hope, "Chewie? Chewie-kitty-kitty? It's *him*! Look, Scooter!" Sarah bubbled, not listening to Scooter's terse, "Can't be him . . . he got car hit. Buried him myself. I couldn't bear to tell—"

But when the rain-sleeked cat began rubbing his bumped nose along Sarah's arms, Scooter told himself, *Must've been a different cat I buried;*

Duffy, a dripping dust mop with huge luminescent eyes,

ran into Brent's field of vision just as his master ran down Lumbermill Drive into town;

As the wind picked up, the rain became a hand, pressing those few people not safe within their homes down to the bubbling sidewalks and streets. To the north, the rides just *stopped*, shook in place, dropped to the ground like shot things, and . . . *dissolved*, while Tony and Adam watched in terrified awe from the fairgrounds building;

Stu Sawyer's office lights went dead, trapping him in a womb of darkness;

The Andersens' car, with Chewie aboard, neared their house, coming within sight of it just across the bridge;

And those few people caught out, exposed, under the mass of scudding, lightning-shattered clouds—

—were all but blinded by the sheets of silver-clear rain and driving winds as the *change* began. . . .

Later, no one admitted remembering, seeing, or recognizing that anything happened at *all*, but there were a few people who found shelter enough to keep them aware and *watching* as it happened; even then, what they saw and heard and felt was something private, never to be confided to another soul;

Pressed against the floor of the HALL OF WONDERS! Tony and Adam each saw distant buildings and trees *vanish*, leaving nothing but a strangely jagged horizon backed with writhing clouds. Both of them felt everything *shift* beneath them, as if they stepped down on the ground only to have their feet go *through* the earth, going down and down;

Stu Sawyer huddled under his desk, peering up through a window that showed *nothing*. Just an empty yawning pit of rainbow-haloed near darkness, as his stomach plummeted;

Wilbur and Treeva clung to each other as the whole Holiday house shuddered, jerked, and *undulated* . . . As the opaque became invisible, everything *compressed* around them, as if something immeasurably huge was trying to squeeze through a narrow crack, all but suffocating them— After they could breathe again, they opened their eyes.

All was as it had been. Calm reigned again . . . Wilbur got up and padded to the window; after he pushed aside the soft lace curtains, he motioned for Treeva to come, too. They hugged in joy as they saw the rain, and the *people* outside, on the living street below;

The tornado-strength winds were too much for the majority of the homes in the Woodlawn Development, most were toppled, empty walls falling in one each other like poorly stacked playing cards. Sarah expected her house to follow suit, but through the sheets of semi-opaque rain, she saw her house standing upright and undamaged, while Scooter trembled in the footwell under the wheel, and the kids screamed and cried in the backseat.

Chewie kneaded her thighs through her soaked dress, as thoughts that were not her own entered her consciousness, imploring in a soft, clear voice, *Stay . . . won't you? Begin again?* Sarah whispered assent;

Brent crawled under a car, Duffy pressed against his heaving chest, only to feel it spin away above him, leaving his bent-over back exposed to the pummeling rain—

[—and as it emerged from that place between, the newly augmented soul-mind of the other Ewerton continued its work. Carefully it chose what was to remain, what was to change, and what was to be eliminated, following a plan beyond mortal understanding. A plan of wholeness *alien to what was before.*

[Without personality, without sex, without true identity, the soul-mind reshaped the town, leaving it a place of both past and *present. Past enough to please that which shaped, present enough to placate those who remained from before.*

[And when all was done, the soul-mind tired, fragmenting. . . .]

The golden lights of the street lamps dimmed, and sputtered out, even as the rain dribbled away to a pattering shower, leaving those outdoors to grope their way home in firefly-lit darkness.

And if the house next door looked *different*, perchance, no one was willing to question Ewerton's good fortune in remaining virtually intact.

Most people were aware that all was not as if *had* been, but were either too scared or too worn out to take note of things, as if grateful that the disruption was as minimal as it was.

The forces that had transmuted their town were beyond their understanding, but they called said forces *nature*.

ONE HUNDRED FIFTEEN

When it was truly over, Brent crawled out from under the car that had *appeared* over him sometime during the storm. In the light from the nearly full moon, he saw that it was his Pacer . . . and it wasn't empty. Someone was slumped in the passenger seat, arms draped around the stuffed Opus toy, head cradled on a black-clad shoulder. Duffy went crazy, squirming and crying as he tried to get into the car. Heart lopping, Brent opened the door; the interior light went on to illuminate Zoe. Only, for some odd reason Brent was at a loss to define, Zoe wasn't quite *Zoe* anymore.

Yet, she *was*. Confused, Brent watched as Duffy jumped onto her lap, kneading her chest and licking her chin. When Zoe stirred, Brent sucked in his breath, as she turned her face to his in the golden car light.

It wasn't quite *her* face . . . but the voice was hers. Sleep-slurred, it asked, "Brent . . . we in Ewerton yet? Changed my mind 'bout the reunion . . . Be mad at me if I want to go home?"

No, the face wasn't Zoe's—if the face she wore for the first twenty-eight years of her life was rightfully hers to begin with. But, it was *hers*; the curve of her cheek was her mother's, and the slight dip of her nose was definitely her father's. Mr. and Mrs. Lawton's features, those that were her birthright . . . only her honey hair remained.

But as Brent circled the car to climb in through the driver's seat, the sparkling gold and reddish-blond highlights dimmed, went soft cocoa brown, along with her eyebrows, as her skin turned soft tan. Duffy didn't care; he purred and kneaded and licked her cheeks with body-shaking cat-abandon. Breathing hard in the silence, Brent reflexively reached for the radio knob, not expecting any *answer* for what he was witnessing, but getting one anyway.

•   •   •

Maeve and Palmer awoke in each other's arms, dry and comfortably situated on the huge grassy expanse to the south of Crescent Lake. His head rested on her shoulder, nestled in the sloping curve where the hardness of shoulder gave way to the rounded softness of breast. Her hair was lying across his cheek when Palmer stirred; she gently lifted a strand of silky taffy hair and ticked him across the tip of his nose with it.

He stroked her face, fingers exploring the smooth warmth of her cheeks, her firm jawline, as he whispered, "What happened? I felt as if I was being dropped—"

Shaking her head, Maeve said, "*That's* not important now . . ." as Palmer helped her to her feet.

Across Crescent Lake to the north, Winston and Mae got to their feet; the former dashing in a crisp, pressed Army uniform, the latter lovely in a black peplumed suit with jet trim. As he rubbed his eyes, Winston said, "Last thing I remember is you, by the car and—"

Mae took his hands away from his face and pressed them on her own cheeks. As she pushed down his long fingers with her small ones, she whispered, "It's all over. . . . We're *home*."

Instead of music or garbled talk on the radio, Brent heard *something*; but the formerly sexless, quiet voice was different now, resonant and masculine as it issued from Brent's car speakers. With parent-to-child patience and firmness, it told Brent:

". . . *that which was taken away from me is mine once more. Just as you now have your own again. . . . Leave now, Brent. Take your wife and your pet and go from here. You play no further part.*

"*I will not permit you to interfere with my children, with their lives. I am sorry about those women, but your wife had her score to settle. The little she 'did' was nothing uncalled-for. Thanks to what I allowed Zoe to do, no one will harm my children. They will not dare, for fear of the consequences.*

"*What should have been will not be. In the place where it should have taken place. So leave us, now—*"

"Like *hell* I will, buster," Brent whispered furiously, as Zoe-not-Zoe shifted in her sleep, hugging both the

stuffed bird and the live cat in her arms. Gathering up all
the anger within him, Brent softly spat out, ''Who the hell
died and left you all gods? These people didn't deserve to
have the town they knew torn out from under them . . .
this is *their* time, too. How do you think they'll take this
come—''

—*Morning?* came the mocking conclusion of Brent's
words, followed by the seething reply, *They will fall to
their pathetic knees and thank God. Despite the changes,
no one will come forward, because they won't want to be
labeled as insane by neighbors who fear they themselves
have gone mad . . . they'll swallow their fear and go on—*
because they have to! *Either that or pick up stakes and
go. Staying will mean accepting.*

*And life will go on here, as it should have . . . before Mr.
Ewert happened along, to sour it all. I've restored your wife
to you; she's been repaid for what Abby did to her.*

*Put simply, your wife was used. You deserve to know what
transpired the night Zoe died. I didn't kill her, nor did my
children.*

My wife had returned to life in the most . . . selfish
sense. She . . . influenced your *wife from the point
of conception. While her lover's soul weakened, was absorbed into the remains of the carnival, Abby's leeched
into the woods where she expired. And she was canny
enough to submerge herself until the time was ripe . . .
before I could discover her in time, her new life in the
womb began.*

*And when the girl's parents brought her into town, I real-
ized what Abby had done, but it was too late. Others already
responded to the* spirit *of Abby within her, tormenting her,
until Zoe left town, never to return . . . I'd hoped, if hope
can be granted to beings such as I.*

Yet, even I was torn . . . I'd loved *Abby, as a goddess, until
that other man lost his miniscule heart to her. She didn't have
to love Otis* back, *she could've warned me, made me throw
him out of town, but she didn't. . . .*

She *brought your wife back here, as if sensing my plans
for my children,* her *children, too. The ones she* loathed
so. *But after your wife was back here, the part of her that
was truly* Zoe *couldn't go through with the prospect of
facing her tormentors again. So . . . after you all left that
night, Zoe took a razor to herself, until the part of her*

*that was Abigail stopped her, so frantic was she to live
again.*

*As I sent my girls over to stop Abby, Zoe overcame my
wife's urge to keep on living, slicing her arms just as the twins
arrived. Zoe was almost gone . . . nonetheless, my girls managed to turn the situation around to their advantage,* Roberts
went on with obscenely quiet pride, *for they needed your
uncle and his brother to join them, Palmer in particular was
so stubborn—*

Squeezing Palmer's hand, Maeve went on, "—was already in your bedroom when Mae and I arrived. Confused, perhaps. There was blood in the hallway . . . we
took care of that. But as Zoe lay between death and *our*
sort of life, I saw the camera on your dresser, and Mae
took that picture. A . . . reminder of the carny days. Then
Mae cut her, to remind you who *else* you were dealing
with. . . .

"For many a year, neither of us were . . . *fond* of you, not
at all. So . . . Zoe was something for you to remember us
by. Something to make you want to assuage your guilt, by
crossing over to us.

"But afterward, I saw something blue-bound poking out
from a pile of magazines. I pulled it out, read it, skimmed it, mostly. I knew the story—" she added, softly,
sadly.

Palmer interrupted, "If you wanted me to cross over, why
didn't you just *come* for me? I'd *missed* you—"

She asked in reply, "How often did you do something
because you were *ordered* to? Willingly, without dobut
and reluctance? You had to *desire* to cross over . . . we
had to all but drag Winston in. He was dying," she added
matter-of-factly. "His liver . . . we could feel the death
coming off him. And he was aging . . . but once we
brought him over, it was up to *him* to want to help
Mae. . . ."

"—and I so wanted you to stay with me, that first time, when
I found myself in that . . . *place*, once I was—*torn* from
Maeve," Mae went on with heart-breaking directness, giving
Winston's fingers a squeeze, "I hoped that *maybe* it would

work, even after everything else had gone wrong that night, that your love would make me really whole, really . . . *real*. Like in a story I read when I was lit-*young*—"

"*The Velveteen Rabbit?*" Winston asked, blinking back tears.

As he helped Mae up the steep rock-studded concrete steps to his house, he added, "When *I* was *young*, my . . . mother's husband used to take my hand, like this, and we'd say—"

Mae's tiny fingers circled his own, as she said in the faintly misty darkness, " 'One, two, buckle my shoe'?" before giggling as Winston picked her up and carried her up the steep flight of stairs.

All around them, the sky was a dome of glittering marcasite set in deepest ebony; Winston thought it matched the glitter of the rhinestones set in Mae's Bakelite stickpin . . . which for all the world now looked like real ivory and genuine diamonds—

—which, as he watched, it *became*. . . .

Blushing, Maeve continued, "—everything about us was so silly . . . ugly and horrible, too. It took Father so long to . . . *create* us, to conceive us in the womb of the woman who more or less killed him—and we didn't turn out right.

"It wasn't intentional, but a reflection of *his* state of being. . . .

"You can't imagine how hideous it was, growing up that way. Yet, it was ironic how Otis . . . *loved* us. We looked so like Mother, but perhaps guilt had an effect, too. Maybe we made his conscience bloom, or, after looking deep into himself to see if *he* was to blame for the way we were . . . formed, he softened. Otis Ewert had been an evil man, a greedy selfish animal with no conscience and no shame, but . . . he *cared* for us, as best he could. More so than *Mother*.

"She blamed him, Wilbur, Treeva . . . *everyone* for our being alive. If Otis had ever left us alone with Mother. . . .

"Otis gave us everything a child—children—could want. But he couldn't buy us everything. . . .

"We saw no one, played with no one but each other, as much as we *could* play together," Maeve said, biting her lower lip, "We never went to school. Otis did hire a tutor, ostensibly for me—his 'sickly' child—and he even took us outside, when it was cool enough for me to wear a cloak.

"Then . . . he took me—*us*—to see *Freaks*, in the balcony, where Mae could peek out too, and afterward, he told us, 'See, there are people out there who will accept you as you are.'

"But we didn't want to be *freaks* . . . and sometimes, at night, I'd lie in bed, pretending that Mae was just . . . *beside* me, and that when we awoke we'd get up off opposite sides of the bed—"

Rubbing her eyes with a fingertip, Maeve went on softly, "When we turned fourteen or so, Otis taught me to drive. At night, when it was difficult to see inside his car. Mae . . . helped hold the wheel when I had to shift. . . .

"One January third, our birthday, he brought home the Pierce-Arrow, and that night he suggested that, for our own good, we'd best prepare to leave, soon.

"Mother was terrified of us. Maybe she saw hints of Father in us, I don't know. Or perhaps she thought what Quigley had said affected us—people believed odd things then.

"So . . . we left home, driving off with ten thousand dollars in my purse. That was the first time we saw *fear*, real fear, in Otis' eyes, as if he knew what might happen to us—and was worried for us.

"Come early summer, we went into the deep south. One night we came across this little carnival—Mae was tired of being hidden away, never breathing outdoor air—so we rigged the doll mask, the gloves, the wires. . . . I feared someone would rip away Mae's mask and expose us, but no one did. We were in a carny, but *we* weren't freaks. We didn't have to be. Or so we told ourselves. . . .

"Admitting things might've been the less selfish thing for *me* to do, but I couldn't. And as the bigger twin, I was used to my own way—" she said, as they walked between the decorated Holiday house and the Woodard house.

(Manther and Blanche were on their porch, seated on comfortable matching wooden out-door chairs, sipping lemonade; the couple waved when Palmer and Maeve went past. Blanche whispered to her husband, "Palmer's such a lucky boy . . . she's the very picture of her mother. I'm so *glad* he stopped seeing that Sawyer girl. Beatrice and Tommy make a much better couple—if Clive'll ever leave

them alone!'' she chuckled, thinking of the battered roadster she'd seen whiz past the house during the trail-end of
the storm.

(''So right, Mother, so right,'' Manther said, clinking the
ice in his glass while pale moths fluttered around the yellow
ball of the porch light. Fire-flies danced and bobbed in the
plush blackness outside the screened-in porch, circling the
heads of the walking couple before flitting off into the darkness. . . .)

''—the time you came, I was of two minds. I knew Harold Shea needed a good freak, yet the illusion of normalcy
was so important to me. . . . I wanted with all my heart
for it to be normal between us. I . . . knew you wanted
me in so many ways. It was a horrible, yet wonderful time
for me.

''I didn't connect your home with my real father until much
later . . . after Quigley came for us.

''You see, Palmer, once we were . . . *forming* inside
Mother, our Father, being part of the place where he was,
realized what went wrong, but couldn't *fix* it. But as we neared
our birth, he figured out that our . . . situation could be
changed by someone who both loved us and *wanted* to see us
whole, changed . . . so *we* could change, for real. Something
like the way we changed after what . . . happened to us *happened* that night so long ago. But it wasn't a permanent
change. Father did the best he could, but it wasn't totally real
because *he* was no longer *real*. But you and Winston . . . you
fell in love with me for more obvious reasons, while Winston
loved Mae because she was a *need* Father *ingrained* in him,
from the time he was young. It almost took over his life, his
sanity . . . but there was no other way for Winston to ever
meet or learn to love Mae. . . .

''And when *that* night came to pass, both you and Winston
were . . . supposed to be there, to help us afterward. . . .
But it all went wrong,'' Maeve said simply, without need for
further explaination, save for—

''For a long time after coming home, we were resting,
dormant, while Father went about *his* business, setting out
after *your* father, for what happened in 1913—''

•   •   •

"Poor Wilbur, vacillating between the pure 'soul of the town' myth of his own design, and the truth of what I had become, what he had helped make me into. He glimpsed part of the truth in his arcane books, but he chose to believe what he could live with sanely.

"I made him alive again, as I let his woman live, only for the sake of Wilbur's sons . . . for the sake of my children."

His voice almost wistful, Roberts continued, *"If someone were to love them for what they were, they would, indeed, become what they should be—"*

Palmer and Maeve passed few people on the street; its wet, uneven surface reflected the renewed brilliance of the street lamps in tiny starbursts of shifting gold, earthbound fireworks they could walk across. As the Happy Wanderer bobbed past, shoving chocolate into his mouth, he managed to smile at the couple nonetheless.

Down the street from the carefree young couple, Stu Sawyer, both confused and bemused, walked through a town that, despite the lack of much *genuine* damage sustained in the freak storm, looked and did not look like the town he last saw. Some changes he understood, but others weren't so easy to rationalize away. . . .

Like the teardrop-shaped golden street lamps, or the old-time slat benches outside the stores. For he'd *seen* those old benches lying broken and warped in the city dump when they hauled away the town's old rides and booths . . . so he had no thought of saying *anything*.

As the couple coming toward him came up to a street lamp, one on each side, they parted their joined hands with the chant, "Bread and Butter!" then grasped hands again, the hackles on Stu's beefy neck rose imperceptibly.

Pressing a finger to his lips, sealing in the screams that bubbled in his throat, Stu told himself, *High time you packed it in, Stu boy . . . if that wasn't Palmer Nemmitz and that girl I saw in the frigging white car, I'll eat my badge and pick my teeth with the pin on the back. . . . And I wouldn't doubt that Bitsy's having a fine time wherever she is—*

Winston set Mae down on the front porch before he went to open the door. It swung open by itself as the hallway lit up to welcome them. He lifted her again and carried her over the threshold, like a Norman Rockwell war bride from a magazine cover of their youth, into the house, to his room upstairs. . . .

Sinking into a state near sleep, Winston pressed Mae closer to him, feeling her silky skin against his own. In his head and in his mouth, it was like an explosion of *green*, of lushness and peace only hinted at in dreams. . . . Only, this time, the dream hugged him back. . . .

"Manther, the lights are on at the movie house." Blanche got up, slowly, making her way to the screened-in wall facing the distant movie theatre, where the flashing bulbs rippled and shimmered against the velvet-upholstery plushness of the sky.

"So they are, Mother," Manther replied, getting up and offering her his arm. Arms linked, they walked down the broad porch steps, and down onto the sidewalk, two fragile moths drawn to the brilliant light. Manther no longer needed his cane by the time they reached Ewert Avenue; he left it propped against a scroll-armed bench. Blanche spit her false teeth out into her cupped palm, and daintily dropped them into the nearest black wire garbage recepticle, covering them with a discarded lace-trimmed hankie.

When his hearing aid began to bother him, Manther plucked it out and tossed it in the nearest storm grate. Blanche unwrapped her shawl and let it dangle from her firm, smooth hand; the ends of the crocheted garment trailing in the inky puddles on Ewert Avenue.

Near the movie house, the air conditioning made the warm sidewalks steam, a misty cloud of pale pink and yellow that swirled up around Manther's baggy trousers and Blanche's athletic legs.

And when they stepped into the lobby, going past the concessions and into the dark pit of the theatre itself, the light from the flickering screen was enough to illuminate their way . . . for their night vision was absolutely perfect. Only when they were seated did the couple look up in awe and remembrance at the screen.

Blanche snuggled close to her husband, resting her dark curly head on his broad shoulder as she sighed, "I was *hop-*

ing they'd play this one . . . I did so miss the movies. Didn't you, Manny?''

Manther nodded, throat too full to speak; *The Best Years of Our Lives* always made his eyes water. In the darkness, he slipped his hand over Blanche's, as they watched the couple on the screen, Wilma and poor Homer who lost his arms, went up to his room, where she tenderly took off his limbs and helped tuck him into bed. . . .

Up in the balcony, Palmer sat close to *his* girl, as tears blurred his eyes. Pulling her closer, he whispered, more to himself than to Maeve, ''I lost my family in that war . . . the old man, Vernilla, Vern, they all went away. And never came home—'' as if he just became aware for the first time that he had, indeed, suffered losses during that long ago war, and finally could acknowledge his guilt for those deaths. . . .

After a long silence from Roberts, Brent leaned back in his seat, thinking, *This* has *to be some sort of nightmare. . . . Zoe and I parked along the road, and—*

In silent answer, Brent suddenly smelled something sweetly corrupt, an effulgence that seeped in darkly and horribly. When he turned to look at Zoe, taffy hair framed a face that sagged *in*, webbed with lines of white moldy decay. Duffy lay stiff and glassy-eyed in her arms, dull fur covering bloated flesh—

Pressing his eyes shut, he started the car and gunned away blindly, thinking frantically, *Okay, okay . . . oh, please, God, all ready, I'll leave, I'll never,* ever *come back, just make them alive again,* please—

The car's interior was briefly lit as it passed under a street lamp. It brought out the dark highlights in Zoe's hair, illuminated the smooth tan curve of her cheek. When her dark brown eyes opened, she murmured, ''Whatsamatter, Brent? Hit a pothole?''

Brent went, ''Uh . . . huh,'' as he reached over to pat her Bill-the-Cat T-shirted shoulder (how she'd changed into *that* he didn't care to know). As he made a U-turn on the water-covered street before heading south, out of Ewerton, he added, ''Yeah, something like that. . . .''

And as Brent sped out of town, his taillights illuminated something new on his rear bumper. The dark green bumpersticker was neatly spliced together, the middle word, "TO" was missing, so the blocky cream letters now read:

"ESCAPE WISCONSIN"

In the fairgrounds storage building, where the last remains of the defunct South-State Enterprises Carnival were stored, all lights out, all secrets hidden under the cloak of blackness, a man named Quigley had to pinch himself just to assure himself that he *was* really real. And still in the town that had killed him—only to become the means of his final resurrection.

His eyes still accustomed to the darkness of death, Quigley could see all the tableau boxes, the Dead Fred machine, and all the rest of the fragments of soul and memory that were still intact, still a *part* of this place. He said out loud, his voice echoing in the hugeness of the building, "Old memories die hard, do they not?" before heading out of the building and carefully locking the door behind him.

ONE HUNDRED SIXTEEN

JULY 29, 1988

In the early morning hours, Stu Sawyer resigned and headed with wife Val for parts unknown; the reporters from Eau Claire, Wausau, and the Twin Cities came and went, seeking a big story about the freak storm but getting only a drizzle of cooperation from the residents of the miraculously unmarred town; a middle-aged man named William Holiday (a grand-nephew of the late Wilbur Holiday), accompanied by his two dark-haired and handsome post-teen sons, paid visits to the banks and realtor's offices in town, quietly claiming properties held in his "great-uncle's" name, and making cash deposits in new banking accounts; and the Happy Wanderer ambled to the movie house.

He liked *this* place. No more looking for the holes in the

air, no more wishing for the pretty while he lived in the ugly. He sniffed as the couple on the screen kissed while the music swelled up and out . . . because the *bad* feeling was gone, replaced by another feeling in the air. An almost palatable emotion, like the way air shimmied and danced above hot pavement.

Sort of happy and sad all at once, like love.

EPILOGUE
"Place of the Green Light"

This is what we really want
Who drink the kingdom of the heart
A toast to the imagination

She is flowering in a doorway
Eyes cheeks haze of hair
Stepping out of time into here

This is what we really have
Who see the one we adore becoming
The two she is in the light

Ah God bounces all the waters
From hand to jubilant hand
He cannot contain himself

But comes over into being
With benediction of painted cloud
The being whom to look at is to become

By fiat of adoration do we reach
The very muscle of miracle
The ease with which beauty is beauty

—Oscar Williams
''By Fiat of Adoration''

From *The Milwaukee Journal*, Tuesday, November 25, 1997, section one, page 4:

MURDER-SUICIDE MARKS START
OF EWERTON HUNTING SEASON
(Special to the Journal)

November 21—The 1997 deer hunting season began not with a deer kill, but with the deaths of a man and a woman in a heavily wooded area north of the Dean County City of Ewerton.

According to local law enforcement personnel, the two bodies were found shortly after noon last Friday. While the Ewerton police and Dean County sheriff's offices offered no further details, the hunter who found the bodies—he declined to be identified—stated that the deceased man held a gun in his hand, and that the woman had a bullet hole in her forehead. The names of the deceased have not been released, pending notification of relatives. . . .

ii

THURSDAY, NOVEMBER 20, 1997

As he drove past the black sign with the cream lettering that stood on the outskirts of Ewerton, Brent Nimitz couldn't help but think of his *last* night in Ewerton . . . the night he promised a dead man that he would leave, never to return. But Zachary Roberts had made an implied promise to Brent . . . one that had been broken.

But no voice, small and sexless, or masculine and cynical, thundered in Brent's head or issued from his car radio speakers that brilliant fall morning, as he steered his rental car through the streets he had hoped never to see again—save for in nightmares. Driving north on Ewert Avenue, until he hit Lumbermill Drive and followed it until he reached Roberts Street, Brent felt as if the buildings were pressing down on him, hovering before the kill.

Which buildings were real and which ones were real-imagined Brent could no longer tell—whatever had been undisturbed during the storm nine years ago had since been revamped, restored to vintage condition—but the whole town was still disquieting.

Save for the modern cars parked near carefully tended lawns, and the occasional child's plastic tricycle parked near a half-open garage door, the town was identical to the *other* Ewerton of Brent's all too painful memory. Even the illusion of the building popping out on him remained . . . if mere illusion it was.

Far off, Brent saw the lush thickness of the Ewert Woods, the virgin pines and spruces offset by the last vestages of the brilliant red and gold leaves of the hardwoods growing among them. A tremor passed through Brent as he remembered the snipe and its consort, and he drove on, disquieted.

On the seat next to Brent was a tourist guide for north central Wisconsin. The glossy booklet was folded over to the section on Dean County; the breeze coming in through the half-open passenger side window made the top page flutter and buzz softly. At the top of the page, an advertisement was circled:

*Where Atmosphere and Hospitality
Come Together For Our Friends—
Old AND New!*

THE HOLIDAY HOUSE * BED & BOARD
(A Historical Register Home)
Open Year Round

''Old Fashion'' Free Breakfasts
Antiques—Only

Furnished Singles
Close by Downtown
Two-Room Plus

Bath Suites
All Major Credit
Cards Accepted
Couples and Families
Welcome!
William and Theresa Holiday
Your Host and Hostess

---

309 Roberts Street, Ewerton, WI

There were pictures, too, but Brent hardly glanced at them. He knew the house too well . . . and its occupants. Idly, he wondered if Treeva's middle name had been Theresa, or if she chose it because it sounded like her old name. The monuments in the cemetery had been of no help . . . there was no middle name indicated under his grandmother's name on the Nemmitz family marker, and there was only an initial, "W.," behind Holiday's first name on his tall granite stone. But the line from Descartes was still there, and as he read it, Brent wondered, *Did you put that there for Roberts' benefit . . . or for your own?*

One thing seemed to be for certain; *this* Ewerton was now of a single mind, and of a unified taste. There wasn't so much as a frayed windsock or weathered redwood hitching post with dangling name plaques . . . the town was perfect, almost unspoiled in its *correctness*, its impeccable taste. As in the perfection of lilies in a funeral spray, or the immobile smile of a corpse resting against blue satin.

Brent passed a telephone pole bearing the sun-bleached remains of an April election poster—"Re-Elect Coroner Holiday," over picture of a man whose features Brent couldn't *quite* make out—

—but one of the Holiday brothers was the subject of that grainy reproduction. . . .

Brent sat outside the Holiday house for a few minutes in his parked car, feet straddling the curb. The hydrangeas had gone the color of twice-used tea bags, brittle rounds of fluttery petals on wire-thin stalks. A cluster of blossoms tore free of the bush near the porch; it rolled across the lawn like a severed child's head, to rest against his booted feet. With a faint "Umph!" he kicked the skull of blossoms into the gutter.

The house loomed above him, sage green and unchanged, save for the ribbon and Indian corn decorated grapevine wreath on the front door. Upstairs, a figured lace curtain rippled; a couple of minutes later the front door opened.

Wilbur—*William*—Holiday was unchanged. True, his blond hair had more soft white strands than when Brent saw him last, and the five or so pounds he'd gained were in all the right places, but his green eyes were still piercing, and when he spoke his voice was still commanding.

"*Brent*. Long time no *see*, young man"—the last was an ironic aside; Brent's brown hair was heavily salted with iron-gray, and his cheeks were slack and jowly—"come in, come in. I'll carry your bags—"

"I haven't any," Brent said stiffly, slamming the car door behind him. As he strode up the walk to meet Holiday, Brent glanced over at the Woodard house—and almost keeled over when he saw the couple wave to him from where they sat rocking in identical Bentwood rockers. Save for the dark hair and the smooth skin, they were the same senile pair Brent last saw in 1988—

Holiday stepped off the porch and hurried over to Brent, whispering, "*Wave*, dammit."

Brent smiled and waved at the couple; they raised glasses of what looked like hot cider at him before turning their attention to each other. By his side, Holiday said softly, in answer to his unspoken question, "Yes, the Woodards are still *lovely* people, if you get my drift," as he ushered Brent through the front door before he had a chance to take another look at the couple on the yellow porch.

Inside, the house was virtually unchanged, save for the unobtrusive registration area in a corner of the front parlor. The Sarouk rug, wallpaper and hardwood floors were all the—

"You shouldn't have returned," Holiday said without pre-amble, startling Brent into attention. They were alone in the parlor; behind them golden light filtered in through the heavy cream lace curtains and thin fringed shade. Up close, Brent saw fine worry lines between Holiday's intense pale eyes, as the older man said, "As I . . . *understood*, you were re-quested by a . . . *mutual* acquaintance not to come back—"

"Eavesdropping that night?" Brent asked, as he stood with his hands on his hips, trying to outstare his host.

Nonplussed, Holiday said, "You know as well as I do it wasn't a matter of *wanting* to know what was said . . . I simply *knew* you had been asked to leave—"

Above him, Brent heard footsteps, and laughter, and realized that Holiday had guests. Crossing his arms, he said, "I want to rent a room—" Holiday's face started to sag, but he recovered his composure and said, "Would a single be all right?" as if the words stuck in his craw. . . .

Brent doubted Holiday's choice of the little room under the second-floor stair landing wasn't accidental, but Brent wasn't about to let Holiday know that the room gave him the willies. Once Holiday left him alone, Brent shut and locked the door, then sat down on the brass bed.

Taking some clippings out of his wallet, he spread them on the quilted comforter, rereading the yellowed bits of paper with penciled dates on the tops:

February, 1991, *St. Paul P. Press*
DIVORCES—Hennepin County:
Amanda Petterson, from Richard Petterson.
Mark Foster, from Gloria Foster.
Zoe Nimitz, from Brent Nimitz.

November, 1993, *Mil. Journ.*

MONSTER SIGHTED IN STATE WOODS
(Journal Madison Bureau)

Ewerton, WI—Two Pewaukee deer hunters claim to have seen a "monster" in a wooded area north of the Dean County seat of Ewerton last Monday morning. The hunters, both of whom requested anonymity, described the "monster" as big, black, and two-horned, but stressed that it was not a buck or a moose. One of the men, a welder in his mid-forties, added, "It was slick-furred, like a bear, but had hooves."

The men stated that the beast was attacking a nude female, but when they approached, both the creature and its "victim" vanished.

After law enforcement personnel in Dean County failed to investigate, the men sought help from Taylor County sheriff's officers, but no evidence of foul play was discovered at the scene of the alleged sighting.

When questioned about the incident, Ewerton Mayor Chris Holiday stated that the woods in question were posted as "off-limits" to hunters, but added that no charges would be filed against the trespassing hunters. Mayor Holiday added that black bear and moose have been sighted in Dean County, but denied the presence of "monsters." Both hunters deny that they were drunk, insane, or trespassing, and they maintain that there were no signs posted in the woods where they sighted the beast.

Ewerton made state headlines when a freak storm hit on July 28, 1988.

And finally, a full-page spread from a 1996 supermarket tabloid. The gist of the article entitled "Death Town Baffles Bikers!" concerned a pair of bikers who lost contact with their fellow riders, only to find themselves tooling along another Wisconsin road, almost identical to the one they'd left . . . except that this road led them to a "dead place" of abandoned and gutted buildings, faithfully re-created by the tabloid's art staff.

While "trapped" there, one of the men drew a rough map of the place, with a lake to the right, and two hills on either side of the river to the north, and dotted with clumps of trees throughout. The reproduced map matched the crumpled Yellow Pages map Brent had torn from the Ewerton phone book almost exactly, down to the abandoned drive-in . . . which Brent *hadn't* seen when he drove into town that day.

One of the bikers swore that the "place" had a "*glow*, like northern lights . . . like it was all comin' down on us." At one point, the two men thought they saw an old model car drive by, with a young man driving and a couple sitting in the back seat, but the vehicle didn't stop when they tried to flag it down. One of the bikers saw something written on a car door, but was unable to read the lettering as the car sped past.

After several hours, the men found a road out of the "dead place," and rejoined their fellow bikers in neighboring Wright county. The pair stated, "It didn't seem right. No people, no animals, no birds, not even a f—ing mosquito, like the whole joint was stuck with posion gas."

Later, the bikers went back to Dean County and found a town almost identical to the one they were trapped in, but when contacted, the Mayor of Ewerton, Chris Holiday, was at a loss to explain the incident. He claimed the town was "always" as it was now, and proved his contention with old photos of the town culled from "private collections and archives." The Mayor, described as a "dakly handsome young man serving his second term," asked, "Do *you* see desolation here," hinting that the men had been stoned or drunk when passing through the town earlier.

The article continued, but Brent was more interested in the photos of Ewerton taken by the tabloid's staff photographers. Specifically, he was interested in a figure in one of the pictures . . . a woman with dark hair and skin, and direct, candid eyes, who walked with her face turned toward the camera. There was a faint, satisfied smile on her lips . . . lips whose contours were most familiar to Brent.

Even though he hadn't seen his ex-wife in years, he'd recognize her anywhere. No matter which face she wore. . . .

Briskly walking through town, Brent noted that despite the presence of modern merchandise in the store windows, the place might have been an old-time postcard come to life. Although he recognized a few people, they did not return his halfhearted waves, or nod their heads in his direction. After a couple of blocks, he quit looking people in the eye.

Despite the coolness of the air, and the fall mildness of the sun, Brent was soon roasting in his corduroy jacket. He leaned against the outer brick wall of the former Coast-to-Coast store, eyes closed, breathing fast and hard, until a voice startled him.

"Looking for someone, mister?"

Opening his eyes, Brent saw a couple of old men sitting on the bench his uncle and half brother used to claim for their own each morning. Wondering why he hadn't noticed them before, Brent ran his fingers through his thinning hair and replied, "Not really. I'm just looking around, enjoying the weather."

The heavier of the pair of old duffs crossed his leg, pulling up his trousers at the knee as he did so, before saying, "Don't pay any attention to old Wayne here, he just likes to nose. Should've kept on with the distributorship. Now that he's re-

A. R. MORLAN

tired he has to bug every Tom, Dick an' Harry that comes down the—''

"Aw shaddup, Arlin, you're as bad as that old man of yours was—''

A strange expression passed over the face of the heavier man, like clouds sending rippling shadows across a field ready for harvest. Brent smiled weakly, and was about to bolt away from Wayne and Arlin—when his subconscious dredged up their surnames.

"Come to think of it, you can help me. Do you happen to know where the mayor's brother, uhm, I forget his name—''

"Eddie?" Wayne Mesabi volunteered.

Palmer's middle name was Edmund . . . I think.

"Yeah, Eddie. Such a hard name it slipped my mind—do either of you know where I might find him this time of day?''

Arlin Winston pointed a shockingly liver-spotted hand to the south. "Eddie bought Lenny's Place when Len and Millie retired and moved down to Appleton. Eddie fixed up the building real nice, better than when Lenny—''

"Bought the coroner's job from Lenny, too—''

"No he *didn't*, Wayne, he was elected last—''

"Only 'cause Lenny's boy Jeffrey couldn't hack it—''

"Jeff couldn't 'hack it' if he used both hands and the toes of his left foot.'Sides, he's got his hands full taking care of his wife—''

Brent hightailed it away from there before he found himself hearing something he did not *want* to know—not until he could ask Zoe about it face-to-face. . . .

Cars of all makes and years surrounded the newly rechristened "Ewerton Amusement," but Brent didn't see a classic Pierre-Arrow among them. But he did see someone through the double glass doors who set his heart to thumping arhythmically in his chest . . . Quigley. Nonetheless, Brent walked into the building, telling himself, *I've come this far*. . . .

The neat revolving racks of videocassettes and shelves of laser-discs near the door quickly dispelled some of Brent's fear, despite the presence of Quigley behind the counter. Beyond the door, pin ball and computer games—most of them in use—clanked and *ponged*. In the distance, he heard bowling balls thunder across the alley, followed by the lightning cracks of balls hitting stacked pins.

Once his eyes adjusted to the dim light, Brent noticed some small glassed-in boxes along one wall. With halting steps, he went over to to inspect them, reluctantly bending down to get a better look, until he was startled by a familiar voice close behind him, "No, Brent, they aren't the ones you saw. Same principle, though."

Wheeling around, Brent found himself face-to-face with his uncle—who looked to be in his late twenties, if that. Putting his arm around Brent's shoulders, he yelled, "I'll be back in a while, Jon, okay?"

From his spot behind the counter, Quigley—still pale, but now dressed casually in jeans and a cotton shirt rolled up at the elbows—grinned, saying, "No problem," before turning his attention to a guy who wanted quarters in exchange for a rumpled dollar bill. But before Brent's uncle steered him down a hallway partially hidden by a curtain of tightly strung beads, Quigley managed to give Brent a knowing *wink*.

Brent let his uncle guide him down a short hallway, until they came to a door marked "Private." While his uncle fumbled with the keys on his brass ring, Brent found himself thinking, for no good reason at all, *I should kill him—kill them all*, but then his uncle opened the door and guided Brent into darkness. After locking the door behind him, "Eddie" felt around on the wall for the light switch. And with the coming of the light, Brent, wide-eyed and numb, sucked in his breath.

A riot of color, pattern and terrible shape assaulted Brent's eyes. The tableau boxes, the bloated Fat Lady in the water-filled tank, the Tarot Wheel, the Dead Fred machine. All the hideous amusements were crowded there.

Unable to face the *things* again, Brent rested his eyes on his uncle, whom he'd last seen as a fading old man. But the man who stood by the Tarot Wheel, uncertainty in his green eyes, was *young*—

The wrinkles of experience, of remembered pain, were gone, replaced only with the faint traces of lines across the smooth brow, the corners of the mouth. The fingers that nervously fiddled with the collar of his blue plaid L.L. Bean shirt were unbent by age, smooth and neatly manicured. And as a final blow of Brent's memories of the Palmer-who-was,

"Eddie" wore expensive leather walking shoes, the hundred and fifty dollar kind sold only in sports shops. . . .

Quickly, the young man said in a voice that sounded slightly *off* to Brent's ears, "You needn't worry about these things . . . they don't work any more. Only the Dead Fred talks, if you put money in, and I don't waste mine on what I had too much of for free. . . ." His voice trailed off with a mixture of uncertainty and plaintiveness which softened Brent, until Eddie went on, "The rest stopped not long after Zachary told you to leave."

My banishment was known to one and all, he thought glumly, dropping his gaze down to the hands his uncle had shoved in his jeans pockets. The pale orange Black Hills gold ring around Eddie's left ring finger told Brent that something had *finally* gone right for his uncle.

As if sensing his *faux pas*, Eddie made small talk, asking Brent how the cat was (Duffy was fine, staying with Brent's landlady over in the Cities), until the tension in the room was a palatable hum.

Casually, Brent said, "I see Ewerton's made the papers a couple of times since. . . . I'm glad Win-*Chris* finally became Mayor."

Sitting down on a small wooden stool Brent hadn't noticed before, Eddie said in a tired voice, "He wasn't glad when those bikers brought in those reporters. You see . . . after *things* became more or less normal, we all thought the other place was *gone*. Even the Happy Wanderer didn't go there . . . but when Chris found out that it's still *out* there, it put everything in a different light—

"Poor Chris really freaked out over the *snipe*—hurried up and put up those post-dated signs. No one goes in those woods now. . . ."

Oddly, his uncle's voice didn't sound convincing, but before Brent could point that out, Eddie continued, "Of course none of us *want* to really know what's still out there in that place. All of us—the girls and Chris especially—had enough—"

For a second, Brent thought he saw the Palmer of old— scared, stooped and dejected—so he quickly asked, pointing at Eddie's hand, "I couldn't help but notice—when did the two of you?—"

Brightening, Eddie held out his hand in a curiously feminine way, admiring the orange-gold band around his finger. "We were married that August. I know, I know, bad month for weddings, but Chris and the girls couldn't wait. And since I'd seen Bitsy and Tom that day . . . I figured she wasn't going to be coming back.

"That was the one good thing about the bikers, them seeing Bitsy and Tom. I'm glad they're happy. I . . . wasn't much of a husband. But it's different now. Maeve and I have children—the *change* was complete for me. See?"

Pushing up his sleeve, which had unrolled to slide down his tanned forearm, Eddie showed Brent skin that was free of the circular bite scar of old. Before Eddie retracted his arm, Brent thought he saw something unusual, but as if he realized that Brent had seen more than he should, Eddie got up, and headed for the door, saying, "Almost forgot, I'm to pick Chris up at the newspaper office. He's the owner, but edits the rag, too. We're having lunch out at the farmhouse—care to join us?"

Not getting a chance to object, Brent followed him out to a new four-wheel-drive mini-van ("The 'Arrow's in the garage—kids and the upolstery don't mix"), listening as Eddie prattled on, "—the kids, they're all home from school. Chris and Mae adore 'em, they lost a couple themselves. SIDS. Really broke us all up—"

"I can't imagine him being broken up, he was so hard-shelled—"

Eddie snapped, "You're thinking of *Winston*. The times he spent over *there*, alone, did him a world of good . . . even though the isolation did some damage of its own. I don't suppose *Zoe* was the same, after—"

"She wasn't the girl I married," Brent said simply.

Eddie came to an expert stop in front of the brick and sculptured facade of the *Ewerton Herald* office, where a tall, cream-suited young man leaned against the front wall. Winston's face was shadowed by a Monte Cristo panama hat (like the suit, totally wrong for the season, yet right for *him*), and his eyes were hidden by sunglasses, expensive, classic, deep black shades, but they failed to conceal the terrified shock which washed across his face when he saw who was sitting next to his brother. But apart from the gaping mouth and the limp hand dangling a cigarette, Chris Holiday might've been an extra from *The Great Gatsby*.

After Eddie coaxed Chris into the van—"He won't *bite*, for Christ-all-Friday"—Brent, scrunched in the middle front seat between the two men, noticed that Chris' suit was cut from fine gaberdine, and that his shirt was silk, peach with woven-in stripes.

Both men gave off the simple, regal odor of bay rum, and Chris wore silk hose and a moon watch. If not a genuine Patek Phillipe, most likely a good Swiss copy. His wedding band was gold, with beading along the edges.

The three men rode in silence; Chris was stone-rigid, holding a rolled-up copy of the *Herald* in fingers pearl white from the strain. His mouth formed the familiar crooked tight line Brent remembered, but his eyes were invisible behind his cheaters. As Eddie drove, one of the big muscles in his right thigh jerked under his tight-fitting jeans.

When they reached the farmhouse, Chris bolted without a word, shoulders set and tense under his suit jacket, and let himself into the house.

Behind him, Eddie and Brent stopped short of the door; Eddie pressed his hand against the frame of the screen, the other hand resting on his hip as he said quietly, "No matter what you see, or what you think . . . whatever you suspect is true."

Puzzled, Brent was unable to reply as he followed his uncle into the house—where they were immediately surrounded by several small children who tugged at their legs and grabbed for their hands, all jabbering at once—"Daddy, who's this?" "Is Uncle Chris okay?" "Daddy, Mommy says you're late—" "Did you bring me some candy?"

Scooping up the nearest and youngest girl in his arms, Eddie smiled, saying, "My baby girl. Penny, can you say hello to Brent?"

The child—who was about two and a half—blushed, hiding her face against her father's shoulder, while she clutched a small red rubber doll in one hand and a white doll shoe in the other. Her siblings crowded around, looking up with wide brown eyes and flushed faces at Brent. "Evan, Elizabeth, Missy, and Peter. Peter can say 'hi' *sometimes*, he's sixteen months old."

Putting down Penny, who toddled after the older children, Eddie said, "Go tell Mommy and Aunt Mae to put out another plate." Turning his attention to Brent, Eddie said guardedly, "You do see, don't you?"

Sensing something off kilter in his uncle's voice, Brent thought . . . until his mind supplied the images that made his uncle's cryptic words make sense.

Brent *had* seen the children before. In Bitsy's old photo album. True, there was no child to take the place of little *Palmer*, but there was no need—

When he looked into Eddie's eyes again, he was already staring at Brent; as he motioned for them to go into the kitchen, he said, "Winston lost two sons, before Arlin . . . and Mae is pregnant again."

Lunch was nothing short of bedlam; with five children under nine years old at the table, there wasn't much of a chance for anyone to remind Brent that his presence in town wasn't welcome. But to their credit, the twins were gracious. And sure enough, Mae was expecting.

The past nine years had been good to the twins; if anything, they were more beautiful than before. The way Zoe should have looked. . . .

Once dessert was over, Eddie shooed the children outside, save for little Peter, who dozed off in his mother's arms. Coming back to the table, Eddie said, "I . . . didn't want to sound inhospitable, but Brent, you *must* leave—"

Around him at the table, the brothers and their wives stared at Brent, their faces both somber and slightly fearful, their eyes unwavering. For the first time that afternoon, Brent noticed that Chris' almond-shaped eyes were green. Bright, pale, leaf-green. . . .

Leaning forward, Brent asked, "Because a . . . disembodied *spirit* said I should?"

Chris spoke up for the first time since lunch began. "It isn't *that*." He laced his nicotine-stained fingers together and rested his chin on them as he stared down at the table.

His wife leaned over, stroking his glossy brown hair, as she finished for him, "We thought all of *this* was over, done with . . . our mother was no longer a threat. Things have been very good for all of us, save for a few *incidents*"—Chris made a small hurt noise in his throat at that—"and no one had suspected that we're who we are, or *what* we are. And we have friends, the Woodards, the Andersens—so we don't want for companionship, but . . . well, we couldn't help but notice that things were—"

"—coming *around* again," Maeve finished, as she smoothed down the baby's soft hair. Hugging her son, she said, "We all *hope* that it's coincidence, but . . . your coming

here only makes our suspicions stronger. Eddie, *show* him."
She turned to her husband, who fished a small credit-card-
sized plastic calendar out of his breast pocket, and handed it
to Brent.

It was from the Holiday Bed and Board, an old-fashioned
design on a sage-green background. Glancing at it, Brent
frowned and was about to hand the calendar back when
Chris said in a strangled, blatty voice, "Look at the *date*,
the *year*—"

The months were the same as the ones in 1997, but the
year written on the top was *1913*.

Eddie took the card back, saying, "Naturally, Father was
the first to notice it. . . . He called me after you arrived at
the bed and board. He said you hadn't told him why you
returned, but . . . It's Zoe, isn't it?"

"How did you—"

The twins exchanged looks, while Eddie said, "It all *fit*.
Zoe moved back to town, last spring—"

"We recognized her," Maeve added tersely as she bit the
inside of her cheek. Mae rested her hands on her ample abdomen as she went on, "Since her looks changed, we thought
that Abby was gone, so we kept hoping her return was just a
coincidence—"

Eyes downcast, Eddie added, "Lately, she's been . . . well,
we're not *sure*, but I think she's been trying to carry on with
Scott Andersen, With him being sheriff, we can't question
him . . . or her. Yet—"

As his uncle spoke, Brent pulled the tabloid article out of
his wallet and slowly slid it along the oilcloth toward him.
Eddie only had to take one glance at the exposed picture
before saying, "You know why Zoe left you, don't you?"

Wondering if any of them had seen the divorce notice, Brent
said, "You aren't insinuating—"

"Abby's come back after *dying* . . . Returning after a short
absence would be nothing for *her*," Maeve said dryly as the
baby stirred in her arms.

Chris broke the ensuing silence with a halting, "Do you
know what this reminds me of? What with Zoe and Brent
and everything?" His green eyes held a strange light Brent
was only now able to comprehend, as Mae put a hand on his
arm and asked gently, "What dear?" as if anticipating his
answer.

In a stilted voice, the man who once had been Palmer

Winston, teacher of English, said, "It's in the *book* . . . at the end," and began to quote:

" 'Gatsby believed in the green light, the orgiastic future that year by year receeds before us. It eluded us then, but that's no matter—tomorrow we will run faster, stretch out our arms further . . . And one fine morning—So we beat on, boats against the current, bourne back ceaselessly into the past.' "

Eddie reached over to pat his brother's arm; as he did so, Brent saw what his uncle had tried to hide on his right arm. A scar. Along one of the major veins in the forearm. Noticing that his nephew was looking at his arm, Eddie said, "At times . . . I've thought . . . ending it all would be better than living through it all again. *But this place*—"

Abruptly Chris got up and left the room; the pound of his footsteps running upstairs was deafening. Once her husband was out of earshot, Mae leaned forward, belly straining against the edge of the table. "He . . . tried to shoot himself in the chest. I came upon him as the wound *sealed itself up*. I . . . don't know what will happen tomorrow. It's the anniversary day, you know."

"Zoe arrived in the springtime, just as Otis did . . . my father-in-law remembers it well. So well, in fact, he won't help us now. He claims he 'did' his part—" The utter helplessness and anguish in Mae's voice mollified Brent; looking from her face to that of her sister, then at that of his uncle, Brent asked himself, *After all they've suffered, surely they shouldn't have to go through all of this again*—

Folding his hands before him, Brent said, "Would it help if I took Zoe away from here? I don't know where she is, but—"

"Her number is in the book," Maeve spat out, but Mae added, "You might find her at the little bookstore she bought—"

As Eddie drove Brent into town, he said to his nephew, "None of us can thank you enough for . . . helping us."

"Yeah . . . I just hope it doesn't happen again."

"Amen." Eddie pulled down the sun flap as he spoke. "I hope so, too, but that doesn't stop us from being scared.

What comes around goes around, as my father likes to say. Only he thinks of that in terms of a circle . . . nooses are round, too. And I can feel this one tightening—''

The mini-van stopped in front of a small brick building on Wisconsin Street, with ''FINE BOOKS'' painted on the lone window. Inside, Brent could just make out a woman moving around, her back to the window. But that cocoa-brown hair was familiar enough to him—as was the hair of the other woman inside the store, helping Zoe. Sarah Andersen, blond hair as brittle and fly-away as ever.

Leaning in close, his uncle said, ''Full of nerve, isn't she? Zoe and Sarah are best buddies. . . .''

As his uncle prattled on, Brent thought, *Funny, how I wanted to see those cream couples of the good old days . . . and now I can't wait to leave these people. . . .*

''—Don't take this as an insult, 'cause you'll always be kin to me, but please, get her the hell out of here and *stay* out.''

Taking a last look at his uncle, before he got out of the van, Brent said, ''I promise, Palmer, I'll take Zoe away from here. For good.'' The two men awkwardly hugged each other, then Brent got out of the van and walked into Zoe's bookstore.

Through the tinted van window, Palmer Edmund Nemmitz Holiday watched his nephew for a few seconds as the young man chatted with Sarah and the creature who called herself Zoe, then pulled away from the curb and drove away, praying with all his heart that he'd done the right thing . . . but doubting it nonetheless.

iii

FRIDAY, NOVEMBER 21

Zoe parked Brent's rental car at the tip of Willow Street's dead end, then got out and began walking toward the Ewert Woods. After coming this far just to convince Zoe to come back to him, Brent supposed he could follow her a little while longer—but he still hung back at the beginning of the posted woods, the remembrance of what he'd seen there nine years before still fresh in his mind.

It was almost ridiculously easy getting Zoe to realize that the divorce had been a hasty mistake, that he still loved her, and was willing to make a go of it again. Brent realized that his uncle and the others had nothing to worry about; Zoe was just plain *Zoe*, not a vengeful dead woman come back again. And the thing with Scooter was *nothing*, just the renewal of an old, old friendship. Sarah wasn't worried, so Brent shouldn't be either, Zoe had assured him that night.

Today, he even let Zoe do the driving—anything to *keep* her happy until they were out of this town—but her decision to stop for a last look at the woods worried him now. Zoe shouted back at him as she entered the woods, "Oh, c'mon, one last look, the fall colors are still holding. The trees aren't *like* this in the Cities. See, the woods are posted. . . ."

Thinking, *We'll gather a couple of leaves, then scram,* Brent shrugged and entered the woods.

A few minutes later, a station wagon pulled up next to the small rental car, and a woman got out . . . a short, tanned woman, who carried a purse that seemed to be *quite* heavy. She wasn't worried about being seen; if anyone remembered seeing her car parked there, later, when questions were bound to be asked, no one would dare question the presence of a car belonging to the *sheriff's* wife.

Even if people aren't *aware that he's a two-timing son of a bitch,* Sarah Andersen thought, before entering the woods in search of her husband's lover.

Zoe was strangely quiet as she and Brent walked in the fragrant woods; finally, he could stand her silence no longer, and asked, "Penny for your thoughts, kid."

Without turning to face him, she replied, "I just needed to see the woods again . . . I wanted to see what Zach saw, before he—"

But before Brent had a chance to digest what she'd just said, Sarah Andersen aimed her husband's gun at Zoe's head, and slowly squeezed the trigger. . . .

A couple of miles away, in the Winston house on the hill, Mae and Maeve were painting the walls of the nursery—for the third time. Mae insisted on re-doing the walls for each baby, as if the painted walls meant for the *last* baby's eyes might jinx the child she carried now. Not that it worked before . . . but the mayor's wife and her sister had reason to believe in omens.

Mae suddenly let out an "Oh!" and stood up so fast her spine popped.

Maeve turned around, asking, "What was *that*?"

Mae stood there, hands on her stomach, saying, "Nothing . . . the baby just kicked, that's all." She turned to Maeve and said, "I have a definite feeling that *this* baby will live . . . funny, isn't it? It just . . . *came* to me."

"Think that means it's a boy?" Maeve asked.

But her sister said dreamily, "No . . . I followed one of those recipes in a woman's magazine. I thought if this one was a girl, it might change our luck. And Chris was hinting he wants a little girl—

" 'Just like her pretty little mother,' he said."

"Isn't that romantic?"

The bloody legend has haunted three generations. Now Anna Sudek discovers the terrifying reality...

THE AMULET

A.R. Morlan

Nearly sixty years removed from the night when Lucy Miner witnessed her father's murderous rampage—which left her mother dead and her beloved grandmother's body missing—Anna Sudek lives every day with its legacy: dead-end jobs, no friends, and the taunting questions of her family's heritage of evil.

Now Anna is about to learn the answers to those questions...and even more terrifying ones of her own. She will discover deadly truths about the little girl who witnessed her mother's death. Soon she will know that the ax-swinging madman was not the most dangerous entity in the Miner house that night. She will learn the horrifying power of a stolen treasure, waiting to be unleashed....

A dark exploration of one bloody family
tree and its stolen, deadly inheritance,
The Amulet
is a spine-tingling tale of
evil, madness and murder

On sale now wherever Bantam Books are sold.

AN 373 12/91

When the great storm comes,
the good life ends.
And hell on earth begins....

John Skipp & Craig Spector

THE BRIDGE

Boonie and Drew have been providing a vital service to the community for years. They dispose of "problem" waste. They never expected the waste to bite back.

Micki's been in intimate touch with the Other Side for years. The information she received was always good. Now she's not so sure.

Gwen and Gary are preparing to bring their first child into the world, and what they want to know is, will there be a world for her to inherit?

This morning, while we slept,
something woke up.
It's virulent. Malign. Intelligent. Ambitious.
It's in our food, our water, our air.
It's inside our bodies themselves.
And it's not leaving.
We are.

"This is the New Horror at work: fast-paced and passionate, breaking new ground as it uncovers the faces that fear wears in the century's final decade." --Clive Barker

The Bridge.
Now on sale wherever Bantam Books are sold.

AN329 -- 9/91

Bantam Spectra Horror
because every spectrum is shadowed by the colors of the night...

☐ **The Demon by Jeffrey Sackett**
(28596-3 * $4.50/$5.50 in Canada)
An ex-sideshow geek moves into a small New York town, and on his heels follows a string of hideous murders.

☐ **The Horror Club by Mark Morris**
(28933-0 * $4.95/$5.95 in Canada)
Three young horror fans learn the true meaning of fear when they invite a new boy into their club who unleashes upon their hometown a terrifying, consuming evil.

☐ **The Amulet by A.R. Morlan**
(28908-X * $4.95/$5.95 in Canada)
Set in a quiet Wisconsin town, this is the chilling story of a woman's desperate struggle against the terrible power of a talisman which controls and changes the people around her.

☐ **House Haunted by Al Sarrantonio**
(29148-7 * $4.50/$5.50 in Canada)
Five people are seduced into a sinister web of madness, murder and supernatural confrontation by a powerful spirit who longs for a doorway into the physical world.

☐ **The Well by Michael B. Sirota**
(28843-1 * $4.50/$5.50 in Canada)
A man returns to his ancestral home only to reawaken the ancient blood curse that haunts his family line.

Look for these bloodcurdling new titles on sale now wherever Bantam Spectra Books are sold, or use this page for ordering:

Bantam Books, Dept. SF103   414 East Golf Road, Des Plaines, IL 60016

Please send me the items I have checked above. I am enclosing $_____
(please add $2.50 to cover postage and handling). Send check or money order;
no cash or C.O.D.s please.

Mr./Ms._____

Address_____

City/State_____ Zip_____

Please allow four to six weeks for delivery.
Prices and availability subject to change without notice.   SF103 -- 6/91